WYATT'S HURRICANE

BAHAMA CRISIS

Desmond Bagley was born in 1923 in Kendal, Westmorland, and brought up in Blackpool. He began his working life, aged 14, in the printing industry and then did a variety of jobs until going into an aircraft factory at the start of the Second World War.

When the war ended, he decided to travel to southern Africa, going overland through Europe and the Sahara. He worked en route, reaching South Africa in 1951.

Bagley became a freelance journalist in Johannesburg and wrote his first published novel, *The Golden Keel*, in 1962. In 1964 he returned to England and lived in Totnes, Devon, for twelve years. He and his wife Joan then moved to Guernsey in the Channel Islands. Here he found the ideal place for combining his writing and his other interests, which included computers, mathematics, military history, and entertaining friends from all over the world.

Desmond Bagley died in April 1983, having become one of the w
with his 16 books – two
death – translated into

'I've read all Bagley's b   marvellous, the best.'

ALISTAIR MACLEAN

By the same author

DESMOND BAGLEY

Wyatt's Hurricane

AND

Bahama Crisis

HARPER

HARPER
an imprint of HarperCollins*Publishers*
77-85 Fulham Palace Road
Hammersmith, London W6 8JB
www.harpercollins.co.uk

This omnibus edition 2009
1

Wyatt's Hurricane first published in Great Britain by Collins 1966
Landslide first published in Great Britain by Collins 1980
Introduction to *Crime Wave* first published by Collins 1981

Desmond Bagley asserts the moral right to
be identified as the author of these works

Copyright © Brockhurst Publications 1966, 1980, 1981

ISBN 978 0 00 730478 3

Printed and bound in Great Britain by
Clays Ltd, St Ives plc

All rights reserved. No part of this publication may be
reproduced, stored in a retrieval system, or transmitted,
in any form or by any means, electronic, mechanical,
photocopying, recording or otherwise, without the prior
written permission of the publishers.

Mixed Sources
Product group from well-managed
forests and other controlled sources
www.fsc.org Cert no. SW-COC-1806
© 1996 Forest Stewardship Council

FSC is a non-profit international organisation established
to promote the responsible management of the world's forests.
Products carrying the FSC label are independently certified
to assure consumers that they come from forests that are managed
to meet the social, economic and ecological needs
of present and future generations.

Find out more about HarperCollins and the environment at
www.harpercollins.co.uk/green

CONTENTS

WYATT'S HURRICANE

This one is for Jimmy Brown

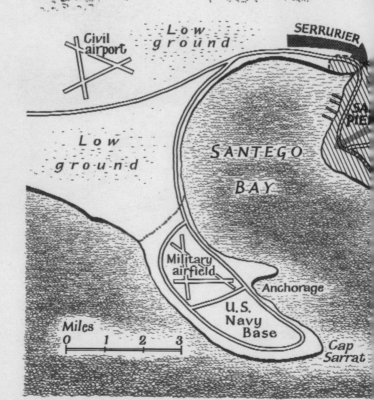

SAN FERNANDEZ
ENVIRONS OF ST. PIERRE

Tour Rambeau

SERRURIER

Civil airport

Low ground

Low ground

SANTEGO

BAY

SA
PIE

Military airfield

Anchorage

U.S.
Navy
Base

Cap
Sarrat

Miles
0   1   2   3

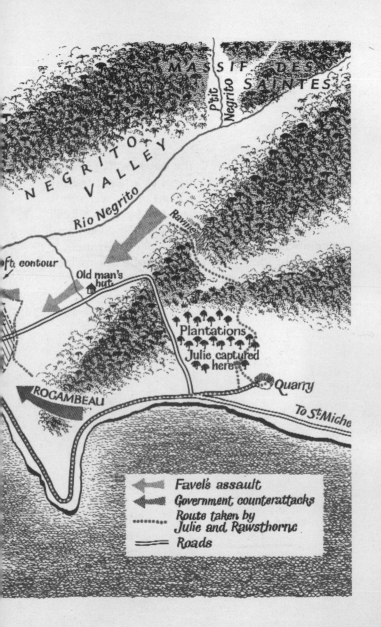

MASSIF DES SAINTES

P'tit Negrito

NEGRITO VALLEY

Rio Negrito

Ravine

ft. contour

Old man's hut

Plantations

Julie captured here

Quarry

ROCAMBEAU

To St. Miche

Favel's assault
Government counterattacks
Route taken by Julie and Rawsthorne
Roads

With the blast of thy nostrils the waters were gathered together, the floods stood upright as a heap, and the depths were congealed in the heart of the sea.

The enemy said, I will pursue, I will overtake, I will divide the spoil; my lust shall be satisfied upon them; I will draw my sword, my hand shall destroy them.

Thou didst blow with thy wind, the sea covered them, they sank as lead in the mighty waters.

EXODUS: ch. 15, vv. 8–10

ONE

The Super-Constellation flew south-east in fair weather, leaving behind the arc of green islands scattered across the crinkled sea, the island chain known as the Lesser Antilles. Ahead, somewhere over the hard line of the Atlantic horizon, was her destination – a rendezvous with trouble somewhere north of the Equator and in that part of the Atlantic which is squeezed between North Africa and South America.

The pilot, Lieutenant-Commander Hansen, did not really know the exact position of contact nor when he would get there – he merely flew on orders from a civilian seated behind him – but he had flown on many similar missions and knew what was expected of him, so he relaxed in his seat and left the flying to Morgan, his co-pilot. The Lieutenant-Commander had over twelve years' service in the United States Navy and so was paid $660 a month. He was grossly underpaid for the job he was doing.

The aircraft, one of the most graceful ever designed, had once proudly flown the North Atlantic commercial route until edged out by the faster jets. So she had been put in mothballs until the Navy had need of her and now she wore United States Navy insignia. She looked more battered than seemed proper in a Navy plane – the leading edge of her wings was pitted and dented and the mascot of a winged

7

cloud painted on her nose was worn and abraded – but she had flown more of these missions than her pilot and so the wear and tear was understandable.

Hansen looked at the sky over the horizon and saw the first faint traces of cirrus flecking the pale blue. He flicked a switch and said, 'I think she's coming up now, Dave. Any change of orders?'

A voice crackled in his earphones. 'I'll check on the display.'

Hansen folded his arms across his stomach and stared ahead at the gathering high clouds. Some Navy men might have resented taking instructions from a civilian, especially from one who was not even an American, but Hansen knew better than that; in this particular job status and nationality did not matter a damn and all one needed to know was that the men you flew with were competent and would not get you killed – if they could help it.

Behind the flight deck was the large compartment where once the first-class passengers sipped their bourbon and joshed the hostesses. Now it was crammed with instruments and men; consoles of telemetering devices were banked fore and aft, jutting into promontories and forming islands so that there was very little room for the three men cramped into the maze of electronic equipment.

David Wyatt turned on his swivel stool and cracked his knee sharply against the edge of the big radar console. He grimaced, reflecting that he would never learn, and rubbed his knee with one hand while he switched on the set. The big screen came to life and shed an eerie green glow around him, and he observed it with professional interest. After making a few notes, he rummaged in a satchel for some papers and then got up and made his way to the flight deck.

He tapped Hansen on the shoulder and gave the thumbs-up sign, and then looked ahead. The silky tendrils of the high-flying cirrus were now well overhead, giving place to the lower flat sheets of cirrostratus on the horizon, and he knew that just over the edge of the swelling earth there would be the heavy and menacing nimbostratus – the rain-bearers. He looked at Hansen. 'This is it,' he said, and smiled.

Hansen grunted in his throat. 'No need to look so god-dam happy.'

Wyatt pushed a thin sheaf of photographs at him. 'This is what it looks like from upstairs.'

Hansen scanned the grained and streaky photographs which had been telemetered to earth from a weather satel-lite. 'These from Tiros IX?'

'That's right.'

'They're improving – these are okay,' said Hansen. He checked the size of the swirl of white against the scale on the edge of the photograph. 'This one's not so big; thank God for that.'

'It's not the size that counts,' said Wyatt. 'It's the pressure gradient – you know that. That's what we're here for.'

'Any change in operating procedure?'

Wyatt shook his head. 'The usual thing – we go in counter-clockwise with the wind, edging in all the time. Then, when we get to the south-west quadrant, we turn for the centre.'

Hansen scratched his cheek. 'Better make sure you get all your measurements first time round. I don't want to do this again.' He cocked his head aft. 'I hope your instrumentation works better than last time.'

Wyatt grimaced. 'So do I.' He waved cheerily and went back aft to check on the big radar display. Everything was normal with no anomalies – just the usual dangerous situa-tion ahead. He glanced at the two men under his command. Both were Navy men, skilled specialists who knew every-thing there was to know about the equipment in their charge, and both had flown on these missions before and

knew what to expect. Already they were checking their
webbing straps to see there would be no chafe when unexpected strain was thrown on them.

Wyatt went to his own place and strapped himself into
the seat. As he snapped down the lever which prevented
the seat turning he at last admitted to himself that he was
frightened. He always felt scared at this stage of the
operation – more scared, he was sure, than any other man
aboard. Because he knew more about hurricanes than even
Hansen; hurricanes were his job, his life study, and he knew
the ravening strength of the winds which were soon to
attack the plane in an effort to destroy it. And there was
something else, something newly added. From the moment
he had seen the white smear on the satellite photographs
back at Cap Sarrat he had sensed that this was going to be a
bad one. It was not something he could analyse, something
he could lay on paper in the cold symbols and formulae of
meteorological science, but something he felt deep in his
being.

So this time he was even more frightened than usual.

He shrugged and applied himself to his work as the first
small buffet of wind hit the plane. The green trace on the
radar screen matched well with the satellite photographs
and he switched on the recorder which would put all that
data on to a coiled strip of plastic magnetic tape to be corre-
lated in the master computer with all the other information
that was soon to come pouring in.

Hansen stared ahead at the blackness confronting the
plane. The oily black nimbostratus clouds heaved tumultu-
ously, driven by the wind, the formations continually building up and shredding. He grinned tightly at Morgan. 'Let's
get on with it,' he said, and gently turned to starboard.
Flying in still air at this particular throttle-setting the Super-
Constellation should have cruised at 220 knots, and so his
air-speed indicator showed, but he was willing to bet that

their ground-speed was nearer 270 knots with this wind behind them.

That was the devil in this job; instruments did not read true and there was no hope of getting a valid ground-sighting because even if the clouds broke – which they never did – merely to see a featureless stretch of ocean would be useless.

Suddenly the plane dropped like a stone – caught in a down-draught – and he fought with the controls while watching the altimeter needle spin like a top. He got her on to an even keel once more and set her into a climb to regain his altitude and, almost before he knew what was happening, the plane was caught in an up-draught just as fierce and he had to push the control column forward to avoid being spewed from the top of the wind system.

Through the toughened glass he saw rain and hail being driven upwards, illuminated by the blue glare of lightning. Looking back, he saw a coruscating flash spreading tree-wise from the wingtip and knew they had been struck. He also knew that it did not matter; there would be a mere pin-hole in the metal to be filled in by the ground staff and that was all – except for the fact that the plane and everything in it was charged up with several thousand volts of electricity which would have to be dissipated when landing.

Carefully he edged the Constellation deeper into the storm, flying a spiral course and finding the stronger winds. The lightning was now almost continuous, the whipcrack of the close discharges drowning out the noise of the engines. He switched on his throat mike and shouted to the flight engineer, 'Meeker, everything okay?'

There was a long pause before Meeker replied. 'Ever . . . . . . ng fine.' The words were half drowned in static.

Hansen shouted, 'Keep things that way,' and started to do some mental arithmetic. From the satellite photograph he had judged the diameter of the hurricane at 300 miles, which would give a circumference of about 950 miles. To get to the south-west quadrant where the winds were least strong and where it was safest to turn inwards to the centre he would have to fly a third of the way round – say, 230 miles. His air-speed indicator was now fluctuating too much to be of any use, but from past experience he judged his ground-speed to be a little in excess of 300 knots – say, 350 miles an hour. They had been in the storm nearly half an hour, so that left another half-hour before the turning-point.

Sweat beaded his forehead.

In the instrument compartment Wyatt felt that he was being beaten black and blue and he knew that when he got back to Cap Sarrat and stripped he would find weals where his harness had bitten into him. The stark functional light-ing dimmed and flared as lightning flashes hit the plane and momentarily overloaded the circuits, and he hoped that the instrumentation held up under the beating.

He cast a glance at the other two men. Smith was hunched in his seat, expertly rolling as the plane lurched and occasionally resetting a knob. He was all right. Jablon-sky's face had a greenish tinge and, as Wyatt looked, he turned and was violently sick. But he recovered quickly and applied himself to his job, and Wyatt smiled briefly.

He looked at the clock set into the panel before him and began to calculate. When they turned in towards the centre of the hurricane they would have to fly a little over a hun-dred miles to get to the 'eye', that mysterious region of calm in the midst of a wilderness of raging air. There would be fierce crosswinds and the ride would be rough and Wyatt estimated it would take nearly three-quarters of an hour. But then they would be able to idle and catch their breaths before plunging into the fray again. Hansen would circle for fifteen minutes in that wondrous stillness while Wyatt did his work, and they would all rub the soreness from their battered bodies and gird themselves for the flight out.

From the moment they turned in to the centre all instruments would be working, recording air pressure, humidity, temperature and all the other variables that go to make up the biggest wind on earth. And on the way through the hurricane they would drop what Wyatt called to himself their 'bomb load' – marvellously complex packages of instruments jettisoned into the storm, some to be tossed for an hour or so in the wind before touching down, some to plunge down to float on the raging sea, others that would sink to a predetermined depth beneath the waves. But all would be sending radio signals to be caught by the complex of receiving instrumentation in the plane and recorded on tape.

He steadied himself in the seat and began to dictate into his throat mike which was hooked up to a small recording machine. He hoped he would be able to disentangle his own voice from the storm noises when he replayed the tape back at base.

Half an hour later Hansen turned in towards the centre, buzzing Wyatt as he did so. Immediately he felt a difference in the quality of the wind's attack on the plane; there was a new set of noises added to the cacophony and the controls reacted differently under his hands. The Constellation became more difficult to control in the crosswinds which he knew were gusting at perhaps 130 miles an hour; she plunged and bucked and his arms began to ache with the constant corrective movements he was forced to apply. The gyro-compass had long since toppled out of action and the card of the magnetic compass was swinging violently in the bowl.

Wyatt and his crew were very busy. Deafened by the murderous sound and shaken like dice in a cup, they still managed to get on with their work. The instrument capsules were dropped with precision at regular intervals and the information which they immediately began to radio back was stored on the inch-wide, thirty-two track tapes which Smith and Jablonsky hovered over solicitously. In the intervals between dropping the capsules Wyatt continued his running commentary on to his private tape; he knew this data was subjective and not to be used for serious analysis, but he liked to have it for his private information and to compare later with the numerical findings.

It was with relief that he heard the racket end with almost shattering abruptness and knew they had penetrated to the eye of the hurricane. The plane stopped bucking and seemed to float through the air and, after the noise of the storm, the roar of the engines seemed to be the most peaceful sound he had ever heard. Stiffly he unbuckled his straps and said, 'How are things going?'

Smith waggled his hand. 'Average score. No humidity readings from number four; no air temperature from number six; no sea temperature from number seven.' He grimaced.

'Not a cheep of anything from number three, and none of the sinkers worked at all.'

'Damn those sinkers!' said Wyatt feelingly. 'I always said that system was too bloody complicated. How about you, Jablonsky? What about direct readings?'

'Everything's okay with me,' said Jablonsky.

'Keep at it,' said Wyatt. 'I'm going to see the skipper.' He made his way forward to the flight deck to find Hansen massaging his arms while Morgan flew the plane in a tight circle. He smiled faintly.

'This one's a bastard,' said Hansen. 'Too rough for this mother's son. How about you?'

'The usual crop of malfunctions – only to be expected. But none of the sinkers worked at all.'

'Have they ever?'

Wyatt smiled ruefully. 'It's asking a bit much, isn't it?' he said. 'We drop a very complicated package into the sea in the middle of a hurricane so that it will settle to a predetermined depth. It broadcasts by sonar a signal which is supposed to be picked up by an equally complicated floating package, turned into a radio wave and picked up by us. There's one too many links in that chain. I'll write a report when I get back – we're tossing too much money into the sea for too little return.'

'*If* we get back,' said Hansen. 'The worst is yet to come. I've never known winds so strong in the south-west quadrant, and it'll be a damn' sight worse heading north.'

'We can scrub the rest of it, if you like,' offered Wyatt. 'We can go out the way we came in.'

'If I could do it I would,' said Hansen bluntly. 'But we haven't the gas to go all the way round again. So we'll bull our way out by the shortest route and you can drop the other half of the cargo as planned – but it'll be a hell of a rough ride.' He looked up. 'This one is really bad, Dave.'

'I know,' said Wyatt soberly. 'Give me a buzz when you're ready to move on.' He returned to the instrument section.

It was only five minutes before the buzzer went and Wyatt knew that Hansen was really nervous because he usually idled for much longer in the eye. He hastily fastened his straps and tensed his muscles for the wrath to come. Hansen had been right – this was a really bad one, it was small, tight and vicious. He would be interested to know what the pressure gradient was that could whip up such high winds.

If what had gone before was purgatory, then this was pure unadulterated hell. The whole fabric of the Constellation creaked and groaned in anguish at the battering it was receiving; the skin sprang leaks in a dozen places and for a time Wyatt was fearful that it was all too much, that the wings would be torn off in spite of the special strengthening and the fuselage would smash into the boiling sea. He was plagued by a stream of water that cascaded down his neck, but managed to get rid of the rest of the capsules with the same well-timed precision.

For nearly an hour Hansen battled with the big wind and, just when he thought he could bear it no longer, the plane was thrown out of the clouds, spat forth as a man spits out an orange pip. He signalled for Morgan to take over and sagged back in his seat completely exhausted.

As the buffeting lessened Wyatt took stock. Half of Jablonsky's equipment had packed up, the tell-tale dials recording zero. Fortunately the tapes had kept working so all was not lost. Smith's tale was even sorrier – only three of a round dozen capsules had returned signals, and those had suddenly ceased half-way through the flight when the recorder had been torn bodily from its mounting with a sputter of sparks and the tapes had stopped.

'Never mind,' said Wyatt philosophically. '*We* got through.'

Jablonsky mopped water from the top of his console. 'That was too goddam rough. Another one like that and I'll take a ground job.'

Smith grunted. 'You and me both.'

Wyatt grinned at them. 'You're not likely to get another like that in a hurry,' he said. 'It was my worst in twenty-three missions.'

He went up to the flight deck and Jablonsky looked after him. 'Twenty-three missions! The guy must be nuts. Ten is my limit – only two more to go.'

Smith rubbed his chin reflectively. 'Maybe he's got the death wish – you know, psychology and all that. Or maybe he's a hurricane lover. But he's got guts, that's for sure – I've never seen a guy look so unconcerned.'

On the flight deck Hansen said heavily, 'I hope you got everything you wanted. I'd hate to go through that again.'

'We'll have enough,' said Wyatt. 'But I'll be able to tell for certain when we get home. When will that be?'

'Three hours,' said Hansen.

There was a sudden change in the even roar and a spurt of black smoke streaked from the port outer engine. Hansen's hand went like a flash to the throttles and then he feathered the airscrew. 'Meeker,' he roared. 'What's wrong?'

'Dunno,' said Meeker. 'But I reckon she's packed in for the rest of the trip. Oil pressure's right down.' He paused. 'I had some bother with her a little while back but I reckoned you didn't feel like hearing about it just then.'

Hansen blew out his cheeks and let forth a long sigh. 'Jesus!' he said reverently and with no intention to swear. He looked up at Wyatt. 'Make it nearly four hours.'

Wyatt nodded weakly and leaned against the bulkhead. He could feel the knots in his stomach relaxing and was aware of the involuntary trembling of his whole body now that it was over.

II

Wyatt sat at his desk, at ease in body if not in mind. It was still early morning and the sun had not developed the power it would later in the day, so all was still fresh and new. Wyatt felt good. On his return the previous afternoon he had seen his precious tapes delivered to the computer boys and then had indulged in the blessed relief of a hot bath which had soaked away all the soreness from his battered body. And that evening he had had a couple of beers with Hansen.

Now, in the fresh light of morning, he felt rested and eager to begin his work, although, as he drew the closely packed tables of figures towards him, he did not relish the

facts he knew he would find. He worked steadily all morning, converting the cold figures into stark lines on a chart –
a skeleton of reality, an abstraction of a hurricane. When he
had finished he looked at the chart with blank eyes, then
carefully pinned it on to a large board on the wall of his
office.

He had just started to fill in a form when the phone rang,
and his heart seemed to turn over as he heard the well-
remembered voice. 'Julie!' he exclaimed. 'What the devil
are you doing here?'

The warmth of her voice triumphed over electronics. 'A
week's vacation,' she said. 'I was in Puerto Rico and a friend
gave me a lift over in his plane.'

'Where are you now?'

'I've just checked into the Imperiale – I'm staying here
and, boy, what a dump!'

'It's the best we've got until Conrad Hilton moves in –
and if he has any sense, he won't,' said Wyatt. 'I'm sorry
about that; you can't very well come to the Base.'

'It's okay,' said Julie. 'When do I see you?'

'Oh, hell!' said Wyatt in exasperation. 'I'll be tied up all
day, I'm afraid. It'll have to be tonight. What about dinner?'

'That's fine,' she said, and Wyatt thought he detected a
shade of disappointment. 'Maybe we can go on to the
Maraca Club – if it's still running.'

'It's still on its feet, although how Eumenides does it is a
mystery.' Wyatt had his eye on the clock. 'Look, Julie, I've
got a hell of a lot to do if I'm to take the evening off; things
are pretty busy in my line just now.'

Julie laughed. 'All right; no telephonic gossip. It'll be
better face to face. See you tonight.'

She rang off and Wyatt replaced the handset slowly, then
swivelled his chair towards the window where he could
look over Santego Bay towards St Pierre. Julie Marlowe, he
thought in astonishment, well, well! He could just distinguish

the Imperiale in the clutter of buildings that made St Pierre, and a smile touched his lips.

He had not known her long, not really. She was an air hostess on a line covering the Caribbean from Florida and he had been introduced to her by a civilian pilot, a friend of Hansen's. It had been good while it lasted – San Fernandez had been on her regular route and he had seen her twice a week. They had had three months of fun which had come to a sudden end when the airline had decided that the government of San Fernandez, President Serrurier in particular, was making life too difficult, so they dropped St Pierre from their schedule.

Wyatt pondered. That had been two years ago – no, nearer three years. He and Julie had corresponded regularly at first, but with the passage of time their letters had become sparser and more widely spaced. Friendship by letter is difficult, especially between a man and a woman, and he had expected at any moment to hear that she was engaged – or married – and that would be the end of it, for all practical purposes.

He jerked his head and looked at the clock, then swung round to the desk and pulled the form towards him. He had nearly finished when Schelling, the senior Navy meteorologist on Cap Sarrat Base, came in. 'This is the latest from Tiros on your baby,' he said, and tossed a sheaf of photographs on to the desk.

Wyatt reached for them and Schelling said, 'Hansen tells me you took quite a beating.'

'He wasn't exaggerating. Look at that lot.' Wyatt waved at the chart on the wall.

Schelling walked over to the board and pursed his lips in a whistle. 'Are you sure your instrumentation was working properly?'

Wyatt joined him. 'There's no reason to doubt it.' He stretched out a finger. 'Eight hundred and seventy millibars in the eye – that's the lowest pressure I've encountered any-where.'

Schelling ran a practised eye over the chart. 'High pres-sure on the outside – 1040 millibars.'

'A pressure gradient of 170 millibars over a little less than 150 miles – that makes for big winds.' Wyatt indicated the northern area of the hurricane. 'Theory says that the wind-speeds here should be up to 170 miles an hour. After flying through it I have no reason to doubt it – and neither has Hansen.'

Schelling said, 'This is a bad one.'

'It is,' said Wyatt briefly, and sat down to examine the Tiros photographs with Schelling looking over his shoulder. 'She seems to have tightened up a bit,' he said. 'That's strange.'

'Makes it even worse,' said Schelling gloomily. He put down two photographs side by side. 'She isn't moving along very fast, though.'

'I made the velocity of translation eight miles an hour – about 200 miles a day. We'd better check that, it's impor-tant.' Wyatt drew a desk calculator and, after checking figures marked on the photographs, began to hammer the keys. 'That's about right; a shade under 200 miles in the last twenty-four hours.'

Schelling blew out his cheeks with a soft explosion of relief. 'Well, that's not too bad. At that rate it'll take her another ten days to reach the eastern seaboard of the States, and they usually don't last longer than a week. That's if she moves in a straight line – which she won't. The Coriolis force will move her eastward in the usual parabola and my guess is that she'll peter out somewhere in the North Atlantic like most of the others.'

'There are two things wrong with that,' said Wyatt flatly. 'There's nothing to say she won't speed up. Eight miles an hour is damned slow for a cyclone in this part of the world – the average is fifteen miles an hour – so it's very probable she'll last long enough to reach the States. As for the Coriolis effect, there are forces acting on a hurricane which cancel that out very effectively. My guess is that a high-altitude jet stream can do a lot to push a hurricane around, and we know damn' little about those and when they'll turn up.'

Schelling began to look unhappy again. 'The Weather Bureau isn't going to like this. But we'd better let them know.'

'That's another thing,' said Wyatt, lifting the form from his desk-top. 'I'm not going to put my name to this latest piece of bureaucratic bumf. Look at that last request – "State duration and future direction of hurricane." I'm not a fortune-teller and I don't work with a crystal ball.'

Schelling made an impatient noise with his lips. 'All they want is a prediction according to standard theory – that will satisfy them.'

'We don't have enough theory to fill an eggcup,' said Wyatt. 'Not that sort of theory. If we put a prediction on that form then some Weather Bureau clerk will take it as gospel truth – the scientists have said it and therefore it *is* so – and a lot of people could get killed if the reality doesn't match with theory. Look at Ione in 1955 – she changed direction seven times in ten days and ended up smack in the mouth of the St Lawrence way up in Canada. She had all the weather boys coming and going and she didn't do a damn' thing that accorded with theory. I'm not going to put my name to that form.'

'All right, I'll do it,' said Schelling petulantly. 'What's the name of this one?'

Wyatt consulted a list. 'We've been running through them pretty fast this year. The last one was Laura – so this one will be Mabel.' He looked up. 'Oh, one more thing. What about the Islands?'

'The Islands? Oh, we'll give them the usual warning.'

As Schelling turned and walked out of the office Wyatt looked after him with something approaching disgust in his eyes.

III

That evening Wyatt drove the fifteen miles round Santego Bay to St Pierre, the capital city of San Fernandez. It was not much of a capital, but then, it was not much of an island. As he drove in the fading light he passed the familiar banana and pineapple plantations and the equally familiar natives by the roadside, the men dingy in dirty cotton shirts and blue jeans, the women bright in flowered dresses and flaming headscarves, and all laughing and chattering as usual, white teeth and gleaming black faces shining in the light of the setting sun. As usual, he wondered why they always seemed to be so happy.

They had little to be happy about. Most were ground down by a cruel poverty made endemic by over-population and the misuse of the soil. At one time, in the eighteenth century, San Fernandez had been rich with sugar and coffee, a prize to be fought over by the embattled colonizing powers of Europe. But at an opportune moment, when their masters were otherwise occupied, the slaves had risen and had taken command of their own destinies.

That may have been a good thing – and it may not. True, the slaves were free, but a series of bloody civil wars engendered by ruthless men battling for power drained the economic strength of San Fernandez and population pressure did the rest, leaving an ignorant peasantry eking out a miserable living by farming on postage-stamp plots and doing most of their trade by barter. Wyatt had heard that some of the people in the central hills had never seen a piece of money in their lives.

Things had seemed to improve in the early part of the twentieth century. A stable government had encouraged foreign investment and bananas and pineapples replaced coffee, while the sugar acreage increased enormously. Those were the good days. True, the pay on the American-owned plantations was small, but it was regular and the flow of money to the island was enlivening. It was then that the Hotel Imperiale was built and St Pierre expanded beyond the confines of the Old City.

But San Fernandez seemed to be trapped in the cycle of its own history. After the Second World War came Serrurier, self-styled Black Star of the Antilles, who took power in bloody revolution and kept it by equally bloody government, ruling by his one-way courts, by assassination and by the power of the army. He had no opponents – he had killed them all – and there was but one power on the island – the black fist of Serrurier.

And still the people could laugh.

St Pierre was a shabby town of jerry-built brick, corrugated iron and peeling walls, with an overriding smell that pervaded the whole place compounded of rotting fruit, decaying fish, human and animal ordure, and worse. The stench was everywhere, sometimes eddying strongly in the grimmer parts of town and even evident in the lounge of the Imperiale, that dilapidated evidence of better times.

As Wyatt peered across the badly lit room he knew by the dimness that the town electricity plant was giving trouble again and it was only when Julie waved that he distinguished her in the gloom. He walked across to find her sitting at a table with a man, and he felt a sudden unreasonable depression which lightened when he heard the warmth in her voice.

'Hello, Dave. I *am* glad to see you again. This is John Causton – he's staying here too. He was on my flight from Miami to San Juan and we bumped into each other here as well.'

Wyatt stood uncertainly, waiting for Julie to make her excuses to Causton, but she said nothing, so he drew up another chair and sat down.

Causton said, 'Miss Marlowe has been telling me all about you – and there's one thing that puzzles me. What's an Englishman doing working for the United States Navy?'

Wyatt glanced at Julie, then sized up Causton before answering. He was a short, stocky man with a square face, hair greying at the temples and shrewd brown eyes. He was English himself by his accent, but one could have been fooled by his Palm Beach suit.

'To begin with, I'm not English,' said Wyatt deliberately. 'I'm a West Indian – we're not all black, you know. I was born on St Kitts, spent my early years on Grenada and was educated in England. As for the United States Navy, I don't work *for* them, I work *with* them – there's a bit of a difference there. I'm on loan from the Meteorological Office.'

Causton smiled pleasantly. 'That explains it.'

Wyatt looked at Julie. 'What about a drink before dinner?'

'That *is* a good idea. What goes down well in San Fernandez?'

'Perhaps Mr Wyatt will show us how to make the wine of the country – Planter's Punch,' said Causton. His eyes twinkled.

'Oh, yes – do,' exclaimed Julie. 'I've always wanted to drink Planter's Punch in the proper surroundings.'

'I think it's an overrated drink, myself,' said Wyatt. 'I prefer Scotch. But if you want Planter's Punch, you shall have it.' He called a waiter and gave the order in the bastard French that was the island *patois*, and soon the ingredients were on the table.

Causton produced a notebook from his breast pocket. 'I'll take notes, if I may. It may come in useful.'

'No need,' said Wyatt. 'There's a little rhyme for it which, once learned, is never forgotten. It goes like this:

> One of sour,
> Two of sweet,
> Three of strong
> And four of weak.

'It doesn't quite scan, but it's near enough. The sour is the juice of fresh limes, the sweet is sugar syrup, the strong is rum – Martinique rum is best – and the weak is iced water. The rhyme gives the proportions.'

As he spoke he was busy measuring the ingredients and mixing them in the big silver bowl in the middle of the table. His hands worked mechanically and he was watching Julie. She had not changed apart from becoming more attractive, but perhaps that was merely because absence had made the heart fonder. He glanced at Causton and wondered where he came in.

'If you go down to Martinique,' he said, 'you can mix your own Planter's Punch in any bar. There's so much rum in Martinique that they don't charge you for it – only for the limes and the syrup.'

Causton sniffed. 'Smells interesting.'

Wyatt smiled. 'Rum does pong a bit.'

'Why have we never done this before, Dave?' asked Julie. She looked interestedly at the bowl.

'I've never been asked before.' Wyatt gave one final stir. 'That's it. Some people put a lot of salad in it like a fruit cup, but 1 don't like drinks I have to eat.' He lifted out a dipperful. Julie?'

She held out her glass and he filled it. He filled the other glasses then said, 'Welcome to the Caribbean, Mr Causton.'

'It's wonderful,' said Julie. 'So smooth.'

'Smooth and powerful,' said Wyatt. 'You wouldn't need many of these to be biting the leg of the table.'

'This should get the evening off to a good start,' said Julie. 'Even the Maraca Club should look good.' She turned to Causton. 'Now there's an idea – why don't you come with us?'

'Thank you very much,' said Causton. 'I *was* wondering what to do with myself tonight. I was hoping that Mr Wyatt, as an old island hand, could give me a few pointers on sightseeing on San Fernandez.'

Wyatt looked blankly at Julie, then said politely, 'I'd be happy to.' He felt depressed. He had hoped that he had been the attraction on San Fernandez, but apparently Julie was playing the field. But why the hell had she to come to San Fernandez to do it?

It turned out that Causton was foreign correspondent for a big London daily and over dinner he entertained them with a hilarious account of some of his experiences. Then they went on to the Maraca, which was the best in the way of a night-club that St Pierre had to offer. It was run by a Greek, Eumenides Papegaikos, who provided an exiguous South American atmosphere with the minimum of service at the highest price he could charge; but apart from the Officers' Club at Cap Sarrat Base it was the only substitute for a civilized evening, and one did get bored with the Base.

As they entered the smoke-filled, dimly-lit room someone waved, and Wyatt waved back as he recognized Hansen, who was whooping it up with his crew. At the far end of the room a loud-voiced American was bellowing, and even at that distance it was easy to hear that he was retailing, blow by blow, his current exploits as a game fisherman. They found a table, and as Causton ordered drinks in perfect and fluent French which the waiter could not understand, Wyatt claimed Julie for a dance.

They had always danced well together but this time there seemed to be a stiffness and a tension between them. It was not the fault of the orchestra, poor though it was, for while the tune was weird, the rhythm was perfect. They danced in silence for a while, then Julie looked up and said softly, 'Hello, Dave. Seen any good hurricanes lately?'

'See one, you've seen them all,' he said lightly. 'And you?'

'About the same. One flight is very like another. Same places, same air, same passengers. I sometimes swear that the air traveller is a different breed from the rest of us common humanity; like Dawson – that man over there.'

Wyatt listened to the raucous voice spinning its interminable fishing yarn. 'You know him?'

'Don't you?' she said in surprise. 'That's Dawson, the writer – Big Jim Dawson. Everyone's heard of him. He's one of the regulars on my flight, and a damn' nuisance he is, too.'

'I've heard of him,' said Wyatt. Julie was right – there could not have been a corner of the world where the name of Big Jim Dawson was not known. He was supposed to be a pretty good writer, although Wyatt did not feel himself equipped to judge; at any rate, the critics appeared to think so.

He looked down at Julie and said, 'You don't appear to find Causton a nuisance.'

'I like him. He's one of these polite, imperturbable Englishmen we're always reading about – you know, the quiet kind with hidden depths.'

'Is he one of your regulars?'

'I met him for the first time on my last flight. I certainly didn't expect to find him here in San Fernandez.'

'You certainly went out of your way to make him feel at home,'

'That was just hospitality – looking after a stranger in a strange land.' Julie looked up with a mischievous glint in her eye. 'Why, Mr Wyatt, I do believe you're jealous.'

'I might be,' said Wyatt bluntly. 'If I had anything to be jealous about.'

Julie dropped her eyes and went a little pale. They danced in stiff silence until the melody was finished, then turned to go back to their table, but Julie was whirled away by the exuberant Hansen. 'Julie Marlowe! What are you doing in this dump? I'm stealing her, Davy Boy, but I'll return her intact.' He swept her on to the floor in a caricatured rumba, and Wyatt returned glumly to Causton.

'Powerful stuff,' said Causton, holding a bottle to the light. He waved it. 'Have one?'

Wyatt nodded. He watched Causton fill his glass, and said abruptly, 'Here on business?'

'Good lord, no!' said Causton. 'I was due for a week's holiday, and since I was in New York, I decided to come down here.'

Wyatt glanced at Causton's shrewd eyes and wondered how far that was true. He said, 'There's not much here for a holiday; you'd have been better off in the Bermudas.'

'Maybe,' said Causton non-committally. 'Tell me something about San Fernandez. Does it have a history?'

Wyatt smiled sourly. 'The same as any other Caribbean island – but a bit more so. First it was Spanish, then English, and finally French. The French made the deepest impression – you can see that in the language – although you do find the natives referring to St Pierre and San Pedro and Peter's Port, and the language is the most mixed-up you've heard.'

Causton nodded ruefully, thinking of his recent difficulties with the waiter.

Wyatt said, 'When Toussaint and Cristophe threw the French out of Haiti at the beginning of the 1800s, the locals here did the same, though it hasn't had the same publicity.'

'Um,' said Causton. 'How did an American base get here?'

'That happened at the turn of this century,' said Wyatt. 'Round about the time the Americans were flexing their muscles. They found they were strong enough to make the Monroe Doctrine stick, and they'd just got over a couple of wars which proved it. There was a lot of talk about "Manifest Destiny" and the Yanks thought they had a big brotherly right to supervise other people's business in this part of the world. San Fernandez was in pretty much of a mess in 1905 with riots and bloody revolution, so the Marines were sent ashore. The island was American administered until 1917 and then the Americans pulled out – but they hung on to Cap Sarrat.'

'Didn't something of the sort happen in Haiti as well?'

'It's happened in most of the islands – Cuba, Haiti, the Dominican Republic'

Causton grinned. 'It's happened more than once in the Dominican Republic.' He sipped his drink. 'I suppose Cap Sarrat is held under some kind of treaty?'

'I suppose you could call it that,' agreed Wyatt. 'The Americans leased the Cap in 1906 for one thousand gold dollars a year – not a bad sum for those days – but depreciation doesn't work in favour of San Fernandez. President Serrurier now gets $1693.' Wyatt paused. 'And twelve cents,' he added as an afterthought.

Causton chuckled. 'Not a bad bit of trading on the part of the Americans – a bit sharp, though.'

'They did the same in Cuba with Guantanamo Base,' said Wyatt. 'Castro gets twice as much – but I think he'd rather have Guantanamo and no Americans.'

'I'll bet he would.'

'The Navy is trying to build up Cap Sarrat as a substitute for Guantanamo in case Castro gets uppity and takes it from them. I suppose there is a possibility that it might happen.'

'There is,' said Causton. 'I don't think he could just take it by force, but a bit of moral blackmail might do it, given the right political circumstances.'

'Anyway, here is Cap Sarrat,' said Wyatt. 'But it's not nearly as good as Guantanamo. The anchorage in Santego Bay is shallow – all it will take is a light cruiser – and the base facilities will take twenty years and a couple of hundred million dollars to even approach Guantanamo. It's very well equipped as an air base, though; that's why we use it as a hurricane research centre.'

'Miss Marlowe was telling me about that –' began Causton, but he was interrupted by the return of Hansen and Julie and he took the opportunity of asking Julie to dance.

'Aren't you going to ask me to have a drink?' demanded Hansen.

'Help yourself,' said Wyatt. He saw Schelling come into the room with another officer. 'Tell me, Harry; how did Schelling come to make Commander in your Navy?'

'Dunno,' said Hansen, sitting down. 'Must be because he's a good meteorologist, because he's an officer like a bull's got tits.'

'Not so good, eh?'

'Hell, one thing an officer's got to do is to lead men, and Schelling couldn't be a Den Mother for a troop of Girl Scouts. He must have got through on the specialist side.'

'Let me tell you something,' said Wyatt, and told Hansen about his conversation that morning with Schelling. He ended up by saying, 'He thinks that meteorology is an exact science and that what the textbooks say is so. People like that frighten me.'

Hansen laughed. 'Dave, you've come across a type of officer that's not uncommon in the good old USN. The Pentagon is swarming with them. He goes by the book for one reason and one reason only – because if he goes by the book he can never be proved wrong, and an officer who is never wrong is regarded as a good, safe man to have around.'

'Safe!' Wyatt almost lost his voice. 'In his job he's about as safe as a rattlesnake.The man has lives in his hands.'

'Most Navy officers have men's lives in their hands at one time or another,' said Hansen. 'Look, Dave, let me tell you the way to handle guys like Schelling. He's got a closed mind, and you can't go through him – he's too solid. So you go round him.'

'It's a bit difficult for me,' said Wyatt. 'I have no status. I'm not a Navy man – I'm not even an American. He's the chap who reports to the Weather Bureau, and he's the chap they'll believe.'

'You're getting pretty steamed up about this, aren't you? What's on your mind?'

'I'm damned if I know,' admitted Wyatt. 'It's just that I've got a funny feeling that things are going to go wrong.'

'You're worried about Mabel?'

'I think it's Mabel – I'm not too sure.'

'I was worried about Mabel when I was rumbling about in her guts,' said Hansen. 'But I'm pretty relaxed about her now.'

Wyatt said, 'Harry, I was born out here and I've seen some pretty funny things. I remember once, when I was a kid, we had news that a hurricane was coming but that we'd be all right, it would miss Grenada by two hundred miles. So nobody worried except the people up in the hills, who never got the warning anyway. There's a lot of Carib Indian in those people and they've had their roots down in the Caribbean for thousands of years. They battened down the hatches and dug themselves in. When that hurricane came up to Grenada it made a right-angle swerve and pretty near sank the island. Now how did those hill people know the hurricane was going to swerve like that?'

'They had a funny feeling,' said Hansen. 'And they had the sense to act on it. It's happened to me. I was once fly-ing in a cloud when I got that feeling, so I pushed the stick forward a bit and lost some height. Damned if a civilian ship – one of those corporation planes – didn't occupy the air space I'd been in. He missed me by a gnat's whisker.'

Wyatt shrugged. 'As a scientist I'm supposed to go by the things I can measure, not by feelings. I can't show my feelings to Schelling.'

'To hell with Schelling,' said Hansen. 'Dave, I don't think there's a competent research scientist alive who hasn't gone ahead on a hunch. I still say you should bypass Schelling. What about seeing the Commodore?'

'I'll see how Mabel behaves tomorrow,' said Wyatt. 'I want to see if she's a really bad girl.'

'Don't forget your feelings about her,' said Hansen.

Julie's cool voice spoke from behind Wyatt. 'Do you really have feelings for this bad girl, Mabel?'

Hansen laughed and began to get up, but Julie waved him down. 'I'm having my feet danced off, and I haven't had a drink yet. Let's sit this one out.' She looked at Wyatt. 'Who's Mabel?'

Hansen chuckled. 'One of Dave's girls. He's got a string of them. Dave, remember Isobel last year? You certainly had fun and games with her.'

Wyatt said, 'She roughed you up a bit, if I remember rightly.'

'Ah, but I escaped from her clutches.'

Causton snapped his fingers and said with sudden perception, 'You're talking about hurricanes, aren't you?'

Julie said with asperity, 'Why must they give girls' names to hurricanes?'

'They're easy to remember,' said Wyatt with a straight face. 'And so hard to forget. I believe the Association of Women's Clubs of America put in an objection to the Weather Bureau, but they were overruled. One round won in the battle of the sexes.'

'I'd be interested to see your work,' said Causton. 'From a professional point of view, that is.'

'I thought you were on holiday.'

'Newspapermen are never really on holiday – and news is where you find it.'

Wyatt discovered that he rather liked Causton. He said, 'I don't see why you shouldn't come up to the Base.'

Hansen grinned. 'Schelling won't object; he's a sucker for publicity – of the right kind.'

'I'd try not to write any unkind words,' said Causton. 'When could I come?'

'What about tomorrow at eleven?' said Wyatt. He turned to Julie. 'Are you interested in my hurricanes? Why don't you come too?' He spoke impersonally.

'Thank you very much,' she said, equally impersonally.

'That's fixed, then,' said Causton. 'I'll bring Miss Marlowe with me – I'm hiring a car.' He turned to Hansen. 'Do you have any trouble with the island government at the Base?'

Hansen's eyes sharpened momentarily, then he said lazily, 'In what way?'

'I gather that Americans aren't entirely popular here. I also understand that Serrurier is a rough lad who plays rough games and he's not too particular about the methods he uses. In fact, some of the stories I've heard give me the creeps – and I'm not a particularly shivery man.'

Hansen said shortly, 'We don't interfere with them and they don't interfere with us – it's a sort of unspoken agreement. The boys on the Base are pretty firmly disciplined about it. There *have* been a few incidents and the Commodore cracked down hard.'

'What kind of – ' Causton began, but a booming voice drowned his question. 'Say, weren't you the hostess on my plane to Puerto Rico?'

Wyatt looked up, shadowed by the bull-like figure of Dawson. He glanced at Julie, whose face was transformed by a bright, professional smile. 'That's right, Mr Dawson.'

'I didn't expect to find you here,' roared Dawson. He seemed incapable of speaking in a normal, quiet tone, but that could have been because he was a little drunk. 'What say you an' me have a drink?' He gestured largely. 'Let's all have a drink.'

Causton said quietly, 'I'm in the chair, Mr Dawson. Will you have a drink with me?'

Dawson bent and looked at Causton, squinting slightly. 'Don't I know you from somewhere?'

'I believe we met – in London.'

Dawson straightened and moved around so he could get a good view of Causton. He pondered rather stupidly for a moment, then snapped his fingers. 'That's right,' he said. 'I know you. You are one of those smart-aleck reporters who roasted me when *The Fire Game* was published in England. I never forget a face, you know. You were one of the guys who came an' drank my liquor, then stuck a knife in my back.'

'I don't believe I had a drink that morning,' observed Causton equably.

Dawson exhaled noisily. 'I don't think I will have a drink with you, Mr Whatever-your-name-is. I'm particular of the company I keep.' He swayed on his feet and his eyes flickered towards Julie. 'Not like some people.'

Both Wyatt and Hansen came to their feet, but Causton said sharply, 'Sit down, you two; don't be damn' fools.'

'Aw, to hell with it,' mumbled Dawson, passing a big hand over his face. He blundered away, knocking over a chair and heading for the lavatories.

'Not a nice man,' said Causton wryly. 'I'm sorry about that.'

Wyatt picked up the fallen chair. 'I thought you were a foreign correspondent?'

'I am,' said Causton. 'But I was in London a couple of years ago when half the staff was down with influenza, and I helped out on local stuff for a while.' He smiled. 'I'm not a literary critic, so I wrote a story on the man, not the writer. Dawson didn't like it one little bit.'

'I don't like Dawson one little bit,' said Hansen. 'He sure is the Ugly American.'

'The funny thing about him is that he's a good writer,' said Causton. 'I like his stuff, anyway; and I'm told that his critical reputation is very high. The trouble is that he thinks that the mantle of Papa Hemingway has fallen on his shoulders – but I don't think it's a very good fit.'

Wyatt looked at Julie. 'How much of a nuisance was he?' he asked softly.

'Air hostesses are taught to look after themselves,' she said lightly, but he noticed she did not smile.

The incident seemed to cast a pall over the evening. Julie did not want to dance any more so they left quite early. After taking Julie and Causton back to the Imperiale, Wyatt gave Hansen a lift back to the Base.

They were held up almost immediately in the Place de la Libération Noire. A convoy of military trucks rumbled across their path followed by a battalion of marching infantry. The troops were sweating under their heavy packs and their black faces shone like shoe-leather in the street lighting.

Hansen said, 'The natives are restless tonight; those boys are in war trim. Something must be happening.'

Wyatt looked around. The big square, usually crowded even at this time of night, was bare except for groups of police and the unmistakable plainclothes men of Serrurier's security force. The cheerful babble of sound that pervaded this quarter was replaced by the tramp of marching men. All the cafés were closed and shuttered and the square looked dark and grim.

'Something's up,' he agreed. 'We had this before – six months ago. I never did find out why.'

'Serrurier always was a nervous type,' said Hansen. 'Frightened of shadows. They say he hasn't been out of the Presidential Palace for over a year.'

'He's probably having another nightmare,' said Wyatt.

The column of marching men came to an end and he let in the clutch and drove round the square, past the impossibly heroic bronze statue of Serrurier and on to the road that led to the Base. All the way to Cap Sarrat he thought of Julie and the way she had behaved.

He also thought a little of Mabel.

TWO

Causton was up early next morning, and after a token breakfast he checked a couple of addresses in his notebook, then went into the town. When he arrived back at the Imperiale to pick up Julie he was very thoughtful and inclined to be absent-minded, so there was little conversation as they drove to Cap Sarrat in the car he had hired. They were halted briefly at the gates of the Base, but a telephone call from the guardroom soon released them, and a marine led them to Wyatt's office.

Julie looked curiously at the charts on the walls and at the battered desk and the scuffed chairs. 'You don't go in for frills.'

'This is a working office,' said Wyatt. 'Please sit down.'

Causton examined a wall chart with some misgivings. 'I'm always baffled by boffins,' he complained. 'They usually make the simplest things sound hellishly complicated. Have mercy on us poor laymen.'

Wyatt laughed, but spoke seriously. 'It's the other way round, you know. Our job is to try to define simply what are really very complex phenomena.'

'Try to stick to words of one syllable,' pleaded Causton. 'I hear you went to look at a hurricane at first hand the other day. It was more than a thousand miles from here – how did you know it was there?'

'That's simple to explain. In the old days we didn't know a hurricane had formed until it was reported by a ship or from an island – but these days we're catching them earlier.' Wyatt spread some photographs on the desk. 'We get photographs from satellites – either from the latest of the Tiros series or from the newer Nimbus polar orbit satellites.'

Julie looked at the photographs uncomprehendingly and Wyatt interpreted. 'This tells us all we need to know. It gives us the time the photograph was taken – here, in this corner. This scale down the edge gives the size of what we're look-ing at – this particular hurricane is about three hundred miles across. And these marks indicate latitude and longi-tude – so we know exactly where it is. It's simple, really.'

Causton flicked the photograph. 'Is this the hurricane you're concerned with now?'

'That's right,' said Wyatt. 'That's Mabel. I've just finished working out her present position and her course. She's a lit-tle less than six hundred miles south-east of here, moving north-west on a course that agrees with theory at a little more than ten miles an hour.'

'I thought hurricanes were faster than that,' said Julie in surprise.

'Oh, that's not the wind-speed; that's the speed at which the hurricane as a whole is moving over the earth's surface. The wind-speeds inside this hurricane are particularly high – in excess of 170 miles an hour.'

Causton had been thinking deeply. 'I don't think I like the sound of this. You say this hurricane is south-east of here, and it's moving north-west. That sounds as though it's heading directly for us.'

'It is,' said Wyatt. 'But fortunately hurricanes don't move in straight lines; they move in curves.' He paused, then took a large flat book from a near-by table. 'We plot the paths of all hurricanes, of course, and try to make sense of them.

Sometimes we succeed. Let me see – 1955 gives an interesting variety.'

He opened the book, turned the leaves, then stopped at a chart of the Western Atlantic. 'Here's 1955. Flora and Edith are textbook examples – they come in from the southeast then curve to the north-east in a parabola. This path is dictated by several things. In the early stages the hurricane is really trying to go due north but is forced west because of the earth's rotation. In the latter stages it is forced back east again because it comes under the influence of the North Atlantic wind system.'

Causton looked closely at the chart. 'What about this one?'

Wyatt grinned. 'I thought you'd spot Alice. She went south and ended up in North Brazil – we still don't know why. Then there's Janet and Hilda – they didn't curve back according to theory and went clear across the Yucatan and into North Mexico and Texas. They killed a lot of people.'

Causton grunted. 'It seems to me there's something wrong with your theory. What about this wiggly one?'

'Ione? I was talking about her only yesterday. It's true she wriggled like a snake, but if you smooth her course you'll see that she fits the theoretical pattern. But we still don't know exactly what makes a hurricane change course sharply like that. I have an idea it may be because it's influenced in some way by a high-altitude jet stream, but that's difficult to tie in because a hurricane is very shallow – it doesn't extend more than a few thousand feet up. That's why contact with land destroys it – it will batter itself to death against a ridge, but it does a lot of damage in the process.'

Julie looked at the lines crawling across the chart. 'They're like big animals, aren't they? You'd swear that Ione wanted to destroy Cape Hatteras, then turned away because she didn't like the land.'

'I wish they were intelligent,' said Wyatt. 'Then we might have a bit of luck in predicting what they're going to do next.'

Causton had his notebook out. 'Next thing – what causes hurricanes?'

Wyatt leaned back in his chair. 'You need a warm sea and still air, and you will find those conditions in the doldrums in the late summer. The warm air rises, heavy and humid, full of water vapour. Its place is taken by air rushing in from the sides, and, because of the earth's rotation, this moving air is given a twist so that the whole system begins to revolve.'

He sketched it on a scrap pad. 'The warm air that is rising meets cooler air and releases its water vapour in the form of rain. Now, it has taken a lot of energy for the air to have lifted that water vapour in the first place, and this energy is now released as heat. This increases the rate of ascent of the air – the whole thing becomes a kind of vicious circle. More water is released and thus more heat, and the whole thing goes faster and faster and becomes much bigger. As much as a million tons of air may be rising each second.'

He drew arrows on the scrap pad, spiralling inwards. 'Because the wind system is revolving, centrifugal force tends to throw the air outwards, and so the pressure in the centre becomes very low, thus forming the eye of the hurricane. But the pressure on the outside is very high and something must give somewhere. So the wind moves faster and faster in an attempt to fill that low pressure area, but the faster it moves the more the centrifugal force throws it outwards. And so we have these very fast circular winds and a fully fledged hurricane is born.'

He drew another arrow, this one moving in a straight line. 'Once established, the hurricane begins to move forward, like a spinning top that moves along the ground. This brings it in contact with more warm sea and air and the process becomes self-sustaining. A hurricane is a vast heat engine, the biggest and most powerful dynamic system on earth.' He nodded to the chart on the wall. 'Mabel, there, has more power in her than a thousand hydrogen bombs.'

'You sound as though you've fallen in love with hurricanes,' said Julie softly.

'Nonsense!' Wyatt said sharply. 'I hate them. All West Indians hate them.'

'Have you had a hurricane here – in San Fernandez?' asked Causton.

'Not in my time.' said Wyatt. 'The last one to hit San Fernandez was in 1910. It flattened St Pierre and killed 6,000 people.'

'One hurricane in nearly sixty years,' mused Causton. 'Tell me – I ask out of personal interest – what is the likelihood of your friend Mabel coming this way?'

Wyatt smiled. 'It *could* happen, but it's not very likely.'

'Um,' said Causton. He looked at the wall chart. 'Still, I'd say that Serrurier is a much more destructive force than any of your hurricanes. At the last count he's caused the death of more than 20,000 people on this island. A hurricane might be pleasanter if it could get rid of him.'

'Possibly,' said Wyatt. 'But that's out of my province. I'm strictly non-political.' He began to talk again about his work until he saw their interest was flagging and they were becoming bored with his technicalities, and then he suggested they adjourn for lunch.

They lunched in the Officers' Mess, where Hansen, who was to join them, was late and apologetic. 'Sorry, folks, but I've been busy.' He sat down and said to Wyatt, 'Someone's got a case of jitters – all unserviceable aircraft to be made ready for flight on the double. They fixed up my Connie pretty fast; I did the ground tests this morning and I'll be taking her up this afternoon to test that new engine.' He groaned in mock pain. 'And I was looking forward to a week's rest.'

Causton was interested. 'Is it anything serious?'

Hansen shrugged. 'I wouldn't say so – Brooksie isn't the nervous type.'

'Brooksie?'

'Commodore Brooks – Base Commander.'

Wyatt turned to Julie and said in a low voice, 'What are you doing for the rest of the day?'

'Nothing much – why?'

'I'm tired of office work.' he said. 'What about our going over to St Michel? You used to like that little beach we found, and it's a good day for swimming.'

'That sounds a good idea,' she agreed. 'I'd like that.'

'We'll leave after lunch.'

'How's Mabel?' asked Hansen across the table.

'Nothing to report.' said Wyatt. 'She's behaving herself. She just missed Grenada as predicted. She's speeded up a bit, though; Schelling wasn't too happy about that.'

'Not with the prediction he made.' Hansen nodded. 'Still, he'll have covered himself – you can trust him for that.'

Causton dabbed at the corner of his mouth with his napkin. 'To change the subject – have any of you heard of a man called Favel?'

'Julio Favel?' said Hansen blankly. 'Sure – he's dead.'

'Is he now!'

'Serrurier's men caught up with him in the hills last year. There was a running battle – Favel wasn't going to be taken alive – and he was killed. It was in the local papers at the time.' He quirked an eyebrow at Causton. 'What's the interest?'

'The rumour is going about that Favel is still alive,' said Causton. 'I heard it this morning.'

Hansen looked at Wyatt, and Wyatt said, 'That explains Serrurier's nightmare last night.' Causton lifted his eyebrows, and Wyatt said, 'There was a lot of troop movement in the town last night.'

'So I saw,' said Causton. 'Who was Favel?'

'Come off it,' said Wyatt. 'You're a newspaperman – you know as well as I do.'

Causton grinned. 'I like to get other people's views,' he said without a trace of apology. 'The objective view, you know; as a scientist you should appreciate that.'

Julie said in bewilderment, 'Who was this Favel?'

Causton said, 'A thorn in the side of Serrurier. Serrurier, being the head of government, calls him a bandit; Favel preferred to call himself a patriot. I think the balance is probably on Favel's side. He was hiding in the hills doing quite a bit of damage to Serrurier before he was reported killed. Since then there has been nothing – until now.'

'I don't believe he's alive,' said Hansen. 'We'd have heard about it before now.'

'He might have been intelligent enough to capitalize on the report of his death – to lie low and accumulate strength unworried by Serrurier.'

'Or he might have been ill,' said Wyatt.

'True,' said Causton. 'That might be it.' He turned to Hansen. 'What do you think?'

'All I know is what I read in the newspapers,' said Hansen. 'And my French isn't too good – not the kind of French these people write.' He leaned forward. 'Look, Mr Causton; we're under military discipline here at Cap Sarrat, and the orders are not to interfere in local affairs – not even to appear interested. If we don't keep our noses clean we're in trouble. If we survive Serrurier's strong-arm boys, then Commodore Brooks takes our hides off. There have been a few cases, you know, mostly among the enlisted men, and they've got shipped back to the States with a big black demerit to spend a year or two in the stockade. I was going to tell you this last night when that guy Dawson busted in.'

'I'm sorry,' said Causton. 'I apologize. I didn't realize the difficulties you people must have here.'

'That's all right,' said Hansen. 'You weren't to know. But I might as well tell you that one thing that is specifically discouraged is talking too freely to visiting newsmen.'

'Nobody likes us,' said Causton plaintively.

'Sure,' said Hansen. 'Everyone has something to hide – but our reasons are different. We're trying to avoid stirring up any trouble. You know as well as I do – where you find a newsman you find trouble.'

'I rather think it's the other way round,' said Causton gently. 'Where you find trouble you find a newsman – the trouble comes first.' He changed the subject abruptly. 'Speaking of Dawson, I find that he's staying at the Imperiale. When Miss Marlowe and I left this morning he was nursing a hangover and breakfasting lightly off one raw egg and the juice of a whisky bottle.'

Wyatt said, 'You're not really on holiday, are you, Causton?'

Causton sighed. 'My boss thinks I am. Coming here was a bit of private enterprise on my part. I heard rumours and rumours of rumours. For instance, arms traffic to this part of the world has been running high lately. The stuff hasn't been going to Cuba or South America as far as I can find out, but it's being absorbed somewhere. I put it to my boss, but he didn't agree with my reasoning, or, as he put it, my non-reasoning. However, I have great faith in myself so I took a busman's holiday and here I am.'

'And have you found what you're looking for?'

'You know, I really fear I have.'

II

Wyatt drove slowly through the suburbs of St Pierre, hampered by the throngs in the streets. The usual half-naked small boys diced with death before the wheels of his car, shrieking with laughter as he blew his horn; the bullock carts and sagging trucks created their usual traffic jams, and the chatter of the crowds was deafening – the situation was normal and Wyatt relaxed as he got out of the town and was able to increase speed.

The road to St Michel wound up from St Pierre through the lush Negrito Valley, bordered with banana, pineapple and sugar plantations and overlooked by the frowning heights of the Massif des Saints. 'It seems that last night's disturbance was a false alarm,' said Wyatt. 'In spite of what Causton said this morning.'

'I don't know if I really like Causton, after all,' said Julie pensively. 'Newspaper reporters remind me of vultures, somehow.'

'I have a fellow feeling for him,' said Wyatt. 'He makes a living out of disaster – so do I.'

She was shocked. 'It's not the same at all. At least you are trying to minimize disaster.'

'So is he, according to his lights. I've read some of his stuff and it's very good; full of compassion at the damn' silliness of the human race. I think he was truly sorry to find out he was right about the situation here – if he is right, of course. I hope to God he isn't.'

She made an impatient movement with her shoulders. 'Let's forget about him, shall we? Let's forget about him and Serrurier and – what's-his-name – Favel.'

He slowed to avoid a wandering bullock cart loaded with rocks and jerked his head back at the armed soldier by the road. 'It's not so easy to forget Serrurier with that sort of thing going on.'

Julie looked back. 'What is it?'

'The *corvé* – forced labour on the roads. All the peasants must do it. It's a hangover from pre-revolutionary France which Serrurier makes pay most handsomely. It has never stopped on San Fernandez.' He nodded to the side of the road. 'It's the same with these plantations; they were once owned by foreign companies – American and French mostly. Serrurier nationalized the lot by expropriation when he came to power. He runs them as his own private preserve with convict labour – and it doesn't take much to become a convict on this island, so he's never short of workers. They're becoming run down now.'

She said in a low voice, 'How can you bear to live here – in the middle of all this unhappiness?'

'My work is here, Julie. What I do here helps to save lives all over the Caribbean and in America, and this is the best place to do it. I can't do anything about Serrurier; if I tried I'd be killed, gaoled or deported and that would do no one any good. So, like Hansen and everyone else, I stick close to the Base and concentrate on my own job.'

He paused to negotiate a bad bend. 'Not that I like it, of course.'

'So you wouldn't consider moving out – say, to a research job in the States?'

'I'm doing my best work here,' said Wyatt. 'Besides, I'm a West Indian – this is my home, poor as it is.'

He drove for several miles and at last pulled off the road on to the verge. 'Remember this?'

'I couldn't forget it,' she said, and left the car to look at the panorama spread before her. In the distance was the sea, a gleaming plate of beaten silver. Immediately below were the winding loops of the dusty road they had just ascended and between the road and the sea was the magnificent Negrito Valley leading down to Santego Bay with Cap Sarrat on the far side and St Pierre, a miniature city, nestling in the curve of the bay.

Wyatt did not look at the view – he found Julie a more satisfying sight as she stood on the edge of the precipitous drop with the trade wind blowing her skirt and moulding the dress to her body. She pointed across the valley to where the sun reflected from falling water. 'What's that?'

'La Cascade de l'Argent – it's on the P'tit Negrito.' He walked across and joined her. 'The P'tit Negrito joins the Gran' Negrito down in the valley. You can't see the confluence from here.'

She took a deep breath. 'It's one of the most wonderful sights I've ever seen. I wondered if you'd show it to me again.'

'Always willing to oblige,' he said. 'Is this why you came back to San Fernandez?'

She laughed uncertainly. 'One of the reasons.'

He nodded. 'It's a good reason. I hope the others are as good.'

Her voice was muffled because she had dropped her head. 'I hope so, too.'

'Aren't you sure?'

She lifted her head and looked him straight in the eye. 'No, Dave, I'm not sure. I'm not sure at all.'

He put his hands on her shoulders and drew her to him. 'A pity,' he said, and kissed her. She came, unresisting, into his arms and her lips parted under his. He felt her arms go about him closer, until at last she broke away.

'I don't know about that,' she said. 'I'm still not sure – but I'm not sure about being not sure.'

He said, 'How would you like to live here – on San Fernandez?'

Julie looked at him warily. 'Is that a proposition?'

'I suppose you could call it a proposal,' Wyatt said, rubbing the side of his jaw. 'I couldn't go on living at the Base, not with you giving up the exotic life of an air hostess, so we'd have to find a house. How would you like to live somewhere up here?'

'Oh, Dave, I'd like that very much,' she cried, and they were both incoherent for a considerable time.

After a while Wyatt said, 'I don't understand why you were so standoffish; you clung on to Causton like a blood brother last night.'

'Damn you, Dave Wyatt,' Julie retorted. 'I was scared. I was chasing a man and women aren't supposed to do that. I got cold feet at the last minute and was frightened of making a fool of myself.'

'So you did come here to see me?'

She ruffled his hair. 'You don't see much in people, do you, Dave? You're so wrapped up in your hurricanes and formulas. Of course I came to see you.' She picked up his hand and examined the fingers one by one. 'I've been out with lots of guys and sometimes I've wondered if this time it was the *one* – women do think that way, you know. And every time you got in the way of my thinking, so I knew I had to come back to straighten it out. I had to have you in my heart altogether or I had to get you out of my system completely – if I could. And you kept writing those deadpan letters of yours which made me want to scream.'

He grinned. 'I was never very good at writing passion. But I see I've been properly caught by a designing woman, so let's celebrate.' He walked over to the car. 'I filled a Thermos with your favourite tipple – Planter's Punch. I departed from the strict formula in the interests of sobriety and the time of day – this has less rum and more lime. It's quite refreshing.'

They sat overlooking the Negrito and sampled the punch. Julie said, 'I don't know much about you, Dave. You said last night that you were born in St Kitts – where's that?'

Wyatt waved. 'An island over to the south-east. It's really St Christopher, but it's been called St Kitts for the last four hundred years. Christophe, the Black Emperor of Haiti, took his name from St Kitts – he was a runaway slave. It's quite a place.'

'Has your family always lived there?'

'We weren't aborigines, you know, but there have been Wyatts on St Kitts since the early sixteen hundreds. They were planters, fishermen – sometimes pirates, so I'm told – a motley crowd.' He sipped the punch. 'I'm the last Wyatt of St Kitts.'

'That's a shame. What happened?'

'A hurricane in the middle of the last century nearly did for the island. Three-quarters of the Wyatts were killed; in fact, three-quarters of the population were wiped out. Then came the period of depression in the Caribbean – competition from Brazilian coffee, East African sugar and so on, and the few Wyatts that were left moved out. My parents hung on until just after I was born, then they moved down to Grenada where I grew up.'

'Where's Grenada?'

'South along the chain of islands, north of Trinidad. Just north of Grenada are the Grenadines, a string of little islands which are as close to a tropical paradise as you'll find in the Caribbean. I'll take you down there some day. We lived on one of those until I was ten. Then I went to England.'

'Your parents sent you to school there, then?'

He shook his head. 'No, they were killed. There was another hurricane. I went to live with an aunt in England; she brought me up and saw to my schooling.'

Julie said gently, 'Is that why you hate hurricanes?'

'I suppose it is. We've got to get down to controlling the damn' things some time, and I thought I'd do my bit. We can't do much yet beyond organizing early warning systems and so on, but the time will come when we'll be able to stop a hurricane in its tracks, powerful though it is. There's quite a bit of work being done on that.' He smiled at her. 'Now you know all about David Wyatt.'

'Not all, but there's plenty of time for the rest,' she said contentedly.

'What about your life story?'

'That will have to wait, too,' she said, pushing away his
questing hand and jumping up. 'What about that swim you
promised?'

They got into the car and Julie stared up at the viridian-
green hills of the Massif des Saints. Wyatt said, 'That's bad
country – infertile, pathless, disease-ridden. It's where Favel
held out until he was killed. An army could get lost up
there – in fact, several have.'

'Oh! When was this?'

'The first time was when Bonaparte tried to crush the
Slave Revolt. The main effort was in Haiti, of course, but as
a side-issue Le Clerc sent a regiment to San Fernandez to
stifle the slave rebellion here. The regiment landed without
difficulty and marched inland with no great opposition.
Then it marched up there – and never came out.'

'What happened to it?'

Wyatt shrugged. 'Ambushes – snipers – fever – exhaus-
tion. White men couldn't live up there, but the blacks could.
But it swallowed another army – a black one this time – not
very long ago. Serrurier tried to bring Favel to open battle
by sending in three battalions of the army. They never came
out, either; they were on Favel's home ground.'

Julie looked up at the sun-soaked hills and shivered. 'The
more I hear of the history of San Fernandez, the more it ter-
rifies me.'

Wyatt said, 'We West Indians laugh when you Americans
and the Europeans think the Antilles are a tropical paradise.
Why do you suppose New York is flooded with Puerto Ricans
and London with Jamaicans? They are the true centres of
paradise today. The Caribbean is rotten with poverty and
strife and not only San Fernandez, although it's just about as
bad here as it can get.' He broke off and laughed embarrass-
edly. 'I was forgetting you said you would come here to live –
I'm not giving the place much of a build-up, am I?' He was
silent for a few minutes, then said thoughtfully, 'What

you said about doing research in the States makes sense, after all.'

'No, Dave,' said Julie quietly. 'I wouldn't do that to you. I wouldn't begin our lives together by breaking up your job – it wouldn't be any good for either of us. We'll make our home here in San Fernandez and we'll be very happy.' She smiled. 'And how long do I have to wait before I have my swim?'

Wyatt started the car and drove off again. The country changed as they went higher to go over the shoulder of the mountains, plantations giving way to thick tangled green scrub broken only by an occasional clearing occupied by a ramshackle hut. Once a long snake slithered through the dust in front of the slowly moving car and Julie gave a sharp cry of disgust.

'This is a faint shadow of what it's like up in the mountains,' observed Wyatt. 'But there are no roads up there.'

Suddenly he pulled the car to a halt and stared at a hut by the side of the road. Julie also looked at it but could see nothing unusual – it was merely another of the windowless shacks made of rammed earth and with a roughly thatched roof. Near the hut a man was pounding a stake into the hard ground.

Wyatt said, 'Excuse me, Julie – I'd like to talk to that man.'

He got out of the car and walked over to the hut to look at the roof. It was covered by a network of cords made from the local sisal. From the net hung longer cords, three of which were attached to stakes driven into the ground. He went round the hut twice, then looked thoughtfully at the man who had not ceased his slow pounding with the big hammer. Formulating his phrases carefully in the barbarous French these people used, he said, 'Man, what are you doing?'

The man looked up, his black face shiny with sweat. He was old, but how old Wyatt could not tell – it was difficult with these people. He looked to be about seventy years of age, but was probably about fifty. '*Blanc,* I make my house safe.'

Wyatt produced a pack of cigarettes and flicked one out. 'It is hard work making your house safe,' he said carefully.

The man balanced the hammer on its head and took the cigarette which Wyatt offered. He bent his head to the match and, sucking the smoke into his lungs, said, 'Very hard work, *blanc,* but it must be done.' He examined the cigarette. 'American – very good.'

Wyatt lit his own cigarette and turned to survey the hut. 'The roof must not come off,' he agreed. 'A house with no roof is like a man with no woman – incomplete. Do you have a woman?'

The man nodded and puffed on his cigarette.

'I do not see her,' Wyatt persisted.

The man blew a cloud of smoke into the air, then looked at Wyatt with blood-flecked brown eyes. 'She has gone visiting, *blanc.*'

'With all the children?' said Wyatt quietly.

'Yes, *blanc.*'

'And you fasten the roof of your house.' Wyatt tapped his foot. 'You must fear greatly.'

The man's eyes slid away and he shuffled his feet. 'It is a time to be afraid. No man can fight what is to come.'

'The big wind?' asked Wyatt softly.

The man looked up in surprise. 'Of course, *blanc,* what else?' He struck his hands together smartly and let them fly up into the air. 'When the big wind comes – *li tomber boum*'

Wyatt nodded. 'Of course. You do right to make sure of the roof of your house.' He paused. 'How do you know that the wind comes?'

The man's bare feet scuffled in the hot dust and he looked away. 'I know,' he mumbled. 'I know.'

Wyatt knew better than to persist in that line of questioning – he had tried before. He said, 'When does the wind come?'

The man looked at the cloudless blue sky, then stopped and picked up a handful of dust which he dribbled from his fingers. 'Two days,' he said. 'Maybe three days. Not longer.'

Wyatt was startled by the accuracy of this prediction. If Mabel were to strike San Fernandez at all then those were the time limits, and yet how could this ignorant old man know? He said matter-of-factly, 'You have sent your woman and children away.'

'There is a cave in the hills,' the man said. 'When I finish this, I go too.'

Wyatt looked at the hut. 'When you go, leave the door open,' he said. 'The wind does not like closed doors.'

'Of course,' agreed the man. 'A closed door is inhospitable.' He looked at Wyatt with a glint of humour in his eyes. 'There may be another wind, *blanc,* perhaps worse than the hurricane. Favel is coming down from the mountains.'

'But Favel is dead.'

The man shrugged. 'Favel is coming down from the mountains,' he repeated, and swung the hammer again at the top of the stake.

Wyatt walked back to the car and got into the driving seat.

'What was all that about?' asked Julie.

'He says there's a big wind coming so he's tying down the roof of his house. When the big wind comes – *li tomber boum.*'

'What does that mean?'

'A very free translation is that everything is going to come down with a hell of a smash.' Wyatt looked across at the hut and at the man toiling patiently in the hot sun. 'He knows enough to leave his door open, too – but I doubt if I could tell you why.' He turned to Julie. 'I'm sorry, Julie, but I'd like to get back to the Base. There's something I must check.'

'Of course,' said Julie. 'You must do what you must.'

He turned the car round in the clearing and they went down the road. Julie said, 'Harry Hansen told me you were worried about Mabel. Has this anything to do with it?'

He said, 'It's against all reason, of course. It's against everything I've been taught, but I think we're going to get slammed. I think Mabel is going to hit San Fernandez.' He laughed wryly. 'Now I've got to convince Schelling.'

'Don't you think he'll believe you?'

'What evidence can I give him? A sinking feeling in my guts? An ignorant old man tying on his roof? Schelling wants hard facts – pressure gradients, adiabatic rates – figures he can measure and check in the textbooks. I doubt if I'll be able to do it. But I've got to. St Pierre is in no better condition to resist a hurricane than it was in 1910. You've seen the shanty town that's sprung up outside – how long do you suppose those shacks would resist a big wind? And the population has gone up – it's now 60,000. A hurricane hitting now would be a disaster too frightening to contemplate.'

Unconsciously he had increased pressure on the accelerator and he slithered round a corner with tyres squealing in protest. Julie said, 'You won't make things better by getting yourself killed going down this hill.'

He slowed down. 'Sorry, Julie; I suppose I'm a bit worked up.' He shook his head. 'It's the fact that I'm helpless that worries me.'

She said thoughtfully, 'Couldn't you fake your figures or something so that Commodore Brooks would have to take notice? If the hurricane *didn't* come you'd be ruined professionally – but I think you'd be willing to take that chance.'

'If I thought it would work I'd do it,' said Wyatt grimly. 'But Schelling would see through it; he may be stupid but he's not a damn' fool and he knows his job from that angle. It can't be done that way.'

'Then what are you going to do?'

'I don't know,' he said. 'I don't know.'

III

He dropped Julie at the Imperiale and headed back to the Base at top speed. He saw many soldiers in the streets of St Pierre but the fact did not impinge on his consciousness because he was busy thinking out a way to handle Schelling. When he arrived at the main gate of the Base he had still not thought of a way.

He was stopped at the gateway by a marine in full battle kit who gestured with a submachine-gun. 'Out, buddy!'

'What the devil's going on?'

The marine's lips tightened. 'I said, "out".'

Wyatt opened the door and got out of the car, noticing that the marine backed away from him. He looked up and saw that the towers by the gateway were fully manned and that the ugly snouts of machine-guns covered his car.

The marine said, 'Who are you, buster?'

'I'm in the Meteorological Section,' said Wyatt. 'What damned nonsense is all this?'

'Prove it,' said the marine flatly. He lifted the gun sharply as Wyatt made to put his hand to his breast pocket. 'Whatever you're pulling out, do it real slow.'

Slowly Wyatt pulled out his wallet and offered it. 'You'll find identification inside.'

The marine made no attempt to come closer. 'Throw it down.'

Wyatt tossed the wallet to the ground, and the marine said, 'Now back off.' Wyatt slowly backed away and the marine stepped forward and picked up the wallet, keeping a wary eye on him. He flicked it open and examined the contents, then waved to the men in the tower. He held out the wallet and said, 'You seem to be in the clear, Mr Wyatt.'

'What the hell's going on?' asked Wyatt angrily.

The marine cradled the submachine-gun in his arms and stepped closer. 'The brass have decided to hold security exercises, Mr Wyatt. I gotta go through the motions – the Lieutenant is watching me.'

Wyatt snorted and got into his car. The marine leaned against the door and said, 'I wouldn't go too fast through the gate, Mr Wyatt; those guns up there are loaded for real.' He shook his head sadly. 'Someone's gonna get killed on this exercise for sure.'

'It won't be me,' Wyatt promised.

The marine grinned and for the first time an expression of enthusiasm showed. 'Maybe the Lieutenant will get shot in the butt.' He drew back and waved Wyatt on.

As Wyatt drove through the Base to his office he saw that it was an armed camp. All the gun emplacements were manned and all the men in full battle kit. Trucks roared through the streets and, near the Met. Office, a rank of armoured cars were standing by with engines ticking over. For a moment he thought of what the old man had said – Favel is coming down from the mountains. He shook his head irritably.

The first thing he did in his office was to pick up the telephone and ring the clearing office. 'What's the latest on Mabel?'

'Who? Oh – Mabel! We've got the latest shots from Tiros; they came in half an hour ago.'

'Shoot them across to me.'

'Sorry, we can't,' said the tinny voice. 'All the messengers are tied up in this exercise.'

'I'll come across myself,' said Wyatt, and slammed down the phone, fuming at the delay. He drove to the clearing

office, picked up the photographs and drove back, then settled down at his desk to examine them.

After nearly an hour he had come to no firm conclusion.
Mabel was moving along a little faster – eleven miles an
hour – and was on her predicted course. She would
approach San Fernandez no nearer than to give the island a
flick of her tail – a few hours of strong breezes and heavy
rain. That was what theory said.

He pondered what to do next. He had no great faith in
the theory that Schelling swore by. He had seen too many
hurricanes swerve on unpredictable courses, too many
islands swept bare when theory said the hurricane should
pass them by. And he was West Indian – just as much West
Indian as the old black man up near St Michel who was
guarding his house against the big wind. They had a common feeling about this hurricane; a distrust which evi-
denced itself in deep uneasiness. Wyatt's people had been in
the Islands a mere four hundred years, but the black man
had Carib Indian in his ancestry who had worshipped at the
shrine of Hunraken, the Storm God. He had enough faith in
his feelings to take positive steps, and Wyatt felt he could do
no less, despite the fact that he could not prove this thing in
the way he had been trained.

He felt despondent as he went to see Schelling.

Schelling was apparently busy, but then, he always was
apparently busy. He raised his head as Wyatt entered his
office, and said, 'I thought you had a free afternoon.'

'I came back to check on Mabel,' said Wyatt. 'She's
speeded up.'

'Oh!' said Schelling. He put down his pen and pushed the
form-pad away. 'What's her speed now?'

'She's covered a hundred miles in the last nine hours –
about eleven miles an hour. She started at eight – remember?'
Wyatt thought this was the way to get at Schelling – to
communicate some unease to him, to make him remember

that his prediction sent to the Weather Bureau was now at variance with the facts. He said deliberately, 'At her present speed she'll hit the Atlantic Coast in about six days; but I think she'll speed up even more. Her present speed is still under the average.'

Schelling looked down at the desk-top thoughtfully. 'And how's her course?'

This was the tricky one. 'As predicted,' said Wyatt carefully. 'She could change, of course – many have.'

'We'd better cover ourselves,' said Schelling. 'I'll send a signal to the Weather Bureau; they'll sit on it for a couple of days and then announce the Hurricane Watch in the South-Eastern States. Of course, a lot will depend on what she does in the next two days, but they'll know we're on the ball down here.'

Wyatt sat down uninvited. He said, 'What about the Islands?'

'They'll get the warning,' said Schelling. 'Just as usual. Where exactly is Mabel now?'

'She slipped in between Grenada and Tobago,' said Wyatt. 'She gave them a bad time according to the reports I've just been reading, but nothing too serious. She's just north of Los Testigos right now.' He paused. 'If she keeps on her present course she'll go across Yucatan and into Mexico and Texas just like Janet and Hilda did in 1955.'

'She won't do that,' said Schelling irritably. 'She'll curve to the north.'

'Janet and Hilda didn't,' pointed out Wyatt. 'And supposing she *does* curve to the north as she's supposed to do. She only has to swing a little more than theory predicts and we'll have her right on our doorstep.'

Schelling looked up. 'Are you seriously trying to tell me that Mabel might hit San Fernandez?'

'That's right,' said Wyatt. 'Have you issued a local warning?'

Schelling's eyes flickered. 'No, I haven't. I don't think it necessary.'

'You don't think it necessary? I would have thought the example of 1910 would have made it very necessary.'

Schelling snorted. 'You know what the government of this comic opera island is like. We tell them – they do precisely nothing. They've never found it necessary to establish a hurricane warning system – that would be money right out of Serrurier's own pocket. Can you see him doing it? If I warn them, what difference would it make?'

'You'd get it on record,' said Wyatt, playing on Schelling's weakness.

'There is that,' said Schelling thoughtfully. Then he shrugged. 'It's always been difficult to know whom to report to. We have told Descaix, the Minister for Island Affairs, in the past, but Serrurier has now taken that job on himself – and telling Serrurier anything is never easy, you know that.'

'When did this happen?'

'He fired Descaix yesterday – you know what that means. Descaix is either dead or in Rambeau Castle wishing he were dead.'

Wyatt frowned. So Descaix, the chief of the Security Force, was gone – swept away in one of Serrurier's sudden passions of house-cleaning. But Descaix had been his right arm; something very serious must have happened for him to have fallen from power. *Favel is coming dawn from the mountains.* Wyatt shook the thought from him – what had this to do with the violence of hurricanes?

'You'd better tell Serrurier, then,' he said.

Schelling smiled thinly. 'I doubt if Serrurier is in any mood to listen to anything he doesn't want to hear right now.' He tapped on the desk. 'But I'll tell someone in the Palace – just for the record.'

'You've told Commodore Brooks, of course,' said Wyatt idly.

'Er . . . he knows about Mabel. . . yes.'

'He knows *all* about Mabel?' asked Wyatt sharply. 'The type of hurricane she is?'

'I've given him the usual routine reports,' said Schelling stiffly. He leaned forward. 'Look here, Wyatt, you seem to have an obsession about this particular hurricane. Now, if you have anything to say about it – and I want facts – lay it on the line right now. If you haven't any concrete evidence, then for God's sake shut up and get on with your job.'

'You've given Brooks "routine" reports,' repeated Wyatt softly. 'Schelling, I want to see the Commodore.'

'Commodore Brooks – like Serrurier – has no time at the present to listen to weather forecasts.'

Wyatt stood up. 'I'm going to see Commodore Brooks,' he said obstinately.

Schelling was shocked. 'You mean you'd go over my head?'

'I'm going to see Brooks,' repeated Wyatt grimly. 'With you or without you.'

He waited for the affronted outburst and for a moment he thought Schelling was going to explode, but he merely said abruptly, 'Very well, I'll arrange an appointment with the Commodore. You'd better wait in your office until you're called – it may take some time.' He smiled grimly. 'You're not going to make yourself popular, you know.'

'I haven't entered a popularity contest,' said Wyatt evenly. He turned and walked out of Schelling's office, puzzled as to why Schelling should have given in so easily. Then he chuckled bleakly. The reports that Schelling had given Brooks must have been very skimpy, and Schelling couldn't afford to let him see Brooks without getting in his version first. He was probably with Brooks now, spinning him the yarn.

The call did not come for over an hour and a half and he spent the time compiling some interesting statistics for

Commodore Brooks – a weak staff to lean on but all he had, apart from the powerful feeling in his gut that disaster was impending. Brooks would not be interested in his emotions and intuitions.

Brooks's office was the calm centre of a storm. Wyatt had to wait for a few minutes in one of the outer offices and saw the organized chaos that afflicts even the most efficient organization in a crisis, and he wondered if this was just another exercise. But Brooks's office, when he finally got there, was calm and peaceful; Brooks's desk was clean, a vast expanse of polished teak unmarred by a single paper, and the Commodore sat behind it, trim and neat, regarding Wyatt with a stony, but neutral, stare. Schelling stood to one side, his hands behind his back as though he had just been ordered to the stand-easy position.

Brooks said in a level voice, 'I have just heard that there is a technical disputation going on among the Meteorological Staff. Perhaps you will give me your views, Mr Wyatt.'

'We've got a hurricane, sir,' said Wyatt. 'A really bad one. I think there's a strong possibility she may hit San Fernandez. Commander Schelling, I think, disagrees.'

'I have just heard Commander Schelling's views,' said Brooks, confirming the suspicions Wyatt had been entertaining. 'What I would like to hear are your findings. I would point out, however, that pending the facts you are about to give me, I consider the possibility of a hurricane hitting this island to be very remote. The last one, I believe, was in 1910.'

It was evident that he had been given a quick briefing by Schelling.

Wyatt said, 'That's right, sir. The death-roll on that occasion was 6,000.'

Brooks's eyebrows rose. 'As many as that?'

'Yes, sir.'

'Continue, Mr Wyatt.'

Wyatt gave a quick résumé of events since Mabel had been discovered and probed. He said, 'All the evidence shows that Mabel is a particularly bad piece of weather; the pressure gradient is exceptional and the winds generated are remarkably strong. Lieutenant-Commander Hansen said it was the worst weather he had ever flown in.'

Brooks inclined his head. 'Granted that it is a bad hurricane, what evidence have you got that it is going to hit this island? I believe you said that there is a "strong possibility"; I would want more than that, Mr Wyatt – I would want something more in the nature of a probability.'

'I've produced some figures,' said Wyatt, laying a sheaf of papers on the immaculate desk. 'I believe that Commander Schelling is relying on standard theory when he states that Mabel will not come here. He is, quite properly, taking into account the forces that we know act on tropical revolving storms. My contention is that we don't know enough to take chances.'

He spread the papers on the desk. 'I have taken an abstract of information from my records of all the hurricanes of which I have had personal knowledge during the four years I have been here – that would be about three-quarters of those occurring in the Caribbean in that time. I have checked the number of times a hurricane has departed from the path which strict theory dictates and I find that forty-five per cent of the hurricanes have done so, in major and minor ways. To be quite honest about it I prepared another sheet presenting the same information, but confining the study to hurricanes conforming to the characteristics of Mabel. That is, of the same age, emanating from the same area, and so on. I find there is a thirty per cent chance of Mabel diverging from the theoretical path enough to hit San Fernandez.'

He slid the papers across the desk but Brooks pushed them back. 'I believe you, Mr Wyatt,' he said quietly. 'Commander, what do you say to this?'

Schelling said, 'I think statistics presented in this way can be misused – misinterpreted. I am quite prepared to believe Mr Wyatt's figures, but not his reasoning. He says there is a thirty per cent chance of Mabel diverging from her path, and I accept it, but that is not to say that if she diverges she will hit San Fernandez. After all, she *could* go the other way.'

'Mr Wyatt?'

Wyatt nodded. 'That's right, of course; but I don't like it.'

Brooks put his hands together. 'What it boils down to is this: the risk of Mabel hitting us is somewhere between vanishing point and thirty per cent., but even assuming that the worst happens, it's still only a thirty per cent risk. Would that be putting it fairly, Mr Wyatt?'

Wyatt swallowed. 'Yes, sir. But I would like to point out one or two things that I think are pertinent. There was a hurricane that hit Galveston in 1900 and another that hit here in 1910; the high death-roll in each case was due to the same phenomena – floods.'

'From the high rainfall?'

'No, sir; from the construction of a hurricane and from geographical peculiarities.'

He stopped for a moment and Brooks, said, 'Go on, Mr Wyatt. I'm sure the Commander will correct you if you happen to err in your facts.'

Wyatt said, 'The air pressure in the centre of a hurricane drops a lot; this release of pressure on the surface of the sea induces the water to lift in a hump, perhaps ten feet in a normal hurricane. Mabel is not a normal hurricane; her internal air pressure is very low and I would expect the sea level at her centre to rise to twenty feet above normal – perhaps as much as twenty-five feet.'

He turned and pointed through the window. 'If Mabel hits us she'll be coming from due south right into the bay. It's a shallow bay and we know what happens when a tidal wave hits shallow water – it builds up. You can expect flood waters to a height of over fifty feet in Santego Bay. The highest point on Cap Sarrat is, I believe, forty-five feet. You'd get a solid wall of water right over this Base. They had to rebuild the Base in 1910 – luckily there wasn't much to rebuild because the Base hadn't really got going then.'

He looked at Brooks, who said softly, 'Go on, Mr Wyatt. I can see you haven't finished yet.'

'I haven't, sir. There's St Pierre. In 1910 half the population was wiped out – if that happened now you could count on thirty thousand deaths. Most of the town is no higher than Cap Sarrat, and they're no more prepared for a hurricane and floods than they were in 1910.'

Brooks twitched his eyes towards Schelling. 'Well, Commander, can you find fault with anything Mr Wyatt has said?'

Schelling said unwillingly, 'He's quite correct – theoretically. But all this depends on the accuracy of the readings brought back from Mabel by Mr Wyatt and Lieutenant-Commander Hansen.'

Brooks nodded. 'Yes, I think we ought to have another look at Mabel. Commander, will you see to it? I want a plane sent off right away with the best pilot you've got.'

Wyatt said immediately, 'Not Hansen – he's had enough of Mabel.'

'I agree,' said Schelling just as quickly. 'I want a different flight crew and a different technical staff.'

Wyatt stiffened. 'That remark is a reflection on my professional integrity,' he said coldly.

Brooks slammed the palm of his hand on the desk with the noise of a pistol shot. 'It is nothing of the kind,' he rasped. 'There's a difference of opinion between the doctors and I want a third opinion. Is that quite clear?'

'Yes, sir,' said Wyatt.

'Commander, what are you waiting around for? Get that flight organized.' Brooks watched Schelling leave, and as Wyatt visibly hesitated he said, 'Stay here, Mr Wyatt, I want to talk to you.' He tented his fingers and regarded Wyatt closely. 'What would you have me do, Mr Wyatt? What would you do in my position?'

'I'd get my ships out to sea,' said Wyatt promptly, 'loaded with all the Base personnel. I'd fly all aircraft to Puerto Rico. I'd do my damnedest to convince President Serrurier of the gravity of the situation. You should also evacuate all American nationals, and as many foreign nationals as you can.'

'You make it sound easy,' observed Brooks.

'You have two days.'

Brooks sighed. 'It would be easy if that's all there were to it. But a military emergency has arisen. I believe a civil war is going to break out between insurgents from the mountains and the government. That's why this Base is now in an official state of emergency and all American personnel confined to Base. In fact, I have just signed a directive asking all American nationals to come to Cap Sarrat for safety.'

'Favel is coming down from the mountains,' said Wyatt involuntarily.

'What's that?'

'It's what I heard. Favel is coming down from the mountains.'

Brooks nodded. 'That may well be. He may not be dead. President Serrurier has accused the American Government of supplying the rebels with arms. He's a pretty hard man to talk to right now, and I doubt if he'd listen to me chitchatting about the weather.'

'Did the American Government supply the rebels with arms?' asked Wyatt deliberately.

Brooks bristled and jerked. 'Definitely not! It has been our declared policy, explicitly and implicitly, not to interfere with local affairs on San Fernandez. I have strict instructions from my superiors on that matter.' He looked down at the backs of his hands and growled, 'When they sent in the Marines in that affair of the Dominican Republic it set back our South American diplomatic efforts ten years – we don't want that to happen again.'

He suddenly seemed to be aware that he was being indiscreet and tapped his fingers on the desk. 'With regard to the evacuation of this Base: I have decided to stay. The chance of a hurricane striking this island is, on your own evidence, only thirty per cent at the worst. That sort of a risk I can live with, and I feel I cannot abandon this Base when there is a threat of war on this island.' He smiled gently. 'I don't usually expound this way to my subordinates – still less to foreign nationals – but I wish to do the right thing for all concerned, and I also wish to use you. I wish you to deliver a letter to Mr Rawsthorne, the British Consul in St Pierre, in which I am advising him of the position I am taking and inviting any British nationals on San Fernandez to take advantage of the security of this Base. It will be ready in fifteen minutes.'

'I'll take the letter,' said Wyatt.

Brooks nodded. 'About this hurricane – Serrurier may listen to the British. Perhaps you can do something through Rawsthorne.'

'I'll try,' said Wyatt.

'Another thing,' said Brooks. 'In any large organization methods become rigid and channels narrow. There arises a tendency on the part of individuals to hesitate in pressing unpleasant issues. Awkward corners spoil the set of the common coat we wear. I am indebted to you for bringing this matter to my attention.'

'Thank you, sir.'

Brooks's voice was tinged with irony. 'Commander Schelling is a *reliable* officer – I know precisely what to expect of him. I trust you will not feel any difficulty in working with him in the future.'

'I don't think I will.'

'Thank you, Mr Wyatt; that will be all. I'll have the letter for Mr Rawsthorne delivered to your office.'

As Wyatt went back to his own office he felt deep admiration for Brooks. The man was on the horns of a dilemma and had elected to take a calculated risk. To abandon the Base and leave it to the anti-American Serrurier would certainly incur the wrath of his superiors – once Serrurier was in it would be difficult, if not impossible, to get him out. On the other hand, the hurricane was a very real danger and Boards of Inquiry have never been noted for mercy towards naval officers who have pleaded natural disasters as a mitigation. The Base could be lost either way, and Brooks had to make a cold-blooded and necessary decision.

Unhappily, Wyatt felt that Brooks had made the wrong decision.

IV

Under an hour later he was driving through the streets of St Pierre heading towards the dock area where Rawsthorne had his home and his office. The streets were unusually quiet in the fading light and the market, usually a brawl of activity, was closed. There were no soldiers about, but many police moved about in compact squads of four. Not that they had much to do, because the entire town seemed to have gone into hiding behind locked doors and bolted shutters.

Rawsthorne's place was also locked up solid and was only distinguishable from the others by the limp Union Jack which someone had hung from an upper window. Wyatt hammered on the door and it was a long time before a tentative voice said, 'Who's that?'

'My name's Wyatt – I'm English. Let me in.'

Bolts slid aside and the door opened a crack, then swung wider. 'Come in, come in, man! This is no time to be on the streets.'

Wyatt had met Rawsthorne once when he visited the Base. He was a short, stout man who could have been typecast as Pickwick, and was one of the two English merchants on San Fernandez. His official duties as British Consul gave him the minimum of trouble since there was only a scattering of British on the island, and his principal consular efforts were directed to bailing the occasional drunken seaman out of gaol and half-hearted attempts to distribute the literature on Cotswold villages and Morris dancing which was sent to him by the British Council in an effort to promote the British Way of Life.

He now put his head on one side and peered at Wyatt in the gloom of the narrow entrance. 'Don't I know you?'

'We met at Cap Sarrat,' said Wyatt. 'I work there.'

'Of course; you're the weatherman on loan from the Meteorological Office – I remember.'

'I've got a letter from Commodore Brooks.' Wyatt produced the envelope.

'Come into my office,' said Rawsthorne, and led him into a musty, Dickensian room dark with nineteenth-century furniture. A portrait of the Queen gazed across at the Duke of Edinburgh hung on the opposite wall. Rawsthorne slit open the envelope and said, 'I wonder why Commodore Brooks didn't telephone as he usually does.'

Wyatt smiled crookedly. 'He trusts the security of the Base but not that of the outside telephone lines.'

'Very wise,' said Rawsthorne, and peered at the letter. After a while he said, 'That's most handsome of the Commodore to offer us the hospitality of the Base – not that there are many of us.' He tapped the letter. 'He tells me that you have qualms about a hurricane. My dear sir, we haven't had a hurricane here since 1910.'

'So everyone insists on telling me,' said Wyatt bitterly. 'Mr Rawsthorne, have you ever broken your arm?'

Rawsthorne was taken aback. He spluttered a little, then said, 'As a matter of fact, I have – when I was a boy.'

'That was a long time ago.'

'Nearly fifty years – but I don't see . . .'

Wyatt said, 'Does the fact that it is nearly fifty years since you broke your arm mean that you couldn't break it again tomorrow?'

Rawsthorne was silent for a moment. 'You have made your point, young man. I take it you are serious about this hurricane?'

'I am,' said Wyatt with all the conviction he could muster.

'Commodore Brooks is a very honest man,' said Rawsthorne. 'He tells me here that, if you are right, the Base will not be the safest place on San Fernandez. He advises me to take that into account in any decision I might make.' He looked at Wyatt keenly. 'I think you had better tell me all about your hurricane.'

So Wyatt went through it again, with Rawsthorne showing a niggling appreciation of detail and asking some unexpectedly penetrating questions. When Wyatt ran dry he said, 'So what we have is this – there is a thirty per cent chance at worst of this hurricane – so grotesquely named Mabel – coming here. That is on your *figures*. Then there is your overpowering conviction that it *will* come, and I do not think we should neglect that. No, indeed! I have a very great regard for intuition. So what do we do now, Mr Wyatt?'

'Commodore Brooks suggested that we might see Serrurier. He thought he might accept it from a British source when he wouldn't take it from an American.'

Rawsthorne nodded. 'That might very well be the case.'
But he shook his head. 'It will be difficult seeing him, you
know. He is not the easiest man to see at the best of times,
and in the present circumstances . . .'

'We can try,' said Wyatt stubbornly.

'Indeed we can,' Rawsthorne said briskly. 'And we must.'
He looked at Wyatt with brightly intelligent eyes. 'You are a
very convincing young man, Mr Wyatt. Let us go immediately. What decisions I make regarding the safety of British
nationals must inevitably depend on what Serrurier
will do.'

The Presidential Palace was ringed with troops. Fully two
battalions were camped in the grounds and the darkness
was a-twinkle with their camp-fires. Twice the car was
stopped and each time Rawsthorne talked their way
through. At last they came to the final hurdle – the guardroom at the main entrance.

'I wish to see M. Hippolyte, the Chief of Protocol,'
Rawsthorne announced to the young officer who barred
their way.

'But does M. Hippolyte want to see you?' asked the officer insolently, teeth flashing in his black face.

'I am the British Consul,' said Rawsthorne firmly. 'And if
I do not see M. Hippolyte immediately he will be very dis-
pleased.' He paused, then added as though in afterthought,
'So will President Serrurier.'

The grin disappeared from the officer's face at the mention of Serrurier and he hesitated uncertainly. 'Wait here,'
he said harshly and went inside the palace.

Wyatt eyed the heavily armed troops who surrounded
them, and said to Rawsthorne, 'Why Hippolyte?'

'He's our best bet of getting to see Serrurier. He's big
enough to have Serrurier's ear and small enough for me to
frighten – just as I frightened that insolent young pup.'

The 'insolent young pup' came back. 'All right; you can see M. Hippolyte.' He made a curt gesture to the soldiers. 'Search them.'

Wyatt found himself pawed by ungentle black hands. He submitted to the indignity and was then roughly pushed forward through the doorway with Rawsthorne clattering at his heels. 'I'll make Hippolyte suffer for this,' said Rawsthorne through his teeth. 'I'll give him protocol.' He glanced up at Wyatt. 'He speaks English so I can really get my insults home.'

'Forget it,' said Wyatt tightly. 'Our object is to see Serrurier.'

Hippolyte's office was large with a lofty ceiling and elaborate mouldings. Hippolyte himself rose to greet them from behind a beautiful eighteenth-century desk and came forward with outstretched hands. 'Ah, Mr Rawsthorne; what brings you here at a time like this – and at such a late hour?' His voice was pure Oxford.

Rawsthorne swallowed the insults he was itching to deliver and said stiffly, 'I wish to see President Serrurier.'

Hippolyte's face fell. 'I am afraid that is impossible. You must know, Mr Rawsthorne, that you come at a most inopportune time.'

Rawsthorne drew himself up to the most of his insignificant height and Wyatt could almost see him clothing himself in the full awe of British majesty. 'I am here to deliver an official message from Her Britannic Majesty's Government,' he said pompously. 'The message is to be delivered to President Serrurier in person. I rather think he will be somewhat annoyed if he does not get it.'

Hippolyte's expression became less pleasant. 'President Serrurier is . . . in conference. He cannot be disturbed.'

'Am I to report back to my Government that President Serrurier does not wish to receive their message?'

Hippolyte sweated slightly. 'I would not go so far as to say that, Mr Rawsthorne.'

'Neither would I,' said Rawsthorne with a pleasant smile. 'But I would say that the President should be allowed to make up his own mind on this issue. I shouldn't think he would like other people acting in his name – not at all. Why don't you ask him if he's willing to see me?'

'Perhaps that would be best,' agreed Hippolyte unwillingly. 'Could you tell me at least the . . . er . . . subject-matter of your communication?'

'I could not,' said Rawsthorne severely. 'It's a Matter of State.'

'All right,' said Hippolyte. 'I will ask the President. If you would wait here . . .' His voice tailed off and he backed out of the room.

Wyatt glanced at Rawsthorne. 'Laying it on a bit thick, aren't you?'

Rawsthorne mopped his brow. 'If this gets back to Whitehall I'll be out of a job – but it's the only way to handle Hippolyte. The man's in a muck sweat – you saw that. He's afraid to break in on Serrurier and he's even more afraid of what might happen if he doesn't. That's the trouble with the tyranny of one-man rule; the dictator surrounds himself with bags of jelly like Hippolyte.'

'Do you think he'll see us?'

'I should think so,' said Rawsthorne. 'I think I've roused his curiosity.'

Hippolyte came back fifteen minutes later. 'The President will see you. Please come this way.'

They followed him along an ornate corridor for what seemed a full half mile before he stopped outside a door. 'The President is naturally . . . disturbed about the present critical situation,' he said. 'Please do not take it amiss if he is a little . . . er . . . short-tempered, let us say.'

Rawsthorne guessed that Hippolyte had recently felt the edge of Serrurier's temper and decided to twist the knife. 'He'll be even more short-tempered when I tell him how we were treated on our arrival here,' he said shortly. 'Never have I heard of the official representative of a foreign power being searched like a common criminal.'

Hippolyte's sweat-shiny face paled to a dirty grey and he began to say something, but Rawsthorne ignored him, pushed open the door and walked into the room with Wyatt close behind. It was a huge room, sparsely furnished, but in the same over-ornate style as the rest of the palace. A trestle-table had been set up at the far end round which a number of uniformed men were grouped. An argument seemed to be in progress, for a small man with his back to them pounded on the table and shouted, 'You will find them, General; find them and smash them.'

Rawsthorne said out of the corner of his mouth, 'That's Serrurier – with the Army Staff – Deruelles, Lescuyer, Rocambeau.'

One of the soldiers muttered something to Serrurier and he swung round. 'Ah, Rawsthorne, you wanted to tell me something?'

'Come on,' said Rawsthorne, and strode up the length of the room.

Serrurier leaned on the edge of the table which was covered with maps. He was a small, almost insignificant man with hunched shoulders and hollow chest. He had brown chimpanzee eyes which seemed to plead for understanding, as though he could not comprehend why anyone should hate or even dislike him. But his voice was harsh with the timbre of a man who understood power and how to command it.

He rubbed his chin and said, 'You come at a strange time. Who is the *ti blanc*?'

'A British scientist, Your Excellency.'

Serrurier shrugged and visibly wiped Wyatt from the list of people he would care to know. 'And what does the British Government want with me – or from me?'

'I have been instructed to bring you something,' said Rawsthorne.

Serrurier grunted. 'What?'

'Valuable information, Your Excellency. Mr Wyatt is a weather expert – he brings news of an approaching hurricane – a dangerous one.'

Serrurier's jaw dropped. 'You come here at this time to talk about the weather?' he asked incredulously. 'At a time when war is imminent you wish to waste my time with weather forecasting?' He picked up a map from the table and crumpled it in a black fist, shaking it under Rawsthorne's nose. 'I thought you were bringing news of Favel. Favel! Favel – do you understand? He is all that I am interested in.'

'Your Excellency – ' began Rawsthorne.

Serrurier said in a grating voice, 'We do not have hurricanes in San Fernandez – everyone knows that.'

'You had one in 1910,' said Wyatt.

'We do not have hurricanes in San Fernandez,' repeated Serrurier, staring at Wyatt. He suddenly lost his temper. 'Hippolyte! Hippolyte, where the devil are you? Show these fools out.'

'But Your Excellency – ' began Rawsthorne again.

'We do not have hurricanes in San Fernandez,' screamed Serrurier. 'Are you deaf, Rawsthorne? Hippolyte, get them out of my sight.' He leaned against the table, breathing heavily. 'And, Hippolyte, I'll deal with you later,' he added menacingly.

Wyatt found Hippolyte plucking pleadingly at his coat, and glanced at Rawsthorne. 'Come on,' said Rawsthorne bleakly. 'We've delivered our message as well as we're able.'

He walked with steady dignity down the long room, and after a moment's hesitation Wyatt followed, hearing Serrurier's hysterical scream as he left. 'Do you understand, Mr British Scientist? *We do not have hurricanes in San Fernandez!*'

Outside, Hippolyte became vindictive. He considered Rawsthorne had made a fool of him and he feared the retribution of Serrurier. He called a squad of soldiers and Wyatt and Rawsthorne found themselves brutally hustled from the palace to be literally thrown out of the front door.

Rawsthorne examined a tear in his coat. 'I thought it might be like that,' he said. 'But we had to try.'

'He's mad,' said Wyatt blankly. 'He's stark staring, raving mad.'

'Of course,' said Rawsthorne calmly. 'Didn't you know? Lord Acton once said that absolute power corrupts absolutely. Serrurier is thoroughly corrupted in the worst possible way – that's why everyone is so afraid of him. I was beginning to wonder if we'd get out of there.'

Wyatt shook his head as though to clear cobwebs out of his brain. 'He said, "We do not have hurricanes in San Fernandez," as though he has forbidden them by presidential decree.' There was a baffled look on his face.

'Let's get away from here,' said Rawsthorne with an eye on the surrounding soldiers. 'Where's the car?'

'Over there,' said Wyatt. 'I'll take you back to your place – then I must call at the Imperiale.'

There was a low rumble in the distance coming from the mountains. Rawsthorne cocked his head on one side. 'Thunder,' he said. 'Is your hurricane upon us already?'

Wyatt looked up at the moon floating in the cloudless sky. 'That's not thunder,' he said. 'I wonder if Serrurier has found Favel – or vice versa.' He looked at Rawsthorne. 'That's gunfire.'

THREE

It was quite late in the evening when Wyatt pulled up his
car outside the Imperiale. He had had a rough time; the
street lighting had failed or been deliberately extinguished
(he thought that perhaps the power-station staff had
decamped) and three times he had been halted by the suspicious police, his being one of the few cars on the move in
the quiet city. There was a sporadic crackle of rifle fire,
sometimes isolated shots and sometimes minor fusillades,
echoing through the streets. The police and the soldiers
were nervous and likely to shoot at anything that moved.
And behind everything was the steady rumble of artillery
fire from the mountains, now sounding very distinctly on
the heavy night air.

His thoughts were confused as he got out of the car. He did
not know whether he would be glad or sorry to find Julie at
the Imperiale. If she had gone to Cap Sarrat Base then all
decision was taken out of his hands, but if she was still in the
hotel then he would have to make the awkward choice. Cap
Sarrat, in his opinion, was not safe, but neither was getting
mixed up in a civil war between shooting armies. Could he,
on an unsupported hunch, honestly advise anyone – and
especially Julie – not to go to Cap Sarrat?

He looked up at the darkened hotel and shrugged
mentally – he would soon find out what he had to do. He

was about to lock the car when he paused in thought, then he opened up the engine and removed the rotor-arm of the distributor. At least the car would be there when he needed it.

The foyer of the Imperiale was in darkness, but he saw a faint glow from the American Bar. He walked across and halted as a chair clattered behind him. He whirled, and said, 'Who's that?' There was a faint scrape of sound and a shadow flitted across a window; then a door banged and there was silence.

He waited a few seconds, then went on. A voice called from the American Bar, 'Who's that out there?'

'Wyatt.'

Julie rushed into his arms as he stepped into the bar. 'Oh, Dave, I'm glad you're here. Have you brought transport from the Base?'

'I've got transport,' he said. 'But I've not come directly from the Base. Someone was supposed to pick you up, I know that.'

'They came,' she said. 'I wasn't here – none of us were.'

He became aware he was in the centre of a small group. Dawson was there, and Papegaikos of the Maraca Club and a middle-aged woman whom he did not know. Behind, at the bar, the bar-tender clanged the cash register open.

'I was here,' said the woman. 'I was asleep in my room and nobody came to wake me.' She spoke aggressively in an affronted tone.

'I don't think you know Mrs Warmington,'Julie said.

Wyatt nodded an acknowledgement, and said, 'So you're left stranded.'

'Not exactly,' said Julie. 'When Mr Dawson and I came back and found everyone gone we sat around a bit wondering what to do, then the phone rang in the manager's office. It was someone at the Base checking up; he said he'd send a truck for us – then the phone cut off in the middle of a sentence.'

'Serrurier's men probably cut the lines to the Base,' said Wyatt. 'It's a bit dicey out there – they're as nervous as cats. When was this?'

'Nearly two hours ago.'

Wyatt did not like the sound of that but he made no comment – there was no point in scaring anybody. He smiled at Papegaikos. 'Hello, Eumenides, I didn't know you favoured the Imperiale.'

The sallow Greek smiled glumly. 'I was tol' to come 'ere if I wan' to go to the Base.'

Dawson said bluffly, 'That truck should be here any time now and we'll be out of here.' He waved a glass at Wyatt. 'I guess you could do with a drink.'

'It would come in handy,' said Wyatt. 'I've had a hard day.'

Dawson turned. 'Hey, you! Where d'you think you're going?' He bounded forward and seized the small man who was sidling out of the bar. The bartender wriggled frantically, but Dawson held him with one huge paw and pulled him back behind the bar. He looked over at Wyatt and grinned. 'Whaddya know, he's cleaned out the cash drawer, too.'

'Let him go,' said Wyatt tiredly. 'It's no business of ours. All the staff will leave – there was one sneaking out when I came in.'

Dawson shrugged and opened his fist and the bartender scuttled out. 'What the hell! I like self-service bars better.'

Mrs Warmington said briskly, 'Well, now that you're here with a car we can leave for the Base.'

Wyatt sighed. 'I don't know if that's wise. We may not get through. Serrurier's crowd is trigger-happy; they're likely to shoot first and ask questions afterwards – and even if they do ask questions we're liable to get shot.'

Dawson thrust a drink into his hand. 'Hell, we're Americans; we've got no quarrel with Serrurier.'

'We know that, and Commodore Brooks knows it – but Serrurier doesn't. He's convinced that the Americans have supplied the rebels with guns – the guns you can hear now – and he probably thinks that Brooks is just biding his time before he comes out of the Base to stab him in the back.'

He took a gulp of the drink and choked; Dawson had a heavy hand with the whisky. He swallowed hard, and said, 'My guess is that Serrurier has a pretty strong detachment of the army surrounding the Base right now – that's why your transport hasn't turned up.'

Everyone looked at him in silence. At last Mrs Warmington said, 'Why, I *know* Commodore Brooks wouldn't leave us here, not even if he had to order the Marines to come and get us.'

'Commodore Brooks has more to think of than the plight of a few Americans in St Pierre,' said Wyatt coldly. 'The safety of the Base comes first.'

Dawson said intently, 'What makes you think the Base isn't safe, anyway?'

'There's trouble coming,' said Wyatt. 'Not the war, but –'

'Anyone home?' someone shouted from the foyer, and Julie said, 'That's Mr Causton.'

Causton came into the bar. He was limping slightly, there was a large tear in his jacket and his face was very dirty with a cut and a smear of blood on the right cheek. 'Damn' silly of me,' he said. 'I ran out of recording tapes, so I came back to get some more.' He surveyed the small group. 'I thought you'd all be at the Base by now.'

'Communications have been cut,' said Wyatt, and explained what had happened.

'You've lost your chance,' said Causton grimly. 'The Government has quarantined the Base – there's a cordon round it.' He knew them all except Mrs Warmington, and regarded Dawson with a sardonic gleam in his eye. 'Ah, yes,

Mr Dawson; this should be just up your street. Plenty of material here for a book, eh?'

Dawson said, 'Sure, it'll make a good book.' He did not sound very enthusiastic.

'I could do with a hefty drink,' said Causton. He looked at Wyatt. 'That your car outside? A copper was looking at it when I came in.'

'It's quite safe,' said Wyatt. 'What have you been up to?'

'Doing my job,' said Causton matter-of-factly. 'All hell's breaking loose out there. Ah, thank you,' he said gratefully, as Papegaikos handed him a drink. He sank half of it in a gulp, then said to Wyatt, 'You know this island. Supposing you were a rebel in the mountains and you had a large consignment of arms coming in a ship – quite a big ship. You'd want a nice quiet place to land it, wouldn't you? With easy transport to the mountains, too. Where would such a spot be?'

Wyatt pondered. 'Somewhere on the north coast, certainly; it's pretty wild country over there. I'd go for the Campo de las Perlas – somewhere round there.'

'Give the man a coconut,' said Causton. 'At least one shipload of arms was landed there within the last month – maybe more. Serrurier's intelligence slipped up on that one – or maybe they were too late. Oh, and Favel *is* alive, after all.' He patted his pockets helplessly. 'Anyone got a cigarette?'

Julie offered her packet. 'How did you get that blood on your face?'

Causton put his hand to his cheek, then looked with surprise at the blood on his fingertips. 'I was trying to get in to see Serrurier,' he said. 'The guards were a bit rough – one of them didn't take his ring off, or maybe it was a knuckle-duster.'

'I saw Serrurier,' said Wyatt quietly.

'Did you, by God!' exclaimed Causton. 'I wish I'd known; I could have come with you. There are a few questions I'd like to ask him.'

Wyatt laughed mirthlessly. 'Serrurier isn't the kind of man you question. He's a raving maniac. I think this little lot has finally driven him round the bend.'

'What did you want with him?'

'I wanted to tell him that a hurricane is going to hit this island in two days' time. He threw us out and banished the hurricane by decree.'

'Christ!' said Causton. 'As though we don't have enough to put up with. Are you serious about this?'

'I am.'

Mrs Warmington gave a shrill squeak. 'We should get to the Base,' she said angrily. 'We'll be safe on the Base.'

Wyatt looked at her for a moment, then said to Causton in a low voice, 'I'd like to talk to you for a minute.'

Causton took one look at Wyatt's serious face, then finished his drink. 'I have to go up to my room for the tapes; you'd better come with me.'

He got up from the chair stiffly, and Wyatt said to Julie, 'I'll be back in a minute,' then followed him into the foyer. Causton produced a flashlight and they climbed the stairs to the first floor. Wyatt said, 'I'm pretty worried about things.'

'This hurricane?'

'That's right,' said Wyatt, and told Causton about it in a few swift sentences, not detailing his qualms, but treating the hurricane as a foregone conclusion. He said, 'Somehow I feel a responsibility for the people downstairs. I think Julie won't crack, but I'm not too sure about the other woman. She's older and she's nervous.'

'She'll run you ragged if you let her,' said Causton. 'She looks the bossy kind to me.'

'And then there's Eumenides – he's an unknown quantity but I don't know that I'd like to depend on him. Dawson is different, of course.'

Causton's flashlight flickered about his room. 'Is he? Put not your faith in brother Dawson – that's a word to the wise.'

'Oh,' said Wyatt. 'Anyway, I'm in a hell of a jam. I'll have to shepherd this lot to safety somehow, and that means leaving town.'

A cane chair creaked as Causton sat down. 'Now let me get this straight. You say we're going to be hit by a hurricane. When?'

'Two days,' said Wyatt. 'Say half a day either way.'

'And when it comes, the Base is going to be destroyed.'

'For all practical purposes – yes.'

'And so is St Pierre.'

'That's right.'

'So you want to take off for the hills, herding along these people downstairs. That's heading smack into trouble, you know.'

'It needn't be,' said Wyatt. 'We need to get about a hundred feet above sea-level and on the northern side of a ridge – a place like that shouldn't be too difficult to find just outside St Pierre. Perhaps up the Negrito on the way to St Michel.'

'I wouldn't do that,' said Causton definitely. 'Favel will be coming down the Negrito. From the sound of those guns he's already in the upper reaches of the valley.'

'How do we know those are Favel's guns?' said Wyatt suddenly. 'Serrurier has plenty of artillery of his own.'

Causton sounded pained. 'I've done my homework. Serrurier was caught flat-footed. The main part of his artillery was causing a devil of a traffic jam just north of the town not two hours ago. If Favel hurries up he'll capture the lot. Listen to it – he's certainly pouring it on.'

'That shipment of arms you were talking about must have been a big one.'

'Maybe – but my guess is that he's staking everything on one stroke. If he doesn't come right through and capture St Pierre he's lost his chips.'

'If he does, he'll lose his army,' said Wyatt forcibly.

'God, I hadn't thought of that.' Causton looked thought-ful. 'This is going to be damned interesting. Do you suppose he knows about this hurricane?'

'I shouldn't think so,' said Wyatt. 'Look, Causton, we're wasting time. I've got to get these people to safety. Will you help? You seem to know more of what's going on out there than anybody.'

'Of course I will, old boy. But, remember, I've got my own job to do. I'll back you up in anything you say, and I'll come with you and see them settled out of harm's way. But after that I'll have to push off and go about my master's business – my editor would never forgive me if I wasn't in the right place at the right time.' He chuckled. 'I dare say I'll get a good story out of Big Jim Dawson, so it will be worth it.'

They went back to the bar and Causton called out, 'Wyatt's got something very important to tell you all, so gather round. Where's Dawson?'

'He was here not long ago,' said Julie. 'He must have gone out.'

'Never mind,' said Causton. 'I'll tell him myself – I'll look forward to doing that. All right, Mr Wyatt; get cracking.' He sat down and began to thread a spool of tape into the minia-ture recorder he took from his pocket.

Wyatt was getting very tired of repeating his story. He no longer attempted to justify his reasons but gave it to them straight, and when he had finished there was a dead silence. The Greek showed no alteration of expression – perhaps he had not understood; Julie was pale, but her chin came up; Mrs Warmington was white with two red spots burning in her cheeks. She was suddenly voluble. 'This is ridiculous,' she exploded. 'No American Navy Base can be destroyed. I demand that you take me to Cap Sarrat immediately.'

'You can demand until you're blue in the face,' said Wyatt baldly. 'I'm going nowhere near Cap Sarrat.' He turned to Julie. 'We've got to get out of St Pierre and on to high ground, and that may be difficult. But I've got the car and we can all cram into it. And we've got to take supplies – food, water, medical kit and so on. We should find plenty of food in the kitchens here, and we can take soda- and mineral-water from the bar.'

Mrs Warmington choked in fury. 'How far is it to the Base?' she demanded, breathing hard.

'Fifteen miles,' said Causton. 'Right round the bay. And there's an army between here and the Base.' He shook his head regretfully. 'I wouldn't try it, Mrs Warmington; I really wouldn't.'

'I don't know what's the matter with you all,' she snapped. 'These natives wouldn't touch *us* – the Government knows better than to interfere with Americans. I say we should get to the Base before those rebels come down from the hills.'

Papegaikos, standing behind her, gripped her shoulder. 'I t'ink it better you keep your mout' shut,' he said. His voice was soft but his grip was hard, and Mrs Warmington winced. 'I t'ink you are fool woman.' He looked across at Wyatt. 'Go on.'

'I was saying we should load up the car with food and water and get out of here,' said Wyatt wearily.

'How long must we reckon on?' asked Julie practically.

'At least four days – better make it a week. This place will be a shambles after Mabel has passed.'

'We'll eat before we go,' she said. 'I think we're all hungry. I'll see what there is in the kitchen – will sandwiches do?'

'If there are enough of them,' said Wyatt with a smile.

Mrs Warmington sat up straight. 'Well, I think you're all crazy, but I'm not going to stay here by myself so I guess I'll have to come along. Come, child, let's make those sandwiches.' She took a candle and swept Julie into the inner recesses of the hotel.

Wyatt looked across at Causton who was putting away his tape-recorder. 'What about guns?' he said. 'We might need them.'

'My dear boy,' said Causton, 'there are more than enough guns out there already. If we're stopped and searched by Serrurier's men and they find a gun we'll be shot on the spot. I've been in some tough places in my time and I've never carried a gun – I owe my life to that fact.'

'That makes sense,' said Wyatt slowly. He looked at the Greek standing by the bar. 'Are you carrying a gun, Eumenides?'

Papegaikos touched his breast and nodded. He said, 'I keep it.'

'Then you're not coming with us,' said Wyatt deliberately. 'You can make your own way – on foot.'

The Greek put his hand inside his jacket and produced the gun, a stubby revolver. 'You t'ink you are boss?' he asked with a smile, balancing the gun in his hand.

'Yes, I am,' said Wyatt firmly. 'You don't know a damn' thing about what a hurricane can do. You don't know the best place to shelter nor how to go about finding it. I do – I'm the expert – and that makes me boss.'

Papegaikos came to a fast decision. He put the gun down gently on the bar counter and walked away from it, and Wyatt blew out his cheeks with a sigh of relief. Causton chuckled. 'You'll do, Wyatt,' he said. 'You're really the boss now – if you don't let that Warmington woman get on top of you. I hope you don't regret taking on the job.'

Presently Julie came from the kitchen with a plate of sandwiches. 'This will do for a start. There's more coming.' She jerked her head. 'We're going to have trouble with that one,' she said darkly.

Wyatt suppressed a groan. 'What's the matter now?'

'She's an organizer – you know, the type who gives the orders. She's been running me ragged in there, and she hasn't done a damned thing herself.'

'Just ignore her,' advised Causton. 'She'll give up if no one takes notice of her.'

'I'll do that,' said Julie. She vanished from the bar again.

'Let's organize the water,' said Wyatt.

He walked towards the bar but stopped when Causton said, 'Wait! Listen!' He strained his ears and heard a whirring sound. 'Someone's trying to start your car,' said Causton.

'I'll check on that,' said Wyatt and strode into the foyer. He went through the revolving door and saw a dim figure in the driving seat of his car and heard the whine of the starter. When he peered through the window he saw it was Dawson. He jerked the door open and said, 'What the devil are you doing?'

Dawson started and turned his head with a jerk. 'Oh, it's you,' he said in relief. 'I thought it was that other guy.'

'Who was that?'

'One of those cops. He was trying to start the car, but gave up and went away. I thought I'd check it, so I came out. It still won't start.'

'You'd better get out and come back into the hotel,' said Wyatt. 'I thought that might happen so I put the rotor-arm in my pocket.'

He stood aside and let Dawson step out. Dawson said, 'Pretty smart, aren't you, Wyatt?'

'No sense in losing the car,' said Wyatt. He looked past Dawson and stiffened. 'Take it easy,' he said in a low voice. 'That copper is coming back – with reinforcements.'

'We'd better get into the hotel pretty damn' fast,' said Dawson.

'Stay where you are and keep your mouth shut,' said Wyatt quickly. 'They might think we're on the run and follow us in – we don't want to involve the others in anything.'

Dawson tensed and then relaxed, and Wyatt watched the four policemen coming towards them. They did not seem in too much of a hurry and momentarily he wondered about that. They drew abreast and one of them turned. '*Blanc*, what are you doing?'

'I thought a thief was stealing my car.'

The policeman gestured. 'This man?'

Wyatt shook his head. 'No, another man. This is my friend.'

'Where do you live?'

Wyatt nodded towards the hotel. 'The Imperiale.'

'A rich man,' the policeman commented. 'And your friend?'

'Also in the hotel.'

Dawson tugged at Wyatt's sleeve. 'What the hell's going on?'

'What does your friend say?' asked the policeman.

'He does not understand this language,' said Wyatt. 'He was asking me what you were saying.'

The policeman laughed. 'We ask the same things, then.' He stared at them. 'It is not a good time to be on the streets, *blanc*. You would do well to stay in your rich hotel.'

He turned away and Wyatt breathed softly in relief, but one of the other men muttered something and he turned back. 'What is your country?' he asked.

'You would call me English,' said Wyatt. 'But I come from Grenada. My friend is American.'

'An American!' The policeman spat on the ground. 'But you are English – do you know an Englishman called Manning?'

Wyatt shook his head. 'No.' The name rang a faint bell but he could not connect it.

'Or Fuller?'

Something clicked. Wyatt said, 'I think I've heard of them. Don't they live on the North Coast?'

'Have you ever met them?'

'I've never seen them in my life,' said Wyatt truthfully.

One of the other policemen stepped forward and pointed at Wyatt. 'This man works for the Americans at Cap Sarrat.'

'Ah, Englishman; you told me you lived in the hotel. Why did you lie?'

'I didn't lie,' said Wyatt. 'I moved in there tonight; it's impossible to get to Cap Sarrat – you know that.'

The man seemed unconvinced. 'And you still say you do not know the men, Fuller and Manning?'

'I don't know them,' said Wyatt patiently.

The policeman said abruptly, 'I'm sorry, *blanc*, but I must search you.' He gestured to his colleagues who stepped forward quickly.

'Hey!' said Dawson in alarm. 'What are these idiots doing?'

'Just keep still,' said Wyatt through his teeth. 'They want to search us. Let them do it – the sooner it's over the better.'

For the second time that day he suffered the indignity of a rough search, but this time it was more thorough. The palace guards had been looking for weapons but these men were interested in more than that. All Wyatt's pockets were stripped and the contents handed to the senior policeman.

He looked with interest through Wyatt's wallet, checking very thoroughly. 'It is true you work at Cap Sarrat,' he said. 'You have an American pass. What military work do you do there?'

'None,' said Wyatt. 'I'm a civilian scientist sent by the British Government. My work is with the weather.'

The policeman smiled. 'Or perhaps you are an American spy?'

'Nonsense!'

'Your friend is American. We must search him, too.'

Hands were laid on Dawson and he struggled. 'Take your filthy hands off me, you goddam black bastard,' he shouted. The words meant nothing to the man searching him, but the tone of voice certainly did. A revolver jumped into his hand as though by magic and Dawson found himself staring into the muzzle.

'You damn' fool,' said Wyatt. 'Keep still and let them search you. They'll turn us loose when they don't find anything.'

He almost regretted saying that when the policeman searching Dawson gave a cry of triumph and pulled an automatic from a holster concealed beneath Dawson's jacket. His senior said, 'Ah, we have armed Americans wandering the streets of St Pierre at a time like this. You will come with me – both of you.'

'Now, look here – ' began Wyatt, and stopped as he felt the muzzle of a gun poke into the small of his back. He bit his lip as the senior policeman waved them forward. 'You bloody fool!' he raged at Dawson. 'Why the hell were you carrying a gun? Now we're going to land in one of Serrurier's gaols.'

II

Causton came out of the deep shadows very slowly and stared up the street to where the little group was hurrying away, then he turned and hurried back into the hotel and across the foyer. Mrs Warmington and Julie had just come in from the kitchen bearing more sandwiches and a pot of coffee, and Papegaikos was busy stacking bottles of soda-water on top of the bar counter.

'Wyatt and Dawson have been nabbed by the police,' he announced. 'Dawson was carrying a gun and the coppers didn't like it.' He looked across at the Greek, who dropped his eyes.

Julie put down the coffee-pot with a clatter. 'Where have they been taken?'

'I don't know,' said Causton. 'Probably to the local lock-up – wherever that is. Do you know, Eumenides?'

'La Place de la Libération Noire,' said the Greek. He shook his head. 'You won't get them out of there.'

'We'll see about that,' said Causton. 'We'll bloody well have to get them out – Wyatt had the rotor-arm of the car engine in his pocket, and now the cops have got it. The car's useless without it.'

Mrs Warmington said in a hard voice, 'There are other cars.'

'That's an idea,' said Causton. 'Do you have a car, Eumenides?'

'I 'ad,' said Eumenides. 'But the Army took all cars.'

'It isn't a matter of a car,' said Julie abruptly. 'It's a matter of getting Dave and Dawson out of the hands of the police.'

'We'll do that, too; but a car's a useful thing to have right now.' Causton rubbed his cheek. 'It's a long way to the docks from here – a bloody long walk.'

Eumenides shrugged. 'We wan' a car, not a sheep.'

'Not a what?' demanded Causton. 'Oh – a ship! No, I want the British Consul – he lives down there. Maybe the power of the state allied to the power of the press will be enough to get Wyatt out of the jug – I doubt if I could do it on my own.' He looked regretfully at the sandwiches. 'I suppose the sooner I go, the sooner we can spring Wyatt and Dawson.'

'You've got time for a quick coffee,' said Julie. 'And you can take a pocketful of sandwiches.'

'Thanks,' said Causton, accepting the cup. 'Does this place have cellars?'

'No – no cellars,' said Eumenides.

'A pity,' said Causton. He looked about the bar. 'I think you'd better get out of here. This kind of party always leads to a lot of social disorganization and the first thing looters go for is the booze. This is one of the first places they'll hit. I suggest you move up to the top floor for the time being; and a barricade on the stairs might be useful.'

He measured the Greek with a cold eye. 'I trust you'll look after the ladies while I'm gone.'

Eumenides smiled. 'I see to ever't'ing.'

That was no satisfactory answer but Causton had to put up with it. He finished off the hot coffee, stuffed some sandwiches into his pocket and said, 'I'll be back as soon as I can – with Wyatt, I hope.'

'Don't forget Mr Dawson,' said Mrs Warmington.

'I'll try not to,' said Causton drily. 'Don't leave the hotel; the party's split up enough as it is.'

Eumenides said suddenly, 'Rawst'orne 'as a car – I seen it. It got them – them special signs.' He clicked his fingers in annoyance at his lack of English.

'Diplomatic plates?' suggested Causton helpfully.

'Tha's ri'.'

'That should come in handy. Okay, I hope to be back in two hours. Cheerio!'

He left the bar and paused before he emerged into the street, carefully looking through the glass panels. Satisfied that there was no danger, he pushed through the revolving doors and set off towards the dock area, keeping well in to the side of the pavement. He checked on his watch and was surprised to find that it was not yet ten o'clock – he had thought it much later. With a bit of luck he would be back at the Imperiale by midnight.

At first he made good time, flitting through the deserted streets like a ghost. There was not a soul in sight. As he got nearer the docks he soon became aware that he was entering what could only be a military staging area. There were many army trucks moving through the dark streets, headlights blazing, and from the distance came the tramp of marching men.

He stopped and ducked into a convenient doorway and took a folded map from his pocket, inspecting it by the carefully shaded light of his torch. It would be the devil of a job getting to Rawsthorne. Close by was the old fortress of San Juan which Serrurier had chosen to use as his arsenal – no wonder there were so many troops in the area. It was from here that his units in the Negrito were being supplied with ammunition and that accounted for the stream of trucks.

Causton looked closer at the map and tried to figure out a new route. It would add nearly an hour to his journey, but there was no help for it. As he stood there the faraway thunder of the guns tailed off and there was dead silence. He looked up and down the street and then crossed it, the leather soles of his shoes making more noise than he cared for.

He got to the other side and turned a corner, striking away from San Juan fortress and, as he hurried, he wondered what the silence of the guns presaged. He had covered many bushfire campaigns in his career – the Congo, Vietnam, Malaysia – and he had a considerable fund of experience to draw upon in making deductions.

To begin with, the guns were indubitably Favel's – he had seen the Government artillery in a seemingly inextricable mess just outside St Pierre. Favel's guns had been firing at something, and that something was obviously the main infantry force which Serrurier had rushed up the Negrito at the first sign of trouble. Now the guns had stopped and that meant that Favel was on the move again, pushing his own infantry forward in an assault on Serrurier's army. That army must have been fairly battered by the barrage, while Favel's men must be fresh and comparatively untouched. It was possible that Favel would push right through, but proof would come when next the artillery barrage began – if it was nearer it would mean Favel was winning.

He had chosen to attack at night, something he had specialized in ever since he had retreated to the mountains. His men were trained for it, and probably one of Favel's men was equal to any two of Serrurier's so long as he was careful to dictate the conditions of battle. But once get boxed in open country with Serrurier's artillery and air force unleashed and he'd be hammered to pieces. He was taking a considerable risk in coming down the Negrito into the plain around Santego Bay, but he was minimizing it by clever strategy and the unbelievable luck that Serrurier had a thick-headed artillery general with no concept of logistics.

Causton was so occupied with these thoughts that he nearly ran into a police patrol head on. He stopped short and shrank into the shadows and was relieved when the squad passed him by unseen. He wanted to waste no time in futile arguments. By the time he got to Rawsthorne's house he had evaded three more police patrols, but it took time and it was very late when he knocked on Rawsthorne's door.

III

James Fowler Dawson was a successful writer. Not only was he accepted by the critics as a man to be watched as a future Nobel Prizewinner, but his books sold in enormous numbers to the public and he had made a lot of money and was looking forward to making a lot more. Because he liked making money he was very careful of the image he presented to his public, an image superbly tailored to his personality and presented to the world by his press agents.

His first novel, *Tarpon*, was published in the year that Hemingway died. At the time he was a freelance writer concocting articles for the American sporting magazines on the glory of rainbow trout and what it feels like to have a grizzly in your sights. He had but average success at this and so was a hungry writer. When *Tarpon* hit the top of the best-seller lists no one was more surprised than Dawson. But knowing the fickleness of public taste he sought for ways to consolidate his success and decided that good writing was not enough – he must also be a public personality.

So he assumed the mantle that had fallen from Hemingway – he would be a man's man. He shot elephant and lion in Africa; he game-fished in the Caribbean and off the Seychelles; he climbed a mountain in Alaska; he flew his own plane and, like Hemingway, was involved in a spectacular smash; and it was curious that there were always photographers on hand to record these events.

But he was no Hemingway. The lions he killed were poor terrified beasts imprisoned in a closing ring of beaters, and he had never killed one with a single shot. In his assault on the Alaskan mountain he was practically carried up by skilled and well-paid mountaineers, and he heartily disliked flying his plane because he was frightened of it and only flew when necessary to mend his image. But game-fishing he had actually come to like and he was not at all bad at it. And, despite everything else, he remained a good writer, although he was always afraid of losing steam and failing with his next book.

While his image was shiny, while his name made headlines in the world press, while the money poured into his bank, he was reasonably happy. It was good to be well-known in the world's capitals, to be met at airports by pressmen and photographers, to be asked his opinion of world events. He had never yet been in a situation where the mere mention of his name had not got him out of trouble, and

thus he was unperturbed at being put into a cell with Wyatt.
He had been in gaol before – the world had chuckled many
times at the escapades of Big Jim Dawson – but never for
more than a few hours. A nominal fine, a donation to the
Police Orphans' Fund, a gracious apology and the name of
Jim Dawson soon set him free. He had no reason to think it
was going to be different this time.

'I could do with a drink,' he said grumpily. 'Those bastards took my flask.'

Wyatt examined the cell. It was in an old building and
there was none of the modernity of serried steel bars; but
the walls were of thick and solid stone and the window was
small and set high in the wall. By pulling up a stool and
standing on it he could barely see outside, and he was a
fairly tall man. He looked at the dim shapes of the buildings
across the square and judged that the cell was on the second
floor of the building in which the Poste de Police was
housed.

He stepped down from the stool and said, 'Why the hell
were you carrying a gun?'

'I always carry a gun,' said Dawson. 'A man in my position meets trouble, you know. There are always cranks who
don't like what I write, and the boys who want to prove
they're tougher than I am. I've got a licence for it, too. I got
a batch of threatening letters a couple of years ago and there
were some funny things happening round my place so I got
the gun.'

'I don't know that that was a good idea, even in the
States,' said Wyatt. 'But it certainly got us into trouble here.
Your gun licence won't cut any ice.'

'Getting out will be easy,' said Dawson angrily. 'All I have
to do is to wait until I can see someone bigger than one of
those junior grade cops, tell him who I am, and we'll both
be sprung.'

Wyatt stared at him. 'Are you serious?'

'Sure I'm serious. Hell, man; everyone knows me. The Government of this tin-pot banana republic isn't going to get in bad with Uncle Sam by keeping me in gaol. The fact that I've been picked up will make world headlines, and this Serrurier character isn't going to let bad change to worse.'

Wyatt took a deep breath. 'You don't know Serrurier,' he said. 'He doesn't like Americans in the first place and he won't give a damn who you are – if he's heard of you, that is, which I doubt.'

Dawson seemed troubled by the heresy Wyatt had uttered. 'Not heard of me? Of course he'll have heard of me.'

'You heard those guns,' said Wyatt. 'Serrurier is fighting for his life – do you understand that? If Favel wins, Serrurier is going to be very dead. Right now he doesn't give a damn about keeping in with Uncle Sam or anyone else – he just doesn't have the time. And, like a doctor, he buries his mistakes, so if he's informed about us there'll probably be a shooting party in the basement with us as guests; that's why I hope to God no one tells him. And I hope his boys don't have any initiative.'

'But there'll have to be a trial,' said Dawson. 'I'll have my lawyer.'

'For God's sake!' exploded Wyatt. 'Where have you been living – on the moon? Serrurier has had twenty thousand people executed in the last seven years without trial. They just disappeared. Start praying that we don't join them.'

'Now that's nonsense,' said Dawson firmly. 'I've been coming to San Fernandez for the last five years – it makes a swell fishing base – and I've heard nothing of this. And I've met a lot of government officials and a nicer bunch of boys you couldn't wish to meet. Of course they're black, but I think none the less of them for that.'

'Very broad-minded of you,' said Wyatt sarcastically. 'Can you name any of these "nice boys"? That information might come in useful.'

'Sure; the best of the lot was the Minister for Island Affairs – a guy called Descaix. He's a – '

'Oh, no!' groaned Wyatt, sitting on the stool and putting his head in his hands.

'What's the matter?'

Wyatt looked up. 'Now, listen, Dawson; I'll try to get this over in words of one syllable. Your nice boy, Descaix, was the boss of Serrurier's secret police. Serrurier said, "Do it," and Descaix did it, and in the end it added up to a nice pile of murders. But Descaix slipped – one of his murders didn't pan out and the man came back to life, the man responsible for all those guns popping off up in the hills. Favel.'

He tapped Dawson on the knee. 'Serrurier didn't like that, so what do you think happened to Descaix?'

Dawson was looking unhappy. 'I wouldn't know.'

'Neither would anyone else,' said Wyatt. 'Descaix's gone, vanished as though he never existed – expunged. My own idea is that he's occupying a hole in the ground up in the Tour Rambeau.'

'But he was such a nice, friendly guy,' said Dawson. He shook his head in bewilderment. 'I don't see how I could have missed it. I'm a writer – I'm supposed to know something about people. I even went fishing with Descaix – surely you get to know a man you fish with?'

'Why should you?' asked Wyatt. 'People like Descaix have neatly compartmented minds. If you or I killed a man it would stay with us the rest of our lives – it would leave a mark. But Descaix has a man killed and he's forgotten about it as soon as he's given the order. It doesn't worry his conscience one little bit, so it doesn't show – there's no mark.'

'Jesus!' said Dawson with awe. 'I've been fishing with a mass murderer.'

'You won't fish with him ever again,' said Wyatt brutally. 'You might not fish with anyone ever again if we don't get out of here.'

Dawson gave way to petulant rage. 'What the hell is the American Government doing? We have a base here – why wasn't this island cleaned up long ago?'

'You make me sick,' said Wyatt. 'You don't know what's going on right in front of your nose, and when your nose gets bitten you scream to your Government for help. The American Government policy on this island is "hands off", and rightly so. If they interfere here in the same way they did in the Dominican Republic they'd totally wreck their diplomatic relations with the rest of the hemisphere and the Russians would laugh fit to burst. Anyway, it's best this way. You can't hand freedom to people on a plate – they've got to take it. Favel knows that – he's busy taking his freedom right now.'

He looked at Dawson who was sitting huddled on the bed, strangely shrunken. 'You were trying to take the car, weren't you? There was no policeman trying to drive it away at all. But you were.'

Dawson nodded. 'I went upstairs and heard you and Causton talking about the hurricane. I got scared and figured I'd better get out.'

'And you were going to leave the rest of us?'

Dawson nodded miserably.

Wyatt stretched out his legs. 'I don't understand it,' he said. 'I just don't understand it. You're Dawson – "Big Jim" Dawson – the man who's supposed to be able to outshoot, out-fight, out-fly any other man on earth. What's happened to you?'

Dawson lay on the bed and turned to the wall. 'Go to hell!' he said in a muffled voice.

IV

The police came for them at four o'clock in the morning, hustling them out of the cell and along a corridor. The office into which they were shown was bare and bleak, the archetype of all such offices anywhere in the world. The policeman at the desk was also archetypal; his cold, impersonal eyes and level stare could be duplicated in any police office in New York, London or Tokyo, and the fact that his complexion was dark coffee did not make any difference.

He regarded them expressionlessly, then said, 'Fool, I wanted them one at a time. Take that one back.' He pointed his pen at Wyatt, who was immediately pushed back into the corridor and escorted to the cell again.

He leaned against the wall as the key clicked in the lock and wondered what would eventually happen to him – perhaps he would join Descaix, an unlikely bedfellow. He had not heard the guns for some time and he hoped that Favel had not been beaten, because Favel was his only chance of getting clear. If Favel did not take St Pierre then he would either be shot or drowned in the cell when the waters of Santego Bay arose to engulf the town.

He sat on the stool and pondered. The policeman who had arrested them had shown a keen interest in Manning and Fuller, the two Englishmen from the North Coast, and he wondered why so much trouble should be taken over them in the middle of a civil war. Then he recalled Causton's questioning earlier about shipments of arms and wondered if Manning and Fuller lived in the Campo de las Perlas, the area in which Causton had said the arms had been landed. If they were involved in that, no wonder Serrurier's police were taking an interest in their doings – and in the doings of all other English people on San Fernandez.

Then, because he was very tired and had sat on the stool all night, he stretched out on the bed and fell asleep.

When he was aroused the first light of dawn was peering through the high window. Again he was taken down the corridor to the bleak room at the end and pushed through the doorway roughly. There was no sign of Dawson, and the policeman behind the desk was smiling. 'Come in, Mr Wyatt. Sit down.'

It was not an invitation but an order. Wyatt sat in the hard chair and crossed his legs. The policeman said, in English, 'I am Sous-Inspecteur Roseau, Mr Wyatt. Do you not think my English is good? I learned it in Jamaica.'

'It's very good,' acknowledged Wyatt.

'I'm glad,' said Roseau. 'Then there will be no misunderstandings. When did you last see Manning?'

'I've never seen Manning.'

'When did you last see Fuller?'

'I've never seen him, either.'

'But you knew where they lived; you admitted it.'

'I didn't "admit" a damned thing,' said Wyatt evenly. 'I told your underling that I'd *heard* they lived on the North Coast. I also told him that I'd never seen either of them in my life.'

Roseau consulted a sheet of paper before him. Without looking up he asked, 'When were you recruited into American Intelligence?'

'Well, I'll be damned!' said Wyatt. 'This is all a lot of nonsense.'

Roseau's head came up with a jerk. 'Then you are in British Intelligence? You are a *British* spy?'

'You're out of your mind,' said Wyatt disgustedly. 'I'm a scientist – a meteorologist. And I don't mind telling you something right now – if you don't get the people out of this town within two days there's going to be the most godawful smash-up you've ever seen. There's a hurricane coming.'

Roseau smiled patiently. 'Yes, Mr Wyatt, we know that is your cover. We also know that you British and the Americans are working hand in hand with Favel in an attempt to overthrow the lawful government of this country.'

'That'll do,' said Wyatt. 'I've had enough.' He slapped the desk with the flat of his hand. 'I want to see the British consul.'

'So you want to see Rawsthorne?' enquired Roseau with a malicious smile. 'He wanted to see you – he was here trying to get you out, together with another Englishman. It is unfortunate that, because of his official position, we cannot arrest Rawsthorne – we know he is your leader – but my government is sending a strong protest to London about his conduct. He is *non persona grata*.' Roseau's smile widened. 'You see I have Latin, too, Mr Wyatt. Not bad for an ignorant nigger.'

'Ignorant is exactly the right word,' said Wyatt tightly.

Roseau sighed, as a teacher sighs when faced with the obtuseness of a particularly stubborn pupil. 'This is not the time to insult me, Wyatt. You see, your companion – your accomplice – the American agent, Dawson, has confessed. These Americans are not really so tough, you know.'

'What the devil could he confess?' asked Wyatt. 'He's as innocent of anything as I am.' He moved his hand and felt a slight wetness on the palm. Turning his hand over he saw a smear of blood, and there were a few more drops spattered along the edge of the desk. He lifted his eyes and looked at Roseau with loathing.

'Yes, Wyatt; he confessed,' said Roseau. He drew a blank piece of paper from a drawer and placed in neatly before him. 'Now,' he said with pen poised. 'We will begin again. When did you last see Manning?'

'I've never seen Manning.'

'When did you last see Fuller?'

'I've never seen Fuller,' said Wyatt monotonously.

Roseau carefully put down his pen. He said softly, 'Shall we see if you are more stubborn than Dawson? Or perhaps you will be less stubborn – it is more convenient for you as well as for me.'

Wyatt was very conscious of the two policemen standing behind him near the door. They had not moved or made a sound but he knew they were there. He had known it ever since Dawson's blood had stained his hand. He decided to take a leaf out of Rawsthorne's book. 'Roseau, Serrurier is going to have your hide for this.'

Roseau blinked but said nothing.

'Does he know I'm here? He's a bad man when he's crossed – but who should know that better than you? When I saw him yesterday he was giving Hippolyte a going over – had Hippolyte shaking in his shoes.'

'You saw our President yesterday?' Roseau's voice was perhaps not as firm as it had been.

Wyatt tried to act as though he was always in the habit of meeting Serrurier for afternoon drinks. 'Of course.' He leaned over the desk. 'Don't you know who Dawson is – the man you've just beaten up? He's the famous writer. You must have heard of Big Jim Dawson – everyone has.'

Roseau twitched. 'He tried to make me believe he was –' He stopped suddenly.

Wyatt laughed. 'You've put Serrurier right in the middle,' he said. 'He has his hands full with Favel but that's all right – he can handle it. He told me so himself. But he was worried about the Americans at Cap Sarrat; he doesn't know whether they're going to come out against him or not. Of course you know what will happen if they do. The Americans and Favel will crack Serrurier between them like a nut.'

'What has this got to do with me?' asked Roseau uncertainly.

Wyatt leaned back in his chair and looked at Roseau with well-simulated horror. 'Why, you fool, you've given the

Americans the chance they've been waiting for. Dawson is an international figure, and he's American. Commodore Brooks will be asking Serrurier where Dawson is in not too many hours from now, and if Serrurier can't produce him, alive and unhurt, then Brooks is going to take violent action because he knows he'll have world opinion behind him. Dawson is just the lever the Americans have been waiting for; they can't take up arms just because a few Americans got mixed up in your civil war – that's not done any more – but a potential Nobel Prizewinner, a man of Dawson's stature, is something else again.'

Roseau was silent and twitchy. Wyatt let him stew for a few long seconds, then said, 'You know as well as I do that Dawson told you nothing about Manning and Fuller. I know that because he knows nothing, but you used him to try to throw a scare into me. Now let me tell you something, Sous-Inspecteur Roseau. When Commodore Brooks asks Serrurier for Dawson, Serrurier is going to turn St Pierre upside down looking for him because he knows that if he doesn't find him, then the Americans will break in the back door and stab him in the back just when he's at grips with Favel. And if Serrurier finds that Sous-Inspecteur Roseau has stupidly exceeded his duty by beating Dawson half to death I wouldn't give two pins for your chances of remaining alive for five more minutes. My advice to you is to get a doctor to Dawson as fast as you can, and then to implore him to keep his mouth shut. How you do that is your business.'

He almost laughed at the expression on Roseau's face as he contemplated the enormity of his guilt. Roseau finally shut his mouth with a snap and took a deep breath. 'Take this man to his cell,' he ordered, and Wyatt felt a firm grip on his shoulder, a grip more welcome now than it would have been five minutes earlier. After being thrust into the cell it was a long time before he stopped shaking. Then he sat down to contemplate the sheer, copper-bottomed brilliance of the idea he had sold Roseau.

He thought that he and Dawson were safe from Roseau. But there was still the problem of getting out before the hurricane struck and that would not be easy – not unless he could manage to work on Roseau's fears some more. He had an idea that he would be seeing Roseau before long; the Sous-Inspecteur would remember that Wyatt had claimed acquaintance with Serrurier and he would want to know more about that.

He looked at his watch. It was seven o'clock and the sunlight was streaming through the small window. He hoped that Causton would have sense enough to get the others out of St Pierre – even by walking they could get a long way.

The noise outside suddenly came to his attention. It had been going on ever since he had been pushed into the cell but he had been so immersed in his thoughts that it had not penetrated. Now he was aware of the racket in the square outside – the revving of heavy engines, the clatter of feet and the murmur of many men interspersed by raucous shouts – sergeants have the same brazen-voiced scream in any army; it sounded as though an army was massing in the square.

He kicked the stool across to the window and climbed up, but the angle was wrong and he could not see the ground at all, merely the façade of the buildings on the opposite side of the square. He stood there for a long time trying to make sense of the confused sounds from below but finally gave up. He was just about to step off the stool when he heard the sudden bellow of guns from so close that the hot air seemed to quiver.

He stood on tiptoe, desperately trying to see what was happening, and caught a glimpse of a deep red flash on the roof of the building immediately opposite. There was a *slam* and the front of the building caved in before his startled eyes, seeming to collapse in slow motion in a billowing cloud of dust.

Then the blast of the explosion caught him and he was hurled in a shower of broken glass right across the cell to thud against the door. The last thing he heard before he collapsed into unconsciousness was the thump of his head against the solid wood.

FOUR

The drumfire of the guns jerked Causton from a deep sleep. He started violently and opened his eyes, wondering for a moment where he was and relieved to find the familiarity of his own room at the Imperiale. Eumenides, to whom he had offered a bed, was standing at the window looking out.

Causton sat up in bed. 'God's teeth!' he said, 'those guns are near. Favel must have broken through.' He scrambled out of bed and was momentarily disconcerted to find he was still wearing his trousers.

Eumenides drew back from the window and looked at Causton moodily. 'They will fight in town,' he said. 'Will be ver' bad.'

'It usually is,' said Causton, rubbing the stubble on his cheeks. 'What's happening down there?'

'Many peoples – soldiers,' said Eumenides.'Many 'urt.'

'Walking wounded? Serrurier must be in full retreat. But he'll do his damnedest to hold the town. This is where the frightful part comes in – the street fighting.' He wound up a clockwork dry shaver with quick efficient movements. 'Serrurier's police have been holding the population down; that was wise of him – he didn't want streams of refugees impeding his army. But whether they'll be able to do it in the middle of a battle is another thing. I have the feeling this is going to be a nasty day.'

The Greek lit another cigarette and said nothing.

Causton finished his shave in silence. His mind was busy with the implications of the nearness of the guns. Favel must have smashed Serrurier's army in the Negrito and pushed on with all speed to the outskirts of St Pierre. Moving so fast, he must have neglected mopping-up operations and there were probably bits of Serrurier's army scattered in pockets all down the Negrito; they would be disorganized now after groping about in the night, but with the daylight they might be a danger – a danger Favel might be content to ignore.

For a greater danger confronted him. He had burst on to the plain and was hammering at the door of St Pierre in broad daylight, and Causton doubted if he was well enough equipped for a slugging match in those conditions. So far, he had depended on surprise and the sudden hammer blow of unexpected artillery against troops unused to the violence of high explosives – but Serrurier had artillery and armour and an air force. True, the armour consisted of three anti-quated tanks and a dozen assorted armoured cars, the air force was patched up from converted civilian planes and Favel had been able to laugh at this display of futile moder-nity when still secure in the mountains. But on the plain it would be a different matter altogether. Even an old tank would be master of the battlefield, and the planes could see what they were bombing.

Causton examined his reflection in the glass and won-dered if Favel had moved fast enough to capture Serrurier's artillery before it had got into action. If he had, he would be the luckiest commander in history because it had been sheer inefficiency on the part of the Government artillery general that had bogged it down. But luck – good and bad – was an inescapable element on the field of battle.

He plunged his head into cold water, came up spluttering and reached for a towel. He had just finished drying himself

when there was a knock on the door. He held up a warning
hand to Eumenides. 'Who's that?'

'It's me,' called Julie.

He relaxed. 'Come in, Miss Marlowe.'

Julie looked a little careworn; there were dark circles
under her eyes as though she had had very little sleep and
she was dishevelled. She pushed her hair back, and said,
'That woman will drive me nuts.'

'What's La Warmington doing now?'

'Right now she's dozing, thank God. That woman's got a
nerve – she was treating me like a lady's maid last night and
got annoyed because I wouldn't take orders. Then in the
middle of the night she got weepy and nearly drove me out
of my mind. I had to fill her full of luminol in the end.'

'Is she asleep now?'

'She's just woken up, but she's so dopey she doesn't
know what's going on.'

'Perhaps it's just as well,' said Causton, cocking his head as
he listened to the guns. 'It might be just as well to keep her
doped until we get out of here. I hope to God Rawsthorne
can make it in time.' He looked at Julie. 'You don't look too
good yourself.'

'I'm beat,' she confessed. 'I didn't sleep so well myself. I
was awake half the night with Mrs Warmington. I got her
off to sleep and then found I couldn't sleep myself – I was
thinking about Dave and Mr Dawson. When I finally got to
sleep I was woken up almost immediately by those damned
guns.' She folded her arms about herself and winced at a
particularly loud explosion. 'I'm scared – I don't mind
admitting it.'

'I'm not feeling too good myself,' said Causton drily.
'How about you, Eumenides?'

The Greek shrugged eloquently, gave a ferocious grin and
passed his fingers across his throat. Causton laughed. 'That
about describes it.'

Julie said, 'Do you think it's any good trying to get Dave out of that gaol again?'

Causton resisted an impulse to swear. As a man who earned his living by the writing of the English language, he had always maintained that swearing and the use of foul language was the prop of an ignorant mind unable to utilize the full and noble resources of English invective. But the previous night he had been forced to use the dirtiest language he knew when he came up against the impenetrably closed mind of Sous-Inspectéur Roseau. He had quite shocked Rawsthorne, if not Roseau.

He said, 'There's not much hope, I'm afraid. The walls of the local prison may be thick, but the coppers' heads are thicker. Maybe Favel may be able to get him out if he hurries up.'

He put his foot up on the bed to lace his shoe. 'I had a talk with Rawsthorne last night; he was telling me something about Wyatt's hurricane. According to Rawsthorne, it's not at all certain there'll be a hurricane here at all. What do you know about that?'

'I know that Dave was very disturbed about it,' she said. 'Especially after he saw the old man.'

'What old man?'

So Julie told of the old man who had been tying his roof down and Causton scratched his head. He said mildly, 'For a meteorologist, Wyatt has very unscientific ways of going about his job.'

'Don't you believe him?' asked Julie.

'That's the devil of it – I do,' said Causton. 'I'll tell you something, Julie: I *always* depend on my intuition and it rarely lets me down. That's why I'm here on this island right now. My editor told me I was talking nonsense – I had no real evidence things were going to blow up here – so that's why I'm here unofficially. Yes, I believe in Wyatt's wind, and we'll have to do something about it bloody quickly.'

'What can we do about a hurricane?'

'I mean we must look after ourselves,' said Causton. 'Look, Julie; Wyatt's immediate boss didn't believe him; Commodore Brooks didn't believe him, and Serrurier didn't believe him. He did all he can and I don't think we can do any better. And if you think I'm going to walk about in the middle of a civil war bearing a placard inscribed "Prepare To Meet Thy Doom" you're mistaken.'

Julie shook her head. 'I know,' she said. 'But there are sixty thousand defenceless people in St Pierre – it's terrible.'

'So is civil war,' said Causton gravely. 'But there's still nothing we can do apart from saving ourselves – and that's going to be dicey.' He took his map from the pocket of his jacket and spread it on the bed. 'I wish Rawsthorne had been ready to leave last night, but he said he had to go back to the consulate. I suppose even a lowly consul has to burn the codebooks or whatever it is they do when you see smoke coming from the Embassy chimney on the eve of crisis. What time is it?'

'Nearly 'alf pas' seven,' said Eumenides.

'He said he'd be here by eight, but he'll probably be late. Neither of us expected Favel to be so quick – I don't suppose Serrurier expected it, either. Rawsthorne might be held up, even in a car with diplomatic plates. Damn that bloody fool Dawson,' he said feelingly. 'If he hadn't messed things up we'd have been away in Wyatt's car hours ago.'

He looked at the map. 'Wyatt said we should find a place above the hundred-foot mark and facing north. This damned map has no contour lines. Eumenides, can you help me here?'

The Greek looked over Causton's shoulder. 'There,' he said, and laid his finger on the map.

'I dare say it is a nice place,' agreed Causton. 'But we'd have to go through two armies to get there. No, we'll have to go along the coast in one direction or another and then strike inland to get height.' His finger moved along the coast road. 'I don't think there's any point in going west towards Cap Sarrat. There are units of the Government army strung along there, and anyway, it's pretty flat as I remember it. The civil airfield is there and Favel will probably strike for it, so altogether it'll be a pretty unhealthy place. So it'll have to be the other way. What's it like this road, Eumenides? The one that leads east?'

'The road goes up,' said Eumenides. 'There is . . . there is . . .' He snapped his fingers in annoyance. 'It fall from road to sea.'

'There are cliffs on the seaward side – this side?' asked Causton, and the Greek nodded. 'Just what we're looking for,' said Causton with satisfaction. 'What's the country like inland – say, here?'

Eumenides waved his hand up and down expressively. ''Ills.'

'Then that's it,' said Causton. 'But you'd better discuss it further with Rawsthorne when he comes.'

'What about you?' asked Julie. 'Where are you going?'

'Someone has to do a reconnaissance,' said Causton. 'We have to find if it's a practicable proposition to go that way. I'm going to scout around the east end of town. It's safe enough for one man.'

He rose from his knees and went to the window. 'There are plenty of civilians out and about now; the police haven't been able to bottle them all up in their houses. I should be able to get away with it.'

'With a white skin?'

'Um,' said Causton. 'That's a thought.' He went over to his bag and unzipped it. 'A very little of this ought to do the trick.' He looked with distaste at the tin of brown boot-polish in his hand. 'Will you apply it, Julie? Just the veriest touch – there are plenty of light-coloured Negroes here and I don't want to look like a nigger minstrel.'

Julie smeared a little of the boot-polish on his face. He said, 'Don't forget the back of the neck – that's vital. It isn't so much a disguise as a deception; it only needs enough to darken the skin so that people won't take a second look and say "Look at that *blanc*".'

He rubbed some of the polish on his hands and wrists, then said, 'Now I want a prop.'

Julie stared at him. 'A what?'

'A stage property. I've wandered all through the corridors of power in Whitehall and got away with it because I was carrying a sheaf of papers and looked as though I was going somewhere. I got a scoop from a hospital by walking about in a white coat with a stethoscope dangling from my pocket. The idea is to look a natural part of the scenery – a stethoscope gives one a *right* to be in a hospital. Now, what gives me a right to be in a civil war?'

Eumenides grinned maliciously, and said, 'A gun.'

'I'm afraid so,' said Causton regretfully. 'Well, there ought to be plenty of those outside. I ought to be able to pick up a rifle and maybe a scrap of uniform to make it look convincing. Meanwhile, where's that pop-gun of yours, Eumenides?'

'In the bar where I lef' it.'

'Right – well, I'll be off,' said Causton. There was a heavy explosion not far away and the windows shivered in their frames. 'It's warming up. A pity this place has no cellars. Eumenides, I think you'd all better move downstairs – actually under the stairs is the best place. And if that Warmington woman gets hysterical, pop her one.'

Eumenides nodded.

Causton paused by the door. 'I don't think I'll be long, but if I'm not back by eleven I won't be coming back at all, and you'd better push off. With the townspeople coming out now the road might be difficult, so don't wait for me.'

He left without waiting for a reply and ran down the stairs and into the bar. There were soda-water bottles stacked on the counter but no sign of the gun. He looked about for a couple of minutes then gave up, vaguely wondering what had happened to it. But he had no time to waste so he crossed the foyer and, with a precautionary glance outside, stepped boldly into the street.

II

Mrs Warmington was still drugged with sleep, for which Julie was thankful. She opened one drowsy eye and said, 'Wha' time is it?'

'It's quite early,' said Julie. 'But we must go downstairs.'

'I wanna sleep,' said Mrs Warmington indistinctly. 'Send the maid with my tea in an hour.'

'But we must go now,' said Julie firmly. 'We are going away soon.' She began to assemble the things she needed.

'What's all that *noise*?' complained Mrs Warmington crossly. 'I declare this is the noisiest hotel I've ever slept in.' This declaration seemed to exhaust her and she closed her eyes and a faint whistling sound emanated from the bed – too ladylike to be called a snore.

'Come on, Mrs Warmington.' Julie shook her by the shoulder.

Mrs Warmington roused herself and propped up on one elbow. 'Oh, my head! Did we have a party?' Slowly, intelligence returned to her eyes and her head jerked up as she recognized the din of the guns for what it was. 'Oh, my God!' she wailed. 'What's happening?'

'The rebels have started to bombard the town,'Julie said.

Mrs Warmington jumped out of bed, all traces of sleep gone. 'We must leave,' she said rapidly. 'We must go now.'

'We have no car yet,' said Julie. 'Mr Rawsthorne hasn't come.' She turned to find Mrs Warmington pushing her overfed figure into a tight girdle. 'Good grief!' she said, 'don't wear that – we might have to move fast. Have you any slacks?'

'I don't believe in women of . . . of my type wearing pants.'

Julie surveyed her and gave a crooked smile. 'Maybe you're right at that,' she agreed. 'Well, wear something sensible; wear a suit if it hasn't got a tight skirt.'

She stripped the beds of their blankets and folded them into a bundle. Mrs Warmington said, 'I *knew* we ought to have gone to the Base last night.' She squeezed her feet into tight shoes.

'You know it was impossible,' said Julie briefly.

'I can't imagine what Commodore Brooks is thinking of – leaving us here at the mercy of these savages. Come on, let's get out of here.' She opened the door and went out, leaving Julie to bring the large bundle of blankets.

Eumenides was at the head of the stairs. He looked at the blankets and said, 'Ver' good t'ing,' and took them from her.

There was a faint noise from downstairs as though someone had knocked over a chair. They all stood listening for a moment, then Mrs Warmington dug her finger into the Greek's ribs. 'Don't just stand there,' she hissed. 'Find out who it is.'

Eumenides dropped the blankets and tiptoed down the stairs and out of sight. Mrs Warmington clutched her bag to her breast, then turned abruptly and walked back to the bedroom. Julie heard the click as the bolt was shot home.

Presently Eumenides reappeared and beckoned. 'It's Rawst'orne.'

Julie got Mrs Warmington out of the bedroom again and they all went downstairs to find Rawsthorne very perturbed. 'They've started shelling the town,' he said. 'The Government troops are making a stand. It would be better if we moved out quickly before the roads become choked.'

'I agree,' said Mrs Warmington.

Rawsthorne looked around. 'Where's Causton?'

'He's gone to find the best way out,' said Julie. 'He said he wouldn't be long. What time is it now?'

Rawsthorne consulted a pocket watch. 'Quarter to nine – sorry I'm late. Did he say when he'd be back?'

She shook her head. 'He didn't think he'd be long, but he said that if he wasn't back by eleven then he wouldn't be coming at all.'

There was a violent explosion not far away and flakes of plaster drifted down from the ceiling. Mrs Warmington jumped. 'Lead the way to your car, Mr Rawsthorne. We must leave now.'

Rawsthorne ignored her. 'A little over two hours at the most,' he said. 'But he should be back long before that. Meanwhile . . .' He looked up meaningly at the ceiling.

'Causton said the best place for us was under the stairs,' said Julie.

'You mean we're staying here?' demanded Mrs Warmington. 'With all this going on? You'll get us all killed.'

'We can't leave Mr Causton,' said Julie.

'I fix,' said Eumenides. 'Come.'

The space under the main staircase had been used as a store-room. The door had been locked but Eumenides had broken it open with a convenient fire axe, tossed out all the buckets and brooms and had packed in all the provisions they were taking. Mrs Warmington objected most strongly to sitting on the floor but went very quietly when Julie said pointedly, 'You're welcome to leave at any time.' It was cramped, but there was room for the four of them to sit, and if the door was kept ajar Rawsthorne found he had a view of the main entrance so that he could see Causton as soon as he came back.

He said worriedly, 'Causton should never have gone out – I've never seen St Pierre like this, the town is starting to boil over.'

'He'll be all right,' said Julie. 'He's experienced at this kind of thing – it's his job.'

'Thank God it's not mine,' said Rawsthorne fervently. 'The Government army must have been beaten terribly in the Negrito. The town is full of deserters on the run, and there are many wounded men.' He shook his head. 'Favel's attack must have come with shocking suddenness for that to have happened. He must be outnumbered at least three to one by the Government forces.'

'You said Serrurier is making a stand,' said Julie. 'That means the fighting is going to go on.'

'It might go on for a long time,' said Rawsthorne soberly. 'Serrurier has units that weren't committed to battle yesterday – Favel didn't give him time. But those fresh units are digging in to the north of the town, so that means another battle.' He clicked deprecatingly with his tongue. 'I fear Favel may have overestimated his own strength.'

He fell silent and they listened to the noise of the battle. Always there was the clamour of the guns from the out-skirts of the town, punctuated frequently by the closer and louder explosion of a falling shell. The air in the hotel quivered and gradually became full of a sifting dust so that the sunlight slanting into the foyer shone like the beams of searchlights.

Julie stirred and began to search among the boxes which Eumenides had packed at the back. 'Have you had break-fast, Mr Rawsthorne?'

'I didn't have time, my dear.'

'We might as well eat now,' said Julie practically. 'I think I can cut some bread if we rearrange ourselves a little. We might as well eat it before it becomes really stale.'

They breakfasted off bread and canned pressed meat, washing it down with soda-water. When they had finished Rawsthorne said, 'What time is it? I can't seem to get at my watch.'

'Ten-fifteen,' said Julie.

'We can give Causton another three-quarters of an hour,' said Rawsthorne. 'But then we *must* go – I'm sorry, but there it is.'

'That's all right,' said Julie quietly. 'He did tell us to go at eleven.'

Occasionally they heard distant shouts and excited cries and sometimes the clatter of running boots. Eumenides said suddenly, 'Your car . . . is in street?'

'No,' said Rawsthorne. 'I left it at the back of the hotel.' He paused. 'Poor Wyatt's car is in a mess; all the windows are broken and someone has taken the wheels; for the tyres, I suppose.'

They relapsed into cramped silence. Mrs Warmington hugged her bag and conducted an intermittent monologue which Julie ignored. She listened to the shells exploding and wondered what would happen if the hotel got a direct hit. She had no idea of the damage a shell could do apart from what she had seen at the movies and on TV and she had a shrewd idea that the movie version would be but a pale imitation of the real thing. Her mouth became dry and she knew she was very frightened.

The minutes dragged drearily by. Mrs Warmington squeaked sharply as a shell exploded near-by – the closest yet – and the windows of the foyer blew in and smashed. She started to get up, but Julie pulled her back. 'Stay where you are,' she cried. 'It's safer here.'

Mrs Warmington flopped back and somehow Julie felt better after that. She looked at Eumenides, his face pale in the dim light, and wondered what he was thinking. It was bad for him because, his English being what it was, he could not communicate easily. As she looked at him he pulled up his wrist to his eyes. 'Quar' to 'leven,' he announced. 'I t'ink we better load car.'

Rawsthorne stirred. 'Yes, that might be a good idea,' he agreed. He began to push open the door. 'Wait a minute – here's Causton now.'

Julie sighed. 'Thank God!'

Rawsthorne pushed the door wider and then stopped short. 'No, it's not,' he whispered. 'It's a soldier – and there's another behind him.' Gently he drew the door closed again, leaving it open only a crack and watching with one eye.

The soldier was carrying a rifle slung over one shoulder but the man behind, also a soldier, had no weapon. They came into the foyer, carelessly kicking aside the cane chairs, and stood for a moment looking at the dusty opulence around them. One of them said something and pointed, and the other laughed, and they both moved out of sight.

'They've gone into the bar,' whispered Rawsthorne.

Faintly, he could hear the clinking of bottles and loud laughter, and once, a smash of glass. Then there was silence. He said softly, 'We can't come out while they're there; they'd see us. We'll have to wait.'

It was a long wait and Rawsthorne began to feel cramp in his leg. He could not hear anything at all and began to wonder if the soldiers had not departed from the rear of the hotel. At last he whispered, 'What time is it?'

'Twenty past eleven.'

'This is nonsense,' said Mrs Warmington loudly. 'I can't hear anything. They must have gone.'

'Keep quiet!' said Rawsthorne. There was a ragged edge to his voice. He paused for a long time, then said softly, 'They *might* have gone. I'm going to have a look round.'

'Be careful,' whispered Julie.

He was about to push the door open again when he halted the movement and swore softly under his breath. One of the soldiers had come out of the bar and was strolling through the foyer, drinking from a bottle. He went to the door of the hotel and stood for a while staring into the street through the broken panes in the revolving door, then he suddenly shouted to someone outside and waved the bottle in the air.

Two more men came in from outside and there was a brief conference; the first soldier waved his arm towards the bar with largesse as though to say 'be my guests'. One of the two shouted to someone else outside, and presently there were a dozen soldiers tramping through the foyer on their way to the bar. There was a babel of sound in hard, masculine voices.

'Damn them!' said Rawsthorne. 'They're starting a party.'

'What can we do?' asked Julie.

'Nothing,' said Rawsthorne briefly. He paused, then said, 'I think these are deserters – I wouldn't want them to see us, especially . . .' His voice trailed away.

'Especially the women,' said Julie flatly, and felt Mrs Warmington begin to quiver.

They lay there in silence listening to the racket from the bar, the raucous shouts, the breaking glasses and the voices raised in song. 'All law in the city must be breaking down,' said Rawsthorne at last.

'I want to get out of here,' said Mrs Warmington suddenly and loudly.

'Keep that woman quiet,' Rawsthorne hissed.

'I'm not staying here,' she cried, and struggled to get up.

'Hold it,' whispered Julie furiously, pulling her down.

'You can't keep me here,' screamed Mrs Warmington.

Julie did not know what Eumenides did, but suddenly Mrs Warmington collapsed on top of her, a warm, dead weight, flaccid and heavy. She heaved violently and pushed the woman off her. 'Thanks, Eumenides,' she whispered.

'For God's sake!' breathed Rawsthorne, straining his ears to hear if there was any sudden and sinister change in the volume of noise coming from the bar. Nothing happened; the noise became even louder – the men were getting drunk. After a while Rawsthorne said softly, 'What's the matter with that woman? Is she mad?'

'No,' said Julie. 'Just spoiled silly. She's had her own way all her life and she can't conceive of a situation in which getting her own way could cause her death. She can't adapt.' Her voice was pensive. 'I guess I feel sorry for her more than anything else.'

'Sorry or not, you'd better keep her quiet,' said Rawsthorne. He peered through the crack. 'God knows how long this lot is going to stay here – and they're getting drunker.'

They lay there listening to the rowdy noise which was sometimes overlaid by the reverberation of the battle. Julie kept looking at her watch, wondering how long this was going to go on. Every five minutes she said to herself, they'll leave in another five minutes – but they never did. Presently she heard a muffled sound from Rawsthorne. 'What is it?' she whispered.

He turned his head. 'More of them coming in.' He turned back to watch. There were seven of them this time, six troopers and what seemed to be an officer, and there was discipline in the way they moved into the foyer and looked about. The officer stared across into the bar and shouted something, but his voice was lost in the uproar, so he drew his revolver and fired a shot in the air. There came sudden silence in the hotel.

Mrs Warmington stirred weakly and a bubbling groan came from her lips. Julie clamped her hand across the woman's mouth and squeezed tight. She heard an exasperated sigh from Rawsthorne and saw him move his head slightly as though he had taken one quick look back.

The officer shouted in a hectoring voice and one by one the deserters drifted out of the bar and into the foyer and stood muttering among themselves, eyeing the officer insolently and in defiance. The last to appear was the soldier with the rifle – he was very drunk.

The officer whiplashed them with his tongue, his voice cracking in rage. Then he made a curt gesture and gave a quick command, indicating that they should line up. The drunken soldier with the rifle shouted something and unslung the weapon from his shoulder, cocking it as he did so, and the officer snapped an order to the trooper standing at his back. The trooper lifted his submachine-gun and squeezed the trigger. The stuttering hammer of the gun filled the foyer with sound and a spray of bullets took the rifleman across the chest and flung him backwards across a table, which collapsed with a crash.

A stray bullet slammed into the door near Rawsthorne's head and he flinched, but he kept his eye on the foyer and saw the officer wave his arm tiredly. Obediently the deserters lined up and marched out of the hotel, escorted by the armed troopers. The officer put his revolver back into its holster and looked down at the man who had been killed. Viciously he kicked the body, then turned on his heel and walked out.

Rawsthorne waited a full five minutes before he said cautiously, 'I think we can go out now.'

As he pushed open the door and light flooded into the store-room Julie released her grip of Mrs Warmington, who sagged sideways on to Eumenides. Rawsthorne stumbled out and Julie followed, then they turned to drag out the older woman. 'How is she?' asked Julie. 'I thought I would suffocate her, but I had to keep her quiet.'

Rawsthorne bent over her. 'She'll be all right.'

It was twenty minutes before they were in the car and ready to go. Mrs Warmington was conscious but in a daze, hardly aware of what was happening. Eumenides was white and shaken. As he settled himself in the car seat he discovered a long tear in his jacket just under the left sleeve, and realized with belated terror that he had nearly been shot through the heart by the stray bullet that had frightened Rawsthorne.

Rawsthorne checked the instruments. 'She's full up with petrol,' he said. 'And there are a couple of spare cans in the back. We should be all right.'

He started off and the car rolled down the narrow alley at the back of the hotel heading towards the main street. The Union Jack mounted on the wing of the car fluttered a little in the breeze of their passage.

It was a quarter to two.

III

When Causton stepped out into the street he had felt very conspicuous as though accusing eyes were upon him from every direction, but after a while he began to feel easier as he realized that the people round him were intent only on their own troubles. Looking up the crowded street towards the Place de la Libération Noire he saw a coil of black smoke indicating a fire, and even as he watched he saw a shell burst in what must have been the very centre of the square.

He turned and began to hurry the other way, going with the general drift. The noise was pandemonium – the thunder of the guns, the wail of shells screaming through the air and the ear-splitting blasts as they exploded were bad enough, but the noise of the crowd was worse. Everyone seemed to find it necessary to shout, and the fact that they were shouting in what, to him, was an unknown language did not help.

Once a man grasped him by the arm and bawled a string of gibberish into his face and Causton said, 'Sorry, old boy, but I can't tell a word you're saying,' and threw the arm off. It was only when he turned away that he realized that he himself had shouted at the top of his voice.

The crowd was mainly civilian although there were a lot of soldiers, some armed but mostly not. The majority of the soldiers seemed to be unwounded and quite fit apart from their weariness and the glazed terror in their eyes, and Causton judged that these were men who had faced an artillery barrage for the first time in their lives and had broken under it. But there were wounded men, trudging along holding broken arms, limping with leg wounds, and one most horrible sight, a young soldier staggering along with his hands to his stomach, the red wetness of his viscera escaping through his slippery fingers.

The civilians seemed even more demoralized than the soldiery. They ran about hither and thither, apparently at random. One man whom Causton observed changed the direction of his running six times in as many minutes, passing and repassing Causton until he was lost in the crowd. He came upon a young girl in a red dress standing in the middle of the street, her hands clapped to her ears and her prettiness distorted as she screamed endlessly. He heard her screams for quite a long time as he fought his way through that agony of terror.

He finally decided he had better get into a side street away from the press, so he made his way to the pavement and turned the first corner he came to. It was not so crowded and he could make better time, a point he noted for when the time came to drive out the car. Presently he came upon a young soldier sitting on an orange box, his rifle beside him and one sleeve of his tunic flapping loose. Causton stopped and said, 'Have you got a broken arm?'

The young man looked up uncomprehendingly, his face grey with fatigue. Causton tapped his own arm. 'Le bras,' he said, then made a swift motion as though breaking a stick across his knee. 'Broken?'

The soldier nodded dully.

'I'll fix it,' said Causton and squatted down to help the soldier take off his tunic. He kicked the orange box to pieces to make splints and then bound up the arm. 'You'll be okay now,' he said, and departed. But he left bearing the man's tunic and rifle – he now had his props.

The tunic was a tight fit so he wore it unbuttoned; the trousers did not match and he had no cap, but he did not think that mattered – all that mattered was that he looked approximately like a soldier and so had a proprietary interest in the war. He lifted the rifle and worked the action to find the magazine empty and smiled thoughtfully. That did not matter, either; he had never shot anyone in his life and did not intend starting now.

Gradually, by a circuitous route which he carefully marked on the map, he made his way to the eastern edge of the city by the coast road. He was relieved to see that here the crowds were less and the people seemed to be somewhat calmer. Along the road he saw a thin trickle of people moving out, a trickle that later in the day would turn to a flood. The sooner he could get Rawsthorne started in the car, the better it would be for everyone concerned, so he turned back, looking at his watch. It was later than he thought – nearly ten o'clock.

Now he found he was moving against the stream and progress was more difficult and would become even more so as he approached the disturbed city centre. He looked ahead and saw the blazon of smoke in the sky spreading over the central area – the city was beginning to burn. But not for long, he thought grimly. Not if Wyatt is right.

He pressed on into the bedlam that was St Pierre, pushing against the bodies that pressed against him and ruthlessly using the butt of his rifle to clear his way. Once he met a soldier fighting his way clear and they came face to face; Causton reversed his rifle and manipulated the bolt with a sharp click, thinking, what do I do if he doesn't take the hint? The soldier nervously eyed the rifle muzzle pointing at his belly, half-heartedly made an attempt to lift his own gun but thought better of it, and retreated, slipping away into the crowd. Causton grinned mirthlessly and went on his way.

He was not far from the Imperiale when the press of the crowd became so much that he could not move. Christ! he thought; we're sitting ducks for a shell-burst. He tried to make his way back, but found that as difficult as going forward – something was evidently holding up the crowd, something immovable.

He found out what it was when he struggled far enough back, almost to the corner of the street. A military unit had debouched from the side street and formed a line across the main thoroughfare, guns pointing at the crowd. Men were being hauled out of the crowd and lined up in a clear space, and Causton took one good look and tried to duck back. But he was too late. An arm shot out and grabbed him, pulling him bodily out of the crowd and thrusting him to join the others. Serrurier was busy rounding up his dissolving army.

He looked at the group of men which he had joined. They were all soldiers and all unwounded, looking at the ground with hangdog expressions. Causton hunched his shoulders, drooped his head and mingled unobtrusively with them, getting as far away from the front as possible. After a while an officer came and made a speech to them. Causton couldn't understand a word of it, but he got the general drift of the argument. They were deserters, quitters under fire, who deserved to be shot, if not at dawn, then a damn' sight sooner. Their only hope of staying alive was to go and face the guns of Favel for the greater glory of San Fernandez and President Serrurier.

To make his point the officer walked along the front row of men and arbitrarily selected six. They were marched across to the front of a house – poor, bewildered, uncomprehending sheep – and suddenly a machine-gun opened up and the little group staggered and fell apart under the hail of bullets. The officer calmly walked across and put a bullet into the brain of one screaming wretch, then turned and gave a sharp order.

The deserters were galvanized into action. Under the
screams of bellowing non-coms they formed into rough
order and marched away down the side street, Causton
among them. He looked at the firing squad in the truck as
he passed, then across at the six dead bodies. *Pour encourager
les autres*, he thought.

Causton had been conscripted into Serrurier's army.

IV

Dawson was astonished at himself.

He had lived his entire life as a civilized member of the
North American community and, as a result, he had never
come to terms with himself on what he would do if he got
into real trouble. Like most modern civilized men, he had
never met trouble of this sort; he was cosseted and protected
by the community and paid his taxes like a man, so that this
protection should endure and others stand between him and
primitive realities such as death by bullet or torture.

Although his image was that of a free-wheeling, all-
American he-man and although he was in danger of believ-
ing his own press-clippings, he was aware in the dim recesses
of his being that this image was fraudulent, and from time
to time he had wondered vaguely what kind of a man he
really was. He had banished these thoughts as soon as they
were consciously formulated because he had an uneasy
feeling that he was really a weak man after all, and the
thought disturbed him deeply. The public image he had
formed was the man he wanted to be and he could not bear
the thought that perhaps he was nothing like that. And he
had no way of proving it one way or the other – he had
never been put to the test.

Wyatt's hardly concealed contempt had stung and he felt
something approaching shame at his attempt to steal the

car – that was not the way a *man* should behave. So that when his testing-time came something deep inside him made him square his shoulders and briskly tell Sous-Inspecteur Roseau to go to hell and make it damn' fast, buddy.

So it was that now, lying in bed with all hell breaking loose around him, he felt astonished at himself. He had stood up to such physical pain as he had never believed possible and he felt proud that his last conscious act in Roseau's office had been to look across at the implacable face before him and mumble, 'I still say it – go to hell, you son of a bitch!'

He had recovered consciousness in a clean bed with his hands bandaged and his wounds tended. Why that should be he did not know, nor did he know why he could not raise his body from the bed. He tried several times and then gave up the effort and turned his attention to his new and won-drous self. In one brief hour he had discovered that he would never need a public image again, that he would never shrink from self-analysis.

'I'll never be afraid again,' he whispered aloud through bruised lips. 'By God, I stood it – I need never be afraid again.'

But he *was* afraid again when the artillery barrage opened up. He could not control the primitive reaction of his body; his glands worked normally and fear entered him as the hail of steel fell upon the Place de la Libération Noire. He shrank back on to the bed and looked up at the ceiling and wondered helplessly if the next shell would plunge down to take away his new-found manhood.

V

Not far away, Wyatt sat in the corner of his cell with his hands over his ears because the din was indescribably deafening. His face was cut about where broken glass had driven at him, but luckily his eyes were untouched. He had spent some time delicately digging out small slivers of glass from his skin – a very painful process – and the concentration needed had driven everything else out of his mind. But now he was sharply aware of what was going on.

Every gun Favel had appeared to be firing on the Place de la Libération Noire. Explosion followed explosion without ceasing and an acrid chemical stink drifted through the small window into the cell. The Poste de Police had not yet been hit, or at least Wyatt did not think so. And he was sure he would know. As he crouched in the corner with his legs up, grasshopper fashion, and his face dropped between his knees, he was busy making plans as to what he would do when the Poste was hit – if he still remained alive to do anything at all.

Suddenly there was an almighty *clang* that shivered the air in the cell. Wyatt felt like a mouse that had crawled into a big drum – he was completely deafened for a time and heard the tumult outside as though through a hundred layers of cloth. He staggered to his feet, shaking his head dizzily, and leaned against the wall. After a while he felt better and began to look more closely at the small room in which he was imprisoned. The Poste had been hit – that was certain – and surely to God something must have given way.

He looked at the opposite wall. Surely it had not had that bulge in it before? He went closer to examine it and saw a long crack zigzagging up the wall. He put his hand out and pushed tentatively, and then applied his shoulder and pushed harder. Nothing gave.

He stepped back and looked around the cell for something with which to attack the wall. He looked at the stool and rejected it – it was lightly built of wood, a good enough weapon against a man but not against the wall. There remained the bed. It was made of iron of the type where the main frame lifts out of sockets in the head and foot. The bed head, of tubular metal, was bolted together, but the bolts had rusted and it was quite a task to withdraw them. However, at the end of half an hour he had a goodly selection of tools with which to work – two primitive crowbars, several scrapers devised from the bed springs and an object which was quite unnameable but for which, no doubt, he could find a use.

Feeling rather like Edmond Dantes, he knelt before the wall and began to use one of the scrapers to detach loose mortar from the crack. The mortar, centuries old, was hard and ungiving, but the explosion had not done the wall any good and gradually he excavated a small hole, wide enough and deep enough to insert the end of his crowbar. Then he heaved until his muscles cracked and was rewarded with the minutest movement of the stone block which he was attacking.

He stood back to inspect the problem and became conscious that the intense shellfire directed at the square had ceased. The shell which had cracked the wall must have been one of the last fired in that direction, and all that could be heard now was a generalized battle noise away to the north of the town.

He dismissed the war from his mind and looked thoughtfully at his improvised crowbar. A crowbar is a lever, or rather, part of a lever – the other part is a fulcrum, and he had no fulcrum. He took the foot of the bed and placed it against the wall; it could be used as a fulcrum but not in the place he had made the hole. He would have to begin again and make another hole.

Again it took a long time. Patiently he scraped away at the iron-hard mortar, chipping and picking it to pieces, and when he had finished his knuckles were bruised and bleeding and his fingertips felt as though someone had sandpapered them raw. He was also beginning to suffer from thirst; he had drunk the small carafe of water that had been in the cell, and no one had come near since that last colossal explosion – a good sign.

He inserted the tip of his crowbar into the new hole and heaved again. Again he felt the infinitesimal shift in the wall. He took the bed foot and placed it within six inches of the wall and then plunged his crowbar into the hole. It rested nicely just on top of the metal frame of the bed. Then he took a deep breath and swung his whole weight on to the crowbar. Something had to give – the crowbar, the bed, the wall – or – maybe – Wyatt. He hoped it would be the wall.

He felt the metal tube of the crowbar bending under his weight but still bore down heavily, lifting his feet from the floor. There came a sudden grating noise and a sharp shift in pressure and he found himself abruptly deposited on the floor. He turned over and coughed and waved his hand to disperse the dust which eddied and swirled through the cell illuminated by a bright beam of sunlight which shone through the gaping hole he had made.

He rested for a few minutes, then went to look at the damage. By his calculations, he should merely have broken through to the next cell and it had been a calculated risk whether he would find the door to that cell locked. But to his surprise, when he looked through the hole he could see, though not very clearly, a part of the square partly obscured by a ragged exterior wall.

The shell that had hit the Poste had totally destroyed the next cell and it was only by the mercy of the excellent and forgotten builders of his prison that he had not been blown to kingdom come.

He had dislodged only two of the heavy ashlar blocks that made up the wall and the hole would be a tight fit, but luckily he was slim and managed to wriggle through with nothing more than a few additional scrapes. It was tricky finding a footing on the other side because half the floor had been blown away, leaving the ground-floor office starkly exposed to the sky. A man looked up at him from down there with shocked brown eyes – but he was quite dead, lying on his back with his chest crushed by a block of masonry.

Wyatt teetered on the foot-wide ledge that was his only perch and supported himself with his hands while he looked across the square. It was desolate and uninhabited save for the hundreds of corpses that lay strewn about, corpses dressed in the light blue of the Government army uniform. The only movement was from the smoke arising from the dozen or so fiercely burning army trucks grouped round what had been the centrepiece – the heroic statue of Serrurier. But the statue was gone, blown from its plinth by the storm of steel.

He looked down. It would be quite easy to descend to the ground and to walk away as free as the air. But then he looked across and saw the door of the ruined cell hanging loose with one hinge broken, and although he hesitated, he knew what he must do. He must find Dawson.

He picked his way carefully along the narrow ledge until he came to a wider and safer part near the door. From then on it was easy and inside thirty seconds he was in the corridor of the cell block. It was strange; apart from the heavy layer of dust which overlay everything, there was not a sign that the building had been hit.

Walking up the corridor, he called, 'Dawson!' and was astonished to hear his voice emerge as a croak. He cleared his throat and called again in a stronger voice, 'Dawson! Dawson!'

A confused shouting came from the cells around him, but he could not distinguish Dawson's voice. Angrily, he shouted, '*Taisez-vous!*' and the voices died away save for a faint cry from the end of the corridor. He hastened along and called again. 'Dawson! Are you there?'

'Here!' a faint voice said, and he traced it to a room next to Roseau's office. He looked at the door – this was no cell, it would be easy. He took a heavy fire-extinguisher, and, using it as a battering ram, soon shattered the lock and burst into the room.

Dawson was lying in bed, his head and hands bandaged. Both his eyes were blackened and he seemed to have lost some teeth. Wyatt looked at him. 'My God! What did they do to you?'

Dawson looked at him for some seconds without speaking, then he summoned up a grin. 'Seen yourself lately?' he asked, speaking painfully through swollen lips.

'Come on,' said Wyatt. 'Let's get out of here.'

'I can't,' said Dawson with suppressed rage. 'The bastards strapped me down.'

Wyatt took a step forward and saw that it was true. Two broad straps ran across Dawson's body, the buckles well under the bed far beyond the reach of prying hands. He ducked under the bed and began to unfasten them. 'What happened after you were beaten up?' he asked.

'That's the damnedest thing,' said Dawson with perplexity. 'I woke up in here and I'd been fixed up with these bandages. Why in hell would they do that?'

'I threw a scare into Roseau,' said Wyatt. 'I'm glad it worked.'

'They still didn't want to lose me, I guess,' said Dawson. 'That's why they strapped me down. I've been going through hell, waiting for a shell to bust through the ceiling. I thought it had happened twice.'

'Twice? I thought there was only one hit.'

Dawson got out of bed. 'I reckon there were two.' He nodded to a chair. 'Help me with my pants; I don't think I can do it myself – not with these hands. Oh, how I'd like to meet up with that son of a bitch, Roseau.'

'How are your legs?' asked Wyatt, helping to dress him.

'They're okay.'

'We've got a bit of climbing to do; not much – just enough to get down to street level. I think you'll be able to do it. Come on.'

They went out into the corridor. 'There's a cell a bit further along that's been well ventilated,' said Wyatt. 'We go out that way.'

A shot echoed in the corridor shockingly noisily and a bullet sprayed Wyatt with chips of stone as it ricocheted off the wall by his head. He ducked violently and turned to find Roseau staggering down the corridor after them. He was in terrible shape. His uniform was hanging about him in rags and his right arm was hanging limp as though broken. He held a revolver in his left hand and it was perhaps that which saved Wyatt from the next shot, which went wide.

He yelled, 'That cell there,' and pushed Dawson violently. Dawson ran the few yards to the door and dashed through to halt, staggering, in an attempt to save himself falling over the unexpected drop.

Wyatt retreated more slowly, keeping a wary eye on Roseau who lurched haltingly down the passage. Roseau said nothing at all; he brushed the blood away from his fanatical eyes with the back of the hand that held the gun, and his jaw worked as he aimed waveringly for another shot. Wyatt ducked through the cell door as the gun went off and heard a distinct thud as the bullet buried itself in the door-jamb.

'Over here!' yelled Dawson, and Wyatt hastily trod over the rubble and on to the narrow ledge. 'If that crazy bastard comes out we'll have to jump for it.'

'It's as good a way to break a leg as any,' Wyatt said. He felt his fingers touch something loose and they curled round a fist-sized piece of rock.

'Here he comes,' said Dawson.

Roseau shuffled through the door, seemingly oblivious of the drop at his feet. He staggered forward, keeping his eyes on Wyatt, until the tips of his boots were overhanging space, and he lifted the gun in a trembling hand.

Wyatt threw the rock and it hit Roseau on the side of the head. The gun fired and he spun, losing his footing, to crash face down in the ruins below. His arm lay across the shoulder of the dead man as though he had found a lost comrade, and the newly disturbed dust settled again on the dead man's open and puzzled eyes.

Dawson took a deep breath. 'Jesus! Now there was a persistent son of a bitch. Thanks, Wyatt.'

Wyatt was shaking. He stood on the ledge with his back to the wall and waited for the quivers to go away. Dawson looked down at Roseau and said, 'He wanted to implicate you – I didn't, Wyatt. I didn't tell him anything.'

'I didn't think you had,' said Wyatt quietly. 'Let's get down from here. There's nothing happening here now, but that could change damn' quickly.'

Slowly they made their way down to the street. It was difficult for Dawson because his hands hurt, but Wyatt helped him. When they stood on the pavement Dawson asked, 'What do we do now?'

'I'm going back to the Imperiale,' said Wyatt. 'I must find Julie. I must find if she's still in St Pierre.'

'Which way is it?'

'Across the square,' said Wyatt, pointing.

They set off across the Place de la Libération Noire and Dawson stared at the carnage in horror. There were bodies everywhere, cut down in hundreds. They could not walk in a straight line for more than five yards without having to deviate and they gave up trying and stepped over the corpses. Suddenly Dawson turned and retched; he had not drunk or eaten for a long time, and his heavings were dry and laboured.

Wyatt kicked something which rang with a hollow clang. He looked down to see the decapitated head of a man; the eyes stared blankly and there was a ghastly hole in the left temple.

It was the bronze head of the statue of Serrurier.

FIVE

Causton marched to the sound of the guns.

He sweated in the hot sun as he stepped out briskly in response to the lashing voice of the sergeant and wondered how he was going to get out of this pickle. If he could get out of the ranks for a few minutes, all he had to do was to rip off the tunic, drop the rifle and he would be a civilian again; but there did not seem much chance of that. The erstwhile deserters were watched carefully by troopers armed with submachine-guns and the officer, driven in a jeep, passed continually from one end of the column to the other.

He stumbled a little, then picked up the step again, and the man next to him turned and addressed him in the island *patois*, obviously asking a question. Causton played dumb – quite literally; he made some complicated gestures with his fingers, hoping to God that the soldier would not know he was faking. The man let out a shrill cackle of laughter and poked the soldier in front in the small of the back. He evidently thought it a good joke that they should have a dumb soldier in their midst and curious eyes were turned on Causton. He hoped the sweat was not making the boot-polish run.

Not far ahead he could hear the sound of small-arms firing – the tac-a-tac of machine-guns and the more

uncoordinated and sporadic rattle of rifles – much closer
than he had expected. Favel had pushed the firing line far
into the suburbs of St Pierre and, from the sound of it, was
expending ammunition at a fantastic rate. Causton winced
as a shell burst a hundred yards to the right, ruining a shack,
and there came a perceptible and hesitant slowing down of
the column of men.

The sergeant screamed, the officer cursed, the column
speeded up again. Presently they turned off into a side street
and the column halted. Causton looked with interest at the
army trucks which were parked nose to tail along the street,
noting that most of them were empty. He also saw that men
were siphoning petrol from the tanks of some of the trucks
and refilling the tanks of others.

The officer stepped forward and harangued them again.
At what was apparently a question several of the men in the
ranks lifted rifles and waved them, so Causton did the same.
At a curt command from the officer, those men broke ranks
and lined up on the other side of the street, Causton with
them. The officer was evidently sorting out the armed men
from those who had thrown away their rifles.

A sergeant passed along the thin line of armed men. To
every man he put a question and doled out ammunition
from a box carried by two men who followed along behind.
When he came to Causton and snapped out his question
Causton merely snapped open the breech of his rifle to
show that the magazine was empty. The sergeant thrust two
clips of ammunition into his hands and passed on.

Causton looked across at the trucks. Rifles were being
unloaded from one of them and issued to the unarmed
men. There were not nearly enough to go round. He tossed
the two clips of ammunition in his hand thoughtfully and
looked at one lorry as it pulled away, replenished with
petrol at the sacrifice of the others. Serrurier was running
short of petrol, guns and ammunition, or, more probably, he

had plenty but in the wrong place at the wrong time. It was very likely that his supply corps was in a hell of a mess, disrupted by Favel's unexpectedly successful thrust.

He loaded the rifle and put the other clip in his pocket. Serrurier's logistic difficulties were likely to be the death of a good foreign correspondent; this was definitely not a good place to be. Despite his aversion to guns, he thought it would be as well to be prepared. He looked about and weighed his chances of getting away and decided dismally that they were nil. But who knew what a change in the fortunes of war would bring?

More orders were barked and the men tramped off again, this time at right angles to their original march from the centre of the town, and Causton judged that they were moving parallel to the firing line. They entered one of the poorest areas of St Pierre, a shanty town of huts built from kerosene cans beaten flat and corrugated iron. There were no civilians visible; either they were cowering in the ramshackle dwellings or they had hurriedly departed.

The line of march changed again towards the noise of battle and they emerged on to an open place, an incursive tongue of the countryside licking into the suburbs. Here they were halted and spread out into a long line, and Causton judged that this was where they would make their stand. The men started to dig in, using no tools but their bayonets, and Causton, with alacrity, followed suit.

He found that a malodorous spot had been picked for him to die in. This open ground, so near to the shanty town, was a rubbish dump in which the unhygienic citizens deposited anything for which they had no further use. Incautiously he stabbed a borrowed bayonet into the bloated corpse of a dead dog which lay half-buried under a pile of ashes – the gases burst from it with a soft sigh and a terrible stench and Causton gagged. He moved away slightly and attacked the ground again, this time with better results, and found that digging in a rubbish dump did have advantages – it was very easy to excavate a man-sized hole.

Having got dug-in, he looked around, first to the rear in search of an avenue of escape. Directly behind him was the sergeant, tough-looking and implacable, the muzzle of whose rifle poked forward, perhaps intentionally, right at Causton. Behind the sergeant and just in front of the first line of shacks were the captain's bully-boys spread in a thin line, their submachine-guns ready to cut down any man who attempted to run; and behind the troopers was the captain himself, leading from the rear and sheltering in the lee of a shack. Beside the shack the jeep stood with idling engine and Causton judged that the captain was ready to take off if the line broke. No joy there.

He turned his attention to the front. The strip of open ground stretched as far as he could see on either side, and was about a quarter of a mile across – maybe four hundred yards. On the other side were the better constructed houses of the more prosperous citizens of St Pierre whose exclusiveness was accentuated and protected from the shanties by this strip of no-man's-land. A battle seemed to be going on across there; shells and mortar bombs were exploding with frightful regularity, tossing pieces of desirable residence about with abandon; the fusillade of small-arms fire was continuous, and once a badly aimed projectile landed only fifty yards to Causton's front and he drew in his head and felt the patter of earth fragments all about him.

He judged that this was the front line and that the Government forces were losing. Why else would the army have whipped together a hasty second line of ill-equipped deserters? Still, the position was not badly chosen; if the front line broke then Favel's men would have to advance across four hundred yards of open ground. But then he thought of the meagre two clips of ammunition with which he had been issued – perhaps Favel's men would not find it too difficult, after all. It depended on whether the Government troops over there could retreat in good order.

Nothing happened for a long time and Causton, lying there in the hot sun, actually began to feel sleepy. He had been informed by soldiers that war is a period during which long stretches of boredom are punctuated by brief moments of fright, and he was quite prepared to believe this, although he had not encountered it in his own experience. But then, his own job had mainly consisted of flitting from one hot spot to another, the intervals being filled in by a judicious sampling of the flesh-pots of a dozen assorted countries. He definitely found this small sample of soldiering very dreary.

Occasionally he turned to see if his chance of escape had improved, but there was never any change. The sergeant stared at him, stony-faced, and the rearguard troopers were always in position. The captain alternated between smoking cigarettes with quick puffs and gazing across at the front line through field glasses. Once, in order to ingratiate himself with the sergeant and in hope of future favours, Causton tossed him a cigarette. The sergeant stretched out an arm, looked at the cigarette in puzzlement, then smiled and lit it. Causton smiled back, then turned again to his front, hoping that a small bond of friendship had been joined.

Presently the uproar in the front line rose to a crescendo and Causton caught the first sight of human movement – a few distant figures flitting furtively on the nearside of the distant houses. He strained his eyes and wished he had the captain's binoculars. From behind him he heard the captain's voice issuing sharp orders and the nearer brazen scream of the sergeant, but he took no notice because he had just identified the distant figures as Government troops and they were running as hard as they could – the front line had broken.

The man nearest to him pushed his rifle forward and cocked it, and Causton heard a series of metallic clicks run down the line, but he did not take his eyes from the scene before him. The nearest blue-clad figure was half-way across – about two hundred yards away – when he suddenly threw up his hands and pitched helplessly forward as though he had stumbled over something. He collapsed into a crumpled heap, heaved convulsively and then lay still.

The field was now filled with running men, retreating in no form of order. Some ran with experience born of battle in short, scuttling zigzags, constantly changing direction in order to throw the marksmen behind off their aim; these were the more intelligent. The stupid ones, or those crazed with fear, ran straight across, and it was these who were picked off by the rattling machine-guns and the cracking rifles.

Causton was abruptly astonished to find himself under fire. There was a constant twittering in the air about him which, at first, he could not identify. But when the dog in the periphery of his vision suddenly jerked its hind leg as though chasing rabbits in its sleep and the dry ground ten yards ahead of him fountained into a row of spurts of dust, he drew himself into his foxhole like a tortoise drawing into its shell. However, his journalist's curiosity got the better of him, and he raised his head once more to see what was going on.

Mortar shells were beginning to drop into the field, raising huge dust plumes which drifted slowly with the wind. The first of the retreating men was quite near and Causton could see his wide-open mouth and staring eyes and could hear the hard thud of his boots on the dry earth. He was not ten yards away when he fell, a flailing tangle of arms and legs, and as he lurched into stillness Causton saw the gaping hole in the back of his head.

The soldier behind him swerved and came on, legs working like pistons. He jumped clear over Causton and disappeared behind in a panic of terror. Then there was another

– and another – and still more – all bolting in panic through the second line of defence. The sergeant's voice rose in a scream as the men in the foxholes nervously twitched as though to run, and there was a near-by shot. We get killed if we run and killed if we don't – later on, thought Causton. Better not to run – yet.

For over half an hour the demoralized survivors of the front line passed through and soon Causton heard scattered shots coming from the rear. The survivors were being whipped back into shape. He stared across the field, expecting to see the assault of Favel's army, but nothing happened except that the mortar fire lifted briefly and then plunged down again, this time directly on their position. In that small moment of time, when the smoke of battle was drifting away, Causton saw dozens of bodies scattered over the field and heard a few distant cries and wails.

Then he had no time even to think of anything else as the shells began to rain down in an iron hail. He crouched in his foxhole and dug his fingers into the nauseous detritus as the ground shook and heaved underneath him. It seemed to go on for an eternity although, on later recollection, he supposed it to have lasted for not more than fifteen minutes. But at the time he thought it would never end. Jesus, God! he prayed; let me get out of here.

The barrage lifted as suddenly as it had started. Causton was stunned and lay for a while in the foxhole before he was able to raise his head. When he did so, he expected to see the first wave of Favel's assault upon them and strained to peer through the slowly dispersing dust and smoke. But there was still nothing – merely the field empty but for the crumpled bodies.

Slowly he turned his head. The tin shacks immediately behind the position had been destroyed, some of them totally, and the ground was pitted with craters. The captain's jeep, its rear wheels blown off, was burning furiously, and of the captain himself there was no sign. Near-by lay the torso of a man – no head, arms or legs – and Causton wondered drearily if it was the sergeant. He stretched his legs painfully and thought that if he was going to run for it, then this was the time to do it.

From the next foxhole a man emerged, his face grey with dust and fear. His eyes were glazed and blank as he levered himself up and began to stagger away. The sergeant appeared from beneath the level of the ground and shouted at him, but the man took no notice, so the sergeant lifted his rifle and fired and the man collapsed grotesquely.

Causton sank back as a tirade of mashed French broke from the sergeant's foxhole. He had to admire the man – this was a tough, professional soldier who would brook no nonsense about desertion in the face of the enemy – but he was confoundedly inconvenient.

He looked about at the heads which were lifted, did a rough count and was surprised at the number of men who had survived the bombardment. He had read that troops well dug in could survive an enormous amount of punishment in the way of shelling – it had been the thing that had kept the First World War going – but experiencing the fact personally was quite a different thing. He looked across the field but could detect no movement that would presage an assault. Even the small-arms fire had ceased.

He turned to see the sergeant clamber out of his hole and walk boldly along the line to check on the men. Still not a shot came from across the field and Causton began to wonder what had happened. He looked uneasily at the steely blue sky as though expecting another storm of metal, and scratched his cheek reflectively as he watched the sergeant.

Suddenly the small-arms fire started up again. A machine-gun opened up shockingly closely and from an unexpected direction. A hail of bullets swept across the position and the sergeant spun like a top, punched by bullets, to fall sprawling and disappear into a foxhole. Causton ducked his head and listened to the heavy fire coming from the *left* and to the rear.

The position had been outflanked.

He heard the yells and the running steps as the rest of the men broke and ran, but he stayed put. He had a hunch they were running into trouble, and anyway be was fed up with being a part of Serrurier's army; the further that unit and he wcrc scparated, the better he would feel. So he lay in the foxhole and played dead.

The machine-gun fire stopped abruptly, but he lay there for fifteen minutes more before even poking his nose above the level of the ground. When he did so, the first thing he saw was a long line of men emerging from the houses on the other side of the field – Favel's men were coming over to mop up. Hastily he wormed his way out of the foxhole and crawled on his belly back towards the shacks, expecting to feel the thud of bullets at any moment. But there was plenty of cover since the ground had been churned up by the mortar fire and he found he could crawl from shell-hole to shell-hole with the minimum of exposure.

Finally he got to the cover of the shacks and looked back. Favel's men were nearly across the field and he had the notion they would shoot anything that moved and he had better find somewhere safer. He listened to the racket coming from the left flank – someone was putting up a fight there, but that would collapse as soon as these oncoming troops hit them. He began to move to the right, dodging from the cover of one shack to another, and always trying to move back.

As he went he ripped off the tunic he was wearing and rubbed at his face. Perhaps the sight of a white skin would cause hesitation of the trigger-finger – at least it was worth trying. He saw no sign of the Government army and all the indications were that Favel was on the verge of punching a hole right through the middle – there did not seem much to stop him.

Presently he had an idea and tried the door of one of the shacks. It had occurred to him that there was no point in running away; after all, he did not *want* to catch up with Serrurier's forces, did he? It would be much better to hide and then emerge in the middle of Favel's army.

The door was not barred, so he pushed it open with a creak and went inside. The shack was deserted; it consisted merely of two rooms and needed a minimum of inspection to show there was no one there. He looked about and saw a wash-basin on a rickety stand below a fly-blown and peeling mirror, which was flanked on one side by a highly coloured oleograph of the Madonna and on the other by the standard official portrait of Serrurier.

Hastily he pulled down the idealized photograph of Serrurier and kicked it under the bed. If anyone interrupted him, he did not want them getting any wrong ideas. Then he poured tepid water into the basin and began to wash his face, keeping a sharp ear cocked for anything going on outside. At the end of five minutes he realized in despair that he was still a light-complexioned Negro; the boot-polish was waterproof and would not come off, no matter how hard he rubbed. Many of the inhabitants of San Fernandez were even lighter complexioned and also had European features.

He was struck by an idea and unbuttoned the front of his shirt to look at his chest. Two days earlier he had been somewhat embarrassed at his pallidity, but now he thanked God that he had not felt the urge to sunbathe. As he stripped off his shirt he prepared for a long wait.

What brought him out was the sound of an engine. He thought that anyone driving a vehicle around there would be civilized enough not to shoot him on sight, so he came

out of the cupboard and into the front room and looked
through the window. The Land-Rover that was passing was
driven by a white man.

'Hey – you!' he shouted, and dashed to the door. 'You
there – *arrêtez*!'

The man driving the Land-Rover looked back and the
vehicle bumped to a halt. Causton ran up and the man
looked at him curiously. 'Who the devil are you?' he asked.

'Thank God!' said Causton. 'You speak English – you *are*
English. My name's Causton – I suppose you could call me
a war correspondent.'

The man looked at him unbelievingly. 'You got off the
mark pretty quickly, didn't you? The war only started yesterday afternoon. You don't look much like a war correspondent – you look more like a nigger minstrel who got on
the wrong side of his audience.'

'I'm genuine enough,' assured Causton.

The man hefted a submachine-gun which was on the
seat next to him. 'I think Favel had better have a look at
you,' he said. 'Get in.'

'Just the man I want to see,' said Causton, climbing into
the Land-Rover and keeping a careful eye on the submachine-gun. 'You a friend of his?'

'I suppose you could say so,' said the man. 'My name is
Manning.'

II

'It's too hot,' said Mrs Warmington querulously.

Julie agreed but did not say so aloud – Mrs Warmington
was the last person she felt like agreeing with about anything. She wriggled slightly, trying to unstick her blouse
from the small of her back, and looked ahead through the
windscreen. She saw exactly what she had seen for the last

half-hour – a small handcart piled perilously high with trumpery household goods being pushed by an old man and a small boy who obstinately stuck to the crown of the road and refused to draw to the side.

Rawsthorne irritably changed down again from second gear to first. 'The engine will boil if we carry on like this in this heat,' he said.

'We mustn't stop,' said Julie in alarm.

'Stopping might prove more difficult than moving,' said Rawsthorne. 'Have you looked behind lately?'

Julie twisted in her seat and looked through the back window of the car, which was now cresting a small rise. Behind, as far as she could see, stretched the long line of refugees fleeing from St Pierre. She had seen this kind of thing on old newsreels but had never expected to see it in actuality. This was a people on the move, trudging wearily from the coming desolation of war, carrying as much of the material minutiæ of their lives as they could on an incredible variety of vehicles. There were perambulators loaded not with babies but with clocks, clothing, pictures, ornaments; there were carts pushed by hand or drawn by donkeys; there were beat-up cars of incredible vintage, buses, trucks and the better cars of the more prosperous.

But primarily there were people: men and women, old and young, rich and poor, the hale and the sick. These were people who did not laugh or speak, who moved along quietly like driven cattle with grey faces and downcast eyes, whose only visible sign of emotion was the quick, nervous twitch of the head to look back along the road.

Julie turned as Rawsthorne blasted on the horn at the obstinate old man ahead. 'The damned fellow won't move aside,' he grumbled. 'If he'd move just a little to the side I could get through.'

Eumenides said, 'The road – it drop on side.' He pointed to the cart. ' 'E fright 'e fall.'

'Yes,' said Rawsthorne. 'That cart is grossly overloaded and there *is* a steep camber.'

Julie said, 'How much farther do we have to go?'

'About two miles.' Rawsthorne nodded ahead. 'You see where the road turns round that headland over there? We have to get to the other side.'

'How long do you think it will take?'

Rawsthorne drew to a halt to avoid ramming the old man. 'At this rate it will be another two hours.'

The car crept on by jerks and starts. The refugees on foot were actually moving faster than those in vehicles and Rawsthorne contemplated abandoning the car. But he rejected the idea almost as soon as he thought of it; there was the food and water to be carried, and the blankets, too – those would be much too valuable in the coming week to leave behind with the car. He said, 'At least this war is having one good result – it's getting the people out of St Pierre.'

'They won't all get out,' said Julie. 'And what about the armies?'

'It's damn' bad luck on Favel,' said Rawsthorne. 'Imagine taking a town and then being smashed by a hurricane. I've read a lot of military history but I've never heard of a parallel to it.'

'It will smash Serrurier, too,' said Julie.

'Yes, it will,' said Rawsthorne thoughtfully. 'I wonder who'll pick up the pieces.' He stared ahead. 'I like Wyatt, but I hope he's wrong about this hurricane. There's a chance he might be, you know; he's relying a lot on his intuition. I'd like Favel to have a fighting chance.'

'I hope he's wrong, too,' said Julie sombrely. 'He's trapped back there.'

Rawsthorne glanced at her drawn face, then bit his lip and lapsed into silence. The time dragged on as slowly as the car. Presently he pointed out a group of young men who were passing. They were fit and able-bodied, if poorly dressed; one had a fistful of bank-notes which he was counting, and another was twirling a gleaming necklace on his forefinger. He said meditatively, 'I wish Causton hadn't taken your gun, Eumenides; it might have come in handy. Those boys have been looting. They've taken money and jewellery but soon they'll get hungry and try to take food from whoever has it.'

Eumenides shrugged. 'Too late; 'e took gun – I look.'

At last they rounded the headland and Rawsthorne said, 'Another few hundred yards and we'll pull off. Look for a convenient place to run the car off the road – what we really need is a side turning.'

They ground on, still in bottom gear, and after a while Eumenides said, 'Turn 'ere.'

Rawsthorne craned his neck. 'Yes, this looks all right. I wonder where it leads.'

'Let's try,' said Julie. 'There's no one going up there.'

Rawsthorne turned the car on to the unmetalled side road and was immediately able to change up to second gear. They bumped along for a few hundred yards and then came into the wide space of a quarry. 'Damn!' he said. 'It's a dead end.'

Julie wriggled in her seat. 'At least we can get out and stretch our legs before going back. And I think we ought to eat again while we have the chance, too,' she said.

The bread was stale, the butter melted and going rancid, the water tepid and, on top of that, the heat had not improved their appetites, but they ate a little while sitting in the shade of the quarry huts and discussed their next move. Mrs Warmington said, 'I don't see why we can't stay here – it's a quiet place.'

'I'm afraid not,' said Rawsthorne. 'We can still see the sea from here – to the south. According to Wyatt, the hurricane will come from the south.'

Mrs Warmington made an impatient noise. 'I think that young man is a scaremonger; I don't think there is going to be a hurricane. I looked back when we could still see the Base and there are still ships there at anchor. Commodore Brooks doesn't think there'll be a hurricane, so why should we?'

'We can't take the chance that he'll be wrong,' said Julie quietly. She turned to Rawsthorne. 'We'll have to go back to the road and try again.'

'I don't think so,' said Rawsthorne. 'I don't really think we can. This track left the road at an acute angle – I don't see how we could turn the car into the traffic stream. Nobody would stop to let us through.' He looked up at the quarry face. 'We've got to get on the other side of that.'

Mrs Warmington snorted. 'I'm not even going to try to climb that. I'm staying here.'

Rawsthorne laughed. 'We don't have to climb it – we go round it. There's a convenient place to climb a little farther back down the track.' He chewed the stale bread distastefully. 'Wyatt said we must get on the north side of a ridge, didn't he? Well, that's what we're going to do.'

Eumenides asked abruptly, 'We leave car?'

'We'll have to. We'll take all we need from it, then park it behind these huts. With a bit of luck no one will find it.'

They finished their brief meal and began to pack up. Julie looked at the wilting Mrs Warmington and forced some humour into her voice. 'Well, there's no dish-washing to be done.' But Mrs Warmington was past caring; she just sat in the shade and gasped, and Julie thought cattily, this is better than a diet for reducing her surplus poundage.

Rawsthorne ran the car down the track and they unpacked all the supplies. He said, 'It's better we do this here; it's a nice out-of-the-way spot with none of those young thugs snooping at us.' He looked up the hill. 'It's not far to the top – I suppose this ridge isn't much more than two hundred feet high.'

He took the car back to the quarry. Mrs Warmington said pettishly, 'I suppose we must, although I think this is nonsense.' She turned to Eumenides. 'Don't just stand there; pick up something.'

Julie looked at Mrs Warmington with a glint in her eye. 'You'll have to do your share of carrying.'

Mrs Warmington looked doubtfully at the scrub-covered hill. 'Oh, but I can't – my heart, you know.'

Julie thought that Mrs Warmington's heart was as sound as a bell and just as hard. 'The blankets aren't heavy,' she said. 'Take some of those.' She thrust a bundle of blankets into Mrs Warmington's unready arms and she dropped her bag. It fell with a dull thud into the dust and they both stooped for it.

Julie picked it up and found it curiously heavy. 'Whatever have you got in here?'

Mrs Warmington snatched the bag from her, dropping the blankets. 'My jewels, darling. You don't suppose I'd leave *those* behind.'

Julie indicated the blankets. 'Those might keep you alive – your jewels won't.' She stared hard at Mrs Warmington. 'I suggest you concentrate more on doing work and less on giving orders; you haven't been right about a damn' thing so far, and you're just a dead weight.'

'All right,' said Mrs Warmington, perhaps alarmed at the expression on Julie's face. 'Don't drive so. You're too mannish, my dear; it's no wonder you haven't caught yourself a husband.'

Julie ignored her and lifted a cardboard box full of bottled water. As she climbed the hill, she smiled to herself. A few days ago that gibe might have rankled, but not now. At one time she had thought that perhaps she was too self-reliant to appeal to a man; perhaps men *did* like the clinging ultra-feminine type, which she herself had always regarded as parasitic and not giving value for value received. Well, to hell with it! She was not going to disguise her natural intelligence for any man, and a man who was fooled by that sort of thing wasn't worth marrying, anyway. She would rather be herself than be a foolish, ineffectual, overstuffed creature like the Warmington woman.

But her heart turned over at the thought that she might not see Wyatt ever again.

It took them a long time to transport their supplies to the top of the ridge. Rawsthorne, although willing, was not a young man and had neither the strength nor the stamina for the sustained effort. Mrs Warmington was totally unfit for any kind of work and after she had toiled to the top with her small load of blankets, she sat back and watched the others work. Julie was fit enough, but she was not used to the intense heat and the strong sun made her head swim. So it was Eumenides who carried the bulk of the supplies, willingly and without complaint. All he allowed himself was a contemptuous glance at Mrs Warmington each time he deposited a load at the top.

At last all the stores had been moved and they rested for a while on the ridge-top. On the seaward side they could see the main coast road, still as warm with refugees heading east away from St Pierre. The city itself was out of sight behind the headland, but they could hear the distant thud of guns and could see a growing smudge of smoke in the western sky.

On the other side of the ridge the ground sloped down into a small green valley, heavily planted with bananas in long rows. Over a mile away was a long, low building with a few smaller huts scattered about it. Rawsthorne looked at the banana plantation with satisfaction. 'At least we'll have plenty of shade. And the ground is cultivated and easy to dig. And a banana plant blowing down on one wouldn't hurt.'

'I've always liked bananas,' said Mrs Warmington.

'I wouldn't eat any you find down there; they're unripe and they'll give you the collywobbles.' Rawsthorne meditated for a moment. 'I'm no expert on hurricanes like Wyatt, but I do know something about them. If the hurricane is coming from the south, then the wind will blow from the east to begin with – so we must have protection from that side. Later, the wind will come from the west, and that makes things complicated.'

Eumenides pointed. 'Over there – lil 'ollow.'

'So there is,' said Rawsthorne. He arose and picked up a spade. 'I thought these might come in useful when I put them in the car. Shall we go? We can leave all this stuff here until we're sure we know where we're going to take it.'

They descended into the plantation, which was quite deserted. 'We'll keep away from that building,' said Rawsthorne. 'That's the barracks for the convict labour. I imagine Serrurier has given orders that the men be kept locked up, but there's no point in taking chances.' He poked at the ground beneath a banana plant and snorted in disgust. 'Very bad cultivation here; these plants need pruning – if they're not careful they're going to get Panama disease. But it's the same all over the island since Serrurier took over – the whole place is running down.'

They reached the hollow and Rawsthorne adjudged it a good place. 'It's nicely protected,' he said, and thrust his spade into the earth. 'Now we dig.'

'How dig?' asked Eumenides.

'Foxholes – as in the army.' Rawsthorne began to measure out on the ground. 'Five of them – one for each of us and one for the supplies.'

They took it in turns digging – Rawsthorne, Eumenides and Julie – while Mrs Warmington panted in the shade. It was not very hard work because the ground was soft as Rawsthorne had predicted, but the sun was hot and they sweated copiously. Near the end of their labours Julie paused for a drink of water and looked at the five . . . *graves*?

She thought sombrely of the unofficial motto of the Seabees – 'First we dig 'em, then we die in 'em.' In spite of the hot sun, she shivered.

When they had finally completed the foxholes and had brought down the supplies it was near to sunset, although it seemed hotter than ever. Rawsthorne cut some of the huge leaves from some near-by plants and strewed them over the raw earth. 'In the middle of a civil war camouflage does no harm. Anyway, these plants need cutting.'

Julie lifted her head. 'Talking of the war – don't the guns sound louder . . . closer?'

Rawsthorne listened intently. 'They do, don't they?' He frowned. 'I wonder if. . .' He clicked his tongue and shook his head.

'If what?'

'I thought the battle might come this way,' he said. 'But I don't think so. Even if Favel takes St Pierre he must attack Serrurier's forces between St Pierre and Cap Sarrat – and that's on the other side.'

'But the guns *do* sound nearer,' said Julie.

'A trick of the wind,' said Rawsthorne. He said it with dubiety. There was no wind.

As the sun dipped down they prepared for the night and arranged watches. Mrs Warmington, by common consent, was left to sleep all night as being too unreliable. They talked desultorily for a while and then turned in, leaving Julie to stand first watch.

She sat in the sudden darkness and listened to the sound of the guns. To her untutored ear they sounded as though they were just down the valley and round the corner, but she consoled herself with Rawsthorne's reasoning. But there was a fitful red glare in the west from the direction of St Pierre – there were fires in the town.

She searched her pockets and found a crumpled cigarette, which she lit, inhaling the smoke greedily. It had been a bad day; she was tense and the cigarette relaxed her. She sat with her back against a banana tree – or plant, or whatever it was – and thought about Wyatt, wondering what had happened to him. Perhaps he was already dead, caught up in the turmoil of war. Or maybe raging in a cell, waiting for the deadly wind he alone knew was going to strike. She wished with all her heart they had not been separated – whatever was going to happen, she wanted to be with him.

And Causton – what had happened to Causton? If he found his way back to the hotel he would find the note they had pinned on the door of the store-room under the stairs and know they had fled to safety. But he would not know enough to be able to join them. She hoped he would be safe – but her thoughts dwelt longer on Wyatt.

The moon had just risen when she awoke Eumenides as planned. 'Everything quiet,' she said in a low voice. 'Nothing is happening.'

He nodded and said, 'The guns ver' close – more close than before.'

'You think so?'

He nodded again but said nothing more, so she went to her own foxhole and settled down for the night. It is like a grave, she thought as she stretched on the blanket which lay on the bottom. She thought of Wyatt again, very hazily and drowsily, and then fell asleep before she had completed the thought.

She was awakened by something touching her face and she started up, only to be held down. 'Ssssh,' hissed a voice. 'Keep ver' still.'

'What's wrong, Eumenides?' she whispered.

'I don' know,' he said in a low voice. 'Man' peoples 'ere – lis'en!'

She strained her ears and caught an indefinable sound which seemed to emanate from nowhere in particular and everywhere at once. 'It's the wind in the banana leaves,' she murmured.

'No win',' said Eumenides definitely.

She listened again and caught what seemed to be a far-away voice. 'I don't know if you're right or wrong,' she said. 'But I think we ought to wake the others.'

He went to shake Rawsthorne, while Julie woke Mrs Warmington, who squealed in surprise. 'Damn you, be quiet,' snapped Julie, and clapped her hand over Mrs Warmington's mouth as it opened again. 'We might be in trouble. Just stay there and be prepared to move in a hurry. And don't make a sound.'

She went over to where Rawsthorne and Eumenides were conferring in low tones. 'There's something going on,' said Rawsthorne. 'The guns have stopped, too. Eumenides, you go up to the top and see what's happened on the sea-ward side of the ridge; I'll scout down the valley. The moon's bright enough to see for quite a distance.' His voice held a note of perplexity. 'But these damn' noises are coming from all round.'

He stood up. 'Will you be all right, Julie?'

'I'll be fine,' she said. 'And I'll keep that damned woman quiet if I have to slug her.'

The two men went off and she lost sight of them as they disappeared in the plantation. Rawsthorne flitted among the rows, edging nearer and nearer to the convict barracks. Soon he came to a service road driven through the planta-tion and paused before he crossed – which was just as well for he heard a voice from quite close.

He froze and waited while a group of men went up the road. They were Government soldiers and from the sound of their voices they were weary and dispirited. From a word and a half-heard phrase he gathered that they had been

defeated in a battle and had not liked it at all. He waited
until they had gone by, then crossed the road and penetrated the plantation on the other side.

Here he literally fell over a wounded man lying just off
the road. The man cried aloud in anguish and Rawsthorne
ran away, afraid the noise would attract attention. He blundered about in the plantation, suddenly aware that there
were men all about him in the leaf-shadowed moonlight.
They were drifting through the rows of plants from the
direction of St Pierre in no form of order and with no discipline.

Suddenly he saw a spurt of flame and then the growing
glow of a newly lit fire. He shrank back and went another
way, only to be confronted by the sight of another fire being
kindled. All around the fires sprang into being like glow-
worms, and as he cautiously approached one of them he
saw a dozen men sitting and lying before the flames, toast-
ing unripe bananas on twigs to make them palatable
enough to eat.

It was then that he knew he was in the middle of
Serrurier's defeated army, and when he heard the roar of
trucks on the service road he had just crossed and the sharp
voice of command from close behind him, he knew also
that this army was beginning to regroup for tomorrow's battle, which would probably be on the very ground on which
he was standing.

III

Dawson felt better once he had left the Place de la
Libération Noire and the sights that had sickened him.
There was nothing wrong with his legs and he had no trou-
ble keeping up with Wyatt who was in a great hurry.
Although the town centre was not being shelled any more

the noise of battle to the north had greatly intensified, and Wyatt felt he had to get to the Imperiale before the battle moved in. He had to make certain that Julie was safe.

As they moved from the square and the area of government administrative buildings they began to encounter people, at first in ones and twos, and then in greater numbers. By the time they got near to the Imperiale, which fortunately was not far, the press of people in the streets was great, and Wyatt realized he was witnessing the panic of a civilian population caught in war.

Already the criminal elements had begun to take advantage of the situation and most of the expensive shops near the Imperiale had been sacked and looted. Bodies lying on the pavement testified that the police had taken strong measures, but Wyatt's lips tightened as he noted two dead policemen sprawled outside a jewellery shop – the streets of St Pierre were fast ceasing to be safe.

He pushed through the screaming, excited crowds, ran up the steps of the hotel and through the revolving doors into the foyer. 'Julie!' he called. 'Causton!'

There was no answer.

He ran across the foyer and stumbled over the body of a soldier which lay near an overturned table just outside the bar. He shouted again, then turned to Dawson. 'I'm going upstairs – you see what you can find down there.'

Dawson walked into the bar, crunching broken glass underfoot, and looked about. Someone had a hell of a party, he thought. He nudged at a half-empty bottle of Scotch with one bandaged hand and shook his head sadly. He would have liked a drink, but this was not the time for it.

He turned away, feeling a surge of triumph within him. Not long before he would have taken a drink at any time, but since he had survived the attentions of Sous-Inspecteur Roseau he felt a growing strength and a breaking of bonds. As he defied Roseau, stubbornly keeping his mouth shut, so he now defied what he recognized to be the worst in himself and, in that, found a new freedom, the freedom to be himself. 'Big Jim' Dawson was dead and young Jimmy Dawson reborn – maybe a little older in appearance and a bit shrivelled about the edges, but still as new and shining and uncorrupted as that young man had been so many years ago. The only added quality was wisdom, and perhaps a deep sense of shame for what he had done to himself in the name of success.

He searched the ground floor of the hotel – discovered nothing, and returned to the foyer, where he found Wyatt. 'Nothing down there,' he said.

Wyatt's face was gaunt. 'They've gone.' He was looking at the dead soldier sprawled with bloody chest near the upturned table. There was a buzzing of flies about him.

Dawson said tentatively, 'You think – maybe – the soldiers took them?'

'I don't know,' said Wyatt heavily.

'I'm sorry it happened,' said Dawson. 'I'm sorry it happened because of me.'

Wyatt turned his head. 'We don't know it was because of you. It might have happened anyway.' He felt suddenly dizzy and sat down.

Dawson looked at him with concern. 'You know what?' he said. 'I think we could both do with some food. When did we eat last?' He held out his bandaged hands and said apologetically, 'I'd get it myself but I don't think I can open a can.'

'What did they do to you?'

Dawson shrugged and put his hands behind his back. 'Beat me up – roughed me around a bit. Nothing I couldn't take.'

'You're right, of course,' said Wyatt. 'We must eat. I'll see what I can find.'

Ten minutes later they were wolfing cold meat stew right out of the cans. Dawson found he could just hold a spoon in his left hand and by holding the can in the crook of his right arm he could feed himself tolerably well. It was painful because his left hand hurt like hell when he gripped the spoon, but the last thing he wanted was for Wyatt to feed him like a baby – he could not have borne that.

He said, 'What do we do now?'

Wyatt listened to the guns. 'I don't know,' he said slowly. 'I wish Causton or Julie had left a message.'

'Maybe they did.'

'There was nothing in their rooms.'

Dawson thought about that. 'Maybe they weren't in their rooms; maybe they were in the cellar. The guns were firing at the square, and that's not very far away – maybe they sheltered in the cellar.'

'There is no cellar.'

'Okay – but they might have sheltered somewhere else. Where would you go in a bombardment?' He shifted in his chair and the cane creaked. 'I know a guy who was in the London blitz; he said that under the stairs was the best place. Maybe those stairs there.'

Awkwardly he put down the spoon and walked over to the staircase. 'Hey!' he called. 'There's something pinned on this door.'

Wyatt dropped his can with a clatter and ran after Dawson. He ripped the note from the door. 'Causton's vanished,' he said. 'But the others got away in Rawsthorne's car. They've gone east – out of the bay area.' He drew a deep breath. 'Thank God for that.'

'I'm glad they got away,' said Dawson. 'What do we do – follow them?'

'You'd better do that,' said Wyatt. 'I'll give you all the necessary directions.'

Dawson looked at him in surprise. 'Me? What are you going to do?'

'I've been listening to the guns,' said Wyatt. 'I think Favel is making a breakthrough. I want to see him.'

'Are you out of your cotton-picking mind? You hang round in the middle of a goddam war and you'll get shot. You'd better come east with me.'

'I'm staying,' said Wyatt stubbornly. 'Someone's got to tell Favel about the hurricane.'

'What makes you think Favel will listen to you?' demanded Dawson. 'What makes you think you'll even get to see him? There'll be bloody murder going on in this city when Favel comes in – you won't have a chance.'

'I don't think Favel is like that. I think he's a reasonable man, not a psychopath like Serrurier. If I can get to him I think he'll listen.'

Dawson groaned, but one look at Wyatt's inflexible face showed the uselessness of argument. He said, 'You're a goddam, pigheaded, one-track man, Wyatt; a stupid dope with not enough sense to come in out of the rain. But if you feel like that about it, I guess I'll stick around long enough to see you get your come-uppance.'

Wyatt looked at him in surprise. 'You don't have to do that,' he said gently.

'I know I don't,' complained Dawson. 'But I'm staying, anyway. Maybe Causton had the right idea – maybe there's the makings of a good book in all this.' He slanted a glance at Wyatt, half-humorous, half-frowning. 'You'd make a good hero.'

'Keep me out of anything you write,' warned Wyatt.

'It's all right,' said Dawson. 'A dead hero can't sue me.'

'And a dead writer can't write books. I think you'd better get out.'

'I'm staying,' said Dawson. He felt he owed a debt to Wyatt, something he had to repay; perhaps he would get the chance if he stayed around with him.

'As you wish,' said Wyatt indifferently, and moved towards the door.

'Wait a minute,' said Dawson. 'Let's not get shot right away. Let's figure out what's going on. What makes you think Favel is making a breakthrough?'

'There was a heavy barrage going on not long ago – now it's stopped.'

'Stopped? Sounds just the same to me.'

'Listen closely,' said Wyatt. 'Those guns you hear are on the east and west – there's nothing from the centre.'

Dawson cocked his head on one side. 'You're right. You think Favel has bust through the middle?'

'Perhaps.'

Dawson sat down. 'Then all we've got to do is to wait here and Favel will come to us. Take it easy, Wyatt.'

Wyatt looked through a glassless window. 'You could be right; the street is deserted now – not a soul in sight.'

'Those people have brains,' said Dawson. 'No one wants to tangle with a driving army – not even Favel's. He may be as reasonable as you say, but reasonableness doesn't show from behind a gun. It's wiser to wait here and see what happens next.'

Wyatt commenced to pace up and down the foyer and Dawson watched him, seeing the irritability boiling up. He said abruptly, 'Got a cigarette – the cops took mine.'

'They took mine, too.' Wyatt stopped his restless pacing. 'There should be some in the bar.'

He went into the bar, found a pack of cigarettes, stuck one in Dawson's mouth and lit it. Dawson drew on it deeply, then said, 'When are you expecting this hurricane of yours?'

'It could be tomorrow; it could be the day after. I'm cut off from information.'

'Then take it easy, for Christ's sake! Favel's on his way, and your girl-friend is tucked away safely.' Dawson's eyes crinkled as he saw Wyatt's head swing round. 'Well, she *is* your girl-friend, isn't she?'

Wyatt did not say anything, so Dawson changed the subject. 'What do you expect Favel to do about the hurricane? The guy's got a war on his hands.'

'He won't have,' promised Wyatt. 'Not in two days from now. And if he stays in St Pierre he won't have an army, either. He's *got* to listen to me.'

'I surely hope he does,' said Dawson philosophically. 'Because he's the only chance we have of getting out of here.' He lifted his left hand clumsily to take the cigarette from his mouth and knocked it against the edge of the table. He winced and a suppressed sound escaped his lips.

Wyatt said, 'We'd better have a look at those hands.'

'They're all right.'

'You don't want them turning bad on you. Let's have a look at them.'

'They're all right, I tell you,' Dawson protested.

Wyatt looked at Dawson's drawn face. 'I want to look at them,' he said. 'Things that are all right anywhere else go sour in the tropics.' He began to unfasten one of the bandages and his breath hissed as he saw what it covered. 'Good Christ! What did they do to you?'

The hand was mashed to a pulp. As he slowly drew the bandage away he saw, to his horror, two finger-nails come away with it, and the fingers were blue with one huge bruise where they weren't red-raw as beefsteak.

Dawson lay back in the chair. 'They held me down and beat my hands with a rubber hose. I don't think they broke any bones, but I'll not be able to handle a typewriter for quite a while.'

Wyatt had once caught his finger in a door – a trivial thing but the most painful happening of his life. The finger-nail had turned blue but his doctor saved it, and he had been careful of his hands ever since. Now, looking down at Dawson's raw hand, he felt sick inside; he could imagine how painful the battered nerve-endings would be. He said glumly, 'Now I can stop being sorry I killed Roseau.'

Dawson grinned faintly. 'I never was sorry.'

Wyatt was puzzled. There was more to Dawson than he had thought; this was not the same man who had tried to steal a car because he was scared – something must have happened to him. 'You'll need some embrocation on that,' he said abruptly. 'And a shot of penicillin wouldn't do any harm, either. There's a place across the street – I'll see what I can find.'

'Take it easy,' said Dawson in alarm. 'That street is not the safest place in the world right now.'

'I'll watch it,' said Wyatt, and went to the door. Opposite was an American-style drugstore; it had been broken into already but he hoped the drug supplies had not been touched. Before going out, he carefully inspected the street and, finding no movement, he stepped out and ran across.

The drugstore was in a mess but he ignored the chaos and went straight to the dispensary at the back, where he rummaged through the neat drawers looking for what he needed. He found bandages and codeine tablets and embrocation but no antibiotics, and he wasted little time on a further search. At the door of the drugstore he paused again to check the street and froze as he saw a man scuttle across to hide in a doorway.

The man peered out behind the muzzle of a gun, then waved, and three more men ran up the street, hugging the walls and darting from door to door. They were not in uniform and Wyatt thought they must be the forward skirmishers of Favel's army. Gently he opened the door and stepped out, holding his hands above his head and clutching his medical supplies.

Strangely, he was not immediately seen, and had got half-way across the street before he was challenged. He turned to face the oncoming soldier, who looked at him with suspicion. 'There are none of Serrurier's men here,' said Wyatt. 'Where is Favel?'

The man jerked his rifle threateningly. 'What is that?'

'Bandages,' said Wyatt. 'For my friend who is hurt. He is in the hotel over there. Where is Favel?'

He felt the muzzle of a gun press into his back but did not turn. The man in front of him moved his rifle fractionally sideways. 'To the hotel,' he ordered. Wyatt shrugged and stepped out, surrounded by the small group. One of them pushed through the revolving door, his rifle at the ready, and Wyatt called out in English, 'Stay where you are, Dawson – we've got visitors.'

The man in front of him whirled and pressed his gun into Wyatt's stomach. *'Pren' gar','* he said threateningly.

'I was just telling my friend not to be afraid,' said Wyatt evenly.

He went into the hotel, to find Dawson sitting tensely in his chair looking at a soldier who was covering him with a rifle. He said, 'I've got some bandages and some codeine – that should kill the pain a bit.'

Favel's men fanned out and scattered through the ground floor, moving like professionals. Finding nothing, they reassembled in the foyer and gathered round their leader, whom Wyatt took to be a sergeant although he wore no insignia. The sergeant prodded the dead soldier with his foot. 'Who killed this one?'

Wyatt, bending over Dawson, looked up and shrugged. 'I don't know,' he said, and turned back to his work.

The sergeant stepped over and looked at Dawson's hands. 'Who did that?'

'Serrurier's police,' said Wyatt, keeping his eyes down.

The sergeant grunted. 'Then you do not like Serrurier. Good!'

'I must find Favel,' said Wyatt. 'I have important news for him.'

'What is this important news, *blanc*?'

'It is for Favel only. If he wants you to know he will tell you.'

Dawson stirred. 'What's going on?'

'I'm trying to get this man to take me to Favel. I can't tell *him* there's going to be a hurricane – he might not believe it and then I'd never get to see Favel.'

The sergeant said, 'You talk big, *ti blanc;* your so important news had better be good or Favel will tear out your liver.' He paused, then said with a grim smile, 'And mine.'

He turned to issue a string of rapid instructions, and Wyatt sighed deeply. 'Thank God!' he said. 'Now we're getting somewhere.'

SIX

The highest point of Cap Sarrat was a hillock, the top of which was forty-five feet above sea-level. On the top of the hillock was a 400-foot lattice radio mast which supported an array of radar antennae. From the antenna right at the top of the tower accurately machined wave-guides conducted electronic signals to a low building at the base; these signals, amplified many millions of times, were then projected on to a cathode-ray screen to form a green glow, which cast a bilious light on the face of Petty Officer (3rd Class) Joseph W. Harmon.

Petty Officer Harmon was both bored and tired. The Brass had been giving him the run-around all day. He had been standing-to at his battle station for most of the day and then he had been told off to do his usual job in the radar room that night, so he had had the minimum of sleep. At first he had been excited by the sound of gunfire reverberating across Santego Bay from the direction of St Pierre, and even more excited when a column of smoke arose from the town and he was told that Serrurier's two-bit army was surrounding the Base and they could expect an attack any moment.

But a man cannot keep up that pitch of excitement and now, at five in the morning with the sun just about due to rise, he felt bored and sleepy. His eyes were sore, and when he closed them momentarily it felt as though there were many grains of sand on his eyeballs. He blinked them open again and stared at the radar screen, following the sweep of the trace as it swept hypnotically round and round.

He jerked as his attention was caught by a minute green swirl that faded rapidly into nothingness and he had to wait until the trace went round again to recapture it. There it was again, just the merest haze etched electronically against the glass, fading as rapidly as it had arisen. He checked the direction and made it 174 degrees true.

Nothing dangerous there, he thought. That was nearly due south and at the very edge of the screen; the danger – if it came – would be from the landward side, from Serrurier's joke of an air force. There had been a fair amount of air activity earlier, but it had died away and now the San Fernandan air force seemed to be totally inactive. That fact had caused a minor stir among the officers but it meant nothing to Harmon, who thought sourly that anything that interested the officers was sure to be something to keep him out of his sack.

He looked at the screen and again caught the slight disturbance to the south. As an experienced radar operator he knew very well what it was – there was bad weather out there below the curve of the horizon and the straight-line radar beam was catching the top of it. He hesitated for a moment before he stretched out his arm for the telephone, but he picked it up decisively. His instructions were to call the Duty Officer if anything – repeat, *anything* – unusual came up. As he said, 'Get me Lieutenant Moore,' he felt some small satisfaction at being able to roust the Lieutenant from whatever corner he was sleeping in.

So it was that when Commander Schelling checked into his office at eight that morning there was a neatly typed report lying squared-up on his blotting-pad. He picked it up, his mind on other things, and got a jolt as the information suddenly sank into him like a harpoon. He grabbed the telephone and said hoarsely, 'Get me Radar Surveillance – the Duty Officer.'

While he waited for the connection he scanned the report again. It became visibly worse as he read it. The microphone clicked in his ear. 'Lieutenant Moore . . . off duty? . . . who is that, then?. . . All right, Ensign Jennings, what's all this about bad weather to the south?'

He tapped impatiently on the desk as he heard what Jennings had to say, slammed down the telephone and felt the sweat break out on his brow. Wyatt had been right – Mabel had swerved to pay a visit to San Fernandez. His body acted efficiently enough as he selected all the information he had on Mabel and packed the sheets neatly into a folder, but a voice was yammering at the back of his mind: It's goddam unfair; why should Wyatt be right on an unscientific hunch? Why the hell didn't Mabel stick to what she should have done? How in God's name am I going to explain this to Brooks?

He entered the radar section at a dead run and one look at the screen was enough. He swung back on Jennings and snapped, 'Why wasn't I told about this earlier?'

'There was a report sent to your office by Lieutenant Moore, sir.'

'That was nearly three hours ago.' He pointed at the thickening green streaks on the bottom edge of the radar screen. 'Do you know what that is?'

'Yes, sir,' said Jennings. 'There's a bit of bad weather blowing up.'

'A bit of bad weather?' said Schelling thickly. 'Get out of my way, you fool.' He pushed past Jennings and blundered out into the sunlit corridor; He stood there indecisively for a moment, then moistened his lips. The Commodore must be told, of course. He left the radar section like a man heading for his own execution with Ensign Jennings staring after him with puzzlement in his eyes.

The officer in Brooks's outer office was dubious about letting Schelling in to bother the Commodore. Schelling leaned over his desk and said deliberately, 'If I don't get to see the

Commodore within two minutes from now, you'll find your-self pounding the anchor cable for the next twenty years.' A small flame of satisfaction leaped within him as he saw that he had intimidated this officer, a weak flame that drowned in the apprehension of what Brooks would, have to say.

Brooks's desk was as neat as ever, and Brooks himself sat in the same position as though he had never moved during the last two days. He said, 'Well, Commander? I understand you want to speak to me urgently.'

Schelling swallowed. 'Er . . . yes, sir. It's about Mabel.'

Brooks did not move a muscle, nor was there any change in his voice, but an air of tension suddenly enveloped him as he asked evenly, 'What about Mabel?'

Schelling said baldly, 'She seems to have swung off her predicted course.'

'*Seems*? Has she or hasn't she?'

'Yes, sir; she has.'

'Well?'

Schelling looked into Brooks's hard grey eyes and gulped. 'She's heading right for us.' He became alarmed at the Commodore's immobility and his tongue loosened. 'She shouldn't have done it, sir. It's against all theory. She should have passed to the west of Cuba. *I* don't know why she turned and I don't know any other meteorologist who could tell you either. There are so many things we don't . . .'

Brooks stirred for the first time. 'Stop prattling, Schelling. How long have we got?'

Schelling put the folder down on the desk and opened it. 'She's a little over a hundred and seventy miles away now, and she's moving along at eleven miles an hour. That gives us fifteen, maybe sixteen, hours.'

Brooks said, 'I'm not interested in your reasoning – I just wanted a time.' He swung round in his chair and picked up a telephone. 'Give me the Executive Officer . . . Commander

Leary, I want you to put Plan K into action right now.' He glanced at his watch. 'As of 08.31 hours. That's right. . . immediate evacuation.'

He put down the telephone and turned back to Schelling. 'I wouldn't feel too bad about this, Commander. It was my decision to stay, not yours. And Wyatt didn't have any real facts – merely vague intuitions.'

But Schelling said, 'Maybe I was too rigid about it, sir.'

Brooks waved that away. 'I took that into my calcula- tions, too. I know the capabilities of my officers.' He turned and looked out of the window. 'My one regret is that we can't do anything about the people of St Pierre. But that, of course, is impossible. We'll come back as soon as we can and help clear up the mess, but the ships will take a beating and it won't be easy.'

He looked at Schelling. 'You know your station under Plan K?'

'Yes, sir.'

'You'd better get to it.'

He watched Schelling leave the office with something like pity in his eyes, then called for his personal assistant. Things had to be done – all the many necessary things. As soon as he was alone again he walked over to a wall safe and began to pack documents into a lead-weighted briefcase, and it was only when he had completed his last official duties on Cap Sarrat Base that he packed the few personal effects he wanted to take, including a photograph of his wife and two sons which he took from a drawer in his desk.

II

Eumenides Papegaikos was a very frightened man. He was not the stuff of which heroes are made and he did not like the position in which he found himself. True, running a night-club had its difficulties, but they were of the nature which could be solved by money – both Serrurier's corrupt police and the local protection racketeers could be bought off, which partly accounted for the high prices he charged. But he could not buy his way out of a civil war, nor could a hurricane be deflected by the offer of all the gold in the world.

He had hoped to be taken to Cap Sarrat with the American women, but Wyatt and the war had put a stop to that. In a way he was thankful he was among foreigners – he was tongue-tied in English but that served to camouflage his fears and uncertainties. He volunteered for nothing but did as he was told with a simulated willingness which concealed his internal quakings – which was why he was now stealthily creeping through the banana plantation and heading towards the top of the ridge overlooking the sea.

There were noises all about him – the singing cicadas and a fainter, more ominous, series of noises that seemed to come from all around. There was the clink of metal from time to time, and the faraway murmur of voices and the occasional rustle of banana leaves which should have been still in the sultry, windless night.

He reached the top of the ridge, sweating profusely, and looked down towards the coastal road. There was much activity down there; the sound of heavy trucks, the flash of lights and the movement of many men under the bright light of the moon. The quarry, where they had left the car, was now full of vehicles and there was a constant coming and going along the narrow track.

After a while Eumenides withdrew and turned to go back to the others. All over the plantation lights were springing up, the flickering fires of a camping army, and sometimes he could distinguish the movements of individual men as they walked between him and the flames. He walked down the hill, hoping that, if seen, he would only be another soldier stumbling about in the darkness, and made his way with caution towards the hollow where they had dug the fox-holes. He made it with no trouble but at the expense of time, and when he joined Julie and Mrs Warmington nearly an hour had elapsed.

From the bottom of her camouflaged foxhole Julie whispered cautiously, 'Eumenides?'

'Yes. Where's Rawst'orne?'

'He hasn't come back yet. What's happening?'

Eumenides struggled valiantly with the English language. 'Lot peoples. Soldiers. Army.'

'Government soldiers? Serrurier's men?'

'Yes.' He waved his arm largely. 'All aroun'.'

Mrs Warmington whimpered softly. Julie said slowly, 'Serrurier must have been beaten back – kicked out of St Pierre. What do we do?'

Eumenides was silent. He did not see what they could do. If they tried to get away capture would be almost certain, but if they stayed, then daylight would give them away. Julie said, 'Are any of the soldiers near?'

Eumenides pointed. 'Maybe two 'undred feet. You speak loud – they 'ear.'

'Thank goodness we found this hollow,' said Julie. 'You'd better get into your hole, Eumenides. Cover yourself with banana leaves. We'll wait for Mr Rawsthorne.'

'I'm frightened,' said Mrs Warmington in a small voice from out of the darkness.

'You think I'm not?' whispered Julie. 'Now keep quiet.'

'But they'll kill us,' wailed Mrs Warmington in a louder voice. 'They'll rape us, then kill us.'

'For God's sake, keep quiet,' said Julie as fiercely as she could in a whisper. 'They'll hear you.'

Mrs Warmington gave a low moan and lapsed into silence. Julie lay in the bottom of her foxhole and waited for Rawsthorne, wondering how long he would be, and what they could possibly do when he came back.

Rawsthorne was in difficulties. Having crossed the serv-ice road, he was finding it hard to recross it; there was a constant stream of traffic in both directions, the trucks roar-ing along one after the other with blazing headlights so that he could not cross without being seen. And it had taken him a long time to find the road at all. In his astonishment at finding himself in the middle of an army he had lost his way, stumbling about in the leaf-dappled darkness between the rows of plants and fleeing in terror from one group of soldiers, only to find another barring his way.

By the time he had calmed down he was a long way from the road and it took him nearly an hour and a half to get back to it, harried as he was by the dread of discovery. He had no illusions of what would happen to him if discovered. Serrurier's propaganda had been good; he had deceived these men and twisted their minds, and then trained and drilled them into an army. To them all *blancs* were Americans and Americans were bogeymen in the mythology Serrurier had built up – there would be a weird equation in which white man equals Americans equals spy, and he would be shot on the spot.

So he trod cautiously as he threaded his way among the banana plants. Once he had to remain motionless for a full half hour while a group of soldiers conversed idly on the other side of the plant under which he was hiding. He pressed himself against the broad leaves and prayed that one of them would not think to walk round the tree, and he was lucky.

When he was able to go on his way again he thought of what the men had been saying. The troops were tired and dispirited; they complained of the inefficiency of their offi-cers and spoke in awe of the power of Favel's artillery. One recurring theme had been: where are *our* guns? No one had been able to answer. But the news was that the army was regrouping under General Rocambeau and they were going

in to attack St Pierre when the night was over. Although a
lot of their military supplies had been captured by Favel,
Rocambeau's withdrawing force had managed to empty
San Juan arsenal and there was enough ammunition to
make the attack. The men's voices lifted when they spoke
of Rocambeau and they seemed to have renewed hope.

At last he found the road and waited in the shadows for
a gap in the stream of traffic, but none came. He looked desperately at his watch – dawn was not far away and he
would have to cross the road before then. At last, seeing no
hope in a diminution of the traffic, he moved along the edge
of the road until he found a curve. Here he might have a
chance of crossing undetected by headlights. He waited
until a truck went by, then ran across and hurled himself
down on the other side. The lights of the next truck coming
round the bend swept over him as he lay there winded.

There was light in the eastern sky when at last he located
the approximate direction of the hollow in which the others were concealed. He moved along warily, thinking that
this sort of thing might be all right for younger men like
Wyatt and Causton, but might prove the death of an elderly
man like himself.

Julie roused herself from her foxhole as the light grew in
the sky. She sat up cautiously, lifting the huge green leaves,
and looked about, wondering where Rawsthorne was. No
one had come near the hollow and it seemed as though
they might yet evade capture if they kept hidden and silent.
But first she had to look about to see from which direction
danger was most likely to threaten.

She whispered to Eumenides, 'I'm going to the edge of
the hollow.'

There was a stir in the banana leaves. 'All ri'.'

'Don't leave me,' Mrs Warmington pleaded, sitting up.
'Please don't go away – I'm frightened.'

'Ssssh. I'm not going far – just a few yards. Stay here and be quiet.'

She crawled away among the plants and found a place from which she could survey the plantation. In the dim morning light she could see the movement of men and heard a low hum of voices. The nearest group was a mere fifty yards away but the men were all asleep, huddled shapes lying round the dying embers of a fire.

She had come away to check on their camouflage in the light of day and before it was too late, so she looked back down into the hollow to see that the newly turned earth looked dreadfully raw, but it was nothing that could not be disguised by a few more leaves. The holes themselves were quite invisible or would be if that damned woman would keep still.

Mrs Warmington was sitting up and looking about nervously, still clutching her purse to her breast. 'Get down, you fool,' breathed Julie, but to her astonishment Mrs Warmington opened her purse, produced a comb and began to comb her hair. She'll never learn, thought Julie in despair; she's quite unadaptable and habit-ridden. To attend to one's coiffure in the morning was, no doubt, quite laudable in suburbia, but it might mean death on this green hillside.

She was about to slip back and thrust the woman back into her foxhole, by force if necessary, when she was arrested by a movement on the other side of the hollow. A soldier was coming down, stretching his arms as he walked as though he had just risen from sleep, and adjusting the sling of his rifle to his shoulder. Julie stayed very still and her eyes switched to Mrs Warmington, who was regarding herself in a small mirror. She distinctly heard the deprecating and very feminine sound which Mrs Warmington made as she discovered how bedraggled she was.

The soldier heard it too and unslung his rifle and came down into the hollow very cautiously. Mrs Warmington heard the metallic click as he slammed back the bolt, and she screamed as she saw him coming towards her, scrabbling at her purse. The soldier stopped in astonishment and then a broad grin spread over his face and he came closer, putting up his rifle.

Then there were three flat reports that echoed on the hot morning air. The soldier shouted and spun round to flop at Mrs Warmington's feet, writhing like a newly landed fish. Blood stained his uniform red at the shoulder.

Eumenides popped up from his hole like a jack-in-a-box as Julie started to run. When she got down to the bottom of the hollow he was bending over the fallen soldier, who was moaning incoherently. He regarded his bloody hand blankly. 'He was shot!'

'He was coming at me,' screamed Mrs Warmington. 'He was going to rape me – kill me.' She waved a pistol in her hand.

Julie let her have it, putting all her strength into the muscular open-handed slap. She was desperate – at all costs she must silence this hysterical woman. Mrs Warmington was suddenly silent and the gun dropped from her nerveless fingers to be caught by Eumenides. His eyes opened wide as he looked at it. 'This is mine,' he said in astonishment.

Julie whirled as she heard a shout from behind and saw three soldiers running down the slope. The first one saw the prone figure on the ground and the pistol in Eumenides's hand and wasted no time in argument. He brought up his gun and shot the Greek in the stomach.

Eumenides groaned and doubled up, his hands at his belly. He dropped to his knees and bent forward and the soldier lifted his rifle and bayoneted him in the back. Eumenides collapsed completely and the soldier put his boot on him and pulled out the bayonet, to stab and stab again until the body lay in a welter of blood.

Rawsthorne, watching from the edge of the hollow, was sickened to his stomach but was unable to tear his eyes away. He listened to the shouting and watched the women being pushed about. One of the soldiers was ruthlessly pricking them with a bayonet and he saw the red blood running down Julie's arm. He thought they were going to be shot out of hand but then an officer came along and the two women were hustled out of the hollow, leaving behind the lifeless body of Eumenides Papegaikos.

Rawsthorne lingered for some minutes, held in a state of shock before his brain began to work again. At last he moved away, crawling on his belly. But he did not really know where he was going nor what he was going to do next.

III

Wyatt discovered that Favel was a hard man to find. With Dawson, he had been handed over to a junior officer who was too preoccupied with the immediate tactical situation to pay much attention to him. In order to rid himself of an incubus, the officer had passed them up the line, escorted by a single private soldier who was depressed at being taken out of the battle. Dawson looked at him, and said, 'There's nothing wrong with the morale of these boys.'

'They're winning,' said Wyatt shortly. He was obsessed by the urgency of getting to see Favel, but he could see it was not going to be easy. The war had split into two separate battles to the west and east of St Pierre. Favel's hammer blow in the centre had split Serrurier's army into two unequal halves, the larger part withdrawing to the east in a fighting retreat, and a smaller fragment fleeing in disorder to the west to join the as yet unblooded troops keeping a watch on Cap Sarrat.

A more senior officer laughed in their faces when Wyatt demanded to see Favel. '*You* want to see Favel,' he said incredulously. '*Blanc, I* want to see him – everyone wants to see him. He is on the move all the time; he is a busy man.'

'Will he be coming here?' asked Wyatt.

The officer grunted. 'Not if I can help it. He comes only when there is trouble, and I don't want to be the cause of his coming. But he might come,' he prophesied. 'We are moving against Rocambeau.'

'Can we stay here?'

'You're welcome as long as you keep out of the way.'

So they stayed in battalion headquarters and Wyatt relayed to Dawson the substance of what he had learned. Dawson said, 'I don't think you have a hope in hell of seeing him. Would you be bothered by a nutty scientist at a time like this?'

'I don't suppose I would,' said Wyatt despondently.

He listened carefully to all that was going on about him and began to piece together the military situation as it stood. The name of Serrurier was hardly mentioned, but the name of Rocambeau was on everyone's lips.

'Who the hell is this Rocambeau?' demanded Dawson.

'He was one of the junior Government generals,' said Wyatt. 'He took over when old Deruelles was killed and proved to be trickier than Favel thought. Favel was relying on finishing the war in one bash but Rocambeau got the Government army out of the net in a successful disengaging action. He's withdrawn to the east and is regrouping for another attack, and the devil of it is that he managed to scrape together enough transport to empty San Juan arsenal. He's got enough ammunition and spare weapons to finish the war in a way Favel doesn't like.'

'Can't Favel move in and finish him before he's ready? Sort of catch him off balance?'

Wyatt shook his head. 'Favel has just about shot his bolt. He's been fighting continuously against heavy odds. He's fought his way down from the mountains and his men are dropping on their feet with weariness. He also has to stop for resting and regrouping.'

'So what happens now?'

Wyatt grimaced. 'Favel stops in St Pierre – he hasn't the strength to push further. So he'll fight his defensive battle in St Pierre, and along will come Mabel and wipe out the lot of them. Neither army will have a chance on this low ground round Santego Bay. No one is going to win this war.'

Dawson looked at Wyatt out of the corner of his eye. 'Maybe we'd better get out,' he suggested. 'We could go up the Negrito.'

'After I've seen Favel,' said Wyatt steadily.

'Okay,' said Dawson with a sigh. 'We'll stick around and see Favel – maybe.' He paused. 'Where exactly is Rocambeau regrouping?'

'Just off the coast road to the east – about five miles out of town.'

'Holy smoke!' exclaimed Dawson. 'Isn't that where Rawsthorne and the others went?'

'I've been trying not to think of that,' said Wyatt tightly.

Dawson felt depressed. 'I'm sorry,' he said abjectly. 'About pulling that stupid trick with the car. If I hadn't done that we wouldn't have got separated.'

Wyatt looked at him curiously. Something had happened to Dawson; this was not the man he had met in the Maraca Club – the big, important writer – nor was it the grouchy man in the cell who had told him to go to hell. He said carefully, 'I asked you about that before and you bit my ear off.'

Dawson looked up. 'You want to know why I tried to take your car? I'll tell you. I ran scared – Big Jim Dawson ran scared.'

'That's what I was wondering about,' said Wyatt thoughtfully. 'It doesn't fit with what I've heard about you.'

Dawson laughed sourly and there was not a trace of humour about him. 'What you've heard about me is a lot of balls,' he said bluntly. 'I scare easy.'

Wyatt looked at Dawson's hands. 'I wouldn't say that.'

'It's a funny thing,' said Dawson. 'When I came slap-bang against Roseau and knew I couldn't talk my way out of it, I ought to have got scared then, but I got mad instead. That's never happened to me before. As for my reputation, that's a fake, a put-up job – and it was so easy, too. You go to Africa and shoot a poor goddam lion, everyone thinks you're a hero; you pull a fish out of the sea a bit bigger than the usual fish, you're a hero again. I used those things like a bludgeon and I built up Big Jim Dawson – what the Chinese call a paper tiger. And it's wonderful what an unscrupulous press agent can do, too.'

'But why?' asked Wyatt helplessly. 'You're a good writer – all the critics say so; you don't need artificial buttresses.'

'What the critics think and what I think are two different things.' Dawson looked at the point of his dusty shoe. 'Whenever I sit at a typewriter looking at that blank sheet of paper I get a sinking feeling in my guts; and when I've filled up a whole lot of sheets and made a book the sinking feeling gets worse. I've never written anything yet that I've liked – I've never been able to put on paper what I really wanted to. So every time a book came out I was scared it would be a flop and I had to have some support so it would sell, and that's why Big Jim Dawson was invented.'

'You've been trying to do an impossible thing – achieve perfection.'

Dawson grinned. 'I'll still try,' he said cheerfully. 'But it won't matter any more. I think I've got over being scared.'

Many hours later Wyatt was shaken into wakefulness. He had not been aware of falling asleep, and as he struggled into consciousness he was aware of cramped limbs and aching joints. He opened his eyes, to be blinded by a flash-light and he blinked painfully. A voice said, 'Are you Wyatt, or is it the other chap?'

'I'm Wyatt,' he said. 'Who are you?' He threw off the blanket which someone had thoughtfully laid over him and stared at the big bearded man who was looking down at him.

'I'm Fuller. I've been looking all over St Pierre for you. Favel wants to see you.'

'Favel wants to see *me*! How does he even know I exist?'

'That's another story; come on.'

Wyatt creaked to his feet and looked through the door-way. The first faint light of dawn was breaking through and he saw the outline of a jeep in the street and heard the idling engine. He turned and said, 'Fuller? You're the Englishman – one of them – who lives on the North Coast, in the Campo de las Perlas.'

'That's right.'

'You and Manning.'

'You've got it,' said Fuller impatiently. 'Come on. We've got no time for chit-chat.'

'Wait a minute,' said Wyatt. 'I'll wake Dawson.'

'We've got no time for that,' said Fuller. 'He can stay here.'

Wyatt turned and stared at him. 'Look, this man was beaten up by Serrurier's bully-boys because of you – you and Manning. We were both within an ace of being shot for the same reason. He's coming with me.'

Fuller had the grace to be abashed. 'Oh! Well, make it snappy.'

Wyatt woke Dawson and explained the situation rapidly, and Dawson scrambled to his feet. 'But how the hell does he know about you?' was his first question.

'Fuller will no doubt explain that on the way,' said Wyatt. The tone of his voice indicated that Fuller had better do some explaining.

They climbed into the jeep and set off. Fuller said, 'Favel has established headquarters at the Imperiale – it's nice and central.'

'Well, I'm damned,' said Dawson. 'We needn't have moved an inch. We were there this . . . last. . . afternoon.'

'The government buildings took a battering during the bombardment,' said Fuller. 'They won't be ready for occupation for quite a while.'

Dawson said feelingly, 'You don't have to tell us anything about that – we were there.'

'So I'm told,' said Fuller. 'Sorry about that.'

Wyatt had been looking at the sky and sniffing the air. It was curiously hot considering it was so early in the morning, and the day promised to be a scorcher. He frowned and said, 'Why has Favel sent for me?'

'An English newspaperman came in with a very curious story – something about a hurricane. A lot of nonsense really. Still, Favel was impressed enough to send search-parties out looking for you as soon as we settled in the city. You *are* the weather boffin, aren't you?'

'I am,' said Wyatt with no expression in his voice.

'So Causton came through all right,' said Dawson. 'That's good.'

Fuller chuckled. 'He served a term in the Government army first. He told us that you'd landed in the jug – the one on Libération Place. *That* wasn't encouraging because we plastered the Place pretty thoroughly, but there weren't any white bodies in the police station so there was a chance you'd got away. I've been looking for you all night – Favel insisted, and when he insists, things get done.'

Wyatt said, 'When does the war start again?'

'As soon as Rocambeau decides to make his push,' said Fuller. 'We're fighting a defensive action – we're not strong enough to do anything else right now.'

'What about the Government troops to the west?'

'They're still grouped around Cap Sarrat. Serrurier is still afraid the Yanks will come out and stab him in the back.'

'Will they?'

Fuller snorted. 'Not a chance. This is a local fight and the Yanks want none of it. I think they'd prefer Favel to Serrurier – who wouldn't? – but they won't interfere. Thank God Serrurier has a different opinion.'

Wyatt wondered where Fuller came into all this. He spoke as one who was high in the rebel hierarchy and he was definitely close to Favel. But he did not ask any questions about it – he had more important things on his mind. The best thing was that Favel wanted to see him and he began to marshal his arguments once again.

Fuller pulled up the jeep outside the Imperiale and they all climbed out. There was a great coming and going and Wyatt noticed that the revolving door had been taken away to facilitate passage in and out of the hotel. He chalked up another mark to Favel for efficiency and attention to minor detail. He followed Fuller inside to find that the hotel had been transformed; the foyer had been cleared and the American Bar had a new role as a map room. Fuller said, 'Wait here; I'll tell the boss you've arrived.'

He went off and Dawson said, 'This is how I like to view a war – from the blunt end.'

'You might change your mind when Rocambeau attacks.'

'That's very likely,' said Dawson. 'But I refuse to be depressed.'

There was a cry from the stairs and they saw Causton hurrying down. 'Welcome back,' he said. 'Glad you got out of the cooler.'

Wyatt smiled wryly. 'We were blown out.'

'Don't believe it,' said Dawson. 'Wyatt did a great job – he got us both out.' He peered at Causton. 'What's that on your face – boot-polish?'

'That's right,' said Causton. 'Can't get rid of the damn' stuff. I suppose you'd like to clean up and put on some fresh clothing.'

'Where's Julie – and Rawsthorne?' asked Wyatt.

Causton looked grave. 'We got separated quite early. The plan was to head east.'

'They went east,' said Wyatt. 'Now they're mixed up with Rocambeau's army.'

There was nothing anyone could say further about that and, after a pause, Causton said, 'You'd better both take the chance of cleaning up. Favel won't see you yet – he's in the middle of a planning conference, trying to get a quart out of a pint pot.'

He took them up to his room and provided welcome hot water and soap. One glance at Dawson's hands produced a doctor, who hustled Dawson away, and then Causton found a clean shirt for Wyatt and said, 'You can use my dry shaver.'

Wyatt sat on the bed and shaved, already beginning to feel much better. He said, 'How did you get separated from the others?'

Causton told him, then said, 'I got to Favel in the end and managed to convince him you were important.' He scratched his head. 'Either he didn't need much convincing, or my powers of persuasion are a lot better than I thought – but he got the point very quickly. He's quite a boy.'

'Hurricanes excepted – do you think he's got a chance of coming on top in this war?'

Causton smiled wryly. 'That's an unanswerable question. The Government army is far stronger, and so far he's won by surprise and sheer intelligence. He plans for every contingency and the groundwork for this attack was laid months ago.' He chuckled. 'You know that the main force of the Government artillery never came into action at all. The guns got tangled in a hell of a mess not far up the Negrito and Favel came down and captured the lot. I thought it was luck, but I know now that Favel never depends on luck. The whole damn' thing was planned – Favel had suborned Lescuyer, the Government artillery commander; Lescuyer issued conflicting orders and had two columns of artillery meeting head-on on the same road, then he ducked for cover. By the time Deruelles had sorted that lot out it was all over, and Deruelles himself was dead.'

'That must have been when Rocambeau took over,' said Wyatt.

Causton nodded. 'That was a pity. Rocambeau is a bloody efficient commander – far better than Deruelles could ever be. He got the Government army out of the trap. God knows what will happen now.'

'Didn't the Government armour cause Favel any trouble when he came out on the plain?'

Causton grinned. 'Not much. He sorted out the captured artillery in quick time, ruthlessly junking the stuff that was in the way. Then he formed it into six mobile columns and went gunning for Serrurier's armour. The minute a tank or an armoured car showed its nose, up would come a dozen guns and blast hell out of it. He had the whole thing taped right from the start – the Government generals were dancing to *his* tune until Rocambeau took over. Like when he blasted the 3rd Regiment in the Place de la Libération Noire – he had artillery observers already in the city equipped with walkie-talkies, and they caught the 3rd Regiment just when they were forming up.'

'I know,' said Wyatt soberly. 'I saw the result of that.'

Causton's grin widened. 'He disposed of Serrurier's comic opera air force in the same tricky efficient fashion. The planes started flying and bombing all right, but when each plane had flown three attacks they found they'd come to the end of the ready-use petrol, so they broke open the reserve tanks on the airfield. The lot was doctored with sugar – there's plenty of *that* on San Fernandez – and now all the planes are grounded with sticky engines.'

'He certainly gets full marks for effort,' said Wyatt. 'Where do Manning and Fuller come into all this?'

'I haven't got to the bottom of that yet. I think they had something to do with getting his war supplies. Favel certainly knew what he wanted – rifles, machine-guns and mobile artillery, consisting of a hell of a lot of mountain guns and mortars, together with bags of ammunition. It must have cost somebody a packet and I haven't been able to find out who financed all this.'

'Manning and Fuller were in the right place,' said Wyatt slowly. 'And the police seemed to think they had a lot to do with Favel. They beat Dawson half to death trying to find out more.'

'I saw his hands,' said Causton. 'What did he tell them?'

'What could he tell them? He just stuck it out.'

'I'm surprised,' said Causton. 'He has the reputation among us press boys of being a phoney. We know that the air crash he had in Alaska a couple of years ago was a put-up job to boost the sales of his latest book. It was planned by Don Wiseman and executed by a stunt pilot.'

'Who is Don Wiseman?'

'Dawson's press agent. I always thought that every view we've had of Dawson was through Wiseman's magnifying glass.'

Wyatt said gently, 'I think you can regard Wiseman as being Dawson's former press agent.'

Causton lifted his eyebrows. 'It's like that, is it?'

'There's nothing wrong with Dawson,' said Wyatt, stroking his clean-shaven cheek. He put down the dry-shaver. 'When do I get to see Favel?'

Causton shrugged. 'When he's ready. He's planning a war, you know, and right now he may be on the losing end. I think he's running out of tricks; his preliminary planning was good but it only stretches so far. Now he faces a slugging match with Rocambeau and he's not in trim for it. He's got five thousand men against the Government's fifteen thousand, and if he tries a war of attrition he's done for. He may have to retreat back to the mountains.'

Wyatt buttoned his shirt. 'He'll have to make up his mind quickly,' he said grimly. 'Mabel won't wait for him.'

Causton sat in silence for a moment, then he said, almost pleadingly, 'Have you anything concrete to offer him, apart from this hunch of yours?'

Wyatt stepped to the window and looked up at the hot blue sky. 'Not much,' he said. 'If I were back at the Base with my instruments I might have been able to come to some logical conclusions, but without instruments . . .' He shrugged.

Causton looked despondent, and Wyatt said, 'This is hurricane weather, you know. This calm sultriness isn't natural – something has stopped the normal flow of the south-east wind, and my guess is that it's Mabel.' He nodded towards the sea. 'She's somewhere over there beyond the horizon. I can't prove for certain that she's coming this way, but I certainly think so.'

Causton said, 'There's a barometer downstairs; would that be any good?' He sounded half-heartedly hopeful.

'I'll have a look at it,' said Wyatt. 'But I don't think it will be.'

They went downstairs into the hurly-burly of the army headquarters and Causton showed him the barometer on the wall of the manager's office. Wyatt looked at it in astonishment. 'Good God, a Torricelli barometer – what a relic!' He tapped it gently. 'It must be a hundred years old.' Looking closely at the dial, he said, 'No, not quite; "Adameus Copenhans – Amsterdam – 1872." '

'Is it any good?' asked Causton.

Wyatt was briefly amused. 'This is like handing a pickaxe to a nuclear physicist and telling him to split some atoms.' He tapped the dial again and the needle quivered. 'This thing tells us what is happening now, and that's not very important. What I'd like to know is what happened over the last twenty-four hours. I'd give a lot to have an aneroid barograph with a recording over the last three days.'

'Then this is useless?'

'I'm afraid so. It will probably give a wrong reading anyway. I can't see anyone having taken the trouble to correct this for temperature, latitude and so on.'

Causton waxed sarcastic. 'The trouble with you boffins is that you've developed your instruments to such a pitch that now you can't do without them. What did you weathermen do before you had your satellites and all your electronic gadgets?'

Wyatt said softly, 'Relied on experience and instinct – which is what I'm doing now. When you've studied a lot of hurricanes – as many as I have – you begin to develop a sixth sense which tells you what they're likely to do next. Nothing shows on your instruments and it isn't anything that can be analysed. I prefer to call it the voice of experience.'

'I still believe you,' said Causton plaintively. 'But the point is: can we convince Favel?'

'That isn't worrying me,' said Wyatt. 'What is worrying me is what Favel will do when he *is* convinced. He's in a cleft stick.'

'Let's see if he's finished his conference,' said Causton. 'As a journalist, I'm interested to see what he *does* do.' He mopped his brow. 'You know, you're right; this weather is unnatural.'

Favel was still not free and they waited in the foyer watching the comings and goings of messengers from the hotel dining-room where the conference was being held. At last Fuller came out and beckoned. 'You're next,' he said. 'Make it as snappy as you can.' He looked at Wyatt with honest blue eyes. 'Personally, I think this is a waste of time. We don't have hurricanes here.'

'Serrurier told me the same thing in almost the same words,' said Wyatt. 'He isn't a meteorologist, either.'

Fuller snorted. 'Well, come on; let's get it over with.'

He escorted them into the dining-room. The tables had been put together and were covered with maps and a group of men were conversing in low voices at the far end of the room. It reminded Wyatt irresistibly of the large ornate room in which Serrurier had been holding his pre-battle conference, but there was a subtle difference. There was no gold braid and there was no hysteria.

Causton touched his elbow. 'That's Manning,' he said, nodding to a tall white man. 'And that's Favel next to him.'

Favel was a lean, wiry man of less than average height. He was lighter in complexion than the average San Fernandan and his eyes were, strikingly and incongruously, a piercing blue – something very unusual in a man of Negro stock. He was simply dressed in clean khaki denims with an open-necked shirt, out of which rose the strong corded column of his neck. As he turned to greet Wyatt the crowsfeet round his eyes crinkled and the corners of his mobile mouth quirked in a smile. 'Ah, Mr Wyatt,' he said. 'I've been looking for you. I want to hear what you have to say but – from what Mr Causton tells me – I fear I won't like it.' His English was smooth and unaccented.

'There's going to be a hurricane,' said Wyatt baldly.

Favel's expression did not change. He looked on Wyatt with a half-humorous curve to his lips, and said, 'Indeed!'

The tall white man – Manning – said, 'That's a pretty stiff statement, Wyatt. There hasn't been a hurricane here since 1910.'

'And I'm getting pretty tired of hearing the fact,' said Wyatt wearily. 'Is there some magic about the year 1910? Do hurricanes come at hundred-year intervals, and can we expect the next in 2010?'

Favel said softly, 'If not in 2010, when may we expect this hurricane?'

'Within twenty-four hours,' said Wyatt bluntly. 'I wouldn't put it at longer than that.'

Manning made a noise with his lips expressive of disgust, but Favel held up his hand. 'Charles, I know you don't want anything to interfere with our war, but I think we ought to hear what Mr Wyatt has to say. It might have a considerable bearing on our future course of action.' He leaned comfortably against the table and pointed a brown finger directly at Wyatt. 'Now, then, give me your evidence.'

Wyatt drew in a deep breath. He *had* to convince this slim brown man whose eyes had suddenly turned flinty. 'The hurricane was spotted five days ago by one of the weather satellites. Four days ago I went to inspect it on one of the usual reconnaissance missions and found it was a bad one, one of the worst I've ever encountered. I kept a check on its course, and up to the time I left the Base it was going according to prediction. Since then I haven't had the opportunity for further tracking.'

'The predicted course,' said Favel. 'Does that bring the hurricane to San Fernandez?'

'No,' admitted Wyatt. 'But it wouldn't take much of a swing off course to hit us, and hurricanes do swerve for quite unpredictable reasons.'

'Did you inform Commodore Brooks of this?' asked Manning harshly.

'I did.'

'Well, he hasn't put much stock in your story. He's still sitting there across the bay at Cap Sarrat and he doesn't look like moving.'

Wyatt said carefully, looking at Favel, 'Commodore Brooks is not his own master. He has other things to take into account, especially this war you're fighting. He's taking a calculated risk.'

Favel nodded. 'Just so. I appreciate Commodore Brooks's position – he would not want to abandon Cap Sarrat Base at a time like this.' He smiled mischievously. 'I would not want him to abandon the Base, either. He is keeping President Serrurier occupied by his masterly inactivity.'

'That's beside the point,' said Manning abruptly. 'If he was as certain about this hurricane as Wyatt apparently is, he would surely evacuate the Base.'

Favel leaned forward. '*Are* you certain about this hurricane, Mr Wyatt?'

'Yes.'

'Even though you have been kept from your instruments and so do not have full knowledge?'

'Yes,' said Wyatt. He looked Favel in the eye. 'There was a man up near St Michel – two days ago, just before the battles started. He was tying down the roof of his hut.'

Favel nodded. 'I, too, saw a man doing that. I wondered . . .'

'For God's sake!' exploded Manning. 'This isn't a meeting of a folklore society. The decisions we have to make are too big to be based on anything but facts.'

'Hush, Charles,' said Favel. 'I am a West Indian, and so is Mr Wyatt. Like is calling to like.' He saw the expression on Wyatt's face and burst out laughing. 'Oh yes, I know all about you; I have a dossier on every foreigner on the island.' He became serious. 'Did you talk to him – this man who was tying down the roof of his hut?'

'Yes.'

'What did he say?'

'He said the big wind was coming. He said he was going to finish securing the roof of his house and then he was going to join his family in a cave in the hills. He said the big wind would come in two days.'

'How did that coincide with your own knowledge of the hurricane?'

'It coincided exactly,' said Wyatt.

Favel turned to Manning. 'That man has gone to his cave where he will pray to an old half-forgotten god – older, even, than those my people brought from West Africa. Hunraken, the Carib storm god.'

Manning looked at him blankly and Favel murmured, 'No matter.' He turned back to Wyatt and said, 'I have a great belief in the instincts of my people for survival. Perhaps – ' he wagged a lean, brown finger – ' and only perhaps, there will be a hurricane, after all. Let us *assume* there will be a hurricane – what will be the probable result if it hits us, here in St Pierre?'

'Mabel is a particularly bad . . .' began Wyatt.

'Mabel?' Favel laughed shortly. 'You scientists have lost the instinct for drama. Hunraken is the better name.' He waved his hand. 'But go on.'

Wyatt started again. 'She'll hit from the south and come into Santego Bay; the bay is shallow and the sea will build up. You'll have what is popularly known as a tidal wave.'

Favel snapped his fingers. 'A map. Let us see what it looks like on a map.'

A large-scale map was spread on one of the tables and they gathered round. Causton had watched with interest the interplay between Favel and Wyatt and he drew closer. Manning, in spite of his disbelief, was fascinated by the broad outline of tragedy which Wyatt had just sketched, and watched with as much interest as anyone. The less intellectual Fuller stood by with a half smile; to him this was just a lot of boffin's bumf – everyone knew they didn't have hurricanes in San Fernandez.

Favel laid his hand on the map, squarely in the middle of Santego Bay. 'This tidal wave – how high will be the water?'

'I'm no hydrographer – that's not my line,' said Wyatt. 'But I can give you an informed guess. The low central pressure in the hurricane will pull the sea up to, say, twenty to twenty-five feet above normal level. When that hits the mouth of the bay and shallow ground it will build up. The level will also rise because of the constriction – you'll have more and more water confined in less and less space as the wave moves into the bay.' He hesitated, then said firmly, 'You can reckon on a main wave fifty feet high.'

Someone's breath hissed out in a gasp. Favel handed a black crayon to Wyatt. 'Disregarding the high winds, will you outline the areas likely to be affected by flooding.'

Wyatt stood over the map, the crayon poised in his hand. 'The wind will be driving the sea, too,' he said. 'You'll get serious flooding anywhere below the seventy-foot contour line all around the bay. To be safe, I'd put it at the eighty-foot line.' He dropped his hand and drew a bold sinuous line across the map. 'Everything on the seaward side of this line you can say will be subject to serious flooding.'

He paused and then tapped the map at the head of Santego Bay. 'The Rio Negrito will back up because of the force of the waters coming into the mouth. All that water will have to go somewhere, and you can expect serious flooding up the Negrito Valley for, say, ten miles. The hurricane will also precipitate a lot of water in the form of rain.'

Favel studied the map and nodded. 'Just like before,' he said. 'Have you studied the 1910 hurricane, Mr Wyatt?'

'Briefly. There's a shortage of statistics on it, though; not too much reliable information.'

Favel said mildly, 'Six thousand dead; I consider that a very interesting statistic.' He turned to Manning. 'Look at that line, Charles! It encloses the whole of Cap Sarrat, all the flats where the airfield is and right up to the foot of Mont Rambeau, the whole of the city of St Pierre and the plain up to the beginning of the Negrito. All that will be drowned.'

'*If* Wyatt is right,' emphasized Manning.

Favel inclined his head. 'Granted.' His eyes became abstracted and he stood a while in deep thought. Presently he turned to Wyatt. 'The man near St Michel – did he say anything else?'

Wyatt racked his brains. 'Not much. Oh, he did say there would be another wind, perhaps worse than the hurricane. He said that Favel was coming down from the mountains.'

Favel smiled sadly. 'Do my people think of me as a destructive force? I hardly think I am worse than a hurricane.' He swung on Manning. 'I am going to proceed as though this hurricane were an established fact. I can do nothing else. We will plan accordingly.'

'Julio, we're fighting a war!' said Manning in an agonized voice. 'You can't take the chance.'

'I must,' said Favel. 'These are my people, Charles. There are sixty thousand of them in this city, and this city may be destroyed.'

'Jesus!' said Manning and glared at Wyatt. 'Julio, we can't fight Rocambeau, Serrurier and a hurricane, too. I don't think there is going to be a hurricane and I won't believe it until Brooks moves out. How the hell can we lay out a disposition of troops under these conditions?'

Favel put a hand on his arm. 'Have you ever known me make an error of judgement, Charles?'

Manning gave an exasperated sigh, and it was as though he had yelled out loud in his fury. 'Not yet,' he said tightly. 'But there's a first time for everything. And I've always had a feeling about you, Julio – when you do make a mistake, it'll be a bloody big one.'

'In that case we'll all be dead and it won't matter,' said Favel drily. He turned to Wyatt. 'Is there anything you can do to provide any proof?'

'I'd like to have a look at the sea,' said Wyatt.

Favel blinked, taken by surprise for the first time. 'That is a small matter and easily provided for. Charles, I want you to see that Mr Wyatt has everything he needs; I want you to look after him personally.' He looked at the writhing black line scored on the map. 'I have a great deal of thinking to do about this. I would like to be alone.'

'All right,' said Manning resignedly. He jerked his head at Wyatt and strode towards the door. Wyatt and Causton followed him into the foyer, where Manning turned on Wyatt violently. He grasped him by the shirt, bunching it up in his big hand, and said furiously, 'You bloody egghead! You've balled things up properly, haven't you?'

'Take your damned hands off me,' said Wyatt coldly.

Manning was perhaps warned by the glint of fire in Wyatt's eye. He released him and said, 'All right; but I'll give you a warning.' He stuck a finger under Wyatt's nose. 'If there is no hurricane after all you've said, Favel will let the matter drop – but I won't. And I promise you that you'll be a very dead meteorologist before another twenty-four hours have passed.'

He drew back and gave Wyatt a look of cold contempt. 'Favel says I've got to nurse you; there's my car outside – I'll drive you anywhere you want to go.' He turned on his heel and walked away.

Causton looked after him. 'You'd better be right, Wyatt,' he murmured. 'You'd better be very right. If Mabel doesn't turn up on time I wouldn't like to be in your shoes.'

Wyatt was pale. He said, 'Are you coming?'

'I wouldn't miss any of this for the world.'

Manning was silent as he drove them down to the docks past the looted arsenal of San Juan and on to the long jetty. 'Will this do?'

'I'd like to go to the end,' said Wyatt. 'If it's safe for the car.'

Manning drove forward slowly and stopped the car within a few yards of the end of the jetty. Wyatt got out and stood looking at the oily swells as they surged in from the mouth of the bay and the open seas. Causton mopped his brow and said to Manning, 'God, it's hot. Is it usually as hot as this so early in the morning?'

Manning did not answer his question. Instead, he jerked his head towards Wyatt. 'How reliable is he?'

'I wouldn't know,' said Causton. 'I've only known him four days. But I'll tell you one thing – he's the stubbornest cuss I've ever struck.'

Manning blew out his breath, but said nothing more.

Wyatt came back after a few minutes and climbed into the car. 'Well?' asked Manning.

Wyatt bit his lip. 'There's a strong disturbance out there big enough to kick up heavy swells. That's all I can tell you.'

'For the love of God!' exclaimed Manning. 'Nothing more?'

'Don't worry,' said Wyatt with a crooked smile. 'You'll get your wind.' He looked up at the sky. 'Wherever I am, I want to be told of the first sign of cloud or haze.'

'All right,' said Manning, and put the car into reverse. He was just about to let out the clutch when a heavy explosion reverberated across the water and he jerked his head. 'What the devil was that?'

There came another *boom* even as the first echoed from the hills at the back of St Pierre and Causton said excitedly, 'Something's happening at the Base. Look!'

They had a clear view across the four miles of water of Santego Bay which separated them from the Base. A column of black smoke was coiling lazily into the air and Wyatt knew that it must be tremendous to be seen at that distance. He had a sudden intuition and said, 'Brooks is evacuating. He's getting rid of his surplus ammunition so that Serrurier can't grab it.'

Manning looked at him, startled, and then a big grin broke out on his face as, one after the other, more explosions came in measured sequence. 'By God!' he roared. 'There *is* going to be a hurricane.'

SEVEN

Favel said tolerantly, 'Because Charles seems pleased does not mean that he does not realize the gravity of the situation. It is merely that he likes to face reality – he is no shadow boxer.'

The dining-room of the Imperiale was stiflingly hot and Causton wished that the fans would work. Favel had promised to get the city electricity plant working as soon as possible, but there was no point in it now. He unstuck his shirt from the small of his back and looked across at Wyatt. Manning isn't the only happy man around here, he thought; Wyatt has made his point at last.

But if Wyatt was more relaxed he was not too happy; there was much to do and the time was slipping away, minute by minute, while Favel airily tossed off inconsequential comments. He shrugged irritably and then looked up as Favel addressed him directly, 'What is your advice, Mr Wyatt?'

'Evacuation,' said Wyatt promptly. 'Total evacuation of St Pierre.'

Manning snorted. 'We're fighting a war, dammit. We can't do two things at once.'

'I'm not too sure,' said Favel in a low voice. 'Charles, come over here – I want to show you something.' He took Manning by the arm and led him to a table, where they bent over a map and conversed in a murmur.

Wyatt looked across at Causton and thought of what he had said just before this conference began. He had been a shade cynical about Favel and his concern for 'my people'. 'Naturally he's concerned,' Causton said. 'St Pierre is the biggest town on the island. It's the source of power – that's why he's here now. But the power comes from the people in the city, not the buildings, and, as a politician, he knows that very well.'

Wyatt had said that Favel seemed to be an idealist, and Causton laughed. 'Nonsense! He's a thoroughly practical politician, and there's precious little idealism in politics. Serrurier's not the only killer – Favel has done his share.'

Wyatt thought of the carnage in the Place de la Libération Noire and was forced to agree. But he could not agree that Favel was worse than Serrurier after he had seen them both in action.

Favel and Manning came back, and Favel said, 'We are in trouble, Mr Wyatt. The American evacuation of Cap Sarrat has made my task ten times more difficult – it has released a whole new army of Government troops to assault my right flank.' He smiled. 'Fortunately, we believe that Serrurier has taken command himself and I know of old that he is a bad general. Rocambeau on my left flank is another matter altogether, even though his men are tired and defeated. I tell you – if the positions of Serrurier and Rocambeau were reversed then this war would be over in twelve hours and I would be a dead man.'

He shook his head sadly. 'And in these conditions you want me to evacuate the entire population of our capital city.'

'It must be done,' said Wyatt stolidly.

'Indeed I agree,' said Favel. 'But how?'

'You'll have to make an armistice. You'll have . . .'

Manning threw back his head and laughed. 'An armistice,' he scoffed. 'Do you think Serrurier will agree to an armistice now he knows he can crack us like a nut?'

'He will if he knows there's a hurricane coming.'

Favel leaned forward and said intensely, 'Serrurier is mad; he does not care about hurricanes. He *knows* this island does not have hurricanes. So you told me yourself in your account of your interview with him.'

'He must believe it now,' exclaimed Wyatt. 'How else can he account for the evacuation of Cap Sarrat Base?'

Favel waved his hand. 'He will find that easy to rationalize. The Americans withdrew because they feared an assault from the mighty army of Serrurier, the Black Star of the Antilles. The Americans ran away because they were afraid.'

Wyatt looked at him in astonishment and then knew that Favel was right. Any man who could banish a hurricane would automatically reason in that grandiloquent and paranoiac manner. He said unwillingly, 'Perhaps you're right.'

'I *am* right,' said Favel decisively. 'So what must we do now? Come, I will show you.' He led Wyatt to the map table. 'Here we have St Pierre – and here we have your line which marks the limit of flooding. The population of St Pierre will be evacuated up the Negrito Valley, but keeping away from the river. While this is being done the army must contain the assaults of Serrurier and Rocambeau.'

'And that's not going to be too bloody easy,' said Manning.

'I am going to make it less easy,' said Favel. 'I want two thousand troops to supervise the evacuation. That leaves one thousand to withstand Serrurier on the right, and two thousand to contain Rocambeau on the left. They'll have all the artillery, of course.'

'Julio, have a heart,' yelled Manning. 'It can't be done that way. We haven't the men to spare. If you don't have enough infantry to protect the guns they'll be overrun. You can't do it.'

'It must be done,' said Favel. 'There is not much time. To move a whole population, we will need the men to get the people from their homes, by force if necessary.' He looked at his watch. 'It is now nine-thirty. In ten hours from now I do not want a single living being left in the city apart from the army. You will be in charge of the evacuation, Charles. Be ruthless. If they won't move, prod them with bayonets; if that fails, then shoot a few to encourage the others. But get them out.'

Wyatt listened to Favel's flat voice and, for the first time, knew the truth of what Causton had implied. This was a man who used power like a weapon, who had the politician's view of people as a mass and not as individuals. Perhaps it was impossible for him to be otherwise: he had the ruthlessness of a surgeon wielding a knife in an emergency operation – to cure the whole he would destroy the parts.

'So we get them out,' said Manning. 'Then what?'

Favel gestured at the map, and said softly, 'Then we let Serrurier and Rocambeau have St Pierre. For the first time in history men will use a hurricane as a weapon of war.'

Wyatt drew in his breath, shocked to the core of his being. He stepped forward and said in a cracked voice, 'You can't do that.'

'Can't I?' Favel swung on him. 'I've been trying to kill those men with steel, and if I had my way I would kill every one of them. And they want to kill me and my men. Why shouldn't I let the hurricane have them? God knows how many of my men will be lost saving the inhabitants of St Pierre; they'll be outnumbered five to one and a lot of them will die – so why shouldn't the hurricane exact my revenge?'

Wyatt momentarily quailed before those blazing blue eyes and fell back. Then he said, 'I gave you the warning to save lives, not to take them. This is uncivilized.'

'And the hydrogen bomb is civilized?' snapped Favel. 'Use your brains – what else *can* I do? This afternoon, when the evacuation is complete, my men will be in sole possession of St Pierre. I am certainly not going to leave them there. When they withdraw the Government forces will move in, thinking we are in retreat. What else would they think? I am not *asking* them to be drowned in St Pierre – they enter the city at their own risk.'

'How far will you withdraw?' asked Wyatt.

'You drew the line yourself,' said Favel remorselessly. 'We will hold, as far as we can, on the eighty-foot contour line.'

'You could withdraw further,' said Wyatt heatedly. 'They'd follow you on to higher ground.'

Favel's hand came down on the table with the sound of a pistol shot. 'I have no wish to fight further battles. There has been enough of killing men. Let the hurricane do its work.'

'This is murder.'

'What else is war but murder?' asked Favel, and turned his back on Wyatt. 'Enough, we have work to do. Charles, let us see which men I can spare you.'

He walked to the end of the room, leaving Wyatt shattered. Causton came over and put his hand on his shoulder. 'Don't worry your head about the policies of princes,' he advised. 'It's dangerous.'

'This is against all I've ever worked for,' said Wyatt in a low voice. 'I never intended this.'

'Otto Frisch and Lise Meitner didn't mean trouble when they split the uranium atom back in 1939.' Causton nodded up the room towards Favel. 'If you find a way of controlling hurricanes, it's men like that who'll decide what they'll be used for.'

'He could save everyone,' said Wyatt in a stronger voice. 'He could, you know. If he retreated up into the hills the Government forces would follow him.'

'I know,' said Causton.

'But he's not going to do that. He's going to pen them in St Pierre.'

Causton scratched his head. 'That may not be as easy as it sounds. He's got to stand off Rocambeau and Serrurier until the evacuation is completed, then he has to conduct a controlled retreat without being smashed while he's doing it. Next, he has to establish his perimeter on the eighty-foot line and that's a hell of a long line to hold with five thousand men – less what he'll have lost while all this has been going on. And on top of all that he'll have to dig in against the wind.' He shook his head doubtfully. 'A tricky operation altogether.'

Wyatt looked at Favel. 'I think he's as power-mad as Serrurier.'

'Look, laddie,' said Causton. 'Start thinking straight. He's doing what he has to do in the circumstances. He's begun something he's got to go through with and in the dicey position he's in now, he'll use any weapon at hand – even a hurricane.' He paused thoughtfully. 'Maybe he's not as bad as I thought. When he said he didn't want any more battles, I think he meant it.'

'He might well,' said Wyatt. 'As long as he comes out on top.'

Causton grinned. 'You're getting an education in the political facts of life. Damn it, some of you scientists are bloody naive.'

Wyatt said, with something of despair in his voice, 'I'd have liked to have gone into atomic physics – my tutor wanted me to – but I didn't like the end results of what they were doing. Now it's happening to me anyway.'

'You can't live in an ivory tower all your life,' said Causton roughly. 'You can't escape the world outside.'

'Perhaps not,' said Wyatt, frowning. 'But there's something I've got to do. What about Julie and Rawsthorne and the others? We must do something about them.'

Causton made a strangled noise. 'What were you thinking of doing?' he asked with caution.

'We've got to do *something*,' said Wyatt angrily. 'I want transport – a car or something – and an escort for part of the way.'

Causton struggled for a while to sort out his emotions. At last he said, 'You weren't intending – by any chance – going into the middle of Rocambeau's army, were you?'

'It seems to be the only way,' said Wyatt. 'I can't think of anything else.'

'Well, I wouldn't worry Favel about it now,' advised Causton. 'He's busy.' He regarded Wyatt thoughtfully, trying to decide if he could be entirely sane. 'Besides, Favel won't want to lose you.'

'What do you mean by that?' demanded Wyatt.

'He'll expect you to consult the skies and give him a timetable for his operations.'

'I'm not lending myself to that sort of thing,' said Wyatt through his teeth.

'Now, look here,' said Causton in a hard voice. 'Favel has over sixty thousand people to think of. You have only four – and you're really only thinking of one. He *is* getting the people out of St Pierre, you know – and that is not essential to his military plans. In fact, the effort might damn' well cripple him. I'll leave it to you to see where your duty lies.' He turned on his heel and walked away.

Wyatt looked after him with a sinking feeling in his stomach. Causton was right, of course; too damnably right. He was caught up in this thing whether he liked it or not – in saving the population of St Pierre he would help to destroy the Government army. Perhaps it would be better to think of it the other way round – in helping to destroy the army he would save the people. He thought about that, but it did not make him feel much better.

II

At eleven o'clock the city of St Pierre boiled over. Manning's plan was brutally simple. Starting simultaneously in the eastern and western suburbs, just behind the troops drawn up ready for battle, his evacuating force pitched the inhabitants into the streets, going systematically from house to house. The people could take the clothes they stood up in and as much food as they could carry – nothing else. The result was as though someone had thrust a stick into an ants' nest and given it a vicious twist.

Manning issued maps of the city to his officers, scored with red and blue lines. The red lines indicated the lines of communication of the army; no civilians were allowed on those streets at all on pain of death – at all costs the army must be protected and serviced and nothing must stand in the way of that. The blue lines led to the main road leading up through the Negrito Valley, the road along which Wyatt had driven with Julie what seemed a hundred years before.

There were incidents. The blue lines indicated one-way traffic only, a traffic regulation enforced with violence. Those attempting to go against the stream were brusquely ordered to turn round, and if this failed, then the point of a bayonet was a convincing argument. But sometimes, against a frantic father looking for his family, even the bayonet was not convincing enough and the rifle beyond the bayonet spoke a louder word. The body would be dragged to the side of the road so as not to impede the steady shuffle of feet.

It was brutal. It was necessary. It was done.

Causton, wearing the brassard of a rebel officer, roamed the city. In all the hot spots of a troubled world he had covered in the course of his work he had never seen anything like this. He was simultaneously appalled and exultant – appalled at the vast scale of the tragedy he was witnessing, and exultant that he was the only newspaperman on the spot. The batteries of his tape recorder having run down, he wrote the quick, efficient shorthand he had learned as a cub reporter in notebooks looted from a stationery shop, and recorded the scene for a news-hungry world.

The people were apathetic. For years Serrurier had systematically culled the leaders from among them and all that were left were the sheep. They resisted vocally on being told to get out of their homes but the sight of the guns silenced them, and, once in the street, they fell into the long line obediently and shuffled forward with Favel's men at their heels chivvying them to greater speed. Inevitably there were confusions and bottlenecks as the greater mass of the populace came on to the streets; at one corner where two broad streets debouched into a third at a narrow angle there was chaos – a tangled inextricable mass of bodies crushed against one another which took Favel's bawling non-coms two hours to straighten out, and when at last this traffic jam was eased it left a couple of dozen crushed and suffocated corpses as evidence of anarchy.

Causton, in his borrowed car, toured the city and finally turned to the Negrito, checking on his map to find the quickest way on a red-lined route. He arrived by means of a side road at the main road leading into the Negrito Valley quite close to where Serrurier's artillery had been captured, and saw the long line of refugees streaming away in the distance. Here there was a sizeable force of rebel soldiers, about two hundred strong. They were weeding out able-bodied men from the passing stream, forming them into squads and marching them away. Curious, Causton followed one of these squads to see where they were going and saw them set to digging under the rifles of Favel's men.

Favel was establishing his final defence line on the eighty-foot contour.

When Causton returned to his car he saw a little pile of bodies tossed carelessly into a heap by the roadside behind the rebel troops – the conscientious objectors, the men who would not dig for victory.

Sickened by death, he contemplated driving up the Negrito to safety. Instead, he turned the car and went back into the city because he still had his job to do and because his job was his life. He drove back to general headquarters at the Imperiale and asked for Wyatt, finding him eventually on the roof, looking at the sky.

He looked up too, and saw a few feathery clouds barely veiling the furnace of the sun. 'Anything doing yet?' he asked.

Wyatt turned. 'Those clouds,' he said. 'Mabel's on her way.'

Causton said, 'They don't seem much. We get clouds like that in England.'

'You'll see the difference pretty soon.'

Causton cocked an eye at him. 'Got over your bloody-mindedness?'

'I suppose so,' said Wyatt gloomily.

'I have a thought that might console you,' Causton said. 'The people who are going to get it in the neck are Serrurier's soldiers, and soldiers are paid to get killed. That's more than you can say for the women and children of St Pierre.'

'What's it like out there?'

'Grim,' said Causton. 'There was a bit of looting, but Favel's men soon put a stop to that.' He deliberately refrained from mentioning the methods being used to get the people on the move; instead, he said, 'The devil of it is that there's only one practicable road out of town. Have you any idea how much road-space a city full of people takes up?'

'I've never had occasion to work it out,' said Wyatt sourly.

'I did some quick mental arithmetic,' said Causton. 'And I came up with the figure of twelve miles. Since they're not moving at more that two miles an hour, it takes six hours for the column to pass any given spot.'

'I spent an hour looking at maps,' said Wyatt. 'Favel wanted me to outline safe areas for the people. I did my best, looking at bloody contours, but – ' he thumped a fist into the palm of his hand – 'safe? I don't know. This town ought to have had a hurricane plan ready for lifting from a pigeon-hole and putting into action,' he said savagely.

'That's not Favel's fault,' pointed out Causton reasonably. 'You can blame Serrurier for that.' He looked at his watch. 'One o'clock and Rocambeau hasn't made a move yet. He must have been mauled more seriously than we thought. Have you eaten yet?'

Wyatt shook his head, so Causton said, 'Let's see what we can rustle up. It might be the last time we'll eat for quite a while.'

They went downstairs and were buttonholed by Manning, who had just walked in. 'When's that hurricane due?' he asked abruptly.

'I can't tell you yet,' said Wyatt. 'But give me another couple of hours and I'll tell you exactly.'

Manning looked disgusted, but said nothing. Causton said, 'Is there anything to eat around here? I'm getting peckish.'

Manning grinned. 'We did find a few stray chickens. You'd better come with me.'

He took them into the manager's office, which had been converted into an officers' mess, and they found Favel just finishing a meal. He also questioned Wyatt, going into it much more thoroughly than Manning had, and then he went back to his map room, leaving them to eat in peace.

Causton gnawed on a chicken leg and then paused, pointing it at Manning. 'Where do you come into all this?' he asked. 'How did you get tangled up with Favel?'

'A matter of business,' said Manning offhandedly.

'Such as professional advice on how to organize a war?'

Manning grinned. 'Favel doesn't need any teaching about that.'

Causton looked profound. 'Ah,' he said, as though enlightenment had suddenly come to him. 'Your business is AFC business.'

Wyatt looked up. 'What's that?'

'The Antilles Fruit Corporation – very big business in this part of the world. I was wondering where Favel got his finance.'

Manning put down a bone. 'I'm not likely to tell you, am I? I wouldn't shoot off my mouth to a reporter.'

'Not in the normal way,' agreed Causton. 'But if the reporter had the smell of the right idea and he was good enough at his job to ferret out the rest of it, you'd want him to get the right story, wouldn't you? From your angle, I mean.'

Manning laughed. 'I like you, Causton; I really do. Well, I can give you some kind of story – but it's off the record and don't quote me on it. Let's say I'm having a quiet talk with Wyatt here, and you're eavesdropping with those long ears.' He looked at Wyatt. 'Let's say there was a big American corporation which had a lot of capital invested in San Fernandez at one time, and all its holdings were expropriated by Serrurier.'

'AFC,' said Causton.

'Could be,' said Manning. 'But I'm not saying so out loud. The officers of this corporation were as mad as hornets, naturally – their losses were more than twenty-five million dollars – and the shareholders weren't pleased, either. That's one half of it. The other half is Favel – he's the chap who could do something about it – for reasons of his own. But he had no money to buy arms and train men, so what more natural than they get together?'

'But why pick you as a go-between?' asked Causton.

Manning shrugged. 'I'm in the business – I'm for hire. And they didn't want an American; that might not have looked right. Anyway, I went shopping with the corporation's money – there's a chap in Switzerland, an American, who has enough guns to equip the British army, let alone our piddling little effort. Favel knew exactly what he wanted – rifles, machine-guns, mortars to pack a big wallop and yet be easily moved, recoilless rifles and a few mountain guns. He got his best men off the island and set up a training school – and I'd better not tell you where. He hired a few artillery instructors to train his men and then gradually started to recruit again on the island. When he had enough men we shipped in the arms.'

Wyatt said incredulously, 'Do you mean to tell me that all this has been done so that a fruit company can make a few dollars more profit?'

Manning looked at him sharply and his hand curled into a ball. 'It has not,' he said crisply. 'Where do you get that idea?'

Causton said hastily, 'Pray forgive my young friend. He's still wet behind the ears – he doesn't understand the facts of life, as I've had occasion to tell him.'

Manning pointed his finger at Wyatt. 'You say that to Favel and you'll get your head chopped off. Somebody had to get Serrurier out and Favel was the only one with guts enough. And it couldn't be done constitutionally because Serrurier abolished the constitution, so it had to be done with blood – a surgical operation. It's a pity, but there it is.'

He relaxed and grinned at Causton. 'Our hypothetical fruit corporation might have caught a tiger by the tail – Favel is no one's dummy. He's a bit of a reformer, you know, and he'll hold out for fair pay and good working conditions on the plantations.' He shrugged. 'I'm no company man; it's no skin off my nose if Favel bites the hand that's fed him.'

Wyatt winced. It seemed that Causton was right again. Nothing in this topsy-turvy world of politics made sense to him. It was a world in which black and white merged into an indeterminate grey, where bad actions were done for good reasons and good reasons were suspect. It was not his world and he wished he were out of it, in his own uncomplicated sphere of figures and formulae where all he had to worry about was whether a hurricane would behave itself.

He was about to apologize but he saw that Manning was still talking to Causton. '. . . will be better when San Fernandez can build up a fund of development capital instead of it being siphoned off into Serrurier's pocket. A bit of spare money round here would make all the difference – it could be a good place.'

Causton said, 'Can Favel be trusted?'

'I think so. He's liberally inclined, but he's not a milk-and-water liberal, and he's got no inclination to be taken over by the Russians like Castro. He'll stand up to the Americans, too.' Manning grinned. 'He'll make them pay a hell of a lot more for Cap Sarrat Base than they've been paying.' He became serious. 'He'll be a dictator because he can't be anything else right now. Serrurier beat the stuffing out of these people, killed their natural leaders and drained them of guts – they're not fit for government yet. But I don't think he'll be a bad dictator, certainly not as bad as Serrurier.'

'Um,' said Causton. 'He'll have to take a lot of criticism from well-meaning fools who don't know what's been going on here.'

'That won't worry him,' said Manning. 'He doesn't give a damn about what people say about him. And he can give as good as he gets.'

The table shook and there came a roll of thunder rumbling from the east. Manning lifted his head. 'The party's started – Rocambeau has begun his attack.'

III

Julie looked through a crack in the door of the corrugated iron hut, paying no attention to the shrill voice of Mrs Warmington who sat crouched on a box behind her. There still seemed to be a lot of trucks in the quarry, although she had heard many drive away. And there were still many soldiers about, some standing in groups, talking and smoking, and others moving about intent on their business. She was thankful that the officer had not considered it necessary to post a guard on the hut; he had merely tested the bolt on the outside of the door before pushing them inside.

She had had a hard time with Mrs Warmington – the woman was impossible. When they were captured and brought down to the quarry Mrs Warmington had tried to talk her way out of it, raising her voice in an attempt to get her point over – which was that she was an American and not to be treated like a criminal when she had merely been defending her life and honour. It had not worked because no one understood English, no matter how loudly shouted, and they had been thrust into the hut and, Julie hoped, forgotten.

She turned from the door, irritated with Mrs Warmington's monologue. 'For God's sake, will you be quiet?' she said wearily. 'What do you want them to do – come in here and shut you up with a gun? They will, you know, once they get as tired of you as I am.'

Mrs Warmington's mouth shut with a snap – but not for long. 'This is intolerable,' she said with the air of a victim. 'The State Department will know of this when I get home.'

'*If* you get home,' said Julie cruelly. 'You shot a man, you know. You shot him with Eumenides's gun.' She cocked her head at the door. 'They're not going to like that.'

'But they don't know,' said Mrs Warmington craftily. 'They think it was that Greek.'

Julie looked at her in disgust for a long moment. 'They don't know,' she agreed. 'But they will if I tell them.'

Mrs Warmington gulped. 'But you wouldn't do that . . . would . . . you?' Her voice tailed away as she saw the expression on Julie's face.

'I will if you don't keep your big trap shut,' said Julie callously. 'You killed Eumenides – you killed him as surely as if you'd shot him and pushed a bayonet into his back yourself. He was a nice guy; not very brave maybe – who is? – but a nice guy. He didn't deserve that. I'm not going to forget it, you know, so you'd better watch yourself. If I killed you here and now it wouldn't be murder, just decent execution.'

She spoke levelly and without emphasis, but her words were chilling and Mrs Warmington shrank into a corner with horror in her eyes. Julie said, 'So walk carefully round me, you big bag of wind, or I might be tempted. I *could* kill you, it shouldn't be too difficult.' Her voice was detached, but when she looked down at her hands she saw they were shaking violently.

She turned and looked again through the crack in the door, astonished at herself. Never before had she struck at another person with such deadly intent to hurt, never before had she trembled in such fury. For too long she had exercised the tact drilled into her as an air hostess and it felt good to let rip at this futile and dangerous woman. She felt a surge of strength and knew she had done the right thing.

She felt a warm trickle run down her thigh, and looked at her arm and saw the drying blood where she had been jabbed by a bayonet. There was much activity outside but no one seemed to be taking particular note of the hut, so she stripped off her slacks and examined the wounds in her legs.

Incredibly, Mrs Warmington had retained her purse when they were dragged down the hill, and now Julie picked it up and dumped the contents on to the floor. It contained no more than the usual rat's nest found in a woman's purse; lipstick, compact, comb, money in notes and coins – quite a lot of that, traveller's cheques, pen, note-book, a packet of tissues, a bottle of aspirin, a small flask of spirit which proved to be bourbon, an assortment of hair-pins, several loose scraps of paper and a cloying scent of spilled face powder.

She stirred the heap with her finger and said sardonically, 'You've lost your jewels.' She took the tissues and began to stanch her wounds. They were not too bad; the worst was not a quarter of an inch deep, but they bled freely and she knew that when they stopped bleeding her legs would become very stiff and painful to move. She took two of the aspirin tablets and dumped half of the contents of the bottle into her shirt pocket. As she swallowed the aspirins she wished they had water, and wondered what could be done about that. Then she donned her slacks and tossed the remainder of the tissues to Mrs Warmington. 'Clean yourself up,' she ordered abrupt-ly, and went to the door again.

She stayed to observe the scene for a long time. The quarry apparently formed a convenient military park close to the main road but not in the way of traffic. There were many trucks moving in and out but she noted that the general trend was to lessen the number of vehicles standing idle. She hoped briefly, but with no great assurance, that everyone would go away, forgetting the white women imprisoned in the hut, and wondered how much chance there was of that happening.

After a while she tired of the changing scene that always remained the same and began to explore the hut. Mrs Warmington sat mutely in her corner, looking at Julie with frightened eyes, and Julie ignored her. Most of the boxes were empty, but behind a large tea-chest filled with bits and pieces of scrap iron she found a sledge-hammer and a pick-axe, both in reasonably good condition.

Julie hefted the hammer and then explored the walls of the hut. The wooden framework was rotten and the nails that held the rusty iron sheets were corroded, and she thought she would have no difficulty in battering her way out provided there was no one within earshot – an unlikely eventuality. She put the tools close to hand behind the door where they would not be easily seen and settled down again to her vigil.

The morning wore on and slowly the quarry emptied of vehicles. As the sun rose higher in the sky the hut warmed to an oven-like heat and the iron walls were too hot to touch. The two women sat there and sweated, listening to the noisy clash of gears and the roar of engines as trucks drove to and fro – and they became very thirsty.

She wondered what had happened to Rawsthorne and concluded that he must also have been taken prisoner, or perhaps killed. It had only been the fortunate arrival of the Negro officer that had saved them, and maybe Rawsthorne had not been so lucky. She coldly contemplated the grim fact that if she did not get out of this hut she would die. Rawsthorne had already rejected the quarry as being safe from the hurricane, and however the fortunes of the civil war she would die if she could not escape.

Her thoughts again turned to Wyatt. It was a great pity that now they had come together at last they should be parted and that both would probably die. At the moment she did not give much for her own chances, and while she was ignorant of what had happened to Wyatt, she was doubtful of his having survived the war that had washed over St Pierre.

She was aroused from her reverie by Mrs Warmington. 'I'm thirsty.'

'So am I,' said Julie. 'Shut up!'

Something was happening – or rather, not happening – and she made a quick gesture with her hand, pressing Mrs Warmington to silence. It had suddenly gone very quiet. True, there was the noise of traffic from the main coast road, but the closer rumble of trucks from the quarry had ceased. She looked through the crack in the door again and found the quarry empty except for one soldier, who squatted in the shade a dozen yards away and seemed to be dozing. There had been a guard, after all.

Julie turned and snatched the purse from Mrs Warmington's grasping hand and took out the wad of notes. Mrs Warmington flared up. 'Don't take that – it's mine.'

'You want water, don't you?' asked Julie. 'We might be able to buy some.' She looked at the thick bundle of money. 'We might even be able to buy our way out of here – if you keep quiet.' Mrs Warmington closed her mouth abruptly, and Julie said, 'I don't know my way around in this language, but I'll try; the money will speak loud enough, anyway.'

She went to the door and looked through the crack. 'Hey you, there!'

The soldier turned round lazily and blinked at the door. He saw what appeared to be a bank-note of large denomination protruding through the door of the hut and moving gently up and down. He scrambled to his feet, seized his rifle, and approached the hut with circumspection diluted with avarice. The bank-note flashed from sight as he made a grab for it, and a feminine voice said, *'L'eau . . . agua.* Can you get us some?'

Julie watched the puzzlement on the man's face, and said urgently, 'Bring us water. Water . . . *l'eau* . . . *agua*. You can have the money.'

The soldier scratched his head, and then his face cleared. 'Ah – *l'eau*!.'

'That's right. You can have the money – the money, see when you bring *l'eau*.'

He broke into a jabber of incomprehensible *patois*, finally ending with, '*L'argent* . . . *la monnaie* . . . *pour l'eau?*'

'That's right, buster; you've got it.'

He nodded and went away and Julie breathed a sigh of relief. Her throat was parched and felt like sand-paper, and the thought of cool water made her feel dizzy for a moment. But there was something that had to be done before the soldier returned. It was not likely he would unlock the door – he probably had no key – and how would he get the water into the hut?

She seized the sledge-hammer and prodded tentatively at the bottom of the door where it seemed to be weakest. Then she swung the hammer like a golf club and crashed it once against the rotten wood. A piece gave way leaving a small opening, and she dared not do more. She did not know how far the soldier had gone and he could still be within earshot – one sharp noise he might dismiss, but not the constant repetition necessary to break down the door.

She saw him coming back bearing a bottle and a tin cup and he paused a moment and looked helplessly as she rattled the door. He said something and shrugged his shoulders and she knew he could not open the door, so she bent down and put her hand through the hole she had made. 'Down here,' she shouted, hoping he did not realize the opening was new.

He squatted before the door and put the bottle and cup just out of her reach. '*L'argent*,' he said in a bass growl. '*La monnaie*.'

She cursed him and pushed a bank-note through the hole. He grabbed it and pushed the tin cup within her reach. She drew it through the hole gently, careful not to spill it, and passed it to Mrs Warmington. When she reached for the bottle it was still beyond her grasp. The soldier grinned and said cheerfully, *'L'argent?'* and she was forced to give him more money before he would let her have the bottle.

The water, tepid though it was, was a benison to her dry throat. She drank half the bottle in one swallow and then paused, looking at Mrs Warmington who was licking the last drop from the rim of the dirty cup. She said, 'Take it easy; this stuff is expensive – it's costing you over four dollars a cup.' She put the bottle in the corner and looked at her watch. It was twelve-thirty.

The soldier had gone back to sitting in the shade, but he kept his eye on the hut, hoping for more easy money. Julie said, 'I wish to hell he'd go away.'

She heard a tapping sound from behind her and turned to look at Mrs Warmington, who was gazing hopefully into the cup as though she expected it to fill up by magic. The tapping continued and came from the back of the hut, so Julie went to the back wall and listened closely. There was a familiar but incomplete rhythm which she recognized as the old shave-and-a-haircut of her childhood days, so she gave the two taps necessary to complete the phrase and said in a low voice, 'Who's that?'

'Rawsthorne – don't make a noise.'

Her heart leaped in her breast. 'How did you get here?'

'I followed you when you were brought down here. I've been watching from the top of the quarry. I was only able to get down when that bloody guard went away just now.'

'Where did he go?' asked Julie urgently.

'Up the track and out of sight,' said Rawsthorne. 'I think he went as far as the main road.'

'Good!' said Julie. 'I think I can make him do it again. If he goes that far we can get out of here. Can you wait there?'

'Yes,' said Rawsthorne. He sounded very much his age and as though he was desperately tired. 'I can wait.'

Julie went back and found that Mrs Warmington had finished the bottle of water. She looked up defiantly, and said, 'Well, it was my money, wasn't it?'

Julie snatched the bottle from her hands. 'It doesn't matter now; we're getting out of here. Get ready – and keep quiet.'

She went to the door and called out, '*L'eau* . . . more *l'eau*, please,' and fluttered another bank-note through the crack. This time she wasn't quick enough and the soldier snatched it from her before she could withdraw it. He grinned in satisfaction as he stuffed it into his pocket but made no objection to taking the bottle and cup.

She watched him walk out of sight and forced herself to wait two full minutes, then she swung at the door with the hammer and with her full strength. One of the planks split along its length; it was rotten with age and lack of paint and another blow shattered it. Rawsthorne called, 'Wait!' and stuck his head through the opening she had made. 'Hit it down there,' he said, indicating the area of the lock.

She swung the hammer again and the hasp and staple burst out of the rotten wood and the door creaked open. 'Come on,' she said. 'Make it fast.' And ran outside, not really caring if Mrs Warmington followed or not.

'Over here,' called Rawsthorne, and she ran after him round a corner of rock and out of sight of the hut. 'We're still in a trap,' Rawsthorne told her. 'This quarry is a dead-end, and if we go along the track we'll meet that guard coming back.'

'How did you get down?'

Rawsthorne pointed upwards. 'I came down there – and nearly broke my neck. But we can't get up that way – not before the guard comes back – he'd pick us off the cliff like ducks in a shooting gallery.' He looked around. 'The only thing we can do is to hide.'

'But where?'

'There's a ledge up there,' said Rawsthorne. 'If we lie flat we should be out of sight of anyone down here. Come on, Mrs Warmington.'

It was an awkward climb. Julie and Rawsthorne gave the ungainly Mrs Warmington a boost, and then Rawsthorne went up and turned to give Julie his hand. She rolled on to the narrow ledge with skinned knees and flattened herself out. Although she kept her head down she could still see the corner of the hut in the distance and expected to see the guard return with the water at any moment.

She whispered, 'Supposing we do get on top of the quarry – what then?'

'All the troops have gone from the top,' said Rawsthorne. 'They moved out of the plantation back towards St Pierre. I think General Rocambeau is going to attack very soon. I thought we could cut across country behind his army, moving over the hills until we reach the Negrito. We should be safe enough there.' He paused. 'But we might not have time; have you looked at the sky?'

Julie twisted her neck and looked up, wincing as the sun bit into her eyes. 'I don't see much – just a few high clouds. Feathery ones.'

'There's a halo round the sun,' said Rawsthorne. 'I think the hurricane will be here soon.'

Julie saw a movement near the hut. 'Hush, he's come back.'

The soldier looked at the hut in astonishment and dropped the bottle and the cup, spilling the water carelessly

on the dusty ground. He unslung his rifle and Julie heard
quite clearly the snap of metal as he slipped off the safety-
catch. He looked around the quarry and she froze – if she
could see him, then he could see her if he looked carefully
enough in the right direction.

Slowly the soldier walked around the hut; he walked
with deliberation, his rifle held ready to shoot, and
she heard the dry crunch of his boots on the ground. He
came forward intent on searching the quarry, and cast in a
wide circle, peering into all the nooks and crannies left by
the blasting. As he came closer he vanished from sight and
Julie held her breath and hoped the Warmington woman
would keep quiet, because now the man was very close –
she could even hear the rasp of his breath as he stood
below the ledge.

And he stood there for a long time. There was no
movement of his feet at all, and Julie pictured him looking up at the ledge and wondering if it was worthwhile
climbing up to investigate. There was a clink and a scrap-
ing sound as of metal on rock, and she thought: he's put
down his gun; he needs both hands for climbing. He's
coming up!

She jerked at the sound of a shattering explosion, and
then there was another – and another. She heard the thud of
boots and, after a few seconds, saw the man running across
the quarry away from them to stand looking up the track
with his hand shielding his eyes from the glare of the sun.
The explosions continued in rapid succession. It was a noise
Julie was becoming familiar with – an artillery barrage.
Rocambeau had attacked and Favel was laying down protective fire.

The soldier hesitated and looked about the quarry again,
then slung his rifle on his shoulder and disappeared from
her view at a rapid trot, heading towards the track. 'I think
he's gone,' she said after a long moment.

Rawsthorne lifted himself up and looked about. 'Then we must go too,' he said. 'We must strike for the high ground.'

IV

Favel's force in the east resisted the first assault, shattering the wave of Government troops that tried to cross the open ground before the furthest suburbs with a deluge of shells and mortar bombs. Rocambeau had no artillery and was impotent in the face of this onslaught of fire, but he had the men – seven thousand to Favel's two thousand – and he used them ruthlessly.

He lost five hundred in that first attack, but when it was beaten off he occupied a line within two hundred yards of the nearest houses, his men burrowing into the shell-holes that pitted the ground; and he filtered in reinforcements from the rear, crawling on their bellies from crater to crater, until his position was unassailable.

Not that Favel meant to counter-attack – or could attack. Over half his force was serving the guns and he had only nine hundred infantrymen to cover them – a dangerously small force. But his infantry were exceptionally well equipped to fight a decisive battle; they had all the automatic weapons which had been withdrawn from the men now evacuating the city and they had had time to site them well. Rocambeau was going to lose a lot more men before he had a chance of getting at those murderous guns which were hammering his force – if he ever could get at them. For the guns were prepared to retreat at a moment's notice; their limbers and transport lay close at hand and they could retreat in echelon to already prepared positions when the order was given, and Rocambeau would be left to go through the whole futile, man-killing process again.

Favel did not even leave his headquarters. His officers knew what was expected of them and he knew he could rely on them to carry out the master plan, so he was left free to concentrate on the coming attack from the west. That morning he had gone down to the docks and watched the American evacuation of Cap Sarrat Base, powerful binoculars shortening the distance across the water. One by one the ships went and the aircraft roared towards the northeast in the direction of Puerto Rico and safety. A hazy pall of black smoke covered the Cap as the oil tanks went up in flames. Commodore Brooks was not leaving anything behind that would do anyone any good.

Favel thought of what Serrurier would do. Putting last things first, he would immediately occupy the Base. The American occupation of Cap Sarrat had always been a sore point with him and several times he had sought to break the agreement, only to be faced with the inflexible refusal of the American Government to be thrown out. Now it was open for him to take and take it he would – an empty victory with the promise of defeat lurking in the background. He would waste time on Cap Sarrat instead of organizing an attack on St Pierre with his reserve of fresh and unblooded troops now freed from the irrational fear of a stab in the back by the Americans.

So when Favel heard the guns from the east bellow in response to Rocambeau's assault he smiled thinly. Rocambeau with his defeated and demoralized army had come into action first and Serrurier was still wallowing in his fool's paradise on Cap Sarrat. Good! Let him stay there. If he knew there were but a thousand men to oppose his eight thousand perhaps he might change his mind – but there was no one to tell him, and if anyone did he would not believe it. He was a suspicious man and, fearing a trap, he would not believe anything so ridiculous.

Favel called an orderly and instructed him to bring Manning and Wyatt as soon as they could be found. Then he sat back in his chair and placidly lit a long thin cigar.

Wyatt was again on the roof when the orderly found him, scanning the horizon with binoculars. The high cirrus clouds, feathery and fragile, now covered the sky and were giving place to cirrostratus from the south, extending in a great flat sheet. It was still intensely hot and the air was still and sultry without the trace of a breeze. The sun was haloed – an ominous sign to Wyatt as he checked the time again.

He went down to see Favel and found Manning giving a progress report. 'We're moving along as fast as we can,' he said. 'But it takes time.'

Wyatt said abruptly, 'Time is something we haven't got. Mabel is moving faster than I thought.'

'How long?' asked Manning.

'She'll hit about five o'clock.'

'Christ!' said Manning. 'It can't be done.'

'It must be done,' said Favel curtly. He turned to Wyatt. 'What do you mean when you say it will hit at five o'clock?'

'You'll have winds of sixty miles an hour.'

'And the flooding?'

Wyatt shrugged. 'I don't know,' he said honestly. 'That's one aspect of hurricanes I haven't studied. I don't really know when you can expect the tidal wave – but I wouldn't put it much after six o'clock.'

Favel said reflectively, 'It is two o'clock now – that gives us four hours, or three at the worst. What is likely to happen between now and then?'

'Not much,' said Wyatt. 'The clouds will thicken very perceptibly in the next hour and a breeze will spring up. From then on it just gets worse.'

'Charles, how is the evacuation going in the east? Can we withdraw to the second prepared line?'

Manning nodded unwillingly. 'I've got all that area cleared – but you'll be pushing it a bit hard. If Rocambeau breaks through – and he could if we aren't careful on this retreat – he'll be right in the middle of us and we won't have a chance.'

Favel pulled a telephone towards him. 'We retreat,' he said firmly. 'Speed things up, Charles. I want every effort made.'

'All right, Julio,' said Manning wearily. 'I'll do my best.' He strode out. Wyatt hesitated, wondering if he should go too, but Favel held up his hand while speaking into the telephone, so he leaned on the edge of the table and waited.

Favel put down the handset gently, and said, 'You mentioned rain, Mr Wyatt. Is this going to be a serious factor?'

'You can expect a lot of rain – more than you've ever seen before; it will add to the flooding problem in the Negrito but I took it into account when you asked me to outline the safe areas. The worst rainfall will occur in the right front quadrant of the hurricane, but I think that will be to the west of here. Still, you can expect between five and ten inches spread over twenty-four hours.'

'A lot of rain,' observed Favel. 'That is likely to preclude serious military operations.'

Wyatt laughed grimly. 'I hope you aren't thinking of doing *any* military operations during the next day or so. The wind will stop you if the rain doesn't.'

Favel said, 'I was thinking of afterwards. Thank you, Mr Wyatt. Keep me informed of any serious developments.'

So Wyatt went back on the roof and watched the dark line of nimbostratus gather on the horizon.

Rocambeau's second blow fell on thin air. True, the shelling was just as severe as before but there was no small-arms fire until his men had penetrated over half a mile into the city. They rushed into this sudden vacuum and became over-extended, and when they came up against opposition they were thin on the ground. The stragglers were lucky, but the enthusiasts in the forefront suffered heavy casualties from strong machine-gun fire and retreated a little way to lick their wounds.

But they did not mind because they heard the sudden rumble of guns from the other side of the city and knew that Serrurier had begun his attack at last. Now Favel and his rebels would surely be crushed.

Serrurier was even more brutal and callous about losses than Rocambeau. His bull-headed rush against the pitiful thin line of defenders was overwhelming. Despite the artillery and the plentiful machine-guns he cracked Favel's line in three places, threatening to split the small force into fragments. Favel took over decisively and ordered an immediate retreat into the city. In the open he had no chance against eight-to-one odds, but street fighting was another matter.

The fighting became brisk on both fronts and Favel's men gave way slowly, suffering many losses but not nearly as many as the Government armies. There was a constant coming and going at the Imperiale as Favel demanded news and yet more news of the evacuation, carefully timing his withdrawals on both flanks to accommodate the slow ebbing of the human tide from St Pierre, and grudgingly trading ground for enemy casualties. It was a risky business and it lost him more good men than he liked, but he stubbornly kept to his plan and somehow made it work.

The city was in flames to east and west as he withdrew. His men had orders to set all buildings on fire to put a barrier of flame before the advancing and victorious Government troops. The flames, fanned by the brisk breeze that had sprung up, roared to the sky and the smoke drifted north to lie over the Negrito.

At four o'clock he decided that he could not possibly save his artillery and gave orders for the guns to be spiked and abandoned as his commanders thought fit. The road to the Negrito was jammed with refugees and it was impossible to push the guns through at the same time, and he knew the guns would not be needed when the hurricane had passed. Already more than fifteen hundred of the troops Manning had used to evacuate the city were in position in the defence line on the eighty-foot contour, and Serrurier and Rocambeau were pushing in faster and pressing harder.

Five minutes later he gave the order to abandon head-quarters, and an orderly passed the news to Wyatt, who cast one more glance at the dark horizon and hurried down-stairs. Favel was waiting in the foyer, watching maps being loaded into a truck standing outside the hotel and seemingly more intent on the lighting of his cigar than on the din of battle.

'We will let Serrurier and Rocambeau join hands,' he said. 'I think they will waste time greeting each other, and perhaps they'll split a bottle of rum together. We will also form one line – but we are united.' He smiled. 'I do not think Rocambeau will take kindly to being superseded by Serrurier.'

A soldier shouted from the truck and Favel, after making sure his cigar was lit, applied the still-burning match to a twist of paper. 'Excuse me,' he said, and walked back into the bar. As he came back Wyatt saw the quick glow of fire behind him.

'Come, we must go,' said Favel, and pushed Wyatt through the door and into the street. As the truck pulled off Wyatt looked back at the Imperiale and saw smoke pouring through the windows to be whipped away in the rising wind.

It was four-thirty in the afternoon.

EIGHT

Wyatt had advocated evacuation – now he saw the reality and was shocked.

The truck travelled through the deserted streets in the centre of the town, while all around the clamour of battle echoed from the blank faces of the buildings as the rebel army grimly retreated in their narrowing circle. The sky was darkening and a wind had risen which blew tattered papers along dirty pavements. The city smelled of fire and the smoke, instead of rising, was now driven down into the streets to catch in the throat.

Wyatt coughed and stared at a body lying on the pavement. A little way along the street he saw another, then another – all male, all civilian. He jerked his head round and said to Favel, 'What the devil has been going on?'

Favel stared straight ahead. He asked tonelessly, 'Have you any conception of what is needed to evacuate a city in a few hours? If the people will not move, then they must be made to move.'

The truck slowed to swerve round another corpse in the middle of the street – a woman in a startlingly patterned red floral dress and a yellow bandanna about her head. She was sprawled like a toy abandoned by a child, her limbs awry in the indecency of violent death. Favel said, 'We share the guilt, Mr Wyatt. You had the knowledge; I had the power.

Without your knowledge this would never have happened, but you brought your knowledge to one who had the power to make it happen.'

'Need there have been killing?' asked Wyatt in a low voice.

'There was no time to explain, no plans already made, no knowledge in the people themselves.' Favel's face was stern. 'Everyone knows we do not have hurricanes in San Fernandez,' he said as though he were quoting. 'The people did not *know*. That is another crime of President Serrurier – perhaps the worst of all. So the people had to be forced.'

'How many dead?' asked Wyatt grimly.

'Who knows? But how many shall be saved? Ten thousand? Twenty – thirty thousand? One must make a balance in these things.'

Wyatt was silent. He knew he would have to live with this thing and that it would hurt. But he could still try to sway Favel in his decision to contain and destroy the Government army. He said, 'Need there be more killing? Must you still stand and fight around St Pierre? How many will you kill in the city, Julio Favel? Five thousand? Ten – fifteen thousand?'

'It is too late,' said Favel austerely. 'I cannot do otherwise if I wished. The evacuation took a long time – it is not yet complete – and my men will be lucky if they can get to their prepared positions in time.' His voice became sardonic. 'I am not a Christian – it is a luxury few honest politicians can afford – but I have justification in the Bible. The Lord God parted the waters and let the Israelites through the flood dry-shod; but he stayed his hand and drowned the pursuing Egyptians – every soldier, every horse, every chariot was destroyed in the Red Sea.'

The truck pulled up at a checkpoint, beyond which Wyatt could see a long line of refugees debouching from a side road. A rebel officer came up and conferred with Favel, and a white man waved and hurried over. It was Causton. 'You took your time,' he said. 'How far has the Government army got into the city?'

'I don't know,' said Wyatt. He climbed out of the truck. 'What's happening up here?'

Causton indicated the refugees. 'The last of the many,' he said. 'They should be all through in another fifteen minutes.' He stretched his arms wide. 'This is where Favel makes his stand – this is the eighty-foot contour line.' The rising wind plucked at his shirt-sleeves. 'I've got a hole already picked out for us – unless you want to push on up the Negrito.'

'You're staying here, then?'

'Of course,' said Causton in surprise. 'This is where the action will be. Dawson is here, too; he said he was waiting for you.'

Wyatt turned and looked back at the city. In the distance he could see the sea, no longer a beaten silver plate but the dirty colour of uncleaned pewter. The southern sky was filled with the low iron-grey mass of the coming nimbostratus, bringing with it torrential rain and howling wind. Already it was perceptibly darker because of the lowering clouds and the smoke from the city.

Above the faint keening of the wind he could hear the sound of battle, mostly small-arms fire and hardly any artillery. The noise fluctuated as the wind gusted, sometimes seeming far away and sometimes very close. The ground sloped away down to the city, and between the top of the low ridge on which he was standing and the nearer houses there was not a soul to be seen.

'I'll stay here,' he said abruptly. 'Though I'm damned if I know why.' Of course he *did* know. His desire was a curious amalgam of professional interest in the action of a hurricane on the sea in shallow waters and a macabre fascination at the sight of a doomed city and a doomed army. He looked up the road. 'Where exactly is Favel making his stand?'

'On this ridge. There are positions dug in on the reverse slope – the men can nip down there when the weather gets really bad.'

'I hope those holes are well drained,' said Wyatt grimly. 'It's going to rain harder than you've seen it rain before. Any hole dug without provision for drainage is going to get filled up fast.'

'Favel thought of that one,' said Causton. 'He's pretty bright.'

'He asked me about rainfall,' said Wyatt. 'I suppose that was why.'

Favel called, 'Mr Wyatt, headquarters has been established about three hundred yards up the road.'

'I'm staying with Causton,' said Wyatt, moving nearer the truck.

'As you wish.' Favel's lips quirked. 'There is nothing more you or I can do now, except perhaps to send a prayer to Hunraken or any other appropriate god.' He spoke to his driver and the truck pulled into the thinning line of refugees.

'Let's join Dawson,' said Causton. 'We've established our new home just over there.'

He led the way off the road and down the reverse side of the ridge, where they found Dawson sitting cross-legged by the side of a large foxhole. He looked pleased when he saw Wyatt, and said, 'Well, hello! I thought you'd been captured again.'

Wyatt looked at the foxhole. It had a drainage trench at the rear which was obviously going to be inadequate. 'That wants deepening – and there should be two. Are there any spades around?'

'Those are in short supply,' said Dawson. 'But I'll see what I can find.'

Wyatt looked along the ridge and saw that it was alive with men, a long, thin line of them burrowing into the earth like moles. At the top of the ridge overlooking the city others were busy, siting machine-guns, excavating more foxholes for cover against enemy fire rather than the coming wind, and keeping careful watch on the city in case Serrurier's men broke through. Causton said, 'I hope you're right about the flooding. If it doesn't happen all hell will break loose. Favel abandoned his guns – he couldn't bring these out and the refugees, too.'

Wyatt said, 'Mabel is going to hit us head-on. There'll be floods.'

'There'd better be. From a military point of view Serrurier is right on top. I'll bet he's crowing.'

'He won't if he looks behind him – out to sea.'

Dawson came back carrying a thin piece of sheet metal under his arm. 'No spades; but this might do it.'

Causton and Wyatt deepened the drainage trench and scooped out another while Dawson watched them. Wyatt looked up. 'How are your hands?'

'Okay,' said Dawson. 'A doctor fixed them up.'

'What are you hanging round here for?' asked Wyatt. 'You should get away up the Negrito while you have the chance.'

Dawson shook his head. 'Have you seen those people? I've never seen a more beaten, dispirited crowd. I'm scared that if I joined them I'd get to feeling like that. Anyway, maybe I can help out here, somehow.'

'What do you think you can do?' asked Causton. 'You can't use your hands, so you can't fire a gun or dig a hole. I don't see the point of it.'

Dawson shrugged. 'I'm not running any more,' he said stubbornly. 'I've been running like hell for a long time, a lot of years. Well, I'm stopping right here on top of this ridge.'

Causton looked across at Wyatt and raised his eyebrows, then smiled faintly, but he merely said, 'I think that's all we can do here. Let's go up and see what trouble is coming.'

The last of the people of St Pierre had passed by on their way up into the Negrito Valley, but the road in the far distance was speckled with trudging figures making their way to high ground. The verdant greenness of the sugar-cane fields looked like a raging sea as the strengthening wind blew waves across the springy canes. Only the soldiers were left, and very few of those in the thin line of trenches scored across the ridge, but there would soon be more as the embattled army in St Pierre retreated on this position.

Wyatt strode to the top of the ridge and dropped flat near a rebel soldier, who turned and grinned at him. He said, 'What is happening, soldier?'

The man's grin widened. 'There,' he said, and stabbed out a finger. 'They come soon – maybe ten minutes.' He checked the breech of his rifle and laid some clips of ammunition before him.

Wyatt looked down the bare slope of the ridge towards the city. The sound of firing was very close and an occasional stray bullet whistled overhead. Soon he saw movement at the bottom of the slope and a group of men began to trudge up the hill, unhurriedly but making good time. From behind him an officer called out an order and the three men grouped round a machine-gun a dozen yards away got busy and swivelled the gun in the direction of the officer's pointing finger.

The men climbing the ridge reached the top and passed over. They were carrying a mortar which they assembled quickly on the reverse slope. Causton watched them and said critically, 'Not many mortar bombs left.'

More men were climbing the ridge now, moving steadily in disciplined retreat and covered by their comrades still fighting the confused battle among the houses below. Causton guessed he was witnessing the last jump in the controlled and planned leap-frogging movement which had brought Favel's defending force across St Pierre, and he was impressed by the steady bearing of the men. This was no rout in undisciplined panic like the debacle he had been involved in earlier, but an orderly withdrawal in the face of the enemy, one of the most difficult of military operations.

Wyatt, after casting a brief glance at the retreating men, had lifted his eyes to the south. The horizon was dark, nearly black, lit only by the dim flickering of distant lightning embedded in thick cloud, and the nearer nimbo-stratus was a sickly yellow, seemingly illuminated from the inside. The wind was backing to the west and was now much stronger. He estimated it to be a force seven verging on force eight – about forty miles an hour and gusting up to fifty miles an hour. It was nothing to worry anyone who did not know what was coming and was merely a gale such as San Fernandez had known many times. Probably Rocambeau, if he was still in command, would welcome it as bringing rain to extinguish the many fires in the city.

The retreating soldiers were now streaming over the ridge and were marshalled by their non-coms into the firing line and issued with more ammunition. They lay on the crest of the ridge in the shallow foxholes that had been dug for them and again set their faces towards the oncoming enemy.

Causton nudged Wyatt. 'Those houses down there – how high are they above sea-level?'

Wyatt considered. The ridge was not very high and the slope to the city was long. He said, 'If this ridge is on the eighty-foot contour, then they shouldn't be more than fifty feet up.'

'Then the tidal wave should wash as high as that, then?'

'It will,' said Wyatt. 'It will probably wash half-way up the slope.'

Causton pulled at his lower lip. 'I think the idea here is to pin the Government troops against those houses. They're three hundred yards away and the troops will have to attack uphill and across open ground. Maybe Favel will be able to do it, after all. But it'll be tricky disengaging the last of his men.'

Dawson said, 'I hope you're right, Wyatt. I hope this tidal wave of yours doesn't come boiling over this ridge. It would drown the lot of us.' He shook his head and grinned in wonder. 'Christ, what a position to be in – I must be nuts.'

'Perhaps we're all light-headed,' said Causton. 'We're seeing something that's never been tried before – the use of a hurricane to smash an army. What a hell of a story this will be when – and if – I get out of here.'

'It has been done before,' said Wyatt. 'Favel quoted a precedent – when Moses crossed the Red Sea with the Egyptians after him.'

'That's right,' said Causton. 'I hadn't thought of that one. It's a damned good – ' He pointed suddenly. 'Look, something's happening down there.'

A long line of men had emerged on to the slope, flitting about and on the move all the time, stopping only briefly to fire back at the houses. The machine-gun near-by cleared its throat in a coughing burst, then settled down to a steady chatter, and all the men along the ridge began to shoot, giving covering fire to the last of the rebel army retreating towards them. They had the advantage of height, little though it was, and could fire over the heads of their own men.

There was a sharp crack from behind as the mortar went off, and seconds later the bomb burst just short of the nearest house. There were more explosions among the houses, and from the rear came a louder report and the whistle of a shell as one of the few remaining guns fired. Again Causton heard that unearthly twittering in the air about him and pulled down his head below the level of the ridge. 'The bastards haven't any *politesse*,' he said. 'They're shooting back.'

The last of Favel's men came pouring over the ridge, to stumble and collapse in the shelter of the reverse slope. They had left some of their number behind – Wyatt could see three crumpled heaps half-way up the slope, and he thought of the sacrifices these men must have made to hold back the Government army until the city had been evacuated. The men rested and got back their breath and then, after a drink of water and a quick snack which was waiting for them, they rejoined the line.

Meanwhile there was a pause. Desultory and sporadic firing came from the houses, which had little or no effect, and the rebels did not fire at all under strict instructions from their officers – there was little enough ammunition left to waste any of it. It was obvious that the Government general was regrouping in the cover of the city for the assault on the ridge.

In spite of the rapidly cooling air Causton sweated gently. He said, 'I hope to God we can hold them. When the attack comes it's going to be a big one. Where's that damned hurricane of yours, Wyatt?'

Wyatt's eyes were on the horizon. 'It's coming,' he said calmly. 'The wind is rising all the time. There are the rain clouds coming up – the nimbostratus and the fractonimbus. The fighting will stop pretty soon. No one can fight a battle in a hurricane.'

The wind was now fifty miles an hour, gusting to sixty, and the smoke clouds over St Pierre had been broken down into a diffused haze driving before the wind. This made it difficult to see the sea, but he managed to see the flecks of white out there which indicated even higher winds.

'Here they come,' said Causton, and flattened himself out as the shooting from the houses suddenly increased to a crescendo. A wave of soldiers in light blue uniforms emerged at the foot of the slope and began to advance, the individual men zigzagging and changing direction abruptly, sometimes dropping on one knee to fire. They came on quickly and when they had advanced a hundred yards another wave broke from the houses to buttress the assault.

'Jesus!' said Dawson in a choked voice. 'There must be a couple of thousand of them down there. Why the hell don't we shoot?'

Not a shot came from the top of the ridge as the flood of blue-clad men surged up the slope. The wind was now strong enough to hamper them and Wyatt could see the fluttering of their clothing, and twice the black dot of a uniform cap as it was blown away. Some of the men lost their footing and, taken off balance, were pushed by the gusting wind, but still they came on, scuttling at the crouch and continually climbing higher.

It was not until the first of them were half-way up that a Very light soared up from the top of the ridge, to burst in red stars over the slope. Immediately pandemonium broke loose as the rebels opened up a concentrated fire. The rifles cracked, the machine-guns hammered, and from behind came the deeper cough of the few guns and mortars.

The oncoming wave of men shivered abruptly and then stopped dead. Causton saw a swathe of them cut down like wheat before the scythe as a defending machine-gun swivelled and chopped them with a moving blade of bullets, and all over that open ground men were falling, either dead, wounded or desperately seeking cover where there was none. He noted that half of Favel's machine-guns were firing on fixed lines so that the attackers were caught in a net stitched in the air with bullets – they would die if they advanced and they would die if they ran because in either event they would run right into the line of fire of the angled machine-guns.

Mortar bombs and shells dropped among the trapped men – Favel was firing his last ammunition with extravagant prodigality, staking everything on the coming hurricane. The earth shook and fountained with darkly blossoming trees and the clouds of smoke and dust were snatched by the wind and blown away. A pitifully thin fire came from below, perhaps there were few to shoot or perhaps those alive were too shattered to care.

For five minutes that seemed an eternity the uproar went on and then, suddenly, as though on command, the line of attackers broke and ebbed away, leaving a wrack of bodies behind to mark the highest level of the assault, a bare hundred yards from the crest of the ridge. And as they ran back in panic, so they still died, hit by rifle bullets, cut in two by the murderous machine-guns and blown to pieces by the mortar bombs. When all was still again the ground was littered with the shattered wreckage of what had been men.

'Oh, my God!' breathed Dawson. His face was pale and sickly and he let out his breath with a shuddering sigh. 'They must have lost a quarter of their men.'

Causton stirred. 'Serrurier must have taken over,' he said quietly. 'Rocambeau would never have made a damn'-fool frontal attack like that – not at this stage of the game.' He turned and looked back at the mortar team just behind. 'These boys have shot their bolt – they have no ammunition left. I don't know if we can stand another attack.'

'There'll be no more attacks,' said Wyatt with calm certitude. 'As far as the fighting goes this war is over.' He looked down the slope at the tumbled heaps of corpses. 'I wish I could have said that half an hour ago, but it doesn't really make any difference. They'll all die now.' He withdrew from the ridge and walked away towards the foxhole.

Down in St Pierre thousands of men would be killed in the next few hours because he had told Favel of the approaching hurricane, and the guilt weighed heavily upon him. But he could not see what else he could have done.

And there was something else. He could not even look after the safety of a single girl. He did not know where Julie was – whether she was dead or alive or captured by Rocambeau's men. He had not properly seen her in his pre-occupation with the hurricane, but now he saw her whole, and he found the tears running down his cheeks – not tears of self-pity, or even tears for Julie, but tears of blind rage at his stupidity and impotent futility.

Wyatt was very young for his years.

Causton listened to the fire-fight still crackling away to the left. 'I hope he's right. When Favel was faced with a sim-ilar problem he outflanked the position.' He jerked his head towards the distant sound of battle. 'If Serrurier breaks through along there he'll come along the ridge rolling up these rebels like a carpet.'

'I think Wyatt's right, though,' said Dawson. 'Look out to sea.'

The city was lost in a writhing grey mist through which the fires burned redly, and the horizon was black. Streamers of low cloud fled overhead like wraiths in the blustering wind which had sharply increased in violence and was already raising its voice in a devil's yell. Lightning flickered briefly over the sea and a single drop of rain fell on Causton's hand. He looked up. 'It does look a bit dirty. God help sailors on a night like this.'

'God help Serrurier and his army,' said Dawson, staring down at St Pierre.

Causton looked back to where Wyatt was sitting at the edge of the foxhole. 'He's taking it badly – he thinks he's failed. He hasn't yet realized that perfection doesn't exist, the damned young fool. But he'll learn that life is a matter of horse-trading – a bit of bad for a lot of good.'

'I hope he never does learn,' said Dawson in a low voice.
'I learned that lesson and it never did me any good.' He
looked Causton in the eye and, after a moment, Causton
looked away.

II

Rawsthorne was not a young man and two days of exertion
and life in the open had told on him. He could not move fast
over the hilly ground – his lungs had long since lost their
elasticity and his legs their driving power. The breath in his
throat rasped painfully as he tried to keep up a good pace
and the muscles of his thighs ached abominably.

But he was in better shape than Mrs Warmington, whom
the years of cream cakes and lack of exercise had softened
to a doughy flesh. She panted and floundered behind him,
her too generous curves bouncing with the effort, and all
the time she moaned her misery in a wailing undertone, an
obbligato to the keening of the rising wind.

In spite of her wounds, Julie was the fittest of the three.
Although her legs were stiff and sore because of the bayonet jabs, her muscles were hard and tough and her breath
came evenly as she followed Mrs Warmington. The brisk
sets of hard-played tennis now paid off and she had no difficulty in this rough scramble over the hills.

It was Rawsthorne who had made the plan. 'It's no use
going further west to escape the army,' he said. 'The ground
is low about St Michel – and we certainly can't stay here
because Rocambeau might be beaten back again. We'll have
to cut across the back of his army and go north over the
hills – perhaps as far as the Negrito.'

'How far is that?' asked Mrs Warmington uneasily.

'Not far,' said Rawsthorne reassuringly. 'We'll have to
walk about eight miles before we're looking into the Negrito

Valley.' He did not say that those eight miles were over rough country, nor that the country would probably be alive with deserters.

Because Rawsthorne had doubts about his ability to climb the quarry cliff – and private, unexpressed doubts about Mrs Warmington's expertise as a climber – they went down the track towards the main road, moving stealthily and keeping an eye open for trouble. They did not want to meet the guard who had disappeared in that direction. They left the track at the point where they had originally climbed up to the banana plantation, and Julie got a lump in her throat when she saw the imprint of Eumenides's shoe still visible in the dust.

The plantation seemed deserted, but they went with caution all the same, slipping through the rows of plants as quietly as they could. Rawsthorne led them to the hollow where they had dug the foxholes in the hope of finding a remnant of food and, more important, water. But there was nothing at all, just four empty holes and a litter of cans and bottles.

Julie looked at the hole that had been filled in and felt a great sorrow as she thought of the Greek. First we dig 'em, then we die in 'em. Eumenides had fulfilled the prophecy.

Rawsthorne said, 'If it wasn't for the war I would recommend that we stay here.' He cocked his head on one side. 'Do you think the fighting is going away or not?'

Julie listened to the guns and shook her head. 'It's difficult to say.'

'Yes, it is,' said Rawsthorne. 'If Rocambeau is defeated again he'll be thrown back through here and we'll be back where we started.'

Mrs Warmington surveyed the hollow and shuddered. 'Let's get away from this horrible place,' she said in a trembling voice. 'It frightens me.'

And well it might, thought Julie; you killed a man here.

'We'll go north,' said Rawsthorne. 'Into this little valley and over the next ridge. We must be very careful, though; there may be desperate men about.'

So they went through the plantation, across the service road and, carefully avoiding the convict barracks, pushed on up the ridge on the other side. At first Rawsthorne kept up a cracking pace, but he did not have the stamina for it and gradually his pace slowed so that even Mrs Warmington could keep up with him. The going was not difficult while they were on cultivated ground and in spite of their slower pace they made good time.

At the top of the first ridge they left the banana plantations and entered pineapple fields, where all was well as long as they walked between the rows and avoided the sharp, spiky leaves. But then they came to sugar-cane and, finding the thicket too hard to push through, had to cast about to find a road leading in the right direction. It was a narrow dusty track between the high green canes, which rustled and crackled under the press of the breeze. In spite of the breeze and the high feathery clouds which veiled and haloed the sun it was still very hot, and Julie fell into a daze as she mechanically plodded behind Mrs Warmington.

They saw no one and seemed to be travelling through an empty land. The track dipped and rose but climbed higher all the time, and Julie, when she looked back, saw huts in the distance, but no smoke arose from these small settlements nor was there any sign of life. Where the tracks came out of the cane-fields they came upon more huts, and as soon as he saw them Rawsthorne held up his hand. 'We must be careful,' he whispered. 'Better safe than sorry. Wait here.'

Mrs Warmington sat down on the spot and clutched her feet. 'These shoes are crippling me,' she said.

'Hush!' said Julie, looking at the huts through the cane. 'There may be soldiers here – deserters.'

Mrs Warmington said no more, and Julie thought in astonishment: she is capable of being taught, after all. Then Rawsthorne came back. 'It's all right,' he said. 'There isn't a soul here.'

They emerged from the cane and moved among the huts, looking about. Mrs Warmington stared at the crude rammed earth walls and the straw roofs and sniffed. 'Pigsties, that's all these are,' she announced. 'They're not even fit to keep pigs in.'

Rawsthorne said, 'I wonder if there's any water here. I could do with some.'

'Let's look,' said Julie, and went into one of the huts. It was sparsely furnished and very primitive, but also very clean. She went into a small cubicle-like room which had obviously been a pantry, to find it like Mother Hubbard's cupboard – swept bare. Going into another hut, she found it the same and when she came out in the central clearing she found that Rawsthorne had had no luck either.

'These people have run away,' he said. 'They've either taken all their valuables with them or buried them.' He held up a bottle. 'I found some rum, but I wouldn't recommend it as a thirst-quencher. Still, it may come in useful.'

'Do you think they've run away from the war?' asked Julie. 'Or the hurricane – like that old man near St Michel?'

Rawsthorne rubbed his cheek and it made a scratchy sound. 'That would be difficult to say. Off-hand, I'd say because of the war – it doesn't really matter.'

'These people must have got their water from somewhere,' said Julie. 'What about from down there?' She indicated a path that ran away downhill along the edge of the cane-field. 'Shall we see?'

Rawsthorne hesitated. 'I don't think we should hang about here – it's too dangerous. I think we should push on.'

From the moment they entered the scrub the going was harder. The ground was poor and stony and the tormented trees clung to the hillside in a frozen frenzy of exposed roots over which they stumbled and fell continually. The hillside was steeper here and what little soil there had been had long since been washed to the bottom lands where the fertile plantations were. Underfoot was rock and dust and a sparse sprinkling of tough grass clinging in stubborn clumps wherever the stunted trees did not cut off the sun.

They came to the top of a ridge to find themselves confronted by yet another which was even higher and steeper. Julie looked down into the little depression. 'I wonder if there's a stream down there.'

They found a watercourse in the valley but it was dry with not a drop of moisture in it, so they pushed on again. Mrs Warmington was now becoming very exhausted; she had long since lost her ebullience and her propensity for giving instructions had degenerated into an aptitude for grumbling. Julie prodded her relentlessly and without mercy, never allowing herself to forget the things this woman had done, and Rawsthorne ignored her complaints – he had enough to do in dragging his own ageing body up this terrible dusty hill.

When they got to the top they found the ground levelling into a plateau and it became less difficult. There was a thin covering of dubious soil and the vegetation was a little lusher. They found another small gathering of huts in a clearing cut out of the scrub – this was deserted too, and again they found no water. Rawsthorne looked about at the small patch of maize and cane, and said, 'I suppose they rely on rainfall. Well, they're going to get a lot of it presently – look back there.'

The southern sky was dark with cloud and the sun was veiled in a thicker grey. It was perceptibly cooler and the breeze had increased to a definite wind. In the distance, seemingly very far away, they could still hear the thudding of the guns, and to Julie it seemed very much less impressive, although whether this was the effect of distance or whether there was less firing she had no way of knowing.

Rawsthorne was perturbed by the oncoming weather. 'We can't stop now. All we have to do is to get over that.' He pointed to an even higher ridge straight ahead. 'On the other side of that is the Negrito.'

'Oh, God!' said Mrs Warmington. 'I can't do it – I just *can't* do it.'

'You must,' said Rawsthorne. 'We have to get on a northern slope, and it's on the other side. Come on.'

Julie prodded Mrs Warmington to her feet and they left the huts. She looked at her watch – it was four-thirty in the afternoon.

By five-thirty they had crossed the plateau and were halfway up the ridge, and the wind had strengthened to a gale. It seemed to be darkening much earlier than usual – the clouds were now thick overhead but no rain had fallen as yet. The wind plucked at them as they scrambled up, buffeting them mercilessly, and more than once one or other of them lost his footing and slid down in a miniature landslide of dust and small stones. The wind whipped the branches of the stunted trees, transforming them into dangerous flails, and the dry leaves were swept away along the ridge on the wings of the gale.

It seemed an eternity before they got to the top, and even then they could not see down into the Negrito. 'We must . . . get down . . . other side,' shouted Rawsthorne against the wind. 'We mustn't . . . stay . . .' He choked as the wind caught him in the mouth, and staggered forward in a crouch.

Julie followed, kicking Mrs Warmington before her, and they stumbled across the top of the hill, exposed to the raging violence of the growing hurricane. There was a thick, clabbery yellow light about them which seemed almost tangible, and the dust swirled up from the barren earth in streaming clouds. Julie could taste it as she ran, and felt the grittiness between her teeth.

At last they began to descend and could see the floor of the Negrito Valley a thousand feet below dimly illuminated in that unwholesome light. As soon as they dropped below the crest of the hill there was some relief from the wind and Rawsthorne stopped, looking down in amazement. 'What the devil's happening down there?'

At first Julie could not see what he meant, but then she saw that the lower slopes were alive with movement and that thin columns of people were moving up from the valley. 'All those people,' she said in wonder. 'Where did they come from?'

Rawsthorne gave an abrupt laugh. 'There's only one place they could have come from – St Pierre. Someone must have got them out.' He frowned. 'But the battle is still going on-I think. Can you hear the guns?'

'No,' said Julie. 'But we wouldn't – not in this wind.'

'I wonder . . .' mused Rawsthorne. 'I wonder if . . .' He did not finish his sentence but Julie caught the implication and her heart lifted. All the people down there must have left St Pierre long before there was any indication that there was going to be a hurricane, and as far as she knew, there was only one man who believed the hurricane was on its way – an undeviating, obstinate, stubborn, thick-headed man – David Wyatt. He's alive, she thought, and found an unaccountable lump in her throat. *Thank God, he's alive!*

'I don't think we'd better go right down,' said Rawsthorne. 'Isn't that a ravine over there?'

There was a cleft in the hillside, an erosion scored deep by weather and water which would give shelter from the wind on three sides. They crossed the hillside diagonally and clambered down the steep sides of the ravine. Here the blast of wind was even less although they could hear it howl above their heads on the open hill, and they found a little hollow carved beneath a large rock, almost a cave, in which they could sit.

It was here that Rawsthorne finally collapsed. He had only been held together by his will to get the women to safety, and now, having done what he had set out to do, his body rebelled against the punishment it had been forced to take. Julie looked at his grey face and slack lips in alarm. 'Are you all right, Mr Rawsthorne?'

'I'll be all right, my child.' He managed a pallid smile and moved his hand weakly. 'In my pocket . . . a bottle . . . rum. Think we all . . . deserve . . . drink.'

She found the rum, uncorked the bottle and held it to his lips. The raw spirit seemed to do him good for some colour came back to his cheeks, or so she thought, for it was difficult to see in the fading light. She turned to Mrs Warmington, who was equally prostrated, and forced some of the rum through her clenched teeth.

She was about to have some herself when there was an ear-splitting crash and a dazzle of vivid blue light, followed by the steady rolling of thunder. She rubbed her eyes and then heard the rain, the heavy drops smacking the dusty ground. Wriggling out of the little shelter she let it pour on her face and opened her mouth to let the drops fall in. Thirstily she soaked up the rain, through her mouth and through her skin, and felt her shirt sticking wetly to her body. The water did her more good than the rum would ever do.

III

The wind roared across St Pierre, fanning the flames of the burning buildings so that the fires jumped broad streets and it seemed as though the whole city would be engulfed in an unquenchable furnace.

Then the rain came and quenched it in fifteen minutes.

It rained over two inches in the first hour, a bitter, painful downpour, the heavy drops driven by the wind and bursting like shrapnel where they hit. Causton had never been *hurt* by rain before: he had never thought that a water drop could be so big, nor that it could hit with such paralysing force. At first he mistook it for hail, but then he saw the splashes exploding on the ground before the fox-hole, and each drop seemed to be as much as would fill a cup. He blinked and shook the hair from his eyes, and then a drop hit him on the side of the face with frightening force and he ducked to the bottom of the hole.

Dawson moaned in pain and turned over on his side, holding his bandaged hands under his body to shield them. No one heard his sudden cry, not even Causton who crouched next to him, because the noise of the wind had risen to a savage howl drowning all other sounds.

Wyatt listened to the wind with professional and knowl-edgeable interest. He estimated that the wind-speed had suddenly risen to force twelve, the highest level on the Beaufort Scale. Old Admiral Beaufort had designed the scale for the use of sailing-ship captains and had been sensible about it – his force twelve was the wind-speed at which, in his opinion, no reasonable seaman would be found at sea if he could help it. Force twelve is sixty-five knots or seventy-four miles an hour, and the Admiral was not concerned about wind-speeds greater than that because to a sailing captain caught *in extremis* it would not matter either. There are no degrees in sudden death.

But times have changed since Admiral Beaufort and Wyatt, who had helped to change them, knew it very well. His concern here was not for the action of the wind on a sailing ship but on an island, on the buildings of the towns. A force twelve wind exerts a pressure of seventeen pounds on each square foot, over three tons on the sides of an

average house. A reasonably well-built house could withstand that pressure, but this hurricane was not going to be
reasonable.

The highest estimated wind-speed in Mabel's gusts had
been 170 miles an hour, producing pressures of well over a
hundred pounds a square foot. Enough to pick a man off his
feet and hurl him through the air as far as the wind cared to
take him. Enough to lean on the side of a house and cave it
in. Enough to uproot a strong tree, to rip the surface soil
from a field, to destroy a plantation, to level a shanty town
to the raw earth from which it had sprung.

Wyatt, therefore, listened to the raging of the wind with
unusual interest.

Meanwhile, he held his head down and sat with Causton
and Dawson in a hole full of water. The two drains spouted
like fire hoses at full pressure, yet the hole never emptied.
It was like sitting in the middle of a river. All around them
streams of water gushed down the slope of the ridge, inches
deep, carving courses in the soft earth. Wyatt knew that
would not last long – as the wind-speed increased it would
become strong enough to lift up that surface water and
make it airborne again in a driving mist of fine spray. That
was one thing – no one he had heard of had died of thirst
in a hurricane.

This rain, falling in millions of tons, was the engine which
drove the monster. On every square mile over which the
hurricane passed it would drop, on average, half a million
tons of water, thus releasing vast quantities of heat to power
the circular winds. It was a great turbine – three hundred
miles in diameter and with almost unimaginable power.

Causton's thoughts were very different. For the first time in
his life he was really frightened. In his work he covered the
activities of men, and man, the political animal, he thought
he understood. His beat was the world and he found himself

in trouble-spots where students rioted in the streets of big cities and where bush wars flared in the green jungles. Other men covered the earthquakes, the tidal waves, the avalanches – the natural disasters.

He had always known that if he got into trouble he could somehow talk his way out of it because he was dealing with men and men could be reasoned with. Now, for the first time in his life, he found himself in trouble where talking was futile. One could no more reason with a hurricane than with a Bengal tiger; in fact, it was worse – one could at least shoot the tiger.

He had listened with vague interest to Wyatt's lecture on hurricanes back at Cap Sarrat Base, but he had been more curious about Wyatt than about the subject under discussion. Now he wished he had listened more closely and taken a keener interest. He nudged Wyatt, and shouted, 'How long will this go on?'

The dark shape of Wyatt turned towards him and he felt warm breath in his ear. 'What did you say?'

He put his mouth next to Wyatt's ear, and bellowed, 'How long will this go on?'

Wyatt turned again. 'About eight hours – then we'll have a short rest.'

'Then what happens?'

'Another ten hours, but coming from the opposite direction.'

Causton was shocked at the length of time he would have to undergo this ordeal. He had been thinking in terms of three or four hours only. He shouted, 'Will it get worse?'

It was difficult to detect any emotion in Wyatt's answering shout, but he thought he heard a cold humour. 'It hasn't really started yet.'

Causton crouched deeper in the hole with the rain flailing his head and thought in despair, how *can* it get worse?

* * *

The sun had set and it was pitchy black, the impenetrable darkness broken only by the lightning flashes which were becoming more frequent. Any thunder there might have been was lost in the general uproar of the gale, which, to Wyatt's ear, was taking on a sharper edge – the wind-speed was still increasing, although it was impossible to tell without instruments any reasonably exact speed. One thing was certain, though – it was pushed well over the further edge of the Beaufort Scale.

Wyatt thought with grim amusement of Causton's question: will it get worse? The man had no conception of the forces of nature. One could explode an atomic bomb in the middle of this hurricane and the puny added energy would be lost – swallowed up in the greater cataclysm. And this was not too bad. True, Mabel was a bad bitch, but there had been worse – and there had been far greater wind-speeds recorded.

He closed his mind to the howling of the wind. Now what was it – oh, yes – two hundred and thirty-one miles an hour recorded at Mount Washington before the instrument smashed – that was the record reading. And then there were the theoretical speeds of the tornadoes. No chance of recording those, of course – the very fast winds in excess of six hundred miles an hour – but it took a fast wind to drive a straw through an inch-thick plank of wood.

And yet tornadoes were small. Comparing a tornado with a hurricane was like comparing a fighter plane with a bomber – the fighter is faster, but the bomber has more total power. And a hurricane has immeasurably more power than any tornado, more power than any other wind system on earth. He remembered the really bad one that crossed the Atlantic when he had been a student in England back in 1953. It had been the very devil in the west Atlantic, but then it had crossed and passed to the north of England, choking up the waters of the North Sea very much as Mabel was doing down there in Santego Bay. The dykes of Holland had been overwhelmed and the waters had surged over East Anglia, bringing the worst weather disaster Europe had known for hundreds of years. The hurricane was the devil among winds.

Dawson held his hands to his chest. He was soaked to the skin and felt that he would never be dry again. Had he not liked game fishing, he thought that he would have spent the rest of his life in some nice desert which never knew a wind like this – say, Death Valley. But he did like fishing and these were the waters for it and he knew that if he survived this experience he would come back. On the other hand – why go away at all? Why not settle in San Fernandez? There was nothing to keep him in New York now and he might as well live where he liked.

He grinned tightly as he thought that even in this he would be continuing the programme mapped out for him by his press agent, Wiseman, who had plotted mightily to cut Hemingway's mantle to fit Dawson's different figure. Hadn't Hemingway lived in Cuba? To hell with that! It was what he wanted to do and he would do it.

Curiously enough, he was not frightened. The unexpected courage he had found in facing up to Roseau and his thugs followed by the catharsis of his confession to Wyatt had released something within him, some fount of manhood that had been blocked and diverted to corrupt ends. He should have been frightened because this was the most frightening thing that had ever happened to him, but he was not and the knowledge filled him with strength.

Smeared with viscous mud, he lay in a water-filled hole with the wind and the rain lashing him cruelly and was very content.

*   *   *

The hurricane achieved its greatest strength just after midnight. The very noise itself was a fearsome thing, a malignant terrifying howl of raw power that seared the mind. The rain had slackened and there were no large drops, just an atomized mist driving level with the ground at over a hundred miles an hour, and, as Wyatt had predicted, the flooding ground water had been lifted in the wind's rage.

Lightning now flashed continuously, illuminating the ridge in a blue glare, and once, when Wyatt lifted his eyes, he saw the dim outlines of the mountains, the Massif des Saints. They would resist the terrible wind; standing there rooted deep in the bowels of the earth they were a match for the hurricane which would batter its life away against them. Perhaps this slight barrier would take the vicious edge off Mabel and she would go on her way across the Caribbean only to die of the mortal wound she had received. Perhaps. But that would not help the agony of San Fernandez.

Again in a lightning flash he saw something huge and flat skim overhead like a spinning playing card. It struck the ground not five yards away from the foxhole and then took off again in sharply upward flight. He did not know what it was.

They lay in their hole, hugging to the thick, viscous mud at the bottom, deafened by the maniacal shriek of the storm, sodden to the skin and becoming colder as the wind evaporated the moisture from their clothing, and with their minds shattered by the intensity of the forces playing about them. Once Causton inadvertently lifted his arm above ground level and the wind caught his elbow and threw his arm forward with such power that he thought it was broken, and if the arm had been thrown against the shoulder joint instead of with it, it very well might have been.

Even Wyatt, who had a greater understanding of what was happening than the others, was astonished at this violence. Hitherto, when he had flown into the depths of hurricanes, he had felt a certain internal pride, not at his own bravery but at the intrepidity and technical expertise of mankind who could devise means of riding the whirl-wind. But to encounter a hurricane without even the thin Duralumin walls of an aircraft to enfold a shrinking and vulnerable body was something else again. This was the first hurricane he had experienced from the ground and he would be a better meteorologist for it – if he lived through it, which he doubted.

Gradually they fell into a stupor. The brain – the mind – can only take so much battering and then it automatically raises its defences. Over the hours the incredible noise became so much a part of their environment that they ceased to hear it, their tensed bodies relaxed when the adrenalin stopped being pumped into the bloodstream and, beaten into tiredness, they fell into an uneasy doze, their limbs flaccid and sprawled in the mud.

At three in the morning the wind began to ease slightly and Wyatt, his expert ear attuned to the noise even in his unquiet inertness, noticed the change immediately. The rain had stopped completely and there was only the cruel wind left to hurt them, and even the wind was pausing and hesitating, sometimes gusting a little harder as though regretting a slight check, yet always dying a little more.

At four o'clock he stirred and looked at his watch, rub-bing away the slimy mud from the dial so that he could see the luminous figures. It was still pitch dark and there was less lightning, but now he could hear the thunder rolling among the clouds, which meant the wind was not as intense. He stirred his limbs and tentatively thrust his hand above ground-level. The wind pushed hard at it but not so much that he could not resist and he concluded that the wind-strength was now just back on the Beaufort Scale – a nice, comfortable storm.

Once roused, his mind was active again. He had an intense curiosity about what was happening on the other side of the ridge, and the itch to know got the better of him. He tested the strength of the wind again and thought it was not too bad, so he turned over and eased himself out of the foxhole on his belly and began to crawl up the slope. The wind plucked at him as he inched his way through the mud and it was worse than he thought it would be. There was a great difference between sitting in a hole and being caught in the open, and he knew that but for the foxhole they would not have survived. However, driven by the need to know, he persevered and, although it took him fifteen minutes to traverse the twenty yards to the top of the ridge, he made it safely and tumbled into water two feet deep in a foxhole that had been dug to protect against a storm of steel rather than a storm of air.

He rested for a few minutes in this shelter, glad to be out of the worst of the wind, then lifted his head and peered into the darkness, his hands cupped blinkerwise about his eyes. At first he saw nothing, but in a momentary lull before a gust he heard something that sounded very much like the sea and the splash of waves. He blinked and stared again and, in the glare of a lightning flash, he saw a terrifying sight.

Not more than two hundred yards away was a storm-driven sea with short and ugly waves, the tops sheered off by the fierce wind to blow horizontally across the waste of water. An eddy of wind blew spray into his face and he licked his lips and tasted salt water.

St Pierre had been totally engulfed.

NINE

As the first grey light of dawn touched the sky Julie eased her cramped legs. She had tucked them under her body in an attempt to keep them reasonably dry and she had failed, but at least they were not lying under a running torrent of water. The wind had dropped with the coming of day; no longer did it howl ferociously nor did it fling cascades of water at them, but still the water ran in a muddied flood down the ravine.

It had been a bad night. In their little cave under the great rock they were well protected from the wind; it had roared about them but they were untouched by it. The water was something else. It came from above, slowly at first, and then in an increasing rush, pouring over the rock that protected them in a dirty brown waterfall which splashed with increasing violence at their feet, and carried with it the tree-fallen detritus which littered the ravine above.

As the wind grew in strength the wall of water before their faces was torn and shredded, blowing away in a fine spray across the hillside, and when the wind backed and eddied they were deluged as though someone had thrown a bathful of water into the cave. This happened a dozen times an hour with monotonous regularity.

Their shelter was cramped, small – and safe. The walls of the ravine rose sheer on each side and the wind, tearing over the open hillside, sometimes actually sucked the air out of this cleft at the height of the storm and left them gasping for breath for the space of a couple of heart-beats. But this did them no harm and indeed helped, because the water also went with the air, giving them momentary respite.

They could either sit with their legs outstretched and have the waterfall pouring over their feet and the danger of bruises or worse as the flood swept down tree branches and stones, or they could sit on them and get cramp. They alternated between these methods, extending their legs when the cramp became too bad. The water was not too cold, for which Julie was thankful, and she thought hysterically that she was being washed so clean that she would never need to take another shower ever again. The very thought of the hissing spray of water in her bathroom at home made her feel physically sick.

At first they could talk quite comfortably. Rawsthorne was feeling better for the rum. He said, 'We might get a bit wet here, but I think we'll be safe with this rock behind us.'

'It won't move?' said Mrs Warmington nervously.

'I doubt it. It seems to be firmly embedded – in fact, I think it's an outcropping of the bedrock.' He looked through the waterfall before him. 'And there's a good runoff for the water down there. It won't back up and drown us. All we have to do is sit here until it's all over.'

Julie listened to the rising shriek of the wind overhead. 'It seems as though the whole island will blow away.'

Rawsthorne chuckled weakly. 'It didn't in 1910 – I see no reason why it should now.'

Julie pulled her legs in from under the waterfall and tucked them underneath herself. 'We've got enough water now – more than enough.' She paused. 'I wonder how all those people got out of St Pierre in the middle of a battle.'

'My guess is that Favel had something to do with it,' said
Rawsthorne thoughtfully. 'He must have had because they
are in the Negrito – his line of communication with the
mountains.'

'You think Dave Wyatt told him about the hurricane?'

'I hope so. It will mean that that young man is alive. But
perhaps Favel had other sources of information; perhaps
there was a message from the Base, or something like that.'

'Yes,' she said slowly, and lapsed into silence.

The rainfall increased and the torrent coursing down the
ravine became a flood swirling over the top of the big rock.
The wind strengthened and now it was that the eddies
hurled back water into the cave, to leave them gasping for
breath and clutching at the stone around them for fear of
being washed away. Mrs Warmington was very frightened
and wanted to leave to find a safer place, but Julie held her
back.

Rawsthorne was not feeling well. The events of the last
two days had been too much for him, and his heart, not too
good in normal circumstances, was beginning to act up. He
doubted if he could have gone on any longer on their flight
from the coast and was thankful for this respite, unpleasant
though it was. He thought of Julie; this was a good girl,
strong and tough when the necessity arose and not frightened of taking a chance. He could tell that young Wyatt was
on her mind, and hoped that both of them would be pre-
served during this terrible night so that they could meet
again and pick up their normal lives. But neither of them
would be the same again, not in their approach to the world
and, especially, to each other. He hoped they would find
each other again.

As for that damned Warmington woman with her eternal nagging moan, he did not care if she was washed out of
the cave there and then. It would at least leave more room
and they would be rid of a strength-sapping incubus. He

gasped as he was soaked by a solid wall of water, and all thought left him save for the one desire for survival.

So the night went on, a terror measured in hours, a luke-warm hell of raging wind and blowing water. But the wind died towards the morning and the cave became drier, no longer inundated every few minutes. Julie eased her cramped legs and thought that, incredibly enough, they were going to survive. She roused Rawsthorne, who said, 'Yes, the wind is dropping. I think we'll be all right.'

'My God, I'll be glad to get out of here,' said Julie. 'But I don't know if I'll be able to stand. The way I feel now I'll have to learn to walk all over again.'

'Can we go out?' asked Mrs Warmington with the first animation she had shown for a long time.

'Not yet. We'll wait until it's lighter, and the wind will have dropped even more by then.' Rawsthorne hunched his shoulders and peered forward. 'I have the idea it would be easy to get drowned out there, especially stumbling around in the dark.'

So they stayed in their cramped shelter until the dim light revealed the sides of the ravine and then they went out into the glorious daylight, first Julie, ducking cautiously through the rapidly flowing curtain of water, then Mrs Warmington, and finally Rawsthorne, who moved slowly and painfully as though his joints were seized up. Julie's hair streamed in the wind that swooped boisterously down the ravine – it was blowing hard by any standards but it was no hurricane.

She waded knee deep through the rushing water and gained the bank, then turned to give a hand to Mrs Warmington, who squeaked and slipped. 'My shoe,' she cried. 'I've lost my shoe.'

But it was gone, washed swiftly down into the valley in the fast water. 'Never mind,' said Julie. 'It doesn't really matter. Maybe we won't have to do much walking from now on.'

Rawsthorne joined them, and said, 'I wonder what's happening down in the valley. I think it's important we should find out.'

Julie glanced at him. 'If we climb out of here on to the hillside we should be able to see. I think we can get up that way.'

The earth had turned to mud, thick and slimy, and it was not easy to climb out of the ravine. They floundered and slid on the slippery surface, but eventually reached the top by tugging on convenient branches and tough tufts of grass. Everything they grasped to pull themselves up by held firm – only the strong was left, the weak had been destroyed by the wind.

Even the barren hillside had been wrecked. Most of the low, gnarled trees showed white wood where branches had been ripped off, and there were raw scars in the red earth to show where entire trees had been uprooted. Hardly a tree had a leaf left on it, and the whole slope had been scraped free of everything that could be moved.

Rawsthorne looked down into the valley. 'My God!' he exclaimed. 'Look at the Gran Negrito – the river!'

The whole floor of the valley was covered with a leaden sheet of water. The Negrito Valley drained most of the southern slopes of the Massif des Saints and the vast runoff of water from the mountains had met the floods pressing in from the mouth of the river in Santego Bay. The river had burst its banks, flooding the rich plantations, destroying roads and bridges and drowning farms. Even from where they stood, so high above the valley, and despite the dying wind, they could hear the murmur of the flood waters.

Mrs Warmington was white-faced. 'Isn't there *anyone* alive down there?'

'The people we saw were climbing the slopes,' said Rawsthorne. 'There's no reason to suppose they were caught in the floods.'

'Let's go down and find out,' suggested Julie.

'No!' said Rawsthorne sharply, and Julie looked at him in surprise. 'I don't think we've finished with the hurricane yet.'

'That's nonsense,' said Mrs Warmington. 'The wind's dropping all the time. Of course it's over.'

'You don't understand,' said Rawsthorne. 'I think we're in the eye of the hurricane. We've got the other half to go through yet.'

'You mean we've got to go through all that again?' asked Julie in alarm.

Rawsthorne smiled ruefully. 'I'm afraid we might have to.'

'But you don't really know,' said Mrs Warmington. 'You don't really know, do you?'

'Not really, but I don't think we ought to take a chance on it just yet. It all depends on whether we encountered the hurricane dead centre or whether it just caught us a glancing blow. If it hit us dead centre, then we're in the eye and we've still got to go through the other half. I'm not a good enough weather expert to tell, though; Wyatt could tell us if he were here.'

'But he's not,' said Mrs Warmington. 'He landed himself in gaol.' She hobbled along the hillside and looked down. 'There are people down there – I can see them moving.'

Rawsthorne and Julie crossed over to where she was standing and saw the hillside crawling with people on the lower slopes. Rawsthorne scratched his chin. 'It's a good thing the valley is flooded, in a way,' he said. 'They can't get down into the bottom again where they might be caught in the winds next time round.'

'Well, I'm going down there,' said Mrs Warmington with unexpected decision. 'I'm sick and tired of being pushed around by you two. Besides, I'm *hungry*.'

'Don't be a fool,' said Julie. 'Mr Rawsthorne knows more about it than you do. You're safer up here.'

'I'm going,' said Mrs Warmington, stepping out of arm's reach. 'And you're not going to stop me.' Her chin quivered with foolish obduracy. 'I think it's nonsense to say that we'll have another storm like the one we've just gone through – things don't happen that way. And there'll be food down there and I'm starving.'

She edged away as Julie stepped forward. 'And you blame me for everything, I know you do. You're always bullying me and hitting me – you wouldn't do it if I were stronger than you. I think it's disgraceful the way you hit a woman older than yourself. So I'm going – I'm going down to those people down there.'

She darted away as Julie made a grab for her and went stumbling down the hill in an awkward limping gait due to the loss of her shoe. Rawsthorne called Julie back. 'Oh, let the damned woman go; she's been a bloody nuisance all along and I'm glad to see her back.'

Julie halted in mid-step and slowly walked up the hill again. 'Do you think she'll be all right?' she asked doubtfully.

'I don't give a damn,' said Rawsthorne tiredly. 'She's meant nothing but trouble all along and I don't see why we should get ourselves killed trying to save her neck. We've done our best for her and we can't do more.' He sat down on a rock and put his head in his hands. 'God, but I'm tired.'

Julie bent over him. 'Are you all right?'

He lifted his head and gave her a wan smile. 'I'm all right, my dear. There's nothing wrong with me but too many years of living. Sitting about in wet clothing isn't too good at my age.' He looked down the hill. 'She's out of sight now. She went in the wrong direction, too.'

'What?'

Rawsthorne smiled and waved his hand in the direction of St Pierre. 'The St Michel road is over there; it leaves St Pierre and sticks to the upper slopes of the Negrito Valley before it climbs over to join the coast road. If we were leaving I would suggest going that way – I don't think that road would be flooded.'

'But you don't think we ought to leave,' Julie said in a flat statement.

'I don't. I fear we're going to have more wind. We've found a safe place here and we might as well stick to it as long as we're not entirely sure. If the wind doesn't blow up in another three or four hours then it will be safe to move.'

'All right – we'll stay,' said Julie. She moved over and looked down into the ravine at the smooth sheet of water flowing over the big rock. The cave was completely hidden behind that watery curtain. She laughed and turned back to Rawsthorne. 'There's one good thing – we'll have a lot more room now that fat bitch has left us.'

II

Wyatt stood on the top of the ridge overlooking St Pierre and looked down over the city. The waters had ebbed since his first startled vision in the flash of lightning, yet half the city was still flooded. The climacteric wave had left nasty evidence of destruction, the wrack of a broken city at the high-water mark half-way up the ridge. The houses at the bottom from which the battle assault had been made just a few hours before had disappeared completely, as had the wide stretches of shanties in the middle distance. Only the core of the city was left standing – the few modern towers of steel and concrete and the older stone buildings which had already withstood more than one hurricane.

Away in the distance the radar tower that marked Cap Sarrat Base had vanished, cut down by the wind as a sickle cuts a stalk of grass. The Base itself was too low-lying and too far away to see if much more damage had been done, although Wyatt saw the glint of water where no water should be.

And of the Government army there was no sign – no movement at all from the ruined city.

Causton and Dawson walked up the slope behind Wyatt and joined him. 'What a mess!' said Causton, and blew out his cheeks expressively. 'I'm glad we got the population out.' He dug into his pocket and produced a cigarette-lighter and a soggy packet of disintegrating cigarettes. 'I always pride myself on being prepared. Here I have a waterproof lighter guaranteed to work under any conditions.' He flicked it and a steady flame sprang forth. 'But look at my damned cigarettes.'

Dawson looked at the flame which burned without a flicker in the still air. 'Are we really in the middle of this hurricane?'

Wyatt nodded. 'Right in the eye. Another hour or so and we'll be in the thick of it again. I don't think Mabel will drop much more rain, though, not unless the bitch decides to stand still. They do that sometimes.'

'Don't pile on the agony,' pleaded Causton. 'It's enough to know that we have another packet of trouble coming.'

Dawson rubbed his ear awkwardly with a bandaged hand. 'I've got a hell of an earache.'

'That's funny,' said Causton. 'So have I.'

'It's the low pressure,' said Wyatt. 'Hold your nose and blow to equalize the pressure in the sinuses.' He nodded towards the flooded city. 'It's the low pressure that's keeping all that water there.'

As the others made disgusting snorting sounds he looked up at the sky. There was a layer of cloud but he had no means of knowing how thick it was. He had heard that sometimes one could see blue skies in the eye of a hurricane, but he had never seen it himself nor had he ever encountered any who had, and he was inclined to dismiss it as one of the tall tales so often found in weather lore. He felt the sleeve of his shirt and found it was nearly dry. 'Low pressure,' he said. 'And low humidity. You'll dry off quickly. Look at that.' He nodded to where the ground was beginning to steam gently.

Causton was watching a group of men march down the slope towards St Pierre. 'Are you sure Favel knows that more wind is due?' he asked. 'Those boys are in for trouble if they don't get back here smartly.'

'He knows it,' said Wyatt. 'We discussed it. Let's go and see him – where did he say headquarters were?'

'Just up the road – it's not far.' Causton chuckled suddenly. 'Are we dressed to go visiting?'

Wyatt looked at the others – they were caked with sticky mud from head to foot and he looked down at himself to find the same. 'I doubt if Favel will be in better condition,' he said. 'Come on.'

They walked back, skirting their foxhole, and suddenly Causton stopped dead. 'Good grief!' he breathed. 'Look at that.'

In the next foxhole lay a body with an outflung arm. The back of the hand which would normally be a rich brown in colour was dirty grey as though all the blood had been drained from it. But what had made Causton pause was the fact that the body had no head, nor was there a head anywhere to be seen.

'I think I know what did that,' said Wyatt grimly. 'Something came over when the wind was really bad and I think it was a sheet of corrugated iron. It hit the ground just about there, then took off again.'

'But where's the goddam head?' said Dawson wildly.

'That will have blown away, too. It was a strong wind.'

Dawson looked sick and walked away. Causton said with a catch in his breath, 'That . . . that could have happened to any of us.'

'It could,' agreed Wyatt. 'But it didn't. Come on.'

His emotions were frozen. The sight of violent death did not affect him and he found himself unstirred by the sight. He had seen too much killing, too many men shot dead and blown to bits. He had killed a man himself. Admittedly Roseau deserved killing if ever a man did, but Wyatt was a product of his environment and killing did not come easily to him. The sight of an accidental death in a hurricane meant nothing to him and left him untouched because he compared it to the death of a whole army of men – also killed in a hurricane, but not accidentally.

Headquarters was a series of holes in the ground. Headquarters was a hurry of officers. Headquarters was a widening circle of effects with Favel as the calm centre.

Wyatt could not get to see him right away. He did not mind because he had weighed up Favel and knew that he was not forgotten and that Favel would see him in time. There were priorities and Wyatt was not among the first. With Dawson, he hovered on the outskirts of the busy group and watched the activity. Men were being sent up into the Negrito in ever increasing numbers and Wyatt hoped that Favel knew what he was doing.

Causton had vanished, presumably about his work, although what greater disasters he could find for his eager readers Wyatt could not imagine. Dawson was impatient. 'I don't see the point in waiting round here,' he grumbled. 'We might as well just sit back there in our hole.'

'I wouldn't want Favel to make a mistake now,' said Wyatt. 'I'll stick around. You can go back if you like, and I'll join you later.'

Dawson shrugged. 'It's the same here as anywhere else.' He did not move away.

After a while a tall Negro walked over to Wyatt and he was astonished to see, on closer inspection, that it was Manning, his face smeared with the all-pervading mud. 'Julio would like to see you,' he said. His face cracked into a grim smile. 'You certainly called the shot on that hurricane.'

'It's not over yet,' said Wyatt shortly.

Manning nodded. 'We know that. Julio is doing a hell of a lot of forward planning to see what we can salvage out of this mess. That's what he wants to talk to you about. After you've seen him I think I can find you a bite to eat; you're not likely to get any more until we've got rid of bloody Mabel.'

Favel received Wyatt with the same quirk of the lips curved in a half smile. Incredibly, he looked smart in a clean shirt and had found time to wash, although his denim pants were stiff with mud. He said, 'You did not exaggerate your hurricane, Mr Wyatt. It was every bit as bad as your prognosis.'

'It still is,' said Wyatt bluntly. 'What about those troops you've sent up the Negrito? They'll get caught if they're not careful.'

Favel waved his hand. 'A calculated risk. I find I am always forced to make these decisions. Let us look at the map.'

It was the same map on which Wyatt had sketched out the supposedly safe areas up the Negrito. It was damp and mud-smeared and the crayon lines had run and blotched. Favel said, 'Messengers were selected to report back here during this break in the hurricane and they've been coming in during the last half hour – not as many as I would have liked, but enough to let me know the broad situation.'

His hand hovered over the map. 'You were right to tell me to get the people off the valley bottom – the whole valley is flooded from the mouth to about here.' He sketched in the area quickly with a pencil. 'That's about eight miles. The Gran Negrito has broken its banks and there is yet more water coming from the mountains down the Gran Negrito itself and down the P'tit Negrito. The bridges are down and the roads under water.'

'It looks a mess,' said Wyatt.

'It is,' agreed Favel. 'This road, the short cut to St Michel up the Negrito, is pretty clear. At this moment it's the only usable road in or out of St Pierre. Because it hangs on the side of the valley it missed the floods. There are a few blockages such as fallen trees, and the three bridges are not too safe. Men are clearing it now and looking at the bridges. Other men are digging in for protection against the second half of the hurricane. As soon as it is over they will come out and do whatever final repairs are necessary on those bridges.'

Wyatt nodded. That sounded reasonable.

'Now, Mr Wyatt, how long is St Pierre going to be flooded?'

Wyatt looked at the map. 'What's this line you've drawn here?'

'That's the extent of flooding that exists now – as far as we can tell.'

'That's on the twenty-foot contour – we can extend that.' He took the pencil and drew a quick, curved line. 'It takes in half the city, a lot of Cap Sarrat, all the flat ground here including your airfield, but there's not much east of here because of the higher ground by this headland. All that area is under water because of the present low pressure, but as soon as Mabel moves on things will return to normal very quickly.'

'So we can go down into St Pierre as soon as the hurricane passes.'

'Yes, there'll be nothing to stop you.'

'What about the flooding in the Negrito – how long will that take to subside?'

Wyatt hesitated. 'That's a different matter. The river has backed up from the mouth and it's still blocked by the floods here, in Santego Bay. Then there's all the water coming down from the mountains to make things worse and it will all have to drain to the sea on the original river course. That's going to take a long time, but I couldn't tell you exactly how long.'

'That is what I thought,' said Favel. 'My estimate is a week, at least.' His finger traced a line on the map. 'I've sent a regiment up the St Michel road with instructions to spread out along the ridge over the Negrito and dig in. When the hurricane has gone they will go down and conduct the people over the hills to the St Michel road, bringing them back that way to avoid the floods.'

He looked up. 'Others of that regiment will push on to St Michel and down the coast. There are other towns on San Fernandez besides St Pierre. Sending those men now is risky but it will save two hours, and a lot of lives can be saved in two hours, Mr Wyatt.' He shook his head. 'We will need medical supplies, blankets, clothing; we will need everything it takes to keep men alive.'

'The Americans will be coming back,' said Wyatt. 'Commodore Brooks will have radioed for assistance. I'll bet they're loading up rescue planes in Miami right now.'

'I hope so,' said Favel. 'Do you think the airfields will be usable?'

'That's hard to say. I should think your own airfield will be written off, but the military airfield at the Base is built for heavy weather so it may be all right.'

'I will have it checked as soon as the hurricane is past,' said Favel. 'Thank you, Mr Wyatt – you have been of great service. How much longer have we got?'

Wyatt stared at the grey sky, then looked at his watch. He felt the faintest of zephyrs blowing on his cheek. 'Less than an hour,' he said. 'Call it three-quarters of an hour, then the wind will come again. I don't think there'll be much rain this time.'

Favel smiled gently. 'A small blessing.'

Wyatt withdrew a little way and Manning thrust an open can into his hand. 'You'd better eat while you can.'

'Thanks.' Wyatt looked about. 'I don't see your pal Fuller around.'

A look of pain crossed Manning's face. 'He was killed,' he said in a low voice. 'He was wounded in the last attack and died during the hurricane.'

Wyatt did not know what to say. To say that he was sorry would be inadequate, so he said nothing.

Manning said, 'He was a good chap – not too good with his brains but dependable in a tight corner. I suppose you could say I killed him – I got him into this.'

It came to Wyatt that others had their guilts as well as he. It did not make him feel any better, but it gave him more understanding. He said, 'How did it all happen?'

'We were in the Congo,' said Manning. 'Working for Tshombe – mercenaries, you know. That job was coming to an end when I got on to this job and I asked Fuller if he'd like to come along. The pay was so bloody good that he jumped at it, not that good pay will do him much good now.' He shrugged. 'But that's in the game.'

'What will you do now?'

'There's not much left here,' said Manning. 'Julio asked me to stay on, but I don't think he really wants a white man to play any big part in what's going to come next. I hear that there are jobs open in the Yemen, working for the Royalists – maybe I'll go across there.'

Wyatt looked at this big man who spoke of working when he meant fighting. He said, 'For God's sake, surely you can find easier ways of making a living?'

Manning said gently, 'I don't think you've got it, after all. Sure, I get paid for fighting – most soldiers do – but I pick the side I fight for. Do you think I'd have fought for Serrurier?'

Wyatt groped for an apology and was glad to be interrupted by Dawson, who came over and said excitedly, 'Hey, Dave, I think there's something you ought to know. One of these guys has just come down from the Negrito – he says there's an American woman up there. At least, that's what I think he says; this is a bastard of a language.'

Wyatt swung round. 'Which man?'

'That guy there – the one who's just finished talking to Favel.'

Wyatt strode over and grasped the man's arm. 'Did you see an American woman in the Negrito?' he asked in the island *patois*.

The man turned an exhausted face towards him and shook his head. 'I was told of her. I did not see her.'

'Where was this?'

'Beyond the St Michel road – down in the valley.'

Wyatt tugged at him urgently. 'Can you show me on the map?'

The soldier nodded tiredly and suffered himself to be led. He bent over the map and laid down a black finger. 'About there.'

Wyatt looked at the map blankly and his heart sank. Julie would not be there, so far down in the Negrito. The party had gone along the coast road. He said, 'Was this an old woman? – A young woman? – What colour hair? – How tall?'

The soldier blinked at him stupidly, and Dawson cut in, 'Wait a minute, Dave. This guy's beat, he can hardly stand up.' He pushed a bottle into the man's hand. 'Have a snort of that, buster; it'll wake you up.'

As the man drank from the neck of the rum bottle Dawson looked at the map. 'If this guy has come from where he says he has, he's come a hell of a long way in double-quick time.'

'It can't be Julie,' said Wyatt in a depressed voice. 'That note she left in the Imperiale said they were going up the coast road.'

'Maybe they didn't,' said Dawson. 'Maybe they couldn't. There was a war going on at the time, remember.' He stared at the map. 'And if they did go to where they said, they'd get mixed up with Rocambeau's army when it retreated. If Rawsthorne had any sense he'd move them out of there fast. Look, Dave; if they travelled in a straight line over the hills they could get into the Negrito. It would be one hell of a tough trip, but it could be done.'

Wyatt turned again to the man and questioned him again but it was no use. He had not seen the woman himself, he did not know her age or her colouring or anything more about her than that an American woman had been seen up the Negrito. And Wyatt knew that this meant nothing, not even that she was American; to these people all whites were American.

He said drearily, 'It could be anybody, but I can't take a chance. I'm going up there.'

'Hey!' said Dawson in alarm, and made a grab at him but could not get a grip because of his ruined hands. Wyatt threw him off and began to run for the road.

Manning came up behind and said, 'What's the matter?'

Dawson choked. 'All hell's going to break loose in half an hour and that obstinate guy is taking off for the Negrito – he thinks his girl's up there.'

'The Marlowe girl?'

Dawson looked after Wyatt. 'That's the one. I'll be seeing you – someone's got to look after that crazy idiot.'

He began to run after Wyatt, and Manning began to run too. They caught up with him and Manning said, 'I'm a fool, but I think I can get you up there faster. Follow me.'

That brought Wyatt up short. He stared at Manning, then followed, as Manning led the way back to a place further along the ridge where there was a low stone structure. 'This is where I've been hiding during the hurricane,' said Manning. 'I've got my Land-Rover inside; you can take it.'

Wyatt went inside and Dawson said, 'What is this thing?'

'An old gun casemate – perhaps three hundred years old. It was part of the harbour fortifications in the old days. Favel wouldn't come in here – he said he wouldn't have better protection than his men. But I had Fuller to look after.'

They heard the engine roar as Wyatt started up and the Land-Rover backed out. Dawson jumped in, and Wyatt said, 'There's no need for you to come.'

Dawson grinned. 'I'm a goddam lunatic, too. I've got to look after you – see you safely back to the nuthouse.'

Wyatt shrugged and rammed the gear-lever home. Manning shouted, 'Try not to bend it; it belongs to me, not the corporation.' He waved as the Land-Rover lurched past him, its wheels slipping in the mud, and he looked after it with a thoughtful expression. Then he went back to headquarters because Favel would need him.

When they got on to the road the going was easier, and Dawson said, 'Where exactly are we going?'

The Land-Rover bounced as Wyatt pressed on the accelerator. 'We go as high up overlooking the Negrito as we can,' he said. 'To where the road turns off to go down to the coast and St Michel.' That was where he and Julie had admired the view and drunk weak Planter's Punch. 'I hope the bridges are all right.'

Dawson tried to wedge himself in as the Land-Rover swung recklessly round a corner. 'How far is it?'

'We ought to get there in half an hour if we can keep moving fast. Favel said the road was blocked by fallen trees but he was having it cleared.'

They began to climb and Dawson looked over to the left. 'Look at that goddam river. It's like a sea – the whole valley is under water.'

Wyatt concentrated on the road. 'That'll be salt water, or very brackish. It won't do the agriculture any good.' He did not even give it a glance; all his attention was on his driving. He was going too fast for this road with all its bends and climbing turns, and he tended to swing wide at the corners. It was unlikely there would be anything coming the other way but the chance was there. It was a chance he was prepared to take for the sake of speed.

Dawson twisted and looked back anxiously at the sea. It was too far away for him to see the waves but he caught a glimpse of the distant horizon before the Land-Rover slid round the next corner. It was boiling with clouds – great black masses of them splintered with lightning. He looked sideways at Wyatt's set face and then up at the wet road coiling and climbing along the southern slopes of the Negrito Valley. This was going to be a near thing.

The plantations on each side were ruined, the soft banana plants hammered flat into a pulpy mass on the ground by the blast. The few plants left standing waved shredded leaves like forlorn battle flags, but it was doubtful if they would survive the next few hours. The sugar-cane was tougher; the stiff canes still stood upright, rattling together in the rising wind, but the verdant green top leaves had been stripped away completely and the plants would die.

They turned another corner and came upon men marching stolidly up the road. Wyatt swerved to avoid running them down, lost speed and cursed as he had to change gear. The soldiers waved as they passed and Dawson waved back. He hoped they found shelter soon – this was no time to be on an open road.

Then they came to the first bridge spanning a water-course which was normally dry but which now gushed water, a spouting torrent that filled the narrow gash in the hillside and streamed under the bridge to hurl itself in a waterfall down the almost sheer drop on the other side of the road. There were men standing by the bridge who looked up in amazement as the Land-Rover came up and Wyatt made a gesture with his arm to indicate he was going to cross. A sergeant shrugged and waved him forward and Wyatt drove slowly on to the bridge.

Dawson looked over the side and held his breath. He thought he could feel a vibration as the fast-moving water slapped at the underside of the bridge and he hoped fervently that it had not been weakened. There was a sheer drop down there of over a hundred feet and he had never had a head for heights. He closed his eyes and opened them a few seconds later when he heard Wyatt change gear to find the bridge was behind and they were continuing the long climb.

Every minute or so Wyatt flicked his eyes to the sky. The clouds were thickening as the southern edge of the hurricane drew closer. The few remaining banana plants still standing streamed their tattered leaves and he knew the big winds were not far away. He said, 'We'll probably get to the top just in time.'

'Then what?'

'Then we take shelter below the crest of the ridge. We should have company – Favel pushed a regiment up there.'

'That seems goddam stupid to me,' commented Dawson. 'What good can it do?'

'It's a matter of organization. The people down in the valley don't have it – they're undisciplined and fragmented, and they'll be worse after the hurricane. If Favel can get a disciplined group among them as soon as the wind dies he can save a lot of lives. Ever heard of disaster shock?'

'I can't say I have.'

'When a disaster hits a community the survivors come out in a state of shock. They're absolutely helpless. It's not merely a question of not wanting to help themselves – they're not capable of it. They just sit around, absolutely numb, while hundreds of them die for lack of minimal attention – things as elementary as putting a blanket over an injured man just don't get done even if the blanket's there. It's a sort of mass catalepsy.'

'That sounds bad.'

'It is bad. It happens in war, too, in cases of heavy bombing or shelling. The rescue organizations like the Red Cross or the special alpine teams they have in Switzerland know that the only thing to do is to get people in from the outside as fast as possible.'

'But Favel's men aren't coming in from the outside,' objected Dawson. 'They'll have taken as big a battering as anyone else – apart from having just fought a war.'

'Disaster shock doesn't have as great an effect on disciplined groups which have the backbone of an existing organization, but it hits civilian populations seriously. Favel's men can do a hell of a lot to help.'

They crossed the second bridge. This was an old stone structure which stood as firm as the rock of which it was built.

Then, a few miles further on, they ran into water on the road, just a skim at first, but deepening to over six inches, which made the steering groggy. Wyatt cursed. 'Favel told me this bloody road wasn't flooded.'

The water was surging down the open hillside and flowing across the road, and the wind flickered across the surface of the water blowing away a fine mist. Wyatt drove slowly and came to the last bridge with the usual army squad about it. 'What's happened?' he asked.

A sergeant turned and pointed upwards. '*Blanc*, there has been a landslide in the ravine.'

'How's the bridge?'

The soldier shook his head. 'Not good. You must not cross.'

'Be damned to that,' said Wyatt, and put the Land-Rover into gear. 'I'm going over.'

'Hey!' said Dawson, looking forward. 'It doesn't look too good to me.' This was a wooden trestle bridge and it seemed decidedly rickety. 'That thing has moved – it's been slung sideways.'

Wyatt drove forward and stopped just short of the bridge. The whole structure was leaning and the road bed was tilted at a definite angle. He put his head out of the side window and stared down at the supports in the gorge below and saw the raw wood where baulks had broken. The wind blew his hair into his eyes and he drew back and glanced at Dawson. 'Shall we chance it?'

'Why not leave the truck here?' asked Dawson. 'You said it wasn't far to the top.'

'We might need the truck on the other side. I'll take it across – you get out and walk.'

'Oh, nuts!' said Dawson. 'Get on with it.'

The Land-Rover crept forward on to the bridge and leaned the way the bridge was tilting. There was an ominous and long-drawn creak from somewhere beneath and then a sudden loud crack, and the whole bridge shuddered. Wyatt kept moving at the same slow pace even though the tilt was perceptibly worse. He eased out his breath as the front wheels touched solid ground and permitted his foot to press a little harder on the accelerator. The Land-Rover jolted and there came a rending crash from behind, and Wyatt frantically fed fuel to the engine. He felt the rear wheels spin under the sudden surge of power and then they were bowling along the road too fast for safety.

Dawson looked back and saw the gap where the bridge had been and he heard the tearing and rending sounds coming from the gorge. There were beads of sweat on his forehead as he said, 'Favel isn't going to like that – you busted a bridge.'

'It would have gone anyway,' said Wyatt. His face was pale. 'We haven't far to go.'

III

When the wind strengthened again after that incredible calm Julie said dully, 'You were right – it's coming again.'

'I'm afraid so,' said Rawsthorne. 'A pity.'

She grimaced. 'Just when I'd got dry. Now we have to sit under that damn' waterfall again.'

'It's better in the ravine,' said Rawsthorne tiredly. 'At least we have more protection than the people down there.'

It had been so quiet during the lull that they had been able to hear the murmur of voices from the multitude below quite clearly. Sometimes it had been more than a murmur; when the wind dropped they heard a woman screaming at the top of her voice, in long, sobbing wails. She had screamed for a long time, and then had stopped, her voice suddenly cut short. Julie looked at Rawsthorne, but neither of them made any comment.

She had expected the people to move, to come up the hill since the floods had made the valley impassable, but nothing like that happened. 'They are West Indians,' said Rawsthorne. 'They know hurricanes – they know it is not over yet.'

'I wonder what's happened to the war,' said Julie.

'The war!' Rawsthorne gave a short laugh. 'There will be no more war. Did Wyatt tell you what would happen to St Pierre in the event of a hurricane?'

'He said there'd be flooding.'

'We English have a fatal gift for understatement. If the armies were fighting in St Pierre when the hurricane struck then there are no more armies. No Government army – no rebel army; a complete solution of conflict. There might be a few remnants left, of course; scattered and useless and in no condition to fight, but the war is over.'

Julie looked up at the grey sky through leafless branches. She hoped Wyatt had got out of the city. Perhaps he was somewhere down there – on the lower slopes of the Negrito. She said, 'What about the Base?'

Rawsthorne shook his head. 'The same,' he said. 'Young Wyatt estimated that the big wave would completely cover the Base.' He tried to cheer her up. 'Commodore Brooks might have reconsidered and evacuated, you know. He's no fool.'

'Dave tried to tell him, but he wouldn't listen. He couldn't get past that fool Schelling. I don't think he would evacuate; he's too stiff-necked – a real Navy man with his "Damn the torpedoes!" and "Damn the hurricanes!"'

'I didn't get that impression of Brooks,' said Rawsthorne quietly. 'And I knew him very well. He had a very difficult decision to make, and I'm sure he made the right one for all concerned.'

Julie looked up at the tall tree on the edge of the ravine and saw the topmost branches straining in the wind. It would soon be time to take shelter again. She knew it was futile to worry about Wyatt – there was nothing she could do – and there was someone closer at hand to trouble her.

Rawsthorne looked very ill. His breathing was bad and, when he spoke, it seemed to strain him. His face had lost its floridity and turned the colour of dirty parchment and his eyes were shrunk into dark smudges in his head. He also had trouble in moving; his actions were slow and uncertain and there was a trembling palsy in his hands. To be soaked to the skin for the next few hours would be the worst thing that could happen to him.

She said again, 'Wouldn't it be wiser to go down the hill?'

'There is no better shelter there than we have here. The ravine provides complete shelter from the wind.'

'But the water . . .'

He smiled gently. 'My dear, one would get just as wet anywhere else.' He closed his eyes. 'You're worried about me, aren't you?'

'I am,' said Julie. 'You don't look too good.'

'I don't feel too well,' he confessed. 'It's an old complaint which I thought I'd got rid of. True, my doctor said I mustn't exert myself, but he didn't take account of wars and hurricanes.'

'It's your heart, isn't it?'

He nodded. 'Running over these hills is all very well for younger men. Don't worry, my dear; there is nothing you can do. I certainly don't intend to do any more running. I shall sit placidly under that waterfall and wait for the wind to stop.' He opened his eyes and looked at her. 'You have a great capacity for love, child. Wyatt is a very lucky man.'

She coloured, then said softiy, 'I don't know if I'll ever see him again.'

'Wyatt is a very stubborn man,' said Rawsthorne. 'If he has something to work towards he will not permit himself to be killed – it would interfere with his plans. He was very concerned about you, you know, the night the battle began. I don't know which was on his mind more, the hurricane or your safety.' He patted her hand and she felt the tremble of his fingers. 'He will be looking for you still.'

The wind gusted among the leafless trees, drying the sudden tears that ran down her cheeks. She gulped and said, 'I think it's time to go back into our hole; the wind's getting stronger.'

Rawsthorne looked up. 'I suppose we must go. It won't be pleasant out here when the wind really starts.' He got to his feet, creaking almost audibly, and his steps were uncertain. He paused for a moment, and said, 'A few minutes longer won't hurt. I don't relish that waterfall at all.'

They walked over to the edge of the ravine, and looked down. The water still coursed over the big rock, although perhaps not as strongly. Rawsthorne sighed. 'It's not a comfortable bed for old bones like mine.' The wind blew his sparse hair.

'I think we ought to go down,' said Julie.

'In a moment, my dear.' Rawsthorne turned to look over the windy hillside. 'I thought I heard voices quite close – from up there.' He pointed towards the top of the ridge in the direction of St Pierre.

'I didn't hear anything,' said Julie.

The wind rose to a greater violence, singing crazily among the branches of the trees. 'Perhaps it was just the wind,' said Rawsthorne. He smiled tightly. 'Did you hear what I said then? Just the wind! Rather silly of me to say that about a hurricane, don't you think? All right, my dear; we'll go down now. The wind *is* very strong.'

He walked over to the tall tree and used it to lean on while he felt for his footing on the edge of the ravine. Julie came forward. 'I'll give you a hand.'

'It's all right.' He lowered himself over the edge and started to climb down, and Julie prepared to follow. There was a roar like an express train as a squall of wind passed overhead and an ominous creaking came from the tree.

Julie whirled and looked up. 'Watch out!' she screamed.

The tree was not securely rooted; water pouring from above had undercut the roots and the sudden hard pressure of the wind was too much for them. The tree began to topple, the roots wrenched themselves from the side of the ravine and the bole of the tree came forward like a battering ram straight at Rawsthorne.

Julie dashed forward and cannoned into him and, caught off balance, he lost his footing and fell down among the rocks. As it dropped the tree twisted and turned and a branch caught Julie a glancing blow on the head. She staggered back and the tree fell on top of her, crushing her legs painfully. The world was suddenly a twisting, turning chaos of red pain, and there were many crackling and popping noises as twigs and branches snapped off short on violent contact with the ground. Then all the noise faded away, even the howling of the wind, and the redness became grey and finally a total black.

At first, Rawsthorne did not know what had happened. He heard Julie's shout and then found himself thrust into space. He was thoroughly winded by his fall into the ravine and lay for a while struggling for breath. There was a tightness in his chest, an old enemy which presaged no good, and he knew he must not move very much or his heart would begin to go back on him. But after a while, when he began to breathe more easily, he sat up and looked at the tangle of branches on the edge of the ravine.

'Julie!' he called. 'Are you all right?'

His voice was painfully thin and lost in the suddenly risen wind. He shouted again and again but heard no reply. He looked up in despair at the wall of ravine, knowing that he must force himself to climb it, and wondered hazily if he would make it. Slowly he began to climb, nursing his ebbing strength and resting often when he found a firm footing.

He nearly made it to the top.

As he stretched out his hand to grasp a firm rock on the lip of the ravine he cried out in pain. It felt as though some vicious enemy had thrust a red-hot sword into his chest and his heart seemed to swell and break asunder. He cried out once more at the awful agony and fell back into the ravine, where he lay with the torrent of water lapping at his hair.

TEN

It seemed to Dawson that the second half of the hurricane was not as bad as the first half, but perhaps that was because there was little rain. Still, it was bad enough. When Wyatt left the road he had driven the Land-Rover into the rough bush on the hillside and had found an almost imperceptible dip in the ground. This was the best he could do to ensure the safety of their vehicle.

Dawson said, 'Why not stay inside?'

Wyatt disillusioned him. 'It wouldn't take much to push it over on to its side even though I've jammed it among the trees. We can't risk it.'

So Dawson gave up hope of being out of the wind and rain and they began looking for personal shelter further along the hillside. The wind was already bad and steadily increased in strength and in the more violent gusts they were hard put to it to retain their footing. Presently they encountered the outlying flank of the regiment that Favel had sent to the ridge above the Negrito. The men were digging in and Wyatt was able to borrow an entrenching tool to do a bit of burrowing himself.

Digging in was harder than it had been outside St Pierre; the ground was hard and stony with bedrock not far beneath the thin layer of poor soil and all he could manage was a shallow scrape. But he took as much advantage of inequalities of the ground as he could and chose a place where there was an outcropping of rock to windward which would give immovable protection.

When he had finished he said to Dawson, 'You stay here. I'm going to see if I can find one of the officers of this crowd.'

Dawson huddled behind the rock and looked apprehensively at the sky. 'Take it easy – that's no spring zephyr you're walking in.'

Wyatt crept away, keeping very close to the ground. The wind closed about him like a giant's hand and tried to pick him up and shake him, but he flattened out to elude its grip and crawled on his belly to the nearest foxhole, where he found a curled-up bundle of clothing which, when straightened out, would be a soldier.

'Where's your officer?' he yelled.

A thumb jerked, indicating that he should go further along the hillside.

'How far?'

Spread fingers said three hundred feet – or was it metres? A long way in either case. Puzzled brown eyes watched Wyatt as he crawled away and then were shrouded in a coat as the wind blew harder.

It took Wyatt a long time to find an officer, but when he did so he recognized him as one he had seen in Favel's headquarters. Better still, the officer recognized Wyatt and welcomed him with a white-toothed grin. ' '*Allo, ti blanc,*' he shouted. 'Come down.'

Wyatt dropped into the foxhole and jammed himself next to the officer. He regained his breath, then said, 'Have you seen a white woman round here?'

'I have seen no one. There is no one this high up the hillside but the regiment.' He grinned widely. 'Just unfortunate soldiers.'

Wyatt was disappointed even though he had not really expected good news. He said, 'Where are the people – and how are they taking this?'

'Down there,' said the officer. 'Near the bottom of the valley. I don't know how they are – we didn't have time to find out. I sent some men down there but they didn't come back.'

Wyatt nodded. The regiment had done a magnificent job – a forced march of nearly ten miles and then a frantic burrowing into the ground, all in two hours. It was too much to expect them to have done more.

The officer said, 'But I expected to find some of them up here.'

'It's more exposed at this height,' said Wyatt. 'They're safer down there. I don't suppose they'll get a wind much above eighty or ninety miles an hour. Up here it's different. How do you think your men will take it?'

'We will be all right,' said the officer stiffly. 'We are soldiers of Julio Favel. There have been worse things than wind.'

'No doubt,' said Wyatt. 'But the wind is bad enough.'

The officer nodded his agreement vigorously, then he said, 'My name is André Delorme. I had a plantation higher up the Negrito – I will get it back now that Serrurier is gone. You must come and see me, *ti* Wyatt, when this is over. You will always be welcome – you will be welcome anywhere in San Fernandez.'

'Thank you,' said Wyatt. 'But I don't know if I'll stay.'

Delorme opened his eyes wide in surprise. 'But why not? You saved the people of St Pierre; you showed us how to kill Serrurier. You will be a great man here – they will make you a statue better than the one of Serrurier in the Place de la Libération Noire. It is better to make a statue of one who saves lives.'

'Saves lives?' echoed Wyatt sardonically. 'But you say I showed you how to kill Serrurier – and his whole army.'

'That is different.' Delorme shrugged. 'Julio Favel told me you saw Serrurier and he did not believe you when you said there would be a hurricane.'

'That is so.'

'Then it is his own fault he is dead. He was stupid.'

'I must get back,' said Wyatt. 'I have a friend.'

'Better you stay here,' said Delorme, raising his head to listen to the wind.

'No, he is expecting me.'

'All right, *ti* Wyatt; but come and see me at La Carrière when this is over.' He held out a muscular brown hand which Wyatt gripped. 'You must not leave San Fernandez, *ti* Wyatt; you must stay and show us what to do when the hurricane comes again.' He grinned. 'We are not always fighting in San Fernandez – only when it is necessary.'

Wyatt climbed out of the foxhole and gasped as the wind buffeted him. He had been tempted to stay with Delorme but he knew he had to get back. If Dawson got into trouble he could not do much to help himself with his injured hands and Wyatt wanted to be with him. It took him over half an hour to find Dawson and he was exhausted as he climbed round the outcrop and tumbled into the shallow hole.

'I thought you'd been blown away,' shouted Dawson as he rearranged his limbs. 'What's going on?'

'Nothing much. There's been no sign of Julie or Mrs Warmington. They're probably down on the lower slopes, and it's just as well.'

'How far are we from the map position that guy gave us back in St Pierre?'

'It's a little over a mile up the valley.'

Dawson pulled his jacket about his chest and huddled against the rock. 'We'll just have to sit this one out, then.'

He had been doing a lot of thinking in Wyatt's absence, planning what to do when the hurricane was over. He would not stay in St Pierre; he would go right back to New York and rearrange his affairs. Then he would come back to San Fernandez, buy a house overlooking the sea, and buy a boat and do a lot of fishing. And write a book once in a while. His last three books had not been too good; they had sold because of Wiseman's jazzy publicity, but in his heart he knew they were not good books even though the critics had let them by. He wondered why he had lost his steam and had been troubled about it, but now he knew he could write again as well, or better, than he had ever done.

He smiled slightly as he thought of his agent. Wiseman would have already written a lot of junk about Big Jim Dawson, the great hero, practically saving San Fernandez single-handed, but he wouldn't really give a damn whether Dawson was alive or dead – in fact, if Dawson had been killed it would be a red-hot story. Dawson would take great pleasure in reading all the press releases and then tearing them up and littering Wiseman's desk with the fragments. This was one episode in his life that wasn't going to be dirtied and twisted for profit by a conniving press agent. Or a conniving and dastardly writer, for that matter.

Maybe he would write the story of the last few days himself. He had always wanted to tackle a great non-fiction subject and this was it. He would tell the story of Commodore Brooks, of Serrurier and Favel, of Julie Marlowe and Eumenides Papegaikos, and of the thousands of people caught in the double disaster of war and wind. And, of course, it would be the story of Wyatt. There would be little, if anything, in it of himself. He had done nothing but get Wyatt in gaol and cause trouble all round. That would go in the book – but no false heroics, none of Wiseman's synthetic glorification. It would be a good book.

He twisted and lay closer to the ground in an effort to avoid the driving wind.

The day wore on and again San Fernandez was subject to the agony of the hurricane. Once more the big wind tormented the island, sweeping in from the sea like a destroying

angel and battering furiously at the central core of mountains as though it would sweep even those back into the sea
from where they had come. Perhaps the hurricane did con-
tribute towards the time when this small piece of land
would be finally obliterated – a landslide here, a new water-
course gouged in the earth there, and a fraction of a
millimetre removed from the top of the highest mountain in
the Massif des Saints. But the land would survive many
more hurricanes before being finally defeated.

Life was more vulnerable than inanimate rock. The soft
green plants were uprooted, torn from the soil to fly on the
wind; the trees broke, and even the tough grasses, stubbornly clumped with long spreading roots, felt the very
earth dissolve beneath. The animals of the mountains died
in hundreds; the wild pig was flung from the precipice to
spill its brains against the stone, the wild dog whimpered in
its rocky shelter and scratched futilely against the earthfall
that sealed the entrance, and the birds were blown from the
trees to be whirled away in the blast and to drown in the
far sea.

And the people?

On the slopes of the Negrito alone were almost 60,000
exposed men, women and children. Many died. The old and
tired died of exposure, and the young and fit died of the violence of air. Some died of stupidity, not having the sense to
find proper shelter, and some died in spite of their intelligence through mere ill-luck. Others died of illness – those
with weak hearts, weak chests and other ailments. Some,
even, died of shock; perhaps one can say that these died of
surprise at the raw violence of the world in which they
lived.

But not as many died as would have perished if they had
stayed in the ruined city of St Pierre.

For ten hours the storm raged at the island – the
hurricane – the big wind. Ten hours, every minute of which

was a stupefying eternity of shattering noise and hammering air. There was nothing left to do except to cower closer to the earth and hope to survive. Wyatt and Dawson crouched in their shallow trench behind the rock and, as Dawson had said, they 'sat this one out'.

At first Wyatt thought in some astonishment of what Delorme had said, and he smiled sardonically. So this was how legends were created. He was to be cast as a saviour, a hero of San Fernandez – the man who had saved a whole population and won a war. He would be praised for the good he had done and the bad he had been unable to prevent. Obviously Delorme had been quite sincere. To him, Serrurier and all who followed him had been devils incarnate and deserved no better than they had received. But to Wyatt, Serrurier had been sick with madness, and his followers, while misguided, had been men like any others, and he had been the one who had shown Favel the trap into which they might be led. Others might forgive him, or even not realize there was anything to forgive, but he would never forgive himself.

And then the hurricane drowned all thought and he lay there supine, waiting patiently for the time when he would be allowed to rouse himself to action and go down into the valley in search of the one person in the world he wanted to bring out in safety – Julie Marlowe.

The hurricane reached its height at eleven in the morning and from that time the wind began to decrease in violence very slowly. Wyatt knew there would not be any sudden drop in wind-speed as when the eye of the hurricane came over the island; the wind would quieten over a period of hours and would remain blustery for quite a long time.

It was not until three in the afternoon that it became safe enough for a man to stand in the open, and even then it was risky but Wyatt was in no mood for waiting any longer. He said to Dawson, 'I'm going into the valley now.'

'Think it's safe?'

'Safe enough.'

'Okay,' said Dawson, sitting up. 'Which way do we go?'

'It will be best to go right down, and then across the lower slopes.' Wyatt turned and looked across the hillside in the direction of Delorme's foxhole. 'I'm going to have a word with that officer again.'

They walked gingerly across the slope and Wyatt bent down and shouted to Delorme, 'I'd wait another hour before you get your men out.'

Delorme looked up. His face was tired and his voice was husky as he said, 'Are you going down now?'

'Yes.'

Then so will we,' said Delorme. He heaved himself up and groped in his pocket. 'Those people down there might not be able to wait another hour.' He blew shrilly on a whistle and slowly the hillside stirred as his men emerged from a multitude of holes and crevices. One of his sergeants came up and Delorme issued a rapid string of instructions.

Wyatt said, 'I'd take it easy on the way down – it's not so difficult to break a leg. If you come across any white people I'd be glad to know.'

Delorme smiled. 'Favel said we were to watch for a Miss Marlowe. He said you were worried about her.'

'Did he?' said Wyatt in surprise. 'I wonder how he knew.'

'Favel knows everything,' said Delorme with pride. 'He misses nothing. I think he talked with the other Englishman – Causton.'

'I'll have to thank him.'

Delorme shook his head. 'We owe you a lot, *ti* Wyatt; what else could we do? If I find Miss Marlowe I will let you know.'

'Thanks.' Wyatt looked at Delorme and knew he had changed his mind. 'And I'll certainly come to see you at your plantation. Where did you say it was?'

'Up the Negrito – at La Carrière.' Delorme grinned. 'But wait until I have cleaned it up and replanted – it will not look good now.'

'I'll wait,' promised Wyatt, and turned away.

It was not easy going down the hill. The wind plucked at them viciously and the surface had been loosened at the height of the storm so that small landslides were easy to start. There were many fallen trees round which they had to make their way, and the ripped-up trees left gaping holes. It was three-quarters of an hour before they reached the first of the survivors, a huddle of bodies lying in a small depression. The wind was still fierce and they had not yet stirred.

Dawson looked at them with an expression of horror. 'They're dead,' he said. 'The whole lot of them are dead.' hugging a child in her arms; the child was obviously dead – the head hung unnaturally on one side like that of a broken-jointed doll – but the woman seemed not to be aware of it. 'What can you do about a thing like that?' he asked.

'We can't do anything,' said Wyatt. 'It's best to leave her to her own people.'

Dawson looked back along the hill. 'But there are thousands here – what can one regiment of men do? There are no medical supplies, no doctors, no hospitals left standing in St Pierre. A lot of these people are going to die – even those who have survived so far.'

'There are a lot of people on the other side of the valley, too,' said Wyatt, pointing across the flood. 'It's like this all along the Negrito – on both sides.'

The hillside heaved with slow, torpid movement as the inhabitants of St Pierre came to the tired realization that their agony was over. Favel's men were now among them, but there was little they could do beyond separating the living from the dead, and the men who had enough first-aid knowledge to be able to splint a broken limb were kept very busy.

Wyatt said hopelessly, 'How can we find one person in this lot?'

'Julie's white,' said Dawson. 'She ought to stand out.'

'A lot of these people are as white as we are,' said Wyatt glumly. 'Let's get on.'

They took to the slopes again where an incursion of the flood crept inland, and Wyatt paused constantly to ask the more alert-seeming survivors if they had seen a white woman. Some did not answer, others replied with curses, and others were slow and incoherent in their replies – but none knew of a white woman. Once Wyatt yelled, 'There she is!' and plunged back down the hill to grasp a woman by the arm. She turned and looked at him, revealing the creamy skin of an octoroon, and he let her arm fall limply.

At last they arrived at their goal and started a more systematic search, patrolling up and down the hill and looking very closely at each group of people. They searched for nearly an hour and did not find Julie or any other white person, male or female. Dawson was sickened by what he saw, and estimated that if what he saw was a fair sample there must have been a thousand killed on the one side of the Negrito alone – and the injured were beyond computation.

The people seemed unable to fight their way clear of the state of shock into which they had been plunged. The air was alive with the moaning and screaming of the injured, while the fit either just sat looking into space or moved aimlessly with the gait of tortoises. Only a minute few seemed to have recovered their initiative enough to leave the hillside or help in the rescue work.

Wyatt and Dawson met again and Dawson shook his head heavily in response to Wyatt's enquiring and wild-eyed look. 'The man can't have made a mistake,' said Wyatt frantically. 'He *can't* have.'

'All we can do is keep on looking,' said Dawson. 'There's nothing else we can do.'

'We *could* go over to the coast road. That's where they went in the first place. That we *know*.'

'We'd better finish checking here first,' said Dawson stolidly. He looked over Wyatt's shoulder. 'Hey, there's one of Favel's boys coming this way – it looks as though he wants us.'

Wyatt spun on his heel as the soldier ran up. 'You looking for a *blanc?*' asked the man.

'A woman?' asked Wyatt tersely.

'That's right; she's over there – just over the rise.'

'Come on,' shouted Wyatt and started to run, with Dawson close behind. They came to the top of the slight rise and looked down at the couple of hundred people, some of whom raised enquiring black faces and rolling eyes in their direction.

'There!' jerked out Dawson. 'Over there.' He stopped and said quietly, 'It's the Warmington woman.'

'She'll know where Julie is,' said Wyatt exultantly, and ran down the slope. He pushed his way among the people and reached out to grasp Mrs Warmington's arm. 'You're safe,' he said. 'Where's Julie – Miss Marlowe?'

Mrs Warmington looked up at him and burst into tears. 'Oh, thank God – thank God for a white face. Am I glad to see you!'

'What happened to Julie – and the others?'

Her face crumpled. 'They killed him,' she said hysterically. 'They shot him and stabbed a bayonet in his back . . . again . . . and again. My God . . . the blood . . .'

Wyatt went cold. 'Who was killed? Rawsthorne or Papegaikos?' he demanded urgently.

Mrs Warmington looked at the backs of her hands. 'There was a lot of blood,' she said with unnatural quietness. 'It was very red on the grass.'

Wyatt held himself in with an effort. 'Who . . . was . . . killed?'

She looked up. 'The Greek. They blamed me for it. It wasn't my fault; it wasn't my fault at all. I had to do it. But they blamed me.'

Dawson said, 'Who blamed you?'

'That girl – that chit of a girl. She said I killed him, but I never did. He was killed by a soldier with a gun and a bayonet.'

'Where is Julie now?' asked Wyatt tensely.

'I don't know,' said Mrs Warmington shrilly. 'And I don't care. She kept on hitting me, so I ran away. I was frightened she'd kill me – she said she would.'

Wyatt looked at Dawson in shocked surprise, then he said dangerously softly, 'Where did you run from?'

'We came from the other side, near the sea,' she said. 'That's where we were locked up. Then I ran away. There was a river and a waterfall – we all got wet.' She shivered. 'I thought I'd get pneumonia.'

'Is there a river between here and the coast?' asked Dawson.

Wyatt shook his head. 'No.' Mrs Warmington was obviously in a state of shock and would have to be treated with kid gloves if they were going to get anything out of her. He said gently, 'Where was the river?'

'On the top of a hill,' said Mrs Warmington incomprehensibly. Dawson sighed audibly and she looked up at him. 'Why should I tell you where they are? They'll only tell you a lot of lies about me,' she said spitefully. 'I'm not going to tell you anything.' She clenched her fists and the nails dug into her palms. 'I hope she dies like she meant me to.'

Dawson tapped Wyatt on the shoulder. 'Come over here,' he said. Wyatt was looking horrified at Mrs Warmington, but he backed away under Dawson's pressure until they stood a few paces away from her. Dawson said, 'I don't know what this is all about. I think that woman has gone crazy.'

'She's raving mad,' said Wyatt. He was trembling.

'Maybe – but she knows where Julie is all right. Something's thrown a hell of a scare into her, and it wasn't the hurricane, although that might have tipped her over the edge. Maybe she *did* kill Eumenides and Julie saw her do it – that means she's scared of a murder charge. She may be crazy, but I think she's crazy like a fox – faking it up, I mean.'

'We've got to get it out of her,' said Wyatt. 'But how?'

'Leave it to me,' said Dawson savagely. 'You're an English gentleman – you wouldn't know how to handle her kind. Now, me – I'm an eighteen-carat diamond-studded American son-of-a-bitch – I'll get it out of her even if I have to beat her brains in.'

He walked back to her and said in a deceptively concilia-tory manner, 'Now, Mrs Warmington; you'll tell me where Julie Marlowe and Mr Rawsthorne are, won't you?'

'I'll do no such thing. I don't like people tattling and telling lies about me.'

Dawson's voice hardened. 'Do you know who I am?'

'Sure. You're Big Jim Dawson. You'll get me out of here, won't you?' Her voice broke pathetically into a wail. 'I want to go back to the States.'

He said dangerously, 'So you'll know my reputation. I'm supposed to be a bad bastard. You've got one chance to get back to the States quick. Tell me where Rawsthorne is or I'll have you held here pending the enquiry into the disappear-ance of the British consul. There's sure to be an enquiry – the British are conservative, they don't like losing officials, even minor ones.'

'On top of the hill,' she said sullenly. 'There's a gully up there.'

'Point it out.' His eyes followed the direction of her wavering hand, then he looked back at her. 'You've come

out of this hurricane pretty well,' he said grimly. 'Someone
must have been looking after you. You should be thankful,
not spiteful.'

He went back to Wyatt. 'I've got it. There's a gully
up there somewhere.' He waved his hand. 'Over in that
direction.'

Without a word Wyatt left at a run and started to climb
the hill. Dawson grinned and moved after him at a slower,
more economical pace. He heard a noise in the air and
looked up to see a helicopter coming over the brow of the
hill like a huge grasshopper. 'Hey!' he shouted. 'Here comes
the Navy – they've come back.'

But Wyatt was far ahead, climbing the hill as though his
life depended on it. Perhaps it did.

II

Causton stood on the concrete apron near the ruined control
tower of the airfield on Cap Sarrat Base and watched the
helicopters come in from the sea in a straggling and wavering line. Commodore Brooks had been quick off his mark –
the aircraft carrier under his command must have been
idling just on the outskirts of Mabel and he had sent off his
helicopters immediately the weather was fit for flying. And
this was only the first wave. Planes would soon pour into
San Fernandez, bringing much-needed medical aid.

He looked across at the small group of officers surrounding Favel and grinned. The Yanks were due for a surprise –
but perhaps not just yet.

Favel had been quite clear about it. 'I am going to occupy
Cap Sarrat Base,' he said. 'Even if only with a token force.
This is essential.'

So a platoon of men had made the dangerous trip across
the flooded mouth of the Negrito and here they were,

waiting for the Americans. It all hinged on the original treaty of 1906 in which Favel had found a loophole. 'The position is simple, Mr Causton,' he said. 'The treaty states that if the American forces voluntarily give up the Base and it is thereafter claimed by the government of San Fernandez, then the treaty is abrogated.'

Causton raised his eyebrows. 'It'll look a pretty shabby gesture,' he said. 'The Americans come in to bring you unstinting aid, and you reciprocate by taking the Base.'

'The Americans will bring us nothing they do not owe already,' said Favel drily. 'They have rented eight square miles of valuable real estate for sixty years at a pittance, on a lease forced at a time when they occupied San Fernandez as though it were an enemy country.' He shook his head seriously. 'I do not want to take the Base away from them, Mr Causton. But I think I will be in a position to negotiate another, more equitable lease.'

Causton took a notebook from his pocket and refreshed his memory. 'One thousand, six hundred and ninety-three dollars a year. I think it's worth more than that, and I think you ought to get it.'

Favel grinned cheerfully. 'You forgot the twelve cents, Mr Causton. I think the International Court at The Hague will give us just judgement. I would like you to be at the Base as an independent witness to the fact that the San Fernandan government has assumed control of Cap Sarrat.'

So now he was watching the first helicopter touch down on the territory of the sovereign government of San Fernandez. He watched men climb out and saw the gleam of gold on a flat cap. 'My God, I wonder if that's Brooks,' he murmured, and began to walk across the apron. He saw Favel move forward and watched the two men meet.

'Welcome back to Cap Sarrat,' said Favel, offering his hand. 'I am Julio Favel.'

'Brooks – Commodore in the United States Navy.'

The two men shook hands and Causton wondered if Brooks knew about the flaw in the treaty. If he did, he showed no awareness of his changed position, nor did he evince any surprise as he flicked his eyes upwards at the sodden green and gold flag of San Fernandez which hung limply from an improvised mast on the control tower. He said, 'What do you need most, Mr Favel, and where do you need it? Anything we've got, you just have to ask for it.'

Favel shook his head sadly. 'We need everything – but first, doctors, medical supplies, food and blankets. After that we would like some kind of large-scale temporary housing – even tents would do.'

Brooks indicated the helicopters landing on the runways. 'These boys are going to check the airfield to see if it's safe for operation. We'll set up a temporary control tower over there. When that's done the big planes can start to move in – they're already waiting for a signal in Miami and Puerto Rico. In the meantime, we have five choppers full of medics. Where do you want them to go?'

'Up the Negrito. They will have plenty of work.'

Brooks raised his eyebrows. 'The Negrito? Then you got your people out of St Pierre.'

'With the help of your Mr Wyatt. That is a very forceful and persuasive young man.'

They began to move away. 'Yes,' said Brooks. 'I wish I had . . .' His voice was lost to Causton as they walked up the runway.

III

Dawson caught up with Wyatt when he was nearly at the top of the hill. 'Take it easy,' he gasped. 'You'll bust a gut.'

Wyatt kept silent, reserving his breath to power his legs which were working like pistons. They reached the crest and he looked around, his chest heaving and the muscles of his legs sore with the effort he had made. 'I don't . . . see . . . a gully.'

Dawson looked over the other side towards the sea and saw a line of welcome blue sky on the horizon. He turned back. 'Suppose they had come up from the coast – where would they go from here?'

Wyatt shook his head in irritation. 'I don't know.'

'My inclination would be to edge in towards St Pierre,' said Dawson. 'So I wouldn't have so far to go home when it was all over.' He pointed to the left. 'That way. Let's have a look.'

They walked a little way along the crest of the hill, and Wyatt said, 'That's it – I suppose you'd call that a gully.'

Dawson looked down at the cleft cut into the hillside. 'It's our best bet so far,' he said. 'Let's go down.'

They climbed down into the ravine and looked about. Pools of water lay trapped among the rocks, and Wyatt said, 'There'd be quite a bit of water coming down here during the hurricane. That's what Mrs Warmington meant when she talked of a river on the top of a hill.' He filled his lungs with air. 'Julie!' he shouted. 'Julie! Rawsthorne!'

There was no answer. Everything was silent save for the distant roar of a helicopter landing at the bottom of the valley.

'We'll go a bit further,' said Dawson. 'Perhaps they're lower down. Perhaps they've left already – gone down to the valley.'

'They wouldn't do that,' objected Wyatt. 'Rawsthorne knows that the St Michel road is easier.'

'Okay, perhaps they've gone that way.'

'We'll look down here first,' said Wyatt. He began to climb among the tumbled rocks at the bottom of the ravine, wading through pools, heedless of the water. Dawson followed him, and kept a careful watch all round. From time to time Wyatt shouted, and then they paused to listen but heard no answering cry.

After a while Dawson said, 'That Warmington cow said something about a waterfall. You see anything that could have been a waterfall?'

'No,' said Wyatt shortly.

They went further down the ravine and found them-selves enclosed within its sheer walls. 'This would be as good a place to sit out a hurricane as any,' commented Dawson. 'Better than the goddam holes we had.'

'Then where the hell are they?' demanded Wyatt, losing his temper.

'Take it easy,' said Dawson. 'We'll find them if they're here. I'll tell you what; you carry on down the ravine, and I'll get up on the hillside. I can move faster up there and still see most of what there is to be seen down here.'

He climbed up the ravine wall and regained the open hillside, and as he thought, he was immediately able to keep up a better speed. Even though he was hampered by fallen trees, they were easier to negotiate than the jumble of rocks in the ravine. He carried on down the hill, outstripping Wyatt, and returned to the lip of the ravine frequently to scan the bottom very carefully. It was quite a while before he found anything.

At first he thought it was some kind of animal moving very slowly, and then his breath hissed as he saw it was a man crawling painfully on his belly. He climbed down to the bottom and stumbled across the rocks to where the crawl-ing figure had stopped. When he turned the man over he lifted his head and yelled, 'Wyatt, come here – I've found Rawsthorne!'

Rawsthorne was in a bad way. His face was deathly pale, accentuating the blood streaks on the side of his head. His right side appeared to be completely paralysed and he made ineffectual pawing movements with his left arm as Dawson gently cradled him. His eyes flickered open and his lips moved but he made no sound.

'Take it easy,' said Dawson. 'You're safe now.'

Rawsthorne's breath rasped and he whispered, 'Heart . . . heart. . . attack.'

'Don't worry,' said Dawson. 'Relax.'

Small stones clattered as Wyatt came up, and Dawson turned his head. 'The poor guy's had a heart attack. He's not too good.'

Wyatt took Rawsthorne's wrist and felt the faint thread of pulse and then looked into the glazing eyes which seemed focused an infinity away. The grey lips moved again. 'Waterfall. . . tree . . . tree . . .'

Rawsthorne suddenly sagged and lay in Dawson's arms, gazing vacantly at the sky, his jaw dropped open.

Dawson eased him down on to the rocks. 'He's dead.'

Wyatt stared down at the body and his face looked haggard. 'Was he crawling?' he whispered.

Dawson nodded. 'He was going down the ravine. I don't know how he expected to make it.'

'Julie would never have left him,' said Wyatt in an over-controlled voice. 'Not if he was sick. Something must have happened to her.'

'He said something about a waterfall, too – just like Warmington.'

'It must be higher up,' said Wyatt. 'And I think I know where it is.' He rose to his feet and stumbled away, moving much too fast for the broken ground and reckless of twisted or broken ankles. Dawson followed him more cautiously and found him beneath an outcrop of rock too hard and stubborn to be worn away. He stooped and picked up something from the cleft in the base of the rock. It was a woman's purse.

'This was Warmington's,' he said. 'This is the waterfall.' His head jerked upwards to the tangle of tree roots above his head on the edge of the ravine. 'And that's the tree – he said "tree", didn't he?'

He scrambled up the side of the ravine and then turned to give a hand to Dawson. 'Let's have a closer look at this bloody tree.'

They walked around the tree and saw nothing, and then Wyatt pushed in among the branches and suddenly gave a choked sound. 'She's here,' he said brokenly.

Dawson pushed his way through and looked over Wyatt's shoulder, then turned away. He said heavily, 'Well – we found her.'

She was lying with the trunk of the tree across her legs and hips and a branch across her right arm, pinning it to the ground. The fingertips of her left hand were scraped bloodily raw where she had scrabbled at the trunk in her efforts to move it. Her face, smudged with dirt, was otherwise marble-white and drained of blood, and the only thing about her that moved was a strand of her hair that waved gently in the wind.

Wyatt stepped back away from the tree and looked at it calculatingly. He said in a repressed voice, 'Let's move this tree. Let's shift this damned tree.'

'Dave,' said Dawson quietly, 'she's dead.'

Wyatt turned in a flash, his face furious. 'We don't know,' he shouted. *'We don't know that.'*

Dawson fell back a step, intimidated by the controlled violence emanating from this man. He said, 'All right, Dave. We'll move the tree.'

'And we'll do it carefully, do you hear?' said Wyatt. 'We'll do it very carefully.'

Dawson looked at the tree dubiously. It was big and heavy and awkward. 'How do we start?'

Wyatt attacked a broken branch and wrenched it free by sheer force. He stepped back panting. 'We take the weight off her . . . her body, then one of us can draw her out.'

That did not look so easy to Dawson, but he was willing to give it a try. He took the branch which Wyatt offered and walked round the tree looking for a convenient place to wedge it under the trunk. Wyatt collected some rocks and followed him. 'There,' he said abruptly. 'That's the place.' His face was very white. 'We must be careful.'

Dawson rammed the branch beneath the trunk and cautiously tested the leverage. He doubted if the trunk would move but said nothing. Wyatt pushed him out of the way and swung his weight on to the branch. There was a creak, but otherwise nothing. 'Come on,' he said. 'You can push on this, too.'

'Who is going to push the stones under?' asked Dawson reasonably. 'Neither of us can do it if we're both heaving on that branch.'

'I can do it with my foot,' said Wyatt impatiently. 'Come on.'

Both of them leaned heavily on the branch and Dawson felt an agony of pain in his hands. The trunk of the tree moved fractionally and he set his teeth and held on. Slowly the trunk lifted, inch by inch, and Wyatt, both his feet off the ground, nudged one of the rocks with the tip of his shoe until it slid underneath. Then another, a larger one, went under, and he gasped, 'That's enough – for now.'

Slowly they released the branch and the trunk settled again, but it was slightly raised on the rocks. Dawson staggered back, his hands aflame with pain, and Wyatt looked up and saw his face. 'What's the matter?' Then he caught on. 'Oh, my God, I'm sorry. I didn't realize.'

Dawson suppressed the sickness that welled up within him and grinned weakly. 'It doesn't matter,' he said, trying to keep his voice steady. 'There's nothing to it. I'm all right.'

'Are you sure?'

'I'm fine,' he said nonchalantly.

Wyatt switched his attention back to the tree. 'I'll see if I can pull her out now.' He crawled under the branches and was silent for some minutes, then said in a muffled voice, 'It needs one more swing.' He came out. 'If you can get under there and pull her out while I lift this damned tree, I think we'll do it.'

He carefully chocked in the rocks he had already inserted under the trunk while Dawson got in position, and when Dawson shouted that he was ready he swung again on the lever. Nothing happened, so he swung harder, again and again, leaning his whole weight on the branch and pushing down until he thought his bones would crack. The thought entered his mind dizzily that he had gone through all this before in the prison cell. Well, he had done it before and he would do it again.

The tree-trunk did not move.

Dawson called a halt and came out from under the branches. He had been close to Julie's body and was now certain that she was dead, but whatever he privately thought of the uselessness of all this did not show on his face for one moment. He said, 'What we need here is weight – not strength. I'm sixty pounds heavier than you are – it may not be all muscle, but that doesn't matter. You pull her out while I do the lifting.'

'What about your hands?'

'They're my hands, aren't they? Get under there.'

He waited until Wyatt was ready, then leaned on the branch and thrust down with all his force and weight. He almost screamed at the cruel torment in his hands and sweat beaded his forehead. The trunk moved and Wyatt gave a shout. 'Keep it up! For God's sake, keep it up!'

Dawson went through an eternity of purgatory and for a fraction of a second he wondered if he would ever be able to use his hands again – say, on a typewriter. Hell! he grunted to himself, I can always dictate – and pressed down harder. Out of the corner of his eye he saw Wyatt backing out, drawing something with him, and it was with exquisite relief that he heard a faint and faraway voice say, 'Okay, you can let it go.'

He released the branch and flopped to the ground, thankfully feeling the flaming hell centred in his hands dying to a welcome numbness. With lacklustre eyes he watched Wyatt bend over Julie, rip open her shirt and apply his ear to her chest. And it was with something approaching shock that he heard him shout exultantly, 'She's alive! She's still alive! It's faint, but it's there.'

It took a long time for them to signal a helicopter, but when they did action was swift. The chopper hovered over them and swirled the dust while Wyatt lay over Julie and protected her from the blast. A man was lowered by a winch and dropped to the ground, and Dawson lurched up to him. 'We need a doctor.'

The man gave a brief grin. 'You've found one – what's the trouble?'

'This woman.' He led the way to where Julie was lying and the doctor dropped to one knee beside her and produced a stethoscope. After a few seconds he fumbled in a cartouche at his waist and drew forth a hypodermic syringe and an ampoule. While Wyatt watched anxiously he gave Julie an injection. Then he waved back the helicopter and, speaking through a microphone at the bottom of the dangling hoist, he gave terse instructions.

The hoist was reeled in and presently another man came down, bearing a folded stretcher and a bundle of splints, and the helicopter retreated again to continue its circling. Julie was tenderly bound in a complex of splints and given another injection. Wyatt said, 'How is . . . will she . . .?'

The doctor looked up. 'We got to her in time. She'll be all right if we can get her off this hillside real fast.' He waved to the helicopter which came in again, and Julie was hoisted up on the stretcher.

The doctor surveyed them. 'You coming?' He looked at Dawson. 'What's the matter with your hands?'

'What hands?' asked Dawson with tremulous irony. He thrust bandaged claws forward. 'Look, doc, no hands!' He began to laugh hysterically.

The doctor said, 'You'd better come with us.' He looked at Wyatt. 'You, too; you look half beat to death.'

They were hoisted up by the winch one at a time, and the doctor followed and tapped the pilot once on the shoulder. Wyatt sat next to the stretcher and looked at Julie's white face. He wondered if she would consider marrying a man who had failed her, who had let her go into the storm to die. He doubted it – but he knew he would ask her.

He stared down blindly at the receding hillside and at the broad waters of the flooded Negrito and felt a touch on his hand. He turned quickly and saw that Julie was awake and that her hand touched his. Two tears ran down her cheeks and her lips moved, but all sound was lost in the roar of the aircraft.

Quickly he bent down with his ear to her lips and caught the faint thread of sound. 'Dave! Dave! You're alive!' Even in the thin whisper there were overtones of incredulity.

He smiled at her. 'Yes, we're alive. You'll be back in the States today.'

Her fingers tightened weakly on his hand and she spoke again. He missed something of what she said, but caught the gist of it.'. . . come back. I want house . . . overlooking sea . . . St Pierre.'

Then she closed her eyes but her fingers still held his hand and he felt half his burden taken from him. She was going to be all right and they were going to be together.

*   *   *

And so he went back to Cap Sarrat Base and into fame and history. He did not know that the headlines of the world's newspapers would blazon his name in a hundred languages as the man who saved a whole city's people – as the man who had destroyed an army. He did not know that honours awaited him, to be bestowed by lesser men. He did not know that one day, when he was a very old man, he would be the one who was to show the way to the taming of the big wind – the hurricane.

He knew nothing of all this. All he knew was that he was very tired and that he was a professional failure. He did not know how many soldiers had died in the trap of St Pierre – many hundreds or many thousands – but even if only one had died it would serve to proclaim to the world his failure in his work and he felt miserable.

David Wyatt was a dedicated scientist, unversed in the ways of the world and very young for his years.

BAHAMA CRISIS

To Valerie and David Redhead
with much affection

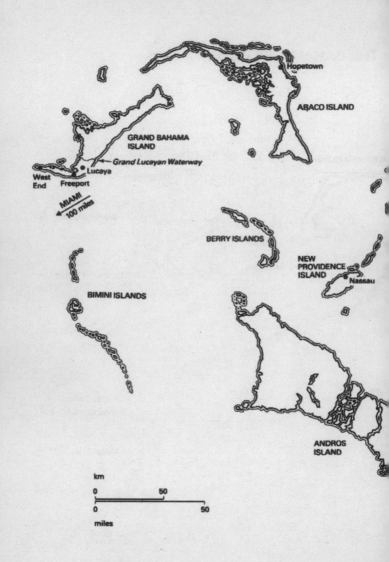

HopetownＡ

ABACO ISLAND

GRAND BAHAMA
ISLAND

← *Grand Lucayan Waterway*

West
End　Freeport　Lucaya

MIAMI
100 miles

BERRY ISLANDS

NEW
PROVIDENCE
ISLAND

Nassau

BIMINI ISLANDS

ANDROS
ISLAND

km

0　　　　　　50

0　　　　　　50

miles

THE BAHAMA ISLANDS

N

ATLANTIC OCEAN

ELEUTHERA ISLAND

CAT ISLAND

SAN SALVADOR

EXUMA SOUND

CONCEPTION ISLAND

RUM CAY

LONG ISLAND

GREAT EXUMA

STOREY CAY

WATER CAY

JUEMENTOS CAYS

FLAMINGO CAY

Duncan Town

RAGGED ISLAND RANGE

PROLOGUE

My name is Tom Mangan and I am a Bahamian – a white Bahamian. This caused some comment when I was up at Cambridge; it is surprising how ill-informed even supposedly educated people can be about my home islands. I was told that I could not be a Bahamian because Bahamians are black; that the Bahamas are in the Caribbean, which they are not; and many confused the Bahamas with Bermuda or even Barbados. For these reasons and because an understanding of the geographical and political nature of the Bahamas is essential to my story it seems to me that I must describe them and also give a brief account of my family involvement.

The Bahamas are a chain of islands beginning about fifty miles off the coast of Florida and sweeping in an arc 500 miles to the south-east to a similar distance off the coast of Cuba. They consist of 700 islands (called cays locally, and pronounced 'keys') and about 2000 lesser rocks. The name is derived from the Spanish *baja mar* which means 'shallow sea'.

I am descended from one of the Loyalists who fought in the American War of Independence. Surprisingly few people are aware that more Americans fought in that war on the side of the British than ever did under the rebel generals, and that the war was lost more by the incompetence of

the British than any superiority on the part of George
Washington. Be that as it may, the war was lost by the
British, and the American nation was born.

Life in the new United States was not comfortable for the
erstwhile Loyalists. Reviled by their compatriots and abandoned by the British, many thought it prudent to leave, the
northerners going mostly to Nova Scotia and the southern-
ers to the Bahamas or to the sugar islands in the Caribbean
beyond Cuba. So it was that in 1784 John Henry Mangan
elected to settle with his family on the island of Abaco in the
Bahamas.

There was not much to Abaco. Shaped something like a
boomerang, Great and Little Abaco Islands stretch for about
130 miles surrounded by a cluster of lesser cays. Most of
these smaller cays are of coral, but Abaco itself is of limestone and covered with thick, almost impenetrable, tropical
bush. Sir Guy Carleton intended to settle 1500 Loyalists on
Abaco, but they were a footloose and fractious crowd and
not many stayed. By 1788 the total population was about
400, half of whom were black slaves.

It is not hard to see why Carleton's project collapsed.
Abaco, like the rest of the Bahamian islands, has a thin,
infertile soil, a natural drawback which has plagued the
Bahamas throughout their history. Many cash crops have
been tried – tomatoes, pineapples, sugar, sisal, cotton – but
all have failed as the fertility of the soil became exhausted.
It is not by chance that three settlements in the Bahamas
are called Hard Bargain.

Still, a man could survive if he did not expect too much;
there were fish in the sea, and one could grow enough
food for one's immediate family. Timber was readily available for building, the limestone was easily quarried, and
palmetto leaf thatch made a good waterproof roof. John
Henry Mangan not only survived but managed to flourish,
along with the Sands, the Lowes, the Roberts and other

Loyalist families whose names are still common on Abaco today.

The Mangans are a thin line because, possibly due to a genetic defect, they tend to run to girls like the Dutch royal family. Thus they did not grow like a tree with many branches but in a straight line. I am the last of the male Mangans and, as far as I know, there are no others of that name in the Islands.

But they survived and prospered. One of my forebears was a ship-builder at Hope Town on Elbow Cay; most of the local ships sailing the Bahamian waters were built on Abaco and the Mangan family built not a few and so became moderately well-to-do. And then there was the wrecking. As the United States grew in power there was much maritime traffic and many ships were wrecked on the Islands of the Shallow Sea. The goods they contained contributed greatly to the wealth of many an island family, the Mangans not excepted. But the great turning point in the family fortunes came with the American Civil War.

The Confederate south was starved of supplies because of the northern blockade, and cotton rotted on the docks. Any ship putting into Charleston or Wilmington found a ready market for its cargo; quinine costing $10 in Nassau brought in excess of $400 in Charleston, while cotton costing $400 at the dockside was worth $4000 in Liverpool. It was a most profitable, if risky, two-way trade and my great-grandfather saw his opportunity and made the family rich in half a decade.

It was his son, my grandfather, who moved the family from Abaco to Nassau on New Providence – Nassau being the capital of the Bahamas and the centre of trade. Yet we still own land on Abaco and I have been building there recently.

If my great-grandfather made the family rich it was my father who made it really wealthy. He became a multi-millionaire which accounts for the fact that a Bahamian was

educated at Cambridge. Again, it was running an American
blockade which provided the profit.

On 15 January 1920 the United States went dry and, as
in the Civil War, the Bahamas became a distribution centre
for contraband goods. The Nassau merchants known as the
Bay Street Boys, my father among them, soon got busy
importing liquor. The profit margin was normally one hundred per cent and the business was totally risk-free; it was
cash on the barrel and the actual blockade-running was
done by the Americans themselves. It was said that there
was so much booze stacked at West End on Grand Bahama
that the island tipped by several degrees. And, for a
Bahamian, the business was all legal.

All good things come to an end and the 18th
Amendment was repealed by Franklin Roosevelt in 1933,
but by then my father was sitting pretty and had begun to
diversify his interests. He saw with a keen eye that the
advent of aircraft was going to have an impact on the tourist
industry and would alter its structure. Already Pan-
American was pioneering the Miami-Nassau route using
Sikorsky seaplanes.

Bahamian tourism in the nineteenth and early twentieth
centuries was confined to the American rich and the four-
month winter season. An American millionaire would bring
his family and perhaps a few friends to spend the whole season on New Providence. This, while being profitable to a
few, was of little consequence to the Bahamian economy,
millionaires not being all that plentiful. My father took the
gamble that aircraft would bring the mass market and
invested in hotels. He won his gamble, but died before he
knew it, in 1949.

I was eleven years old when my father died and had as
much interest in money and business as any other boy of
eleven, which is to say none. My mother told me that a
trust fund had been set up for me and my two sisters and

that I would come into my inheritance on my twenty-fifth birthday. She then continued to run the family affairs which she was quite capable of doing.

I went to school in Nassau but spent my holidays on Abaco under the watchful eye of Pete Albury, a black Abaconian whom I thought was old but, in fact, was about thirty at the time. He had worked for the family since he was a boy and looked after our property on Abaco. He had taught me to swim – a non-swimming Bahamian being as common as a wingless bird – and taught me to shoot, and we hunted the wild pig which are common on Abaco. He acted *in loco parentis* and tanned my hide when he thought I needed it. He stayed in my employ until his death not long ago.

Those early years were, I think, the most enjoyable of my life. In due course I went to England to study at Cambridge, and found England uncomfortably cold and wet; at least in the Bahamas the rain is warm. I took my degree and then went to the United States for a two-year course in business studies at Harvard to prepare myself for the administration of my inheritance. It was there I met Julie Pascoe who was to become my wife. In 1963 I was back in Nassau where, on my twenty-fifth birthday, there was much signing of documents in a lawyer's office and I took control of the estate.

Many things had changed in the Bahamas by then. My father's hunch had proved correct and the coming of the big jets brought the mass tourist market he had predicted. In 1949, the year he died, 32,000 tourists came to the Islands; in 1963 there were over half a million. It is worth adding that next year the estimated total is over two million. My mother had looked after our interests well, but now she was getting old and a little frail and was glad to relinquish responsibility into my hands. I found that one of the things she had done was to become involved in the development of Grand Bahama. At the time that worried me very much because Grand Bahama was turning sour.

Wallace Groves was an American who had a dream and that dream was Freeport on the island of Grand Bahama. He persuaded Sir Stafford Sands, then Minister of Finance in the Bahamian Government, to sell him over 200 square miles of government land on Grand Bahama upon which he would build a city – Freeport. His intention, not actually realized in his lifetime, was to create a duty-free area for the benefit of American corporations where they could avoid American taxes. In 1963 the scheme was not working; no immediate enthusiasm was being shown by any corporation anywhere. Groves switched the emphasis to tourism, recreation and residential housing, and twisted Sands's arm to allow the building of a casino to attract custom.

Sands was a quintessential Bay Street Boy who could catch a dollar on the fly no matter how fast it went. It was he who was primarily responsible for the vast increase of tourist traffic. Reasoning that the tourist needs much more than mere sun and sand he saw to it that the whole infrastructure of the tourist industry was built and maintained. He acceded to Groves's request and the casino opened in 1964.

It was the worst mistake Sands could ever have made. The shadowy figure supervising the running of the casino was Meyer Lansky who used to run casinos in Havana until he was tossed out of Cuba by Castro. Having put out a contract on Castro for $1 million Lansky looked for somewhere else to operate and found Grand Bahama. The gangsters had moved in.

Politics and economics walk hand in hand, largely revolving around the question of who gets what, and the black Bahamians saw the wealth created by the tourist industry going into the pockets of the white Bay Street Boys who also controlled the House of Assembly and ran the country in the interest of the whites. Something had to give, and in 1967 the largely black Progressive Liberal Party led by Lynden Pindling squeaked into power with a two-seat majority. The following year Pindling unexpectedly held another election and the PLP got in with twenty-nine seats out of the thirty-eight.

This landslide came about because of the mistake made by Stafford Sands. As soon as Pindling came to power he decided to take a closer look at Freeport and, in particular, the casino. He found that Groves and Lansky were giving kick-backs to Sands and others in the form of dubious 'consultancy fees' and that Sands himself was reputed to have taken over $2 million. When this was disclosed all hell broke loose; Sands was discredited and fell, bringing his party down with him.

But Groves had been right – the casino had brought prosperity to Grand Bahama, and Freeport had boomed and was thriving. There were plans for vast residential developments – great areas were already laid out in streets, complete with sewerage and electricity. The streets even had names; all that was missing were the houses on the building plots.

But investors were wary. To them a Caribbean revolution had taken place and what would those crazy blacks do next? They ignored the fact that it had been a democratic election and that the composition of the Assembly now compared with the ethnic composition of the Bahamas; they just pulled out and took their money with them and the economy of Grand Bahama collapsed again and is only now recovering.

And what was I doing while this was going on? I was trying to keep things together by fast footwork and trying not to get my hands too dirty. To tell the truth I voted for Pindling. I could see that the rule of the Bay Street Boys' oligarchy was an anachronism in a fast changing world and that, unless the black Bahamian was given a share in what was going, there would be a revolution and not a peaceful election.

And among other things I got married.

Julie Pascoe was the daughter of an American doctor and lived in Maryland. When I left Harvard we kept up a correspondence. In 1966 she visited the Bahamas with her parents and I took them around the Islands; showing off, I suppose. We married in 1967 and Susan was born in 1969. Karen came along in 1971. The propensity of the Mangans to breed daughters had not failed.

Although I had been worried about the investments on Grand Bahama, three years ago I decided that an upswing was due. I floated a company, the West End Securities Corporation, a holding company which I control and of which I am President. More importantly I moved my base of operations from Nassau to Freeport, and built a house at Lucaya on Grand Bahama. Nassau is an old town, a little stuffy and set in its ways. Brave new ideas do not sprout in an environment like that so I left for Grand Bahama where Wally Groves's dream seems about to come true.

I suppose I could have been pictured as a very lucky man – not worrying where my next dollar was coming from, happily married to a beautiful wife with two fine children, and with a flourishing business. I *was* a lucky man, and I thought nothing could go wrong until the events I am about to recount took place.

Where shall I begin? I think with Billy Cunningham who was around when it happened just before the Christmas before last. It was the worst Christmas of my life.

ONE

Billy Cunningham was a scion of the Cunningham clan; his father, uncle, brother and assorted cousins jointly owned a fair slice of Texas – they ran beef, drilled for oil, were into shipping, newspapers, radio and television, hotels, supermarkets and other real estate, and owned moderate tracts of downtown Dallas and Houston. The Cunningham Corporation was a power to be reckoned with in Texas, and Prince Billy was in the Bahamas to see what he could see.

I had first met him at Harvard Business School where, like me, he was being groomed for participation in the family business, and we had kept in touch, meeting at irregular intervals. When he telephoned just before Christmas asking to meet me on my own ground I said, 'Sure. You'll be my guest.'

'I want to pick your brains,' he said. 'I might have a proposition for you.'

That sounded interesting. The Cunningham Corporation was the kind of thing I was trying to build West End Securities into, though I had a long way to go. I had a notion that the Cunninghams were in a mind for expansion and Billy was coming to look over the chosen ground. I would rather cooperate than have them as competitors because they were a tough crowd, and I hoped that was what Billy had in mind. We fixed a date.

I met him at Freeport International Airport where he arrived in a company jet decked in the Cunningham colours. He had not changed much; he was tall, broad-shouldered and blond, with a deep tan and gleaming teeth. The Cunninghams seemed to run to film star good looks, those of them I had met There was nothing about him to indicate he was American, no eccentricity of style which might reasonably be expected of a Texan. Texans are notorious, even in the United States, for their unselfconscious and nostalgic frontier rig. If he ever wore them, then Billy had left his ten-gallon hat, string tie and high-heeled boots at home, and was dressed in a lightweight suit of obviously English cut. Being a Cunningham he would probably order them casually by the half-dozen from Huntsman of Savile Row.

'How's the boy?' he said as we shook hands. 'I don't think you've met Debbie – this is my little cousin.'

Deborah Cunningham was as beautiful as the Cunningham menfolk were handsome; a tall, cool blonde. 'Pleased to meet you, Miss Cunningham.'

She smiled. 'Debbie, please.'

'Tell me,' said Billy. 'How long is the runway?'

That was a typical Billy Cunningham question; he had an insatiable curiosity and his questions, while sometimes apparently irrelevant, always had a bearing on his current train of thought. I said, 'The last time I measured it came to 11,000 feet.'

'Just about handle everything,' he commented. He turned and watched the Cunningham JetStar take off, then said, 'Let's move.'

I drove them through Freeport on my way to the Royal Palm Hotel. I was proud of the Royal Palm; for my money it was the best hotel in the Bahamas. Of course, it had been my money that had built it, and I was looking forward to seeing Billy's reaction. On the way I said, 'Is this your first time in the Bahamas, Debbie?'

'Yes.'

'Mine, too,' said Billy. That surprised me, and I said so. 'Just never gotten around to it.' He twisted in his seat. 'Which way is Freeport?'

'Right here. You're in downtown Freeport.' He grunted in surprise, and I knew why. The spacious streets, lawns and widely separated low-slung buildings were like no other city centre he had seen. 'It shows what you can do when you build a city from scratch. Twenty years ago this was all scrubland.'

'Oh, look!' said Debbie. 'Isn't that a London bus?'

I laughed. 'The genuine article. There seems to be a mystique about those all over the English-speaking world – I've seen them at Niagara, too. I think the London Transport Board makes quite a profit out of selling junk buses as far-flung tourist attractions.'

In the foyer of the Royal Palm Billy looked around with an experienced eye. The Cunningham Corporation ran its own hotels and knew how they ticked. He glanced upwards and gave a long, slow whistle. The foyer rose the entire height of the hotel, a clear eight storeys with the bedrooms circling it on mezzanines. 'Wow!' he said. 'Isn't that a lot of wasted space?'

I smiled; even the Cunninghams had a lot to learn. 'It might be in a city hotel, but this is a resort hotel. There's a difference.'

Jack Fletcher, the hotel manager, was standing by and I introduced him to the Cunninghams. He booked them in with as few formalities as possible, then said, 'Here are your room keys – Mr Cunningham, Miss Cunningham.' He gave Billy another key. 'Your car's in the garage.'

I said, 'Find another car for Miss Cunningham; she might like to do some sightseeing by herself.'

'Hey!' said Billy. 'No need for that.'

I shrugged. 'No sweat; we run a car hire company and the season hasn't topped out yet. We have a few cars spare.'

He took me by the elbow and led me to one side. 'I'd like to talk with you as soon as possible.'

'You always were in a hurry.'

'Why not? I get things done that way. Say, fifteen minutes?'

'I'll be in the bar.' He nodded in satisfaction.

He was down in ten minutes and strode into the bar at a quick clip. After ordering him a drink I said, 'Where's Debbie?'

Billy smiled crookedly. 'You know women; she'll take a while to prettify herself.' He accepted the bourbon on the rocks. 'Thanks.'

'Your room all right?'

'Fine.' He frowned. 'But I still say you're wasting a hell of a lot of space.'

'You're thinking in terms of city downtown hotels. Space is cheap here and the clientèle is different.' I decided to push. 'What are you here for, Billy? You mentioned a proposition.'

'Well, we have a few dollars going spare and we're looking for somewhere to invest. What's your idea of the future of the Bahamas?'

'My God, Billy, but you have a nerve! You want to come in here as a competitor and you're asking my advice?'

He laughed. 'You won't lose out on it. You've already said a couple of things that have set me thinking. We think we know how to run hotels back home, but it might be different here. Maybe we could set up a partnership of sorts and use your local expertise.'

'A consortium?' He nodded, and I said contemplatively, 'A few dollars. How few would they be?'

'About forty million few.'

The bartender was standing close by, polishing an already over-polished glass. I said, 'Let's go and sit at that corner table.' We took our drinks and sat down. 'I think the future of the Bahamas is pretty good. Do you know much of our recent history?'

'I've done my homework.' He gave me a swift and concise résumé.

I nodded. 'That's about it. You Americans are now coming to the realization that Pindling isn't an ogre and that he runs a fairly stable and conservative government. He's safe. Now, let's come to your hotels and the way you run them. Your clientèle consists of businessmen and oil men, fast on their feet and on the move. They want fast service and good service, and they're here today and gone tomorrow. Because your land values in the city are so enormous you pack them in tight and charge them the earth because you have to. If you didn't the operation wouldn't pay; it would be more profitable to sell up and move into some other business. Have I got it right?'

'Just about. Those guys can pay, anyway; we don't get many complaints.'

I waved my arm. 'What do you think of this place?'

'Very luxurious.'

I smiled. 'It's intended to look that way; I'm glad you think it succeeds. Look, Billy; your average tourist here isn't a jet-setter and he doesn't have all that many dollars to spend. He's a man and his wife, and maybe his kids, from Cleveland, Ohio. Perhaps he's done one trip to Europe, but he can't go again because Europe is too damned expensive these days and the dollar is bloody weak. So he comes here because he's going foreign and economizing at the same time. Big deal.'

'What about the Europeans? Lots of those about here.' Billy jerked his thumb towards the lobby. 'Out there I heard German, French and Spanish.'

'The Spanish would be coming from the Argentine,' I said. 'We get lots of those. They, and the Europeans, come for the same reason – because it's cheaper here. But they don't come first class or even tourist. They come on charter flights in package deals organized by the travel agents – mostly German and Swiss. Neither the Americans nor the Europeans, with few exceptions, have a lot of money to throw around. So how do we handle the operation?'

'You tell me.'

'Okay.' I spread my hands. 'We give them the semblance of luxury – stuff they can't get at home. Palm trees are cheap to buy, easy to plant and grow quickly; and you don't get many of those in Cleveland or Hamburg. And they look damned good. We have a few bars dotted about the place; one on the beach, one by the pool, a couple inside. We hire a local guitarist and a singer to give the live mood music – Bahamian and Caribbean calypso stuff – very romantic. We have a discothèque. We have a place to serve junk food and another for gourmet dining – both are equally profitable. We have shops in the lobby; jewellery, clothing, local hand-icrafts, a news-stand and so on. So far those have been con-cessions, but now we're tending to operate them ourselves; I've just started a merchandising division. And, as I said, we run a car hire outfit; that's part of the tours division. On the beach we have a few sailboats and wind-surfing boards, and we hire a beach bum to act as life-guard and to show the clients how to use the stuff. That's free. So are the tennis courts. There's also use of an eighteen-hole golf course for a concessionary fee. There's a marina linked to the hotel so we also pull in the boating crowd.'

'It seems a customer can get most of what he wants on his vacation without ever leaving the hotel,' Billy hazarded.

'That's it,' I said. 'That's why they're called resort hotels. But what we *don't* have in the lobby is a liquor store; if a tourist wants his booze he pays bar prices. We want to squeeze as many dollars and cents out of these people as we can while they're in our tender care. And they *are* in our care, you know; they have a good time and they're not

cold-decked. We have a crêche and a children's play-
ground – that's more to keep the kids out of people's hair
than for anything else – and we have a doctor and a nurse.
And there's no drill or razzmatazz – they're just left alone to
do as they please which seems to be mostly roasting in the
sun.'

Billy grimaced. 'Not the kind of vacation I'd fancy.'

'Neither would I, but we're not tourists. So what happens
when our man goes home? His friends look at that deep tan
and ask him about it. "Gee!" he says. "I had the greatest
time. Free sailboating, free tennis, cheap golf on the most
superb course you can imagine. It was marvellous." Then he
does a hip shimmy around the office. "And, gee, that calypso
beat!" That's what he tells his friends when the snow is two
feet deep in the street outside the office, and they like the
idea, so they come, too. Maybe the year after.'

Billy mused. 'Fast turnover and small margins.'

'That's the name of the game,' I said. 'That's why room
occupancy is critical; we keep filled up or go broke.'

'Any trouble in that direction?'

I smiled. 'We're doing just fine,' I said lightly.

He grunted. 'I'd like to see your profit and loss account
and your balance sheet.'

'If you come up with a firm offer I might give you a quick
look.' I thought for a moment. 'I'll introduce you to a few
people and you can get a feel of the place. David Butler is a
good man to talk to; he's top man in the Ministry of Tourism
here on Grand Bahama.' I hesitated. 'There might be a problem there.'

'What problem?'

'Well, you're a southerner. Would you have any problem
dealing with a black on equal terms?'

'Not me,' said Billy. 'Billy One might, and Jack certainly
would; but they won't be involved out here.' Billy One was
Billy's father, so called to distinguish him from Billy. Jack

was his uncle and head of the Cunningham clan. 'Is this guy, Butler, black?'

'He is. There's another thing. Any hotels you build here must be Bahamian-built and Bahamian-staffed.'

'The Bahamas for the Bahamians – is that it?'

'Something like that. No one else can hold down a job here if it can be done by a Bahamian.'

Billy jerked his head towards the lobby. 'Your hotel manager – Fletcher; he's white.'

'So am I,' I said evenly. 'We're both white Bahamians. But the manager of the Sea Gardens – that's our hotel on New Providence – is black.'

Billy shrugged. 'It doesn't worry me as long as we have an efficient operation.'

'Oh, we're efficient.' I looked up and saw Debbie Cunningham coming into the bar. 'Here's your cousin.'

She was wearing a halter top and a pair of shorts which were well named – a long-stemmed American beauty. 'I hope this is okay,' she said, and looked down at herself. 'I mean, do you have *rules*?'

'Not so as you'd notice. Our visitors can dress pretty much as they like – up to a point.' I inspected her. 'I don't think you've reached the point yet, though. Will you have a drink?'

'Something soft; a Coke, maybe.' I signalled a waiter and she sat down. 'Isn't this quite a place? Have you seen the pool, Billy?'

'Not yet.'

I checked the time. 'I'm going to be busy for the next hour. Why don't you give the place the once-over lightly and I'll meet you at the desk. We'll have lunch at home. If you need to know anything ask Jack Fletcher.'

'That's fine,' said Billy. 'You've told me enough already so I know what to look for.'

I left them and went to my office to do some hard thinking. When Billy had told me the size of his proposed investment it had given me quite a jolt, although I had tried not to show it. Forty million dollars is a hell of a lot of money and that much injected into West End Securities could provide for a lot of expansion. The problem would be to avoid being swamped by it, and it was going to be quite a puzzle to put together a suitable package which would keep both me and the Cunningham Corporation happy.

If Billy had been surprised by the Royal Palm Hotel he was equally surprised by my home and he showed it. I took him through into the atrium where the swimming pool was. He looked around and said, 'My God!'

I laughed. 'Ever been in Rome in August?'

'Who goes to Rome in August?' He shrugged. 'But yes, I have – once,' and added feelingly, 'Goddamn hot. I got out of there fast.'

'And humid – just like here. When I built this place I had an architect dig into the plans of Roman villas; the ancient Romans, I mean. I had a feeling they'd be building for the climate. This is not a reproduction of a villa – more an adaptation. With modern conveniences, of course; air-conditioning included. But my air-conditioning costs less to run than any of my neighbours' because the building design helps. We used some of that know-how when we built the Royal Palm; that big, tall lobby is a natural cooling tower.'

Billy was about to say something when Julie walked out of the house. I said, 'Here's Julie now. Julie, you've met Billy, but I don't think you know Debbie, his cousin.'

'Hi, Billy, welcome to Grand Bahama. Glad to meet you, Debbie.'

'You have a beautiful home,' said Debbie.

'We like to think so.' Julie turned and called, 'Come out of there, Sue. We have guests; come and meet them.'

My elder daughter emerged from the pool as sinuously as an otter. 'Say "hello" to Mr Cunningham,' commanded Julie.

'To Billy,' I amended.

Sue shook hands gravely. She had an impish look as she said, 'Hello, Mr Billy Cunningham.'

Billy laughed. 'A regular little towhead, aren't you?'

'And this is Debbie.' Sue curtsied, something that would have looked better done in a crinoline instead of a minimal bathing suit.

'How old are you, Sue?' asked Debbie.

'Eleven years, two months, three weeks and six days,' said Sue promptly.

'You swim very well,' said Debbie. 'I bet you swim better than I can.'

Julie looked pleased – Debbie had said exactly the right thing. 'Yes, she swims well. She came second in the Marathon in her class.'

I said, 'It's a two-mile course in the open sea.'

Debbie was visibly startled and looked at my daughter with new respect. 'That's really something; I doubt if I can swim a quarter-mile.'

'Oh, it's nothing,' said Sue airily.

'All right, fish,' I said. 'Back into your natural element.' I turned to Julie. 'Where's Karen?'

'She's running a temperature. I put her to bed.'

'Nothing serious?'

'Oh, no.' Julie looked at Debbie. 'She's been having school problems and might even be faking it. Come and see her; it might buck her up.'

The women went into the house, and I said to Billy, 'I think drinks are indicated.'

'Yeah, something long and cold.'

'A rum punch, but easy on the rum.' As I mixed the drinks I said, 'Air-conditioning in hotels is important if we're to have a year-round season. We don't want the tourists frying even if it is good for the bar trade.'

Billy took off his jacket and sat in a recliner. 'You forget I'm a Texan. Ever been in Houston in summer? You know what Sherman said about Texas?' I shook my head. 'He said, "If I owned Hell and Texas, I'd rent out Texas and live in Hell."'

I laughed. 'Then you'll see the problems, although we're not as bad as Texas. There's always a sea breeze to cut the heat.'

We chatted while Luke Bailey, my general factotum, laid the table for lunch. Presently the women came back and accepted cold drinks. 'You have two very nice girls,' said Debbie.

'Julie must take the praise for that,' I said. 'I get any of the blame that's going.'

Talk became general over lunch and I was pleased to see that Julie and Debbie got on well together. If the women-folk of business associates are bitchy it can upset things all round, and I have known several sweet deals fall down because of that.

At one point Julie said, 'You know Mom and Pop are coming for Christmas.'

'Yes.' It was an arrangement that had been made earlier in the year.

'I thought I'd do my Christmas shopping in Miami and meet them there.'

I said, 'Why don't you give them a sea trip? Take *Lucayan Girl* and bring them back by way of Bimini. I'm sure they'd enjoy it.'

She said, 'It's a good idea. Would you come?'

'Afraid not, I'll be too busy. But I'll have a word with Pete; he'll need an extra hand for that trip.'

'Still a good idea,' said Julie meditatively. 'I think I'll take Sue – and Karen, if she's better.'

'Take me where?' Sue had joined us draped in a towel. She helped herself to ice-cream.

'How would you like to go to Miami to meet Grandma and Grandpop? We'd be going in the *Girl*.'

Ice-cream went flying and Sue's squeal of delight was an adequate answer.

After lunch Julie took Sue back to school and Debbie went along because Julie said she would show her the International Bazaar where you can walk from France to China in one stride. When they had gone Billy said, 'How big is your boat?'

'Fifty-two feet. Come and look at her.'

His eyebrows lifted. 'You have her here?'

'Sure. This way.' I led him through the house to the lagoon on the other side where *Lucayan Girl* was moored at the quayside. Pete Albury was on board and when he heard us talking he appeared on deck. 'Come and meet Pete,' I said. 'He's skipper, but sometimes he thinks he's the owner.'

'Tom, I heard that,' called Pete, his face cracking into a seamed black grin. 'But I'll allow you on board anyway.'

We went aboard. 'Pete, this is Billy Cunningham, an old friend from the States.'

Pete stuck out his hand. 'Glad to know you, Mr Cunningham.'

I was watching Billy carefully. He did not know it, but this was a minor test; if he had hesitated, even fractionally, in spite of what he had said I would have been worried because no one who is a nigger-hater, even in a minor way, can get along successfully in the Bahamas. Billy grasped Pete's hand firmly. 'Glad to know you, Mr . . . er . . .'

'Albury,' said Pete. 'But I'm just Pete.'

'I'm Billy.'

I said, 'Julie wants to go to Miami next week to do the Christmas shopping and to pick up her parents. She'll be taking Sue and maybe Karen, and you'll be touching in at Bimini on the way home. Is everything okay for that?'

'Sure,' said Pete. 'Are you comin'?'

'Sorry. I can't make it.'

'Then I'll need a hand. Don't worry; there's always youngsters around the marinas. I'll pick a good one who'll be glad of the ride for a few dollars.'

'That's it, then,' I said.

Billy was looking at the lagoon. 'This is artificial,' he said abruptly.

'I hoped you'd notice.' I pointed. 'The channel out to sea is there – by the Lucayan Beach Hotel. That's where the BASRA Marathon begins.'

'BASRA?' he said interrogatively.

'The Bahamas Air-Sea Rescue Association. The Marathon is run by and for BASRA to raise funds. It's a voluntary organization – a good crowd. If you're coming in here it wouldn't do you any harm to donate a few dollars or offer facilities.'

'Do you do that?'

'Yes. We have the company planes . . .' I broke off and laughed. 'Not big jets like yours, but we have four Piper Navajos – seven-seaters we use to take tourists to the Out Islands, part of our tours division. And they're used on other company business, of course. But if a boat is lost and BASRA wants an air search the planes are available.'

He nodded. 'Good public relations.' He switched his attention back to the lagoon. 'So this has been dredged out?'

'That's it. This lagoon, and others like it, stretches for about three miles up the coast.'

Billy looked at the lagoon and then back at the house. 'Not bad,' he said, 'having a house with a water frontage. And it's protected, too; no big waves.'

'You've got it. Now I'll show you something weird. Let's take a drive.' We said farewell to Pete, left the house, and

I drove about four miles east into Lucaya. 'Notice anything?'

Billy looked around. 'Just trees – and the traffic is light.'

That was an understatement; there was no traffic. I had
not seen a car for the last two miles. But there were many
trees. I pointed. 'That's a street. See the name plate? Now
keep your eyes open.'

I drove on and presently the trees thinned out and we
came on to a plain dotted with mounds of limestone. I said,
'We're coming to the Casuarina Bridge. It crosses the Great
Lucayan Waterway.'

'So?'

'So we're going to cross it.'

'I don't get it,' said Billy.

I said, 'We've been passing streets, all named and paved.
Those poles carry power lines. Now, I don't know how it is
in the States where any wide place in the road can call itself
a city, but to me a road is something that goes from one
place to another, but a street *is* a place, and it usually has
houses on it.'

Billy was momentarily startled. 'Houses!' he said blankly.
'No goddamn houses! Nary a one.'

'That's it. But I've more to show you or, rather, not show
you. We'll get a better view from Dover Sound.' I carried on
driving, following the signposts to Dover Sound and
Observation Hill. It is not really a hill – just a man-made
mound with the road leading up and a turning circle at the
top. I stopped the car and we got out. 'What do you think
of that?'

Billy looked at the view with a lack of comprehension. I
knew why because I had been baffled by the sight when
first I saw it. There was land and there was water and it was
not easy to see where one stopped and the other began. It
was a maze of water channels. Billy shrugged helplessly. 'I
don't know. What am I supposed to think?'

I said, 'Think of my house and the lagoon. This is the Grand Lucayan Waterway – it cuts right across Grand Bahama, nearly eight miles from coast to coast. But it has forty-five miles of water frontage.' I flapped open the map I held. 'Look at this. You can see where the streets and waterways fit together like fingers in a glove.'

Billy studied the map then took out a calculator and began punching buttons. 'At a hundred feet of water frontage to a house that's nearly 2500 houses. Where the hell are they?'

'There's more. Look at the map.' I swept my hand over an area. 'Twenty square miles of land all laid out in paved streets with utilities already installed – the unfleshed skeleton of a city of 50,000 people.'

'So what happened?'

'An election happened. Pindling got in and the investors ran scared. But they're coming back. Take a man who runs his own business in Birmingham, Alabama, or Birmingham, England, come to that. He sells out to a bigger company at, say, the age of fifty-five when he's still young enough to enjoy life and now has the money to indulge himself. He can build his house on the canal and keep his fishing boat handy, or he can take one of the dry land plots. There's sun and sea, swimming and golf, enough to keep a man happy for the rest of his life. And the beauty of it is that the infrastructure already exists; the power station in Freeport is only working to a tenth of its capacity.'

Billy looked over the expanse of land and water. 'You say the investors are coming back. I don't see much sign.'

'Don't be fooled.' I pointed back the way we had come. 'You can see the landscaping has begun – tree planting and flower beds. And that big parking lot, all neatly laid out. It looks a bit silly, but it's probably earmarked for a supermarket. There are houses being built right now, but you don't see them because they're scattered over twenty square miles.

Give this place a few years and we'll have a thriving community. That's one answer to a question you asked – what's the future of the Bahamas?'

He rubbed his jaw. 'Yeah, I see what you mean.'

'Don't take my word for it – look for yourself. I'll lend you a plane and my chief pilot, Bobby Bowen, and you can do some island hopping. Go to Abaco; we have a hotel there – the Abaco Sands at Marsh Harbour. Go on to Eleuthera where we're building a hotel. Have a look at some of the other islands and don't leave out New Providence. I'll give you a list of people you can talk to. Then come back and tell me what you think.'

'Okay,' he said. 'I'll do just that.'

TWO

Billy went on his tour a couple of days later after looking around Grand Bahama, but Debbie stayed on at the Royal Palm. Billy confided in me that he had brought her along in an attempt to cure a fit of the blues; apparently Debbie had been having man trouble – an affair had turned sour. Anyway, she fell into the habit of going to the house and using the pool, and she and the children became friends in jig time. Debbie would pick up the kids from school and take them home and then stay on to lunch with Julie. Julie must have liked her because she put off her trip to Florida until Billy came back.

As for me, I was damned busy. I rousted Jamieson, the chief accountant, who fairly set the computer smoking as we figured the net worth of the company as at the end of that month. I wanted to have all my ammunition ready and dry for Billy when he came back because I had the notion he would be ready to talk turkey.

One evening after Julie had put the girls to bed I told her about Billy's proposition and asked what she thought of it. She was ambivalent. She saw the possibilities for expansion, but on the other hand she said, 'I don't know if it would be good for you – you're too independently minded.'

I knew what she meant. 'I know I like to run my own show and that's my problem – how to extract forty million bucks from the Cunninghams without losing control. I have a few ideas about that and I might be able to swing it.'

She laughed at me. 'I always knew I married a genius. All right, if you can do that then it won't be a bad thing.'

I had to consult my sisters, Peggy and Grace. Both had stock in the West End Securities Corporation, enough for them to have a say in any decision as big as this. Peggy lived on Abaco with her son and daughter and her husband, Bob Fisher, who ran the Abaco Sands Hotel for the corporation. Grace had married an American called Peters and lived in Orlando, Florida, with their three sons. It seemed that the tendency of the Mangans to produce girls was confined to the males. It meant some flying around because this was not something that could be settled on the telephone, but I had written agreements by the time Billy came back.

He returned to Grand Bahama after eight days, having gone through the Bahamas like a whirlwind. He was armed with so many facts, figures and statistics that I wondered how he had assembled them all in the time, but that was like Billy – he was a quick student.

'You were right,' he said. 'The Bahamas have potential, more than I thought. You didn't tell me about the Hotels Encouragement Act.'

I laughed. 'I left you to find out yourself. I knew you would.'

'My God, it's like stumbling across a gold mine.' He ticked the points off on his fingers. 'No customs duty on anything imported to build or equip a hotel; no property taxes for the first ten years; no company taxes for the first twenty years. And that applies to hotels, marinas, golf courses, landscaping – anything you can damn near think of. It's incredible.'

'It's why we're going to have two million tourists next year.'

He grunted. 'I've been thinking about that. I was talking to that tourism guy, Butler. He told me that eighty per cent of your economy and two-thirds of your population are supported by tourism. That's a hell of a lot of eggs in one basket, Tom.' His voice was serious. 'What if something happens like war breaking out?'

Something told me I had better come up with the right answer. I said lightly, 'If World War III breaks out everybody's eggs get broken.'

'I guess you're right at that.'

'Are you ready to talk business yet?'

'No. I'll be speaking to Billy One and Jack today. I'll let you know the decision tomorrow.'

I grinned. 'I promise I won't bug the switchboard. I won't be coming in to the office tomorrow. Julie is leaving for Miami and I like to see them off. Why don't you come to the house and bring Debbie along?'

'I'll do that.'

So Billy and Debbie arrived at the house next morning at about ten o'clock. Debbie joined the girls in the pool and I winked at Julie and took Billy into my study. He said, 'I think we're in business.'

'You may think so, but I'm not so sure. I don't want to lose control.'

He stared at me. 'Oh, come on, Tom! Forty million bucks swings a lot of clout. You don't want us busting in as competitors, do you?'

'I'm not afraid of competition. I have plenty of that, anyway.'

'Well, you can't expect us to put up all that dough and not have control. That's ridiculous. Are you joking or something?'

'I'm not joking,' I said. 'I'm perfectly serious. But I'd like to point out that there are different kinds of control.'

Billy looked at me speculatively. 'Okay, I'll buy it. What's on your mind?'

'I take it you'd be setting up a corporation here.'

'That's right, we would. I've been talking to some of your corporate lawyers over in Nassau and they've come up with some great ideas, even though they'd be illegal back in the States. This sure is a free-wheeling place.'

'Rest easy,' I said. 'As an offshore tax haven we're positively respectable, not like some others I could mention. What would you call your corporation?'

'How would I know? Something innocuous, I guess. Let's call it the Theta Corporation.'

I said, 'I run three hotels with a fourth building for a total of 650 rooms. That's a lot of bed linen, a lot of crockery and cutlery, a lot of kitchenware and ashtrays and anything else you care to name. Now, if the Theta Corporation is going to build and equip hotels it would be better to consolidate and keep the economy of scale. You get bed sheets a damn sight cheaper if you order by the 5000 pair rather than the 500 pair, and that applies right down the line.'

'Sure, I know that.' Billy flapped his hand impatiently. 'Come to the point.'

'What I'm suggesting is that the Theta Corporation take over West End Securities in return for stock.'

'Ha!' he said. 'Now you're saying something. How much stock?'

'One-fifth.'

'We put in $40 million, you put in West End and take a fifth of the stock. That makes it a $50 million corporation, so you estimate West End as being worth $10 million. Is it? What's the book value?'

I said, 'Jamieson and I have been working it out. I put it at $8 million.'

'So you put in $8 million and take stock worth $10 million. What kind of a deal is that? What do we get for the other two million bucks?'

'Me,' I said evenly.

Billy burst out laughing. 'Come on, Tom! Do you really think you're worth that?'

'You're forgetting quite a few things,' I said. 'If you come in here on your own you come in cold. I know you've picked up your facts and statistics and so on, but you don't know the score – you don't know the way things get done here. But if you come in with me you begin with a firm base ready for expansion, eager for expansion. And you don't only get me, but you get my staff, all loyal to me personally. And don't forget the Bahamas for the Bahamians bit. Call it goodwill, call it know-how, call it what you like, but I reckon it's worth two million.'

Billy was silent for a long time, thinking hard. 'Maybe you're right,' he said at last.

I gave him another jolt. 'And I get to be President of the Theta Corporation,' I said calmly.

He nearly choked. 'Jesus, you don't want much! Why don't you just pick my pocket of forty million bucks and have done with it?'

'I told you. I don't want to lose control. Look, Billy; you'll be Chairman and I'll be President – the Cunninghams retain financial control but I have operational control. That's the only way it can work. And I want a five-year contract of service; not a cast iron contract – that fractures too easily – an armour plate contract.'

Billy looked glum, but nodded. 'Billy One might go for it, but I don't know about Jack.' He drummed his fingers on the desk and said cautiously, 'If we take over West End we get everything? Not just the hotels part of it?'

'You get all the trimmings,' I assured him. 'Tours division, car hire fleet, merchandising division – the lot.'

'Before we go any further into this,' he said, 'I'd like to have your ideas about expansion. Have you given it any thought?'

I pushed a folder across the desk. 'There are a few ideas here. Just a beginning.'

He studied the papers I had put together and we discussed them for a while. At last he said, 'You've obviously been thinking hard. I like your idea of a construction division.' He checked the time. 'I need the telephone. Will you give me half an hour? I might have to do some tough talking.'

I pushed the telephone towards him. 'Best of luck.'

I found Julie holding Karen in her arms and looking faintly worried. Karen was sniffling and wailing. 'But I *want* to go!'

'What's the matter?'

'Oh, Karen's not well,' said Julie. 'I don't think she should come with us. That cold in the head has sprung up again and she's got a temperature.'

'It's not *fair*!' cried Karen. 'Sue's going.'

I put out my hand and felt her forehead; Julie was right about the rise in temperature, but it was not much. 'Maybe we should cancel the trip,' said Julie.

'Put her to bed and we'll talk about it.' I looked around. 'Where's Sue?'

'On *Lucayan Girl* helping Pete or, rather, getting in his way. I'll be back soon.' Julie walked into the house carrying Karen who had burst into tears.

I found Debbie relaxing by the pool and dropped into a chair next to her. 'Poor kid,' she said. 'She's so disappointed. How ill is she?'

'Not very. You know how kids are; their temperature goes up and down for no apparent reason. She'll probably be all right in a couple of days. But Julie is thinking of cancelling the trip.'

'I've noticed something about this household,' said Debbie. 'Apart from Julie and the girls there are no women in it. If Julie wants someone to look after Karen I could do that.'

'It's a kindly thought,' I said. 'But if it comes to the push I'll take Karen to the Royal Palm. We have a very efficient and charming young nurse there whom Karen knows very well. I've done it before when Julie has been away.'

'Then talk Julie out of cancelling. It would disappoint Sue so much.'

'I'll do my best.' Presently Julie came out of the house, and I asked, 'How is she?'

'Rebellious.'

'You don't have to cancel the trip. I don't want *two* gloomy kids sulking about the house. Debbie has offered to look after Karen, and there's always Kitty Symonette at the hotel.'

'Thanks, Debbie. That's good of you.' Julie thought for a moment. 'Very well – we'll go.' She looked at Debbie. 'Don't let Karen play you up; that little minx is full of tricks.'

I stood up. 'If everything's aboard I'll come and see you off.'

Just then Billy came striding out of the house and beckoned me with a jerk of his head. He said, 'There'll be a squad of lawyers and auditors flying in to look at your books. If everything checks we have a deal.' He laughed and put out his hand.

So it was with a light heart that I saw Julie and Sue away on *Lucayan Girl*. I told Julie about the deal and she was delighted, and then we went out to the lagoon where the *Girl* was ready to cast off, her engines already ticking over. Sue was running about taking photographs with the camera I had given her for her birthday; her teacher had set her the exercise of a photo-essay as her homework for the Christmas vacation. By the look of her both she and her stock of film would be exhausted before the voyage began.

I had a word with Pete who was coiling a rope in the bows. 'Got a crewman?'

'Sure.'

'How is he?'

'He'll do,' said Pete laconically. Knowing Pete that meant the young fellow was pretty good.

'Where is he?'

'Below – greasing the shafts.' Pete raised his voice. 'All right, then; all aboard that's goin' aboard.'

Sue scampered aboard and Julie kissed me and followed more sedately. 'Cast off the after line, Miss Mate,' said Pete. He cast off the forward line and quickly went to the helm on the flying bridge. The engines growled and *Lucayan Girl* moved slowly away.

We watched as the *Girl* went down the lagoon and turned into the channel which led to the open sea and so out of sight. I said to Billy, 'I think we have work to do.' I stooped to pick up Sue's camera which she had left on a chair. 'Sue will be mad enough to bust. When Julie rings tonight I'll tell her to buy another. We mustn't disappoint teacher.'

THREE

It was late in the day when it went bad – an hour from midnight. Billy and I had worked late, sorting out the details of the proposed merger and outlining future plans, and were having a final drink before he went back to the Royal Palm. Suddenly he broke off what he was saying in mid-sentence. 'What's the matter? You got ants in your pants? That's the third time you've checked your watch in five minutes. I hope I'm not that unwelcome.'

'Julie hasn't telephoned,' I said shortly. 'That's not like her.'

I picked up the telephone and rang the Fontainbleu in Miami where she usually stayed. The call took an annoyingly long time to place and Billy occupied himself with shuffling his papers together and putting them into his briefcase. Finally I got through and said, 'I'd like to speak to Mrs Mangan.'

There was a pause. 'Do you know the room number, sir?'

'No.'

Another pause. 'There's no one of that name in the hotel, sir.'

'Put me through to the desk clerk, please.' Again that took a bit of time but I finally got him. I said, 'My name is Mangan. Has my wife checked in yet?'

A rustle of papers. 'No, sir.'

'But she did make a reservation?'

'Yes, sir; two rooms. Mrs Mangan and Miss Mangan, and Mr and Mrs Pascoe.'

'Have the Pascoes checked in?'

'No, sir.'

'Thank you.' I put down the telephone and said blankly, 'She's not there.'

'What time was she supposed to get into Miami?' asked Billy.

'Before dark; say, eight o'clock. Pete has standing instructions from me to get into port in daylight if possible, especially with the family aboard. She's a fast boat for her type and he'd have no trouble about that.'

'She's only three hours overdue, Tom. Anything could have happened. Engine trouble, perhaps.'

'Boats with Pete aboard don't have engine trouble,' I said sharply. 'Besides, the *Girl* has two engines.'

'If one was knocked out it would slow her down.'

'Not by a lot – not by three hours.' I picked up the telephone again. 'I'll ring the marina in Miami.' Ten minutes later I knew that *Lucayan Girl* had not arrived. I said to Billy, 'I've got a feeling about this. I'm going over to BASRA – they can raise the US Coast Guard.'

'How long will you be?'

'Fifteen – twenty minutes. It's quite close.'

'I'll stick around until you get back. Julie might ring.'

'Thanks. I'll check that Karen's safely asleep before I go.'

BASRA headquarters on Grand Bahama are in the building which also holds the Underwater Exploration Society. Five minutes later I was climbing the stairs to the Tide's Inn, a tavern which supports both the Society and BASRA. The place was noisy with vacationers and I found Joe Kimble of BASRA employed in his favourite occupation – chatting up a couple of nubile females. I crossed to his table. 'Sorry to interrupt, Joe, but *Lucayan Girl* is overdue in Miami.'

He looked up. 'How much overdue?'

'Over three hours now.' I met his eye. 'Julie and Sue are aboard.'

'Oh!' He stood up. 'Sorry, girls, but business comes first.'

We went down to the BASRA office and I said, 'What's the weather like in the Florida Straits?'

'Calm – no problems there.' He sat behind a desk and took a pen. 'When did she leave?'

'Dead on eleven this morning.'

'Give me the number of the marina in Miami.' He scribbled it down, then said, 'You'd better go home, Tom, and stick by your telephone. But don't use it. I'll do any telephoning that's necessary – you keep an open line. I'll ring the marina and tell them to notify BASRA if she comes in.'

'What about the Coast Guard?'

'I'll radio them but there's not much they can do at night – you know that.'

'Can I use the phone here?' At Joe's nod I picked it up and rang Bobby Bowen at his home. I outlined the situation, then said, 'There may be nothing in it, but if there's no report in the next few hours I'll need planes in the air at first light. How many can we raise?'

'Just two here,' said Bowen. 'There's one in Nassau and the other has its engine stripped for the 300-hour check.'

'Get that plane back from Nassau as fast as you can. You'll liaise with Joe Kimble of BASRA who will be coordinator. Unless the order is cancelled you'll rendezvous at . . .' I twitched an eyebrow at Joe who said, 'Lucayan Beach Air Services.'

I passed that on, and added, '. . . at five-thirty a.m.' I put down the phone. 'I'm going home, Joe. Julie might ring.'

He nodded. 'If I'm going to fly tomorrow I'll need some shuteye. I'll get one of the groundlings to stand by here as soon as I've raised the Coast Guard.'

I had an argument with Billy which he won. 'I'll stay by the telephone,' he said. 'You've got to sleep. If anything comes through I'll wake you.' He raided the kitchen and made me warm milk laced with brandy. Afterwards he told me that he had roused Luke Bailey who found Julie's sleeping pills and he dissolved one into the milk.

So it was that when he woke me at five in the morning I felt doped and muzzy. At first I did not know what he was doing there in my bedroom, but then the knowledge hit me. 'Any news?' I demanded.

He shook his head. 'Just a call from BASRA; the Coast Guard are putting helicopters out of Miami as soon as it's light enough to see.'

I got up and found Debbie in the living-room; Billy had rung her and she had immediately come from the hotel. None of us did much talking because there was nothing much to say, but Debbie insisted that she was going to stay to look after Karen. Luke Bailey made an early breakfast and I drove to the airport feeling like hell.

Joe Kimble was in the office of Lucayan Beach Air Services, allocating areas on a map. Bobby Bowen was there, and Bill Pinder, another Corporation pilot, and there were three other pilots, volunteers from BASRA. Joe said, 'Now, remember we're tying in with the US Coast Guard on this. Stick to your own areas and watch your altitude. And watch for the choppers – we don't want a mid-air collision to complicate things.'

We walked out to the tie-down lines and the sky was just lightening in the east as we took off. I flew with Bobby Bowen and, as we flew west and gained altitude, the panorama in the rising sun was achingly beautiful.

Lucayan Girl was of a type which the Americans call a trawler. Because of recurrent oil crises a demand has arisen for a boat, not particularly fast, but with range and sea-keeping qualities, and light on fuel. These boats, no matter who the designer, all look pretty much alike because they were all trying to solve the same problems and inevitably came up with the same results. And our problem was that in Florida and Bahamian waters they are as thick as fleas on a dog.

Not many people make night passages in power boats in the Islands but we spotted our first twenty miles out and heading our way. We were flying at 2500 feet, adhering strictly to regulations for the course we were on, and Bowen dropped us 1000 feet, again going by the book. I looked at the boat through glasses as we went by and shook my head. Bowen took us up again.

It was a long and futile search. We found six boats but not *Lucayan Girl.* From the intermittent chatter on the radio no one else was having any luck either. Visibility so early in the morning was generally good but, as the sun rose, cloud began to form. Presently Bowen said, 'Got to go back.' He tapped the fuel gauge.

So we went back, the engine coughing as we landed, and found that all the others had already returned. No one had seen the *Girl* and neither had the US Coast Guard. Joe Kimble reamed out Bobby Bowen. 'You cut that too damn fine.'

Bowen managed a tired smile. 'No problem; I emptied my cigarette lighter into the tank.'

'I sure as hell don't want to go out there looking for plane wreckage because some damn fool has run out of gas. Don't do it again.'

I said, 'Refuel, Bobby.'

One of the BASRA pilots stirred. 'I'll take you out again, Mr Mangan. I'm fuelled up.'

So I went out again. They all went out again. They were a good crowd. And we all came back, but not *Lucayan Girl*.

The next few days were grim. People pussyfooted around me, not knowing what to do or say, and work went to hell. I felt as numb as though I had been mentally anaesthetized and I suppose I acted like a zombie, one of the walking dead. I wished I was dead.

Billy said, 'This is no time to talk business, Tom. Let me know when we can get together again.' He went back to Houston, but Debbie refused to go home and stayed on to look after Karen. I was in no mood to argue.

Looking back I can see that this was worse than a normal death in the family. There was no funeral, no assuaging ceremonial – nothing to do. There was the ever-present expectation of a telephone call which would magically solve everything and restore my wife and daughter to me and bring back my old friend, Pete Albury. I jerked every time a phone rang – anywhere.

The house was haunted. Although the pool was mirror-like in its quietness there was still held in the mind's eye the image of a lithe young body, sleek as an otter, breaking the surface with a shout of joy, and I expected, on turning a corner, to find at any moment the dark beauty of Julie, perhaps going about some domestic chore like watering the roses.

I suppose I was a haunted man.

Debbie was very good. At first she sought to cheer me up, but I was impervious so she desisted and contented herself with acting as a barrier between me and the world of the newspapers. And she saw that I ate regularly and did not drink too much or, at least, drink alone. She need not have worried about that; I have never considered that diving into a bottle could solve any problems.

She looked after Karen and played with her and stopped my little daughter from worrying me too much in those awful first days. Once I overheard Karen say to her, 'What's wrong with Daddy?'

'Your father has some problems,' said Debbie. 'Don't bother him now – he'll be all right soon.'

Karen had not been told, but sooner or later I would have to tell her that her mother and sister were dead. I wondered if the idea of death would mean much to a nine-year-old. I sweated at the thought of telling her.

And then there were Julie's parents, Mike and Ellen Pascoe. I did not know how to contact them because they were on the move, driving from Maryland to Miami where they expected to meet Julie at the Fontainbleu. I left a message at the Fontainbleu asking that they ring me immediately on arrival.

The call came two days later and Ellen was on the line. 'Julie isn't here,' she said. 'Has she been held up?'

'Can I speak to Mike?'

'Of course.' Her voice sharpened. 'Is anything wrong, Tom?'

'Just let me talk to Mike for a moment.' Mike came on and I told him what had happened, and I heard his breath hiss in my ear.

He said, 'Is there no . . . hope?'

'Oh, God! Hope is the only thing that's been keeping me going. But it's been nearly three days, and every hour that goes by . . . Look, I'll send a plane for you. It'll be there this afternoon. Just wait at the hotel for Bobby Bowen. Okay?'

'All right,' he said heavily.

Half an hour after that telephone call Debbie came into my study. 'There are two men to see you. Policemen.'

I jerked around. 'With news?' She shook her head sadly and I sighed. 'All right; show them in.'

Debbie led them into the study and then left. I stood up and looked at Perigord in some perplexity. Deputy-Commissioner Perigord, a black Bahamian, was the top-ranking police officer on Grand Bahama and I knew him slightly, having met him at social functions. His companion was also black but unknown to me. Both were in uniform.

Perigord said, 'I'm sorry to have to intrude at this time, Mr Mangan; I assure you I wish it were otherwise. I put it off for as long as possible but . . .' He shrugged.

'I know,' I said. 'Won't you sit down?'

He took off his uniform cap and laid it on my desk together with his swagger stick. 'This is Inspector Hepburn.'

I nodded in acknowledgement and sat down. Perigord said, 'I knew Mrs Mangan slightly; we met at PTA meetings – our daughters attend the same school. If there is anything my wife and I can do to help then please call on us. However, I am here on a different errand. You must know that in circumstances like this there are questions to be asked.'

'Yes,' I said. 'Just get on with it.'

He took out a notebook. 'The name of your boat is *Lucayan Girl?*'

'Yes.'

'Where did she sail from?'

'Here.' I pointed through the window towards the atrium. 'Her mooring is just through that archway.'

'Would you mind if Inspector Hepburn looks at the mooring?'

'No – but what does he expect to find?'

'I don't know. Police work consists of looking at a lot of things, most of which turn out to be useless in the end. But sometimes we get lucky.' He nodded to Hepburn who got up and left the room.

'I don't see how the police come into it.' I saw Hepburn walk by the pool and disappear through the arch.

'There is more to police work than crime; we fulfil many social functions. Were you present when *Lucayan Girl* sailed?'

'Yes.'

'Who was on board?'

'Julie, my wife; my daughter, Susan; Pete Albury, the skipper; and a crewman.'

'What is the crewman's name?'

'I don't know.'

Perigord frowned. 'You don't know!' he said with a tinge of perplexity in his voice.

'Pete Albury hired him. I didn't want my wife and daughter to sail with only Pete aboard so I asked Pete to hire a hand just for this trip.'

'I see. But if you hired him you were obviously going to pay him. Was it to be by cash or cheque?'

'I don't know,' I said to Perigord's obvious bafflement. As he made a disapproving clicking sound with his tongue I said, 'That was Pete's business. He ran *Lucayan Girl;* he had a bank account from which to draw funds, and I checked the account monthly. He'd have paid, but whether in cash or by cheque I wouldn't know.'

'You must have trusted Mr Albury,' said Perigord.

'I did,' I said evenly.

'Now, then; what did this man – this crewman – look like?'

'I don't know; I didn't see him.'

Perigord definitely lost his composure. 'You mean you hired a man you didn't even *see*!'

'I didn't hire him,' I said. 'Pete did. I had every confidence in Pete to pick a good man. Look, I run a business. I don't hire personally everyone who works for me, neither do I necessarily know them by name or sight. That's known as delegation of authority.'

'And so you bring your business practices into your household.'

'I trusted Pete,' I said stubbornly.

'How do you know that this . . . this stranger was on board when the boat sailed?'

'Pete told me. I asked him and he said the crewman was below greasing the shafts.'

'But you don't know it of your own knowledge.'

'I can't say that I do.'

Perigord pondered for a moment, then asked, 'Is there anyone else to whom I can refer who would know it from his own knowledge?'

I thought about that, casting my mind back to the scene by the lagoon. Billy, Debbie and I had walked through the archway together and if I had not seen the crewman then neither could they. I shook my head. 'No, I don't think so.'

Inspector Hepburn came back and Perigord glanced at him. 'So what it comes to is this – we have a man, probably dead, whose name we don't know and whom we can't describe. We don't even know his colour. In fact, Mr Mangan, we might even be wrong about the sex – this crew member *could* be a woman for all we know.'

'No,' I said definitely. 'I asked Pete about him, and Pete said, "*He*'ll do."'

'Well, that's something,' said Perigord. 'Where does Mr Albury live?'

'Here,' I said. 'There are some work rooms and store rooms for ship's chandlery with an apartment over. Pete moved in here when his wife died last year.'

'There may be something in the apartment to give us a lead. Do you mind if Inspector Hepburn looks?'

'Of course not.' I opened the wall safe and took out the key to Pete's rooms and gave it to Hepburn, then rang for Luke who appeared with suspicious alacrity. 'Show the Inspector where Pete's rooms are.'

They left and I turned to Perigord. 'There's something here which may possibly be useful.' I took a small book from the safe. 'I record the serial numbers of any important equipment I own, and there's a section for *Lucayan Girl* in here – her engine numbers, radar, radio and so on. Even the binoculars and the cameras we routinely carry aboard.'

'Ah, that's better!' Perigord took the book and flicked through it. 'And the numbers carried on certain documents, I see. Is the boat insured?'

'Of course.'

'And you, Mr Mangan; do you carry life insurance?'

'Certainly.'

'And Mrs Mangan? Was her life insured?'

I stared at him. 'I'm a rich enough man not to want to benefit by my wife's death. What the hell are you getting at?'

He held up his hand in a conciliatory gesture. 'I'm sorry; in my work we are forced to intrude at inopportune moments with questions which may be construed as tactless – tactless but necessary. I did not wish to offend, sir.'

'I'm sorry,' I said. 'I'm under a bit of strain. No apology is necessary.'

There were more questions, the answers to most of which appeared to satisfy him, and presently Hepburn came back and Perigord picked up his cap and swagger stick. 'That will be all for now, sir. There'll be an enquiry; I'll let you know where and when it will be held. May I offer my profound sorrow and my . . . condolences. I did like Mrs Mangan.'

'Condolences!' I said in a choked voice.

'It *has* been two and a half days,' said Perigord gravely.

I took a grip on myself. 'Commissioner, what do you think happened?'

'I doubt if we'll ever know. Perhaps a gas leak in the bilges leading to an explosion – that's rather common. Or the boat could have been run down by a supertanker.'

'In daylight!'

'We don't know that it was daylight,' he pointed out, and shrugged. 'And those ships are so big they could run down a moderately small craft and no one would feel a thing. A ship carrying 300,000 tons of oil has a lot of momentum. We'll do our best to find out what happened, but I offer no certainties.' With that he and Hepburn left.

He had not been gone two minutes when Luke Bailey came in wearing a worried frown. 'I'd like to tell you something.' He jerked his head at the door. 'That policeman . . .'

'Who – Perigord?'

'No, the other one – the Inspector. He's on the Narcotics Squad. I thought you'd like to know.'

FOUR

That evening I had to cope with the Pascoes who, oddly enough, were more philosophical about it than I was. I was in a cold, helpless, miserable rage; wanting to strike out at something but finding nothing to hit – no target. The Pascoes were more equable. Nearing the end of their own days I suppose that death was a not unexpected figure lurking over the horizon, something with which they had come to terms on a personal level. Besides, Mike was a doctor and death had been a factor in his professional life. They did their best to comfort me.

I had a long talk with Mike after Ellen had gone to bed. 'I know how you feel,' he said. 'I lost a boy – killed in Vietnam. Did Julie ever tell you about that?' I nodded. 'It hit me hard. Allen was a good boy.' He wagged his head sagely. 'But it wears off, Tom; you can't grieve for ever.'

'I suppose so,' I said moodily. Deep in my heart I knew he was wrong; I would grieve for Julie and Sue for the rest of my life.

'What are you going to do now?' he asked.

'I don't know.'

'For God's sake, wake up! You can't just let everything slide. You're running a corporation and you have folk depending on you. You're still a young man, too. How old? Forty what?'

'Forty-two.'

'You can get married again,' he said.

'Let's not talk about that now,' I said sharply. 'Julie's not been gone three days. And maybe . . .'

'Maybe she'll come back? Don't set your heart on that, Tom, or you'll drive yourself nuts.' I said nothing to that and there was a long silence. After a while Mike stirred. 'What are you going to do about Karen?'

'I haven't thought about it yet.'

'Then you'd better put your mind to it. Debbie Cunningham's a good girl from what I've seen of her, but she won't be around for ever. You'll have to make some arrangements. Bringing up a daughter aged nine *and* running a corporation could be a mite tough – tough on Karen, I mean.'

'I'll get a woman in to look after her, I suppose.'

'Humph!' Evidently he did not think much of that idea. I did not think much of it myself. He said, 'Ellen and I have been talking. We'd like to take Karen until you've got things settled in your mind.'

'That's generous of you.'

'No; just plain horse sense. Karen should be with her own kin.' He smiled slowly. 'But I thought I'd gotten past the age of child-raising.'

'I agree,' I said. 'I had a call from my sister, Peggy, this morning. She wants to take Karen to Abaco, at least until I get settled and can make other arrangements. She has two kids of her own, and that might be better for Karen.'

Mike looked a shade relieved. 'It would be better,' he said positively. 'Children brought up by old folk sometimes turn out funny. You're starting to think, Tom.'

We talked about it some more and then I changed the subject. 'There's something I can't understand. I don't see why Perigord should be conducting this investigation personally. He's a Deputy-Commissioner, the top cop on the island. I shouldn't have thought this would warrant it.'

'You're running yourself down,' said Mike. 'You're a prominent citizen on Grand Bahama. And you say he knew Julie?'

'So he says. He says he met her at the school, at PTA meetings. I didn't go to many of those.'

'Maybe he feels he has a personal obligation.'

'Perhaps. But then there's Hepburn. Luke Bailey tells me Hepburn is a narcotics officer, and he did give Pete's rooms a good shakedown. There's something behind all this, Mike.'

'Imagination!' he scoffed. 'Probably Hepburn was the only officer handy in the precinct house at the time.' He got up and stretched. 'I'm going to bed; I'm not as young as I was.' He looked down at me. 'Tom, I've been a doctor all my life until I retired three years ago. I've seen a lot of people die and a lot of grief in families. Tell me; have you shed one single tear since Julie went?'

'No,' I said flatly.

He walked to the corner cupboard, poured four fingers of brandy into a glass, and brought it back to me. 'Drink that, relax, and let yourself go. There's no fault in a man crying, and bottling it up can harm you.' He turned and walked out of the room.

Mike was a kindly man and a good man. He had once said that being a doctor made a man a fair jackleg psychologist and he was right about this. I sat for a long time holding the glass and just looking into its brown depths. Then I swallowed the lot in two long gulps. The brandy burned going down and I gasped. Fifteen minutes later I was sprawled on the settee and crying my heart out. I cried myself to sleep and awoke in the early hours of the morning when I went to bed after turning out the lights.

It was acceptance that Julie and Sue were dead; and Pete and an unknown man. The acceptance brought a curious

kind of peace; I still felt numbed in my mind, but I felt better and was a functioning man. Mike had known what he
was doing.

Four days later I took Karen to Abaco, and Debbie came
with us. It was then, in the presence of Peggy and Bob, that
I told Karen that her mother and sister were dead and that
she would be staying with her aunt and uncle for a while.
She looked at me, wide-eyed, and said, 'They won't be coming home? Ever?'

'I'm afraid not. You remember when Timmy died?'
Timmy was a pet kitten who had been run over by a car,
and Karen nodded. 'Well, it's something like that.'

Tears welled in her eyes and she blinked them away.
'Timmy didn't come back,' she agreed. 'Does that mean I
won't see Mommy and Susie – not ever?' Suddenly she bust
loose. She burst into tears and tore herself away. 'I don't
believe you,' she cried, and began to wail, 'I want my
Mommy. I want my Mommy.'

Peggy caught her up in her arms and comforted her, then
said over her shoulder to me, 'I think a mild sedative and
bed is the best thing now.' She took Karen away.

Bob said awkwardly, 'It's hard to know what to say.'

'I know – but the world goes round as usual. It'll take me
a bit of time to get used to this, but I'll pull through. Where's
Debbie?'

'On the patio.'

I looked at my watch. 'We'll have to get back; the plane
is needed. I'll come across as often as I can – at least once a
week.'

Debbie and I did not talk much at first on the flight back to
Grand Bahama; both of us were immersed in our private
thoughts. It was a long time before I said, 'I suppose you'll
be going back to Houston.'

'Yes,' she said colourlessly. Presently she said, 'And I thought I had troubles.'

'What happened?'

She laughed shortly. 'Would you want to know?'

'Why not? We can cry on each other's shoulder.'

'A man happened – or I thought he was a man. I thought he loved me, but he really loved my money. I happened to pick up a telephone at the wrong time and I heard a really interesting conversation about the big deals he was going to make and the life he was going to lead as soon as he'd married me. The trouble was that he was talking to another woman, and she was included in his plans.'

'That's bad,' I said.

'I was a damned fool,' she said. 'You see, I'd been warned. Billy was against it all along because he didn't trust the guy and he made that very clear. But would I listen? Not me. I was grown up – a woman of the world – and I knew it all.'

'How old are you, Debbie?'

'The ripe old age of twenty-five.'

'I had my fingers burned, too, when I was your age,' I said. 'That was before I met Julie. You'll get over it.'

'You think so? But, God, it's taught me something and I don't think I like what it's taught me. Here I am – a poor little rich girl – and from now to eternity I'll be looking at every guy I meet and wondering if he wants me or all that lovely dough. That's no way to have to go through life.'

'Other rich people cope,' I said.

'Yes?' she said challengingly. 'Examined the divorce statistics lately?'

Her voice was bitter and I could see that she had been badly hurt. And coming to Grand Bahama and seeing how happily Julie and I were married could not have helped much. Presently she said quietly, 'But you don't want to be burdened with my problems even though you do seem to have got over the worst of your blues. Was it the talk you had with Mike Pascoe the other day?'

'Yes,' I said. 'He dutch-uncled me, and it helped. It could help you.'

'All right, Tom,' she said. 'What would you do if you were me? I know you can't possibly put yourself in my position, but I've told you enough to know about me. I'd like your advice. You know, Billy thinks a lot of you and I respect Billy's judgement – now.'

I scratched the angle of my jaw and thought about it. 'Well, I wouldn't get rid of your money, if that's what you're thinking about. It's too useful; you can do a lot of good if you have enough dollars.'

'Buying my way out?'

'Not exactly. Are you thinking of being a missionary in Calcutta or something like that?'

Her laugh was rueful. 'You know more about me than I thought.'

'Forget it,' I said. 'It doesn't work. Besides, charity begins at home. Now, you're a Texan. I'll bet there are poor black kids in Texas who have never even seen the sea.'

'That's a thought. What are you getting at?'

'I'm working it out,' I said slowly. 'Starting from the fact that we're in the Bahamas with plenty of black faces around. Your black Texan kids wouldn't stand out if you brought them here, and we've no colour bar to speak of. Teach them to swim, scuba-dive, sail a boat – things they've only been able to dream about back home. If you brought them out of season I could give you cheap rates in the hotels. They could go to Abaco and Eleuthera; real desert island stuff.'

'My God!' she said. 'What a marvellous idea. And there are poor white kids, too.'

'All right, mix 'em up.' I saw she was caught up in enthusiasm, and warned, 'But you'll have to do more than pay for it, Deb, if it's going to work – I mean for you personally. You'll have to participate and bring the kids yourself, with perhaps a couple of assistants. It's something to think about.'

'It surely is.'

My eye was caught by Bill Pinder, the pilot, who was waving at me. I leaned forward and took the piece of paper he held. It was a message that had been radioed through Freeport air control and told me that Perigord wanted to see me urgently in his office.

I took Debbie along to the police station which was on the corner of Pioneer's Way and East Mall. I suppose I could have driven her to the Royal Palm and then gone back, but there was something about Perigord's message which made me want to see him fast, so I asked Debbie if she minded stopping off. It was a hot day and I did not want to leave her sitting in the car so I took her inside with me.

I happened to catch Perigord walking through the entrance hall so I introduced them, and added, 'Miss Cunningham and her brother were present when *Lucayan Girl* left for Miami.'

Perigord looked at her thoughtfully. 'You'd better come into my office – both of you,' he said abruptly, and led the way. In his office he turned to Debbie and asked without preamble, 'Are you a good friend of Mr Mangan?'

She was startled and shot me a swift look. 'I would say so.'

I said, 'I haven't known Miss Cunningham long but I would certainly consider her my friend. Her cousin and I have been friends for many years.'

For a moment Perigord looked undecided, then he waved at a chair. 'Please sit down.' He sat opposite us and said, 'I am not certain that Miss Cunningham should be here at this point, but you might need some support from a friend.'

'You've found them,' I said with certainty.

He took a deep breath. 'A fisherman found the body of a small, female child on a beach on Cat Island.'

'Cat Island!' I said incredulously. 'But that's impossible! *Lucayan Girl* was going south-west to Miami – Cat Island is 200 miles south-east. It *can't* be Sue!'

'I'm sorry, Mr Mangan, but there is no doubt.'

'I don't believe it. I want to see her.'

'I would advise against it.' Perigord shook his head. 'You wouldn't recognize her.'

'Why not?'

Perigord was unhappy. 'I don't have to explain to a fellow Bahamian what happens to a body in our seas in a very short time.'

'If I wouldn't recognize her how in hell can *you* be so sure?' I was becoming angry at the impossibility of all this. 'How could Sue have got to Cat Island?'

Perigord took a card from his desk drawer and laid it flat. 'This is your daughter's dental record; we obtained it from the school. Dr Miller, your daughter's dentist, has done a comparison and it fits in every respect. We took no chances; we had another evaluation from a dentist who does not know your daughter. He confirmed Dr Miller's identification.'

I suddenly felt sick and a little dizzy. It must have shown in my colour because Debbie put her hand on my arm. 'Are you all right, Tom?'

'Yes,' I said thickly. I raised my head and looked at Perigord. 'And Julie? And the others?'

'Nothing, I'm afraid.' He cleared his throat. 'There'll be an inquest, of course.'

'How do you explain Cat Island? You know it's bloody impossible. Anything abandoned in the Florida Straits would be swept north-east in the Gulf Stream.'

'I can't explain it; at least, not to your satisfaction.' He held up his hand as I opened my mouth. 'It might help if you could identify the crewman.'

I said dully, 'I didn't see him.'

Perigord said, 'We have asked questions at the marinas with no luck at all. The trouble is that the marinas have, literally, a floating population.' He repeated that, appreciating the double edge. 'Yes, a floating population – here today and gone tomorrow. Nobody has been reported missing because everybody is missing, sooner or later. It makes police work difficult. We have also checked from the other end by asking Mr Albury's friends if he had been seen talking to a stranger. Again, no luck.'

Debbie said, 'He might not have been a stranger.'

'Oh, yes, I think he was,' said Perigord confidently. 'I think he was a beach bum, one of the young Americans who hitchhike around the islands on the cheap and are willing to crew for anyone if it gives them a leg further. I think this one was going home.'

'Then he might be on an American missing persons list,' she remarked.

'Why should he be?' asked Perigord. 'He's only been gone a week, and he's probably a footloose young man, a social drop-out. In any case, in which American city do we ask? And with no name and no face how do we operate?'

My brain started to work creakily. Perigord had said something which aroused my ire. 'You said you couldn't explain how Sue came to be on Cat Island *to my satisfaction*. Does that mean that you are satisfied?' I was becoming enraged at Perigord because I knew he was holding something back.

That got to him. 'By God, Mr Mangan, I am not satisfied. It gives me no satisfaction to sit here and pass on bad news, sir.'

'Then what's all the bloody mystery? Is it because I am a suspect? If I am then say so. Am I to be accused of blowing up my own boat?'

My voice had risen to a shout and I found myself shaking. Again Debbie held my arm, and said, 'Take it easy, Tom.'

'Take it easy? There's been something damn funny going on right from the start.' I stabbed a finger at Perigord. 'No one can tell me that a Deputy-Commissioner of Police does his own legwork when a boat goes missing. Especially when he brings a narcotics officer with him. Perigord, I'm well-known in Government circles, and if you don't come across I'll be over in Nassau talking to Deane, your boss, and a few other people and you won't know what hit you.'

Perigord made a curious gesture as though to brush away an irritating fly. 'I assure you that the police are treating this with the utmost seriousness. Further, the Government is serious. And alarmed, I might add. The Attorney General, acting under direct instruction from the Prime Minister, is putting very heavy pressure on me – as much as I can stand – and I don't need any more from you.'

'But you'll damn well get it,' I said. 'Good Christ, this is my family we're talking about!'

He stopped being impervious and his voice softened. 'I know – I know.' He stood up and went to the window, looking out on to East Mall in silence and with his hands clasped tightly behind his back. He stood there for a long time evidently having difficulty in making up his mind about something.

Presently he turned and said quietly, 'I suppose if I were in your position I would feel and act as you do. That's why I'm going to tell you something of what is happening in the Bahamas. But I'll want your discretion. I don't want you going off half-cocked and, above all, I want your silence. You must not talk about what I'm about to tell you.'

Debbie rose to her feet. 'I'll leave.'

'No,' said Perigord. 'Stay, Miss Cunningham.' He smiled. 'Mr Mangan will want to talk to someone about this; he wouldn't be human if he didn't, and his confidante might as well be you. But I'll need the same assurance of your silence.'

Debbie said, 'You have it.'

'Mr Mangan?'

I thought Perigord was every bit as good an amateur psychologist as Mike Pascoe. 'All right.'

He returned to his seat at the desk. 'It is not normal for a well-found boat to vanish in a calm sea, and the enquiries made before I took over the case gave us the assurance that *Lucayan Girl* was a very well-found boat with more than the usual complement of safety equipment. She was very well-equipped, is that not so?'

'I made it so,' I said.

Perigord examined the backs of his hands. 'There have been too many boats going missing these past few years. There has been much ill-informed and mischievous talk about the so-called Bermuda Triangle of which we are in the centre. The Bahamian Government, however, does not believe in spooks – neither do the insurance companies. The Government is becoming most worried about it.'

'Are you talking about piracy?' said Debbie unbelievingly.

'Just that.'

I had heard the rumours, as I suppose every other Bahamian had, and it had been a topic in some of the American yachting magazines. I said, 'I know there was piracy around here in the old days, but these boats aren't treasure ships – they're not carrying gold to Spain. I suppose you could sell off bits and pieces – radar, radio, engines, perhaps – but that's chicken feed, and dangerous, too. Easy to detect.'

'You're right. Your boat is probably on the sea bed by now, with all its equipment intact. These people are not going to risk selling a few items for a few dollars.

Mr Mangan, I think we're dealing with coke smugglers, and I don't mean Coca-Cola – I mean cocaine. It comes through here from South America and goes to the States. Some heroin, too, but not much because we're not on that route. Some marijuana, also, but again not much because it's too bulky.'

He nodded and gestured towards the large map of the Bahamas on the wall. 'Look at that – 100,000 square miles of which only five per cent is land. If the land were conveniently in one place our task would be easier, but there are thousands of cays. An area the size of the British Isles with a population of 220,000. That's what we have to police.'

He walked over to the map. 'Take only one small group.' His arm slashed in an arc. 'The Ragged Island Range and the Jumentos Cays – 120 miles long with a total population of 200, mostly concentrated in Duncan Town in the south. Anyone could bring a boat in there with a nine nines certainty of not being seen even in daylight. They could land on Flamingo Cay, Water Cay, Stoney Cay – or any one of a hundred others, most of which don't even have names. And that's just one small chain of islands among many. We could turn our whole population into police officers and still not have enough men to cover.'

Debbie said, 'How does piracy come into this?'

'It's not called piracy any more, although it is,' said Perigord tiredly. 'It's become prevalent enough to have aquired its own name – yacht-jacking. They grab a boat and sail it out of the local area, fast. A quick paint spray job of the upperworks takes care of easy identification. They head for the cay where the cocaine is hidden and then run it to the States. Once the cocaine is ashore they usually sink the boat; sometimes they may use it for a second run, but not often. And you know how many we've caught?' He held up a single finger.

'And for that they murder the crew?' I demanded.

'Do you know what the profits are, Mr Mangan? But normally the boats are stolen from a marina and there are no deaths. That's easy enough considering the informality of most boat owners and the laxity of the average marina.'

'*Lucayan Girl* wasn't stolen from a marina.'

Perigord said deliberately, 'When a man like you sends his wife and small daughter to sea with a crewman he has never seen and whose name he doesn't know he's asking for trouble.'

He had not come right out and said it, but he was implying that I was a damn fool and I was inclined to agree with him. I said weakly, 'But who could have known?'

Perigord sighed. 'We hand out circulars, put posters in marinas – watch your boat – know your crew – use your keys – and no one apparently takes a damn bit of notice.' He paused. 'I wouldn't say that the case of *Lucayan Girl* is the norm. Boats *are* lost at sea for other than criminal reasons; storm damage, fire, explosions, run down, and so on. But if they're taken by piracy and then sunk who's to know the difference? That's our problem; we don't *know* how many acts of piracy are occurring. All we know is that too many boats are being lost.'

Debbie said, 'Are you implying that the crewman on *Lucayan Girl* might be alive?'

Perigord spread his hands. 'Miss Cunningham, if this is a simple matter of sinking, which we can't discount, then he's probably dead. If it is piracy, which is more than likely because of what we found on Cat Island, then he is probably alive. And that's why I want your silence. If he's still here I don't want him to know he's being looked for.' He pursed his lips in a dubious manner. 'But without a name or description he's going to be difficult to find.'

I said, 'Commissioner, find the bastard. If it's a matter of a reward to be offered I'll put it up, no matter how much.'

'I mentioned discretion,' said Perigord softly. 'Offering a public reward is hardly being discreet.' He clasped his hands in front of him. 'This is a professional matter, Mr Mangan; a matter for the police. I don't want you butting in, and you did give me your word.'

'He's right, Tom,' said Debbie.

'I know.' I stood up and said to Perigord, 'I'm sorry if I blew my top.'

'No apology is necessary. I understood.'

'You'll keep me informed of developments?'

'Insofar as I can. You must understand that I may not be able to tell all I know, even to you. Discretion also applies to the police when in the public interest.'

He stood up and we shook hands, and with that I had to be satisfied. But, as Perigord had warned, it was not to my entire satisfaction.

FIVE

And so there was a funeral after all, but before that, the inquest. I attended, but before the proceedings began Perigord had a word with me. 'Regardless of the findings of this inquest we're treating this as a murder case.'

I looked at him sharply. 'New evidence?'

'Not really. But your daughter didn't die by drowning; there was no salt water in the lungs. Of course, in the event of an explosion on the boat she could have struck her head hard enough to kill her before entering the water. The head injuries are consistent with that.' He paused. 'It might help you to know that, in the opinion of the forensic pathologist, death was instantaneous.'

Debbie sat with me at the inquest – she was staying until after the funeral. The inquest was beautifully stage-managed; by Perigord, I suspect. The coroner had obviously been briefed and knew all the questions he was not supposed to ask, and he guided witnesses skilfully. As I gave my evidence it occurred to me that one of the factors in Perigord's decision to tell me what he had was to prevent any awkward questions coming from me at the inquest.

The verdict was death by unknown causes.

The family was at the funeral, of course. Grace came from Florida, and Peggy and Bob from Abaco, bringing Karen with them. Karen had regained most of her spirits but the funeral subdued her a little. In Peggy's opinion it was a good thing for Karen to attend. She was probably right. Also present were some of my Bahamian friends and a surprising number of Corporation employees.

It was sad to see the pathetically small coffin being lowered into the sandy earth. Karen cried, so I picked her up and held her close during the brief ceremony. A few last words were said and then it was all over and the crowd drifted away.

Debbie left for Houston the next day and I drove her to the airport. I picked her up at the Royal Palm and, on the way, she asked me to stop at the International Bazaar as there was something she wanted to pick up. I parked outside, and she said, 'Don't bother to come in; I won't be long.' So I sat in the car and waited, and she was back in five minutes.

At the airport we had coffee after we had got rid of her luggage and were waiting for her flight announcement. I said, 'You can tell Billy I'm willing to talk business as soon as he's ready.'

She looked at me closely. 'You're sure?'

'Mike was right,' I said. 'Life goes on, and the Corporation doesn't run itself. Yes, I'm sure.'

'I've been thinking of what you suggested when we were coming back from Abaco. You know, when I think of it I've lived a pretty useless life.' She smiled wryly. 'The Cunningham family doesn't believe in women in business. They're supposed to be ornamental, be good in bed and make babies – preferably boys to carry on the line. Damned misplaced southern chivalry. So I've been ornamental and that's about all.'

I smiled. 'What about the bed bit?'

'You won't believe this, but I was a virgin until I met that bastard back in Houston.' She shook the thought from her. 'Anyway, I think all that's going to change, and it's going to give a hell of a shock to my father – me mixing with black kids and poor white trash. I think I can get it past Billy One though.'

'Stick at it. It's time the Cunninghams made something besides money. Making people happy isn't a bad aim.'

We talked about it some more, and then she excused herself and walked across the concourse to the toilets. When she came back she was hurrying, her heels clicking rapidly on the hard floor. She stopped in front of me and said, 'There's something I have to show you, Tom. I wasn't going to, but . . .' She stopped and bit her lip nervously, then thrust an envelope into my hand. 'Here!'

'What is it?'

'You remember Sue left her camera behind. Well, I took out the film and had it developed. I just picked up the prints at the International Bazaar and I went into the John to have a look at them.'

'I see,' I said slowly. I was not sure I wanted to see them. There would be too many memories of that last day.

'I think you ought to look at them,' Debbie urged. 'It's important.'

I took the prints out of the envelope and shuffled through them. There were a couple of pictures of the *Girl* in one of which Pete posed in the bows, striking a mock-heroic attitude; three pictures of Sue herself, probably taken by Julie, which damn near broke my heart to see; and the rest were of Julie herself in various locations – by the pool, by the boat, and on board supervising the loading of luggage. There was one picture of Debbie and also four duds, out of focus and blurred. Sue had not yet got the hang of the camera and now never would. I got a lump in my throat and coughed.

Debbie was watching me closely. 'Look again.'

I went through the pictures again and suddenly Debbie said, 'Stop! That one.' In the picture where Pete was in the bows there was a dim figure in the stern – a man just coming on deck from below. He was in the shade and his face was indistinct.

'Well, I'll be damned!' I put down the print and took out the negative. A 110 film negative is damned small – it will just about cover your thumbnail – and the bit which showed the man was about as big as a pinhead. 'The crewman!' I said softly.

'Yes. You'll have something to show Perigord.'

'But I'll have it enlarged first. I'm not letting this into Perigord's hands without having a few copies for myself. His ideas of discretion might get in my way. I have a shrewd idea that once he gets this I'll never see it again.'

Debbie's flight was announced, garbled by bad acoustics, and I accompanied her to the barrier where we said our goodbyes. 'I'll write to you about our scheme,' she said. 'Look after yourself, Tom.' She kissed me, a chaste peck on the cheek.

Then she was gone and I went back into Freeport to find a photographer.

Two days later I had what I wanted. I sat in my office and examined the duplicate negative, the copies of the colour print, and the six glossy black-and-white blow-ups of the pinhead-sized area of the negative which was the head of the crewman. The darkroom technician had done a good job considering the size of the image he had to work with. It could not be said to be a good portrait, being very grainy and slightly out of focus, but it was not all that bad.

The man was youngish – I would say under thirty – and he appeared to be blond. He had a broadish forehead and narrow chin, and his eyes were deepset and shadowed. One hand was up by his face as though he intended to hide it, and the head was slightly blurred as though it was in motion when the picture was taken. On the colour print it looked as though he was emerging from below, and perhaps he had suddenly been aware that he was on candid camera. If so, he had not beaten the speed of a camera shutter and a fast film.

I studied the face for a very long time. Was this a callous murderer? What did a murderer look like? Like anyone else, I suppose.

I was about to ring Perigord when the intercom buzzed so I flicked the switch. 'Yes, Jessie?'

'Mr Ford to see you.'

I had forgotten about Sam Ford. I pushed the photographs to one side of my desk, and said, 'Shoot him in.'

Sam Ford was a black Bahamian, and manager of the marina which was attached to the Sea Gardens Hotel on New Providence. He was an efficient manager, a good sailor, and did a lot for the branch of BASRA over there. Ever since the talk in Perigord's office and his expressed views on marina security I had been thinking about ours, and I had a job for Sam.

He came in. 'Morning, Mr Mangan.'

'Morning, Sam. Take a chair.'

As he sat down he said, 'I was real sorry to hear about what happened. I'd have come to the funeral, but we had problems that day at the marina.'

There had been a wreath from Sam and his family. 'Thanks, Sam. But it's over now.' He nodded and I leaned back in my chair. 'I've been reviewing our policy on marinas. We have three, and soon we'll have another when the hotel is finished on Eleuthera. If things turn out as I hope we'll have more. So far the marinas have been attached to the hotels with the marina manager being responsible to the hotel manager. It's worked well enough, but there's been a certain amount of friction, wouldn't you say?'

'I've had trouble,' said Sam. 'I don't know about the other marinas but my boss, Archie Bain, knows damn all about boats. The times he's asked me to put a quart in a pint pot I swear he thinks boats are collapsible.'

I had heard similar comments from other marina managers. 'All right, we're going to change things. We're going to set up a marinas division with the marina managers responsible to the divisional manager, not to the hotel managers. He'd be running the lot with the centralized buying of ship's chandlery and so on. How would you like the job?'

His eyebrows rose. 'Divisional manager?'

'Yes. You'd get the pay that goes with the job.'

Sam took a deep breath. 'Mr Mangan, that's a job I've been praying for.'

I smiled. 'It's yours from the first of the month – that's in two weeks. And as divisional manager you get to call me Tom.' We talked about his new job for some time, settling lines of demarcation, his salary, and other details. Then I said, 'And I want you to beef up on security in the marinas. How many boats have you had stolen, Sam?'

'From the Sea Gardens?' He scratched his head. 'One this year, two last year, and two the year before. The one this year was recovered on Andros, found abandoned. I think someone just took it for a joyride.'

Five in three years did not sound many out of all the boats Sam had handled, but multiply that by the number of marinas in the Bahamas and it was a hell of a lot. I began to appreciate Perigord's point of view. I said, 'Go back over the records of all our marinas for the last five years. I want to know how many boats went missing. And, Sam, we don't want to lose any more.'

'I don't see we're responsible,' said Sam. 'And there's a clause in the marina agreement which says so. You know boat people. They reckon they've gotten the freedom of the seas. Maybe they have because no one has gotten around to licensing them yet, but some are downright irresponsible.'

I winced because Sam had hit a raw nerve; I had been a boat owner. 'Nevertheless, beef up security.'

'It'll cost,' Sam warned. 'That means watchmen.'

'Do it.'

Sam shrugged. 'Anything more, Mr . . . er . . . Tom?'

'I think that's all.'

He stood up, then hesitated. 'Excuse me, but I've been wondering. What are you doing with those pictures of Jack Kayles?'

'Who?'

Sam pointed to the black-and-white photographs. 'There. That's Jack Kayles.'

'*You know this man?*'

'Not to say know like being friends, but he's been in and out of the marina.'

'Sam, you've just earned yourself a bonus.' I pushed a photograph across the desk. 'Now, sit down and tell me everything you know about him.'

Sam picked it up. 'Not a good picture,' he commented. 'But it's Kayles, all right. He's a yacht bum; got a sloop – a twenty-seven footer, British-built and glass fibre. Usually sails single-handed.'

'Where does he keep her?'

'Nowhere and everywhere. She's usually where he happens to be at the time. Kayles can pitch up anywhere, I reckon. He was in New Providence two years ago and told me he'd comes up from the Galapagos, through the Panama Canal, and had worked his way through the islands. He was going on to look at the Florida keys. He's pretty handy with a boat.'

'What's she called?'

Sam frowned. 'Now that's a funny thing – he changed her name, which is mighty unusual. Most folk are superstitious about that. Two years ago she was called *Seaglow*, but when I saw her last she was *Green Wave*.'

'Maybe a different boat,' I suggested.

'Same boat,' said Sam firmly.

I accepted that; Sam knew his boats. 'When was he last in your marina?'

'About three months ago.'

'How does Kayles earn his living?'

Sam shrugged. 'I don't know. Maybe he crews for pay. I told you; he's a yacht bum. There's plenty like Kayles about. They live on their boats and scratch a living somehow.' He thought for a moment. 'Come to think of it, Kayles never seemed short of cash. He paid on the nail for everything. A few bits of chandlery from the shop, fuel, marina fees and all that.'

'Credit card?'

'No. Always in cash. Always in American dollars, too.'

'He's an American?'

'I'd say so. Could be Canadian, but I don't think so. What's all this about, Tom?'

'I have an interest in him,' I said uninformatively. 'Any more you can tell me?'

'Not much to tell,' said Sam. 'I just put diesel oil in his boat and took his money. Not much of that, either. He has a pint-sized diesel engine which he doesn't use much; he's one of those guys who prefers the wind – a good sailor, like I said.'

'Anything at all about Kayles will be useful,' I said. 'Think hard, Sam.'

Sam ruminated. 'I did hear he was awful quick-tempered, but he was always civil to me and that's all I cared about. He never made trouble in the marina but I heard he got into a fight in Nassau. Like all yachtsmen he carries a knife, and he used it – he cut a guy.'

'Were the police in on that?'

Sam shook his head. 'It was a private fight,' he said dryly. 'No one wanted police trouble.'

I was disappointed; it would be useful if Kayles already had a police record. 'Did he have any particular friends that you know of?'

'No, I'd say Kayles is a loner.'

'When he left your marina three months ago did he say where he was going?'

'No.' Sam suddenly snapped his fingers. 'But when I met him last month in the International Bazaar he said he was going to Florida. I forgot about that.' Then he added, 'The International Bazaar here – not the one in Nassau.'

I stared at Sam. 'Are you telling me you saw Kayles here on Grand Bahama a month ago?'

'Not a month ago,' corrected Sam. 'Last month. It would be a little over two weeks ago. I'd brought a boat over for a client to give to Joe Cartwright here.' Sam tugged his ear. 'Chances are that Kayles had his boat here, too. I didn't see her, but I wasn't looking. He knew about the discount.'

We had a system whereby a yachtsman using one of our marinas got a ten per cent discount in any of the others; it helped keep the money in the family. I rang my secretary. 'Jessie, get Joe Cartwright up here fast. I don't care what he's doing but I want him here.' I turned back to Sam. 'Did Kayles say how he was going to Florida?'

'He didn't tell me and I didn't ask. I assumed he'd be going in *Green Wave.*'

I hammered at Sam for quite a while, but could get nothing more out of him. Presently Joe Cartwright arrived. He was the marina manager for the Royal Palm. 'You wanted me, Mr Mangan?' He flicked his hand in a brief salute. 'Hi, Sam!'

I pushed forward the photograph. 'Did this man bring a boat into the marina about two weeks ago?'

Sam said, 'His name is Kayles.'

'The face and the name mean nothing to me,' said Joe. 'I'd have to look at the records.'

I pointed to the telephone. 'Ring your office and have someone do it now.'

As Joe spoke into the mouthpiece I drummed my fingers restlessly on the desk. At least I had something for Perigord and I hoped it would prove to be a firm lead.

Joe put down the telephone. 'He was here, but I didn't see him. He came in a British sloop with a red hull.'

'Green,' said Sam.

'No, it was red. Her name was *Bahama Mama*.'

'He changed the name again,' said Sam in wonder. 'Now why would a man do that?'

My upraised hand silenced him. I said to Joe, 'Is the boat still here?'

'I'll find out.' Joe picked up the telephone again and I held my breath. If the boat was still here then Kayles, in all likelihood, was dead with Julie, Sue and Pete. If not . . .? Joe said, 'She left on the twenty-fifth – Christmas Day.'

I let out my breath with a sigh. That was six days after *Lucayan Girl* had disappeared. Joe said, 'No one saw her leave; suddenly she wasn't there.' He shrugged. 'It didn't bother anyone; the marina fee had been paid in advance to the end of the month. We made a profit on that one.'

I said, 'I want both of you to wait in the outer office until you're wanted.' They left and I rang Perigord. 'I've got a name and a face for you. That crewman.'

He did not sound surprised. All he said was 'Who?'

I told him.

'Where are you?'

'My office at the Royal Palm.'

'Ten minutes,' he said, and rang off.

SIX

Perigord put Sam Ford and Joe Cartwright through the wringer, but did not get much more out of them than I had, then he took the negative and photographs and departed. But he did not take all of them; I had retained some, locked in the office safe. I spoke to Sam and Joe. 'If you see or hear of this man I want to know, but don't alarm him – just contact me.'

Sam said, 'What's all this about, Tom?'

I hesitated, half inclined to tell him, but said briefly, 'You don't have to know. It's a police matter.' I changed the subject. 'We're organizing the marinas into a division, Joe; and Sam will be boss. Spread the word that we're expanding. There'll be no firings and a lot of hirings. Sam will tell you all about it. All right, that's it.'

And that was that.

Jack Kayles did not come to the surface, not then, but Billy Cunningham arrived a couple of weeks later with a platoon of lawyers and accountants and they started to go through the books of West End Securities, finding not much wrong and a lot that was right. After a few days Billy came to me and said with a crooked smile, 'You under-estimated your value by about a quarter-million – but you're still not going to get more than a fifth of Theta stock.'

'Suits me.'

'The Corporation will be set up by the end of the week; I've had the Nassau lawyers working on it. Then we can sign papers.'

'You'd have done better to have consulted me on that,' I said.

'Perhaps, but I thought that maybe you weren't in any condition to think straight.'

'You could have been right,' I admitted.

He stood up and stretched. 'Gee, it's been a hard week. I could do with a drink. Where do you keep your office bottle?'

I opened the cabinet, poured drinks, and handed him a glass. 'Here's to the Theta Corporation.'

We drank the toast, and Billy said, 'You sure put a burr under Debbie's saddle. What the hell did you do?'

'Just a bit of fatherly advice.'

Billy's lips quirked. 'Fatherly!' He sat down. 'My revered uncle, Jack Cunningham, Chairman of the Cunningham Corporation and something of a prime bastard, thinks you're some kind of subversive nut. He says you've been putting leftist ideas into his daughter's head.'

'What do you think?'

'I think it's the best thing that ever happened to her,' he said frankly. 'She's been spoiled silly all her life and it's time she thought of something other than herself. Maybe this will do it.'

'I hope so.'

He hesitated. 'She told me about Sue, and the funeral. Why didn't you let me know?'

'Not your problem.' I tasted the whisky. 'Did she tell you about the photograph?'

'What photograph?'

So Debbie was keeping her promise to Perigord; she had not even told her family. I was not as honourable. 'I'll tell you about it, but keep it under your hat.'

So I told him and it was long in the telling, and when I had finished he said, 'Jesus, I've never heard of anything like that!' He picked up the photograph I had taken from the safe. 'You mean this son of a bitch killed your family?'

'That's the general theory. If he's still alive he did, and if he's dead who took his boat from the marina here?'

'This is a crummy picture,' said Billy. 'I think we can do better than this?'

'How?'

'You know we have the Space Center in Houston. I know a lot of the guys there because we do business with NASA. When they shoot pictures back from space they're pretty blurred so they put them through a computer which sharpens them up; makes a computer-enhanced image, as they call it.' He tapped the photograph. 'I think they could do the same with this, and if they can't you're no worse off. Mind if I take this back to Houston?'

I thought it was a good idea. 'Take it.'

Three days later we signed papers and I was President of a $50 million corporation.

Time passed.

I had a heavy workload as I buckled down to making the Theta Corporation work. I began by activating some of the suggestions I had outlined to Billy, beginning with the construction division. Jack Foster was a childless widower who ran a construction company based in Nassau. He was past sixty and wanted to get out, not seeing the point of working himself into the grave when he had no one to leave the company to, so I flew to Nassau and we did a deal, and I got the company for a quarter-million less than I expected to pay. Since this was the company that was building the hotel on Eleuthera things started to move faster there because I saw to it that the Theta Corporation got first choice of materials and manpower. The sooner the hotel was completed the sooner the cash flow would turn from negative to positive.

The quarter-million I saved I put into a geographical and economic survey of the Bahamas, hiring an American outfit to do it. I did not expect them to come up with anything that would surprise me, but what they found would buttress my ideas with the Cunninghams.

I flew to Abaco at least once a week to see Karen, even if only to stay an hour. She seemed to have settled down completely and seemed none the worse for her bereavement. I wished I had her resilience; I stopped myself from brooding only by hard work and keeping occupied. But there were times in the small hours . . .

I discussed the question of taking Karen home but Peggy counselled against it. 'Tom, you're working all the hours God sends. How do you expect to look after a little girl? Let her stay here until things ease off for you. She's no trouble.'

Peggy and Bob were over the moon because I was funding them to a golf course to compete with the one at Treasure Cay. I also told them I was having joint meetings with the Ministry of Finance, the Ministry of Tourism and the Department of Public Works to see if anything could be done about the God-awful road between Marsh Harbour and Treasure Cay. I told them I had produced the Pilot's Bahamas Aviation Guide – the bit where it says that if anyone wants to get from Treasure Cay to Marsh Harbour they'd better fly. 'I asked them, "What sort of tourist advertising is that?" I think we'll get our improved road.'

'It would help our lunch trade a lot,' said Bob. 'People coming on day tours from Treasure Cay.'

'The hell with lunch. You'll be running a car hire service.'

So I was keeping busy and the time passed a little less painfully.

I made a point of dropping in to see Perigord from time to time. The computer-enhanced pictures of Kayles came back from NASA and I gave them to him. He took one look at them and blinked. 'How did you do this?' he demanded.

'Ask no questions,' I said. 'Remember discretion.'

There was no sign of Kayles. 'If he's still alive he could be anywhere,' said Perigord. 'Yachtsmen are mobile and there's no control over them at all. For all I know he's in Cape Town right now.'

'And he'll have changed the name of his boat again.'

'And perhaps his own,' said Perigord.

'He'd surely have passport difficulties there.'

Perigord looked at me a little sorrowfully. 'It may come as a surprise to you to know that the skipper of a boat, no matter how small the boat, doesn't need a passport; all he needs are ship's papers and those are easily forged. In any case, getting a passport is easy enough if you know where to look.'

Perigord was stymied.

Three months passed and Debbie came back bringing with her two black American girls of about her own age. She blew into my office like a refreshing breeze and introduced them. 'This is Cora Brown and Addy Williams; they're both teachers, and Addy has nursing qualifications. We're an advance scouting party.'

'Then I'd better fix you up with rooms.' I stretched for the telephone.

'No need,' she said airily. 'I made reservations.'

I made a mental note to tell Jack Fletcher to inform me any time Debbie Cunningham made a reservation. 'So you're going ahead.'

They told me about it, extensively and in detail. They were going to bring twenty children each month for a two-week stay. 'I had a bit of trouble with the school boards about that,' said Debbie. 'But I pointed out that both Cora and Addy are teachers and the whole thing is one big geography lesson, anyway – with sport thrown in. They went for it.'

Cora and Addy were to give the kids lessons in basic arithmetic and English, and they were to learn the history of the Bahamas in relationship to the United States. That took care of the education bit. Debbie said tentatively, 'You said something about the Family Islands. I thought a week here and a week on one of those . . .'

'Sure,' I said. 'That's easy. While they're here those kids who can swim can go along to the Underwater Exploration Society and learn scuba-diving. They'll give you a low rate. Those who can't swim can have lessons here in the hotel pool. We have an instructor.'

'That's great,' said Cora. 'I can't swim – maybe I'll take lessons, too.'

And so it went with much enthusiasm. I took time off to introduce them to people I thought they ought to know and then let them loose in Freeport. Before they went back to the States I took Debbie to dinner at the Xanadu Princess. I had engineered that tête-à-tête by sending Cora and Addy to Abaco with an introduction to Peggy.

As we got out of the car Debbie looked up at the hotel. 'Does this belong to the Theta Corporation?'

I laughed. 'No, I just like to keep tabs on what the opposition is up to.'

Over cocktails I said, 'I like Cora and Addy. Where did you find them?'

'Oh, I just asked around and came up with the jackpot.' She smiled. 'Neither of them is married. From what I've observed in the last few days they could very well marry Bahamian boys. Your menfolk sure move in fast.' The smile left her face and she said soberly, 'How are you doing, Tom?'

'All right. The Theta Corporation is keeping me busy. So much so that I'm thinking of selling the house. I don't spend much time there now; usually I sleep at the hotel.'

'Oh, you mustn't sell that beautiful house,' she said impulsively.

'I rattle around in it. And there are too many memories.'

She put her hand on mine. 'I hope it's not too bad.' We were quiet for a while, then she said, 'Billy talked to me. He said you'd told him about Kayles. Any more news?'

'Nothing. Kayles seems to have vanished completely. If it weren't for all the inconsistencies I'd be inclined to believe he went down with *Lucayan Girl* – that it was a genuine accident.'

I changed the subject deliberately and we talked of other and lighter matters, and it was pretty late when I took her back to the Royal Palm. As we walked towards the parking lot, something flashed out of the darkness and Debbie ducked, and gasped, 'What was that!'

'Don't worry, it's harmless – it won't hurt you. It was just a bat. We call them money bats.'

Debbie looked up doubtfully and I could see she did not altogether believe my claim that the bats were harmless. 'That's an odd name? Why *money* bats?'

I chuckled. 'Because the only time you see them is when they're flying away from you.'

That night, lying sleepless in bed, I had a curious thought. Could the mind play tricks on one? Had I given Debbie Cunningham the idea of bringing American kids to the Bahamas just so I could see more of her? It had not been a conscious decision, of that I was sure. With Julie and Sue just dead a week I would not, could not, have made such a decision. But the mind is strange and complex, and perhaps it had put those words in my mouth, the idea into Debbie's mind, for reasons of its own.

All the same I felt happier than I had felt for a long time, knowing that I would be seeing Debbie Cunningham monthly for the foreseeable future.

The months went by. Seven months after I became President of the Theta Corporation we had the Grand Opening of the Rainbow Bay Hotel on Eleuthera. I invited a crowd of notables: Government ministers, a couple of film stars, a golf champion and so on. I also invited Deputy-Commissioner Howard Perigord and his wife, Amy. And the Cunninghams came; Billy and his father, Billy One; Jack Cunningham, who looked upon me with some mistrust, and, of course, daughter Debbie.

To make sure that everything went like clockwork I pulled the best of the staff from the other three hotels. The service in those hotels might have suffered a little at that time, but not much because, in general, the quality of our staff was high. In the event all went well.

Before we flew to Eleuthera the Cunninghams and I had an informal board meeting. I handed out copies of the survey made by the American company, and added my report with its detailed recommendations. 'You're not expected to read all this now, but I'll give you a brief summary.'

I ticked off the points on my fingers. 'We go into the Family Islands . . .' I paused, and said in parentheses, 'They used to be known as the Out Islands but the Minister of Tourism thinks that the Family Islands sounds more cosy.'

'He's right,' said Billy. 'And Shakespeare was wrong. There's a lot to names.'

'Anyway, the future lies in the Family Islands. We go into real estate in a big way on Crooked Island, Acklins Island, Mayaguana and Great Inagua. And we buy a couple of cays in the Ragged Island Range. All this is undeveloped and we get in there first, especially before the Swiss moneymen move in and send the prices up.'

I tapped another finger. 'We put together our own package deals and farm them out to travel agents in the States and in Europe. In order to do that we either make deals with a couple of airlines or charter planes ourselves to fly our customers into Grand Bahama or New Providence. From there we'll either have to do a deal with Bahamasair or set up our own islands airline.'

Another finger went up. 'Next I want one really top-class luxury hotel; not for the package tourist but for the people with money.' I grinned. 'Simple folks like yourselves. Ten per cent of the visitors to the Islands come in their own aircraft and I want to capture that market.'

'Sounds good,' said Billy.

Billy One said, 'Yeah, it seems to make sense.'

Jack Cunningham had been flipping through the pages of my report. 'What's this about you wanting to start a school?'

I said, 'If we're building hotels we'll need staff to run them. I want to train them my way.'

'The hell with that!' said Jack roundly. 'We pay for training, then they leave and go to some other goddamn hotel like a Holiday Inn. No way are we doing that.'

'The Ministry of Tourism is putting up half the cost,' I said.

'Oh, well,' said Jack grudgingly. 'That may be different.'

Billy said, 'Jack, I'm Chairman of this corporation and as far as I'm concerned you're the seventeenth Vice-President in Charge of Answering Stupid Questions. Don't stick your oar in here.'

'Don't talk to your uncle like that,' said Billy One. But his voice was mild.

'I've gotten my money in here,' snapped Jack. 'And I don't want this guy throwing it away. He's already filled Debbie's head with a lot of communistic nonsense.'

Billy grinned. 'Show me another commie with over ten million bucks.'

'Two million of which we gave him,' snapped Jack. He tossed the report aside. 'Billy, you damn near swore a Bible oath that the Government of the Bahamas was stable.' He pointed at me. 'You believed him. He gives us a report which makes nice reading, but I've been reading other words – in newspapers, for instance. There was a goddamn riot in Nassau three days ago. What's so stable about that?'

I knew about the riot and was at a loss to account for it. It had flashed into being from nowhere and the police had had a hard time in containing the disturbance. I said, 'An American outfit pulled out and closed down a factory. They did it too damned fast and without consultation. People don't like being fired, especially when it's done without so much as a by-your-leave. I think that started the trouble. It's just a local difficulty, Jack.'

He grunted. 'It had better be. Some American tourists got hurt, and that's not doing the industry any good; an industry, I might point out, which we're into for fifty million dollars.'

I could see that any relationship I had with Jack would be uneasy and I determined to steer clear of him as far as I could. As for the riot, I had given a glib enough explanation, but I was not sure it was the right one.

Billy One said, 'Let's cool it, shall we?' He looked at me. 'Would you happen to have any sour mash around?'

So it was smoothed over and next day we flew to Eleuthera. Eleuthera is 120 miles long but at the place where I had built the hotel it was less than two miles wide, so that from the hotel one could see the sea on both sides. Billy One looked at this in wonder. 'I'll be goddamned!'

I said, 'We get two beaches for the price of one. That's why I built here.'

Even Jack was impressed.

During the course of the day I had a few words with Perigord and asked him about the riot in Nassau. 'What caused it?' I asked.

He shrugged. 'I don't really know. It's not in my jurisdiction. It's in Commissioner Deane's lap – and he's welcome to it.'

'Any chance of a similar occurrence on Grand Bahama?'

He smiled grimly. 'Not if I have anything to do with it.'

'Was it political?'

He went opaque on me and deliberately changed the subject. 'I must congratulate you on this very fine hotel. I wish you every success.'

That reaction worried me more than anything else.

But the Grand Opening was a tremendous success and I danced with Debbie all night.

And so it went. The Theta Corporation was a success after its first year although more money was going out than coming in. After all, that was the point – we were still in the stage of expansion. Billy was satisfied with the way I was handling things and so, largely, was Billy One. How Jack felt I did not know; he kept his nose out of things and I did not care to ask. Everything was going fine in my business life, and my private life was perking up, too, to the point where I asked Debbie to marry me.

She sighed. 'I thought you'd never ask.'

So I took her to bed and we were married three weeks later over the protests of Jack, whose open objection concerned the disparity in our ages, but he did not like me, something I knew already. Billy and, I think, Billy One were for it, but Debbie's brother, Frank, followed Jack's line. Various members of the family took sides and the clan was split to some extent on this issue. But none of them could say that I was a fortune-hunter marrying her for her money – I had enough of my own. As for my own feelings about it, I was marrying Debbie, not Jack.

We married in Houston in a somewhat tense atmosphere and then went back to the Bahamas to honeymoon briefly at the new Rainbow Bay Hotel. Then we went back to Grand Bahama via Abaco where we picked up Karen who seemed dubious about having a new mother. Debbie and Karen moved into the house at Lucaya and I went back to running the Corporation. Two months later she told me she was pregnant which made both of us very happy.

But then things began to go wrong again because people who were coming to the Bahamas on vacation were going home to die.

SEVEN

Legionella pneumophila.

I learned a lot about that elusive bug with the pseudo-Latin name in the next few months. Anyone connected with the hotel industry had to learn, and learn fast. At first it was not recognized for what it was because those afflicted were not dying in the Bahamas but back home in the States or in England or Switzerland or wherever else they came from. It was the World Health Organization that blew the first warning whistle.

Most people might know it as Legionnaires' disease because it was first discovered at the convention of the American Legion held at the Bellevue-Stratford Hotel in Philadelphia in 1976 where there was an almost explosive outbreak of pneumonia among those who had attended. Altogether 221 people became ill and thirty-four of them died. Naturally, Legionnaires' disease is bad news for any hotelier. No one is likely to spend a carefree vacation in a resort hotel from which he may be carried out feet first, and the problem is compounded by the fact that even those hotels which are well kept and disease-free feel a financial draught. Once the news gets around that a particular holiday resort is tainted then everybody gets hurt.

So it was that a lot of people, me among them, were highly perturbed to hear that Legionnaires' disease was loose in the Parkway Hotel in Nassau. I flew to New Providence to talk to Tony Bosworth, our Corporation doctor. He had his base at the Sea Gardens Hotel because New Providence is fairly central and he could get to our other hotels reasonably quickly, using a Corporation plane in an emergency. A company doctor was another of my extravagances of which Jack Cunningham did not approve, but he earned his salary on this, and other, occasions.

When I told him what was happening at the Parkway he gave a low whistle. 'Legionellosis! That's a bad one. Are you sure?'

I shrugged. 'That's what I hear.'

'Do you know which form? It comes in two ways – Pontiac fever and Legionnaires' disease.'

That was the first time I had heard of Pontiac fever, but not the last. I shook my head. 'I wouldn't know. You're the doctor, not me.'

'Pontiac fever isn't too bad,' he said. 'It hits fast and has a high attack rate, about ninety-five per cent, but usually there are no fatalities. Legionnaires' disease is a killer. I'll get on to the Department of Public Health. Give me fifteen minutes, will you?'

I went away to look at the kitchens. I often make surprise raids on the kitchens and other departments just to keep the staff up to the mark. All departments are equally important but, to paraphrase George Orwell, the kitchen is more equal than others. Every hotelier's nightmare is an outbreak of salmonella. It was nearer half an hour before I got back to Tony and he was still nattering on the telephone, but he laid it down a couple of minutes after my arrival.

'Confirmed,' he said gloomily. 'Legionnaires' disease. Suspected by a smart young doctor in Manchester, England, it was confirmed by the Communicable Disease Surveillance Centre. The World Health Organization has identified a man dead in Paris and two more in Zurich;

there's a couple of cases in Buenos Aires and a rash of them across the States.'

'All these people stayed at the Parkway?'

'Yes. How many rooms there?'

I had all the statistics of my competition at my fingertips. 'A hundred and fifty.'

'What would you say the year-round occupation rate is?'

I considered. 'It's a reasonably good hotel. I'd say between seventy-five and eighty per cent.'

Tony's lips moved silently as he made a calculation. 'They'll have to contact about 12,000 people, and they're spread all over the bloody world. That's going to be a job for someone.'

I gaped at him. 'Why so many?'

'There's been some work done on this one since 1976. Studies have shown that this deadly little chap can live in water for over a year, so that's how far back it's standard to check. One will get you ten that the bacteria are in the air-conditioning cooling tower at the Parkway, but we don't know how long they've been in there. Look, Tom, this is pretty serious. The attack rate among those exposed is between one and five per cent. Let's split the difference and call it two-and-a-half. That means three hundred casualties. With a death rate among them of fifteen per cent that gives us forty-five deaths.'

In the event he was not far out. When the whole scare was over the final tally came to 324 casualties and 41 deaths.

'You seem to know a lot about it.'

He gave me a lopsided grin. 'I'm a hotel doctor; this is what I get my salary for. Those casualties who don't die won't be good for much for a few months, and there's a grave risk of permanent lung damage, to say nothing of the kidneys and the liver.'

I took a deep breath. 'All right, Tony; what do we do?'

'Nothing much. These outbreaks tend to be localized – usually restricted to a single building. They've turned off the air-conditioning at the Parkway so there'll be nothing blown out.'

'So you think our hotels are safe?'

He shrugged. 'They should be.'

'I'd like to make sure.'

'Testing for *L. pneumophila* is a finicky business. You need a well-equipped laboratory with livestock – guinea pigs, fertilized eggs and so on. That's why the damned creature only turned up as late as 1976. And it takes a long time, too. I'll tell you what; I'll take samples of the water from the air-conditioners in the four hotels and send them to Miami – but don't expect quick results.'

'What about the room conditioners?' I asked. The lobby and the public rooms of the Sea Gardens were handled by a central air-conditioner, but each room had its own small one which could be set individually by the occupier. The same system worked at the Royal Palm because those two were our older hotels. The Abaco Sands and the brand-new Rainbow Bay had completely centralized air-conditioning.

Bosworth raised his eyebrows. 'You're taking this a bit far, aren't you?' He turned and took a fat medical book from a shelf next to his desk and flipped through the pages. 'We haven't developed an anti-bacterial agent for this one yet; nothing specific, anyway. Heavy chlorination would appear to be the answer.'

'Tell me how it's done.'

So he told me and I got busy. In the two hotels we had 360 rooms and that meant 360 air-conditioners to be emptied, filled with chlorinated water, left to soak for twenty-four hours, emptied again and refilled with guaranteed pure water. A big job.

I did not wait for Bosworth to report on the samples he sent to Miami, but got working on the big air-conditioners in each hotel, taking them out of service one at a time and using the same technique. But there was a difference. An air-conditioner in a moderately big hotel can handle up to 1000 gallons of water a minute and the cooling is effected by evaporation as the water pours over splash bars and has air blown through it.

A cooling tower will lose about ten gallons of water a minute as water vapour and there is another gallon a minute lost in what is known technically in the trade as 'drift'; very finely divided drops of water. Attempts are made to control the emission of drift by drift eliminators, but some always gets out. Tony Bosworth told me that any infectious bacteria would probably be escaping in the drift. I chlorinated that water to a fare-thee-well.

I supervised it all myself to make sure it was done properly. It might seem odd that the boss would do it personally but I had to make sure it was done in the right way. There was a lot riding on this, apart from the fact that I did not want anyone to die just because he had patronized one of my hotels. *L. pneumophila* had a nasty habit of not only killing people, but hotels, too.

Tony Bosworth was also pretty busy flitting from island to island attending suspected cases of Legionnaires' disease which turned out to be the common cold. Our hotels were clean but the tourists were jittery and the whole of the Bahamas ran scared for a little while. It was not a good year for either the Bahamas or the Theta Corporation, and the Ministry of Tourism and I sat back to watch the people stay away. Tourism fell off by fifteen per cent in the next three months. The Parkway Hotel was cleaned up and certified safe, but I doubt if the room occupancy even reached ten per cent in the months that followed. The company that owned it later went broke.

Another thing it meant was that I was away from home more often than I was there. Debbie grew fractious and we had our first rows. It had never been that way with Julie but now, with hindsight, I remember that when Julie was expecting Sue I had been always careful to stay close. That had been my first baby, too.

So, perhaps, in a sense our quarrels were equally my fault even if I did not recognize it at the time. As it was I took umbrage. I was working very hard, not only protecting against this damned disease which was worrying the hell out of me, but also taking the usual workload of the President of the Theta Corporation, and I did not see why I should have to be drained of my energies at home, too. So the quarrelling became worse. It is not only jealousy that feeds on itself.

Debbie was still doing her thing with Cora, Addy and the Texan kids, but operating mainly from the Bahamian end. But then I noticed that she was spending more and more time back home in Texas. Her excuse was that Cora and Addy were hopeless at organization and she had to go back to iron out problems. I accepted that, but when her visits became more frequent and protracted I had the feeling I was losing a wife. It was not good for young Karen, either, who had lost one mother and looked like losing the surrogate. It was a mess and I could not see my way out of it.

My feelings were not improved when I saw the headlines in the *Freeport News* one morning. There had been a fire in Nassau and the Fun Palace had burned down. The Fun Palace was a pleasure complex built, I think, to rival Freeport's International Bazaar as a tourist trap. It contained cinemas, restaurants and sporting facilities and had been a shade too gaudy for my taste. As modern as the day, it had a cheap feel to it of which I did not approve.

And now it was gone. Analysing the newspaper report it would seem that the firemen never had a chance; the place had gone up in flames like a bonfire almost as though it had been deliberately built to burn easily, and it took eighty-two lives with it, most of them tourists and a lot of them children. That, coming on top of Legionnaires' disease, would certainly not help the image of the Bahamas. Come to the Islands and die! Take your pick of method!

Over the next few days I followed the newspaper reports and listened to people talking. There were muttered rumours of arson but that was to be expected; after any big fire there is always talk of arson. The Chief of the Fire Brigade in Nassau was eloquent in his damning of the construction of the Fun Palace and the materials used in its construction. In order to give it a light and airy appearance a lot of plastic had been used and most of the victims had died, not of burning, but of asphyxiation caused by poisonous fumes. He also condemned the use of polyurethane foam as furniture upholstery. 'This is a real killer,' he said. I made a note to check on what we were using in our hotels, and also to tighten up on fire precautions.

And it was at this point that Jack Kayles popped into sight.

EIGHT

Storm signals flew over the breakfast table next morning but I was too preoccupied to notice them until Debbie said, 'I suppose you're going back to the office again today.'

I poured myself a cup of tea. 'I had thought of it.'

'I never see you any more.'

I added sugar. 'You do in bed.'

She flared up. 'I'm a wife – not a harlot. When I married a man I expected all of him, not just his penis.'

It was then I became aware that this was not a mere storm in a tea-cup. 'I'm sorry,' I said. 'Things have been really tough lately.' I reflected. 'I suppose I don't really have to go in today, or even tomorrow. In fact, I can take the rest of the week off. Why don't we take one of Joe Cartwright's sailboats from the marina and cruise to one of the Family Islands? That would take us to the weekend and we could fly back.'

She lit up like a Christmas tree. 'Could we?' Then she frowned. 'But we're going nowhere near any of your damned hotels,' she warned. 'This isn't a disguised business trip.'

'Cross my heart and hope to die.' I was drinking my tea as the telephone rang.

It was Jessie. 'I think you'd better come in early this morning; we've got trouble.'

'What kind of trouble?'

'Something to do with baggage at the airport. I don't really know what it is, but the lobby sounds like a hive of bees. Mr Fletcher's at the dentist and the under-manager isn't coping very well.'

That was all I needed. 'I'll be in.' I hung up and said to Debbie, 'Sorry, darling, but duty calls.'

'You mean you're going in spite of what you just promised? Damn you!'

I left the house with recriminations clanging in my ears, and arrived at the Royal Palm to find that a minor bit of hell had broken loose.

I sat in Jack Fletcher's office listening to him moan. 'Two hundred and eight of them, and without a damned toothbrush between them, not to mention other necessities. All they have is their hand baggage and what they stand up in.'

I winced. 'What happened? Did they arrive here and their baggage end up in Barcelona?'

He looked at me with mournful eyes. 'Worse! You know that new baggage-handling carousel at the airport?' I nodded. It was an innovation for which we had been pressing for a long time. With increased flights of wide-bodied jets the airport had developed a baggage-handling bottleneck which the carousel was intended to alleviate.

Fletcher said, 'It couldn't have done a better job if it had been designed for the purpose.'

'A better job of what?'

'Opening the baggage without benefit of keys. The baggage was put on the conveyor, and somewhere in that underground tunnel something ripped open every suitcase. What spewed out on to the carousel were smashed suitcases and mixed-up contents.'

'Didn't they try to turn it off when they saw what was happening?'

'They tried and couldn't. Apparently it wouldn't stop.
And the telephone link between the carousel and the loading point outside hasn't been installed yet. By the time
they'd fiddled around and sent someone outside to stop
the loading it was too late. They'd pushed in the lot – the
whole plane-load of baggage.'

I nodded towards the lobby. 'Who is this crowd?'

'LTP Industries convention from Chicago. They're
already raising hell. If you want a slice of gloom just go out
into the lobby – you can cut it with a knife. One good thing;
the Airport Authority carries the can for this – not us.'

The Airport Authority might carry ultimate responsibility
but the airport people did not have on their hands over 200
unhappy and discontented Americans – and when
Americans are discontented they let it be known, loud and
clear. Their unhappiness would spread through the hotel
like a plague.

Jack said, 'That Boeing was full, every seat filled. We're
not the only people with grief; Holiday Inn, Atlantik Beach,
Xanadu – we've all got troubles.'

That did not make me feel any better. 'What's the Airport
Authority doing about it?'

'Still trying to make up their minds.'

'Oh, for God's sake!' I said. 'You go out there and give
them a pacifier – $50 each for immediate necessities. I'll ring
the airport to tell them I'll be sending them the bill. And
make it a public relations service on the part of the hotel.
Let them know clearly that we don't have to do it, but we're
full of the milk of human kindness. We have to make some
profit out of this mess.'

He nodded and left, and I rang the airport. There followed
a short but tempestuous conversation in which threats of
legal action were issued. As I put down the telephone it
rang under my hand. Jessie said, 'Sam Ford wants to see
you. By the way he's acting the matter is urgent.'

'I'll be along.' I went back to my office via the lobby, testing the atmosphere as I went. Fletcher had made an announcement and the tension had eased. A queue had already formed at the cashier's desk to receive their dole. I walked through Jessie's office, beckoning to Sam as I went, and sat behind my desk. 'I thought you were down by Ragged Island.'

The Ragged Island project was something I had developed by listening to Deputy-Commissioner Perigord. What he had said about the Ragged Island Range and the Jumento Cays had remained with me. My idea was to buy a couple of the cays and set up camps for those tourists who preferred to rough it for a few days on a genuine desert island. It was my intention to cater for all tastes and, being in the low tourist season, I had sent Sam Ford down in a boat to scout a few locations.

'I was,' said Sam. 'But something came up. You remember that fellow you wanted to know about?

'Who?'

'Kayles. Jack Kayles.'

I jerked. 'What about him? Have you seen him?' It had been over a year and I had almost forgotten.

'No, but I've seen his boat.'

'Where?'

'In the Jumentos – lying off Man-o'-War Cay. Now called *My Fair Lady* and her hull is blue.'

I said, 'Sam, how in hell can you be sure it's the same boat?'

'Easy.' Sam laughed. 'About a year and a half ago Kayles wanted a new masthead shackle for his forestay. Well, it's a British boat and I only had American fittings, so I had to make an adaptor. It's still there.'

'You got that close to her?'

''Bout a cable.' That was 200 yards. 'And I put the glasses on her. I don't think Kayles was on board or he'd have come out on deck. They usually do in those waters because there are not that many boats about and folks get curious. He must have been ashore but I didn't see him.' He looked at me seriously. 'I thought of boarding her but I remembered what you said about not wanting him scared off, so I just passed by without changing course and came back here.'

'You did right. When was this?'

'Yesterday. Say, thirty hours ago. I came back real fast.'

He had indeed; it was over 300 miles to the Jumentos. I pondered for a while. To get there quickly I could fly, but the only place to land was at Duncan Town and that was quite a long way from Man-o'-War Cay and I would have to hire a boat, always supposing there was one to be hired with a skipper willing to make a 100-mile round trip. For the first time I wished we had a seaplane or amphibian.

I said, 'Are you willing to go back now?'

'I'm pretty tired, Tom. I've been pushing it. I haven't had what you'd call a proper sleep for forty-eight hours. I had young Jim Glass with me but I didn't trust his navigation so all I got were catnaps.'

'We'll go by air and see if he's still there, and you can sleep at Duncan Town. Okay?'

He nodded. 'All right, Tom, but you'll get no words from me on the way. I'll be asleep.'

I had completely forgotten about Debbie.

I took the first plane and the first pilot handy, and we flew south-east to the Jumentos, the pilot being Bill Pinder. I sat in the co-pilot's seat next to Bill, and Sam sat in the back. I think he was asleep before take-off. I had binoculars handy and a camera with a telephoto lens. I wanted firm identification for Perigord although how firm it would be was problematical because Kayles's boat changed colour like a bloody chameleon.

Although I use aircraft quite a lot, flying being the quickest way for a busy man to get around the islands, I find that it bores me. As we droned over the blue and green sea, leaving the long chain of the Exumas to port, my eyes grew heavier and I must have fallen asleep because it took a heavy dig in the ribs from Bill to rouse me. 'Man-o'-War Cay in ten minutes,' he said.

I turned and woke Sam. 'Which side of the cay was he?'

Sam peered from a window. 'This side.'

'We don't want to do anything unusual,' I told Bill. 'Come down to your lowest permitted altitude and fly straight just off the west coast of the cay. Don't jink about or circle – just carry on.'

We began to descend and presently Bill said, 'That little one just ahead is Flamingo Cay; the bigger one beyond is Man-o'-War.'

I passed the binoculars back to Sam. 'You know Kayles. Take a good look as we fly past and see if you can spot him. I'll use the camera.'

'There's a boat,' said Bill.

I cocked the camera and opened the side window, blinking as the air rushed in. The sloop was lying at anchor and I could see distinctly the catenary curve of the anchor cable under clear water. 'That's her,' said Sam and I clicked the shutter. I recocked quickly and took another snapshot. Sam said, 'And that's Kayles in the cockpit.'

By then the sloop was disappearing behind us. I twisted my neck to see it but it was gone. 'Did he wave or anything?'

'No, just looked up.'

'Okay,' I said. 'On to Duncan Town.'

Bill did a low pass with his landing gear down over the scattered houses of Duncan Town, and by the time we had landed on the air strip and taxied to the ramp a battered car was already bumping towards us. We climbed out of the Navajo and Sam said, nodding towards the car, 'I know that man.'

'Then you can do the dickering,' I said. 'We want a boat to go out to Man-o'-War – the fastest you can find.'

'That won't be too fast,' he said. 'But I'll do my best.'

We drove into Duncan Town and I stood by while Sam bargained for a boat. I had never been to Duncan Town and I looked around with interest. It was a neat and well-maintained place of the size Perigord had said – less than 200 population, most of them fishermen to judge by the boats. There were signs of agriculture but no cash crops, so they probably grew just enough food for themselves. But there were evaporation pans for the manufacture of salt.

Sam called me, and then led me to a boat. 'That's it.'

I winced at what I saw. It was an open boat about eighteen feet long and not very tidily kept. A tangled heap of nets was thrown over the engine casing and the thwarts were littered with fish-scales. It smelled of rotting fish, too, and would have broken Pete Albury's heart. 'Is this the best you can do?'

'Least it has an inboard engine,' said Sam. 'I don't think it'll break down. I'll come with you, Tom. I know Kayles by sight, and I can get six hours sleep on the way.'

'Six hours!'

'It's forty miles, and I don't reckon this tub will do more than seven knots at top speed.' He looked up at the sun. 'It'll be about nightfall when we get there.'

'All right,' I said resignedly. 'Let's get a seven-knot move on.'

Five minutes later we were on our way with the owner and skipper, a black Bahamian called Bayliss, at the tiller. Sam made a smelly bed of fish nets and went to sleep, while I brooded. I was accustomed to zipping about the islands in a Navajo and this pace irked me. I judged the length of the boat and the bow wave and decided we were not even doing six knots. I was impatient to confront Kayles.

We came to Man-o'-War Cay just as the sun was setting and I woke Sam. 'We're coming to the cay from the other side. How wide is it?'

''Bout half a mile.'

'What's the going like?'

'Not bad.' He peered at me. 'What's all this about, Tom?'

'Personal business.'

He shook his head. 'A year back when I asked why you were interested in Kayles you damn near bit my head off. And then you brought the police in – Commissioner Perigord, no less. This is more than personal business. What are you getting me into?'

It was a fair enough question. If we were going to confront a man I believed to be a murderer then Sam had a right to know. I said, 'How close were you to Pete Albury?'

'I knew him all my life. You know we both came from Abaco. I remember him and you together when I was a little nipper, not more than four years old. You'd be twelve or thirteen then, I reckon.'

'Yes, he was my friend,' I said quietly. 'What about you?'

'Sure, he was my friend. We used to go turtling together. Biggest we ever caught was a 200-pounder. He taught me how to catch bush bugs with a crutch-stick.'

That was Abaconian vernacular for catching land crabs with a forked stick. I said, 'Kayles was on *Lucayan Girl* when she disappeared.'

Sam went very still. 'You mean . . .'

'I don't know what I mean, but I will when I get to the other side of that damn cay. Right now I'm working out the best way to go about it.'

'Wait a minute.' Sam called out to Bayliss, 'Slow down,' then turned back to me, the whites of his eyes reddened by the light of the setting sun. 'If Kayles was on *Lucayan Girl*, if that's Kayles on that boat, then that means murder.' Sam was as quick as any other Bahamian at adding up the facts of life – and death – at sea. 'I read about the inquest in the *Freeport News*. It seemed to me then there was something left out.'

'Perigord put the lid on it; he didn't want to frighten Kayles away. The picture of Kayles you saw was taken by my daughter, Sue, just before the *Girl* left for Miami. Perigord reckons Kayles is a cocaine smuggler. Anyway, that's not the point, Sam. I want to talk to Kayles.'

'And you're thinking of walking across the island.' He shook his head. 'That's not the way. That boat is anchored nearly a cable offshore. You'd have to swim. It wouldn't look right. What we do is to go around and get next to him in a neighbourly way like any other honest boat would.' He pointed to the water keg in the bows. 'Ask him for some water.'

'Are you coming?'

'Sure I'm coming,' said Sam promptly.

'He'll recognize you,' I said doubtfully.

Sam was ironic. 'What do you want me to do? Put on a white face? It doesn't matter if he knows me or not – he's not afraid of me. But he might know your face and that would be different. You'd better keep your head down.'

So we went around Man-o'-War Cay with the engine gently thumping and made a few final plans. Although Sam had seen Kayles from the air through binoculars, it had been but a quick flash and firm identification would only be made when he talked to the man on the sloop. If Sam recognized Kayles he was to ask for water; if it wasn't Kayles he was to ask for fish. From then on we would have to play it by ear.

When we drifted alongside the sloop there was very little light. I took off the engine casing and stood with my back to *My Fair Lady* apparently tinkering with the engine. Bayliss took the way off and Sam bellowed, 'Ahoy, the sloop!' He stood in the bows and held us off with a boathook.

A voice said, 'What do you want?' The accent was American.

I think Sam went more by the voice than by what he could see. 'We've run us a mite short of water. Can you spare us a few drops?'

A light stabbed from the cockpit and played on Sam. 'Don't I know you?' said Kayles. There was a hint of suspicion in his voice.

'You could,' said Sam easily 'I run a marina in New Providence. I know a lot of yachtsmen and they know me. Maybe you've been to my place – at the Sea Gardens Hotel, west of Nassau. I'm Sam Ford.' He held his hand to shade his eyes, trying to see beyond the bright light.

'I remember you. You want water?'

'I'd appreciate it. We're damn thirsty.'

'I'll get you some,' said Kayles. 'Got anything to put it in?'

Sam had taken the precaution of emptying the water keg. He passed it up to Kayles who went below. 'He'll know if we go aboard,' Sam whispered. 'The sloop will rock. If we're going to take him it'll have to be when he comes up now. Get ready to jump him when I shout.'

'You're sure it is Kayles?'

'Damn sure. Anyway, any ordinary yachtsman would have asked us aboard.'

'All right, then.'

The sound of a hand pump came from the sloop and after a few minutes it stopped. 'Ready, now!' said Sam in a low voice.

The sloop rocked as Kayles came up into the cockpit. Sam said cheerfully, 'This is kind of you, sir.' He had shortened his grip on the boathook and when Kayles leaned over the side to hand down the keg, instead of taking it Sam gripped Kayles's wrist and pulled hard. With the other hand he thrust the end of the boathook into Kayles's stomach like a spear.

I heard the breath explode out of Kayles as I jumped for the sloop. Kayles stood no chance; he lay half in and half out of the cockpit fighting for breath and with Sam holding on to his wrist with grim tenacity. I got both knees in the small of his back, grinding his belly into the cockpit coaming. 'Come aboard, Sam,' I said breathily.

Bayliss shouted, 'What's going on there?'

'Stick to your own business,' said Sam, and came aboard. He switched on the compass light which shed a dim glow into the cockpit. 'Can you hold him?'

Kayles's body writhed under mine. 'I think so.'

'I'll get some rope; plenty of that on a boat.' Sam plucked the knife from Kayles's belt and vanished for a moment.

Kayles was recovering his breath. 'You . . . you bastard!' he gasped, and heaved under me and nearly threw me off so I thumped him hard at the nape of the neck with my fist – the classic rabbit punch – and he went limp. I hoped I had not broken his neck.

Sam came with the rope and we tied Kayles's hands behind his back, and I knew Sam knew enough about seaman's knots to let him do it. When we had Kayles secure he said, 'What do we do now?'

Bayliss had allowed his boat to drift off a little way in the gathering darkness. Now I heard his engine rev up and he came alongside again. 'What you doin' to that man?' he asked. 'I'm havin' nothin' to do with this.'

I said to Sam, 'Let's get him below, then you can talk to Bayliss. Cool him down because we might need him again.'

We bundled Kayles below and stretched him on a bunk. He was breathing stertorously. Sam said, 'What do I tell Bayliss?'

I shrugged. 'Why not tell him the truth?'

Sam grinned. 'Who ever believes the truth? But I'll fix him.' He went into the cockpit and I looked around. Sam had been right about Kayles being a good seaman because it showed. Everything was neat and tidy and all the gear was stowed; a place for everything and everything in its place. Nothing betrays a bad seaman more than sloppiness, and if everything below was trim it would be the same on deck. That is the definition of shipshape. Given five minutes' notice Kayles could pull up the hook and sail for anywhere.

But a good seaman is not necessarily a good man; the history of piracy in the Bahamas shows that. I turned and looked at Kayles who was beginning to stir feebly, then switched on the cabin light to get a better look at him. I got a good sight of his face for the first time and was relieved to see that Sam had made no mistake – this definitely was the man whose picture had been taken by Sue.

I sat at the chart table, switched on the gooseneck lamp, and began going through drawers. A good seaman keeps a log, an honest seaman keeps a log – but would Kayles have kept a log? It would be useful to have a record of his movements in the past.

There was no log to be found so I started going through the charts. In recording a yacht's course on a chart it is usual to use a fairly soft pencil so that in case of error it can be easily erased and corrected, or when the voyage is over the course line can be erased and the chart used again. Most yachtsmen I know tend to leave the course on the chart until it is needed for another voyage. A certain amount of bragging goes on amongst boat people and they like to sit around in a marina comparing voyages and swapping lies.

Kayles had charts covering the eastern seaboard of the Americas from the Canadian border right down to and including Guyana, which is pretty close to the equator, and they covered the Bahamas and the whole of the Caribbean. On many of them were course lines and dates. It is normal to pencil in a date when you have established a position by a midday sun sight and you may add in the

month, but no one I know puts in the year. So were these
the records of old or recent voyages?

Sam came below and looked at Kayles. 'Still sleeping?'
He went into the galley, unclipped an aluminium pan, and
filled it with water. He came back and dumped it in Kayles's
face. Kayles moaned and moved his head from side to side,
but his eyes did not open.

I said, 'Sam, take a look at these charts and tell me if they
mean anything.' We changed places and I stood over
Kayles. His eyes opened and he looked up at me, but there
was no comprehension in them and I judged he was suffering from concussion. It would be some time before he
would be able to talk so I went exploring.

What I was looking for I do not know but I looked anyway, opening lockers and boxes wherever I found them.
Kayles's seamanship showed again in the way he had
painted on the top of each food can a record of the contents.
I found the cans stowed in lockers under the bunks and he
had enough to last a long time. If water gets into the bilges
labels are washed off cans, and Kayles had made sure that
when he opened a can of beef he was not going to find
peaches.

I opened his first-aid box and found it well-equipped
with all the standard bandages and medications, including
two throwaway syringes already loaded with morphine.
Those were not so standard but some yachtsmen, especially
single-handers, carry morphine by special permission. If so,
the law requires that they should be carried in a locked box
and these were not. There were also some unlabelled glass
ampoules containing a yellowish, oily liquid. Unlike the
morphine syringes they carried no description or maker's
name.

I picked up one of them and examined it closely. The
ampoule itself had an amateur look about it as though it
was home-made, the ends being sealed as though held in a

flame, and there was nothing etched in the glass to tell the nature of the contents. I thought that if Kayles was in the drug-running scene he could very well be an addict and this was his own supply of dope. The notion was reinforced by the finding of an ordinary reuseable hypodermic syringe. I left everything where it was and closed the box.

I went back to Sam who was still poring over the charts. He had come to much the same conclusion that I had, but he said, 'We might be able to tell when all this happened by relating it to weather reports.'

'We'll leave that to Perigord,' I said.

Sam frowned. 'Maybe we should have left it all to the Commissioner. I think we should have told him about this man before we left. Are we doing right, Tom?'

'Hell, I didn't *know* it was Kayles before we left. It was just a chance, wasn't it?'

'Even so, I think you should have told Perigord.'

I lost my temper a little. 'All right, don't drive it home, Sam. So I should have told Perigord. I didn't. Maybe I wasn't thinking straight. Everything has been going to hell in a handcart recently, from Legionnaires' disease at the Parkway to the fire at the Fun Palace. And we could do without those bloody street riots, too. Do you know what I was doing when you came to my office?'

'No – what?'

'Straightening out a mess caused by the Airport Authority. Their baggage-handling machinery ripped a plane-load of suitcases into confetti and I had over 200 Americans in the lobby looking for blood. Any more of this and we'll all go out of business.' I swung around as Kayles said something behind me. 'What was that?'

'Who the hell are you?' Kayles's voice was stronger than I expected and I suspected he had been feigning unconsciousness for some time while working on his bonds. I did not worry about that – I had seen the knots.

'You know me, Mr Kayles,' said Sam, and Kayles's eyes widened as he heard his own name. 'You're carrying no riding lights. That's bad – you could be run down.' His voice was deceptively mild.

'Goddamn yacht-jackers!' said Kayles bitterly. 'Look, you guys have got me wrong. I can help you.'

'Do you know much about yacht-jacking?' I asked.

'I know it happens.' Kayles stared at me. 'Who are you?'

I did not answer him, but I held his eye. Sam said casually, 'Ever meet a man called Albury? Pete Albury?'

Kayles moistened his lips, and said hoarsely, 'For God's sake! Who are you?'

'You know Sam here,' I said. 'You've met him before. I'm Tom Mangan. You might have heard of me – I'm tolerably well-known in the Bahamas.'

Kayles flinched, but he mumbled, 'Never heard of you.'

'I think you have. In fact I think you met some of my family. My wife and daughter, for instance.'

'And I think you're nuts.'

'All right, Kayles,' I said. 'Let's get down to it. You were hired over a year ago by Pete Albury as crew on *Lucayan Girl* to help take her from Freeport to Miami. Also on board were my wife and daughter. The boat never got to Miami; it vanished without trace. But my daughter's body was found. How come you're still alive, Kayles?'

'I don't know what you're talking about. I don't know you, your wife or your daughter. And I don't know this guy, Albury.' He nodded towards Sam. 'I know him because I put my boat in his marina, that's all. You've got the wrong guy.'

Sam said, 'Maybe we have.' He looked at me. 'But it's easily provable, one way or the other.' He regarded Kayles again. 'Where's your log-book?'

Kayles hesitated, then said, 'Stowed under this bunk mattress.'

Sam picked up Kayles's knife which he had laid on the chart table. 'No tricks or I'll cut you good.' He advanced on Kayles and rolled him over. 'Get it, Tom.'

I lifted the mattress under Kayles, groped about and encountered the edge of a book. I pulled it out. 'Okay, Sam.' Sam released Kayles who rolled over on to his back again.

As I flipped through the pages of the log-book I said, 'All you have to do is to prove where you were on a certain date.' I tossed the book to Sam. 'But we won't find it in there. Where's your last year's log?'

'Don't keep a log more'n one year,' said Kayles sullenly. 'Clutters up the place.'

'You'll have to do better than that.'

'That's funny,' said Sam. 'Most boat folk keep their old logbooks. As souvenirs, you know; and to impress other boat people.' He chuckled. 'And us marina people.'

'I'm not sentimental,' snarled Kayles. 'And I don't need to impress anyone.'

'You'll have to bloody well impress me if you expect me to turn you loose,' I said. 'And if I don't turn you loose you'll have to impress a judge.'

'Oh, Christ, how did I get into this?' he wailed. 'I swear to God you've got the wrong guy.'

'Prove it.'

'How can I? I don't know when your goddamn boat sailed, do I? I don't know anything about your boat.'

'Where were you just before last Christmas but one?'

'How would I know? I'll have to think about it.' Kayles's forehead creased. 'I was over in the Florida keys.'

'No, you weren't,' said Sam. 'I met you in the International Bazaar in Freeport, and you told me you were going to Miami. Remember that?'

'No. It's a hell of a long time ago, and how can I be expected to remember? But I did sail to Miami and then on down to Key West.'

'You sailed for Miami, all right,' I said. 'In *Lucayan Girl*.'

'I sailed in my own boat,' said Kayles stubbornly. 'This boat.' He jerked his head at me. 'What kind of a boat was this *Lucayan Girl*?'

'A trawler – fifty-two feet – Hatteras type.'

'For God's sake!' he said disgustedly. 'I'd never put foot on a booze palace like that. I'm a sailing man.' He nodded towards Sam. 'He knows that.'

I looked towards Sam who said, 'That's about it. Like I told you, he has this tiddy little diesel about as big as a sewing machine which he hardly ever uses.'

For a moment I was disconcerted and wondered if, indeed, we had the wrong man; but I rallied when Sam said, 'Why do you keep changing the name of your boat?'

Kayles was nonplussed for a moment, then he said, 'I don't.'

'Come off it,' I scoffed. 'We know of four names already – and four colours. When this boat was in the marina of the Royal Palm in Freeport just over a year ago she was *Bahama Mama* and her hull was red.'

'Must have been a different boat. Not mine.'

'You're a liar,' said Sam bluntly. 'Do you think I don't know my own work? I put up the masthead fitting.'

I thought back to the talk I had had with Sam and Joe Cartwright in my office a year previously. Sam had seen Kayles in the International Bazaar but, as it turned out, neither Sam nor Joe had seen the boat. But he was not telling Kayles that; he was taking a chance.

Kayles merely shrugged, and I said, 'We know you're a cocaine smuggler. If you come across and tell the truth it might help you in court. Not much, but it might help a bit.'

Kayles looked startled. 'Cocaine! You're crazy – right out of your mind. I've never smuggled an ounce in my life.'

Either he was a very good actor or he was telling the truth, but of course he would deny it so I put him down as a good actor. 'Why did you go to Cat Island?'

'I'm not saying another goddamn word,' he said sullenly. 'What's the use? I'm not believed no matter what I say.'

'Then that's it.' I stood up and said to Sam, 'Where do we go from here?'

'Sail this boat back to Duncan Town and hand him over to the local Government Commissioner. He'll contact the police and they'll take it from there. But not until daylight.'

'Scared of sailing in the dark?' jeered Kayles.

Sam ignored him, and said to me, 'I'd like a word with you on deck.'

I followed him into the cockpit. 'What did you tell Bayliss?'

'Enough of the truth to shut him up. He'd heard of the disappearance of *Lucayan Girl* so he'll stick around and cooperate.' He picked up the flashlamp Kayles had used and swept a beam of light into the darkness in a wide arc. There came an answering flicker from a darker patch of blackness about 200 yards to seaward. 'He's there.'

'Sam, why don't we sail back now? I know it's not true what Kayles said.'

'Because we can't,' said Sam, and there was a touch of wryness in his voice. 'I was a mite too careful. I was figuring on what might happen if Kayles got loose and I wanted to hamstring him, so I got some of Bayliss's fish net and tangled it around the propeller. That engine will never turn over now. Then I cut all the halliards so Kayles couldn't raise sail. Trouble is neither can we. I'm sorry, Tom.'

'How long will it take to fix?'

'Splicing the halliards and re-reeving will take more than an hour – in daylight. Same with the engine.'

'We could take Kayles back in Bayliss's boat, starting right now.'

'I don't think he'd do it,' said Sam. 'Fishermen aren't the same as yachtsmen who sail for fun. They don't like sailing around at night because there's no call to do it, so they don't have the experience and they know it.' He pointed south. 'There are a lot of reefs between here and Duncan Town, and Bayliss would be scared of running on to one. You don't know these folk; they don't work by charts and compasses like pleasure boat people. They navigate by sea colour and bird flight – things they can see.'

'You'd be all right on the tiller,' I said.

'But Bayliss wouldn't know that. It's his boat and he wouldn't want to lose her.'

'Let's ask him anyway,' I said. 'Call him in.'

Sam picked up the lamp and flashed it out to sea. There were a couple of answering winks and I heard the putt-putt of the engine as Bayliss drew near. He came alongside, fending off with the boathook, and then passed his painter up to Sam who secured it around a stanchion. Sam leaned over the edge of the cockpit still holding the light. 'Mr Mangan wants to know if you'll take us back to Duncan Town now.'

Bayliss's face crinkled and he looked up at the sky. 'Oh, no,' he said. 'Might if there was a full moon, but tonight no moon at all.'

I said, 'Sam here is willing to navigate and take the tiller, too. He's a good man at sea.'

It was just as Sam had predicted. Bayliss became mulish. 'How do I know that? This the only boat I got – I don't want to lose her. No, Mr Mangan, better wait for sunrise.'

I argued a bit but it was useless; the more I argued the more Bayliss dug in his heels. 'All right,' I said in the end. 'We wait for sunrise.'

'Jesus!' said Sam suddenly. 'The knife – I left it on the chart table.' He turned and looked below. 'Watch it!' he yelled. 'He's coming through the forehatch.'

I looked forward and saw a dark shape moving in the bows, then there was a flash and a flat report and a *spaaaang* as a bullet ricocheted off metal. Sam straightened and cannoned into me. 'Over the side!'

There was no time to think but it made immediate sense. You could not fight a man with a gun on a deck he knew like the back of his own hand. I stepped on to the cockpit seat and jumped, tripping on something as I did so and because of that I made a hell of a splash. There was another splash as Sam followed, and then I ducked under water because a light flashed from the sloop and the beam searched the surface of the water and there was another muzzle flash as Kayles shot again.

It was then I thanked Pete Albury for his swimming lessons on the reefs around Abaco. Scuba gear had just been introduced in those days and its use was not general; anyway, Pete had a hearty contempt for it. He had taught me deep diving and the breath control necessary so that I could go down among the coral. Now I made good use of his training.

I dribbled air from my mouth, zealously conserving it, while conscious of the hunting light flickering over the surface above. I managed to kick off my shoes, being thankful that I was not wearing lace-ups, and the swimming became easier. I was swimming in circles and, just before I came up for more air, I heard the unmistakeable vibrations of something heavy entering the water and I wondered what it was.

I came to the surface on my back so that just my nose and mouth were above water. Filling my lungs I paddled myself under again, trying not to splash. I reckoned I could stay underwater for two minutes on every lungful of air, and I came up three times – about six minutes. The last time I came up I put my head right out and shook the water from my ears.

Then I heard the regular throb of the engine of Bayliss's boat apparently running at top speed. Ready to duck again if it came my way I listened intently, but the noise died away in the distance and presently there was nothing to be heard. The sound of a voice floated softly over the water. 'Tom!'

'That you, Sam?'

'I think he's gone.'

I swam in what I thought was Sam's direction. 'Gone where?'

'I don't know. He took Bayliss's boat.'

'Where's Bayliss?' I saw the ripples Sam was making and came up next to him.

'I don't know,' said Sam. 'I think he went overboard, too. He may still be in the boat, though.'

'Let's not jump to conclusions,' I said. 'That might have been Bayliss running away, and Kayles might still be around.'

Sam said, 'I was bobbing under the bows and Kayles was swearing fit to bust a gut. First, he tried to start the engine and it seized up. Then he tried to hoist sail and found he couldn't. I think it's fairly certain he took Bayliss's boat.'

'Well, if we're going to find out, let's do it carefully,' I said.

We made a plan, simple enough, which was to come up simultaneously on both sides of the sloop, hoping to catch Kayles in a pincer if he was still there. On execution we found the sloop deserted. Sam said, 'Where's Bayliss?'

We shouted for a long time and flashed the light over the water but saw and heard nothing. Sam said, 'It's my fault, Tom. I botched it. I forgot the knife.'

'Forget it,' I said. 'Which way do you think Kayles went?'

'I don't know, but in his place I'd head north. He has fifty miles of fuel and maybe more, and there are plenty of cays up there to get lost in. He might even have enough fuel to get to Exuma.' He took a deep breath. 'What do we do now?'

I had been thinking about that. 'We wait until sunrise, do the repairs, find Bayliss if we can, go back to Duncan Town and report to the Government Commissioner, and have Bill Pinder make an air search for that son of a bitch.'

It was an uneasy night and a worse morning because, while Sam was repairing the halliards, I went under the stern to cut the fish net from around the propeller and found Bayliss jammed in there. He had been shot through the head and was very dead.

That broke up Sam Ford more than anything else and it did not do me much good.

NINE

Deputy-Commissioner Perigord was thunderous and gave the definite impression that invisible lightning was flashing around his head. 'You had Kayles and you let him go!' he said unbelievingly.

'Not deliberately,' I said. 'There wasn't much we could do about it – he had the gun.'

'But you did go off half-cocked. I warned you about that. Why, in God's name, didn't you tell me you knew where Kayles was?'

'I didn't know where he was. I thought I knew where his boat was. And I wasn't even sure of that. I know that Sam Ford knows his boats but I couldn't be entirely sure. I went down to the Jumentos to make the identification.'

'Instead of which you made a stinking mess,' said Perigord cuttingly. 'Mr Mangan, I told you that this is a professional matter and you were not to butt in. You are responsible for the death of a man; an innocent bystander whom you casually took along on a hunt for a murderer. Fred Bayliss was a married man with a wife and four children. What of them?'

I felt like hell. 'I'll look after the family,' I muttered.

'Oh, you will? Big deal. You know what it's like to lose your family. How do you suppose Mrs Bayliss is feeling

424

now? Do you think you can cure her grief with a few dollars?'

Perigord was a man who knew how to go for the jugular. 'Christ, what can I say beyond that I'm sorry?'

'Neither your sorrow or your money is of much help. And now I have an armed man loose in the Bahamas who knows he is being hunted, and it is my men who will have to do the hunting. How much sorrow will you feel if one of them is killed in the process?'

'Jesus, Perigord, enough is enough!'

He nodded. 'I think so, too. Go back to running your hotels, Mr Mangan. Go back to making money – but stay out of this business.' He paused. 'I may want to question you and Sam Ford further – I'll let you know. That's all.'

I left Perigord's office feeling so low I could walk under a snake's belly wearing a top hat. He was a man who knew how to use words as weapons, and the hell of it was that I knew I had it coming. I had been irresponsible. When Sam had come with the news of Kayles's boat I should have taken him to Perigord immediately and let the police handle it.

My disposition did not improve when I returned to my office and telephoned home. Luke Bailey answered. 'Is Mrs Mangan at home?'

'No, Mr Mangan.'

'Have you any idea where she is?'

'She left for Houston this morning.'

'Thanks, Luke.' I put down the telephone feeling more depressed than ever.

A few days later Perigord asked to see me and Sam Ford and we met him, not in his office, but in the Customs Department at the harbour. He had had Kayles's sloop brought up from Duncan Town and, as I thought he might, he had enlisted the aid of Customs officers to give it a real going-over.

The boat had been taken out of the water and put into a warehouse where she looked enormous. It is surprising how much larger a sailing boat looks out of the water than in; one tends to forget that most of a boat is under water. The Customs officers had taken most of the gear out of her and it was stacked on the floor of the warehouse and on tables in small heaps, each heap labelled as to where it was found. Again, it is surprising how much you can cram into a twenty-seven footer.

Perigord took us into a small glassed-in office in a corner of the warehouse and put us through the hoops again, this time with a tape recorder on the desk. It was a gruelling interrogation and it hit Sam hard because he blamed himself for everything, knowing that if he had not left the knife on the chart table then Bayliss might still be alive.

It was a two-hour grilling, occasionally interrupted by a Customs officer who would come in to show Perigord something or other. At last he switched off the recorder and took us out into the warehouse where he had Sam show him the masthead fitting by which he was able to identify the boat, even with its name and colour changed.

I said, 'Have you found anything useful?'

'Nothing of interest.' There was that in Perigord's voice which told me that even if he had found something he was not going to inform me.

'Not the drugs?' I asked in surprise.

His interest sharpened. 'What drugs?'

'The stuff in the first-aid box.'

He beckoned to a Customs man and the box was produced. It was empty. The Customs man said, 'We've laid out the contents over there.' We walked over to the trestle table and I scanned through the articles. The morphine syringes were there but there were no glass ampoules.

I described them, and said, 'I thought if Kayles was a drug-runner he might be a user, too, and that this was his personal stock.'

'Yes,' said Perigord thoughtfully. 'If he was a user he would certainly take it along, no matter in how much of a hurry he was. It was a liquid, you say?'

'That's right; a faintly yellowish liquid.' I described the ampoules and told of the home-made look they had.

The Customs officer picked up the reuseable hypodermic syringe. 'It's funny he didn't take this.' He shook his head. 'A yellow liquid. That's new to me.'

'They're always coming up with something new to blow their minds,' said Perigord. 'So now we've got a hopped-up gunman. It gets worse, doesn't it, Mr Mangan? Once his supplies run out he might start raiding pharmacies to resupply. Another headache.'

'Have you any idea where he might be?' I asked.

Bayliss's boat had not been found and, according to Perigord's gloomy prediction, it never would be. He thought it had been sunk. A small sailing yacht had been stolen from George Town in the Exumas. 'And it could be anywhere now, with a change of name and colour,' said Perigord. 'If Kayles has any sense he'll be getting clear of the Bahamas.'

I was about to turn away, but thought of something. 'There are rumours floating around that the fire at the Fun Palace was due to arson. Is there anything in that?'

'Not to my knowledge,' he said. 'Squash those rumours, if you can.'

'I do,' I said. 'It's in my interest to do so.'

So I went home and found that Debbie had returned.

She was spoiling for a fight. I was greeted with: 'Where were you? You're never here when I want you.'

'I could say the same for you,' I returned acidly. 'In point of fact I was being shot at down in the Jumentos.'

'Shot at!' I could see her disbelief. 'Who by?'

'A man called Kayles – remember him? He killed a man down there, and damn near killed me and Sam Ford.'

'Who is Sam Ford?'

'If you took more interest in me and my doings you'd know damn well who Sam Ford is. He's boss of the marinas division.'

'So you found Kayles.'

'Sam did, and you're looking at a damn fool. I tried to take him myself and got a poor bloody fisherman killed. I'm beginning to sicken myself.' I poured myself a stiff drink and sat down. 'Commissioner Perigord doesn't think a great deal of me these days. Just about as much as you seem to do.'

'And whose fault is that?' she flared. 'What interest are you taking in me? You're never around any more.'

'My God, you know the problems I've had recently, what with one thing and another. And a new one has just come up – the Fun Palace fire. There's a meeting of the Hoteliers' Association and the Ministry of Tourism in Nassau tomorrow. I'll have to leave early.'

'That was bad,' she said. 'I read about it in the Houston papers.'

'You would. If you were in Timbuctu you'd have read about it. That's the problem.'

'But what has it got to do with you? Why should you fly to Nassau?'

I looked at Debbie thoughtfully and decided to cool it. She was in a worse temper than I had ever seen, but even though she was being unreasonable she deserved an explanation. 'Because I'm in the business,' I said patiently. 'It affects the Theta Corporation. The Bahamas seems to have become a disaster area lately and we're trying to figure out ways of minimizing the damage. My guess is that the Ministry of Tourism will propose a levy on the industry to fund a new advertising campaign.'

'Oh, I see.'

I adopted a more conciliatory tone. 'Debbie, I know I haven't been around much lately, and I'm sorry – truly I am. I'll tell you what. Let me get straightened out here and we'll take a holiday. Maybe go to Europe – London and Paris. We've never had a holiday together, not a real one.'

'A second honeymoon so soon after the first?' she said ruefully. 'But will you get straightened out? Won't there be something else come along to need your personal attention? And then something else? And something else? Won't it be like that?'

'No, it won't be like that. No man is indispensable in a decently run organization, not even the boss. And this run of bad luck can't go on for ever.'

She shook her head slowly. 'No, Tom. I'm going away to think this out.'

'Think what out, for God's sake?'

'Us.'

'There's nothing wrong with us, Debbie. And can't you do your thinking here?'

'I'd rather go home – be among my own family.'

I took a deep breath. 'I wish you wouldn't, Debbie, I really do, but if you must I don't suppose I can stop you.'

'No, you can't,' she said, and left the room.

I poured myself another drink, again a stiff one. As I sat down I reflected that although I had told Debbie I had been shot at, never once had she asked if I had been hurt. We had gone so far down the line. The Mangan marriage appeared to be another part of the Bahamian disaster area.

Bobby Bowen flew me to Nassau early next morning and I spent the day arguing the toss with Ministry of Tourism officials and a crowd of apprehensive and tight-wadded hoteliers. Everyone agreed that something must be done; the argument was about who was going to pay for it. The argument went on all day and ended as I had predicted; there would be a levy on the industry and the Government would put up dollar for dollar.

I got home at about seven in the evening to find that Debbie had gone, but had left a note.

'Dear Tom,

I meant what I said yesterday. I have gone back to Houston and will stay until the baby has come. I don't want to see you until then, but I suppose you will want to come just before the birth. That's all right with me, but I don't want to see you until then.

I have not taken Karen with me because I think it would be unfair to take her from her school and her friends and into what is a foreign country. Besides, she is your daughter.

I can't see clearly what has gone wrong between us, but I will be thinking hard about it, and I hope you do the same. It's funny but I still love you, and so I can end this note with

Love,
    Debbie.'

I read that letter five times before putting it into my wallet, and then sat down to write my own letter asking her to come back. I had no great hopes that she would.

TEN

The week after Debbie left we lost Bill Pinder.

He was taking four American fishermen to Stella Maris on Long Island which they were going to use as a base for hunting marlin and sailfish off Columbus Point and on the Tartar Bank in Exuma Sound. I was going with them, not because I am particularly charmed by American fishermen, but because Bill was flying me on to Crooked Island, 100 miles further south, where I was to look at some property on behalf of the Theta Corporation.

As it chanced I did not go because the previous evening I slipped in the bathroom and broke a toe which proved to be rather painful. To look at property and to walk a few miles on Crooked Island in that condition was not a viable proposition, so I cancelled.

Bill Pinder took off in a Navajo early next morning with the Americans. He was flying over Exuma Sound and was filing his intentions with Nassau radio when suddenly he went off the air in mid-sentence, so we know exactly when it happened. What happened I know now but did not know then. The Bahamas may be the Shallow Sea but there are bits like the Tongue of the Ocean and Exuma Sound which are very deep; the Tartar Bank rises to within seven fathoms of the surface in Exuma Sound but the rest is deep water.

The Navajo was never found, nor any wreckage, and
Bill Pinder disappeared. So did the four Americans, and two
of them were so influential on Wall Street that the event
caused quite a stir, more than I and the Bahamas needed.
After a couple of weeks some bits and pieces of clothing
were washed up on one of the Exuma cays and identified as
belonging to one of the Americans.

The death of Bill Pinder hit me hard. He was a good man,
and the only better light plane pilot I know is Bobby Bowen.
It is hard for blacks like Bill and Bobby to achieve a commercial pilot's ticket, or at least it was when they pulled off
the trick. I suppose it is easier now.

There was a memorial service which I attended and to
which many of the Corporation employees came, as many
as could be spared without actually closing down the hotels.
A lot of BASRA pilots were there, too. After the service I
had a word with Bobby Bowen; I had not had a chance to
talk to him much because, being an aircraft short, he was an
overworked man. I said, 'What happened, Bobby?'

He shrugged. 'Who knows? There'll be no evidence coming out of Exuma Sound.' He thought for a moment. 'He
was filing with Nassau at the time so he'd be flying pretty
high, about 10,000 feet, to get radio range. But why he fell
out of the sky . . . ?' He spread his hands. 'That was a good
plane, Tom. It had just had its 300-hour check, and I flew it
myself three days earlier.' He grimaced a little. 'You'll hear
talk of the Bermuda Triangle; pay no heed – it's just the
chatter of a lot of screwy nuts who don't know one end of
an airplane from the other.'

I said, 'We'll need another plane and another pilot.'

'You won't get one like Bill,' said Bobby. 'He knew these
Islands right well. About another plane – something
bigger?' he said hopefully.

'Perhaps. I'll have to talk it over with the board. I'll let
you know.'

We watched the Pinder family walking away from the church. Bobby said, 'It's bad for Meg Pinder. Bill was a good husband to her.'

'She'll be looked after,' I said. 'The pension fund isn't broke yet.'

'Money won't cure what's wrong with her,' said Bobby, unconsciously echoing what Perigord had said about Bayliss's wife, and I felt a stab of shame.

But how could I know that someone was trying to kill me?

Billy Cunningham paid a flying visit. He came without warning at a weekend and found me at the house where I was packing a few things to take to my suite at the Royal Palm. We talked about Bill Pinder and he said the usual conventional things about what a tragedy it was, and we talked about getting another aircraft. He appeared to be a little nervous so I said, 'Stop pussy-footing, Billy. Sit down, have a drink, and get it off your chest. Are you an emissary?'

He laughed self-consciously. 'I guess so. I've had obligations laid on me.'

'Cunningham obligations?'

'Score one for you – I never did think you were stupid. You had that subtle look in your eye when you were inspecting us back home when you married Debbie. I suppose you didn't miss much.'

'A tight-knit bunch,' I observed.

'Yeah. The advantages are many – one for all and all for one – that stuff. A guy always has someone guarding his back. But there are disadvantages, like now. Old Jack's not been feeling too well lately so he couldn't come himself.'

'I'm sorry to hear that,' I said sincerely.

Billy waved his hand. 'Nothing serious. Frank had a business meeting in California – important. So I was elected.'

I said, 'Tell me one thing. Does Debbie know about this? Does she know you're here?'

He shook his head. 'No. It's just that Jack wants to know what the hell is going on. Personally, I think it's none of our business, but. . .'

'But the Cunninghams look after their own.'

'That's about it. Hell, Tom, I told Jack that interfering between man and wife is pure poison, but you think he'd listen? You know the old man.'

'Not too well,' I said coolly. 'What do you want to know?'

'It's not what I want to know – it's what Jack wants to know. Jack and Frank both. They're both mad at you.' Billy paused, then said meditatively, 'If Frank had come on this mission he might have taken a poke at you. Very protective is Frank.'

'Why should he do that?' I demanded. 'I don't beat up his little sister every Friday night as a regular routine.'

He grinned crookedly. 'It might have been better if you had. The Cunningham women . . .' He stopped short. 'Anyway, Jack wants to know why his little girl has come running home looking as blue as a cold flounder.'

'Didn't he ask her?'

'She clammed up on him – and on Frank. Me – I didn't bother to ask. What is it, Tom?'

'I don't know,' I said. 'It appears that she wants me to stay home and hold her hand. Says I'm neglecting her. But, God, you know what's been happening here. If it hasn't been one bloody thing it's been another. Did she tell you about Kayles?'

'No. What about him?'

I told Billy in some detail, and said, 'I know I made a damn fool of myself and I'm sorry a man was killed – but Debbie didn't even ask if I'd been hurt.'

'Self-centred,' observed Billy. 'She always was, and I've told her so to her face, many times. So where do you go from here?'

I took out my wallet and showed Billy the note Debbie had left and he made a sour face. 'If she wasn't family I'd call her a bitch,' he said. 'What are you doing about Karen?'

'She's staying with me at the hotel for the moment. I doubt if it's good for her but it's the best I can do right now.'

'Do you want me to talk with Debbie?'

'No,' I said. 'Keep out of it. She must work this thing through herself. And tell Jack and Frank to keep out of it, too.'

He shrugged. 'I've already told them, but I'll pass on the message from you.'

'Do that.'

And so we left it there and began to discuss our problems in the Bahamas. Billy said, 'The way things are going you'd better start another division – staffed by morticians. It should show a profit.'

'Not if the bodies aren't found,' I said. 'Anyway, the Theta Corporation was only directly involved in one of these incidents, the air crash.'

'We don't want another like that,' warned Billy. 'The waves are still rocking the New York Stock Exchange. Those guys who were killed weren't ready to die; their financial affairs weren't exactly in order. I hear the Securities and Exchange Commission might start an investigation and that'll cause grief all round. Tom, the name of the Bahamas is coming up too often in headlines and it's beginning to stink. And don't give me that crap about any publicity being good publicity as long as they get the name right.'

'It's just a streak of bad luck. It'll come right.' I told him of the deal made between the Hoteliers' Association and the Ministry of Tourism ending with, 'So we're doing something about it.'

'You'd better do something about it. Jack's getting worried; he's talking about pulling out.'

'Is he chicken-livered? We've had a run of three bad incidents and Jack runs scared?'

'Three incidents and 128 dead,' said Billy. 'Jack's been counting; he's keeping score.' He sighed. 'Trouble is he never really wanted to come into the Bahamas anyway. It was my idea and Billy One backed me. Jack went along but his heart was never really in it.'

'On top of which he's never cottoned on to me,' I said a little bitterly.

'He thinks you run a loose ship,' said Billy frankly. 'That you give too much away. According to Jack at best you're a do-gooder; at worst, when his bile really starts to rise, you're an agent of the Kremlin.'

I gave Billy a level look. 'What do you think?'

'I think Jack is a fossilized dinosaur. Times are changing but he isn't. As for me I'm willing to play along with your plans of operation as long as they show a profit – a reasonable return on a fifty million buck investment, a return comparable to what we'd get anywhere else. I know you're a Bahamian and you want to help your own people; all I ask is that you don't do it *too* much at corporate expense.'

'Fair enough. But, Billy, all those things which Jack thinks are giveaways – the pension fund, the hotel doctor, the hotels' school, and so on – all those are investments for the Corporation. They'll pay off in staff service and corporate loyalty, and that's hard to buy.'

'You're probably right,' acknowledged Billy. 'But Jack's an old-time Texan. He even accused Nixon of being a commie when he pulled out of Vietnam. Sometimes I think he's a nut. But look at you from his side of the fence. You're a foreigner who first subverted his daughter into mixing with black kids, then took her away, and now she's back home looking goddamn unhappy. Add all that together and you'll see he's just looking for an excuse to pull out of here. It won't take much.'

'How much of the Theta Corporation does he control?'

'As an individual, nothing; our eighty per cent of Theta is owned by the Cunningham Corporation. But he has some clout in there. With some fast talking he could line up enough proxies to vote for a pull-out from the Bahamas.'

'That would be a personal disaster for me,' I said slowly. 'I'm too deeply committed now.'   —

'I know. That's why you'd better pray there isn't an earthquake here next week, or an outbreak of infectious dandruff. No more headlines, Tom.'

As though I did not have enough to worry about I now had Jack Cunningham gunning for me. And, as Billy had said, all I could do was pray.

ELEVEN

That was on Saturday. Billy stayed to lunch and then departed, saying that he was going to Miami on business for the Cunningham Corporation, and from there to New York. He gave me telephone numbers where I could find him. On Sunday I caught up with paperwork.

Monday was – well, Monday was Monday – one of those days when nothing goes really wrong but nothing goes really right; a day of niggling futilities and a rapidly shortening temper. I suppose we all have days like that.

I dined in the restaurant and went to my room early, after seeing Karen to bed, intending to go to bed myself and to scan some managerial reports before sleeping. I have never known why one is supposed to be vertical while working, and I can read perfectly well while flat on my back. I had just got settled when the telephone rang and a voice said in my ear, as clear as a bell, 'Mangan? Is that you?'

'Yes. Who's speaking?'

'Jack Cunningham here. Is Debbie there?'

'No, I thought she was with you. Where are you?'

'Houston.' His voice suddenly receded although he was still speaking. I caught a few scattered words and concluded he was consulting with someone else.'. . . not there . . . must be right . . . Billy . . .' He came back full strength. 'Is young Billy there?'

'No,' I said. 'He was here on Saturday. He'll be in Miami if he hasn't gone on to New York.'

Again he withdrew and I heard incomprehensible bits of a conversation nearly 1000 miles away. '. . . Miami . . . airplane . . . both . . .' then Jack said loudly, 'Tom, you pack a bag and be ready to get your ass over here.'

I resented that rasping tone of command. 'Why? What's happening?'

'I'm not going to talk about it now. There's a satellite up there spraying this conversation all over the goddamn planet.'

'I don't see . . .'

'Damn it! Do as I say and don't argue. There'll be a jet at Freeport International in about two hours. Don't keep it waiting, and be prepared to stay over awhile.' The connection broke and silence bored into my ear.

I checked the time. It was 9.30 in the evening.

Much against my will I got out of bed and dressed, impelled by the fizzing urgency in Jack Cunningham's voice. Then I thought of Karen, asleep in the next room. Damn Jack Cunningham! Damn the whole blasted family! I rang the desk and asked the clerk to find Kitty Symonette and send her up to my suite, then I started to pack a bag.

I was just finishing a letter when Kitty Symonette tapped at the door and I let her in. 'Sit down, Kitty. I have problems and I want you to help me.'

She looked slightly surprised. 'I'll do what I can.'

Kitty was the hotel nurse and I liked her very much, and so did Karen. She was totally unflappable and equally reliable. 'I'm not interrupting anything, am I?'

'No. I was going to have an early night.'

'Good. I have to go away and I don't know for how long. Tomorrow I want you to take Karen to stay with my sister on Abaco. I've just spoken to Peggy and Karen is expected.'

I scribbled my signature. 'These are instructions for Bobby Bowen to take you.'

'No problem there,' said Kitty.

'Karen is asleep in that room there. I don't want her to wake alone so you'd better sleep in my room tonight.'

'You're going right away?'

'This minute. I don't want to wake Karen now, but you tell her I'll be back as soon as I can make it.'

Kitty stood up. 'I'll collect some things from my room.'

I gave her the key to the suite, picked up my bag, and went to my office where I collected my passport from the office safe. As an afterthought I took the packet of 2000 American dollars which I kept there for an emergency and put them in my wallet.

The wait at the airport was long and boring. I drank coffee until it sickened me, then had a couple of scotches. It was after midnight when the public address speakers said, 'Will Mr Mangan please go to the enquiry desk?'

I was met by a pretty girl dressed in a yellow uniform trimmed with black and with a badge on her lapel, two letters 'C' intertwined in a monogram. The outfit made her look waspish, about as waspish as I was feeling. 'Mr Mangan?'

'Yes,' I said shortly.

'This way, sir.' She led the way from the concourse and through a side door. Standing on the apron not very far away was a Lockheed JetStar in gold with black trim; on the tailfin was the Cunningham monogram. Around it was a collection of airport vehicles like workers around a queen bee. I followed her up the gangway and paused as she stopped inside the door to take my bag. 'Glad to have you with us, Mr Mangan.'

I could not reciprocate her feelings, but I murmured, 'Thank you,' and passed on into the main cabin.

Billy Cunningham said explosively, 'Now, will you, for Christ's sweet sake, tell me what's going on?'

From Freeport to Houston is about 1000 miles across the Gulf of Mexico. We droned across the Gulf at 500 miles an hour and Billy was morose – sore because he had been yanked out of Miami as unceremoniously as I had from Freeport – and he was irritated when he found I could tell him nothing. 'What bugs me,' he said, 'is that for the first time in my life I'm going somewhere in an airplane and I don't know why. What the hell's got into Jack?'

'I don't know,' I said slowly. 'I think it's something to do with Debbie.'

'Debbie! How come?'

'The first thing Jack asked was if she was with me – in Freeport.'

'He knew she wasn't,' said Billy. 'She was in Houston.'

I shrugged. 'Air travel is wonderful. A girl can get around fast.'

'You think she's taken off again?' He snorted. 'That girl wants her ass spanked – and if you won't do it, then I will. It's time she settled down and learned how to behave.'

There was nothing more to say so we did not say it.

There was a car waiting at Houston airport and an hour later I was at the start of a Cunningham conference. At least it was the start for me; the others had evidently been arguing the toss for a long time – and it showed. Jack Cunningham was at the head of the table, his silver hair making him look senatorially handsome as usual, and Billy One sat next to him. Debbie's brother, Frank, eyed me with arrogant and ill-concealed hostility. As background there were half a dozen other collateral Cunninghams, most of whom I did not know, ready to take their cue from the powerful tribal bosses. This was the Cunningham clan in full deliberation and, predictably, there was not a woman in sight.

Our arrival brought instant silence which did not last long. Billy flipped a hand at his father, surveyed the gathering, and drawled, 'Morning, y'all.' Uproar broke out, everybody talking at once and I could not distinguish a word until Jack hammered the long table with a whisky bottle and yelled, 'Quiet!'

It could have been the traditional smoke-filled room but for the air-conditioning and, indeed, they did look like a crowd of old-time political bosses carving up next year's taxes. Most had their jackets off and had loosened their neckties and the room smelled of good cigars. Only Jack had kept on his coat, and his tie was securely knotted at his neck. Even so he looked decidedly frayed around the edges, and there was a persistent twitch in his left cheek.

He said, 'Tom, do you know what's happened to Debbie?'

The question could have had two meanings – he really wanted to know if I knew, or it was rhetorical – and there was no way of knowing from the inflection of his voice. I said, 'How would I know? She left me.'

'He admits it,' said Frank.

'Admit! I admit nothing – I'm *telling* you, if she hasn't told you already. She's her own woman and she ran away.'

'Ran away from what? That's what I'd like to know.'

Billy casually walked up to the table and picked up a whisky bottle. 'Any clean glasses around?' Then he swung on Frank. 'Button up your mouth.'

'You can't . . .'

'Shut it,' said Billy quietly, but there was a cutting edge to his voice. 'Your sister's a brat. Everything she ever wanted she got, but she wouldn't know a man when she saw one, not a real man. When she found she couldn't handle him she picked up her marbles and wouldn't play any more.' He looked at Jack. 'Nobody's going to hold a kangaroo court on Tom. Hear?'

Billy One stirred. 'Quiet, boy.'

'Sure,' said Billy easily. 'I've said the core of it, y'all know that.' He dropped into a chair. 'Come sit here, Tom; you look as though you need a drink.'

I suppose I did; we both did. And it was half past three in the morning. I took the chair he offered and accepted the drink, then I said, 'If you want to know what happened to Debbie why don't you ask her?'

I was now facing Billy One across the table. He laid his hands flat. 'That's just it, son. She's not around to be asked.'

'Jesus!' said Billy, and stared at Jack. 'Your little girl runs away again, and you jerk me from making the sweetest deal you ever saw?'

The tic convulsed Jack's cheek; he looked defeated. 'Tell him, Billy One,' he said in an old man's voice.

Billy One stared at the back of his hands. He said slowly, 'We weren't sure at first, not really, not even this afternoon when . . .' He looked up at me. 'Now you're here we're pretty sure Debbie's been kidnapped.'

Suddenly it all did not seem real. My head swam for a moment as a host of questions crowded in. I picked the first at random. 'Who by?'

'Who the hell knows?' said Frank disgustedly. 'Kidnappers don't hand out business cards.'

He was right; it was a stupid question. Billy said, 'When?'

'Saturday, we think; maybe Sunday early.' And today was late Monday or, rather, very early Tuesday. Billy One nodded down the table. 'Last one of us to see her was Joe's wife.'

'Yeah,' said Joe. 'Linda and Debbie went shopping Saturday morning – Sakowitz and Nieman-Marcus. They lunched together.'

'Then what?' asked Billy.

Joe shrugged. 'Then nothing. Linda came home.'

'Did she say what Debbie was going to do Saturday afternoon?'

'Debbie didn't tell her.'

This did not seem to be getting anywhere. I cleared my throat, and said, 'How do you know she's been kidnapped? Billy, here, jumped to the conclusion that she'd taken off again. So did I. So how do you *know?*'

'Because the goddamn kidnappers told us,' said Frank.

Billy One said, 'We got a letter this . . . last afternoon – least, Jack did. Tell the truth I don't think we believed it at first, neither of us. Thought it was some kind of hoax until we discovered she really wasn't around.'

'Where was Debbie staying?'

'At my place,' said Jack. He looked at me reproachfully. 'My girl was very unhappy.'

'She was last seen by the family at midday on Saturday and it took you until Monday to find out she'd disappeared?' I looked at Jack. 'Wasn't her bed slept in?'

'Take it easy, Tom,' said Billy One. 'We thought she'd gone back to you.'

'She'd have left word,' I said. 'She may be irresponsible, but she's not that irresponsible. When she left me she at least had the decency to leave a note telling me where she'd gone, if not why. What about her clothes? Didn't you check to see if any were missing? Or, more to the point, not missing?'

'Oh, Christ!' said Frank. 'She'd been living away. Who knew what clothes she had?' He waved an impatient hand. 'This is wasting time.'

'I agree,' I said emphatically. 'Have you notified the police?'

There was silence around the table and Jack evaded my eye. Finally Billy One said quietly, 'Kidnapping is a federal offence.'

I knew that; it had been a federal offence ever since the stink caused by the Lindbergh kidnapping. 'So?'

He tented his fingers. 'If it was just a matter for the State Police we'd be able to keep control – we draw a lot of water here in Texas. But once the Federal Government gets into the act – and that means the FBI – then anything could happen. Since Watergate every Government department has been as leaky as a goddamn sieve, and that damn fool, Carter, calls it open government.' In his voice was the contempt of the old-line Republican for a Democratic administration. 'The FBI is no exception, and if the newspapers get hold of this I wouldn't give a bent nickel for our chances of getting Debbie back safely.'

'We can control our press down here, but those newspapers back east would really screw things up,' said Frank.

'To say nothing of the professional bleeding hearts on TV,' Joe commented.

'So you haven't told the police,' I said bleakly.

'Not yet,' said Billy One.

'Hell, we can pay,' said Billy. He grinned sardonically. 'And stop it out of Debbie's allowance when we get her back.'

'If we get her back,' said Jack. There was agony in his voice. 'You know what kidnappers are like.'

'Right,' said Billy. 'But if you don't call the cops you don't get her back unless you pay – so let's start opening the coffers.'

'It's not as easy as that,' said Billy One. 'Not by a long shot. There are . . . difficulties.'

'What difficulties? These guys want dough, we want Debbie. We give them how many dollars they want and we get Debbie.' Billy's voice turned savage. 'Then we go hunting and we get the money back and maybe some scalps. But I don't see any difficulty.'

'You brought one with you,' said Frank.

'What the hell do you mean by that?'

'I mean that this son of a bitch . . .'

'Shut up!' said Billy One. He sighed. 'These guys don't want money, Billy. They want him.' He was pointing at me. 'He's the ransom.'

TWELVE

Dawn was breaking as I got to bed that morning but I did not sleep much. I just lay there in bed, staring into the darkness of the curtained room, and thinking. The trouble was that I could not think very well; fugitive thoughts chittered about in my skull like bats in an attic. Nothing seemed to connect.

I moved restlessly in bed and again saw the face of Billy One and the finger pointing directly at me. That finger had been a little unsteady; it trembled with age or fatigue – or possibly both. 'Don't ask me why,' said Billy One. 'But they want Tom for Debbie – an even deal.'

'Bullshit!' said Billy. He did not believe it, and neither did I. It made no sense.

'Show him the ransom note,' said Frank.

Jack took a folded letter and tossed it on to the table. I grabbed it and read it with Billy peering over my shoulder. It was in typescript, addressed to Mr John D. Cunningham, and written with a stilted formality which contrasted oddly with the rawness of the contents.

'Dear Mr Cunningham,
    You will have difficulty in believing this but we have in our possession the person of your daughter, Deborah Mangan. In short, we have kidnapped her.

In the belief that you will want her back unharmed
we now give you our terms. They are not subject to
negotiation.

You will cause your son-in-law, Thomas Mangan, to
travel to Houston. How you do this is your concern.
We will know when he has arrived. Our price for your
daughter's safety and, possibly, her life is the person of
Thomas Mangan delivered to us intact and unhurt.
Your daughter will then be returned in fair exchange.
You will be notified as to the manner of this transac-
tion upon the arrival of Mr Mangan in Texas.

It goes without saying that the police should not
be informed of these arrangements nor should any of
those steps be taken which might seem obvious in
such a dramatic situation as this.

You will understand my motives in not signing
this communication.'

'For Christ's sake!' said Billy. He looked at me with a baffled expression. 'Who'd . . .' He stopped and shook his head
in wonder.

'I don't know.' What I did know was the reason for Jack
Cunningham's peremptory summons to Houston.

'You must be quite a guy,' said Frank, his tone belying his
words. He looked around the table. 'Any hoodlum knows a
Cunningham woman is worth hard cash money. How much?
Quarter of a million dollars? Half a million? A million? Christ,
we'd pay five million if we had to. Course, any hoodlum with
sense would know he wouldn't live long enough to spend it,
no matter which way the ball bounced. But this guy would
rather have Mangan than the dough.' He eyed me challengingly. 'So what the hell makes you so valuable?'

'Cut it out,' said Billy.

Billy One said pointedly, 'We want to make friends and
influence people.'

'Yeah,' said Billy. 'Tom hasn't said much yet. He hasn't said he wants any part of this.'

'He's not a man if he runs out,' said Frank hotly.

'Oh, I don't know,' said Billy in a detached voice. 'How much would you do for a wife who's run out on you?'

For some reason that seemed to hit Frank where it hurt. He flushed and was about to say something, but thought better of it and sat back in his chair, drumming his fingers on the table. From which I gathered that Frank had marital troubles of his own.

There was a long silence. Jack Cunningham sat at the head of the table, looking along its length with dead eyes; Billy pulled the letter closer and read it again; Frank fidgeted while Billy One studied him with watchful eyes. The rest, the family underlings, said nothing.

Billy One sat upright, apparently satisfied that Frank had shot his bolt, at least temporarily. 'Okay, Tom.' His voice was neutral but not unfriendly. 'Frank has a point, you know. What makes you so valuable that someone would kidnap a Cunningham to get you?'

That was a good question and I did not have an answer. 'I don't know,' I said flatly. 'You know who I am and what I do. Jack had me thoroughly investigated, didn't he? Twice. Once before the merger and again before the wedding. You don't think I can't recognize private detectives when they're floating around my hotels?'

Billy One smiled slightly. 'You checked out fine,' he said. 'Both times.'

'It wasn't necessary,' I said. 'All you had to do was to come to me and ask. My life is a pretty open book. But I thought that if that's the way you operate, then that's the way you operate, and there was nothing I could do about it. Which isn't to say I liked it.'

'We didn't give a damn if you liked it or not,' said Frank.

Jack said, 'That will be enough, Frank.'

'Jack was dead against the marriage,' said Billy One. 'He had his reasons. Frank was, too; but Billy was for it – he thought you were a right guy. Me, I had no druthers either way. As it turned out, what we all thought didn't matter a damn because Debbie got her own way, as always.'

He reached out and poured a measure of whisky into a glass. 'Now, we've gotten two things here, both separate – I think. Debbie left you, and she's been kidnapped. Can you think of any connection?'

'No,' I said. 'As you know, I've had my hands full lately – you've read the reports – and perhaps I couldn't, or didn't, give Debbie enough of my time. That's what she thought, anyway, so she quit. But I don't know why she should be kidnapped with me as ransom. That fits nowhere.'

'Has anything out of the ordinary happened lately?'

'Yes,' said Billy. 'Tell him about Kayles.'

So I told the story of me and Kayles. When I had finished Frank said, 'And this guy is still loose?'

'Yes – so far.'

'That's it, then,' he said. 'There's your answer.'

'What would Kayles want with me?' I demanded, and prodded at the ransom demand on the table. 'I've met and talked with Kayles – he wouldn't and couldn't write a thing like this. It's way above his head – he's not that much educated.'

Billy One said, 'And where does that leave us? What makes you so goddamn valuable, Tom?'

'I have no idea,' I said tiredly. 'And does it matter? The point at issue here is what to do about Debbie.'

'Mangan, I'd say you lose wives awful easy,' said Frank nastily.

'That does it,' said Billy, and hit Frank before I could get my own hands on him. It was a backhander across the jaw which caught Frank by surprise. He went over backwards and his chair went with him, and he sprawled on the floor with Billy standing over him. He looked up, rubbing his jaw, and Billy said, 'Cousin Frank, I've always been able to whip your ass, and if you don't stay off Tom's back I'm ready to do it again right now.'

Billy One glanced at Jack who was silent. He said, 'That was uncalled for, Frank. Now, you'll stand up and apologize to Tom or you leave this room right now, and maybe you won't be back – ever. Understand? Help him up, Billy.'

Billy hoisted Frank to his feet. Frank rubbed his mouth and looked at the blood on the back of his hand. 'I guess I'm sorry,' he mumbled, then looked at me directly. 'But what are you going to do about my sister?'

'I'm going to make the exchange.' I looked at the expression on his face, and then at Billy One. 'Did you have any doubt I would?'

A suppressed chuckle came from Billy. 'You're damn right they had doubts.'

Billy One exhaled a long sigh. 'Maybe I misjudged you, Tom,' he said quietly.

'Well, now we can plan,' said Billy. He sat down and picked up the letter. 'Frank was talking about hoodlums, but Tom's right; this wasn't written by any illiterate jerk. But he used a typewriter – they can be traced.'

'Typewriters are cheap,' said Frank as he picked up his chair. 'That one is probably at the bottom of Galveston Bay by now.' He sat down. 'And what's to plan? This guy is doing the planning. We can't do a goddamn thing until we get instructions on how we do the deal.'

'You're wrong,' said Billy. 'What's the use of having a security section in the Corporation if we don't use it? Those guys know all about bugs.'

Billy One lifted a shaggy eyebrow. 'So?'

'So we bug Tom. A transmitter in the heel of a shoe, maybe. In a ballpoint pen or sewn into his pants. We bug him until he's crawling.'

'And then?'

'Then we . . .'

Billy One had a sudden thought. He held up his hand and looked about the table. 'Hold it! There are too many damn people in here. Let's do some pruning. Tom stays, of course – and Billy. Jack stays, too, if he wants.' He peered at the far end of the table. 'Jim, you stay. The rest of you clear out.'

There was a general murmur of disapproval but no one objected overtly except Frank. 'What the hell!' he said tightly. 'We're talking about my sister. I'm staying.'

Billy One scowled at him. 'Okay. But quit riding Tom; we're talking about his wife and that's a closer relationship.' He turned to Jack. 'It's after four in the morning and you look beat. You sure you want to stay? You've been grinding at this all night.'

'So has Frank. So have you.'

'Yeah, but Frank is a young guy – and I'm not as close to it as you. I'm more objective. Why don't you catch some sleep and come up tomorrow full of the old moxie?'

'Maybe you're right,' said Jack. His face was grey with fatigue as he stood up slowly. 'Frank, fill me in tomorrow morning. Hear?'

'I'll do that.' A frown creased Frank's forehead as he watched his father walk to the door.

I had a sudden insight into the workings of the Cunningham Corporation. It operated remarkably like the Kremlin – collective leadership. Everybody had a vote but some votes were heavier than others. Every so often the old bulls at the top would do battle over some issue and the weaker would be tossed out. I had the idea that this was happening now; that Billy One was in the process of tossing out Jack, just as Brezhnev had got rid of Podgorny.

Billy and Frank were fighting for second place. Where Jim Cunningham came into this I did not know; probably

Billy One was sealing an alliance with a faction of the clan. Jim was lucky – he had been promoted to top table.

This was confirmed when, as the door closed, Billy One called, 'Jim, come sit up here.' He glowered at us under white eyebrows. 'From now on we operate on "need to know", and what they don't know won't hurt us, or Debbie. Hell, it only needs Joe to drop a loose word at home and Linda would spread it over half Houston. She's a gossip.'

Frank said, 'If she shoots her mouth off about what's happened to Debbie she'll wish she never married a Cunningham. I'll see to it if Joe doesn't.'

Billy One nodded. 'Jim, you know more about the security angle than any of us. Got any ideas on this?'

Jim was a young chap of about twenty-five, dressed casually in jeans. He had a sleepy look about him which was deceptive because he was as sharp as a tack. He said, 'Billy is right.' He turned to me. 'I'll need your clothes – coat, pants, everything you wear down to socks and underwear. The outfit you'll use when you go to make this lousy deal. We'll have you radiating right through the electromagnetic spectrum.' To Billy One he said, 'We'll need cars, light airplanes and maybe choppers. Better lay on a couple of fast boats, too; Tom might be taken out to sea.'

'We'll use my boat,' said Frank. 'Nothing faster in Texas.'

'No!' said Jim quickly. 'We use nothing Cunningham. We rent everything.'

'My job,' said Billy.

I said, 'But no one makes a move until Debbie's safe.'

'That's understood,' said Billy One. 'What about a gun?'

I shook my head. 'No gun. I don't want to kill anybody.'

He looked disappointed; my way was not the Texan way. 'You might need a gun to stop someone killing *you*.'

'A gun wouldn't stop them – not the way I use one,' I said dryly. 'Anyway, they'll search me. The joker who wrote this ransom note doesn't sound like a damn fool.'

Jim agreed. 'Finding a gun might make him nervous; nervous guys are dangerous.'

A telephone beeped discreetly in a corner of the room. Billy One jerked his head and Jim got up to answer it. Even though he had got to the inner cabinet he knew his place on the totem pole; he was still a messenger boy. Presently he said, 'It's the Security Officer speaking from the lobby. He says an envelope has been handed in addressed to Jack.'

Billy One grunted. 'Have him bring it up.'

'Our security force might need beefing up,' said Billy. 'The way this is turning out we might be spread thin. What about a detective agency?'

'I'll fix that,' said Billy One. 'I know a good one.'

Frank said, 'We might not have time for all that. I have a gut feeling trouble is coming up in the elevator right now.'

Billy One looked at his watch. 'If you're right, it's bad news.' He picked up the ransom letter. 'I know this guy said he'd know when Tom arrives, but Tom's been here not much over an hour.'

'Good intelligence service,' said Billy.

'Too goddamn good.' Frank frowned. 'Inside information? From this building, maybe?'

'Who knows?' Billy One irritably threw down the sheet of paper. 'We'll wait and see.'

If the information of my arrival had come from the inside of the building then it was bad news indeed, because we were sitting in the penthouse of the slab-sided glass tower that was the Cunningham Building, the latest addition to the Houston skyline. It would mean the Cunningham Corporation itself had been penetrated.

The long moments dragged by. Billy One must have parallelled my train of thought because he ceased his finger-tapping and said, 'Jim, have security check this room for bugs first thing in the morning.'

'Will do.'

There was a discreet tap at the door and Jim got up. After a brief colloquy he came back carrying a large envelope which he laid on the table. Billy One bent forward to read the superscription, then pulled the ransom letter towards him and compared. 'Could be the same typewriter. Probably is.'

'The guy has confidence,' said Billy with a sideways glance at Frank.

'Lot of stuff in here,' said Billy One, hefting the envelope. 'Who delivered it?'

'A guy who said he'd been given five bucks in a bar.' As Billy One picked up a paper-knife Jim said sharply, 'Let's do this right. Let's not get our fingers all over what's in there.'

'You do it.'

Jim slit open the envelope and shook its contents on to the table. Most of it appeared to be eight-by-ten glossy black-and-white photographs, but there were also a couple of sheets of paper covered with typescript, single-spaced. Jim took a ballpoint pen and separated it all out, being careful not to touch anything with his fingers. He said, 'I'll have these put in glassine envelopes later. You can look at them now, but don't touch.'

The two pages of typescript were complicated instructions of what to do and when to do it. The photographs were of places where certain actions had to be done, and had been annotated with a red fibre pen. On one, for instance, were the instructions, 'Wait here exactly four minutes. Flash headlamps twice at end of each minute.' There were eleven photographs, each numbered, and the eleventh showed the edge of a road with open country beyond and trees in the distance. A red dashed line traced a path from the road to the trees, and an inscription read, 'Mangan goes this way alone. Deborah Mangan comes out same way ten minutes later. No tricks, please.'

It was all very complicated.

Billy was studying the first typed page. 'What a nerve! This one begins: "Mr Thomas Mangan, welcome to Houston, the fastest growing city in America".'

Frank said, 'Well, he gives us until Thursday – three days. Enough time to get ready for the son of a bitch.'

Billy One grunted, but said nothing.

Jim looked down at the photographs. 'I don't think this guy is American. Look here, Billy.' His finger hovered an inch over the table. 'An American wouldn't refer to headlamps – he'd say headlights.'

'Yeah, could be. European usage, maybe.'

'Why not come right out and say British?' Frank looked at me unsmilingly. 'What do you say in the Bahamas, Mangan? Headlamps or headlights?' He could not resist needling me.

I shrugged. 'I use them interchangeably. Both usages are valid. We're being penetrated by the American language because most of our tourists are American.'

Billy One yawned. 'Since we have time to spare I'm going home to bed. I want y'all in my office downstairs at ten a.m. Jim, don't forget to have this room debugged. Where are you sleeping tonight, Tom? I don't believe Jack made arrangements.'

'Come home with me,' said Billy. He rubbed his eyes wearily. 'Jesus, but I'm tired.'

THIRTEEN

Tuesday morning, early but not very bright. I had had about three hours' sleep and my body felt as heavy as my spirits, and even the forceful shower in the guest bathroom did not help. Knowing Houston I dressed lightly; it's like living in a permanent sauna and it was fairly steamy even so early in the morning.

Breakfast was on the patio outside the house, a low rambling structure of stone, timber and glass. I do not know if Billy's wife, Barbara, knew anything about the kidnapping of Debbie; she made no reference to it as she served breakfast so I concluded that probably Billy had not told her. It is a characteristic of Texans, and Cunninghams in particular, not to involve their womenfolk.

Over breakfast we talked of the weather, of baseball, and other mundane matters. A couple of times I caught Barbara giving me a sidelong glance and I knew what she was thinking – why was I there and not at Jack's place with Debbie? The gossiping close-knit Cunningham women would know, of course, that the marriage was in trouble, but Barbara was too disciplined to refer to it and hid her curiosity well if not entirely.

After breakfast I went with Billy to his study where he picked up a red telephone and depressed a button. 'Hi, Jo-Ann; anything I ought to know?' I realized he had a direct line to his office in the Cunningham Building. He listened for a while then said abruptly. 'Cancel all that.' Standing ten feet away I was able to hear the cry of expostulation which came from the earphone.

'No, I can't tell you,' he said. 'But it'll be a week. Damn it, don't argue with me, Jo-Ann. Here's what you do. I want to see Harry Pearson of Texas Aviation and Charlie Alvarez of the Gulf Fishing Corporation – both this morning – *not* at the Cunningham Building, some place else. Sure, the Petroleum Club will do fine. You can tell me when you see me – half an hour.'

He put down the telephone and grinned. 'I have a strong-minded secretary – but efficient.' He became serious. 'If we want helicopters and fast boats to be used in the way we want them used I'll have to tell Harry and Charlie the reason. No chopper jockey or boat skipper will do what we want without their bosses' say-so – we may have to skirt the law. So Harry and Charlie have to know. They'll keep their mouths shut, I promise.'

'I don't mind,' I said. 'It's my skin you're protecting. Just so you don't take action before you have Debbie safe.'

'Right,' he said. 'Have you got the clothing Jim wants?'

'All packed.'

'Then let's go downtown.'

Houston.

Not so much a city as a frame of mind – a tribute to the dynamism of American technology. Too far from the sea? Bring the sea fifty miles to the city and make Houston the third biggest port in the United States. Want to produce gasoline? Build seven refineries and produce a flood of fifteen billion gallons a year. Want to go to the moon? Spend ten years, forty billion dollars, and make Houston the nerve centre of the operation. Want to play baseball when it is too hot and steamy to move? Put a roof over a stadium

which holds 52,000 people and cool it to a constant 74° F. –
cool for Houston – using 7000 tons of air-conditioning
machinery. The grass in the stadium won't grow? For
Christ's sake, man; design a special plastic grass.

The latest proposal was to roof over the entire business
quarter of the city – much simpler than to air-condition
individual buildings.

Houston – Baghdad-on-the-Bayou. I hated the place.

We went downtown in Billy's car which he drove with the
casual ease which comes to Americans by second nature,
through the air they breathe – conditioned, of course. We
went from his house to his office in the Cunningham
Building without once taking a breath of the nasty, polluted,
natural stuff outside. Billy's secretary, I was interested to
note, was a middle-aged lady with a face like a prune. As
we passed through the outer office she said quickly, 'Mr
Pearson and Mr Alvarez – eleven o'clock – Petroleum Club.'

Without breaking stride Billy said, 'Right. Find Cousin
Jim – might be in security.' We went into his office and he
picked up a telephone and stabbed a button. 'Pop, we're
in and ready to go.' He listened for a moment and his
expression changed. 'Oh, God, no!' Pause. 'Yeah, I guess so.
Okay.'

He put down the telephone. 'Jack had a heart attack an
hour ago. He's being taken to the Texas Medical Center.
Frank is with him and Pop is going there now. Of all the
times . . .'

'Because of the times,' I said. 'It probably wouldn't have
happened if Debbie hadn't been kidnapped. He wasn't
looking too good last night.'

He nodded. 'That leaves you, me and Jim to plan and
execute this operation. Not enough – I'll draft a couple
more.'

Jim came in and Billy told him about Jack. 'Tough,' said
Jim. 'Poor old guy.'

'Well, let's get to it,' said Billy. 'Tom's outfit is in that grip there.'

'Fine.' Jim frowned. 'I've been worrying about something. What happens if they strip Tom? His bugged clothes might be going one way and Tom in another direction.'

'That's a chance we have to take,' said Billy.

Jim smiled. 'Not so. I've got something, if Tom will go for it.' He produced a capsule of plastic, about an inch long, three-eighths of an inch in diameter, and with rounded ends. 'You have to swallow it.'

'What!'

'It's a transponder – it returns a signal when interrogated by a pulsed transmitter; not a powerful signal but good enough to get a direction finder on it. It goes into action when the gastric juices work on it, so you swallow it at the last minute.'

Billy inspected it critically. 'Looks like one of those pills they blow down a horse's throat through a tube.'

Jim laughed. 'That's all right if the horse doesn't blow first. How about it, Tom?'

I looked at it distastefully. 'All right – if I have to. Where did you get it?'

'I have a pipeline into the CIA. I borrowed it.'

'Borrowed!' said Billy, grimacing. 'Anyone going to use it afterwards?'

Jim said, 'It's good for thirty-six to forty-eight hours before peristalsis gets rid of it.'

'Just don't crap too much, that's all,' said Billy. 'Anything else?'

'I had the contents of the second letter checked for fingerprints. Result negative. No dice, Billy.'

'Okay,' said Billy. 'I have things to do. Tom, why don't you go along with Jim and watch him ruin your coat and pants? I'm going out to round up some transport.'

So I went with Jim to the security section in the Cunningham Building which meant having my photograph taken in colour by a Polaroid camera and wearing a plastic lapel badge with my name, signature and aforesaid photograph. Jim wore one too, as did everybody else.

I was introduced to an electronics genius called Ramon Rodriguez who displayed and discussed his wares, all miracles of micro-miniaturization. 'Do you wear dentures, Mr Mangan?' he asked.

'No.'

'A pity.' He opened a box and displayed a fine set of false gnashers. 'These are good; they'll transmit anything you say-range over a mile. If you keep your mouth a little open they'll also catch what the guy you're talking to is saying – those two front top incisors are microphones.' He put them away.

'We'll put a bug in the car you'll be driving,' said Jim.

'Two,' said Rodriguez. 'Know anything about bugs, Mr Mangan?'

'Not a thing.'

'There are many kinds. Most fall into one of two categories – active and passive. The active bugs are working all the time, sending out a signal saying, "Here I am! Here I am!" The passive bugs only transmit when asked by a coded impulse, like the dohickey Mr Cunningham showed me this morning.'

Jim chuckled. 'The pill.'

'That's to economize on power where space is limited. Those bugs send out an unmodulated signal, either steady or pulsed. When it comes to modulation, a voice transmission, it becomes a little harder. You'll be wired up with every kind of bug we have.'

Rodriguez put a familiar-looking box on the bench. 'Pack of cigarettes; genuine except for those two in the back right corner. Don't try to light those or the sparks will fly.' Something metallic went next to the cigarette pack. 'Stick-pin for your necktie – will pick up a conversation and transmit it a quarter-mile. Belt to hold up your pants – bug in buckle, but will transmit a mile because we have more room to play with. Try to face the man you're talking with, Mr Mangan.'

'I'll remember that.'

Two identical objects joined the growing heaps. 'These go in the heels of your shoes. This one sends a steady signal so we can get a direction finder on it. But this one has a pressure transducer – every time you take a pace it sends out a beep. If you're being hustled along on foot we'll know it – we might even be able to calculate how fast. And if it stops we know you're static – if you're not in an automobile, that is. Now, this is important. You know the rhythm of shave-and-a-haircut?'

I smiled and knocked it out with my knuckles on the bench.

'Good. If you're being taken for a ride tap it out once for a car, twice for a boat, three times for an airplane. Repeat at five minute intervals. Got that?'

I repeated his instructions. 'Just tap it out with my heel? Which one?'

'The right heel.' Rodriguez picked up my jacket and trousers. 'I'm giving you two antennae – one in your coat sewn into the back seam, the other in your pants. Don't worry; they won't show. And there'll be a few other things – I'll give you a new billfold and there'll be the coins in your pockets – anything I can cook up between now and Thursday. You don't have to know about them, just be glad they're there.'

The Cunninghams were going to a great deal of trouble and it occurred to me that if they had all this stuff ready to hand then they were probably up to their necks in industrial espionage. I wondered if they had used it on me in the course of their admitted investigations.

Rodriguez looked at his watch. 'I have to make a phone call. I won't be long, Mr Cunningham.' He walked away into his office.

Jim said, 'That man once said he could make a working microphone out of three carpenter's nails, a foot of copper wire, and a power cell. I bet he couldn't. I lost.' He laughed. 'He even made his own power cell from a stack of pennies and nickels, a piece of blotting paper and some vinegar.'

'He seems a good man.'

'The best,' said Jim, and added casually, 'Ex-CIA.'

I looked longingly at the packet of cigarettes on the bench. I had run out and I knew Jim did not smoke. 'I'll be back in a minute,' I said. I remembered there was a stand in the lobby of the Cunningham Building which sold cigarettes among other things, so I went down in the elevator to street level.

There was a short line waiting for service but I bought two packets of cigarettes within minutes. As I turned, opening one of them, I bumped heavily into a man. 'Watch it, buster!' he said nastily, and walked past me.

I shrugged and headed towards the elevator. In a climate like that of Houston anyone was entitled to be short-tempered. I stood waiting for the elevator and looked at the half-opened packet in my hand while absently rubbing my thigh. The health warning on the side of the packet shimmered strangely.

'You okay, mister?' The elevator starter was looking at me oddly.

I said distinctly, 'I'm perfectly all right.'

'Hey!' He grabbed my arm as I swayed. Everything was swimming and my legs felt like putty. Slowly and majestically I toppled forward like a falling tree, and yelled 'Timber!' at the top of my voice. Oddly enough, not a sound passed my lips.

The next thing I knew was that I was being turned over. I looked at the ceiling and heard someone say, 'Just fell down right there.' Someone else said, 'A drunk, I guess.' And again: 'At this time of day!'

I tried to speak. My brain worked all right in a somewhat crazy manner – but there seemed to be interference with the connection to my voice box. I experimented with 'Mary had a little lamb', but nothing came through. It was weird.

From a distance a man said, 'I'm a doctor – let me through.' He bent over me and I stared up at him, past a big nose and into his eyes, yellow flecks in green irises. He felt my pulse then put his hand over my heart. 'This man is having a heart attack,' he said. 'He must be taken to hospital immediately.' He looked up. 'Someone help me – my car is outside.'

I was lifted bodily and carried to the entrance, shouting loudly that this was no bloody heart attack and this was no bloody doctor, either. My brain told me I was shouting loudly but not a sound did I hear from my lips, and neither could I move a muscle. They put me on the back seat of a limousine and off we went. The man in the front passenger seat twisted around and took my limp arm. I saw the flash of glass and felt the prick of a needle, and soon the bright world began to go grey.

Just before I passed out I reflected that all the Cunninghams' organization and the painstaking work of Ramon Rodriguez was going for nothing. The kidnappers had jumped the gun.

FOURTEEN

It was dark when I woke up. I was lying on my back and staring into blackness and feeling no pain, at least not much. When I stirred I found that I was naked – lying on a bed and covered by a thin sheet – and my left thigh ached a little. I turned my head and saw a rectangular patch of dim light which, when I propped myself up on one elbow, appeared to be a window.

I tossed aside the sheet, swung my legs out of bed, and tentatively stood up. I seemed to be in no immediate danger of falling so I took a step towards the window, and then another. The window was covered with a coarse-fibred cloth which I drew aside. There was nothing much to see outside, just the darker patches of trees silhouetted against a dark sky. From the west came the faint loom of the setting moon. There were noises, though; the chirping of cicadas and the distant, deeper croaking of bull-frogs.

There were bars on the window.

The breeze which blew through the unglazed window was warm and smelled of damp and rotting vegetation. Even so, I shivered as I made my way back to the bed, and I was glad to lie down again. That brief journey had taken the strength out of me; maybe I could have lasted two seconds with Mohammed Ali, but I doubted it. I pulled the sheet over my body and went back to sleep.

When next I woke I felt better. Perhaps it was because of the sunlight slanting through the room, making a yellow patch at the bottom of the bed. The window was now uncurtained and next to the bed a tray was laid on a table which contained a pitcher of orange juice, an empty glass, a pile of thick-cut bread slices, a pot of butter and a crude wooden spatula with which to spread it.

The orange juice went down well and my spirits rose when I saw the pot of honey which had been hidden behind the pitcher. I breakfasted stickily, sitting on the edge of the bed with the sheet draped around me, and doing an inventory of the room. Against one wall was another table holding a basin and a water jug together with a piece of kitchen soap. And there was a chair with clothing draped over it – not mine. And that, apart from the bed and the bedside table, was all.

After breakfast I washed, but first looked through the uncurtained window. There was nothing much to see – just trees baking under a hot sun. The air was humid and dank and smelled of vegetable corruption.

After washing I turned to the clothing – a pair of jeans, a tee-shirt with the words HOUSTON COUGARS emblazoned across the chest, and a pair of dirty white sneakers. As I was putting on the jeans I examined the bruise on the outside of my thigh; it was livid and there seemed to be a small pin hole in the middle of it. It did not hurt much so I put on the jeans, then the shirt, and sat on the bed to put on the shoes. And there I was – dressed and almost in my right mind.

I might have hammered on the door then, demanding in highfalutin terms to be released, and what the devil is the meaning of this, sir? I refrained. My captors would see me in their own time and I needed to think. There is a manoeuvre in rugby football known as 'selling the dummy', a feint in which the ball goes in an unexpected direction. The Cunningham family had been sold the dummy and I would bet that Billy Cunningham would be spitting bullets.

I mentally reviewed the contents of the first and second ransom letters. The object of the first was to get me to Houston. The second was so detailed and elaborate that no one thought it would be the dummy we were being sold. It was a fake all the way through.

One thing was certain: the Cunninghams would be incensed beyond measure. To kidnap a Cunningham was bad enough, but to add a double-cross was to add insult to injury. Right at that moment the Cunningham Building would be like a nest of disturbed rattlesnakes; all hell would be breaking loose and, perhaps, this time they would bring in the police. Not that it would help me, I thought glumly, or Debbie.

Which brought me to Debbie. Was she here or not? And where the devil was here? There was a frustrating lack of information. I went to the window again and looked out through the bars and again saw nothing but trees. I tested the bars; steel set firmly in concrete, and immoveable.

I turned at a metallic noise at the door. The first man to enter held a shotgun pointing at my belly. He was dressed in jeans and a checkered shirt open almost to the waist, and had a lined grim face. He took one pace inside the room and then stepped sideways, keeping the gun on me. 'On the bed.' The barrel of the gun jerked fractionally.

I backed away and sidled sideways like a crab to the bed. The muzzle of that gun looked like an army cannon.

Another man came into the room and closed the door behind him. He was dressed in a lightweight business suit and could have been anybody. He had hair, two eyes and a mouth, with a nose in the middle – a face-shaped face. He was nobody I had seen before or, if I had, I had not noticed him. He was my most forgettable character.

'Good morning, Mr Mangan. I hope you had a quiet night and slept well.'

English – not American, I thought. I said, 'Where's my wife?'

'First things first.' He gestured sideways. 'This man is armed with an automatic shotgun loaded with buckshot. Anything that will kill a deer will kill a man – men die more easily. At ten feet he couldn't miss; he could put five rounds into you in five seconds. I think you'd be chopped in half.'

'Two seconds,' said the shotgunner flatly and objectively.

I was wrong about him being English; at the back of those perfectly modulated tones was the flavour of something I could not pin down. I repeated, 'Where's my wife?'

'She's quite safe,' he said reassuringly.

'Where? Here?'

He shrugged. 'No harm in you knowing. Yes, she's here.'

'Prove it. I want to see her.'

He laughed. 'My dear Mr Mangan, you are in no position to make demands. Although . . .' He was pensive for a moment. 'Yes, my dear chap, that might be a good idea. You shall see her as soon as we have finished our initial conversation. I trust you are fit and well. No ill effects from the curious treatment we were forced to administer?'

'I'm all right,' I said shortly.

He produced a small cylinder from his pocket and held it up; it looked like a shotgun cartridge. 'It was one of these that did the trick. Issued to NATO soldiers for use in nerve-gas attacks. You put one end against the arm or leg – so – and push. A spring-loaded plunger forces a hypodermic needle right through the clothing and into the flesh, then injects atropine. I admit that the needle going through clothing is not hygienic; there's a small risk of tetanus – but that is preferable to heart failure from nerve gas, so the risk is acceptable. I don't think you even felt the prick of the needle.'

'I didn't.'

'Of course we used something other than atropine,' he said. 'A muscle relaxant derived from curare, I believe; used when giving electric shock therapy. You're lucky I wasn't a Middle Eastern guerilla; they use something totally lethal. Very useful for street assassinations.'

'Very interesting,' I said. 'But I can do without the technical lecture.'

'It has a point,' he said, and laughed. 'Just like the needle. It's to tell you we're most efficient. Remember that efficiency, Mr Mangan, should you be thinking of trying anything foolish.'

'Who are you?'

'Does it matter?' He waved his hand. 'Very well, if you must call me something call me . . . Robinson.'

'Okay, Robinson. Tell me why.'

'Why you're here? Rest assured I shall do so, but in my own time.' He looked at a point over my head. 'I was about to begin your interrogation immediately, but I have changed my mind. Don't you think it is a mark of efficiency to be flexible?'

He had a formal, almost pedantic, way of speech which fitted well with the tone of the ransom letters, and could very well have typed 'headlamps' instead of 'headlights'. I said, 'I couldn't give a damn. I want to see my wife.'

His gaze returned to me. 'And so you shall, my dear chap. What is more, you shall have the privilege of seeing her alone so that you may talk freely. I am sure she will be able to tell you many things of which you are, as yet, unaware. And vice versa. It will make my later interrogation so much easier – for both of us.'

'Robinson, quit waffling and get her.'

He studied me and smiled. 'Quite a one for making demands, aren't you? And in the vernacular, too. But I shall accede to . . . er . . . shall we call it your request?'

He put his hand behind him, opened the door, and backed out. The man with the shotgun went out, gun last, and the door closed. I heard it lock.

I thought about it. The man with the shotgun was local, a Texan. He had spoken only a total of five words but the accent was unmistakeable. Robinson was something else. Those cultured tones, those rolling cadences, were the product of a fairly long residence in England, and at a fairly high social level.

And yet . . . and yet . . . there was something else. As a Bahamian, class differences, as betrayed by accent, had been a matter of indifference to me, but my time in England had taught me that the English take it seriously, so I had learned the nuances. It is something hard to explain to our American cousins. But Robinson did not ring a true sound – there was a flaw in him.

I looked with greater interest at my prison. The walls were of concrete blocks set in hard mortar and white-washed. There was no ceiling so I could look up into the roof which was pitched steeply and built of rough timbers – logs with the bark still on – and covered with corrugated iron. The only door was in a gable end.

From the point of view of escape the wall was impossible. I had no metal to scrape the mortar from between the blocks, not even a belt buckle; and they had carefully not put a knife on the tray with which to spread the butter, just a flat piece of wood. As Robinson had said – efficiency. A careful examination of the furniture told me that I was probably in a rural area. The whole lot had not a single nail in them, but were held together by wooden pegs.

Not that I was intending to escape – not then. But I was looking at the roof speculatively when I heard someone at the door. I sat on the bed and waited, and the door opened and Debbie was pushed in, then it slammed behind her quickly.

She staggered, regained her balance, then looked at me unbelievingly. '*Tom*! Oh, Tom!' The next moment she was in my arms, dampening the front of my Houston Cougars' tee-shirt.

It took some time to get her settled down. She was incoherent with a mixture of relief, remorse, passion and, when she understood that I, too, was a prisoner, amazement, consternation and confusion. 'But how did you get here?' she demanded. 'To Texas, I mean. And why?'

'I was drawn into it by bait,' I said. 'You were the bait. We were all fooled.'

'The family,' she said. 'How are they?'

'Bearing up under the strain.' There were a few things I was not going to tell Debbie. One was that her father had just suffered a heart attack. Others would doubtless occur to me. 'How were you snatched?'

'I don't know. One minute I was looking in the window of a store on Main Street, then I was here.'

Probably Robinson had used his NATO gadget; but it did not matter. 'And where is here? You're the local expert.'

She shook her head. 'I don't know. Somewhere on the coast, I think.'

I disentangled myself, stood up, and turned to look at her. The dress she was wearing certainly had not come from a plushy Main Street store – it was more reminiscent of Al Capp's Dogpatch and went along with my jeans and tee-shirt. From where I stood it seemed to be the only thing she was wearing. 'All right, Daisy-Mae, has anyone told you why you were kidnapped?'

'Daisy-M . . . ?' She caught on and looked down at herself, then involuntarily put a hand to her breast. 'They took my clothes away.'

'Mine, too.'

'I must look terrible.'

'A sight for sore eyes.' She looked up at me and flushed, and we were both silent for a moment. Then we both started to talk at the same time, and both stopped simultaneously.

'I've been a damned fool, Tom,' she said.

'This is not the time – nor place – to discuss our marital problems,' I said. 'There are better things to do. Do you know why you were kidnapped?'

'Not really. He's been asking all sorts of questions about you.'

'What sort of questions?'

'About what you were doing. Where you'd been. Things like that. I told him I didn't know – that I'd left you. He didn't believe me. He kept going on and on about you.' She shivered suddenly. 'Who is this man? What's happening to us, Tom?'

Good questions; unfortunately I had no answers. Debbie looked scared and I did not blame her. That character with the automatic shotgun had nearly scared the jeans off me and I had just arrived. Debbie had been here at least three days.

I said gently, 'Have they ill-treated you?'

She shook her head miserably. 'Not physically. But it's the way some of them look at me.' She shivered again. 'I'm scared, Tom. I'm scared half to death.'

I sat down and put my arm around her. 'Not to worry. How many are there?'

'I've seen four.'

'Including a man whose name isn't Robinson? An English smoothie with a plummy voice?'

'He's the one who asks the questions. The others don't say much – not to me. They just look.'

'Let's get back to these questions. Was there anything specific he wanted to know?'

Debbie frowned. 'No. He asked general questions in a roundabout way. It's as though he wants to find out

something without letting me know what it is. Just end-
less questions about you. He wanted to know what you'd
told the police. He said you seemed to spend a lot of time
in the company of Commissioner Perigord. I said I didn't
know about anything you might have told Perigord, and
that I'd only met Perigord once, before we were married.'
She paused. 'There was one thing. He asked when I'd left
you, and I told him. He then commented that it would be
the day after you'd found Kayles.'

I sat upright. *'Kayles!* He mentioned him by name?'

'Yes. I thought he'd ask me about Kayles, but he didn't.
He went off on another track, asking when we were married. He asked if I'd known Julie.'

'Did he, by God! What did you say?'

'I told him the truth; that I'd met her briefly but hadn't
known her well.'

'What was his reaction to that?'

'He seemed to lose interest. You call him Robinson – is
that his name?'

'I doubt it; and I don't think he's English, either.' I was
thinking of the connection between Robinson and Kayles
and sorting out possible relationships. Was Robinson the
boss of a drug-running syndicate? If so then why should he
kidnap Debbie and me? It did not make much sense.

Debbie said, 'I don't like him, and I don't like the way he
talks. The others frighten me, but he frightens me in a different way.'

'What way?'

'The others are ignorant white trash – corn-crackers –
but they look at me as a woman. Robinson looks at me as
an object, as though I'm not a human being at all.' She
broke down into sobs. 'For God's sake, Tom; who are these
people? What have you been doing to get mixed up in
this?'

'Take it easy, my love,' I said. 'Hush, now.'

She quietened again and after a while said in a small voice, 'It's a long time since you've called me that.'

'What?'

'Your love.'

I was silent for a moment, then said heavily, 'A pity. I ought to have remembered to do it more often.' I was thinking of a divorce lawyer who had told me that in a breaking marriage there were invariably faults on both sides. I would say he was right.

Presently Debbie sat up and dried her eyes on the hem of her dress. 'I must look a mess.'

'You look as beautiful as ever. Cheer up, there's still hope. Your folks will be skinning Texas to find us. I wouldn't like to be anyone who gets on the wrong side of Billy One.'

'It's a big state,' she said sombrely.

The biggest – barring Alaska – and I could not see the Cunninghams finding us in a hurry. The thought that chilled me was that Robinson had made no attempt at disguise. True, his face was not memorable in the normal way, but I would certainly remember it from now on, and so would Debbie. The rationale behind that sent a grue up my spine – the only way he could prevent future identification was by killing us. We were never intended to be released.

It was cold comfort to know that the Cunninghams were roused and that sooner or later, with the backing of the Cunningham Corporation, Robinson would eventually be run down and due vengeance taken. Debbie and I would know nothing of that.

Debbie said, 'I'm sorry about the way I behaved.'

'Skip it,' I said. 'It doesn't matter now.'

'But you could be a son of a bitch at times – a real cold bastard. Sometimes you'd act as though I wasn't there at all. I began to think I was the invisible woman.'

'There was no one else,' I said. 'There never was.'

'No one human.'

'Nor a ghost, Debbie,' I said. 'I accepted Julie's death a long time ago.'

'I didn't mean that – I meant your goddamn job.' She looked up. 'But I ought to have known because I'm a Cunningham.' She smiled slightly. '"For men must work and women must weep." And the Cunningham men do work. I thought it might be different with you.'

'And the sooner it's over, the sooner to sleep.' I completed the quotation, but only in my mind; it was too damned apposite to say aloud. 'Why should it have been different? The Cunningham men haven't taken out a patent on hard work. But maybe I did go at it too hard.'

'No,' she said thoughtfully. 'You did what you had to, as all men do. The pity is that I didn't see it. Looking back, I know there's a lot I didn't see. Myself, for one thing. My God, you married an empty-headed ninny.'

That was a statement it would be politic not to answer. I said, 'You had your problems.'

'And piled them on your back. I swear to God, Tom, that things will be different. I'll make an effort to change if you will. We've both, in our own ways, been damned fools.'

I managed a smile. The likelihood that we would have a future together was minimal. 'It's a bargain,' I said.

She held out her hand and drew me down to her. 'So seal it.' I put my hands on her and discovered that, indeed, she wore nothing beneath the shift. She said softly, 'It won't hurt him.'

So we made love, and it was not just having sex. There is quite a difference.

FIFTEEN

Robinson gave us about three hours together. It was difficult to judge time because neither of us had a watch and all I could do was to estimate the hour by the angle of the sun. I think we had three hours before there was a rattle at the door and the Texan came in, gun first.

He stepped sideways, as before, and Robinson came in with another man who could have been the Texan's brother and possibly was. He was armed with a pistol. Robinson surveyed us and said benignly, 'So nice to see young people getting together again. I hope you have acquainted your husband with the issue at hand, Mrs Mangan.'

'She doesn't know what the hell you want,' I said. 'And neither do I. This is bloody ridiculous.'

'Well, we'll talk about that later,' he said. 'I'm afraid I must part you lovebirds. Come along, Mrs Mangan.'

Debbie looked appealingly at me, but I shook my head gently. 'You'd better go.' I could see the man's finger tightening on the trigger of the shotgun.

And so she was taken from me and escorted from the room by the man with the pistol. 'We won't starve you,' said Robinson. 'That should be an earnest of my good intentions – should you doubt them.'

He stood aside and a woman came in with a tray which she exchanged for the breakfast tray. She was a worn

woman with sagging breasts and hands gnarled and twisted
with rheumatics. I pointed to the pitcher and basin on the
other side of the room. 'What about some fresh water?'

'I see no reason why not. What about it, Leroy?'

The Texan said, 'Belle, git th' water.'

She took the pitcher and basin outside, and I had a
couple more names, for what they were worth. Robinson
looked at the tray from which steam rose gently. 'Not the
best of cuisine, I'm afraid, but edible . . . edible. And it's very
much a case of fingers being made before forks. I think
you'll need the water.'

I said, 'What about coming to the point?'

He wagged a finger at me. 'Later . . . I said later. There is
something which I must think over rather carefully. There's
really plenty of time, my dear chap.'

Belle came back, put the basin on the table and stood the
pitcher in it. When she left Robinson said, '*Bon appetit*,' and
backed out, followed by Leroy.

The meal was fish or, rather, wet cotton wadding mixed
with spiky bones. I ate with my fingers and the flesh tasted
of mud. When I had eaten rather less than my fill, but
could stomach no more, I walked over to the water pitcher
and was about to pour water into the basin to wash my
slimy hands when I stopped and looked at it thoughtfully.
I did not pour the water but dabbled my hands in the
pitcher, then wiped them dry on my jeans.

The pitcher held more than two gallons. That, plus the
weight of the pitcher itself, would be about twenty-five
pounds. I was beginning to get ideas. I went back to the bed,
spread butter on a thick slice of bread, and munched while
looking at the pitcher, hoping it would tell me what to do.
The first faint tendrils of an idea began to burgeon.

Robinson came back about two hours later with his usual
bodyguard, and Leroy took his position just to the left of the
door. Robinson closed the door and leaned on it. 'I'm sorry

to learn of your marital troubles, Mr Mangan,' he said suavely. 'But from what I heard I gather you are on your way to solving them.' He smiled at my startled expression. 'Oh, yes, I listened to your conversation with your wife with great interest.'

I cursed silently. Ramon Rodriguez had shown me what could be done with bugs, and I might have known that Robinson would have the place wired. 'So you're a voyeur, too,' I said acidly.

He sniggered. 'I even recorded your love-play. Though not my main interest it was very entertaining. If set to music it could hit the top twenty.'

'You bastard!'

'Now, now,' he said chidingly. 'That's not the way to speak when you're at the wrong end of a gun. Let us come to more serious matters – the case of Jack Kayles. I noted when listening to the tape that you showed interest when your wife mentioned his name. My interest is in how you tracked him down. I would dearly like to know the answer to that.'

I said nothing but just looked at him, and he clicked his tongue. 'I advise you to be cooperative,' he said. 'In your own interest – and that of your wife.'

'I'll answer that if you tell me why he killed my family.'

Robinson regarded me thoughtfully. 'No harm in that, I suppose. He killed your family because he is a stupid man; how stupid I am only now beginning to find out. In fact, it is essential that I now find the measure of his stupidity, and that is why you are here.'

He took a pace forward and stood with his hands in his pockets. 'Kayles was supposed to sail from the Bahamas to Miami in his own boat. There was a deadline, but Kayles was having problems – something technical to do with boats.' Robinson waved the technicality aside. 'At any rate he found he could not meet the deadline. When he heard that a skipper needed a crewman to help take a boat to Miami the next day he jumped at the chance. Do you follow me?'

'So far.'

'Now, Kayles was carrying something with him, something important.' Robinson waved his hand airily. 'There is no necessity for you to know what it was. As I say, he is stupid and he let your skipper find it, so Kayles killed him with the knife he invariably carries. His intention was to conveniently lose that poor black man overboard but, unfortunately, the killing was seen by your little girl and then . . .' He sighed and shrugged. '. . . then one thing led to another. Now, Mr Mangan, I don't mind telling you that I was very angry about this – very angry, indeed. It was a grievous setback to my plans. Disposing of your boat was a great problem, to begin with.'

'You son of a bitch,' I said bitterly. 'You're talking about my wife, my daughter and my friend.' I stuck my finger out at him. 'And you've no need to be coy about what Kayles was carrying. It was a consignment of cocaine.'

Robinson stared at me. 'Dear me! You do jump to conclusions. Now, I wonder . . .' He broke off and looked up at the roof, deep in thought. After a while his gaze returned to me. 'Well, we can take that up later, can't we? I've answered your question, Mangan. Now answer mine. How did you trace the idiot?'

I saw no reason not to answer, but I was becoming increasingly chilled. If Robinson saw no reason not to gossip about three murders then it meant that he thought he was talking to a dead man, or a man as good as dead. I said, 'I had a photograph of him,' and explained how it had come about.

'Ah!' said Robinson. 'So it *was* the little girl's camera. That really worried Kayles. He was pretty sure she had taken his photograph, but he couldn't find the camera on your boat. Of course, it was a big boat and he couldn't search every nook and cranny, but it still worried him. So he solved his problem – as he thought – by sinking your boat, camera and all. But it wasn't there, was it? You had it. I suppose you gave the photograph to the police.'

'There'll be a copy of it in every police office in the Bahamas,' I said grimly.

'Oh dear!' said Robinson. 'That's bad, very bad. Isn't it, Leroy?'

Leroy grunted, but said nothing. The shotgun aimed at me had not quivered by as much as a millimetre.

Robinson took his hands from his pockets and clasped them in front of him. 'Well, to return to the main thrust of our conversation. You tracked Kayles to the Jumentos. How did you do that? I must know.'

'By his boat.'

'But it was disguised.'

'Not well enough.'

'I see. I told you the man is an idiot. Well, the idiot escaped and reported back to me. He told me a strange story which I found hard to credit. He told me that you knew all my plans. Now, isn't that odd?'

'Remarkable, considering that I don't know who the hell you are.'

'I thought so, too, but Kayles was most circumstantial. Out it all came, information which even he was not supposed to know about – and all quite accurate.'

'And I told him all this?' I said blankly.

'Not quite. He eavesdropped while you were talking to the man, Ford. I must say I was quite perturbed; so much so that I acted hastily, which is uncharacteristic of me. I ordered your death, Mr Mangan, but you fortuitously escaped.' Robinson shrugged. 'However, the four Americans were quite a bonus – I believe the Securities and Exchange Commission is causing quite a stir on Wall Street.'

'The four Am . . .' I broke off. 'You caused that crash? You killed Bill Pinder?'

Robinson raised an eyebrow. 'Pinder?' he enquired.

'The pilot, damn you!'

'Oh, the pilot,' he said uninterestedly. 'Well, by then I had time to think more clearly. I needed to interrogate you in a place of my own choosing – and so here you are. It would have been difficult getting near to you on Grand Bahama; for one thing, you were tending to live in Commissioner Perigord's pocket. But that worried me for other reasons; I want to know how much information you have passed on to him. I must know, because that will influence my future actions.'

'I don't know what you're talking about,' I said, wishing I did.

'I will give you time to think about it; to think and remember. But first I will do you a favour.' He turned and opened the door, saying to Leroy, 'Watch him.'

A couple of minutes later the pistol carrier came in. He jerked his head at Leroy. 'He wants you.' Leroy went out and I was left facing the muzzle of a pistol instead of a shot-gun. Not a great improvement.

Presently Robinson came back. He looked at me sitting on the bed, and said, 'Come to the window and see what I have for you.'

'The only favour I want from you is to release my wife.'

'I'm afraid not,' he said. 'Not for the moment. But come here, Mangan, and watch.'

I joined him at the window and the man with the pistol moved directly behind me, standing about six feet away. There was nothing to be seen outside that was new, just the trees and hot sunlight. Then Leroy came into view with another man. They were both laughing.

'Kayles!' I said hoarsely.

'Yes, Kayles,' said Robinson.

Leroy was still carrying the shotgun. He stooped to tie the lace of his shoe, gesturing for Kayles to carry on. He let Kayles get ten feet ahead and then shot him in the back from his kneeling position. He shot again, the two reports coming so closely together that they sounded as one, and Kayles pitched forward violently to lie in a crumpled heap.

'There,' said Robinson. 'The murderer of your family has been executed.'

I looked at Kayles and saw that Robinson was right – buckshot does terrible things to a man's body. Kayles had been ripped open and his spine blown out. A pool of blood was soaking into the sandy earth.

It had happened so suddenly and unexpectedly that I was numbed. Leroy walked to Kayles's body and stirred it with his foot, then he reloaded the shotgun and walked back the way he had come and so out of sight.

'It was not done entirely for your benefit,' said Robinson. 'From being an asset Kayles had become a liability. Anyone connected with me who has his photograph on the walls of police stations is dangerous.' He paused. 'Of course, in a sense the demonstration *was* for your benefit. An example – it could happen to you.'

I looked out at the body of Kayles and said, 'I think you're quite mad.'

'Not mad – just careful. Now you are going to tell me what I want to know. How did you get wind of what I am up to, and how much have you told Perigord?'

'I've told the police nothing, except about Kayles,' I said. 'I know nothing at all about what other crazy ideas you might have. I know nothing about you, and I wish I knew less.'

'So do I believe you?' he mused. 'I think not. I can't trust you to be honest with me. So what to do about it? I could operate on you with a blunt knife, but you could be stubborn. You could even know nothing, as you say, so the

exercise would be futile. Even if your wife saw the operation with the blunt knife there would be no profit in it. You
see, I believe she knows nothing and so torturing you could
not induce her to speak the truth. In fact, anything she
might say I would discount as a lie to save you.'

I said nothing. My mouth was dry and parched because I
knew what was coming and dreaded it.

Robinson spoke in tones of remote objectivity, building
up his ramshackle structure of crazy logic. 'No,' he said. 'We
can discard that, so what is left? Mrs Mangan is left, of
course. Judging from the touching scene of reconciliation
this morning it is quite possible that you still have an attach-
ment for her. So, we operate on Mrs Mangan with a blunt
knife – or its equivalent. Women have soft bodies, Mr
Mangan. I think you will speak truly of what you know.'

I nearly went for him then and there, but the gunman
said sharply, 'Don't!' and I recoiled from the gun.

'You son of a bitch!' I said, raging. 'You utter bastard!'

Robinson waved his hand. 'No compliments, I beg of
you. You will have time to think of this – to sleep on it. I
regret we can waste no more good food on you. But that is
all for the best – the digestion of food draws blood from the
brain and impedes the thought processes. I want you in a
condition in which you think hard and straight, Mr
Mangan. I will ask you more questions tomorrow.'

He went out, followed by the gunman, and the door
closed and clicked locked, leaving me in such despair as I
had never known in my life.

SIXTEEN

The first thing I did when I had recovered the power of purposive thought was to find and rip out that damned microphone. A futile gesture, of course, because it had already fulfilled Robinson's purpose. It was not even very well hidden, not nearly as subtle as any of Rodriguez's gadgets. It was an ordinary microphone such as comes with any standard tape recorder and was up in the rafters taped to a tie-beam, and the wire led through a small hole in the roof. Not much sense in it, but it gave me savage satisfaction in the smashing of it.

As I hung from the tie-beam, my feet dangling above the floor preparatory to dropping, I looked at the door at the end of the room and then at the roof above it. My first thought was that if I was up in the roof when Leroy came in I might drop something on to his head. That idea was discarded quickly because I had seen that every time he entered he had swung the door wide so that it lay against the wall. That way he made sure that, if I was not in sight, then I would not be hiding behind the door. If he did not see me in that bare room he would know that the only place I could be was up in the roof, and he would take the appropriate nasty action.

If there was anyone watching what I did next he would have thought I had gone around the bend. I stood with my back to the door, imitating the action of a tiger – the tiger being Leroy. I had no illusions about him; he was as deadly as any tiger – possibly more dangerous than Robinson. I do not think that Robinson was the quintessential man of action; he was more the cerebral type and thought too much about his actions. Leroy, however vacant in the head, would act automatically on the necessity for action.

So I imitated Leroy coming in. He booted the door wide open; I had to imagine that bit. The door swung and slammed against the wall. Leroy looked inside and made sure I was on the bed. Satisfied he stepped inside, fixing me with the shotgun. I stood, cradling an imaginary shotgun, looking at an imaginary me on the bed.

Immediately behind came Robinson. In order that he could enter I had to cease blocking the doorway, so I took a step sideways, still holding the gun on the bed. That was what Leroy had done every time – the perfect bodyguard. I looked above my head towards the roof and was perfectly satisfied with what I saw.

Then I studied the water pitcher and basin. I had seen a piece of a similar basin before. As part of my education I had studied the English legal system and, on one Long Vacation, I had taken the opportunity of attending a Crown Court to see what went on. There had been a case of a brawl in a sea-men's hostel, the charge being attempted murder. I could still visualize the notes I took. A doctor was giving evidence:

Prosecutor: Now, Doctor, tell me; how many pints of blood did you transfuse into this young man?
Doctor: Nine pints in the course of thirty hours.
Prosecutor: Is that not a great quantity of blood?
Doctor: Indeed, it is.
Judge (breaking in): How many pints of blood are there in a man?
Doctor: I would say that this man, taking into account his weight and build, would have eight pints of blood in him.

Judge: And you say you transfused nine pints. Surely, the blood must have been coming out of him faster than you were putting it in?

Doctor (laconically): It was.

The weapon used had been a pie-shaped fragment of such a basin as this, broken in the course of the brawl, picked up at random, and used viciously. It had been as sharp as a razor.

I next turned my attention to the window curtain, a mere flap of sackcloth. I felt the coarse weave and decided it would serve well. It was held in place by thumb tacks which would also be useful, so I ripped it away and spent the rest of the daylight hours separating the fibres rather like a nineteenth-century convict picking oakum.

While I worked I thought of what Robinson wanted. Whatever Kayles had told him was a mystery to me. I went back over the time I had spent with Kayles, trying to remember every word and analysing every nuance. I got nowhere at all and began to worry very much about Debbie.

I slept a little that night, but not much, and what sleep I had was shot with violent dreams which brought me up wide awake and sweating. I was frightened of over-sleeping into the daylight hours because my preparations were not yet complete and I needed at least an hour of light, but I need not have worried – I was open-eyed and alert as the sun rose.

An hour later I was ready – as much as I could be. Balanced on a tie-beam in the roof was the pitcher full of water, held only in place by the spatula with which I had spread my butter. I had greased it liberally so that it would slide away easily at the tug of the string I had made from the sackcloth. The string ran across the roof space, hanging loosely on the beams to a point in the corner above my bed where it dropped close to hand. Lacking a pulley wheel to take care of the right-angle bend I had used two thumb tacks and I hoped they, would hold under the strain when I pulled on the string.

The pitcher was just above the place where Leroy usually stood, and I reckoned that a weight of twenty-five pounds dropping six feet vertically on to his head would not do him much good. With Leroy out of action I was fairly confident I could take care of Robinson, especially if I could get hold of the shotgun.

Making my hand weapon had been tricky but fortunately I was aided by an existing crack in the thick pottery of the basin. Afraid of making a noise, and thankful that I had destroyed the microphone, I wrapped the basin in the bed sheet and whacked it hard with a leg I had taken from the table. It had not been difficult to dismantle the table; the wooden pegs were loose with age.

It took six blows to break that damned basin and after each one I paused to listen because I was making a considerable row. On the sixth blow I felt it go and unwrapped the bed sheet to find I had done exactly what I wanted. I had broken a wedge-shaped segment from the basin, exactly like the fortuitous weapon I had seen in that distant court-room in England. The rim fitted snugly into the palm of my hand and the pointed end projected forward when my arm was by my side. The natural form of use would be an upward and thrusting slash.

Then, after gently pulling on the string to take up the slack I sat on the bed to wait. And wait. And wait.

The psychologists say that time is subjective, which is why watched pots never boil. I now believe them. I do not know whether it would have been better to have had a watch; all I know is that I counted time by the pace of shadows creeping across the floor infinitesimally slowly and by the measured beat of my heart.

Debbie had said there were four of them. That would be Leroy, Robinson, Kayles and the man with the pistol – I did not think Debbie had counted Belle. Kayles was now dead and I reckoned that if the pitcher took care of Leroy and I tackled Robinson I would have a chance. I would have the shotgun by then and only one man to fight – I did not expect trouble from Belle. The only thing which worried me was Leroy's trigger finger; if he was hit on the head very hard there might be a sudden muscular contraction, and I wanted to be out of the way when that shotgun fired.

Time went by. I looked up at the pitcher poised on the beam and worked equations in my head. Accelerating under the force of gravity it would take nearly two-thirds of a second to fall six feet, by which time it would be moving at twenty-two feet a second – say, fifteen miles an hour. It might seem silly but that is what I did – I worked out the damned equations. There was nothing else to do.

The door opened with a bang and the man who came in was not Leroy but the other man. He had the shotgun, though. He stood in the doorway and just looked at me, the gun at the ready. Robinson was behind him but did not come into the room. 'All right,' he said. 'What did you tell Perigord?'

'I still don't know what you're talking about.'

'I'm not going to argue,' he said. 'I'm done with that. Watch him, Earl. If you have to shoot, make sure it's at his legs.'

He went away. Earl closed the door and leaned his back against it, covering me with the shotgun. It was all going wrong – he was in the wrong place. A break in the pattern was ruining the plan.

I said, 'What did he say your name was?' My mouth was dry.

'Earl.' The barrel of the shotgun lowered a fraction.

I slid sideways on the bed about a foot, going towards him. 'How much is he paying you?'

'None of your damn business.'

Another foot. 'I think it is. Maybe I could pay better.'
'You reckon?'
'I know.' I moved up again, nearly to the end of the bed.
'Let's talk about it.'

I was getting too close. He stepped sideways. 'Get back or
I'll blow yo' haid off.'

'Sure.' I retreated up the bed to my original position. 'I'm
certain I could pay better.' I was cheering silently because
friend Earl had been manoeuvred into the right place. I
leaned back casually against the wall and felt behind me for
the string. 'Like to talk about it?'

'Nope.'

I groped and could not find the bloody string. The pottery
knife was hidden by my body ready to be grasped by my
right hand, but the string had to be tugged with my left
hand, and not too obviously, either. I had to be casual and
in an apparently easy posture, an appearance hard to main-
tain as I groped behind me.

As my fingertips touched the string there came a scream
from outside, full-throated and ending in a bubbling wail.
All my nerves jumped convulsively and Earl jerked the gun
warningly. 'Steady, mister!' He grinned, showing brown
teeth. 'Just Leroy havin' his fun. My turn next.'

Debbie screamed again, a cry full of agony. 'Christ damn
you!' I whispered and got my index finger hooked around
the string.

'Let's have your hands in sight,' said Earl. 'Both of 'em.'

'Sure.' I put my left hand forward, showing it to him
empty – but I had tugged that string.

I dived forward just as the shotgun blasted. I think Earl
had expected me to move up the bed as I had before, but I
went at right-angles to that expectation. My shoulder hit
the ground with a hell of a thump and I rolled over, struggling to get up before he could get in a second shot. There
was no second shot. As I scooped up the fallen shotgun

I saw that nearly 600 foot-pounds of kinetic energy had cracked his skull as you would crack an egg with a spoon. A fleeting backward glimpse showed the mattress of the bed ripped to pieces by the buckshot.

I had no time for sightseeing. From outside Debbie screamed again in a way that raised the hair on my neck, and there was a shout. I opened the door and nearly ran into a man I had not seen before. He looked at me in astonishment and began to raise the pistol in his right hand. I lashed out at him with my home-made knife and ripped upwards. A peculiar sound came from him as the breath was forcibly ejected from his lungs. He gagged for air and looked down at himself, then dropped the pistol and clapped both hands to his belly to stop his entrails falling out.

As he staggered to one side I ran past him, dropping the pottery blade, and tossed the shotgun from my left hand to my right. It was then I realized I had made a dreadful mistake; this was no small crowd of four people – I could see a dozen, mostly men. I had a hazy impression of clapboard houses with iron roofs arranged around a dusty square, and a mongrel cur was running towards me, snapping and barking. The men were running, too, and there were angry shouts.

Someone fired a gun. I do not know where the bullet went, but I lifted the shotgun and fired back, but nothing happened because I had forgotten to pump a round into the breech. There was another shot so I ducked sideways and ran like hell for the trees I saw in the middle distance. This was no time to stop and argue – I had probably killed two men and their buddies would not be too impressed by exhortations from Robinson to shoot at my legs.

And, as I ran for my life, I thought despairingly of Debbie.

SEVENTEEN

They chased me; by God, how they chased me! The trouble was that I did not know the country and they did. And damned funny country it was, too; nothing like anything I had heard of in Texas. Here were no rolling plains and barren lands but foetid, steaming swamp country, lush with overripe growth, bogs and streams. I had no woodcraft, not for that kind of country, and my pursuers had probably grown up in the place. I think that had it been the Texas we all know from Hollywood movies I would not have stood a chance, but here was no open ground where a man could see for miles, and that saved me.

At first I concentrated on sheer speed. There would be confusion back there for a while. They would find Earl and the other man and there would be a lot of chatter and waste of time if I knew human nature. Those first few minutes were precious in putting distance between me and my nemesis. As I ran I tried not to think of Debbie. Giving myself up would not help her, and I doubted if I *could* give myself up. Leroy would just as soon kill me as step on a beetle – there had been a close resemblance between him and Earl.

So I pressed on through this strange wilderness, running when I could and glad to slow down when I could not run. I considered myself to be a reasonably fit man, but this was the equivalent of going through an army battle course and I soon found I was not as fit as I thought.

My clothing was not really up to the job as I found when I inadvertently plunged into a brier patch. Sharp spines raked my arms and ripped the tee-shirt, and I cursed when I had to go back again, moving slowly. My shoes, too, were not adequate; the rubber soles slipped on mud and one of the sneakers was loose on my foot and I tended to lose it. This also slowed me down because to lose even one shoe would be fatal; my feet were not hardened enough for me to run barefoot.

And so I plunged on. My problem was that I did not know where I was going; I could just as well be running away from help as towards it. What I wanted to find was a house, preferably with a telephone attached to it. Then I could find out where I was and ring Billy Cunningham so that he could send one of his lovely helicopters for me – to ring the police and then go and beat the bejasus out of Robinson. There were no houses. There were no roads which would lead to houses. There were no telephone lines or power lines I could follow. Nothing but tall stands of trees interspersed with boggy meadows.

After half an hour I stopped to get my breath back. I had travelled about three miles over the ground, I reckoned, and was probably within two miles of the place where I had been held captive. I fiddled with the shotgun and opened the magazine to find out what I had – four full rounds and one fired. I reloaded, pushed one up the spout, and set the safety catch.

Then I heard them, a distant shout followed by another. I went on, splashing up a shallow stream in the hope of leaving no trail. Presently I had to leave the stream because it was curving back in just the direction I did not want to go. I jumped on to the bank and ran south, as near as I could estimate by the sun.

I went through a patch of woodland, tall trees dappling the ground with sun and shadow, then I came to a river. This was no brook or stream; it was wide and fast-flowing, too deep to wade and too dangerous to swim. If I was spotted half-way across I would be an easy target. I ran parallel with it for some way and then came to a wide meadow.

There was no help for it so I ran on and, half-way over, heard a shout behind me and the flat report of a shot. I turned in the waist-high grass and saw two men coming from different angles. Raising the shotgun I aimed carefully, banged off two shots, and had the satisfaction of seeing them drop, both of them. I did not think I had hit them because the shouts were not those of pain, but nobody in his right mind would stand up against buckshot. As they dropped into the cover of the grass I turned and ran on, feeling an intolerable itch between my shoulder blades. I was not in my right mind.

I got to the cover of the trees and looked back. There was movement; the two men were coming on and others were emerging on to the meadow. I ejected a spent cartridge and aimed and fired one shot. Again both men dropped into cover but the rest came on so I turned and ran.

I ran until my lungs were bursting, tripping over rocks and fallen trees, slipping into boggy patches, and cannoning off tree trunks. My feet hurt. In this last mad dash I had lost both shoes and knew I was leaving a bloody trail. I was climbing a rise and the pace was too much. I threw myself to the ground beneath a tree, sobbing with the rasping agony of entraining air into my lungs.

This was it. One last shot and they would be upon me. I put my hand out to where the shotgun had fallen and then stopped because a foot pinned down my wrist. I twisted around and looked up and saw a tall man dressed in faded denims. He had a shotgun under his arm.

'All right,' I said, defeated. 'Get it over with.'

'Get what over with?' He turned his head and looked down the hill at the sound of a shout. 'You in trouble?'

Someone else moved into sight – a busty brunette in skintight jeans and a shirt knotted about her middle. I suddenly realized these were not Leroy's people. 'They're going to kill me,' I said, still gasping for breath. 'Chased me to hell and gone.'

He showed polite interest. 'Who are?'

'Don't know all the names. Someone called Leroy. Torturing my wife.'

He frowned. 'Whichaway was this?'

I pointed with my free arm. 'That way.'

He turned to the girl. 'Could be the Ainslees.'

'It is.' She was looking down the hill. 'I see Trace.'

The man released my wrist, then picked up my shotgun. 'Any load in this?'

'One round of buckshot.'

'Enough. Can you climb a tree?' He was looking at my feet.

'I can try.'

'If you admire yo' skin you better climb this tree,' he advised. He tossed my shotgun to the girl. 'Over there, behind that rock. Watch my signal.'

'Okay, Pop.'

The man gave me a boost into the tree. For a skinny old man he was surprisingly strong. 'Stay on the upslope side an' keep yo' haid down.' I managed the rest by myself and got lost in the leafy branches. I could not see down the hill but I had a good view to one side, and I saw him walk out and look towards my pursuers. I heard heavy breathing as someone came up the hill fast, and the old man said sharply, 'Just hold it there, son.'

'Hell, Dade . . .'

'I mean it, Trace. You stop right there.' The shotgun Dade carried was held steady.

Trace raised his voice in a shout. 'Hey, Leroy; here's old Dade.'

There was the sound of more movement and presently Leroy said breathily, 'Hi, there, Dade.'

'What you huntin', Leroy?' asked Dade. 'T'ain't razor-back hog 'cause you ain't gotten dogs. An' yo' makin' too much damn noise for deer.'

'Ah'm huntin' one son of a bitch,' said Leroy. He came into sight.

'I don't care what yo' huntin',' said Dade. 'I told you before. If you came huntin' on my land agin I'd kick yo' ass. I don't care if yo' huntin' a man or Hoover hog – you git offen my land.'

'You don't understand,' said Leroy. 'This guy kilt Earl – smashed his haid in like a water melon. An' Tukey – he's like to die; he ain't hardly got no belly left. Belle's tendin' to him, but ah don't know . . .'

'If Belle's tendin' him he's sure to die,' said Dade flatly. 'Now git the hell outta here.'

Leroy looked around. 'You reckon you can make us?'

'Think I'm crazy?' said Dade. 'I've gotten six of my boys within spittin' distance.'

Leroy eyed him speculatively. 'Prove it.'

'Sure.' Dade took an apple from his pocket. 'I was goin' to enjoy this, an' that's somethin' else I have agin you, Leroy.' He suddenly tossed the apple into the air, and shouted, 'Hit it!'

There was a shotgun blast from the rock behind me and the apple disintegrated in mid-air. Wetness splattered against my cheek.

'Could have been yo' haid, Leroy,' said Dade. 'It's bigger. Mighty fine target is a swelled haid.' His voice sharpened. 'Now, you heard me tellin' you, an' you know I tells no one twice. Move yo' ass.' His hand pointed down the hill. 'That's the shortest way offen my land.'

Leroy looked uncertainly at the shotgun pointing at his belly, then he laughed shortly. 'Okay, Dade. But, listen, old man; you ain't heard the last.'

'An' yo' not the last to tell me that. Better men, too.' Dade spat at Leroy's feet.

Leroy turned on his heel and went out of sight and I heard the sound of many men going down the hill. Dade watched them go, his sparse grey hair moving in the slight breeze. He stood there for a long time before he moved.

From somewhere behind me the girl said, 'They're gone, Pop.'

'Yeah.' Dade came up to the tree. He said, 'I'm Dade Perkins an' this is my girl, Sherry-Lou. Now, suppose you come down outta that tree an' tell me just who the hell you are.'

EIGHTEEN

It nearly went sour even then.

I climbed down from the tree, wincing as the rough bark scraped my bruised and bloody feet. As I reached the ground I said, 'Where's the nearest telephone? I need help.'

Sherry-Lou laughed. She looked me up and down, taking in my bleeding arms, the tattered tee-shirt with its incongruous inscription, the ripped jeans and my bare feet. 'You sure do,' she said. 'You look like you tangled with a cougar.' She saw the expression on my face and the laughter vanished. 'Got a telephone back at the house,' she offered.

'How far?'

'Two – three miles.'

'You won't make that in under an hour,' said Dade. 'Yo' feet won't. Can Sherry-Lou go ahead an' talk for you?'

I was not feeling too well. I leaned against the tree, and said, 'Good idea.'

'Who do I talk with?' she asked. 'What number?'

I had forgotten the number and had no secretary handy to ask. 'I don't know – but it's easy to find. Houston – the Cunningham Corporation; ask for Billy Cunningham.'

There was an odd pause. Sherry-Lou seemed about to speak, then hesitated and looked at her father. He glanced at her, then looked back at me. 'You a Cunningham?' he asked, and spat at the ground. That ought to have warned me.

'Do I sound like a Cunningham?' I said tiredly.

'No,' he admitted. 'You talk funny. I reckoned you was from Californy – some place like that.'

'I'm a Bahamian,' I said. 'My name's Mangan – Tom Mangan.'

'What's the Cunninghams to you?'

'I married one,' I said. 'And Leroy's got her.' Perkins said nothing to that. I looked at his expressionless face and said desperately, 'For Christ's sake, do something! She was screaming her head off when I busted out this morning. I couldn't get near her.' I found I was crying and felt the wetness of tears on my cheek.

Sherry-Lou said, 'Those Ainslees . . .'

'Cunningham or Ainslee – dunno which is worst,' said Dade. 'Ainslee by a short haid, I reckon.' He nodded abruptly. 'Sherry-Lou, you run to the house an' talk to Billy Cunningham.' He turned to me. 'The young sprout or Billy One?'

'Young Billy would be best.' I thought he would be better able to make quick decisions.

Dade said, 'Tell young Billy he'll need guns, as many as he can get. An' tell him he'd better be fast.'

'How far are we from Houston?' I did not even know where I was.

'Mebbe hundred miles.'

That far! I said, 'Tell him to use helicopters – he'll have them.'

'An' tell him to come to my place,' said Dade. 'He sure knows where it is. Then come back an' bring a pair of Chuck's sneakers so as Tom here can walk comfortable.'

'Sure,' said Sherry-Lou, and turned away.

I watched her run up the hill until she was lost to sight among the trees, then I turned to look about. 'Where is this place?'

'You don't know?' said Dade, surprised. 'Close to Big Thicket country.' He pointed down the hill to the right. 'Neches River down there.' His arm swung in an arc. 'Big Thicket that way, an' Kountze.' His thumb jerked over his shoulder. 'Beaumont back there.'

I had never heard of any of it, but it seemed I had just come out of Big Thicket.

Dade said, 'Seems I remember Debbie Cunningham marryin' a Britisher a few months back. That you?'

'Yes.'

'Then it's Debbie Leroy's got,' he said ruminatively. 'I think you'd better talk.'

'So had you,' I said. 'What have you got against Cunninghams?'

'The sons of bitches have been tryin' to run me offen my own land ever since I can remember. Tried to run my Paw off, too. Been tryin' a long time. They fenced off our land an' big city sportsmen came in an' shot our hogs. They reckoned they was wild; we said they belonged to people – us people. We tore down their fences an' built our own, an' defended 'em with guns. They ran a lot of folks offen their land, but not us Perkinscs.'

'The Cunninghams don't want your land just to hunt pigs, do they?'

'Naw. They want to bring in bulldozers an' strip the land. A lot of prime hardwood around here. Then they replant with softwoods right tidy, like a regiment of soldiers marchin' down Pennsylvania Avenue in Washington like I seen on TV once. Ruinin' this country.'

Dade waved his arm. 'Big Thicket was three million acres once. Not much left now an' we want to keep it the way it is. Sure, I cut my timber, but I do it right an' try not to make too many big changes.'

I said, 'I can promise you won't have trouble with the Cunninghams ever again.'

He shook his head. 'You'll never get that past Jack Cunningham – he's as stubborn as a mule. He'll never let go while there's a dollar to be made outta Big Thicket.'

'Jack will be no trouble; he had a heart attack a couple of days ago.'

'That so?' said Dade uninterestedly. 'Then it's Billy One – that old bastard's just as bad.'

'I promised,' I said stubbornly. 'It'll hold, Dade.'

I could see he was sceptical. He merely grunted and changed the subject. 'How come you tangled with Leroy Ainslee?'

'Debbie was kidnapped from Houston,' I said. 'So was I. Next thing I knew I was at the Ainslee place locked up in a hut with Leroy on guard with a shotgun. That one,' I added, pointing to the shotgun leaning against the tree where Sherry-Lou had left it.

'Kidnappin'!' said Dade blankly. He shook his head. 'Ainslees have mighty bad habits, but that ain't one of 'em.'

'They didn't organize it. There was an Englishman; called himself Robinson, but I doubt if that's his real name. I think all the Ainslees provided was muscle and a place to hide. Who are they, anyway?'

'A no account family of white trash,' said Dade. 'No one around here likes 'em. An' they breed too damn fast. Those Ainslee women pop out brats like shelling peas.' He scratched his jaw. 'How much did they ask for ransom?'

'They didn't tell me.' I was not about to go into details with Dade; he would never believe me.

'Did you really kill Earl? An' gut Tukey?'

'Yes.' I told him how I had done it and he whistled softly. I said, 'And Debbie was screaming all the time and I couldn't get near her.' I found myself shaking.

Dade put his hand on my arm. 'Take it easy, son; we'll get her out of there.' He looked down at my feet. 'Think you can walk a piece?'

'I can try.'

He looked down the hill. 'Them Ainslees might take it into their haids to come back. We'll go over the rise an' find us a better place to be.' He picked up Leroy's shotgun and examined it. 'Nice gun,' he said appreciatively.

'You can have it,' I said. 'I doubt if Leroy will come calling for it.'

Dade chuckled. 'Ain't that so.'

Just over an hour later Dade nudged me. 'Here's Sherry-Lou. Got Chuck with her, too.' He put two fingers in his mouth and uttered a peculiar warbling whistle, and the two distant figures changed course and came towards the tumble of rocks where Dade and I were sitting.

Sherry-Lou had brought more than footwear. She produced a paper bag full of chunky pork sandwiches and I suddenly realized I had not eaten for about twenty-four hours. As I ate them she rubbed my feet with a medicament and then bandaged them.

More important than this was the news she brought. When Billy had heard her story he exploded into action and promised all aid short of the US Navy as fast as humanly possible. 'He's flyin' here direct,' she said. 'I told him to bring a doctor.' She avoided my eyes and I knew *my* hurts were not in her mind when she said that.

'What's all this about?' asked Chuck.

I let Dade tell the story – I was too busy eating. When he had finished Chuck said, 'I always knew the Ainslees were bad.' He shook his head. 'But this . . .' He stared at me. 'An' you kilt Earl?'

'He's dead, unless he can walk around with his brains leaking out,' I said sourly.

'Jeez! Leroy will be madder than a cornered boar. What's to do, Pop?'

Dade said, 'Did Billy Cunningham say how long he'd be?'

' 'Bout three o'clock,' said Sherry-Lou.

Dade hauled out an old-fashioned turnip watch and nodded. 'Chuck, you get back to the house right smartly. When Billy drops by in his whirlybird you show him the big meadow near Turkey Creek. We'll be there. No reason for Tom to walk more'n he has to.'

'Jeez!' said Chuck with enthusiasm. 'Never flown in one of them things.' He loped away. I thought that Dade Perkins's kids could stand a chance in the Olympics marathon; they did everything on the dead run.

Sherry-Lou snorted. 'He's never been in the air in his life – in anythin'.' She finished knotting a bandage over the deepest gash on my arm. 'You all right, Tom?'

'I'll be better when I know Debbie's all right.'

She veiled her eyes. 'Sure.'

Dade stood up. 'Take us fifteen minutes to get down to the creek. Might as well start.'

When the helicopter came down in the meadow Billy had the door open before the shock absorbers had taken up the weight, and came running across the grass towards us, stooping as people always do when they know rotors are turning overhead. He took in my condition in one swift glance. 'Christ! How are you? How's Debbie?'

Dade and Sherry-Lou moved tactfully to one side, out of earshot, and were joined by Chuck who was talking nineteen to the dozen and windmilling his arms wildly. I gave Billy the gist of it, leaving out everything unimportant; just outlining the 'whats' and ignoring the 'hows' and 'whys'. He winced. 'Torturing her!' he said incredulously.

'She was screaming,' I said flatly. 'I was being shot at – I had to move fast.' I paused. 'I should have stayed.'

'No,' said Billy, 'you did the best you could.' He looked back at the helicopter. 'The State Police and some of our own security men are coming up behind. We'd better get back to the Perkins place.'

'One more thing,' I said. 'Seems Dade Perkins doesn't like Cunninghams, and from what little he told me I know why. Now, he just saved my life, so from now on you haul off your dogs.'

'It's not up to me,' said Billy. 'Jack won't . . .'

'Jack doesn't matter any more and you know it.'

'Yeah, but Dad won't be buffaloed either.' He frowned. 'Let me think about it. Come on.'

A few minutes later we dropped next to the Perkins's family residence and to two more helicopters with State Police markings. More were in the sky coming in. When all six were on the ground we had a conference – a council of war.

Dade Perkins was in on it, and outlined on a table what the Ainslee place was like, using match books and tobacco tins. Then there was a brief argument when Sherry-Loū announced that she was coming along.

The senior police officer was Captain Booth who was inclined to want to know the whys and wherefores until he was cut down by Billy. 'For Christ's sake, Captain, quit yammering! We can hold the inquest after we've gotten my cousin out of there.' It was a measure of Cunningham influence that Booth stopped right then and there.

Now he said decidedly, 'No place for a woman. There might be shooting.'

'Miz Mangan will need a woman if she's . . .' Sherry-Lou swallowed the words 'still alive', and continued, 'I know Leroy Ainslee.'

Dade turned red in the face. 'Has he interfered with you?'

'No, he hasn't!' she retorted. 'Not since I laid a rock against his head an' then got me a gun an' told him I'd perforate him.'

Dade glowered, and Booth said thoughtfully, 'There'll be one chopper in the air all the time. They might scatter and we'll want to see where they go. I reckon Miss Perkins could be in that one.'

We left in the helicopters and descended like a cloud of locusts on the Ainslee place less than five minutes later with the precision of a military operation. I was in the chopper which dropped right in the middle. No one shot at us because there was no one there to shoot. All the Ainslee menfolk were absent and only the women and a few kids were left. The children were excited by the sudden invasion but the slatternly women merely looked at us with apathetic eyes.

Billy had a gun in his hand when he jumped out, and Dade carried Leroy's shotgun. I looked about and saw cops closing in from all sides. Billy holstered his pistol. 'They're not here.'

'Still out lookin' for Tom, I reckon,' said Dade. He squinted up at the helicopter hovering overhead. 'They'll know somethin's wrong. Been nothin' like this since I seen the Vietnam war on TV. They won't be back in a hurry.'

I said, 'For God's sake, let's find Debbie.' I picked out the biggest house, a ruinous shack, and began to run.

It was Billy who found her. He came out of a smaller shack bellowing, 'A doctor! Where is that goddamn doctor?' He caught me by the shoulders as I tried to go in. 'No, Tom. Let the doctor see to her first. Will you quit struggling?'

A man ran past us carrying a bag and the door of the shack slammed shut. Billy yelled at me, 'She's alive, damn it! Let the doctor tend to her.'

I sagged in his arms and he had to hold me up for a moment, then I said, 'Okay, Billy, I'm all right now.'

'Sure,' he said. 'I know you are.' He turned and saw Booth. 'Hey, Captain, better get the Perkins girl down here.'

'Right, Mr Cunningham.' Booth spoke to one of the pilots standing by, then came over to us. 'Mr Mangan, I'd like you to come with me.' I nodded and was about to follow him, but he was looking at Billy. 'You okay, Mr Cunningham?'

Billy had developed a curious greenish pallor and beads of sweat stood out on his forehead. He sat down on the stoop of the shack. 'I'll be all right. You go with the Captain, Tom.'

I followed Booth to the shack in which I had been held prisoner. Earl's body had been laid out parallel to the wall and beneath the window. The big pitcher was lying on its side, still intact, and a pool of water lay on the floor, as yet unevaporated. Tukey lay on the bed; he was dead and stank of faeces.

Booth said, 'Know anything about this?'

'Yes. I killed them.'

'You admit it,' he said in surprise. I nodded, and he said, 'You'd better tell me more.'

I thought about that, then shook my head. 'No, I'll say what I have to say in a courtroom.'

'I don't think I can accept that,' he said stiffly. 'Not in a case of murder.'

'Who said anything about murder?' I asked. 'When you lift Tukey you'll find the bed has been ripped up by buckshot. I happened to be sitting there when Earl pulled the trigger. I stabbed Tukey when he was going to shoot me. Don't prejudge the case, Captain; it's for a court to decide if it was murder.' He made a hesitant movement, and I said, 'Are you going to arrest me?'

He rubbed his chin and I heard a faint rasping sound. 'You're not an American, Mr Mangan. That's the problem. How do I know you'll stay in State jurisdiction?'

'You can have my passport, if you can find it,' I offered. 'I had it on me when I was snatched. It may be around here somewhere. Anyway, Billy Cunningham will guarantee I'll stay, if you ask him.'

'Yeah, that'll be best.' Booth seemed relieved.

'There *was* a murder.' I nodded towards the window. 'It happened out there. Leroy Ainslee shot a man in the back. I saw it.'

'There's no body.'

'Then have your men look for a new-dug grave.' I turned on my heel and walked out of that stinking room into the clean sunlight. The hovering helicopter had come down, and I saw Sherry-Lou hurrying into the shack the doctor had gone into. I felt curiously empty of all feeling, except for a deep thankfulness that Debbie was still alive. My rage was muted, dampened down, but it still smouldered deep in my being, and I knew it would not take much for it to erupt.

I went over and stood in the shade of a helicopter. Presently I was found by Chuck Perkins. 'Jeez, you sure kilt Earl,' he said. His face sobered. 'Tukey died bad.'

'They deserved it.'

'Pop's been looking for you.' He jerked his thumb. 'He's over there.'

I walked around the helicopter and saw Dade talking to Sherry-Lou. His face was serious. As I approached I heard Sherry-Lou say, '. . . tore up real bad.'

He put his hand on her arm in a warning gesture as he saw me. He swallowed. 'Sherry-Lou's got something to tell you,' he said. 'I'm sorry, Tom, real sorry.'

I said, 'Yes, Sherry-Lou?'

'Did you know Miz Mangan was pregnant?'

'Yes.' I knew what was coming.

'She lost the baby. I'm sorry.'

I stared blindly into the sky. 'Rape?'

'An' worse.'

'God damn their souls to hell!' I said violently.

She put out her hand to me. 'Some women are hurt more in birthin' a baby,' she said. 'She'll be all right.'

'In her body, maybe.'

'She'll need a lot of love . . . lot of attention. She'll need cherishin'.'

'She will be. Thanks, Sherry-Lou.'

They brought her out on a stretcher, the doctor walking alongside, and a nurse holding up a bottle for an intravenous drip. All that could be seen of her was her face, pale and smudgy about the eyes. I wanted to go with her in the helicopter back to Houston, but the doctor said, 'There's no use in it, Mr Mangan. She'll be unconscious for the next twenty-four hours – I guarantee it. Then we'll wake her up slowly. We'll want you there then.'

So the helicopter lifted without me aboard and I turned to find Captain Booth standing close by talking to Dade. I said bitterly, 'If I find Leroy Ainslee before you, Captain, I can guarantee you'll have a murder case.'

'We'll get him,' Booth said soberly, but from the way Dade spat on the ground I judged he was sceptical.

Billy came up. He had recovered something of his colour. 'Dade Perkins, I want to talk with you. You too, Tom.'

Dade said, 'What do you want?'

Billy glanced at Booth, then jerked his head. 'Over here.' He led us out of earshot of Booth. 'I know we've been putting pressure on you, Dade.'

Dade's face cracked in a slow smile. 'An' not gettin' far.'

'All I want to say is that it stops right now,' said Billy.

Dade glanced at me then looked at Billy speculatively. 'Reckon you big enough to make yo' Paw eat crow?'

'This crow he'll eat with relish,' said Billy grimly. 'But there's something I want from you.'

'Never did know the Cunninghams give anything away free,' observed Dade. 'What is it?'

'I want the Ainslees out of here,' said Billy. 'I don't want to feel there's folks like that dirtying up the place.'

'The cops'll do that for you,' said Dade. 'Why pick me?'

'Because I saw your face when Sherry-Lou said what she did about Leroy back at your place. Where do you suppose Leroy is now?'

'Easy. Hidin' out in Big Thicket.'

'Think the cops will find him there?'

'Them!' Dade spat derisively. 'They couldn't find their own asses in Big Thicket.'

'See what I mean.' Billy stuck his forefinger under Dade's nose. 'I don't want that son of a bitch getting away. I'd be right thankful if he didn't.'

Dade nodded. 'There's a whole passel of folks round here that don't like the Ainslees. Never have – but never gotten stirred up enough to do anythin'. This might do it. As for Leroy – well, if the devil looks after his own, so does the Lord. So let's leave it to the Lord.' Dade spat again, and said thoughtfully, 'But mebbe he could do with a little help.'

Billy nodded, satisfied. 'That make you happy?' he said to me.

'It'll do – for now.' I was thinking of Robinson.

'Then let's go home.'

I said goodbye to the Perkinses, and Dade said, 'Come back some time, you hear? Big Thicket ain't all blood. There's some real pretty places I'd like to show you.'

'I'll do that,' I said and climbed up into the helicopter. I slid the door closed and we rose into the sky and I saw Big Thicket laid out below. Then the chopper tilted and there was nothing but sky as we slid west towards Houston.

NINETEEN

Medical science made Debbie's wakening mercifully easy, and when she opened her eyes mine was the first face she saw. She was not fully conscious, lapped in a drug-induced peace, but enough so to recognize me and to smile. I held her hand and she closed her eyes, the smile still on her lips, and slipped away into unconsciousness again. But her fingers were still tight on mine.

I stayed there the whole afternoon. Her periods of semi-consciousness became more frequent and longer-lasting, monitored by a nurse who adjusted the intravenous drip. 'We're bringing her out slowly and smoothly,' the nurse said in a low voice. 'No sudden shocks.'

But Debbie did have the sudden shock of remembrance. In one of her periods of wakefulness her eyes widened and she gave a small cry. 'Oh! They . . . they . . .'

'Hush, my love,' I said. 'I'm here, and I won't leave. It's finished, Debbie, it's all over.'

Her eyes had a look of hazy horror in them. 'They . . .'

'Hush. Go back to sleep.'

Thankfully she closed her eyes.

Much later, when she was more coherent, she tried to talk about it. I would not let her. 'Later, Debbie, when you're stronger. Later – not now. Nothing matters now but you.'

Her head turned weakly on the pillow. 'Not me,' she said. 'Us.'

I smiled then because I knew that she – we – would be all right.

I talked with her doctor and asked bluntly if Debbie would be able to have another baby. His answer was almost the same as Sherry-Lou's. 'Women are stronger than most men think, Mr Mangan. Yes, she'll be able to have children. What your wife has suffered, in terms of physical damage, is no more than some women suffer in childbirth. Caesarean section, for instance.'

'Caesarean section is usually done more hygienically,' I said grimly. 'And with anaesthetics.'

He had the grace to look abashed. 'Yes, of course,' he said hurriedly. 'She may need a great deal of care of the kind that is out of my field. If I could recommend a psychiatrist . . .?'

Sherry-Lou had said Debbie would need cherishing, and I reckoned that was my department; the cherishing that comes from a psychiatrist is of an arid kind. I said, 'I'll be taking her home.'

'Yes,' said the doctor. 'That might be best.'

I was hedged about by the law. The Cunninghams retained a good lawyer, the best trial lawyer in Texas I was assured. His name was Peter Heller and his only command was that I keep my mouth shut. 'Don't talk to anyone about the case,' he said. 'Not to the police and especially not to newsmen.'

One thing troubled him. 'The reef we're going to run on is that of intent,' he said. 'You see, Mr Mangan, you made certain preparations, way ahead of the event, to kill one of the Ainslees – and you did kill Earl Ainslee and, subsequently, Tukey. Now, we might just get away with Tukey because you could have had no knowledge he'd be there when you opened the door, but Earl is a different matter – that was deliberately planned. That pitcher did not walk up into the roof by itself. The jury might not like that.'

Ten days after we came out of Big Thicket Leroy Ainslee's body was found by the track of the Southern Pacific railroad. Apparently he had been run over by a train.

'Where exactly did it happen?' I asked Billy.

'Just north of Kountze. Little town which might be described as the capital of Big Thicket.'

'"Leave him to the Lord",' I quoted ironically.

'I got the pathologist's report,' said Billy. 'Most of the injuries were consistent with tangling with a freight train.'

'Most?'

Billy shrugged. 'Maybe the Lord had help. Anyway the cops have written it down as accidental death. He's being buried in Kountze.'

'I see.' I saw that Texas could be a pretty rough place.

'It's best this way,' said Billy. 'Oh, by the way, Dade Perkins sends his regards.'

The case did not come to trial or, at least, not to the kind of trial we have in the Bahamas where the law is patterned after the British style. It went to the Grand Jury which was supposed to establish if there was a case to be answered at all. I never did get to the bottom of the intricacies of the American legal system, but I suspect that a considerable amount of string-pulling was done by the Cunninghams behind the scenes.

Because it involved kidnapping, a federal offence, the argument before the Grand Jury was not conducted by a local District Attorney from Houston but by a State Attorney from Austin, the State capital. I was represented by Heller and, as far as I could judge, he and the State Attorney – a man called Riker – had no adverse relationship at all. The whole hearing was conducted in such a way as to get a cool assessment of the facts.

There was a tricky moment when I was on the stand and Riker was interrogating me. He said, 'Now, Mr Mangan; you have stated that you made certain preparations – and quite elaborate preparations – involving a pitcher of water to kill Earl Ainslee.'

'No,' I said. 'I thought it would be Leroy Ainslee.'

'I see,' he said thoughtfully. 'Did you have anything against Leroy Ainslee?'

I smiled slightly. 'Apart from the fact that he was keeping me prisoner at gun point, and that he was keeping my wife from me – nothing at all.' There was a rumble of amusement from the jury. 'I'd never met the man before.'

'Yes,' said Riker. 'Now, to return to the man you actually killed – Earl Ainslee. He actually had you at gun point at that time?'

'Yes. It was a 12-bore shotgun.'

Riker looked puzzled. 'Twelve what?'

'I'm sorry,' I said. 'It would be called 12-gauge here.'

'I see. Did you know the gun was loaded?'

'I had been so informed. Robinson said buckshot.'

'The mysterious Mr Robinson said that?'

'Yes. I found his information to be accurate when Earl pulled the trigger.'

'Earl fired a shot at you?'

'That's right. The buckshot ripped up the bed I was sitting on.'

'Now, I want you to answer this question very carefully, Mr Mangan. Did Earl Ainslee pull that trigger involuntarily as a result of being struck on the head with the heavy pitcher, or did he shoot first?'

'I don't know,' I said. 'I was too busy getting out of the way.' Again there came a murmur from the jury.

'But, at all events, you did pull the string which released the pitcher?'

'Yes.'

'Why?'

Into the sudden silence I said, 'My wife was screaming.' I moistened my lips. 'Earl said Leroy was having fun, and that it was his turn next.'

Riker waited until the stir had died away. 'Mr Mangan, had your wife not screamed would you have pulled that string?'

Again there was silence.

'I don't know. I honestly don't know.'

Heller put up his hand. 'Objection. The witness can testify only as to matters of fact. That is a hypothetical question.'

'I withdraw the question,' said Riker.

And that was the worst of it as far as I was concerned. There were more questions concerning the death of Tukey and the chase through Big Thicket, but Heller steered me past all the pitfalls. Then I retired because I was not allowed to hear other witnesses giving evidence.

Debbie told me afterwards that they handled her gently and considerately, and her time on the stand was brief. I believe the evidence of the doctor who had attended Debbie at the Ainslee place, and that of Sherry-Lou, damned Leroy thoroughly.

Anyway the whole thing was tossed out as being no case of murder or culpable homicide to answer at trial. There appeared to be a slight incredulity mixed with gratification that a Britisher, as I was popularly supposed to be, could be as red-blooded as any American and, I suppose, the unwritten law had a lot to do with it. Anyway, it was over and I was a free man.

Afterwards, Heller said, 'I know I objected to that hypothetical question, but I'm damned glad Riker asked it. You'll notice I objected only *after* you had answered it.'

'Yes.'

He grinned. 'I had my heart in my mouth waiting for your answer. I was taking a hell of a chance on that.'

'So was I,' I said dryly.

He looked a bit startled at that, and said, 'You know, Mr Mangan, you're no man's fool. That was a perfect answer. Have you studied law?'

'Not in any depth.'

'Well, there's a peculiar grey area that's not covered in any of the law books, and that answer of yours was right in the middle of it. You did all right.'

Before I went home to Grand Bahama Billy One convened another conference. Again it was confined to his kitchen cabinet; present were Billy, Frank and young Jim. Jack was absent; although out of hospital he was still confined to his home. I was there, too, and waiting to find out why.

Billy One started by saying to Frank, 'Your Pa is a sick man and I don't reckon he'll be attending to business for some time. But decisions have to be made and someone has to make them, and I think it's up to me. Of course, it'll be put to a full meeting of the board as soon as we get around to it, but we don't have time to wait on that.' He looked around the table. 'Any objections?'

Billy smiled and Jim merely shrugged – he was not going to argue with the man who had promoted him to top table – but Frank said, 'I think it should be put to the board.'

'No time,' said Billy One. 'Joe's in Scotland wrapping up that North Sea oil deal and I don't want to pull him from that. Besides, I'd want to have Jack at the meeting and he's not up to it yet.'

Frank nodded and accepted defeat. 'Okay – but what's he doing here?' His finger stabbed at me.

'He's here because he's a Cunningham,' said Billy One flatly. 'And because I want him here.' He ignored Frank's perplexed look and turned to me. 'How's Debbie today?'

'Not too bad,' I said. 'She's mended in body but . . .' I shrugged. 'She has nightmares.'

'Tom, I know you want to get back to her, but this won't take long.' Billy One leaned back and surveyed us. 'I want to remind you young fellows of some history – family history. We Cunninghams originally came from Scotland. Two brothers, Malcolm and Donald, settled here in tidewater Texas when it was still Mexico. They were piss-poor but it was a goddamn sight better than crofting back home.'

He clasped his hands. 'Over the years the family prospered. We helped Sam Houston take Texas from the Mexicans, and the family were among the leaders who pressurized Tyler into admitting Texas to the Union. We grew rich and strong and now we're not only powerful in Texas but over the whole goddamn world. And the way we did it was this.' He raised his clasped hands before him, the knuckles white under firm pressure. 'The family stays together and works as a team.'

Frank said in a bored voice, 'We know all that.'

'Sure,' said Billy One mildly. 'But I want Tom to know the score. It was Billy's idea to bring him into the Bahamas deal. Me, I was neutral but willing to go along. I didn't think all that much of Tom but I had nothing against him. Same when he married Debbie.'

'He cut himself a fair slice in that Bahamas deal,' said Frank.

'Sure he did,' agreed Billy One. 'And my respect for him went up a notch.' He looked at me. 'Why did you set it up that way?'

'I like my independence.'

'That can be good – but solidarity can be better. How would you like to join the Cunningham Corporation?'

'As what?'

'You'll be on the board making policy.'

'The hell he will!' said Frank outraged.

Billy One swung on him. 'You've still got a sister and Jack's still got a daughter on account of this guy, and he killed two men making it that way. He's shed blood and lost some of his own. In my book that makes him family – a Cunningham.' He stared Frank down and then sighed. 'Okay, Tom, what do you think?'

It was a handsome offer but there had to be a catch. As Dade Perkins had remarked, the Cunninghams were not notorious for offering free handouts. There had to be a catch in spite of Billy One's rhetoric, and he confirmed it by saying, 'Before being appointed to the board there's something you'll have to do.'

'And that is?'

'Well, there's something I want. Another thing about us Cunninghams is that we take insults from nobody. Now, my brother nearly died in that damn hospital, and my niece – your wife – was raped, and that's the biggest insult you can offer a woman.' His voice trembled. 'I want this guy, Robinson, and I want him real bad.'

Jim said, 'The State Police haven't gotten far on it.'

'They don't have our reasons,' snapped Billy One. He stared at me. 'You'll have the whole family right behind you, and that means the Cunningham Corporation. You can have any resources we have and, believe me, that's plenty.'

I said, 'Wow!' but not aloud. I did not know how many billions of dollars the Cunningham Corporation controlled, but it was a respectable chunk of the GNP. It was not the biggest corporation in the United States, but it was not the smallest, either, not by a long way.

'It might not be a question of money,' I said. 'In any case, I have plenty of that.' I held Billy One's eye. 'And I don't need any reasons from you why I should find Robinson;

I have plenty of my own.' I leaned back. 'The problem is that we have a total lack of information.'

Jim said, 'We have a pretty fair intelligence unit; you can put that to work.' I nodded, thinking of the ready way Rodriguez had hustled up bugging devices.

'Anything you want you get through Billy or Jim,' said Billy One. 'You'll liaise with them.'

'What about me?' said Frank.

'You and me have the Corporation to run. Have you any immediate ideas, Tom?'

'I think the answer lies in the Bahamas,' I said. 'That's the reason why your State Police have come up with nothing. I don't think Robinson is in Texas, or even in the United States. I think he's in the Bahamas. That's where I'm going to look for him, anyway. I'm leaving tomorrow with Debbie.'

'With Debbie?' said Frank. 'Wouldn't it be better if she stays here?'

I said deliberately, 'We've had enough of separate lives – both of us.' I turned to Jim. 'But I'd like a twenty-four-hour bodyguard on her until this thing is settled. Can you arrange that?'

'Sure, no problem. We have some dandy bodyguards – Treasury-trained.'

I did not see the point of that remark. 'What's that got to do with anything?'

Billy said, 'The Department of the Treasury bodyguards the President of the United States. Those guys are very good.' He smiled. 'We get to hire them because we pay better than the Treasury. But I've had an idea, Tom. I know you did a photofit of Robinson for the cops, but they've gotten no place with it. I have a kissing cousin who is a pretty fair portrait painter. Maybe she can produce something better.'

So it was that I was introduced to Cassie Cunningham, aged about twenty-five and unmarried, who came armed with a sketching block, pencils and water colours. She was quite a good portraitist and, after a few false starts, I began to feel hopeful of success. When we had done Robinson for good measure I asked Cassie to do another of the fake doctor who had whipped me from the lobby of the Cunningham Building.

The next day we flew to Freeport in the Cunningham Corporation JetStar. Apart from Debbie and myself there were six large men with bulges under their arms. 'Six!' I said to Jim Cunningham. 'I'm not going to start a bloody war.'

'Billy thought you ought to have a bodyguard, too. Anyway, allocate them as you choose.'

After thinking that one over I thought that Billy could very well be right. 'One thing,' I said. 'They're not employed by me. The Bahamian Government is very strict about firearms, and if these men are caught they're on their own.'

So we went home and I installed Debbie back in the house, with Kitty Symonette as attendant and companion. After making arrangements to bring Karen back from Abaco I went to see how the Theta Corporation had fared in my enforced absence. But it was just going to be a quick look because I was not going to leave Debbie for long. I had learned that lesson well.

TWENTY

The boss of the bodyguarding team was Steve Walker and
he went with me to the office. I introduced him to Jessie in
the outer office, then we went into my own. Walker looked
around. 'Two doors,' he commented. 'Where does that one
lead?'

'To the corridor.'

The key was in the lock so he turned it, locking the door.
'I'd rather you use just the one door,' he said. 'Can I have a
desk in the corner of your secretary's office?'

'Sure. I'll have Jessie set it up.' So I did, much to her
mystification, and when Walker had settled down I sat
behind my own desk to do some heavy thinking.

I went over everything Robinson had said and latched
on to something. He had said that Kayles had reported
that I knew all about his plans, whatever they were,
and that I had not told Kayles directly, but that
Kayles had overheard a conversation between me and
Sam Ford.

I thought back to the affray on *My Fair Lady*. Kayles could
have listened when Sam and I were talking in the cockpit,
but we had not talked about any mysterious plans, only
about how to get Kayles back to Duncan Town. Anyway,
Kayles would have been too busy cutting himself free and
grabbing his gun to listen to us.

518

The only other time he could have listened to Sam and me was when he was tied up on the bunk. I vaguely remembered that I had a notion he had been feigning unconsciousness at the time, so what had I said to Sam about anyone's plans? I remembered I had been a bit irritable and had blown my top about something, but what it was I could not remember – a lot had happened since then. But perhaps Sam would know.

I snapped on the intercom. 'Jessie, get Sam Ford on the telephone. I don't know where he'll be; you'll have to track him down.'

'But didn't you know?' she said.

'Know what?'

'He's in hospital in Nassau. A boat fell on him.'

'Come in here and tell me more.'

It appeared that Sam had been supervising the removal of a yacht from the water. Half-way up the slip it had fallen sideways from the cradle, and Sam happened to be in the way. It was a ten-ton ketch. 'He's in the intensive care unit of the Princess Margaret Hospital,' said Jessie. 'He was still in a coma the last I heard.'

'When did this happen?'

'About a week ago.'

I was filled with a cold rage. If Robinson had tried to kill me because of what Kayles overheard he would certainly not leave out Sam. This was as much of an ordinary accident as the disappearance of Bill Pinder. I said, 'Ask Mr Walker to come in.'

Jessie stood up, then hesitated. 'Who is he?' she asked. 'He's just sitting there reading magazines. And he asked me to give him a signal if a stranger comes in.'

'Don't worry about him, but do as he says. And I'd appreciate it if you didn't talk about him – to anyone.'

All the same she looked a bit worried as she left. When Walker came in I said, 'We have another bodyguard job,' and filled in the details. 'I don't want anyone getting to Sam.'

Walker tugged his ear. 'That might be tricky. Do we get the cooperation of the hospital?'

'I'll see what I can do about that. In the meantime have a couple of your men on alert, ready to fly to Nassau.'

He nodded and left, and I was about to ask Jessie to put me through to the hospital in Nassau when she buzzed me. 'Commissioner Perigord to see you.'

I had been expecting Perigord but not as soon as this. He was quick off the mark. 'Send him in.'

Perigord came in, as trim and elegant as ever in his well-cut uniform. 'What can I do for you?' I asked. 'Please sit down.'

He took off his cap and laid it on the desk, together with the swagger stick he always carried, and sat in the chair opposite. He regarded me with dark brown eyes set in a dark brown face, and said quietly, 'Don't be bland with me, Mr Mangan. You have much to tell me. When a Bahamian of some eminence is kidnapped in Texas and kills two men in the act of escaping it tends to make headlines in the newspapers. You are a man of some notoriety.'

I should have expected that but it had not occurred to me. True, Jessie had looked at me with big eyes when I had walked into the office, but I had kept her on the run and we had not had time to be chatty. 'I must get the clippings for my scrapbook,' I said ironically.

'Captain Booth of the Texas State Police telephoned me. He wanted to know about you, naturally enough. Your status in the community, had you a criminal record, and so forth. I gave you a clean bill of health.'

'Thanks for the testimonial.'

'We also talked about our common problems – drug-running, for instance. Texas has a long border with Mexico.'

'Do you still think this case has to do with drugs? I'm beginning to wonder about that.'

Perigord shrugged. 'I'm keeping an open mind. I read the transcript of the Grand Jury hearing with great interest.'

I was surprised. 'You did? That hearing was held in private.'

Perigord's lips quirked into a smile. 'Like you, I have friends in Texas. It made . . . how shall I put it? . . . empty reading. For example, there was the mysterious Mr Robinson, your kidnapper, floating about the case with no visible means of support – never found. And there was the body of Kayles which, again, has never been found.'

'It wouldn't be too hard to make a body vanish in Big Thicket,' I said. 'You could toss it into any swamp.'

'True, but Captain Booth is moderately unhappy. You see, he only has your word for it that there was a third body or even a Robinson. He couldn't ask Leroy Ainslee because he was inconsiderately killed by a train.'

I said, 'My wife never saw Kayles, but she did see Robinson. You must have read her evidence.' I took a glossy colour photograph from my desk drawer. 'Meet Mr Robinson.'

Perigord took it from my fingers and examined it critically. 'You did better with Kayles,' he said. 'That was a photograph. This is a photograph of a painting.' He dropped it on to the desk. 'Not what one would call hard evidence for the existence of Robinson.'

'Are you saying you don't believe me – or Debbie?' I demanded.

'No – but I'm dissatisfied. Like Captain Booth I'm moderately unhappy.' He then said what Frank Cunningham had said before Billy hit him, but in a way that robbed it of offence. 'You seem to have problems with your wives, Mr Mangan. I was very sorry when the first Mrs Mangan died because I had a regard for her, and I was equally sorry when

I heard what had happened to your present wife. I ask myself if these events are related in any way, and if your problems are going to continue. Too much has happened around you in the last year or so.' He leaned forward. 'Now let us talk about Robinson.'

So we talked about Robinson for a long time. At last I said, 'I've been racking my brains to think of what Kayles overheard between me and Sam Ford, and I can't ask Sam.' I told him about that, and added pointedly, 'And I don't think that was an accident, either.'

Perigord looked grave. 'I'll ring Commissioner Deane in Nassau, and we'll have that incident investigated.'

'And put a guard on Sam,' I said.

He nodded and picked up the picture of Robinson. 'How accurate is this?'

'I really don't know,' I said candidly. 'But it's the best Cassie Cunningham and I could do. She said it's difficult for a painter to depict an image in someone else's mind's eye.'

'Very well put.' Perigord picked up his hat. 'Now, there is just one last matter. You came back from Texas without a passport. Well, that's all right because we know the reason. But you came back with six Americans, two of whom are in your home though not, I suspect, as house guests; three are billeted in the Royal Palm Hotel, and the sixth is sitting in your outer office at this moment. We checked *their* passports very carefully and what did we find on further enquiry? All six are members of the security section of the Cunningham Corporation. Mr Mangan, if you have fears for your own safety or the safety of your wife you should come to me, and not import a private army.'

'My wife is dear to me.'

'I understand that.' He stood up. 'But I would like to see Mr Walker now.'

I eyed Perigord with respect; he even had the identification down pat. I called in Walker and introduced them.

Perigord said, 'Mr Walker, we encourage Americans to come to our island; you are our bread and butter. But we don't like firearms. Are you armed, sir?'

Walker said, 'Uh . . .' He glanced at me.

'Tell him,' I said.

'Well . . . er . . . yes, I am.'

Perigord held out his hand without saying a word and Walker took a pistol from a holster clipped to his belt and handed it over. Perigord put it into his pocket where it made an unsightly bulge and spoiled the line of his uniform. He picked up his swagger stick. 'You and your friends may stay, Mr Walker, even though I have the power to deport you. But all your firearms must be delivered to my office before midday today.' He raised the swagger stick in a semi salute. 'Good day, Mr Mangan. I'll let you know of any developments.'

As the door closed Walker said, 'A swagger stick, yet! Is he for real?'

'He had you tagged the moment you got off the JetStar. He knows who you are and what you do. I wouldn't underestimate Perigord.'

'What do we do about the guns?'

'You do exactly as he says. What have you got? A pistol each?'

'Yeah. And a couple of Armalite rifles.'

'My God! Let Perigord have the lot. You'll get them back when you leave.' I had the impression that Walker and his friends would feel stripped naked.

While not neglecting Debbie I buckled down to getting the Theta Corporation back into shape. Not that there was much wrong – I had a good staff – but when the boss takes an enforced vacation things tend to loosen and the system becomes sloppy. So I did the necessary tightening here and there to tune the organization.

One of the things I did was to transfer Jack Fletcher to the Sea Gardens Hotel on New Providence. The manager there had broken his leg and was out of action, and Philips, the under manager, was a new boy, so I thought it wise to send Fletcher. The point is that I went with him to introduce him to the staff. It was to be a quick trip because I did not want to spend time away from Debbie. Although Cora and Addy had brought over a crowd of kids and were company for Debbie I wanted to get back quickly.

Bobby Bowen flew us to Nassau and Steve Walker came along, too. During this period he was never more than ten feet away from me at any moment, and there would be only one door between us, if that. If Jack Fletcher noticed that Walker stuck closer to me than my shadow he made no comment.

After the round of introductions were over we sat in the manager's office to tidy up a few last details. There were minor differences in running the two hotels and I wanted to be sure that Fletcher knew of them. The manager's office at the Sea Gardens is immediately behind the reception desk in the lobby and one wall is of glass – glass with a difference.

From the customer's point of view when standing in the lobby the wall behind the reception desk is fitted with a big mirror. Mirrors are important in hotel design because they give a sense of space, spurious though it may be. But this mirror is of trick, one-way glass so that the manager, sitting at his desk, can see what is happening in the lobby while being unobserved himself.

So it was that, while chatting with Fletcher, I happened to look out idly at the reception desk and beyond. There was the usual scene, a combination of idleness and bustle. Small groups of tourists stood about chatting, and bellhops were bringing in the baggage of a newly arrived tour group. Philips said they had just come from Italy. Everything was normal. At the cashier's desk there was a short queue of departing visitors doing what the whole business was about – they were paying.

There was something about the third man in the queue that interested me. I thought I knew him but could not recollect ever having met him. He was tall with greying hair and had a neatly trimmed moustache and a short beard. I stood up, went closer to the window, and stared at him. He did what many do – he looked at his reflection in the mirror and straightened his tie. For a moment he stared directly into my eyes; his own were green flecked with yellow, and I had looked into those eyes before when lying helpless in the lobby of the Cunningham Building.

I swung around. 'Jack, see that man with the beard? I want him held up – delayed until I can find out who he is.'

Fletcher looked surprised. 'How?'

'Double his bill. Say it's a computer error and spend a long time rectifying it. But keep him there.' Fletcher shot off, and I said to Philips, 'Go with him. I want the man's name, room number, home address, where he came from, where he's going, and anything else you can find out about him. But be tactful. And quick.'

Walker joined me at the window. 'What's the panic?'

'That's one of Robinson's friends,' I said grimly. 'He had no beard when I last saw him, but there's no disguising those eyes and that big nose. When he leaves I want you to stick close to him.' I thought for a moment. 'How much money have you got on you?'

'I don't really know. A couple of hundred bucks, maybe.'

'You might need more. There's no knowing where he might go.' I took a cash voucher from the desk, scribbled a figure and added my signature. 'The cashier will honour this.'

Walker took the slip and gave a low whistle. 'Five thousand dollars!'

'He might be flying to Europe, damn it! Ask for American dollars or you might be stuck with Bahamian.'

'If I'm going to tail the guy I'd better not join that line at the desk,' he said.

'True. Stay here until Philips comes back. He can get the cash from behind the desk.'

We watched the comedy at the cashier's desk. My friend, the phoney doctor, moved up to the counter and presented his room key with a smile. There was a bit of dumb show and then the bill was presented. He glanced at it, then frowned, prodded at it with his forefinger, and pushed it back across the counter. The cashier made some chat and called over Jack Fletcher who now came into sight.

Walker said, 'If he pays by credit card we can trace him through the number.'

I nodded. Fletcher was making voluble apologies with much gesturing. He held up one hand in a placatory manner and disappeared from view. Two minutes later he walked into the office followed by Philips. 'His name is Carrasco – Dr Luis Carrasco.'

'So he really is a doctor,' I commented. 'Nationality?'

'Venezuelan.'

'Where is he going?'

'I don't know,' said Fletcher. 'I've only spoken to him for about three minutes. He said he had a plane to catch and would I make it short.'

'I know where he's going,' said Philips. 'He used our inter-hotel booking service. He's flying to Freeport and he's staying at the Royal Palm. He's booked in for a week.'

'Damned cheek!' I said, and looked at Carrasco. He was standing at the desk wearing a preoccupied expression and tapping restlessly with his fingers.

'He'll probably be flying Bahamasair,' said Fletcher, glancing at his watch. 'There's a flight in an hour.'

'He booked a hire car to await him at Freeport International,' said Philips.

'One of ours?'

'Yes.'

I looked at Walker. 'Can we bug that car? I mean, do we have the facilities handy?'

Walker shook his head. 'No, but we can have Rodriguez in Freeport in under four hours.'

'Make the phone call, direct to Billy Cunningham. Tell him it's bloody urgent.'

Walker picked up the telephone, and Fletcher said curiously, 'What's all this about, Tom?'

'Something that Commissioner Perigord will want to know about.' I had made one mistake with Perigord and another was unthinkable. 'What room did Carrasco have?'

Philips said, 'Three-one-six.'

'Have it locked and sealed. We can get fingerprints.' Walker heard that and nodded vigorously. I picked up the voucher which Walker had laid on the desk and tore it up; he would not need that now.

'How long do we keep Carrasco hanging about?' asked Fletcher.

'You can let him go as soon as Walker has finished his call and got a Bahamasair ticket to Freeport.' There was a travel agency in the lobby, so I said to Philips, 'Get that now and debit it to hotel expenses.'

Carrasco had interrupted a transaction between another client and the cashier; he was obviously arguing and was tapping his wristwatch meaningfully. Walker put down the telephone. 'Fixed,' he said. 'Rodriguez is coming over in the JetStar with a bag of gadgets.'

The minutes ticked by and Carrasco was becoming increasingly irritable. When I saw Philips walking across the lobby with an air ticket in his hand I said, 'Okay, let him go now. Many apologies, and tell him his taxi fare to the airport is on us as compensation for the trouble we've caused him. Do a grovel.'

Fletcher shrugged and left as Philips came in and gave Walker the ticket. 'Get a taxi for Mr Walker and have it standing by,' I said, and picked up the telephone to ring Perigord.

As I waited for him to come on the line I saw Jack Fletcher doing his obsequious act in a smarmy manner and I hoped he was not laying it on too thick. He escorted Carrasco to the door and Walker nodded to me and left without saying a word.

I got Perigord and told him what was happening. I said, 'I don't want this man alarmed because we haven't got Robinson yet. Carrasco could lead us to him.'

'At last you are using the brains you undoubtedly possess,' said Perigord, and promised to have a discreet escort awaiting Carrasco at the airport.

I told him that Walker was on the same flight, then said, 'One last thing; there'll be an American called Rodriguez coming in on the Cunningham JetStar later today. I don't want the Customs holding him up by taking a too close interest in his bags. Can you arrange that?'

'Not if he's bringing firearms,' said Perigord. 'You know that.'

'No firearms – my guarantee,' I promised. 'He's an electronics expert – I'll tell you about him later.'

Perigord agreed. I told him I'd be flying back immediately, then hung up and sat at Fletcher's desk and pondered. Was I right? I had seen him only for a matter of seconds, and I had been in a drugged condition at the time. But it had been very close up. Was I right in staking that he was Carrasco? Staking everything on the colour of a man's eyes and the size of his nose?

I thought I was right. The recent painting session with Cassie Cunningham had clarified my mind and etched that face into my mind's eye. But if I was wrong and Perigord laid on an elaborate operation to no good purpose then he would have an even lower opinion of me than ever.

Fletcher came back, and I asked, 'What's Carrasco's credit card number?'

'He paid cash. Just dug out his wallet and paid in hundred dollar bills, American. It didn't empty the wallet, either.'

'How much was the bill?'

'A little over 1100 dollars. He used the restaurant a lot and his bar bill wasn't small. Then there was the car rental charge.'

I leaned back in the chair. 'Jack, you've been in this business quite a time. When was the last time you can remember that a bill like that was paid in cash?'

'It's happened a few times,' he said. 'Not many, though. Usually when a man has cleaned up at the casino – he gets paid out in cash so he pays his bill in cash. But that's usually in Bahamian dollars.'

'I don't think Carrasco is a gambler,' I said meditatively. 'Not that kind, anyway. I'll take a copy of the bill with me.' I felt much more confident and happy.

TWENTY-ONE

I flew back to Freeport and went to see Perigord immediately. He had Inspector Hepburn with him, and he came
quickly to the point. 'Tell us more about this man
Carrasco.'

I did not do that. Instead, I looked at Inspector Hepburn,
and asked, 'Do you still think this is about cocaine?'

Perigord said, 'Yes, we do.'

'Well, I don't. Both Kayles and Robinson seemed surprised when I brought up the subject.'

'They would,' said Hepburn. 'They were not likely to
admit it, were they?'

I said, 'To my mind their surprise was genuine. It took
them aback.'

'But we don't have your mind,' said Perigord. 'I doubt if
you would consider yourself an expert on the way criminals
behave when confronted.'

I saw I was getting nowhere pursuing that line; their
minds were made up. 'What do you want to know about
Carrasco?'

'Everything,' Perigord said succinctly.

'He kidnapped me from the Cunningham Building,' I
said. 'And . . .'   '

Perigord held up his hand. 'You're sure it's the same
man?'

I hesitated. 'Not one hundred per cent, but near enough. I don't trust people who pay large bills in cash.' I told them of what had happened and put a copy of the bill on Perigord's desk.

Perigord, too, found that odd. We thrashed it out a bit, then he said, 'Mr Mangan, can we trust your American friends?'

'In what way?'

'Can we trust them to stick to surveillance, but not to take action in the matter of Carrasco? Our police force is relatively small and I would welcome their help in keeping tabs on Carrasco, but not to the extent of their taking violent action. That I can't permit.'

'They'll do exactly as I tell them.'

'Very well. I have talked to Mr Walker and he has Carrasco under observation at this moment; and is to report to my man at your hotel. Why is Rodriguez coming, and what is he carrying?' I told him and he smiled. 'Yes, I think we can do with scientific aid.'

Hepburn said, 'There's something I don't understand. If Carrasco kidnapped you in Houston isn't he taking a risk by walking openly about your hotels? He could bump into you at any time. In fact, you *did* spot him – or so you think.' He glanced at Perigord. 'To my mind this may be a case of mistaken identification. Mr Mangan admits he only saw the man in Houston for a few seconds.'

'What do you say to that?' asked Perigord.

'It's been puzzling me, too,' I said. 'But I'm ninety-five per cent convinced it's the same man.'

'Nineteen chances out of twenty in favour of you being correct,' he mused. 'Those are odds I can live with. We'll watch Dr Carrasco.'

Driving from the police station to the hotel I thought of what Hepburn had said, and came to the conclusion that it could cut both ways. If Carrasco had been the man in Houston then perhaps he was willing to take the chance of me seeing him *because* I had seen him for only a few seconds. In those circumstances perhaps he thought a beard and moustache were sufficient disguise. As I switched between alternatives my mind felt like a yo-yo.

A good hotel has two circulatory systems, one for the clientele which is luxuriously furnished, and the other for the staff which has a more spartan décor; and in the best hotels the two systems are mutually exclusive because one does not want maintenance traffic to erupt into the public rooms. When I got back to the hotel I stuck to the staff system because I wanted to keep out of the way of Carrasco.

Walker reported on Carrasco and related affairs. 'He's holed up in his room; probably unpacking. Rodriguez will be here in about two hours; I'll have a man at the airport to meet him. Perigord has a man here in the hotel, and he assigned another to your house to guard your wife.' He scratched the angle of his jaw, and added sourly, 'They're both armed.'

'They're entitled to be,' I said. 'You're not.' It was good of Perigord to think of Debbie. 'You're not to lay a finger on Carrasco. Just watch him and report on who he talks to.'

'Can we tap his room telephone?'

'It's probably illegal but we'll do it. I'll have a word with the switchboard operator. Carrasco might speak Spanish; do we have anyone who can cope with that?'

'One – two when Rodriguez comes.'

'That should be enough. Any problems, let me know.' We knocked it around a bit more, trying to find angles we had forgotten, did not find any and left it at that.

For the next three days nothing happened. Carrasco had no visitors to his room and used his telephone only for room service and for restaurant bookings. Rodriguez bugged his Car and his room, and put a tape recorder on the telephone tap so that we had a record of his conversations, but we got little joy out of that. A search of Carrasco's possessions brought nothing; he carried with him just what you would expect of a man on holiday.

Debbie wondered audibly about the muscular young black who had been imported into the house to help Luke Bailey, who did not need it, and who was making good time with Addy Williams. She knew about Walker's crew and I saw no reason to keep from her the knowledge that this addition to the household was one of Perigord's cops. 'I'd like you to keep to the house as much as possible,' I said.

'How long will we have to live like this?' she said desolately. 'Being in a state of siege isn't exactly fun.'

I did not know the answer to that, but I said, 'It will blow over soon, I expect.' I told her about Carrasco. 'If we can use him to nail Robinson I think it will be finished.'

'And if we can't?'

I had no answer to that, either.

I had not expected to go back to New Providence for some time. Jack Fletcher was an experienced manager and did not need his hand held, which is why I had put him into the Sea Gardens. But when he telephoned four days after I had left him in charge he was in a rare panic. 'We've got big trouble, Tom,' he said without preamble. 'Our guests are keeling over in all directions – dropping like flies. Tony Bosworth has his hands full.'

'What is it? Does he know?'

'He's closed down the big air-conditioner.'

'He thinks it's Legionnaires' disease?' I thought quickly. 'But it doesn't work that way – it didn't at the Parkway. Let me talk to him.'

'You can't. He's in a conference with officials from the Department of Public Health.'

'I'll be right over,' I said. 'Have a car waiting for me at the airport.'

During the flight I was fuming so much that I expect
steam was blowing out of my ears. After all the trouble I
had taken to ensure the hotels were clean, this had to happen. Surely Tony must be wrong; the symptoms seemed
quite different to me. This would be enough to give Jack
Cunningham another heart attack.

Fletcher met me at Nassau Airport himself. As we drove
to the Sea Gardens I said, 'How many people ill?'

His answer appalled me. 'A hundred and four – and I'm
not feeling too good myself.' He coughed.

'My God!' I glanced at him. 'Are you really not feeling
well, Jack? Or was that just a figure of speech?'

'I'm feeling lousy. I'm running a temperature and I have
a hell of a headache.'

He was not the only one. I said, 'You're going to bed
when we get back. I'll have Tony look you over. How many
of that figure you gave me are staff?'

'As of this morning we had three on the sick list – four
with me now.' He coughed again convulsively.

'Stop the car,' I said. 'I'll drive.' I found it puzzling that
the number of staff casualties should be so low. As I drove
off again I said, 'How many registrations have you got?'

'Something over three hundred; I'll let you know when
we get to my office.'

'Never mind,' I said. 'I'll ask Philips. You go to bed.' What
he had told me meant that about one-third of the clientèle
had gone down sick. 'Any deaths?'

'Not yet,' he said ominously.

We got to the Sea Gardens and I packed Fletcher off to
his staff flat and then went to look for Philips. I found him
helping out at the cashier's desk where there was a long
line of tourists anxious to leave as quickly as they could –
like money bats. The buzz of conversation in the queue was
low and venomous as though coming from a disturbed hive
of bees. I was in no mood to placate the rats leaving the

sinking ship, to mix the metaphor even further, and I hauled him out of there. 'Someone else can do that. Jack Fletcher's gone down sick, so you're in charge. Where's Bosworth?'

Philips jerked his thumb towards the ceiling. 'Doing his rounds.'

'Has he any help?'

'A load of doctors from Nassau and some nursing staff from the hospital.'

'Track him down; I want to see him in Fletcher's office five minutes ago.'

When I saw Tony Bosworth he looked tired and drawn, his eyes were reddened as though he had not slept, and he swayed a little on his feet. I said, 'Sit down before you fall down, and tell me what the hell we've got.'

He sighed as he sat down. 'The tests aren't through yet, but I'm fairly certain it's legionellosis.'

'Damn!' I mopped the sweat from my brow and loosened my tie. It was hot and humid and I realized why. The air-conditioning in the public rooms was not working. 'It's hitting faster this time, isn't it?'

'It's the Pontiac fever form, I think. It hits sooner and harder, in the sense that more people exposed to it contract the symptoms – ninety-five per cent is the usual rate.'

'My God!' I said. 'Then we still have a long way to go. Did you see what was happening in the lobby as you came through?'

He nodded. 'I'm not sure it's wise to allow those people to leave. They could go away and still come down with the bug.'

'I don't see how we can stop them. You can't expect people to stay in what they think is a pest house. What's the position of the Public Health Department?'

'They're still making up their minds.' Tony's eyes met mine. 'I think they'll close you down.'

I winced. 'How could this happen?' I demanded. 'You know the precautions we took.'

'Tom, I don't know.' He, too, took out a handkerchief and wiped his brow, then ran it around the edge of his collar. 'What's puzzling me is the spotty spread. We're not getting an incidence of ninety-five per cent – it's more like thirty per cent.'

'Then perhaps it's not Pontiac fever.'

'All the symptoms check.' Tony scratched his head. 'But *all* the Italians have gone down, seventy-five per cent of the Americans, but only twenty-five per cent of the British.'

I blinked at that. 'You mean it's attacking by nationality selectively? That's crazy!' I had a thought. 'It's tending to give Bahamians a miss, too. Only four of the staff have gone down.'

'Four? Who's the fourth?'

'Jack Fletcher – I've just packed him off to bed. I'd like you to look at him when you have time. Who are the other three?' He named them, and I said slowly, 'They all live here in the hotel.' Most of the staff had homes of their own, but a select few of the senior staff, like Fletcher, had staff flats.

It was as though I had goosed Bosworth. He jerked visibly and sat up straight from his slumped position, and I could see the Big Idea bursting from him. Someone has christened it the Eureka Syndrome. He leaned forward and grabbed the telephone. A minute later he was saying, 'Nurse, I want you to go to every patient and ask a question – Do you habitually take tub baths or a shower? Make a tabulated list and bring it to the manager's office. Yes, nurse, I'm serious. Get someone to help you; I want it fast.'

He put down the telephone, and I said dryly, 'I'm not surprised the nurse asked if you were serious. What is this?'

'National habits,' he said. 'Do you know the Russians don't have plugs in their wash hand basins? They don't like washing their hands in dirty water so they let the taps run.'

For a moment I thought Tony had gone completely round the bend. 'What the hell have the bloody Russians to do with this?' I said explosively.

He held up both his hands to quieten me. 'I once talked with an Italian doctor. He told me the Italians consider the English to be a dirty race because they bathe in their own filth. He said most Italians take showers. Now, every Italian in the hotel has gone down with this bug – every last one of them.'

'And seventy-five per cent of the Americans, but only twenty-five per cent of the English.'

'Whereas, if the infection had been coming from the air-conditioner as at the Parkway, it should have been ninety-five per cent overall. You know what this means, Tom; it's in the water supply, not the air-conditioner.'

'That's bad.' I sat and thought about it. If the water supply was contaminated the hotel was sure to be shut down. I said, 'It won't work, Tony. Everybody has been drinking the damn water, and they sure as hell don't drink their shower water.'

'But that's the point. You can drink a gallon of water loaded down with this bug and it'll do no harm in the gut. To be infective it must be inhaled into the lungs. At the Parkway the air in the lobby and on the pavement outside was filled with drift from the air-conditioner – an aerosol loaded with *L. pneumophila* which was inhaled. Exactly the same thing happens when you take a shower; the water is broken up into very fine droplets and you inhale some of it.'

'Jack Fletcher takes showers,' I said. 'I was in his apartment once and his wife said he was in the shower. I could hear him; he has a fine bathroom baritone.' I blew out my cheeks. 'So what do I tell those people out there? That everything is okay as long as they don't take a shower? I really don't think that would work.'

'I'm sorry,' said Tony. 'But I really think you'll have to close if my theory turns out to be right. I'll lay in some sodium hypochlorite to flush out the system.'

Three-quarters of an hour later we had the answer; all the patients, without exception, had taken showers. Tony had sent some of the older people to the Princess Margaret Hospital and they were interrogated, too. Same answer. 'That does it,' he said. 'It's in the water supply.'

I said, 'We have to retrieve something out of this mess, so we'll turn it into a public relations exercise. I'll notify the Department of Public Health that we're closing before they tell me I must.' I grinned at Tony and quoted,' "His cause is just who gets his blow in fust." Then there are the customers. We'll get them into other hotels, preferably our own, and stand the expense.' It would break Jack Cunningham's heart, but would be good business in the long run.

'What about all the people still here and sick?'

'They can stay if you and the other medicos can look after them. My worry is how many of them are going to die here.'

'None,' said Tony. 'No one has been known to die of Pontiac fever yet. They'll be up and about in a few days – a week at most.'

'Thank God for that!' I said fervently. 'Now for the big question. I know we can get this bactcrium out of the water system. What I want to know is how it got in.'

'I'll check into that,' said Tony. 'I'll need your maintenance engineer, and I think we should have one of the Public Health people along.'

'And you'll have me,' I said. 'I want to know exactly what I happened so I can make sure it never happens again.'

We began the investigation that night. All afternoon I had been helping Philips and the rest of the managerial staff to organize the future wellbeing of our departing guests. It took a lot of telephoning around but it got done, and although my competitors were pleased enough to take the business they did not really like it. We all knew it would be bad for trade in the future.

Then I had to quell a minor revolt on the part of the staff. Word had somehow got around that there was something wrong with the hotel water and I was in danger of losing some of my best people. It took some straight talking on the part of Tony Bosworth, including a demonstration in which he drank a full glass of water straight from the tap – and so did I. I was glad he believed his own theories but I was not so sure, and it took some effort to drink that water without gagging.

Four of us gathered together at eight that evening – myself, Tony Bosworth, Bethel, the hotel maintenance engineer, and Mackay from Public Health. Tony had a dozen sterilized sample bottles. 'Where do you want to start?' asked Bethel. 'Bottom up or top down?'

'We're nearer to the bottom,' said Tony. 'Might as well begin there.'

So we went down into the basement where the boilers were. A hotel needs a lot of hot water and we had three calorifiers, each of a capacity of three million British Thermal Units. The huge drums of the calorifiers were connected by a tangle of pipes coloured red, blue and green, with arrows neatly stencilled to indicate the direction of flow. Tony asked questions and I looked about. The place was spotless and dry.

Bethel was explaining something technical to Tony when I broke in. 'This place is as dry as a bone, Tony; there have been no leaks recently.' I turned to Bethel. 'When did you last strip down any of this?'

He frowned. 'Must have been eight months ago, Mr Mangan. A normal maintenance check. This equipment is efficient; hardly ever goes wrong.'

'Where does the water come from?'

'Out of the mains supply.' He nodded towards Mackay. 'Mr Mackay can tell you more about that.'

'Then why should we be the only building hit?' I asked Tony.

'That's not exactly true,' said Mackay. 'Isn't the mains water piped into tanks somewhere at the top of the building?'

'That's right,' said Bethel. 'Right at the top to give it a good head.'

'So it could have been contaminated in the tanks after it left the mains,' I said. 'I don't think it could have happened down here. Everything is as tight as a drum.'

'Let's go to the top,' proposed Tony, so we went up in the service elevator.

The water tanks were on the roof and they were big. 'Twenty-five thousand gallons,' said Bethel. 'Five thousand in each tank.' He pointed out the mains piping rising up the side of the hotel. 'The water comes up there and is distributed by this manifold into the tanks. Each tank has a ball valve to control the water level.' He shrugged. 'The whole system is just the same as the one you'll have in your own home; it's just that this is bigger.'

'I've never seen mine,' I said.

Bethel grinned. 'I don't come up here too often myself. The system is automatic.' He pointed. 'You can see that the tanks are all interconnected by that manifold at the bottom.'

That meant that water would flow freely between the tanks. 'Why five?' I asked. 'Why not one big tank?'

'Well, if something happens – a tank springs a leak, say – we can isolate it and go on using the other four.' Bethel was very good at answering stupid questions from a layman.

'And the tanks are sealed?'

'Sure. There's a manhole on the top of each so we can get at a sticky valve if we have to, but the lids are bolted down on a mastic seal.'

'Let's take a look,' said Tony, and began to climb the steel ladder on the side of the nearest tank.

We all followed him. On top of the tank Bethel squatted on his haunches. 'Here's the manhole. I had the tanks repainted about three months ago and we just painted over the manhole covers, bolts and all. You can see this hasn't been opened since then – the paint seal isn't cracked.'

I looked at Mackay. 'Then how did the bug get into the system? It *must* be in the mains water.' Something bright on the roof shot a sun reflection into my eye and I turned slightly to get rid of it.

'Impossible!' said Mackay positively. 'Not if this is the only building affected. Look.' He unrolled the chart he was carrying which proved to be a water distribution map. 'All those houses take the same water. Even the airport is on the same water main.'

'People normally don't shower in airports,' said Tony.

'They do in houses,' retorted Mackay. 'It can't be in the mains water. Of that I'm certain.'

Bethel had wandered away and was standing on the next tank. 'Hey!' he called, and again the reflection stabbed my eye as I turned. 'This one's been opened.' We crossed to the tank and stood around the manhole cover. 'The paint has cracked around the bolts.'

'Opened some time in the last three months,' said Tony.

'Later than that,' said Bethel confidently. He pointed to where bright metal showed where paint had flaked away. 'It hasn't started to rust. I'd say some time in the last week.'

'That adds up,' said Tony.

'Who would have opened it?' I asked.

542   DESMOND BAGLEY

'I didn't,' said Bethel. 'Harry Crossman might have, but if he did he didn't tell me.'

Crossman was Bethel's assistant. 'It will be on his work sheets,' I said. 'I want to see them. I want to see them now.'

Bethel stood up. 'They're in my office.'

'Bring back a wrench,' said Tony. 'I want to take samples from here.'

There was no point in me watching Tony take samples so I went with Bethel. We climbed down on to the roof and walked towards the elevator motor housing, and I kicked something which rolled away and came to a stop with a clink at the edge of a water tank. I stooped and picked it up and found the object that had been sending reflections into my eye.

But it was more than that – much more. It was a cylindrical glass tube broken at one end. The other end was pointed as though it had been sealed in a flame, and I had seen others like it in Jack Kayles's first-aid box on *My Fair Lady.* Suddenly ideas came slamming into my head so hard and so fast that they hurt. Whole areas of mystification suddenly became clear and made sense; a weird and unnatural sense, it is true, but conforming to logic.

I turned and yelled, 'Tony, come down here.'

He clambered down the ladder. 'What's the matter?'

I held out the glass tube. 'Could you take a swab from the inside of there and test it for your damned bug?'

He looked surprised. 'Sure, but. . .'

'How long will it take?'

'Not long. After the last scare they set up a testing facility in the hospital here. Say, four days.'

'I can't wait that long, but take care of it and do your test.' I turned and ran for the staircase.

Five minutes later I was talking to Walker at the Royal Palm on Grand Bahama. He said, 'Where are you, Mr Mangan? I'm supposed to be bodyguarding you.'

'I had to leave in a hurry, but never mind that. I want you to send a man on to the roof. No one is to get near the water tanks up there.'

'The water tanks!' he echoed. 'What the . . .'

'Never mind arguing, just do it,' I said sharply. 'And put another man near the air-conditioning cooling tower. Nobody is to get near that, either. Nobody at all.'

'Not your maintenance crew?'

'Nobody,' I said flatly. I did not know if Carrasco had local assistance or not, but I was taking no chances. 'Where's Carrasco?'

'He spent the day sightseeing in West End,' said Walker a shade wearily. 'Right now he's having dinner at the Buccaneer Club out at Deadman Reef. I have two men with him – Rodriguez and Palmer.'

'You'll probably have police to help you at the hotel as soon as I've talked to Perigord. And after that I'm flying back.'

As I rang off Bethel came in. 'Nothing in Harry's work sheets, Mr Mangan.'

'I know. He didn't do it. Do you know Bobby Bowen, my pilot?' Bethel nodded. 'Chase him up, will you? Tell him we'll be flying to Freeport. Oh, and tell Dr Bosworth he'll be coming with me. Mackay can take the samples to the hospital.' Bethel turned to go, and I added, 'And thanks. You've been a great help.'

When he had gone I rang Perigord. He was not in his office, not entirely unnaturally considering the time of day, but neither was he at home. The telephone was answered by his daughter who told me in a piping voice that Mummy and Daddy were out. Where were they? She was vague about that. They had gone out to dinner. Could be the Stoned Crab or the Captain's Charthouse or possibly the Japanese Steak House in the International Bazaar or the Lobster House in the Mall. Or was it the Lucayan Country Club? I sighed and thanked her, then reached for the Grand Bahama telephone directory.

I found him in none of those places but finally ran him to earth in the Mai Tai. It took me some time to convince him of my sanity and even longer to move him to action. I think I ruined his dinner.

TWENTY-TWO

Tony Bosworth and I walked into the lobby of the Royal Palm and I noticed immediately the two uniformed policemen, one standing by the elevators, the other at the foot of the staircase. I crossed to the desk. 'Is Commissioner Perigord here?'

'In the manager's office.'

I jerked my head at Tony and we went in. Perigord, in plain clothes, was talking on the telephone, and Walker sat on a settee. Perigord said into the mouthpiece, 'I quite agree; I'll check it out thoroughly. I can expect you tomorrow, then.' He looked up. 'He's here now; I'll have it in more detail by then. Yes, I'll meet you. Goodbye.' He put down the telephone. 'Now, Mangan, you'll have to explain – '

I cut him short. 'First things first. I'd like you to get those coppers out of the lobby and out of sight. I don't want Carrasco scared off.'

He leaned forward. 'If your story is correct then Carrasco is the most dangerous man in the Bahamas.'

'No, he's not,' I contradicted. 'Robinson is, and he's the joker I want. He's the boss.' I pulled up a chair and sat down. 'Besides, you can't charge Carrasco with anything. You need hard proof and you've got none. But scare him and he'll skip, and Robinson will send someone else in his place – someone we don't know. Besides, I don't like uniformed policemen cluttering up the public rooms in my hotels. It lowers the tone.'

Perigord nodded and stood up. 'We may be guarding an empty stable,' he said sourly. 'Carrasco may not be back. Your men have lost him.' He walked out.

I turned on Walker. 'For God's sake! Is that true?'

He said heavily, 'He went into the john at the Buccaneer Club and didn't come out. Rodriguez thinks he left by the window. His car is still there but no Carrasco.'

I thought for a moment. 'Maybe he's in Harry's Bar; that's not far from the Buccaneer.'

'No – Palmer checked that out.'

I thought of the topography of Deadman Reef. 'A boat,' I said. 'He's meeting a boat. Have your men thought of that?'

Walker said nothing but reached for the telephone as Perigord came back. He glanced at Tony. 'Who is this?'

'Dr Bosworth. He identified the disease and has been of great help.'

Perigord nodded briefly and sat down. 'Are you really trying to tell me that Carrasco is a maniac – the stereotyped mad doctor of the "B" movies – who is poisoning the water in hotels in these islands?'

'I don't believe him to be mad, but that's what he's doing. And Robinson is directing him.'

'But why?'

'I've had a few thoughts in that direction which I'll come to in a minute. Let's look at the evidence.'

'That I'd be pleased to do,' said Perigord sardonically.

'I know it's all circumstantial, but so is most evidence of murder. When I found that glass tube it all came together suddenly. One, I'd seen others like it on Kayles's boat. Two, I remembered what Kayles must have heard me saying to Sam Ford.'

'Which was?'

'I was blowing my top about the chain of disasters which had hit the Bahamas. Rioting in the streets of Nassau, Legionnaires' disease at the Parkway, the burning of the Fun Palace, even the shredding of the luggage at the airport. Now, I'd knocked Kayles cold and he was just coming to his senses. He must have been muzzy – dislocated enough in his mind to think I was actually describing Robinson's doings to Sam. So when he escaped he reported to Robinson that I knew all.'

I frowned. 'And what convinced Robinson was that there was at least one item on that list that Kayles wasn't privy to. That indicated to Robinson that I did indeed know about his plans – he told me so – and he was as worried as hell because I might have told you.'

Perigord said, 'Are you telling me that Robinson burned down the Fun Palace? And sabotaged the carousel at the airport?'

'Yes, I think he did – but not personally. Another thing: when Robinson admitted to trying to have me killed in an air crash he made a curious remark. He said the death of the Americans was an unexpected bonus, and he went on to say that Wall Street was a bit rocky about it. The idea seemed to please him.'

'Come to the point you are so circuitously making.'

'It was all pulled into place by a remark made by Billy Cunningham,' I said. 'When we put together the Theta Corporation Billy did some research in the course of which he talked to Butler of the Ministry of Tourism. He learned that eighty per cent of the economy and two-thirds of the population are supported by tourism. Billy said to me that it was too many eggs in one basket, and it worried him a little. And that's your answer.'

'Spell it out,' said Perigord.

'Robinson is trying to sabotage the economy of the Bahamas.' Perigord regarded me expressionlessly, and I

said, 'How many tourists have we lost since all this began?
Ask Butler, and I guarantee the answer will startle you.
And it's not long since Billy Cunningham warned me that
if this series of disasters continued the Cunningham
Corporation would think seriously of pulling out. The company which runs the Parkway in Nassau is already nearly
bankrupt.'

'It's all too thin,' complained Perigord. 'Too speculative.
The only hard evidence we have is the glass tube you found,
and that won't be evidence if it's clean. How long will it take
you to make the tests, Dr Bosworth?'

'The hospital in Nassau is doing the testing, and it will
take four days.'

'Not sooner?'

'This bacterium is very elusive,' said Tony. 'The samples
have to go through a guinea pig and then be cultured
on an agar medium supplemented by cysteine and iron.
Then –'

Perigord flapped his hand. 'Spare me the technical
details,' he said irritably. 'All right – four days.'

'I'll tell you something, Commissioner,' said Tony. 'If that
capsule gives a positive result it means someone has found
a way of culturing *Legionella pneumophila* in quantity, and
that implies a well-equipped biological laboratory. It's not
something you can whip up in a kitchen.'

Perigord absorbed that in silence. Walker stirred and said,
'There's something you ought to know. This morning one of
my guys found Carrasco in a place he shouldn't be – on one
of the back stairs used by the cleaning staff. He said he'd got
lost; taken a wrong turning and gone through the wrong
door.'

I slapped the desk with the flat of my hand. 'Perigord,
what more do you want?' I turned on Walker. 'So Carrasco
has given you the slip before. I hope to God he didn't doctor the water tanks here.'

'No way,' said Walker, stung. 'And he didn't give us the slip. He dropped out of sight and my guy went looking for him. He wasn't out of sight for more than three minutes.'

'I could bear to know a lot about who and why,' said Perigord.

'There's a proverb to the effect that fishing is best done in troubled waters,' I said. 'The CIA know it as destabilization. They've been pretty good at it in the past.'

He looked startled. 'You're not suggesting the CIA is behind this?'

'I don't know who is behind it − I didn't say it was the CIA. It's not in the American interest to destabilize a sound capitalist economy in this part of the world. Others do come to mind, though.'

'Five will get you ten that Carrasco is a Cuban,' said Walker. 'Venezuelan my ass.' The telephone rang and he picked it up. 'I'm expecting this.' He held a short conversation, his end of it consisting of monosyllables. As he laid down the handset he said, 'You were right; Carrasco went out in a boat. He's just come back and he's in the Buccaneer Club now, having a drink. We have a picture of him landing on the beach.'

'Taken at night,' I said scornfully. 'A fat lot of good that will be. And what good is a picture? We already know what he looks like.'

'There was another guy in the boat,' said Walker reasonably. 'We might like to know who he is. As for picture quality, if anyone can come up with something good it's Rodriguez; he has some kind of gismo on his camera. That guy is gadget-happy. He says Carrasco came back in a small boat that's probably a tender to a big yacht. After landing Carrasco, the boat went out to sea again.'

'A night rendezvous,' said Perigord. 'I'll have a police boat take a look at Deadman Reef.' He reached for the telephone.

When he had finished we continued to kick the problem around for quite a while. No, Perigord had not investigated the catastrophe of the airport carousel; it had not been considered a police matter at the time. He would look into it next day. The fire at the Fun Palace in Nassau had been investigated for arson, but no firm evidence had come up. It might be possible to borrow a deep-diving submersible from the Americans to look for the remains of Pinder's Navajo in Exuma Sound. Evidence of sabotage would be useful.

'Useful for what?' I asked. 'That's in the past and I'm worried about the future. I'm wondering what Robinson's department of dirty tricks will come up with next.'

It was agreed that Carrasco was our only lead and that he would be closely watched. I looked hard at Walker. 'And don't lose him again.'

'I'll assign some of my own men to him,' said Perigord. 'There are too many whites watching him now. My blacks will blend into the background better.' He looked at his watch. 'Nearly midnight. I suggest that Dr Bosworth will sleep better in a bed than in that chair. And I'm for bed, too.'

I turned and found Tony asleep. I woke him up. 'I'll find you a room. Come on.'

We went into the lobby, but Walker stayed behind to wait for the call which would tell us that Carrasco had left the Buccaneer. He would not have long to wait because the Buccaneer closes at midnight. There were quite a few returning revellers in the lobby and I waited at the desk for a few moments while they collected their keys.

Perigord walked towards the entrance, but turned and came back. 'I forgot to tell you that I have informed Commissioner Deane in Nassau of these developments, and he is flying across to see me tomorrow. He will certainly want to see you. Shall we say my office at ten tomorrow morning?'

Perigord may have been the top copper on Grand Bahama, but there was a bigger gun in Nassau. I said, 'That will be okay.'

The man next to me asked for his key. 'Room two-three-five.'

Carrasco!

I should not have looked at him but I did, in an involuntary movement. He picked up his key and turned towards me. He certainly recognized me because I saw the fractional change in his expression, and he must have seen the recognition in my eyes because he dropped the key, whirled, and ran for the entrance.

'Stop him!' I yelled. 'Stop that man!'

Carrasco turned on me and there was a gun in his hand. He levelled it at me and I flung myself sideways as he fired. Then there was another shot from behind me, and another. When I next looked, Carrasco was pitching forward to fall on the floor. I looked back and saw Perigord in the classic stance – legs apart with knees bent, and his arms straight out with both hands clasped on the butt of the revolver he held.

I picked myself up shakily and found I was trembling all over, and my legs were as limp as sticks of cooked celery and about as much use in holding me up. Perigord came forward and put his hand under my elbow in support. 'Are you all right? Did he hit you?'

'I don't think so. I don't feel anything. He threw a bloody scare into me, though.'

Somewhere in the middle of all that I had heard a woman scream and now there was a babble of excited voices. Perigord's uniformed men appeared from where he had hidden them, and he motioned them forward to break up the mob which was surrounding Carrasco's body. He raised his voice. 'All right, everybody; it's all over. Please clear the lobby and go to your rooms. There's nothing more to see.'

I beckoned to the nearest bellboy. 'Get something to cover the body – a tablecloth or a blanket.' I saw Walker standing in the doorway of the manager's office, and strode over to him. 'What the hell happened?' I was as mad as a hornet. 'How did he get here without warning?'

Walker was bewildered. 'I don't know, but I'll find out. There's Rodriguez.' He ran towards the entrance of the lobby where Rodriguez had just appeared.

Perigord was standing over the body and Tony Bosworth was on his knees beside it. Tony looked up and said something and Perigord nodded, then came over to me. 'He's dead,' he said. 'I didn't want to kill him but I had no option. There were too many innocent bystanders around to have bullets flying. Where can we put him?'

'In the office will be best.'

The policemen carried the body into the office and we followed. 'Where did his bullet go?' I asked. 'Anyone hurt?'

'You'll probably find a hole in the reception desk,' said Perigord.

'Well, thanks. That was good shooting.' Walker returned and I stuck my finger under his nose. 'What happened? He damn near killed me.'

Walker spread his hands. 'The damnedest thing. Rodriguez was in the bar watching Carrasco, and Palmer was in the car outside with the engine running. When Carrasco made his move to go, Rodriguez went to the public phone to make his call and found that some drunken joker had cut the cord. It had been working earlier because I'd talked to him about a possible boat. He didn't have much time because Carrasco was already outside, in his car, and on the move. So he made a judgement – he went after Carrasco.'

Perigord said, 'Perhaps Carrasco knew he was being watched. Perhaps he cut the telephone cord.'

'No way,' said Walker. 'Rodriguez said that Carrasco never went near the public phone when he came back from his sea trip. It was just plain dumb luck.'

'There was no reason for Carrasco to cut the cord,' I said. 'He wasn't going anywhere mysterious; he was coming back here. And now he's dead, and we've lost our lead, to Robinson.'

'Well, let's have a look at him,' said Perigord. He stripped away the tablecloth which covered the body, knelt beside it, and began going through the pockets, starting with the inner breast pocket. 'Passport – Venezuelan.' He opened it. 'Dr Luis Carrasco.' He laid it aside. 'Wallet with visiting cards in the name of Dr Luis Carrasco; address – Avenida Bolivar, 226, Caracas. And money, more than a man should decently carry; there must be 4000 dollars here.'

There were several other items: a billfold containing a few dollars in both American and Bahamian currency, coins, a pen knife, a cigar case containing three Havana cigars – all the junk a man usually carries in his pockets.

From a side pocket of the jacket Perigord took a flat aluminium box. He opened it and there, nestling in cotton wool, were three glass ampoules filled with a yellowish liquid. He held it up. 'Recognize them?'

'They're exactly like those I saw in Kayles's boat,' I said. 'And like the broken one I found on the roof of the Sea Gardens Hotel. My bet is that he picked them up tonight when he went on his little sea trip. He wouldn't want to carry those about too long, and they weren't in his room when we searched it.'

He closed the box and stood up. 'I think you're beginning to make your case. Commissioner Deane will definitely want to see you tomorrow morning.'

I glanced at the clock. 'This morning.' I was feeling

depressed. Later, when the body was removed on a stretcher I reflected gloomily that Carrasco had advanced his bloody cause as much in the manner of his death as in life. A shoot-out in the lobby of a hotel could scarcely be called an added attraction.

TWENTY-THREE

The morning brought news – bad and good.

When I got home I told Debbie what had happened because there was no way of keeping it from her; it was certain to be on the front page of the *Freeport News* and on the radio. She said incredulously, 'Shot him!'

'That's right. Perigord shot him right there in the lobby of the Royal Palm. A hell of a way to impress the guests.'

'And after he shot at you. Tom, you could have been killed.'

'I haven't a scratch on me.' I said that lightly enough, but secretly I was pleased by Debbie's solicitude which was more than she had shown after my encounter with Kayles in the Jumentos.

She was pale. 'When will all this stop?' Her voice trembled.

'When we've caught up with Robinson. We'll get there.' I hoped I put enough conviction into my voice because right then I could not see a snowball's chance in hell of doing it.

So I slept on it, but did not dream up any good ideas. In the morning, while shaving, I switched on the radio to listen to the news. As might have been predicted the big news was of the shooting of an unnamed man in the lobby of the Royal Palm by the gallant and heroic Deputy-Commissioner

Perigord. It was intelligent of Perigord to keep Carrasco's name out of it, but also futile; if Robinson was around to hear the story he would be shrewd enough to know who had been killed.

The bad news came with the second item on the radio. An oil tanker had blown up in Exuma Sound; an air reconnaissance found an oil slick already twenty miles long, and the betting was even on whether the oil would foul the beaches of Eleuthera or the Exuma Cays, depending on which way it drifted.

The Bahamas do not have much going for them. We have no minerals, poor agriculture because of the thin soil, and little industry. But what we do have we have made the most of in building a great tourist industry. We have the sea and sun and beaches with sand as white as snow – so we developed water sports; swimming, scuba-diving, sailing – and we needed oiled water and beaches as much as we needed *Legionella pneumophila*.

I could not understand what an oil tanker was doing in Exuma Sound, especially a 30,000 tonner. A ship that size could not possibly put into any port in any of the surrounding islands – she would draw far too much water. I detected the hand of Robinson somewhere; an unfounded notion to be sure, but this was another hammer blow to tourism in the Bahamas.

I dressed and breakfasted, kissed Debbie goodbye, and checked into my office before going on to see Perigord. Walker, my constant companion, had not much to say, being conscious of the fiasco of the previous night, and so he was as morose as I was depressed. At the office I gave him a job to do in order to take his mind off his supposed shortcomings. 'Ring the Port Authority and find out all you can about the tanker that blew up last night. Say you're enquiring on my behalf.' Then I got down to looking at the morning mail.

At half past nine Billy Cunningham unexpectedly appeared. 'What's all this about a shoot-out at the OK Corral?' he demanded without preamble.

'How do you know about it?'

'Steve Walker works for me,' he said tersely. 'He keeps me informed. Was Debbie involved in any way?'

'Didn't Walker tell you she wasn't?'

'I forgot to ask when he rang last night.' Billy blew out his cheeks and sat down. 'I haven't told Jack about this, but he's sure to find out. He's not in good shape and bad news won't do him any good. We've got to get this mess cleared up, Tom. What's the pitch?'

'If you've talked to Walker you know as much as I do. We've lost our only lead to Robinson.' I held his eye. 'Have you flown a thousand miles just to hold my hand?'

He shrugged. 'Billy One is worried. He reckons we should get Debbie out of here, both for her own sake and Jack's.'

'She's well enough protected,' I said.

'Protected!' Billy snorted. 'Steve Walker is pissed off with your cops; he tells me they've taken his guns. How can he protect her if his guys are unarmed?'

'Perigord seems to be doing all right,' I said. 'And there's an armed police officer at the house.'

'Oh!' said Billy. 'I didn't know that.' He was silent for a moment. 'How will you find Robinson now?'

'I don't know,' I said, and we discussed the problem for a few minutes, then I checked the time. 'I have an appointment with Perigord and his boss. Maybe they'll come up with something.'

It was then that Rodriguez and the good news came in. 'I've got something for you,' he said, and skimmed a black-and-white photograph across the desk.

It was a good photograph, a damned good photograph. It showed Carrasco hopping over the bows of a dory which had its prow dug into a sandy beach. The picture was as sharp as a pin and his features showed up clearly. In the stern of the dory, holding on to the tiller bar of an outboard motor, was another man who was equally sharply delineated. I did not know him.

'You took this last night?' Rodriguez nodded. 'You were crazy to use a flash. What did Carrasco do?'

'He did nothing. And who said anything about a flash? That crazy I'm not.'

I stared at him then looked at the picture. 'Then how . . . ?'

He laughed and explained. The 'gismo' mentioned by Walker was a light amplifier, originally developed by the military for gunsights used at night but now much used by naturalists and others who wished to observe animals. 'And for security operations,' Rodriguez added. 'You can take a pretty good picture using only starlight, but last night there was a new moon.'

I looked at the photograph again, then handed it to Billy. 'All very nice, but it doesn't get us very far. All that shows is Carrasco climbing from a boat on to a beach. We might get somewhere by looking for the man in the stern, but I doubt it. Anyway, I'll give it to Perigord; maybe he can make something of it.'

'I took more than one picture,' said Rodriguez. 'Take a look at this one – especially at the stern.' Another photograph skimmed across the desk.

This picture showed the dory again which had turned and was heading out to sea. And it was a jackpot because, lettered across the stern, were the words: 'Tender to *Capistrano*'.

'Bingo!' I said. 'You might have made up for losing Carrasco last night.' I looked at Billy. 'That's something for you to do while I'm with Perigord. Ring around the marinas and try to trace *Capistrano*.'

Five minutes later I was in Perigord's office. Also present was Commissioner Deane, a big, white Bahamian with a face the colour of mahogany, and the authority he radiated was like a blow in the face. I knew him, but not too well. We had been at school together in Nassau, but I had been a new boy when he was in his last year. I had followed him to Cambridge and he had gone on to the Middle Temple. Returning to the Bahamas he had joined the Police Force, an odd thing for a Bahamian barrister to do, because mostly they enter politics with the House of Assembly as prime target. He was reputed to be tough and abrasive.

Now he said raspily, 'This is a very strange business you've come up with, Mangan.'

'We'd better discuss it later.' I tossed the pictures before Perigord. 'Carrasco probably made a rendezvous with a boat called *Capistrano*. Rodriguez took those last night.'

A little time was wasted while we discussed how Rodriguez could possibly have taken photographs at night without a flash, then Perigord twitched an eyebrow at Deane. 'With your permission?'

'Yes,' said Deane. 'Get busy. But you have a watching brief, that's all.'

Perigord left, and Deane said, 'As I started to say, you have come up with an oddity. You have suggested a crime, or a series of crimes, with no hard evidence – merely a chain of suppositions.'

'No evidence! What about the ampoules taken from Carrasco?'

'Those won't be evidence until we find what is in them, and Perigord tells me that will take four days. We flew an ampoule to Nassau during the night. So far the whole affair is very misty. A lot of strange things have been happening around you, and don't think my deputy has not kept me informed. Now, these events are subject to many interpretations, as all subjective evidence is.'

'Subjective!' I said incredulously. 'My first wife disappeared and my daughter was found dead; there's nothing bloody subjective about that. My second wife and I were kidnapped; I suppose we dreamed it up. There have been two cases of disease in hotels and that's fact, Commissioner, bloody hard fact.'

'What is subjective is your interpretation of these events,' said Deane. 'You have brought in a number of events – the breakdown of a baggage carousel at the airport, a fire, an air crash, and a number of other things, and the only connection you can offer is your interpretation. Just give me one piece of hard evidence, something I can put before a court – that's all I ask.'

'You've got it – the ampoules.'

'I've got nothing, until four days from now. And what's in the ampoules might prove to be a cough cure.'

'You can prove it right now,' I said. 'Just take one of those ampoules, break it, and inhale deeply. But don't ask me to be in the same room when you do it.'

Deane smiled unexpectedly. 'You're a stubborn man. No, I won't do that because you may be right. In fact, I think you *are* right.' He stood up and began to pace the room. 'Your interpretation of events dovetails with a number of mysteries which have been occupying my mind lately.'

I sighed. 'I'm glad to hear it.'

'A lot of telephoning was done during the night. We now know that Dr Luis Carrasco is unknown at 226 Avenida Bolivar in Caracas.'

That was disappointing. 'Another lead gone,' I said dejectedly.

'Negative findings can be useful,' observed Deane. 'It tells us, for instance, that he was bent, that he had something to hide.' He added casually, 'Of course, now we know his real name all becomes clear.'

I sat up. '*You know who he is?*'

'When you sealed his hotel room you did well. We could make nothing of the fingerprints so we passed them on to the Americans, and their report came on that telephone just before you arrived here. Carrasco turns out to be one Serafin Perez.'

That meant nothing to me. 'Never heard of him.'

'Not many people have,' said Deane. 'He liked his anonymity. Perez is – was – a Cuban, a hardline communist and Moscow-trained. He was with Che Guevara when Guevara tried to export the revolution, but he broke with Guevara because he thought Guevara was mishandling the business. As it turned out Perez proved to be right and Guevara wrong. Since then he's been busy and a damn sight more successful than Che. He's been pitching up all over the place – Grenada, Nicaragua, Martinique, Jamaica. Notice anything about that list?'

'The hot spots,' I said. 'Grenada has gone left, so has Nicaragua. Jamaica is going, and the French are holding on to Martinique with their finger tips.'

'I believe Perez was here during the riots in Nassau. There was a certain amount of justification for that trouble, but not to the length of riot. Many of the rioters had no direct connection and I smelled a rent-a-mob. Now I know who rented it.'

'So much for Carrasco-Perez,' I said. 'A white ant.'

Deane looked puzzled. 'What do you mean?'

'When I was at Cambridge I knew a South African. He once said something which had me baffled and I asked him to explain it. He said he had been white-anted; apparently it's a common South African idiom. A white ant is what we would call a termite, Commissioner.'

Deane grunted. 'Don't talk to me about termites,' he said sourly. 'I've just discovered that my house is infested. It's going to cost me five thousand dollars – probably more.'

I said, 'You take a wooden post or a beam in a house. It looks good and solid until you hit it, then it collapses into a heap of powder – the termites have got into it. When the

South African said he'd been white-anted he meant he'd been undermined without his knowledge. In his case it was student politics – something to do with the student union. Commissioner, the Bahamas are being white-anted. We're being attacked at our most vulnerable point – tourism.'

'A good analogy,' said Deane thoughtfully. 'It's true that the Ministry of Tourism is perturbed about the fall in the number of visitors lately. So is the Prime Minister – there was a special Cabinet meeting last week. And there's more political unrest. Fewer tourists means more unemployment, and that is being exploited. But we need evidence – the Prime Minister demands it. Any crack-down without evidence would lead to accusations of police interference in political matters. The Prime Minister doesn't want the Bahamas to have the reputation of being a police state – that wouldn't do much for tourism, either.'

'Then investigate the sinking of that tanker in Exuma Sound last night. The report mentioned a twenty-mile oil slick only eight hours after she went down. If that's true the oil came out awfully fast. If I were you I'd question the skipper closely – if he's still around. Don't wait for the official inquiry; regard it as a police matter.'

'By God!' said Deane. 'I hadn't made *that* connection.'

'And find Robinson,' I said. 'What do you know about *him*?'

'Nothing at all. Your Mr Robinson is an unknown quantity.'

Perigord came in. '*Capistrano* just left Running Mon marina, heading east along the coast.'

East! 'Making for the Grand Lucayan Waterway and the north coast,' I said. 'Florida next stop.'

'What kind of a boat is she?' asked Deane.

'Sixty-foot motor yacht, white hull,' said Perigord. 'I don't think she's all that fast, she's a displacement type according to the management of Running Mon. She put into the marina during the night with engine trouble. Had it fixed this morning.'

I looked at Deane who was sitting immobile. 'What are we waiting for? You have a fast police launch, and *Capistrano* is still in Bahamian waters.'

'So we put men aboard, search her, and find nothing. Then what?' Deane stood up. 'I'll tell you what would happen next. We'd have to let her go – with profuse apologies. If your Mr Robinson is as clever as you say we would certainly not find anything because there would be nothing to be found.'

'But you might find Robinson,' I said. 'He could be aboard and he's wanted for kidnapping in Texas.'

'Not so,' contradicted Deane. 'A man calling himself Robinson is wanted for questioning concerning a kidnapping in Texas. He cannot possibly be extradited merely for questioning. We would have to let him go. He has committed no crime in the Bahamas for which we have evidence – as yet.'

'Robinson might not be on board, anyway,' said Perigord.

'Then aren't you going to do *anything*?' I demanded desperately.

'Oh, yes,' said Deane blandly. He lifted his eyebrows interrogatively at Perigord. 'I hope your contingency planning is working well.'

'It is. A fast Customs boat will pass *Capistrano* and enter the Lucayan Waterway ahead of her. There'll be another behind. Once she's in the Waterway she's bottled up. Then we put the Customs officers aboard her.'

'But I thought you said . . .' I was bewildered.

'We might as well try,' said Deane smoothly. 'Who knows what the Customs officers might find if they search thoroughly enough. Cocaine, perhaps?'

I opened my mouth again, then shut it firmly. If this pair was about to frame Robinson by planting cocaine on his boat they would certainly not admit it to me, but it seemed that Deane was a hard case who was not above providing his own evidence. After all, all he had to do was to keep Robinson in the Bahamas for four days.

'We had better be on hand,' Deane said casually. 'You'll come, too – you can identify Robinson.' He picked up the photograph of Carrasco-Perez. 'And I shall certainly want to question those on board about their association with Perez. We rendezvous at the Casuarina Bridge in thirty minutes.'

'I'll be there,' I said.

Hoping and praying that Robinson would be aboard *Capistrano* I drove the few hundred yards to the Royal Palm knowing that Billy Cunningham would want to be in at the kill. As soon as he saw me he said, '*Capistrano* was in a marina called Running Mon, but she's gone now.'

I said, 'I know. The police are going to pick her up.'

'Is Robinson on board?'

'I hope so. I'm joining Perigord and Deane. They want me to identify Robinson. Want to come along?'

'Try stopping me,' he said. 'I'm looking forward to meeting that son of a bitch.'

I made a decision. 'We'll go by boat. Let's go down to the marina.'

We found Joe Cartwright in the marina office. I popped my head around the door, and said, 'I want the rescue boat, Joe; with a full tank.'

Cartwright looked up. 'Can't be done, Mr Mangan. Got the engine out of her. Tuning her up for the BASRA Marathon next month.'

'Damn! What else have we that's fast and seaworthy?'

'What about the inflatable?' he suggested. 'She's not bad.'

'Get her ready.'

Within minutes we were at sea, roaring east along the south coast towards the Lucayan Waterway. Some people feel uncomfortable about being in a blow-up boat but they are very good. They are unsinkable, and the British even use them as lifeboats for inshore rescue. And they are damned fast even if they do tend to skitter a bit on the surface of the water.

I told Billy about the plan of attack, and presently I pointed. 'There's the Waterway, and that's the Customs launch just turning in. We've got *Capistrano* trapped.'

I slowed as we entered the Waterway. The Casuarina Bridge was nearly two miles ahead, and in the distance I could see the Customs launch lying next to a white-hulled boat. 'They've got her.' We motored on and drew alongside the Customs launch where I tossed the painter to a seaman and cut the engine. 'Let's go aboard.'

As we stepped on to *Capistrano*'s deck I was accosted by a Customs officer. 'Who are you?'

'Tom Mangan.' I looked up at the bridge and saw Perigord and Deane looking down. 'I'm with Commissioner Deane.' Three men stood on the after deck. None of them was Robinson. 'That the crew?'

'Yes; skipper, engineer and seaman-cum-cook.'

'No one else?'

'We're still looking. I've got men searching below.'

One of the three men approached us. 'Hell, Captain, this is crazy. We're not carrying anything illegal. We're just on a cruise.' He was an American.

'Then you have nothing to worry about,' said the Customs man.

'Well, I've gotta get back before the bad weather blows up. Did you hear the weather report? If you don't let me go I'll have to see the American consul here.'

'I'll give you his address,' said the officer blandly.

Another Customs man emerged from a hatch. 'No one below,' he reported.

'Are you sure?' I said.

'We opened up every compartment big enough to hold a man.'

'It's a bust,' said Billy disgustedly.

Deane and Perigord had come down from the bridge and were picking their way along the shore towards us. I looked around the deck of *Capistrano* and stiffened as I noticed that the stern davits were empty. I swung around to face the skipper. 'Where's the dory – your tender?'

'Mr Brown took it.'

'Brown? Who's he?'

'The guy who chartered this boat back in Fort Lauderdale.'

'When was this?'

'Just as soon as we entered this canal. He said he'd have a final spin and he'd meet us at the other end at the north shore.'

'Christ, he's given us the slip.' I looked at the Customs man. 'You must have been following him too closely and he took fright – or an insurance policy. If you weren't going to stop *Capistrano* there'd be no harm done and he'd rejoin her on the north shore. But you did and his insurance has paid off.'

'He won't get far. He'll run into the boat at the other end.'

'I wouldn't bet on it,' said Billy. 'This guy plays real cute.' He gave an exasperated snort. 'Brown, for God's sake!'

The skipper said, 'Will someone tell me what the hell's going on?'

I turned and stepped on to the Customs launch. 'Come on. Let's go after him.' Billy followed me.

We dropped down into the inflatable, and just before I started the engine I heard Deane bellow, 'Mangan, come back!' I ignored him and drowned his voice in a staccato roar as I twisted the throttle. We shot under the bridge and I looked back to see Deane on the deck of *Capistrano*. He was waving frantically.

Billy chuckled. 'I guess he's wondering what will happen to Robinson if we get to him first.' He suddenly had an automatic pistol in his hand.

'Put that damn thing away,' I said. 'If Deane knows you have it you're for the chop. And we don't want murder.'

'Not murder,' said Billy. 'Execution.' But he put the gun back into its holster.

The Lucayan Waterway stretched ahead of us and there was nothing to be seen on its surface. On either side there were occasional inlets leading to the proposed residential estates on which no houses had yet been built – the water maze. It all went by in a blur as I cranked up to top speed.

'Something ahead – coming this way,' said Billy.

It was a small dot in the middle of the Waterway which rapidly grew in size under the influence of our combined speeds. 'The dory!' I said.

'And something coming up behind it,' said Billy. 'The other Customs launch?'

'I hope not,' I said.

There was no time to explain why because I was busy trying to ram the approaching boat. I pulled on the tiller but the dory went the other way in an evading manoeuvre, and as it flashed past I saw the man at the wheel pointing at me. Something hit the side with a thwack and there was the hiss of escaping air.

'Goddamn!' said Billy.

I twisted the boat in the water and cut speed. 'This boat is compartmented. One hole won't make much difference.' I looked around. There was no sign of the dory.

'I didn't mean that,' said Billy. 'But if I'm shot at I'm going to shoot back and to hell with Deane.' The gun was in his hand again.

I could not argue with that. 'It was Robinson; I saw him. Where did he go?'

Billy pointed to an inlet on the port side. 'He shot down that rabbit hole.'

The boat that had chased Robinson from the north shore was almost upon us. I stood up and waved with both hands, and as it approached it slowed. A Customs officer leaned from the wheelhouse, and I yelled, 'Get back to the north shore, you damn fool. Keep the cork in the bloody bottle. If he gets past he can lose you.'

'Who are you to give orders?'

'If you want to argue do it with Commissioner Deane. Now, get the hell back and guard that bloody entrance.'

The officer withdrew and the launch began to turn in the water. There was a metallic click as Billy put a round into the breech of his pistol. 'How to make friends and influence people.' He snapped off the safety catch. 'What do we do now?'

'I don't know.' I wished I had a map. 'Winkling him out of there won't be easy, but if we don't he can ditch the dory and make an escape overland. He could lose himself in the pine barrens to the east, and it would take a damned army to find him.'

Billy pointed down the Waterway. 'A boat's coming. Your friend the Commissioner, no doubt.'

I slipped the clutch on the idling engine and we began to move slowly. 'We're going in – but easy.'

I took the boat into the inlet, the engine putt-putting quietly, and we immediately came to a cross canal. 'Which way?' said Billy.

I tossed a mental coin. 'To starboard,' I said. 'It doesn't really matter.' We turned to the right and went on for about a hundred yards and came to another junction. Straight on or turn to the left? This was impossible – worse than Hampton Court Maze – and there were forty-five miles of it.

From behind came the noise of a rapidly accelerating engine, and Billy shouted, 'We went the wrong way! Go back!'

I spun the throttle and slammed over the tiller, and I was in time to see Robinson's dory shooting across the canal and into the main artery of the Waterway. As it went Billy popped off a shot and then was thrown back as the boat picked up speed and the bow rose into the air.

We slalomed round the corner and nearly ran into a Customs boat in the Waterway, scooting under its stern and missing by the thickness of a playing card. I twisted the throttle to slow, and kicked over the tiller so as to avoid hitting the opposite bank, then I looked around. The damned dory had disappeared again so I hailed the launch. 'Where did he go?'

Deane was on deck. 'Mangan, get out of here, and take your friend. This is no place for heroics from civilians.'

I repeated, 'Where did he go?'

The launch moved so as to be between me and an inlet. 'He moved in here – but it's no business of yours. Perigord is organizing reinforcements. *Is* he Robinson?'

'Yes.'

'Who's your friend?'

'If you want to know, why don't you ask me?' said Billy. 'I'm Billy Cunningham and I want that bastard, Robinson.'

'Mr Cunningham, I see you're holding a gun. You'd better not have it on your person when we meet again. You'd better drop it over the side.'

'In a pig's eye,' said Billy. He pointed to the hole in the rubber and fabric side of the boat. 'Robinson came out shooting.'

'Suit yourself,' said Deane. 'We have excellent jails. Mangan, go away. I want to see you going back down the Waterway.'

'Let's go,' I said quietly, and turned the boat away.

'Your goddamn cops!' said Billy disgustedly. 'You'd think he'd want our help, even thank us for it.'

'Be quiet!' I said. 'I'm thinking.'

Again I wished I had a map. I had used the Waterway many times when I had *Lucayan Girl,* but I had always stuck to the main channel and had not bothered to explore the maze. Now I wished I had. I had a map of Freeport-Lucaya in my office and I tried to visualize the layout of the Waterway.

We went on a mile down the Waterway and came to another inlet on the same side as the one blocked by the Customs launch. I said, 'We're going in here.'

'Is there a through connection?'

'No.'

'Then what's the use?'

I said, 'Billy, every section of this water-riddled bit of real estate has but one connection with the main channel, like the one we're in now. Deane knows that and he's sitting there like a terrier outside a rabbit hole waiting for Robinson to come out. Robinson may *not* know that and if he doesn't he'll be looking for another way out. So what happens when he can't find one?'

'He'll leave the boat and take to land.'

'Yes. And he's on the town side this time. It wouldn't be too hard for him to steal a car, and he stands a sporting chance of getting away. I think Deane is counting on Robinson wasting enough time looking for an exit to allow Perigord to bring up his reinforcements, and I think he's taking a hell of a chance.'

'So?'

'So we're going in to chase him into Deane's arms.'

'How in hell are we going to do that if there's no inter-connection?'

'Portage,' I said. 'Now I'm glad we came in this boat and not the other.'

I had timed the minutes we had taken to get from one inlet to the other, and had kept a constant speed. Now we were going back, parallelling the Waterway on a minor canal. I reckoned that when we got half-way that would be the place to go overland. Presently I said, 'This should be it. We put ashore straight ahead.'

I cut the engine and we drifted until the boat nosed the bank. 'Keep your voice down,' I said. 'Robinson could very well be just on the other side of here.'

We went ashore and hauled out the inflatable. 'We'll take a look across there before carrying the boat over. And keep your head down.' We walked over limestone rubble and then over an unused paved road, built for the traffic that had never come. On the other side of the road I dropped into a crouch and then on to my belly as I neared the edge of the next canal.

I peered over the bank and everything was peaceful. A light breeze ruffled the surface of the water and there was no sign of Robinson's dory. I caught a movement out of the corner of my eye and looked to the left. In the middle distance I was a half-constructed house, and a man was working on the roof. I returned my attention to the canal. 'Okay. Let's bring up the boat.'

Billy looked back. 'A long haul,' he said. 'Nearly two hundred yards.'

'We'll unship the engine,' I said. 'And the inflatable has carrying straps.'

It was hot and heavy work but we finally made the portage and were sitting in the boat with the engine rese-cured on the transom. I was about to start up when Billy said, 'Listen!'

Someone in the half-built house was using a hammer, but under the rhythmic knocking I heard the faraway growl of an outboard engine. It grew louder, and I said, 'He's coming this way. Let's move it.'

I started the engine, hoping that Robinson would not hear it over the noise of his own, and we moved off. I kept the pace slow and, when we had gone about 200 yards and come to a junction, I killed the engine. Again we heard the sound of another outboard motor, this time distinctly louder. Billy was moving his head from side to side to locate the direction. 'To the left,' he said, and took out his gun.

I restarted the engine and pushed over the tiller, and we moved to the left and towards the house in the distance.There was a bend ahead and I moved to the inside curve, still travelling slowly because I wanted to keep quiet. Over the sound of our own engine I heard the noise of another.

'There he is,' said Billy, and I saw the dory coming towards us on the other side of the canal on the outside of the bend. I twisted the throttle and the boat bucked at the sudden application of power. Then we were on to him and Billy was shooting, but so was Robinson. Even as Billy fired, a bullet impacted inboard close to my hand and again there was the hiss of escaping air. Robinson was too damn good with his shooting; he had fired but two shots and had hit us both times, and although I had told Billy the inflatable was compartmented Robinson had punctured two air chambers out of the five.

Then he was past us and I slammed over the tiller, already feeling the difference in the behaviour of the boat; she was slow to come about and not as easily controlled. But Billy shouted, 'He's stopped. I hit his engine.'

I twisted and looked back. The dory was drifting into the bank and, as it touched, Robinson leapt ashore and began to run. He paused and snapped one shot at us before disappearing behind one of the heaps of grey limestone rubble, the spoil left from the dredging of the canal.

'Let's get after him,' urged Billy.

I needed no urging. Already I was heading for the bank and standing, ready to jump. Our feet hit the ground simultaneously, and Billy said, 'We'll tackle him from two sides.' He gestured with his pistol. 'You go that way and keep your head down.' He ran in the other direction.

I ran to the nearest heap of limestone and dropped flat before peering around it cautiously. There was no sign of Robinson. From behind I heard the sound of engines so I looked back to see the Customs launch coming up the canal, fairly boiling along at top speed. Deane must have heard the shots and decided to come in.

I ignored it and turned again to look for Robinson. We were quite close to the house and there were now two men on the roof, and one of them was pointing at something. I followed the direction of his arm, got to my feet, and began to run. Skidding around another heap of rubble I came across Robinson about ten yards away. He had his back to me, and beyond him I saw Billy come into sight.

I was late in the tackle. Before I could get to him Robinson fired and Billy dropped in his tracks. But then I was on to him and I had no mercy. His pistol went flying and it took Deane and two of his men to prise my hands from Robinson's neck.

Deane hauled me to my feet and pushed me away, standing between me and Robinson. 'That's enough!' he said curtly.

I heard a car door slam and saw Perigord walking over from a police car near the house. I regained my breath, and said, 'Then get the bastard out of my sight before I kill him.' I turned and walked towards Billy.

He was sitting up, his hand to his head, and when he took it away it was red with blood. 'He creased me!' he said blankly. 'Jesus, but it hurts!' There was an unfocused look to his eyes, a sign of concussion. I stooped, picked up his gun, and walked to the water's edge and tossed it into the canal. Then I went back and helped him to his feet.

'You're lucky you're not dead,' I said. 'Be glad it hurts; it means you'll live.'

Already he was looking better. He glanced across at Deane and saw Robinson still prostrate on the ground. 'Well, we've got him.'

'Yes,' I said shortly. Deane would not now need any excuse for holding Robinson. Any man who popped off a gun was automatically his prey – including Billy. Still, Deane had not seen Billy shoot, so, as we walked towards him, I said, 'I ditched your gun in the canal.'

'Thanks.'

Robinson sat up and Deane was addressing him in fast, fluent Spanish. Among the spate of words I heard the name Perez, repeated several times. Robinson shook his head and replied in Spanish, and then switched into English, with the same plummy accent I had come to know in Texas. 'I'm a soldier of the revolution,' he said pompously. 'And now a prisoner of war. I will answer no questions.' He got to his feet.

'Prisoner of war?' said Billy unbelievingly. 'The guy's nuts!'

'He's a bloody murderer,' I said.

'But that's for a court to decide, Mr Mangan,' said Perigord.

Deane took out handcuffs and then paused, looking at Billy expressionlessly. 'Search this man,' he said.

Billy grinned widely as Perigord's hands expertly patted his body. 'What gun?' he said. 'I took your advice. It was good.'

It was then that Robinson made his break. He thumped the nearest Customs officer in the gut, sending him to the ground writhing and retching, and took off, running towards the house. He took us all by surprise. Deane dropped the handcuffs and broke into a run, with me at his heels.

The builders at the house had stopped work and were now all on the roof, a good vantage point to view the morning's unexpected entertainment. The sole exception was the driver of a truck which had just arrived. He had got out, leaving the door open and the engine idling, and was calling to the men on the roof. Robinson clouted him in passing and he staggered back to collide with Deane and they both went down in a tangle of arms and legs.

By that time Robinson was in the cab and the engine of the truck roared. I leaped over the sprawled bodies of Deane and the driver and jumped for the cab, but it was too late and the truck was moving. I missed and fell to the ground. By the time I had picked myself up the truck was speeding up the road.

I saw Perigord getting into his car so I ran and piled in next to him just as he drove off with a squeal of rubber and a lot of wheel spin. He drove with one hand while unhooking the microphone of his radio from its bracket. He began to give brief but precise instructions, and I gathered that he was remarshalling his forces.

The truck was still in sight and we were gaining on it. It turned left on to East Sunrise Highway, and I said, 'He'll be going on to Midshipman Road, by the Garden of the Groves.'

'Yes,' said Perigord, and spoke into the microphone again.

The Garden of the Groves is one of the more sedate of our tourist attractions, the name being a punning one because the 100-acre gardens are dedicated to the memory of Wallace Groves, the founder of Freeport. There were always tourists wandering about that area and the chances were that Robinson could kill someone, travelling at the speed he was.

We sped down East Sunrise and turned on to Midshipman, and by then we were within fifty yards of the truck. A car shot out of a side road and hit the truck a glancing blow and Perigord braked hard as it crashed into a palm tree. I fumbled for the door handle as I saw Robinson jump from the cab and run towards the Garden.

Perigord was out before me, and he did something surprising – he threw his swagger stick at Robinson. It flew straight as an arrow and hit Robinson at the nape of the neck and he fell in a tumbled heap in the road.

Perigord was about to go to him but jumped back as a big double-decker London bus came around the corner. The driver swerved to avoid the crashed truck and his brakes squealed, but it was too late. The bus brushed past Perigord but one wheel went over Robinson's head.

EPILOGUE

After the immediate discussion that followed that incident I did not see Perigord to talk with seriously for nearly a month. He was a very busy man, and so was Commissioner Deane over in Nassau. But he did telephone to tell me that the ampoules found on Carrasco-Perez proved to contain a culture of *L. pneumophila*, enough to poison the water in every hotel in the Bahamas.

On the occasion of the annual BASRA Swimming Marathon I invited him and his family back to the house for drinks. Both our daughters had been competitors and Karen, like Sue before her, had won a second prize in her class. Full of pride and ice-cream she cavorted in the pool with Ginnie Perigord, and there did not seem to be much difference between a tanned white hide and a natural brown hide.

Debbie laughed and said to Amy Perigord, 'Where do they get the energy? You wouldn't think they've just swum two miles. Would you like a drink?'

'I'd rather have tea,' said Mrs Perigord. 'I'm not really a drinker.'

'We won't bother Luke,' said Debbie. 'Come into the kitchen and chat while I make it.'

I smiled at Perigord as they went away. Because he had attended the Marathon in his official capacity he was in full fig, swagger stick and all. I said, 'I propose something stronger. What will you have?'

He sat down and laid his cap and swagger stick by the chair. 'Some people think because I'm a black Bahamian that I exist on a liquid diet of rum, but I prefer scotch.'

I went to the poolside bar and held up a bottle of Glenlivet. 'This do?'

He grinned. 'That will do very well.'

I poured two drinks and put a bottle of iced water at his elbow. I said, 'Billy Cunningham rang me this morning. He says he's growing a streak of white hair where that bullet grazed him. He thinks it makes him look distinguished.'

'Did he really lose that pistol in the water?' asked Perigord curiously.

'I'll answer that by asking you a question,' I said. 'Would Deane really have framed the crew of *Capistrano* by planting cocaine?'

Perigord smiled. 'I see.' He ignored the water and sipped the scotch. 'Very good,' he observed.

'Now, tell me – who was Robinson?'

'We sent his fingerprints to the States and the Americans told us, but we could have found out ourselves once we began to dig. He was an Anglo-Cuban, educated in England. His name was Rojas and he was Perez's brother-in-law.'

I contemplated that information which did not mean much to me. 'So what happens now? Do we live in a permanent state of siege?'

'I don't think so,' said Perigord. 'An attempt was made – a covert attack on the Bahamas – and it failed. We have investigated every unusual occurrence since Rojas was killed and have found nothing to indicate that the attack is continuing. In my opinion, an opinion now shared by Commissioner Deane and the Government, the whole idea was conceived, planned and executed by Perez and Rojas. Probably Castro knew nothing about it.'

'You think not?'

'I think it was rather like Henry II and Becket. You know the story?'

'Henry said, "Who will rid me of this turbulent priest?" and the four knights went and slaughtered Becket in the cathedral.'

'Henry did penance for it afterwards,' said Perigord. 'I know Fidel Castro is no saint, but I don't think he'd stoop to what that pair did. He's too vulnerable himself. No, there's been bad blood between Cuba and the Bahamas ever since their jet planes shot up our fishery patrol vessel and killed four men, and matters haven't become any easier since. I think Castro wondered aloud how to solve the Bahamian question, and Perez and Rojas decided to take action.'

'So you now think we can live like reasonable human beings.'

'I would say so.' He smiled. 'But didn't someone say that eternal vigilance is the price of liberty. It has taught us a lesson from which we have benefited. At a cost.'

'I'm not going to relax the security measures in the hotels,' I said.

'Very wise. We also have instituted security measures; they are unobtrusive but they are there.' He held up his hand. 'Don't ask me what they are.'

I grinned at him. 'I wouldn't dream of it.' We sat in silence for a while and Perigord savoured his whisky. I said, 'You know the funniest thing in the whole damn business?'

'What?'

'When you threw that swagger stick. You looked so damned silly, but it worked.'

'Ah, the swagger stick. Do you know the history of this?'

'No.'

'It's the lineal descendant of the ash plant carried by the Roman centurion over two thousand years ago. He used it to discipline his men, but then it became a staff of office.

The line split quite early; one way led to the field marshal's baton, the other to the officer's cane. Catch!' He suddenly tossed it to me.

I grabbed it out of the air and nearly dropped it because it was unexpectedly heavy. I had thought it to be merely a cane encased in leather, but this one was loaded with lead at both ends. Perigord said suavely, 'Not only a staff of office but a weapon against crime. It has saved my life twice.'

I returned the weapon against crime, and he said, 'Amy confided in me this afternoon that your wife is expecting a baby. Is that so?'

'Yes – in about six months.'

'I'm glad she wasn't permanently harmed by what happened in Texas. In view of what I know about your family history may I offer the hope that it will be a boy?'

And six months later Karen had a brother.

INTRODUCTION TO
CRIME WAVE

This short introduction was written for the anthology
Crime Wave: World's Winning Crime Stories 1981. It is
accompanied here by Desmond Bagley's own author
fact sheet, written by him the same year to help promote his books.

INTRODUCTION

The Third Crime Writers' International Congress, known as the CWIC-3, was held in Stockholm under the auspices of the Swedish Academy of Detection at midsummer 1981, and was a resounding success. It was attended by nearly 300 delegates from 25 countries, ranging from Australia to Zimbabwe, and included, besides crime writers, forensic pathologists and scientists, working police officers, academic criminologists, lawyers, historians and other serious students of crime.

As part of the Congress the Swedish Academy of Detection organized a short story competition for which there were over 400 entries from all over the world. The Saab Motor Co. kindly donated a Saab Turbo as first prize and there were cash prizes for the runners-up. This collection represents the cream of the entries.

I suspect I have been asked to write this introduction because I have no axe to grind. I did not enter the competition. My ostensible reason was that I already have a car, but the real reason is that I cannot write short stories. A short story is deceptive in its simplicity and is one of the most difficult forms of literature. So when, in Stockholm, I was approached by Fred Dannay, better known as Ellery Queen, who was twisting my arm to write stories for *Ellery Queen's Mystery Magazine*, I said, 'Fred, I can't write short stories; they're not my metier. But I'll send you a couple providing you sign the rejection slips personally. They'll be valuable.'

Yet I know a good short story when I read one and this anthology is choc-à-bloc with them. The measure of excellence of a crime story does not depend upon the crime; it must be a good story in itself. The characterization must be sharp, the prose unlaboured, the detail accurate, and all must be encompassed within 7,500 words. And so in this book we have humanity in all its variety; its strengths and weaknesses, its brutality and heroism, its humour and sadness, its compassion and ruthlessness.

It is no accident that the three top prize-winners are American. The standard of American crime writing is exceptionally high, due in great measure to the work of Fred Dannay, who has done more for the genre in the English language than any other single man. He has taught two generations of writers by wielding a meticulous editorial pen.

Crime writers are often accused of adding to the violence of the world by depicting it. The truth is that we just hold up a mirror to the world and reflect but a pale image of reality. Truth *is* stranger than fiction. The winning story, *A Visit with Montezuma* by Frank Sisk, is such a reflection of the urban jungle we have ourselves created.

Dwight Steward's *Genesis*, the second prize-winner, goes back to the very roots of crime fiction. A story with an almost fairy-tale quality, it depicts a man at the moment when he decides to create a form of writing then unknown to the world. In addition, it *is* a good detective story.

Tony Hillerman shows his undeniable interest in anthropology when he writes *The Witch, Yazzie, and the Nine of Clubs*, the third prize-winner. He has used his immense knowledge of the ways and folklore of the Navajo Indian to produce a story which is a delight.

There are fifteen other stories. I have not the space here to comment on them and it would be invidious to pick out any to the exclusion of others. Suffice to say that this collection you hold in your hand is not a compilation made by a commercial book editor attempting to judge the level of popular taste. These are the stories written by the crime writers of the world today, judged by an international committee of their peers. Here are the world's crime writers saying, 'This is what crime writing is about.'

DESMOND BAGLEY

Born on October 29th 1923 in Kendal, Westmorland, England, the second son of John and Hannah Marie Bagley. His father was a coal miner but then ran a theatrical boarding house in Kendal and, later, in Blackpool, Lancashire, where DB spent most of his youth.

After a minimum of schooling DB left to begin work at the age of 14 as a printer's devil. At the start of World War II he worked in an aircraft factory in Lancashire making, among other things, Spitfire components and machine gun turrets. After the war he emigrated to Africa, travelling overland, and held a variety of jobs in Uganda, Kenya, Rhodesia (now Zimbabwe) and South Africa before making a start in journalism.

This began when he wrote a series of radio talks on scientific subjects for the South African Broadcasting Corporation in Durban (1950-51). He then went on to Johannesburg where he worked as a freelance reporter for several newspapers – the *Rand Daily Mail, the Sunday Times* and the *Star* – and for several trade journals.

He was for a long time the film critic for the *Rand Daily Mail* and the Johannesburg Film Society; and wrote theatre, concert and record reviews. There were numerous feature articles and emphasis on fact-finding surveys and trade shows from 1956 to 1962.

DB also at this time wrote commercial film scenarios for the cinema and Rhodesian television. Privately he worked on a number of short stories, without marked success.

NOVELS

In 1962 he began to write a novel (not the first he had tried) which he had been planning for a long time, giving up other work while the book was in progress. This was *The Golden Keel* which was submitted to William Collins Ltd and was accepted by them in early 1963 for publication later that year.

On the strength of this acceptance DB and his wife moved to England after a short and abortive attempt to live in Italy, and rented a house in Bishopsteignton, South Devon.

A second novel, *High Citadel*, had been written in South Africa just before the move and was accepted by Collins for publication in 1965. Since then they have published all DB's novels:

1963	The Golden Keel
1965	High Citadel
1966	Wyatt's Hurricane
1967	Landslide
1968	The Vivero Letter
1969	The Spoilers
1970	Running Blind
1971	The Freedom Trap
1973	The Tightrope Men
1975	The Snow Tiger
1977	The Enemy
1978	Flyaway
1980	Bahama Crisis
1981	The Man from Hell's Gate*

*Published as *Windfall* in 1982. It was followed by *Night of Error* (1984) and *Juggernaut* (1985), both published posthumously.

These have all been published in Britain by Collins in hardback and by Fontana in paperback. There have also been English book club editions, radio dramatizations and readings, and serial publication. The books have all come out in Braille and large-print editions and have been read on to tape for the blind and the seriously handicapped. Both Collins and Hutchinson Educational Books Ltd have produced remedial editions.

WORK IN PROGRESS

DB is at present (August 1980) writing his autobiography, and at all times there is at least one novel in the pipeline.

The hardback American editions are published by Doubleday & Co. Inc. of New York. Paperbacks in the US are produced by Bantam and Fawcett. There have been American serials, book club editions and Readers' Digest condensations.

DB's novels have also appeared in hard and soft-covered editions, book clubs, serials and condensations in the following languages:

French, German, Italian, Portuguese, Dutch, Finnish, Danish, Swedish, Norwegian, Icelandic, Flemish, Hebrew, Afrikaans, Hindi, Turkish, Japanese, Czech.

In 1979 the Dutch Publisher, Elsevier, celebrated the occasion of the publication of one million copies of DB's books in the Dutch language.

FILMS AND TV

One book, *The Freedom Trap*, was produced and released under the title *The Mackintosh Man*, starring Paul Newman and James Mason, and directed by John Huston. Other books are being considered for filming. DB spent some time in Hollywood in 1970-71 where he wrote his own script for *Running Blind*. However, the film was not made and he has decided not to tackle scriptwriting in future, preferring to stick to original work. In 1978 *Running Blind* was produced by BBC-Scotland as a three-part serial and this production has been screened in Britain and many other countries.*

PERSONAL

In 1960 DB married Joan Margaret Brown, Johannesburg-born, who was then working in a bookshop in that city. They have no children.

In 1965 they bought a Georgian house in Totnes, South Devon, and lived there until 1976. Then they moved to Guernsey in the Chanel Islands, where they bought a house of similar period, and where they live with three cats and a dog and a steady flow of visitors from the UK and abroad.

DB is a member of several writers' organisations; in Britain the Crime Writers' Association and the Society of Authors; in the US the Mystery Writers of America, the Authors' Guild and the Authors' League. He is a member of the Royal United Services Institute for Defence Studies and, in 1978, was elected a member of The Detection Club.

---

*Since his death in April 1983, other books have been adapted into TV movies: *Landslide* (1992), *The Vivero Letter* (as *Forgotten City*, 2000) and *The Enemy* (2001).

He has travelled extensively in search of material for his books. Apart from two overland crossings of the Sahara and much of the rest of Africa, he has visited Australia and New Zealand, Canada, the United States, and much of Europe, especially liking Scandinavia. He has travelled to Iceland and Greenland. He has explored by boat the waterways of France, Germany and Ireland. In 1968 he went to Antarctica as a guest of the United States Navy, visiting several polar bases including the South Pole itself.

DB is deeply interested in modern technology. He has long owned and programmed his own computer and now composes his books and other writings (including this fact sheet) on a word processor. Outside of writing his interests include recreational mathematics, military history, music, photography and reading. He reads fast and widely on the above subjects and also science. His own ability to read and enjoy fiction has diminished since he began to write fiction himself, and he now prefers non-fiction.

He reads three daily and two weekend newspapers regularly and a large number of weekly and monthly periodicals including *Scientific American* and *New Scientist*, bookselling and computer journals and so on. He is a regular but highly selective TV viewer. He sees fewer new films than he used to and goes to few forms of live entertainment. He has done some sailing and used to be a fencer, but no longer takes part in any sport, actively or as a spectator.

Desmond Bagley
April 1981

DESMOND BAGLEY

'Unbeatable for sheer gripping excitement.'

Daily Telegraph

RUNNING BLIND

The assignment begins with a simple errand – a parcel to deliver. But to Alan Stewart, standing on a deserted road in Iceland with a murdered man at his feet, it looks anything but simple. The desolate terrain is obstacle enough. But when Stewart realises he has been double-crossed and that the opposition is gaining ground, his simple mission seems impossible . . .

THE FREEDOM TRAP

The Scarperers, a brilliantly organised gang which gets long-term inmates out of prison, spring a notorious Russian double agent. The trail leads Owen Stannard to Malta, and to the suave killer masterminding the gang. Face to face at last with his opponents, Stannard must try to outwit both men – who have nothing to lose and everything to gain by his death . . .

'Literate, exciting, knowledgeable adventure stories – Desmond Bagley is incomparable.' *Sunday Mirror*

978-0-00-730474-5

DESMOND BAGLEY

'Sizzling adventure.'   *Evening Standard*

THE TIGHTROPE MEN

When Giles Denison of Hampstead wakes up in an Oslo hotel room and finds the face looking back at him in the mirror is not his own, things could surely get no more bizarre. But it is only the beginning of a hair-raising adventure in which Denison finds himself trapped with no way to escape. One false move and the whole delicately balanced power structure between East and West will come toppling down . . .

THE ENEMY

Wealthy, respectable George Ashton flees for his life after an acid attack on his daughter. Who is his enemy? Only Malcolm Jaggard, his future son-in-law, can guess, after seeing Ashton's top secret government file. In a desperate manhunt, Jaggard pits himself against the KGB and stalks Ashton to the silent, wintry forests of Sweden. But his search for the enemy has barely begun . . .

'Bagley has become a master of the genre – a thriller writer of intelligence and originality.'   *Sunday Times*

978-0-00-730475-2

DESMOND BAGLEY

'Compulsively readable.'   *Guardian*

FLYAWAY

Why is Max Stafford, security consultant, beaten up in his
own office? What is the secret of the famous 1930s aircraft,
the Lockheed Lodestar? And why has accountant Paul
Bilson disappeared in North Africa? The journey to the
Sahara desert becomes a race to save Paul Bilson, a race to
find the buried aircraft, and – above all – a race to return
alive . . .

WINDFALL

When a legacy of £40 million is left to a small college in
Kenya, investigations begin about the true identities of
the heirs – the South African, Dirk Hendriks, and his
namesake, Henry Hendrix from California. Suspicion
that Hendrix is an impostor leads Max Stafford to the Rift
Valley, where a violent reaction to his arrival points to a
sinister and far-reaching conspiracy far beyond mere
greed . . .

'From word one, you're off. Bagley's one of the best.'
                                                        The Times

978-0-00-730476-9

DESMOND BAGLEY

'The best adventure stories I have read for years.'
Daily Mirror

THE GOLDEN KEEL

When the Allies invaded southern Italy in 1943, Mussolini's personal treasure was moved north to safety under heavily armed guard. It was never seen again. Now, an expedition plans to unearth the treasure and smuggle it out of Italy. But their reckless mission is being followed – by enemies who are as powerful and ruthless as they are deadly . . .

THE VIVERO LETTER

Jeremy Wheale's well-ordered life is blasted apart when his brother is murdered. The killer was after a family heirloom – an antique gold tray – which sets Wheale on a trail from Devon to the tropical rainforest of Yucatan. There he joins the hunt for a lost Mayan city. But in the dense cover of the jungle a band of vicious convict mercenaries are waiting to strike . . .

'Bagley has no equal at this sort of thing.'
Sunday Mirror

978-0-00-730477-6

DESMOND BAGLEY

'Tense, heroic, chastening . . . a thumping good story.'
Sunday Express

THE SNOW TIGER

Fifty-four people died in the avalanche that ripped apart a small New Zealand mining town. But the enquiry which follows unleashes more destructive power than the snowfall. As the survivors tell their stories, they reveal a community so divided that all warnings of danger went unheeded. At the centre of the storm is Ian Ballard, whose life depends upon being able to clear his name . . .

NIGHT OF ERROR

When Mark Trevelyan dies on a journey to a remote Pacific atoll, the verdict that it was natural causes doesn't convince his brother, Mike. The series of violent attacks that follows only adds to his suspicions. Just two clues – a notebook in code and a lump of rock – are enough to trigger off a hazardous expedition, and a violent confrontation far from civilization . . .

'The detail is immaculately researched – the action has the skill to grab your heart or your bowels.'   *Daily Mirror*

978-0-00-730481-3

DESMOND BAGLEY

'Bagley in top form.'   *Evening Standard*

THE SPOILERS

When film tycoon Robert Hellier loses his daughter to heroin, he declares war on the drug pedlars, the faceless overlords whose greed supplies the world with its deadly pleasures. London drug specialist Nicholas Warren is called upon to organise an expedition to the Middle East to track down and destroy them – but with a hundred million dollars' worth of heroin at stake, Warren knows he will have to use methods as deadly as his prey . . .

JUGGERNAUT

It is no ordinary juggernaut. Longer than a football pitch, weighing 550 tons, and moving at just five miles per hour, its job – and that of troubleshooter Neil Mannix – is to move a giant transformer across an oil-rich African state. But when Nyala erupts in civil war, Mannix's juggernaut is at the centre of the conflict – a target of ambush and threat, with no way to run and nowhere to hide . . .

'Bagley is a master story-teller.'   *Daily Mirror*

978-0-00-730480-6

DESMOND BAGLEY

'Bagley is one of the best.'   *The Times*

HIGH CITADEL

When Tim O'Hara's plane is hijacked and forced to crash land in the middle of the Andes, his troubles are only beginning. A heavily armed group of communist soldiers intent on killing one of his passengers – an influential political figure – have orders to leave no survivors. Isolated in the biting cold of the Andes, O'Hara's party must fight for their lives with only the most primitive weapons . . .

LANDSLIDE

Bob Boyd is a geologist, as resilient as the British Columbia timber country where he works for the powerful Matterson Corporation. But his real name and his past are mysteries – wiped out by the accident that nearly killed him. Then Boyd reads a name that opens a door in his memory: Trinavant – and discovers that Bull Matterson and his son will do almost anything to keep the Trinavant family forgotten forever . . .

'Very much of the moment. The characters are sympathetic and believable'   *Sunday Times*

978-0-00-730479-0

LEN DEIGHTON

'A stunning spy story'   *Guardian*

XPD

June 11, 1940 – where is Winston Churchill?

A private aircraft takes off from a small town in central France, while Adolf Hitler, the would-be conqueror of Europe, prepares for a clandestine meeting near the Belgian border.

For more than forty years the events of this day have been Britain's most closely guarded secret. Anyone who learns of them must die – with their file stamped: *XPD – expedient demise*

'Exciting and well made.'   *Daily Telegraph*

'Deighton in top form . . . the best kind of action entertainment.'   *Publishers Weekly*

'Deliciously sharp and flawlessly accurate dialogue, breathtakingly clever plotting, confident character drawing . . . a splendidly strongly told story.'   *The Times*

978-0-586-05447-5

LEN DEIGHTON

'A brilliant picture of Britain under German rule.'

Sunday Telegraph

SS-GB

In February 1941 British Command surrendered to the Nazis. Churchill has been executed, the King is in the Tower and the SS are in Whitehall. For nine months Britain has been occupied – a blitzed, depressed and dingy country. However, it's 'business as usual' at Scotland Yard run by the SS when Detective Inspector Archer is assigned to a routine murder case. Life must go on.

But when SS Standartenführer Huth arrives from Berlin with orders from the great Himmler himself to supervise the investigation, the resourceful Archer finds himself caught up in a high level, all action, espionage battle.

'One of Deighton's best. Apart from his virtues as a story-teller, his passion for researching his backgrounds gives his work a remarkable factual authority.'

Anthony Burgess, *Observer*

'Len Deighton is the Flaubert of the contemporary thriller writers . . . there can be little doubt that this is much the way things would have turned out if the Germans had won the war.'

Michael Howard, *Times Literary Supplement*

978-0-586-05002-6

LEN DEIGHTON

'A massively different novel . . . the effect is – quite literally – devastating.'
Sunday Times

BOMBER

Bomber follows the progress of an Allied air raid through a period of twenty-four hours in the summer of 1943. It portrays all the participants in a terrifying drama, in the air and on the ground, in Britain and in Germany. In its documentary style, it is unique. In its emotional power, it is overwhelming.

Len Deighton has been hugely acclaimed both as a novelist and as an historian. In *Bomber* he has combined both talents to produce a masterpiece.

'The magnificent *Bomber* is rich with historical detail.'
The Times

'A massive and superbly mobilised tragedy of the machines which men create to destroy themselves . . . masterly and by far Mr Deighton's best.'
Douglas Hurd, *Spectator*

'A magnificent story . . . the characters lean out of the pages.'
Daily Mirror

978-0-586-04544-2

LEN DEIGHTON

'The sheer charge of the writing swept me into another world.'
H.R.F. Keating, *The Times*

GOODBYE MICKEY MOUSE

In *Goodbye Mickey Mouse* Len Deighton has written a brilliant, multi-dimensional picture of what it is to be at war . . . and what it was to be in love in the England of 1944.

'It is a novel of memory, satisfying on every imaginable level, but truly astonishing in its recreation of a time and place through minute detail. Deighton has written well of the air before, nonfictionally, and he informs us in an afterword that it took six years of research to do this novel. It shows. The only way you could know more about flying a P-51 Mustang, after reading this book, is to have flown one.'
Washington Post

'He writes, as usual, with authority and a superb sense of period.'
Daily Telegraph

978-0-586-05448-2